W9-CMF-074

THE MIND-MURDERS

and two other

GREAT MYSTERIES

THE MIND-MURDERS

and two other

GREAT MYSTERIES

Janwillem van de Wetering

Houghton Mifflin Company
Boston

Contents

THE MIND-
MURDERS

for St. John Nixon

PART I

1

IT WAS FRIDAY NIGHT and the lush heat of summer hung under a clear and starry sky. An old model Volkswagen, dented and rusty on the edges, hesitated before entering the bridge crossing the Emperorscanal at the side of the Brewerscanal. An ordinary car, containing two ordinary men.

Perhaps not too ordinary; the driver had been called handsome, mostly by women, and some of that quality could be seen even through the dirty window that the sergeant was in the process of winding down, unveiling such currently acceptable features as a straight nose above a sweeping mustache, soft, expressive eyes, and thick, carefully combed curls.

"Doesn't work!" Rinus de Gier said. The sergeant, employed by the Amsterdam Municipal Police, criminal investigation department, and veteran of the murder brigade, turned to address his superior. "That window doesn't work. It worked yesterday. Since then you drove the car. You forced it again."

"Yes," Adjutant Grijpstra said, "you're right. Whatever I touch malfunctions. Now drive on."

De Gier concentrated on Grijpstra's face, trying to determine the validity and seriousness of the order. He smiled. The adjutant looked peaceful and solid in the dignity of his crumpled pinstripe suit; a father figure, ten years older than the sergeant who, having passed forty, was aging himself. Grijpstra's body attitude showed what he was: a man of substance, substance of the spiritual variety, an experienced officer,* trustworthy, matured while grumpily serving the abstract state, committed to uphold order so that its millions of wayward citizens could carry on in their egocentric ways. Grijpstra's grizzled heavy head remained impassive under de Gier's scrutiny, but his pale blue eyes reflected restrained impatience.

"Drive on," Grijpstra said, kindly but insistently.

De Gier observed the growing crowd milling about on the bridge. He appraised the crowd's nature and nodded approvingly. He subsequently studied the row of gabled houses displaying their seventeenth-century splendor through the branches of majestic elms lining both canals.

"A lovely spot, Grijpstra. This, I believe, is one of the better locations of the inner city. We are surrounded by decorative and beautiful architecture."

Grijpstra slipped his watch off his wrist and dangled it in front of de Gier's eyes. "It's past ten-thirty, sergeant. We are overdue at Headquarters. The job is done and we aren't working this weekend. The weekend has started."

De Gier didn't respond. Grijpstra sighed.

"We don't have to be here, Rinus, we have to be in a pub. We should be ordering our first drink. You could be telling me a story and I could be listening to you."

De Gier pointed at a café ahead, a little to the right. It occupied the lower story of a proud and delicate building, and its sign, the goal of the sergeant's long and straight index finger, proclaimed BEELEMA in elegant script; the word was surrounded by a garland of iron leaves.

"I haven't been to Beelema's for years, but I believe that it still attracts an intelligent clientele."

Grijpstra's calm persisted, but the wrinkles around his eyes moved.

"Beer!" he said slowly. "But I won't have it there, and you can't have any. It makes you linger near trees and I get tired of waiting for you. I'll buy you a jenever. Let's go."

De Gier's gaze slipped back to the crowd. The crowd had doubled in the last few moments and began to obstruct the quay.

"Go!" Grijpstra's elbow prodded de Gier's sensitive side. "This has nothing to do with us. Crowds are for the uniformed police. They're

---

* The ranks of the Dutch municipal police are constable, constable first class, sergeant, adjutant, inspector, chief inspector, commissaris, and chief constable.

here. See? Their car is parked behind that truck, and there's a constable. He can take care of this. He's an excellent constable. His name is Ketchup. He's of the local station."

De Gier, after a swift glance at the adjutant's face, decided to play for time.

"Ketchup?" he asked politely.

Grijpstra tried to wave the question away.

"Yes. The constable has a somewhat violent reputation, he has been known to occasionally bloody a suspect. His mate is of the same caliber, fellow by the name of Karate. Rough maybe, but you can expect it in this area. Ketchup has been talking into his radio, he must have called for assistance. For the last time, sergeant, let's get away while we still can."

De Gier's even but slightly protruding teeth flashed. He parked the car and got out. "Half a minute, adjutant, I'll be right back."

"Evening," Ketchup said. "Did you hear my radio call for assistance? Quick service, sergeant. I know you. Do you remember that evening on the range the other night? When Karate won all the prizes? Pity that Headquarters couldn't win, but we get more practice, I suppose. You were on the team too, I believe."

"I was?"

"Oh yes. Karate is a real crack shot of course, a winner, but right now he's having a bit of trouble. He's in the canal. He's trying to save a drowning man who prefers to drown." Ketchup had to shout the last of his sentence. The crowd's enthusiasm was increasing. "Goal!" the crowd shouted. "Hurrah!"

De Gier shouldered his way to the bridge. The blue uniform of the swimming policeman contrasted nicely with the deep green color of the slimy and fertile surface of the canal; then the courageous constable became invisible for a moment, as he dived to avoid the splashing attack of the drowning man's stick.

The stick was a crutch. The sergeant addressed Ketchup who had followed him to the railing.

"Is that civilian an invalid?"

"He is, sergeant."

Ketchup smiled eagerly. He was a small man, and de Gier bent down to address his subordinate.

"Explain!"

Ketchup obeyed, immediately and subserviently. Most of his report was lost in the assorted noise produced by the crowd. De Gier frowned.

"Tell me," the sergeant bellowed, "how did this start?"

Ketchup tried to step away, but the crowd pushed him back against the sergeant's chest. He repeated his narrative, shouting, abbreviating his sentences.

"Aha." De Gier had heard. He now fitted the facts together. Karate and Ketchup, driver and observer in a patrol car, were ordered to investigate a disturbance. A street seller, dispensing raw herring and onions from his stall, had telephoned his complaint to Headquarters. Hippies, so the herringman said, were interfering with his trade. The patrol car, delayed by heavy traffic and slowed by many neatly fenced areas where streets were being repaired, arrived late. The herringstall was closed, and there were no hippies in sight. The constables, disappointed, did not return to their car. The evening, so far, was uneventful, and they would welcome some action. Insisting on locating disorder, they were attracted by the sounds coming from café Beelema. The sounds were of breaking glass and raised voices. They charged the café. Karate, who led the charge, was hit by a crutch wielded by a drunk.

The sergeant cupped his hands and aimed his shout at Ketchup's forehead. "So you felt threatened?"

"Right, sergeant!"

"And you removed the threat by depositing your man in the Emperorscanal?"

"Right! So that we could create a temporary point of rest. There were other troublemakers: a fat man dressed in leather, a male model in his nighties, and a younger female who yelled. They supported the crutchclubber. They were ringleaders. There was a dog."

"It attacked you?"

"It growled."

De Gier observed the policeman in the canal, popping up in various places. He shrugged. "You didn't go for your guns?"

Ketchup smiled politely. "No."

The drowning man renewed his attack. His crutch hit the spot that had held Karate's head. The crowd approved. "Olé!"

"Please sergeant, assist Karate. I'll discipline the crowd." Ketchup had found a hole; he slipped away.

De Gier began to undress. He removed the silk scarf from his tapered shirt and looked around. Grijpstra approached and held up his arm. De Gier deposited the scarf. He took off his jacket. He slipped out of the straps that held the gun holstered under his armpit. He stepped out of his trousers. A girl pushed Grijpstra away and admired the stripping sergeant. The girl's girlfriend also pushed Grijpstra.

"Lovely," the first girl said.

"Ooh-ooh!" the second girl said and repeated her statement while de Gier displayed his wide shoulders, his long and muscled back, his narrow waist, and his straight legs.

"The legs are too thin," the first girl said, "not that I mind. Nice, eh?"

The second girl stuck to her original observation. The first girl nudged her.

"Yes," the second girl said, "I like his eyes too, and his curls. Let's wait for him afterward and ask if he is for hire."

De Gier stepped over the railing, hesitated, and jumped. While he jumped he thought it was a pity. The case was not out of the ordinary: a drunk in a canal, it might not happen every day but it certainly happened every week. He had, when he spotted the disturbance, hoped for a little more. He needed work to fill the emptiness of the coming weekend. He saw, while he fell (the mind is fast), an aphorism neatly lettered on the slow green swell of the canal's surface. *Emptiness is the devil's headpillow*. Then a word changed. Emptiness is the *smoker's* headpillow. Not having anything to do for two empty days would surely make him smoke again. He hadn't smoked for five days now. The threatening peace and horrifying quiet of the weekend ahead would break his effort. The weekend would destroy him unless *splash!* The splash exploded both aphorism and reflection. (The mind may be fast, but still moves within time.) De Gier, excused from the duty to think, experienced the sensations of becoming wet and dirty. A condom curled itself around his toe, a soggy newspaper brushed past his mouth, his wrists were linked by a pale green waterweed. He muttered and shook off the condom. The newspaper floated on. He broke the waterweed. He determined his position. His body had turned while it fell, and he no longer saw the constable and the civilian but a row of legs belonging to an orderly line of spectators settled on a tree, felled by age and lying across the canal. The eyes of the spectators were hostile. De Gier breathed out; the rippling water rose to his mouth.

"Watch out!" shouted Karate.

De Gier turned and saw a blond head and a pink hand. The enemy watched him from bloodshot eyes. His spluttering mouth blew a bubble, a balloon that had to be more than mere spittle-film, for it didn't burst, managed to detach itself from the man's extended lips, and wafted away. The crutch was raised, ready to come down, and de Gier spread his arms and propelled himself backward. The crutch came down and shot up again. De Gier's rowing arms provided more distance.

Grijpstra had seen enough. Hindered by jostling bodies and deafened by rough voices the adjutant struggled, liberated himself, and found an abandoned handcart chained to a tree well away from the disturbance. He climbed the cart, careful not to tip it, and admired the view—a perfect square bordered by bridge, quaysides, and the tumbled elm tree—the arena where the law fought its formidable opponent. He averted his eyes. The view might be interesting but he didn't enjoy its irregular motion. He preferred what lay beyond its limits and observed calm water supporting two black geese with fiery red and bulbous beaks, and glittering eyes. Grijpstra thought that he recognized the scene and searched his memory for associations. The requested information appeared promptly. He saw clearly remembered paintings, created by Melchior Hondecoeter, a medieval artist inspired by birds. The adjutant saw pheasants in a snow-covered cemetery, a giant woodcock defending itself with swollen purple throat and half-raised wings against the attack of jealous peacocks, and sooty coots landing on a castle pond surrounded by crumbling moss-grown walls. He nodded, but Hondecoeter had forgotten to portray these exotic geese, floating in arrogant glory on a green swell of luminous water mirroring steeply rising silver-gray mansions, holding on to each other in their great age.

Grijpstra looked up. The narrow gable frames supported golden balls flanking a stonework angel raising his trumpet. The tall trees, carrying heavy loads of leaves, reached for the angel. The adjutant sighed. He would like to do this painting himself, and perhaps he could, but he would need some rest and unlittered space. His small apartment offered neither. He thought of his flat-footed heavy wife and the overflow of furniture, stacked under low ceilings, in a haze of kitchen smells.

He was ready to sigh again, when the rocking cart forced him into a lopsided dance. An old woman climbed the cart, an ugly shape topped by a glistening skull spotted by transparent clusters of gray trailing hair. She peered at him from watery eyes pressed by puffy skinbags. Her teeth clacked as she spoke.

"Isn't it terrible? Yes, it's terrible. That's my neighbor, Frits Fortune. He doesn't do nothing. It's no sin to be drunk. I order more beer and Frits goes to get it and falls. His crutch gets away and breaks the glasses. We jump about, me and the others, to get hold of Frits and save the drink and down he goes again. The fuzz rushes in. It beats us with nightsticks. Frits gets off the floor and his crutch hits the fuzz, right on the smacker. Accident, everybody knows he don't mean it, but the fuzz knows nothing. They drag Frits out and dump him in the canal. We're friends so we put in a word. I did, and Zhaver, he's the barman, and Titania, she's the barmaid, and Borry Beelema, he's the boss, he also runs the hair salon on the other side. Borry always helps, he does, God's other son we call him, you know? So Borry, he grabs a bottle and *hey hey* we all shout and back comes the fuzz. Then we do nothing, for the fuzz has guns." She waved a claw.

"Yes ma'm," Grijpstra said.

The claw pointed. "I'll be the death of him, poor feller, and all by mistake. Because Uncle Harry got scared of the weirdoes. Calls the fuzz and goes home. You know Uncle Harry?"

"No ma'm."

"Sells herring, he's all right. But when he's in his stall he can't get away and the weirdoes come and yell in his face. Got weak nerves, Uncle Harry has. The weirdoes are on junk, they're needlers, that's the worst. It's terrible, ain't it?"

Grijpstra agreed.

The woman clacked her teeth cheerfully. She faced the adjutant and admired his pink clean cheeks sagging heavily over solid jawbones. Eager to increase her contact, she thumped him on the thigh. The cart wobbled.

"Easy, ma'm."

"Yeh. Poor Frits, he don't earn it, not after the other trouble he don't. Like Job, he lost it all."

"Job?"

"Come on," she said coyly. "You're from my time, you read the Bible. Like *Job,* on the shitheap, man who got boils. Lost everything, right? Poor overnight, and sick too, ain't that terrible?"

"Yes ma'm. Mr. Fortune lost it all too?"

"Yeh. Yesterday. Just imagine, he comes home, worked all day, poor man is tired, a good man, opens the door, and *nothing there.*"

"Nothing at all?"

"Nothing. Over there. See Hotel Oberon? Next door. Old warehouse they changed into apartments. He lives on top and I'm underneath. That's how I know. Frits comes home, puts his key in, opens the door and *nothing there.*"

"Thieves?"

She squeaked like a bird in fear. "Never. His own wife. Never surprised me. Rea Fortune, the silly bitch. Frits's too good for a silly bitch. The mister works while the missus sits on her sucker, if nobody holds it for her, that is. When he's home she yells at him, the floor is thick but I can still hear her. He makes the money and she spends it, but she can't do nothing."

"Mrs. Fortune wasn't home?"

The woman cackled. "Not home? Nothing was home. He gets inside and there's nothing but polished floors. That's why he's got the crutch. He slips and hurts himself. I hear it and I go up and help him down the stairs, take him to the doctor. He's in pain. He's lame. Poor Frits. But she'd taken it all, except the phone, can you believe it? Even the dog is gone, nice dog, a poodle, Babette. But Babette comes back late last night, scratching and barking and Frits lets it in and this morning the dog is gone again, ain't that terrible? So I take Frits to the pub and everybody knows and they all buy him a drink and look at it now."

Grijpstra looked and nodded. Righteous power was closing in; Frits Fortune's movements became restricted by the sergeant's and Karate's strategy. The crutch still swung but it had lost both strength and direction. The sight didn't thrill the adjutant. He averted his gaze and admired the geese again. The birds, ungainly as they climbed a board attached to a houseboat, were being fed by a holy-looking old man. Grijpstra no longer concentrated; his mind reverted to duty. He visualized a report and phrased the essential statement: *While removing all household goods.*

"Mrs. Fortune didn't leave a note?"

"Nothing. She leaves space."

"Nobody saw a van?"

"Nobody. Poor Frits goes about asking, but it's busy here during the day, there's always a van somewhere. Nobody notices. He phones his relatives, everybody he knows. Me too, but I am out most of that day."

"Grijpstra!" shouted de Gier.

"Here."

Fortune was pushed up by the sergeant and Karate. Grijpstra left his cart and received the suspect. Ketchup drove the patrol car alongside. The crowd approached and was restrained by other policemen pouring out of a minibus. Frits Fortune, relieved at being on dry ground again and encouraged by friendly faces in the crowd, whacked Ketchup on his cap. The crowd howled and Grijpstra joined his colleagues and addressed the hostile civilians lovingly, peering benevolently, touching softly.

"You're fuzz too!" the old woman shrieked.

"Yes ma'm."

"Take care of poor Frits."

"We will," Ketchup said. "We'll bounce him up and down in the drunks' cell and he can roll in his own filth all night. And if he doesn't call us 'sir' tomorrow, we'll have him for a little while longer."

Grijpstra put an arm around Ketchup's shoulders and walked him away.

"Monkeyface."

"Beg pardon, adjutant."

"I say you're a monkeyface. You shouldn't be throwing invalids into the canal. And you shouldn't be fighting in pubs. When there's pub trouble, you should stay in the open door and wait till it calms down, and then you should go in. Don't you learn that at school anymore?"

"Yes, adjutant, but tonight it was different. Karate was a bit nervous and so was I. We wanted to take care of it quickly."

"You didn't. You aggravated and provoked. I'll be mentioning the matter. I'm telling you now so that you know what's ahead."

"Yes, adjutant."

"Take care of poor Frits."

"Yes, adjutant."

De Gier had dressed. "Strange suspect, you know. Blew bubbles. Like bubble gum, but it wasn't."

"The man was disturbed." Grijpstra passed on his information.

De Gier listened while he dried his hair with his scarf. "Yes? Doesn't sound right to me."

"Doesn't sound right at all," Grijpstra said, "but they can explain it in the café, and pour us a drink meanwhile."

De Gier shook his scarf.

"I don't want to drink, I want to smoke."

"They'll have nicotine."

"Like in cigarettes?"

"Of course, and like in shag tobacco, and like in cigars."

"But I stopped smoking."

Grijpstra entered the pub. De Gier stood and watched a cyclist. The cyclist was a slender but hairy gentleman dressed in a three-piece summer suit complete with an old-fashioned felt hat. The cycle was new but a bent pedal touched the metal chain guard, clanging monotonously. Ducks, awakened by the melancholy repetitive sounds, quacked sleepily. The two red-beaked geese honked briefly. The old man who had been feeding them cleared his throat sadly. A shiny Mercedes, parked in front of the Hotel Oberon which occupied the five finest gable houses on the other side of the canal, emitted a fat man.

Grijpstra came out of the pub again and grabbed the sergeant by the arm, turned him round, and pushed him to the pub.

"I read it somewhere," Grijpstra said, "in a book that gives examples of correct reports, based on true cases: *A gentleman lost his temper because his wife annoyed him. He picked up a vase and broke it on her head, killing her. The body rolled on the carpet and bled profusely. The gentleman rolled the body into the carpet and dug a large hole in his garden. He dropped the bundle into the hole, covered it up with earth, and stated: 'My wife has left me, I don't know where she went.'*"

"Yes," de Gier said, "and in that way he hid both body and the traces of his crime. I remember the report, but it only mentioned a carpet, not everything that goes into a house. This case is different."

"Every case is different, principles are often identical."

"True."

"We're closed," the barman said. He was dressed in bib overalls made out of imitation silk. Downy hair flowed over the bib. His profile was Greek and divine but no longer young.

"Police."

The barman read the two plastic-coated identity cards and noted the stamps, the photographs, and the diagonal red, white, and blue stripes. He put them on the counter and moved his thumb so that they slid toward a short elderly man who was sitting at the bar. "More of the same, Borry."

The man studied the cards and returned them to the detectives. He felt his stomach bulging under a leather waistcoat, pulled his curly sideburns, and smiled convincingly.

"Drinks on the house, gentlemen. My name is Borry Beelema. I own this establishment, and my hair salon across the water is at your service should you wish to look better than you do now. Titania, ask my friends what they would have."

A young woman presented herself behind the bar.

"Titania?" asked Grijpstra.

"Titania, at your service. What would our guests like to imbibe? A triple whisky with a drop of cognac? Ice and whipped cream? A gilded straw? Please state your desires."

Grijpstra's lips twisted.

"Not that sort of desire," the girl said primly.

"Two jenevers, miss."

Grijpstra turned to de Gier. The sergeant offered no support. He wasn't looking at Titania but at the half-revealed upper part of a young lady on a poster. Grijpstra corrected his observation. De Gier was looking at the young lady's hand. The hand held a cigarette.

De Gier cursed.

"Beg pardon?"

De Gier smiled brightly. "Nothing, adjutant. I was thinking. Please proceed."

2

"I REGRET that I have to state that the tradition of the police, born in a noble past, stretching to an enlightened future, does not allow . . ."

"Yes," Sergeant Jurriaans said softly.

". . . for a shoddy present. Two of your men, dressed in the Queen's uniform, disgraced the force last night. I'm here to complain."

"So I gather."

The two men leaned toward each other across a worn counter in the front office of the police station in the inner city. Grijpstra wore his usual crumpled three-piece pinstripe that now contrasted sadly with Sergeant Jurriaans's impeccable uniform. Grijpstra sighed and prepared to match the power of this tall and wide-shouldered colleague and to withstand the steady gaze directed at him from a heavily lined face under a wealth of cropped orange hair.

"Would you like some coffee?" a female constable asked. Grijpstra now sighed with pleasure. He noted that the young constable was well shaped and looked back at him through unusually large and sparkling blue eyes. She was small and slender, but her breasts seemed to exert considerable pressure against the stiff material of her jacket. The intensity of her eyes disconcerted him, however, and he faced the sergeant again. The sergeant was rubbing his face. The stiff hairs on the back of his hand reminded Grijpstra of carrot scrapings.

"Please, dear," Jurriaans said, "and I don't mind if you serve the Revenging Angel too. He's a colleague, after all, and carries a superior rank, and he's probably been sent, he can't help himself."

The girl giggled. The adjutant attempted to ignore her. He couldn't. He saw more in her eyes than he wanted to see. Wise, Grijpstra thought, and lewd. She knows it all. How can she know it all? She's too young.

The constable left, gracefully wobbling her small tight bottom.

"Don't mind her," Sergeant Jurriaans said, "she's amused by older men. She likes them, too. She has a father complex. When you get through with your heavy words, I'll tell you a story about her. It's about time we exchanged the news of the day, we don't see each other much lately."

Grijpstra's eyes were on the girl again. Sergeant Jurriaans coughed politely.

"Ah yes," Grijpstra said. "She's as nice from the rear as the front. Why don't we ever get female assistants? Cardozo doesn't compare with . . . what's her name?"

"Asta."

"Asta. And I haven't been sent, Jurriaans, as you know."

"I know. What happened?"

"Two of your constables, Ketchup and Karate, threw an invalid into the Emperorscanal last night. A dangerous crowd had to be restrained by six uniformed colleagues, my sergeant, and myself. My sergeant even had to swim. An unnecessary and painful commotion. Unreasonable, too. Your constables provoked the trouble. There was no charge against the invalid. There'll probably be a charge against him now. If so, I demand that you withdraw it, apologize to the civilian, and take disciplinary action against the constables."

The sergeant nodded. "Right. But the blame is mine. Not just for this but for everything. I admit it freely so that we can continue on our various paths. Do you know why I should be blamed?"

"Tell me," Grijpstra said and stirred the coffee in his paper cup, handed to him by Asta whose attractiveness he didn't notice this time. He removed the plastic spoon and stuck it into the sergeant's cup. The sergeant held Grijpstra's spoon together with his own and stirred too. Then he removed both spoons and inserted them in Grijpstra's cup. Grijpstra took them out, held them in his hand for a while, and dropped them into a trash can.

Jurriaans smiled. "I won that one. Your turn. But first I'll tell you why the guilt is mine for anything that goes wrong, here and everywhere. It has to do with my birth. I could have slipped back but I did not. By making that initial choice I became part of an unacceptable situation which, and not in my innocence I assure you, I accepted. On that fateful moment I became loaded with universal guilt."

"Quite."

"With that out of the way, I will leave the general for the particular. I am also responsible for the system that channels new blood into the force. You still follow me?"

Grijpstra smiled noncommittally.

"I'm with you."

"Do you know how the system works, now, I mean?"

Grijpstra's smile froze.

"No, because you and I started at the same time, but I'm of the uniformed branch and closer to ground level. I know what goes on now and remember what it used to be like. In our days, a commissaris blew some cigar smoke into your face and if you didn't drop—they weren't really corrupt as you'll recall, they smoked whatever the civilians gave them—you were accepted. It was a strong test, but honest. Now it's different. The aspiring cadet is faced by a psychologist, with a degree from a respected university and a violent facial tic, smoking a pipe that doesn't draw in a small room where flies crash into the window. He has to answer questions that the psychologist reads to him from a form that also lists the correct replies. Sometimes the psychologist also reads the replies."

"What sort of questions?"

"About hobbies. Does the young man have hobbies? The reply should be 'growing flowers' or 'jigsaw-puzzling,' but our fellow doesn't know that yet, so, in his ignorance, he states that he likes to beat people. The psychologist knows what to do. He says, 'Hee hee, I won't write that down, sir, you're joking, of course, but I'll mark down, further along, that you have a sense of humor, and that's something else that is needed in the police force today; the right answer is . . .' What did I say it was just now?"

"Composing poetry."

"Right. So the psychologist helps the fellow along and says, 'You do like making poems, don't you?' and the fellow says, 'I sure do,' and the psychologist says, 'Let's hear some of your art, sir,' and the fellow recites,

> *Swishing swiftly through the sky*
> *for crown and church, I fly . . .*

and the psychologist says; 'Right, right, no more, sir, not in this dismal little room with the flies banging against the window and my pipe poisoning the already polluted air. My, you are a sensitive one, the police should be proud to welcome you. What sports do you prefer?' "

"Shooting dolls," Grijpstra said, "with poisoned arrows."

"Exactly, and the psychologist checks his form, shakes his head, chokes, and finally whispers, 'Balls, sir, balls!' and the fellow doesn't understand right away and shouts, 'What do you mean, what do you mean?' and the psychologist gets up and begins to dribble across the room, pretending to catch and throw balls and in the end the new fellow says, after he has said just about everything, they can get really involved you know, sometimes there are fist fights or they break up the furniture, but in the end the fellow catches on and says that he plays a lot of football, badminton, rugby, pelota, jokari, volleyball, squash, tennis, and so on, and the psychologist puts a lot of v's on his form, for he's a mental cripple and can only work a few hours a day and it's time to go home. So they get to the final question and he asks if the fellow ever dreams about the Queen and the fellow gets that one and says he does."

"So he misses a lot of time at school, but he gets through the year, and they put him in uniform and send him to you," Grijpstra said.

"And what do I do with him? Shoot two holes in his body and file him? Or do I keep him in the refrigerator behind the beer?"

"No."

"I don't do that, I'm glad he came; and I'm glad you came too, adjutant, this is a bad day, and I need a friend. I take the young blighter and I send him on patrol, that's what I do, damn my rotten soul if I don't. I know that he's going to add to the mess, but never mind, out he goes. I've got to be grateful after all, the fellow could have gone on welfare, but he has those ideas about the crown and the church, and the sky, and so forth, and he does dream about the Queen. The colonial attitude, somewhat scarce these days. 'To work,' I say. 'Catch me an invalid and dump the useless son-of-a-whore in the Emperorscanal.' Karate and Ketchup, eh? Who else? I knew it straightaway. Even the marrow in their spines is bad, although they look okay in a way, the despicable little clowns. Asta, darling! See if you can find Karate and his mate. Tell them they are wanted at the counter and don't breathe a word about what has been going on here."

The girl rushed off.

"Morning, sergeant."

"Same to you, Ketchup, and yourself, Karate. Do you know who this officer is?"

Ketchup came to attention, Karate answered the question.

"Adjutant Grijpstra, sergeant. He assisted us last night when we were faced by a hostile gathering and engaged in arresting a troublesome suspect. He and Sergeant de Gier. Assistance to colleagues, sergeant. The operation was successful and the report is on your desk."

Jurriaans bowed so that he could look under Karate's cap.

"Yes, successful." The vein halving his forehead swelled and crinkled up to the hairline. "Is it true that the two of you dashed into café Beelema last night? Nightsticks at the ready?"

"Yes, sergeant."

"And that you, without warning, engaged in a battle with civilians?"

"Yes, sergeant."

"And that you, in the aforementioned establishment, grabbed hold of an invalid, a man who moves along with the help of a crutch, dragged the said individual outside, and threw him into the canal?"

"Yes, sergeant."

Sergeant Jurriaans lifted part of the counter, walked through the opening, and carefully took hold of one ear of each constable. He pulled in opposing directions. The constables pulled back and squeaked. "Eee-ee-ee-ee."

"Louder."

"Eee-ee-ee-ee."

"I won't have this any longer. I won't warn you two again. The next bleeder you introduce into this station, the next suspect who has difficulty walking, the next civilian who doesn't look altogether healthy and happy—do you know what that arrest will do for you?"

"Eee-ee-ee-ee?"

"It will mean a transfer to a certain little village of fishermen that I won't mention, because the whole building may crash down on us if I do. And do you know what those God-fearing fishermen do with constables who haven't learned the meaning of the word *proportion?*"

"Eee?"

"How they treat those officials who have no idea of *human relations?*"

"Eee?"

"How they approach ignorant policemen who cannot *weigh* this against that?"

"Eee?"

"They grind them to dolls' shit. Ground, sieved, purified, refined dolls' shit."

Sergeant Jurriaans let go. The constables tumbled away and came to rest against opposite walls.

"Did I hurt you?"

"Yes, sergeant!"

"Do you wish to apply for sick leave?"

"No, sergeant."

"You may go to the canteen. The brothel on the other side of the street delivered some apple pie, because we haven't interfered with it for the last five years. Madame baked the pies with her own puffy hands. Sometimes all this becomes too much for me. She sent her two prize whores to carry the basket; the handle was decorated with a plastic rose."

"I want some pie too," Grijpstra said.

"Be my guest, and tell me more. Something jolly this time. Tell me about some nice murder."

"Yes," Grijpstra said a little later, before plunging his fork. "A murder, you said. But I can't tell you much about it yet. It's not the right sort of murder, you see."

"Is there a right sort of murder?"

"Oh yes."

"What's wrong with this one?"

"No corpse."

"No," Sergeant Jurriaans said when Grijpstra had finished his story and three helpings of pie. "A murder because some furniture disappeared? And some silly poodle? And a wayward wife? Don't you have anything better to do? You've got a whole weekend ahead of you and the weather happens to be fine. Go fishing. Or count tits on the beach. Another two miles of beach have been set aside for the naked. I can give you directions."

"No."

"You've been doing something wrong, or you are jumping to conclusions. Is superstar de Gier in this too? How is our hero? He caused a few laughs at the range the other night. I always thought he was supposed to be a reasonable shot."

"You fellows gave him a pistol with the sights out of whack. He's doing badly. Nervous, Jurriaans, very. Stopped smoking and lives in pure insanity. Of course he is in this with me, it's my duty to keep him busy. I'm not expecting him to be useful but he can look at Titania while I work. That's a nice girl, although your Asta is better. What's the use of beauty without invitation? Your Asta is friendlier. Do you ever go to café Beelema?"

Jurriaans grinned. "Sure, and I know Titania. Did you happen to look at her sideways?"

Grijpstra ate his last crumb and scraped his plate. "Yes. That blouse must have been specially designed, and they placed the bottles on a high shelf so that she has to reach up all the time. Whoever cut the armholes in that blouse should be decorated. She does have perfect breasts, doesn't she? Never saw anything like it. Sure, on photographs, but that's all tricks. They photograph them upside down or attach nylon threads to their nipples and pull. Titania doesn't need any of that. De Gier thought so too. We changed places a few times so that we could check the other side. Perfect, Jurriaans, perfect."

Jurriaans pursed his lips. "Not quite. Asta looks better."

"Yes? How do you know?"

"How do you think? I told you she has a father complex and I'm the right type for her. I live a strict life, of course, the police is housed in glass; but pressure is pressure, and there are limits, Grijpstra. I could tell you stories."

"Any more apple pie?" asked Grijpstra.

"No."

"Go ahead then."

"Just one story. Some weeks ago. My wife was watching a program I didn't like and we had an argument. I'm a pleasant man, but there are songs I have heard before, they're all the same anyway. So I left the house. There are evenings you're ready for anything and you should stay home. I couldn't stay home for there were those songs. I went to café Beelema, it's the best place around here. I drank a bit but there was nobody there I wanted to be with, until Asta came in, she lives close by. She wears an old T-shirt and no bra when she is out of uniform. She's beautiful, Grijpstra, I tell you she's beautiful. I said hello and she came to sit at my table. I don't know what was the matter with the girl. She was stone cold sober, but she was all over me. Under the table mostly. Beelema is busy on Saturday nights and nobody noticed much but I wanted to get away. She wouldn't let me. She said she likes older men. I got so nervous I had more to drink. She got on my lap and got my hand under her shirt. Wow, Grijpstra, *wow!* I couldn't stand it and I left and she came with me. She has an old car and we went for a drive. She said she had a friend somewhere in the country, a rich divorced woman who gets lonely at times. Dame by the name of Magda. Good-looking, she said. Thirtyish or so. I didn't care, she was bending over and kissing me while she drove, didn't worry much about stoplights. I stopped worrying too. That car is the biggest mess you've ever seen, outside and inside. Half the stuff she owns must be in that car. She kept pushing it aside to reach for me. We got to some town, I can't remember which one, and it was a nice evening and there was a garden party. She stopped and we went inside, didn't know anybody there but it didn't seem to matter. Next thing she's stripping on a table, with a hundred men ogling her. Heavenly body, Grijpstra, moves right, too. She didn't have much on, so it didn't take long to take it off. Pity in a way. I thought I had lost her, but she came back to me and we were on our way again. She driving with her shirt off, breaking the speed limit. We were drinking in the car; if the state cops had stopped us, well, never mind."

Jurriaans, overcome by memory and emotion, pushed at a crumb.

"Yes?"

"Where was I?"

"They didn't get you."

"Who?"

"The state cops."

"No. We got to this Magda, or whatever her name was. The lady was asleep but seemed overjoyed to see us. Broke out the champagne. Served us in a tight black dress that was mostly transparent. I saw it all, even when she wasn't standing with the light behind her. She suggested a game on the Oriental rug in the living room."

"So?" Grijpstra was whispering too. He was leaning across the table. Jurriaans straightened up. "So nothing. The game started, but I don't know how it finished. I woke up eight hours later on that damned rug. Asta and Magda were having breakfast on the porch. I was sick; Asta took me to the bathroom and home afterward. I missed it. Maybe they did it together."

Grijpstra gaped, then frowned. "Yes?"

"That's it."

"No ending?"

"I just told you the ending. You don't think I would go out with that girl again, do you? My wife only talks to me since yesterday. That particular evening spent itself a week ago."

"Tell me another story with a better ending."

Jurriaans raised his voice to a normal level. "No. These are working hours. You tell me about your possible murder, and about what you did since your theory got away with you."

"De Gier and I visited Beelema's last night as part of our preliminary investigation as to the whereabouts of Rea Fortune, wife of the suspect we found in the canal."

"Ha."

"She's missing, isn't she?" Grijpstra asked.

Jurriaans shrugged. "She is not. She isn't home but what does that mean? There have been some lifestyle changes you know; married women sometimes leave their homes without asking permission."

"*While removing all household goods?*"

"So what? Maybe it makes it special but not very special. You still haven't got a case. What does de Gier think about your theory?"

Grijpstra gestured. "Not much, but de Gier is never impressed by subtle reasoning."

"He consents to going ahead?"

"Of course. He's a simple sergeant and I'm an adjutant. I'm telling him what to do. He wants to work, he can't sit still in his present predicament. That's why he wouldn't come in with me. He's outside somewhere, watching tobacconists' windows."

"A murder," Sergeant Jurriaans said. "All right. I'm a simple sergeant too and I can't see your view; you have an elevated position. But I would think that you need serious suspicions. I learned that when I still learned. Nobody can be designated as a suspect without serious suspicions that the person has committed a crime. You don't have any."

Grijpstra grunted. "No? If a lady disappears, suddenly and without leaving a note, *while all household goods are removed*—that's a nice clause, I'm keeping it for my report—then I have serious suspicions."

"No," Jurriaans said.

"No what?"

"It's not a nice clause. Household goods are pots and pans. You're talking about everything, including the thing that keeps the door from slamming against the wall and the chromium nut that prevents the toilet-paper bar from slipping."

"You know better words?"

"All contents of the house."

"Thanks."

"See? I'm quite willing to help you. I can help you too, for I know the suspect."

"Because you've got him in your dungeon here?" Grijpstra asked.

"No, I let him go this morning, with a sermon. But I've known him for years. I know the other actors on your stage too. I've been around for a while, adjutant, the environment is familiar to me and café Beelema is where I go when the universal guilt becomes too much to carry."

"You know," Grijpstra said slowly, "when I hear that a woman has gone completely, and that nobody, except one particular person, has the slightest idea where she may have gone to, if such knowledge comes to me and I notice that the husband of the lady behaves in a most unusual manner . . ."

"What do you mean, unusual?"

"What? You weren't there. Frits Fortune didn't just behave strangely, he *mis*behaved. De Gier was trying to save his life . . . I mean, really . . . and the man was actually trying to brain my sergeant with his crutch."

"Man kills wife," said Jurriaans, "it has happened before in my practice. The other day, for instance. Man goes to his work, to some horrible daily drudge, and just before he leaves the apartment, his wife thrusts a verbal barbed dagger in his neck, liberally dipped in poison. The man wheels around, grabs the shrew by the neck, presses and shakes . . ."

"Dead? No!"

"As dead as a doornail. Man drops the body, telephones us and sits in a chair until my constables rush to him. Ketchup and Karate, of course, there happened to be nobody else available. They were throwing up when they came back. Ketchup had to visit the shrink a few times; he kept breaking into tears. That's odd behavior in a police station, I won't put up with it."

"Were you ever tempted to throttle your wife?" Grijpstra asked.

"Sure. Why?"

"Just thought I'd ask."

A slight tenderness moved the lines on Jurriaans's face. "She isn't too bad, and she's beautiful too, much younger than I am. She's been looking for a last fling lately, but she doesn't dare to make the break. Makes things awkward at times."

Grijpstra coughed.

"I don't help much," Jurriaans continued. "I have similar thoughts myself. As you know."

"Right," Grijpstra said. "Didn't mean to pry really. So you let Frits Fortune go. Pity, in a way. After a night in the drunks' cell, suspects interrogate easily."

"True, weakens their defenses. He didn't look in great shape, a little crumpled and his mouth was all dry and caked with filth."

"De Gier says he was blowing peculiar bubbles, like gum bubbles; they flew away."

"Because of the medication. He explained it to me. That's why I let him go. Extraordinary and extenuating circumstances. The doctor prescribed tranquilizers and they don't mix with alcohol. Probably explains his aggression, but this morning he was peaceful. He said he felt fine, wouldn't even take his crutch, didn't limp when he left."

Grijpstra's jaw hardened. "Really? There we go again, the man behaves in a suspicious manner. First he limps and the next morning he runs like a deer."

"That's correct; I watched him leave, nothing the matter with him."

"You said you knew him before. What's he like? Has he ever been in trouble?"

Jurriaans removed a cigar from Grijpstra's breast pocket and lit it. "He owns a warehouse further along the Brewerscanal where he has his business, and he used to live in one of those concrete blocks in the south. He didn't like it there and bought some horizontal property in a remodeled mansion next to the Oberon. Spent a lot of money to get it right and just when he wanted to move in, a bum broke into the place. Fortune came to see me about it, but you know that there's little we can do. The city fathers are socialists and they feel that a bum who finds an empty living place has a right to grab it. Property is theft and all that. The law states that such an act is illegal, but the authorities who employ us feel differently. A ticklish situation and I do what the chief constable tells me to do. He tells me to do nothing, and besides I'm busy, for the police are corrupt and we spend all our time taking bribes from the drug dealers. Right?"

Grijpstra sucked his cigar.

"That's what the papers say we do," Jurriaans said, "and I've learned not to argue. So I tell Mr. Fortune that regretfully there is nothing I can do to get his bum out of his brand new apartment. But because I know the guy, as I've met him at Beelema's and we've bought each other drinks, I blow into his ear that Beelema is known to be God's other son."

"So Fortune goes to see Beelema."

"He does. Beelema ponders the matter and gives him the address of a certain little pub in a certain little alley where ex-prize fighters meet. But now the fine point of it all. Do you know who the bum was?"

"No."

"Zhaver, the barman at Beelema's. You must have met him last night."

"I met him; lovely looking gent."

"Gent is an understatement. Zhaver is nobility, a count filled with the bluest of bloods, born in a castle that now houses a state committee and its girlfriends."

"You're joking."

"I'm not joking. Xavier Michel d'Ablaing de Batagglia is a count. His father went under with something and didn't come up again, and Zhaver became a bum, a city bum, an Amsterdam city bum, the worst variety. I wouldn't mention what he hasn't done, for it wouldn't be worth the trouble mentioning. But we are the police and we understand that sort of thing."

"Let me see now," Grijpstra said, "pickpocket, drug pushing, prostitution and blackmail, breaking into cars, what else?"

"What else too. He also broke into Fortune's apartment. The turning point in his career, for Zhaver came to see me too, to complain about the ex-prize fighters who threatened to do nasty things to him."

"I can see it," Grijpstra said. "Big lumpy gents with soft voices, one on each side. 'Nice teeth you have, Zhaver,' one of them says and 'Pity they are loose,' says the other, 'we could knock them out in a jiffy, couldn't we, mate?' "

"Those very words. Zhaver drops to his knees, prays and begs for mercy, his tears are cleaning the pavement. 'Please dear bad men, leave my teeth alone.' The teeth stay where they are; Zhaver moves out of the apartment."

"And visits you," Grijpstra said.

"And I see that Zhaver hides some good in his character, but that it won't come out by itself, and that he needs help. I help him."

"Do you help people?"

"Sure, often."

"Why?"

Jurriaans stopped smiling.

"Because it is the task of the police and because I work for the police. I refer you to article 28 of the Police Law. *It is the duty of the police to assist those who are in need of help.* I try to adhere to the law, insofar as the authorities do not restrict me."

"Boy boy boy!" Grijpstra said.

"You want to tell me that I didn't dig that up from the law?"

"You're leaving out the middle piece. I don't recall the exact wording, but that article also tells us that we should maintain order actively. And by *help* the law means that we should help those who have suffered because of some crime perpetrated by another."

"So? Wasn't Zhaver the subject of a crime? Didn't those two gorillas threaten him? And where was our friend supposed to sleep that night? Wouldn't he be stealing or even robbing to obtain the wherewithal to take care of his normal needs?"

"Certainly, but you do go on," Grijpstra said. "You referred the

blighter to Beelema knowing that Beelema would refer him to the gorillas. I've never been accused of perspicacity but it does seem to me
that you are twisting your argumentation."

Jurriaans took a deep breath. Grijpstra jumped up. "All right, you're
nice. Go on. I'm sorry I interrupted."

"And you won't interrupt me again?"

"No."

"You may sit down, adjutant. Zhaver needed help. Also because he
is a nobleman. His grandfather burned native villages in the colonies
and his father made a mint out of creating work for the unemployed
during the depression. We have to respect good deeds performed in the
past, and a son from a noble family cannot sleep in the gutter."

Grijpstra touched Jurriaans's hand. "How right you are."

"I am. And I thought of how I could save Zhaver. Again I happened
to think of Beelema. I went to see him. I had to see him anyway, for a
lady visited me here at the station and stated that she had been bothered
by a gentleman late one evening in one of the alleys, and her description
of the suspect's features and mode of dress reminded me somewhat of
Beelema. Borry Beelema is a good man, of course, and God is his father, but he does tend to forget his manners when out for a stroll, and
has been known to upset civilians, both male and female, by making
certain propositions. The complaints are never too serious as he adheres
to certain limits, so we can usually send the complainants home
but . . ."

"Beelema, eh?"

"Beelema. And I was upset for another reason. He had given me a
bad haircut. Too long. And I felt annoyed for a third reason; another
lady had been complaining, bothering us, us the police, as if we don't
have enough to do, about Beelema's oversexed dog's forceful behavior.
All in all, I was in the proper mood to persuade Beelema . . ."

"The dog!" Grijpstra's hand whacked the table. "You should have
seen that dog with de Gier last night. All over the poor sergeant. 'Hello,
dog,' the sergeant says, and the animal jumps him and doesn't let go. As
if de Gier was the whore of Babylon. The beast went easy at first, but
he does know how to quicken his rhythm. Staring into de Gier's eyes too,
slime dribbling off his jaws, disgusting, absolutely disgusting!"

Jurriaans grinned. "That's what he does. They say owners and their
pets become alike after a while. True in this case, but Beelema isn't as
strong as Kiran and the dog's teeth are bigger. Did you manage to liberate your sergeant or did he get the full dose? About half a liter, I would
guess; that dog likes to finish what it starts."

"Is that his name? Kiran?"

"Named after a Russian prince, couldn't leave anybody alone either."

"We got him off the sergeant, but everybody had to help. Beelema kicked him out after that, for the dog kept watching the sergeant and slavering."

"So that's what I did," Jurriaans said and frowned impatiently. "Got myself worked up and saw Beelema. I knew he needed somebody to tend bar and Zhaver needed a job and a place to sleep. I'm always happy when the pieces fit. Two or three years ago that was. Zhaver still has the job and he gets on with Borry who has obtained more time to look after his hair salon. Fortune visits Beelema's café regularly; so does his wife, Rea. You want to know about Rea? Analysis of the victim, very important in murder cases it seems."

"Please."

Jurriaans shook his head. "Don't know much about her. I believe she used to be on the stage, long time ago, before she married. A quiet woman, arrogant, talks as if she has a mouthful of hot potatoes. Because she comes from The Hague, I believe they all talk like that out there, but they say that The Hague people are real too. I wouldn't know, I've never been there. You?"

"Once or twice. Attractive?"

"The Hague?" Jurriaans asked.

"No! Rea Fortune, an attractive lady?"

"I wouldn't say so. Not unattractive either. Wishy-washy. I preferred her poodle, a woolly rag with a silk collar, known as Babette. I'll say that for Babette, she knew how to deal with Kiran. One yap from Babette and Kiran was scratching at the door. Admirable behavior, even for an animated needlecraft kit."

"Love and friendship," Grijpstra said, "that's what we see when we want to see it. But in reality there's nothing but evil behind the rosy shades. Zhaver grateful to Beelema, what do *we* know? He probably hates the exploiter's guts and curses him daily from his cramped quarters above the bar."

Jurriaans nodded. "Possibly. He does have the smallest room ever, even smaller than Titania's who lives on the same floor."

"And Zhaver hates Frits Fortune because Frits threatened him through the gorillas," Grijpstra said. "And Zhaver has an affair with Rea Fortune, so has Beelema. Fortune and Titania carry on too."

"Who carries on now? Although you're right that Zhaver isn't gay, he only looks gay. I've given you facts, the rest you can imagine and try to prove. Jealousy is a fact of life, but it isn't always everywhere. I wouldn't follow you in any of your accusations. Fortune, for one, is a fine upstanding specimen. All he ever does is work and when he drinks he only has one or two. Last night was an exception. Personally, I like them all, except Rea. She can stay away for all I care and I won't miss Babette either."

Grijpstra got up. "People are no good, Jurriaans. I don't have to stress the point. If you haven't found out by now, you should leave the police. I suspect Fortune of having murdered his wife. Maybe he should have, but that's the court's business. I plan to pursue the man. If only I knew what he did with the corpse. So far, I move in empty space. I don't like that much. All that emptiness, it's eerie. Bah!" He brought out his wallet.

"On the house," Jurriaans said. "Come again. Don't forget to say goodbye to Asta when you leave."

De Gier waited in the street; he was talking to a small black boy. The boy smoked a cigarette.

"I knew it," the boy said, "but I forgot for a moment. Thank you." He dropped his cigarette stub and walked away.

Grijpstra touched de Gier's shoulder. "Weren't preaching, were you? What did that boy know? That smoking is bad for the health?"

"Wrong conclusion, adjutant. I just managed to pull that boy from under an oncoming truck and probably saved his life. Whereupon I said, 'Don't you know that you should look before you cross?' He answered politely. A nice little boy, even if he happens to be pitch black."

"You discriminate," Grijpstra said. "So did your colleague inside, but he was referring to people from The Hague."

"It's impossible to discriminate against people from The Hague," de Gier said when they walked to the car. "Are we going anywhere?"

"To Headquarters. I telephoned the commissaris. He's making a special trip to his office to hear us. He's got the weekend off."

"I don't want to go. The two of you will be smoking."

"You could smoke too."

"I can't, you know I can't." There was agony in the sergeant's voice and Grijpstra took pity.

"So why did you stop, Rinus?"

"For you."

"*Hondecoeter*."

"What?"

"Hondecoeter," Grijpstra said. "If you answer out of context, I can do the same. I say *Hondecoeter* and you can find out what I mean."

De Gier drove on silently. He parked in the courtyard of the gray forbidding police building.

When Grijpstra wanted to enter the elevator, de Gier restrained him. "Now what?"

"I know what you mean by Hondecoeter," de Gier said. "Melchior Hondecoeter was a not-too-well-known painter who liked to portray birds. You took me to see his pictures once, in the municipal museum. They all looked as if they had been painted in the evening. You thought of him last night, when you saw the exotic geese in the canal. I thought of him too. And you mentioned his name because you wanted to draw my attention to the essential beauty of . . ."

"Restrain yourself, sergeant."

"Never mind, don't withdraw at the crucial point. I know exactly what you meant, Grijpstra. You wanted to share your perception with me. Very sweet of you. Really, I'm serious. You're right too, we live in a wonderful world, but we busy ourselves and don't notice."

"I didn't mean anything of the kind."

"Subconsciously," de Gier said. "The true feeling that only comes out in some children and a few artists. I appreciate your true intentions."

"A brothel," Grijpstra said.

"Hey?"

"Apple pie, very tasty. But I would like to know who gets sent to the brothel when there is trouble. There's always trouble in brothels. If he sends Karate and Ketchup, they'll tear the joint apart and he won't get apple pie that way. But he does. So . . ."

De Gier gaped.

"So he sends himself," Grijpstra said triumphantly.

De Gier touched the breast pocket of his shirt. "I forgot to buy cigarettes. I always have cigarettes. Now why did I forget?"

"Sergeant Jurriaans is no good either," Grijpstra said.

3

"WHAT NONSENSE is this?" the commissaris asked. "It's Saturday. Since when do I work Saturdays? Since when do I work at all? Don't you read newspapers? It says so here, in last night's *Courier*. The *Courier* is writing a regular column on the police these days. It's gotten tired of playing up the drug bribes and now it's paying attention to officers above the rank of inspector. It says that high police officers are only concerned about publicity." He waved the newspaper. "In black and white, read all about it, colleagues. We're stupid too, that was in yesterday's issue. We can't remember the simplest details. So why are you wasting your time with me? Whatever you'll tell me will go into one ear, out of the other." The small old man stood in the dead center of the large Oriental rug that decorated his office. Irregularly shaped orange halberds seemed to grow out of the points of his polished shoes.

De Gier laughed.

"I'm glad I amuse you, sergeant."

De Gier stopped laughing. The commissaris's sharp little nose pointed at the sergeant's forehead.

Grijpstra cleared his throat. "He stopped smoking, sir. His behavior is somewhat irregular."

"Is that so? What's this story on the disappeared household goods? You fellows getting into simple theft? Didn't anybody see the van or truck the criminals used? Trucks don't look as identical as cars; they can be traced without too much footwork."

"No sir. We would like to acquaint you with the framework of our case and ask for your advice and permission to go ahead."

The commissaris almost smiled but snorted instead. "Advice? Permission? Really!" He slapped the newspaper. "Read this. I'm here to beautify the building, and as I don't even do that, I've become an appendix that can painlessly be removed. You two are doing the work. The journalist delved deeply and the quality of his research is admirable. He even took some photographs of my colleagues. You should see how dumb they look. No brains anywhere in their oversize skulls. No function either. Filling rooms on the upper stories of police stations."

"We haven't been able to trace the truck, sir, but we haven't done much so far. The only witnesses we interrogated were people who happened to get in our way. On Monday we can telephone the movers."

"Did you say 'murder' just now, Grijpstra?"

"Yes sir."

"Tell me the story again. You can say something too, sergeant. Do you *have* to stare at me like that?"

"Would you have a match, sir?"

"You stopped smoking, didn't you?"

"To chew, sir."

De Gier chewed. Grijpstra reported. The commissaris dropped his newspaper, picked up a watering can and busied himself with the plants on the windowsills.

"That's all, sir."

The commissaris replaced the can in his cupboard. "Yes, the facts, as described by you, don't tally much. But they fit exactly, of course, once you have the pattern and the other facts. Anything that happens consists of intertwining causes and effects and every single one of them can be traced. Some of your missing facts could be criminal, or they could be harmless. They might very well be harmless. Offhand I would say that Sergeant Jurriaans's approach is correct. Mr. Fortune is having a hard time without you two stepping on his toes. If I tell you to consider him as a suspect he loses some of his liberty, and he has already lost his wife and his possessions."

"And his dog," de Gier said, smiling inanely.

"Job," Grijpstra said.

"Beg pardon, adjutant?"

"I said 'Job,' sir. The old woman who shared the handcart with me called him that. Fortune is Job. Not on the dungheap but in an empty apartment. A comparison, sir."

The commissaris was following the edge of his carpet which contained a number of colored squares. He only stepped on the blue squares which were irregularly placed, so that he had to jump here and there.

"Job. Quite. But Job came out fine. He used the right attitude, passive positivity. The man's faith was impeccable. Hey! You can't be serious, Grijpstra. Are you identifying me with the almighty Father? Are you saying that I have the power to plague the unhappy man further because he'll gain the heavenly kingdom anyway?"

De Gier grabbed his throat and coughed harshly. He spat out a sliver of match wood.

"What now?" the commissaris asked, his voice rising. "Are you okay, sergeant?"

"It's the chewing, sir. Haven't got the habit yet. I shouldn't tear so much; just flattening the match is enough."

Grijpstra was halfway out of his chair. "Please start smoking again, Rinus."

"No."

"A fundamental change of a habitual pattern causes critical effects, adjutant. We'll have to harden ourselves. Job, eh? A most interesting comparison. God and the devil gambling and the suspect is the stake. Let's hope he is intelligent and knows he can't lose. Did I ever tell you about the time that I lost my car?"

De Gier suffered another attack of harsh rasping coughs and it took a few minutes before the commissaris could entertain his assistants. He had, a few years back, been issued a new Citroën of the expensive variety and was pleased with the classy vehicle. He thought of an errand, drove into town, and parked the car. When he returned the car was gone. His disappointment was mingled with fear. Not only that something wasn't there that should be there, not only that the missing item was the gleaming auto he had been so proud of owning a few minutes ago—the loss could be related to events of the past, he had attempted to twist his car key into thin air before—no, the emptiness confronting him at that fearful moment was more than he could have expected. The Citroën wasn't there and the ground on which it had rested wasn't there either. The commissaris, abruptly transformed from acting object into suffering subject, stared down into a gaping hole. The bright red bricks were replaced by a black aperture that sucked at his very existence.

"Then," the commissaris declared, "I doubted the benevolence of the creation and I haven't dared to stop doubting since. Another loss that added, in a way, to my liberation. To lose may be frightening, to know that you have nothing can be encouraging."

"And the car, sir?" Grijpstra asked.

"The car? It returned. There is always a superficial explanation. I forget what had happened exactly, maybe the sewer burst, or a gas pipe. They suddenly had to dig a hole and my car happened to be in the way. I telephoned, and a polite lady told me where they had left the Citroën. But who cares? I'm talking about something else. We don't have earthquakes here, which is a pity. To be reminded that even the ground isn't safe, that we are forever suspended in undefinable space; very heartening, adjutant. To assume that we rest on gravity tends to make us dullish. It must be fun to see the planet sway and bubble and crack up into holes, for then we know where we are, and, presumably, what's to become of us."

Grijpstra looked blank, de Gier tittered.

"Very well, adjutant. Pursue your investigation if it makes you happy, but do try to find some serious suspicions before you trip over yourself and others. And, by the way, has it occurred to you that Rea Fortune may just have left? To get away is legal, you know. It's a right guaranteed by our democratic constitution."

4

"LISTEN HERE," Frits Fortune said, "you're really not all that welcome. Why don't you leave?"

The suspect was lying down on his side on an air mattress under the open windows of the largest room in the apartment. De Gier sat opposite him, cross-legged. Grijpstra, unable to find a suitable spot, walked about, becoming visible every now and then through open doors. Fortune still wore the same clothes, a linen suit of good quality, crumpled and stained. He smelled mainly of damp rot but the stench mingled with the fragrances of soap, shampoo, and after-shave. Fortune smoked, spilling ash on the shiny parquet floor.

De Gier admired the glowing cigarette. The pack was within reach of his right hand. It still contained nineteen cigarettes. De Gier wanted to grab it, tear off the paper and silver foil, spread his hand around its entire contents, and light all cigarettes at the same time. He would then inhale the combined smoke into the extreme depths of his lungs. Afterward he would feel better.

"Won't you leave?" Fortune asked again.

"We'd rather not," de Gier said, "but if you insist, we'll have to, for to stay, after having been told to leave by the legal possessor of living space, constitutes a crime and would, in our case, being police officers and having identified ourselves as such, be punishable by a double maximum penalty, or six months in jail. But if we leave, we'll have to return with an order signed by a high-ranking officer. We have a car and it wouldn't take me longer than half an hour to obtain such an order.

With a warrant you'll have to admit us, and if you refuse, *you*'ll be punishable."

"But what do you want of me? Is it because of last night? I remember vaguely that I fought with policemen, including yourself. You were in the canal too, but I don't believe you were in uniform."

"I'm a detective."

"You are? I'm sorry if I hurt you with my crutch. Did I hurt you?"

"You only intended to. Any charges the constables may have come up with have been dropped. We aren't here to remind you of last night, we only want to know the whereabouts of your wife."

Fortune rested his head on his arm. "Gone."

"Gone where?"

"Doesn't a detective detect? I've tried, but being an amateur I failed. I could only think of telephoning everybody who knows Rea. I made a list; here it is. It's been in the water too, which hasn't improved my handwriting. I checked off all the names, which means that I telephoned those people. I borrowed the telephone book of my neighbor downstairs, Mrs. Cabbage-Tonto and . . ."

Grijpstra reappeared and held up his hand.

"Is that her name?" de Gier asked. "Cabbage-Tonto?"

"The lady who lives below this apartment?" Grijpstra asked.

"Yes."

"Cabbage-Tonto," Grijpstra said thoughtfully. "The right name. If I had to name her I couldn't do better."

"Of Italian origin and married to a dead Englishman," Fortune said.

"There's always a superficial explanation."

Fortune nodded at the adjutant's disappearing back.

"How . . ." De Gier extended a hand and pushed the pack of cigarettes away. "How is your leg, Mr. Fortune?"

Fortune laughed. He had good teeth. His face was good too. De Gier thought of a hero he had seen in an old war movie that ended well when the bad enemies surrendered and the good flag was raised.

"My leg? My leg is fine. There's nothing ever wrong with me, really, I only have weak nerves. Or I'm crazy, like most of us. Whenever I have a bad fright, a part of my body goes wrong, but only for a while. Some time ago I was nearly run down by a car and I fainted on the sidewalk. The specialists played snooker with me. I hit every hospital and clinic in town. The doctors agreed in the end that I might have a bad heart and that the next severe shock would knock me down again. But they were wrong, as you can see. When the constables hit me and lost me in the canal, I didn't even faint. The shock repaired the effect of a previous unpleasant experience, when I came home to find nothing." He sat up. "By the way, those little constables are dangerous, they should be restrained. The same goes for that fool sergeant Jurriaans who disciplined me this morning. And to think that I've known him for years and respect him in a way. Another Aunt Coba, appearances mean nothing, a black soul in respectable dress. Arrrgh!" He lay down again.

"Aunt Coba?"

"She has been living on the Emperorscanal for several centuries now. As a child I used to spend time in her house; with her and Uncle Henry. A dignified-looking couple but their valor is lopsided. Only Uncle Henry will go to heaven."

"You stayed with them? You're not Amsterdam born?"

"Of course I am, but my parents lived on the other side of the river and my mother was sickly. I would be sent to Aunt Coba. Aunt Coba would interfere with my mind. Would you like to have coffee?"

They went to the kitchen, finding Grijpstra observing an empty shelf. On the stone sink stood a hot plate and a box filled with groceries.

Fortune talked while he made the coffee. "Never thought Rea could be that thorough. She even took the toilet paper, very bothersome if you notice its absence too late. Had to use the paper in my pocket diary, too thin and too slippery.

"Not that the experience isn't two-sided. Without obstructions one can see far. When the dizziness wore off I went shopping. It happened to be Thursday evening and the stores were open. I could even buy a mattress and lie down and think it out. I used to think in a circle, about the business, about money. More of this to get that, more of that to get this."

"You publish books, we were told."

"I certainly do, or did maybe. A good selection, if I say so myself, nothing but what the public wants. Books on how to grow tomatoes in water, and what the gurus say about coitus and meditation, illustrated. Today's subject today, for those who want to live free in the security of togetherness. The cozy seekers, Holland's hope."

De Gier looked for a match. Grijpstra frowned.

"Coitus?" Grijpstra asked. "Meditation? Separate or simultaneous?" He sipped his coffee, didn't like the taste, and continued to frown, studying miniature swells in his plastic cup.

"Both, the book is in two parts, but I don't know too much about the quality of what I sell. A publisher believes in sales and calculates in profit. There's no choice. Expenses increase and profit diminishes. Only more of this gives more of that, as I explained just now."

Grijpstra's frown dissolved.

Fortune smiled. "The endless circle, but not quite, as I found out on the mattress in the other room. To think that I quarreled with Rea because I refused to sell the circle. To consider that someone, a colleague who lives on the next canal, would buy my garbage on behalf of his company—a hundred times the size of mine, he doesn't own it but he's a director—would offer to free me, and I actually refused." He shook his head.

"At the right price?"

"A little more."

"Your wife wanted you to sell?"

"She did and I wouldn't agree. My colleague invited me to dinner at Beelema's, Rea was asked to come too. Borry Beelema likes to serve meals at request. He serves himself, and Zhaver and Titania dress up as cooks. Beelema believes in perfection. Caviar and champagne. Hyme, my colleague, must have discussed every detail of the party. It was meant as a trap, but I hadn't learned yet how to be caught in order to become free. FREE, damn it! They may not have known how to approach me. I'm a quiet man, or used to be. I worked, and that was all. Hyme sidled up along conventional lines and wined and dined me to soften up my resistance."

"The price?" asked Grijpstra.

Fortune told him.

Grijpstra whistled. "You could retire."

"And I didn't want to."

They had left the kitchen and stood alongside each other, gazing out of the windows. Below them a sea of irregular roof tops was contained by a row of warehouses. A thrush, perched on the head of a gargoyle, initiated a fairly complicated statement. The silver Mercedes with the German number plate that de Gier had seen before slithered to a stop before the striped awning of the Hotel Oberon and the same fat German slammed his car door and waddled across the street.

"You refused outright?"

"No, I asked for time to consider the offer. I was alone, under attack by a wicked monstrosity, horribly eager to rob me of my safe routine, or so I thought. I pretended to laugh a lot, became angry, and went home."

"With your wife."

"Yes, then we fought."

"Did you hit her?" Grijpstra asked pleasantly.

"No. I repeated myself. We didn't sleep that night. She wanted to buy a car, a country house, furnish it in style. She said I could read books. I told her that I manufactured books."

"You don't read?"

"I do, but not too often. I told her I was being useful to society. She tore me to pieces. She proved I wasn't, that the other company could publish my trash better than I."

"Was she right?"

"Of course."

Fortune thought.

"You would sell now?" Grijpstra asked.

Fortune grinned. "Yes, I will. I've been looking at my products again. Goat-wool socks, hallucinating mushrooms, UFO wisdom, Mr. Hyme can have it."

"UFOs may exist."

"Sure, but what do my authors know? They know how to spread ignorance on two hundred pages. They fantasize or lie outright and connect nonsense with fabrication."

The thrush sang on.

"Rea was right, but for the wrong reasons," Fortune said. "And she didn't care. I care now, and I disagree with her motivation. All she wanted was wealth, happiness, some short-range goal like that. She's a silly woman really."

"You won't take her back?"

"No."

"Divorce?"

"Yes."

"What will the neighbors say?" Grijpstra asked solemnly.

Fortune lit another cigarette and puffed placidly.

"Mrs. Cabbage-Tonto? She's the only neighbor I know and she never liked Rea. Sure I'll divorce Rea, but she'll have to show up or write to me through her lawyer. I'll return her money to her; she brought a fair sum into the marriage. I invested it in the business. I'll pay her back with profits."

"You're angry with her?"

Fortune dropped down on the mattress.

"No."

"And what do you plan to do?"

Fortune yawned. "Nothing much. Think more out of the circle, right here. This is a good place to think. Go on a trip afterward, find a quiet place, build my own cabin. I can't do that yet, but somebody may teach me."

"Will you have a car?"

"I'll have to learn to drive again. I could when I was in the army, that's twenty years ago. I don't have a license."

"Your wife can't drive either?"

"No."

De Gier swirled his coffee. "The dog, do you think it will come back again?"

"It did come back and I can't understand where it went. I'm sure I locked the door. It's Saturday today, yesterday I was in the canal, Rea left Thursday. I come home and it's all gone. I fall, Mrs. Cabbage takes me to the doctor. I do some shopping. Babette is at the door when I come back, pleased to see me, yapping, affectionate. I go in with the dog. On Friday I leave the dog in the house. It isn't there when I come home."

"The dog could only leave through the door?"

"Door, communal staircase, front door, there's no other way."

De Gier pointed at a wall built out of rough bricks. "Solid wall."

"Yes, the building used to be a warehouse, everything is solid. You see the holes in that wall? I drilled them and drove in cast-iron bars to support my book shelves. She even removed the bars."

"Do you miss your books?"

"Not really. A few perhaps but they can be replaced. Books become stuffing after a while, something to collect; another circle."

"What subjects did you read yourself?"

"Some novels, travel, horror."

"Any particular horror?"

"Poe."

"Poe," Grijpstra said helpfully. "I've heard of him. What's he like?"

De Gier pressed his hand against the wall. "I'll tell you a Poe story. There was a couple. They weren't happy. They lived in the country on an estate. It cost them all they had to keep the estate going. The estate wasn't profitable and the lady couldn't buy what she wanted. She would screech at her husband and one evening he picked up the poker and brained her."

"That was bad," Grijpstra said.

"Not too bad. It solved the squire's problem. But the corpse was still there, he had to remove that as well. Wait, I almost forgot, they also had a cat. The cat was around. Okay. The gentleman was a handy fellow and he got some tools and made a hole in the wall. A big hole, big enough to hold the corpse. He put the corpse in the hole and closed it up again."

"I've never done any masonry," Fortune said.

"But the squire had, you see. He was handy, as I said just now. He did an excellent job. Another thing about this gentleman, he had a sense of humor. He waited a couple of days, a week maybe, and invited the local constable for a glass of wine. Wait, I forgot that cat again. The cat disappeared. The squire looked for the cat but it had gone. Right. The constable comes and gets his wine and the squire pours himself some, too, and tells jokes. After every joke he laughs, loudly, *haha, hoho,* and knocks on the wall with the poker. Harder and harder." De Gier hit the brick wall with his flat hand. "Like this. The squire kept on laughing, *haha, hoho.*" De Gier shouted. A reaction on the roof became audible. There were screeches and cackles, a rustling and a flapping.

"Sea gulls," Grijpstra said.

"And crows," Fortune added. "There are always crows on the roof, but they are noisier now than usual."

"Let's have a look."

Fortune showed de Gier a trap door and the sergeant stepped into Grijpstra's hand and hoisted himself nimbly through the hole.

"How does that story finish?" Grijpstra asked Fortune. "Or don't you know how it goes?"

"Yes, I know the tale well. When the squire banged the wall with his poker, something inside the wall screeched back at him. An earsplitting screech, unnerving him and the constable. The constable had the wall opened and found the lady's corpse standing up. On her disheveled head sat the cat, the cat that your colleague kept forgetting. The cat was alive, and it screeched."

De Gier's head popped back. "Come up here, I found something."

"A corpse?" Grijpstra asked.

The corpse was on the other side of the roof, partly hidden by a chimney. It had neither ears nor eyes and its skin was badly torn, but it was still recognizable as the remains of a small poodle. Around its neck were the remnants of a red silk collar.

"Babette," whispered Fortune. "Poor little thing. Whatever happened to you?"

Grijpstra sat on his haunches and studied the dog's head. "Got a bit of a blow, the skull is broken. The birds didn't do that, they've only worked on the softer parts of the body."

De Gier walked away until he reached the roof's edge. He looked down and staggered backward.

"I'm nauseous," he said softly, "and dizzy." He held his stomach. "If I don't absorb some nicotine into my blood quickly, I'll lose control. I'll be mumbling and I'll never stop. I'll be gesticulating too. I'll be mentally ill. Maybe they'll let me do something in therapy. I could sweep the path, somewhere in the rear of the asylum, in the cemetery, between the gravestones of the medieval disturbed. Nobody'll come to look for me."

"Talking to me?" Grijpstra asked.

"Yes. I'm telling you that I'm no good as a policeman."

"You never were," Grijpstra said, "or I wouldn't have asked for your transfer to the murder brigade ten years ago. Look at Fortune."

Frits Fortune had cradled Babette's head in his hands and peered into its empty sockets. His pursed lips were whispering endearments. He was also crying.

5

"Now what kind of a man is Frits Fortune?" Grijpstra asked. "If we don't answer that question, we don't answer anything. Is he a comedian? Is he a nice guy? Is he a murderer? He could be a nice guy but I think that he is a murderer."

Grijpstra leaned on the railing of the bridge. De Gier leaned next to him. A municipal barge, its lone skipper using the helm as a support for his back, approached slowly through the Brewerscanal. The skipper's legs were spread, he had his hands in his pockets, and he gazed straight ahead. The bent bodies of the detectives underwent a slight tension. It could just be possible that the barge would turn and sail under the bridge into the Emperorscanal. If it did, it would hit the elm tree straddling the water. The resulting accident would be spectacular and cause considerable damage to houseboats. There would be bodies in the water and appreciable commotion. The all-pervading silence of a late Saturday afternoon in the inner city, underlined by the monotonous growl of the barge, would be ripped into a thousand shreds.

But the barge didn't turn and the detectives returned to their quiet questioning. The red-beaked geese appeared majestically. The hairy well-dressed cyclist turned up; his pedal still clanged against the chain guard. The shiny Mercedes parked in front of Hotel Oberon and the fat German got out. The door of Café Beelema opened and closed. Kiran, the Great Dane, romped about the quayside, slowed down and left drops on trees and lampposts.

"Stupid dog," de Gier said, "I hope he doesn't see me."

Kiran saw him and barked cheerfully.

"What kind of a man is Frits Fortune?" de Gier asked. "And what kind of question do we have here? Is it the right question? What sort of a man are you? What sort of a man am I? Sometimes I've been known to be like this, at other times, however, I'm more like that."

"This and that are limited ideas," Grijpstra said. "They're the extreme limits that hold the habitual behavior of a suspect. If he did something before, we know that he may do it again. If he was a comedian yesterday, chances are he'll be a comedian today."

"I used to smoke but I don't smoke anymore. What does that make me? A nonsmoker who smoked? A former smoker turned the other way? A nonsmoking former smoker who will smoke again? Finished once, done forever? Once started, on forever?"

"You are a nicotineur," Grijpstra said, "and you have a weak character. But as you aren't a suspect, I don't care what sort of a man you are."

"No?" de Gier asked. He raised his voice. The old man, feeding the geese on the board attached to his houseboat, looked up. "Shshsh!"

"What sort of a man are you?" shouted de Gier.

The old man crumbled his last piece of bread.

"What sort of a man am I?" he asked in a clear high voice. "I'm a feeder of red-beaked geese. I am what I do and I do what I am." He sprinkled the crumbs like a stingy farmer sowing his field, nodded, and shuffled back into his boat.

Grijpstra laughed. "He's a shuffler-into-boats. And I'm a haver-of-hunger."

Kiran trotted on to the bridge.

"And so is the dog. Care to join us in a visit to a sandwich shop? Or don't you dare?"

Kiran stood against the door, imploring de Gier. The sergeant opened the door. Kiran fell/jumped inside. The dog placed his front paws on a stool and slobbered two meatrolls off the plate of a client. Then he ate another meatroll out of the hand of another client. The clients objected and the dog growled. He stopped growling and embraced a young woman who entered the shop.

The detectives found a booth in the rear. Protected but invisible behind its high partitioning, Grijpstra shouted for service. He shouted twice again before a square woman with a granite face growing from a starched dazzling white coat inquired after the purpose of his powerful exclamations.

"A roll with warm meat, another with chopped steak, another with ox sausage, and another with *two* meatrolls."

"A hundred," the woman said. "Pay now."

"*What?*"

"You let the dog in. The dog stole twenty guilders' worth and is now outside gobbling a liver worth eighty that I had to give him so that he would leave."

"Are you out of your mind?"

"Out," the woman said.

They walked along for some distance, then they walked back.

"If only we could find somebody who knows Fortune well," Grijpstra said. "I could ask Borry Beelema, and the man who tends bar in his nighties, and Titania, but I believe, with the certainty provided by almost total probability, that they are all interchangeable parts of the same thing and not on my side. I need somebody on the outside, which is my side, outside the lost lady and the dead dog but still within the boundaries of the suspect, if such a person existed."

"A relative?" asked de Gier.

They faced the display window of the sandwich shop. Kiran had returned to his opening position and implored the detectives over his shoulder.

"Again," Grijpstra said. "Shall I . . . ?"

"No, he'll be stealing and raping," de Gier said. "He's done it already, we shouldn't allow him to step into the same river twice."

Grijpstra stopped. "I can find him a similar river. A relative you say. An aunt or an uncle?"

"Both. Aunt Coba and Uncle Henry."

"True. I forgot. I'm getting old. Those people live on the Emperorscanal. This is the Emperorscanal. We need a number. You know what, I think I'll open the door for that dog. Like this he looks pitiful. This is not a normal attitude for a dog, he'll get cramps in his paws. Maybe he won't be so hungry for he ate that liver. The girl has gone so there's nothing to rape. He might communicate with the woman who wasn't polite to us and with the big men sitting at the counter. What do you think?"

"The decision is yours. There's a public telephone over there. I'll find Uncle Henry's house number. Let's hope he's a paternal uncle and that his name is Fortune too." De Gier left.

Grijpstra opened the door. Kiran barked and fell/jumped inside. Grijpstra walked on. A slowly passing coach, filled with Japanese tourists being instructed through loudspeakers, drowned a disharmony of sounds erupting from within the restaurant.

6

AUNT COBA smoked a cigarette, Uncle Henry smoked a pipe, Grijpstra smoked a small cigar, and de Gier didn't smoke. The four protagonists sat on armchairs, upholstered with green velvet, on the back porch of a mansion built and kept in an exuberance that would surely have been liberating if Calvinism and the urge to make both spiritual and material profit hadn't imposed certain limits. The open garden doors offered a view of rhododendron bushes gracefully curving around a sea of lowly flowers. A choir of invisible songbirds engaged in a fairly steady melody embellished with trills and twitters. Aunt Coba and Uncle Henry were stately miniatures, and their faces were nicely chiseled by age and determination. They looked alike, under silvery hair cut and combed in identical fashion, and wore about the same clothes. Antique unisex, the sergeant thought, observing and admiring their narrow trousers and flowing jackets of old shiny velours.

Uncle Henry talked around the stem of his pipe.

"Nephew Frits did something wrong?"

"No, Mr. Fortune, not that we know of. But we're looking for his wife, who seems to have disappeared. All household goods, I beg your pardon, the contents of the house, disappeared as well. So did the dog, we retrieved the dog; it was dead, however."

"Still had its head?" Aunt Coba asked.

Grijpstra stared.

Aunt Coba repeated her question loudly, articulating the syllables.

"Yes ma'm. But somebody knocked it on the head. The skull broke. The dog was on the roof."

Aunt Coba nodded happily.

"Never was much good."

"The dog?"

"Nephew Frits. If you *knew* what experiences we had with him! But how could you know?"

Uncle Henry coughed painfully. Aunt Coba's beady eyes pierced her husband's forehead. He coughed again and patted his chest.

"You want a glass of water?"

"No. Isn't it coffee time yet?"

"Not for a long while. Why don't you go and write some checks? You always write checks on Saturdays. I'll take care of these gentlemen."

Uncle Henry didn't move. Aunt Coba's steady gaze increased in strength. He got up, excused himself and left the room.

Aunt Coba sighed. She restrained her hands that were about to rub each other.

"So Rea has gone, has she? Doesn't surprise me, no, not at all. What isn't needed anymore is put away. Such a nice woman too, serving, servile even. And married to Frits!" She sighed again, sadly this time, also a little longer and deeper. "Ah well."

"Yes ma'm."

"But that's the way it had to go. His father was a Fortune and his mother was crazy too. Whenever she got too crazy, the child came here. *Little Frits is going to spend some time with Coba.* She always said that with such conviction. I was never asked whether I wanted to put up with that child, the child just came."

Empathy flooded Grijpstra's face.

"And what would little Frits do, when he stayed with you, ma'm?"

"What wouldn't he do?"

"What wouldn't your nephew do, ma'm?"

"He would wet the bedclothes. He wouldn't eat cauliflower, with or without white sauce, the sauce didn't matter to him. He would use half a roll of toilet paper at a time. If that garden fence was locked, it always was locked, and if he wanted to get his pushbike into the garden, he would break the lock, again and again. He picked his nose, at mealtimes preferably. He didn't do well at school. He stole money."

"Your money, ma'm?"

"No. He stole at home. But he wasn't home much, he was mostly here."

Aunt Coba gazed at the garden. De Gier kicked Grijpstra's ankle, too
hard, because his leg jumped out of control. Grijpstra began to get up,
but de Gier pushed him back. De Gier's lips formed the word 'home.'

"What else did he do at home, ma'm?"

"He read. He wasn't allowed to read, the doctor said he shouldn't.
He had to play. He was given a box of toy bricks, an electric train, and
a teddy bear. He refused to play, although he would pretend to play. He
attached strings to the bricks and kicked the string while he read, and
meanwhile the train moved around and around. They gave him another
train with a clockwork he would have to wind now and then, but he
worked out a defense. Do you know what he did with that train?"

"What did he do, ma'm?"

"My sister-in-law came into the room one evening, and there were no
lights in the room. The curtains were drawn. Frits had inserted match-
heads into the locomotive and the little carts and wagons, and lit them.
A big flame rushed around the carpet. It frightened his mother and she
tripped over the rail. Half the house burned down."

"Is that it, ma'm?"

Aunt Coba shrank in her armchair. Her eyes glistened behind her
gleaming glasses.

"You know what he did with his teddy bear?"

"No ma'm."

"The teddy bear was called Brom. It was a big bear, of good quality
and expensive. One day Brom disappeared. Frits's parents couldn't understand what had happened to it, and they didn't trust Frits's peculiar
answers to their straightforward questions. Do you know where Brom
was found?"

"No ma'm."

"Buried in the garden in a shallow grave. And do you know what
else Frits had done?"

"No ma'm."

"He had beheaded Brom."

7

GRIJPSTRA DANCED. Two little steps ahead, a little step to the right, then to the left, to the rear, and repeat. He sang sidewards and backwards.

"*Weedeeho. Weedeeha.*"

"Don't do that," de Gier said, "or do you want me to dance too? I will if you insist, although I see nothing but misery. What *is* the matter with you?"

"Good luck comes to those who keep on trying," Grijpstra said, performing a fresh set of steps with care, "and whoever insists will win in the end. I've been trying for a long time. So here it comes. A chance encounter, you will say, providing incidental information. In a way you are right, but I see more. Bull's eye I see, thanking fate meanwhile, and you too. If you hadn't stopped last night . . . I don't want to think about what would have happened then. But you stopped the car, dear friend, and activated yourself and handed me the murderer, solemnly in your inimitable way. You raised him from the water for me to receive and appreciate your gift, decorated with weeds. 'There you are,' you said, and 'thank you kindly,' I replied. And you made your gesture so *naturally.*"

"Are you done?"

"*Weedeeho. Weedeeha.*"

A patrol car rode by with a tall male constable at the wheel and a young female, impeccably uniformed, most of her long dark blonde hair tucked away under a small round cap, in the observer's seat. She observed Grijpstra's dance and waved. De Gier waved back.

"Nice girl," de Gier said, "but very young for a constable. I think she knows you."

Grijpstra no longer sang and lowered his foot. He stood.

"Her name is Asta. She's not so nice. She seduces older men. Men like you, sergeant. From forty years old upward. She would even seduce me. Sergeant Jurriaans told me about her. He managed to escape her clutches, but she wounded him, I think."

"Ah."

"Ah what?"

"Interesting," de Gier said.

Grijpstra's heavy forefinger pressed against the sergeant's chest.

"For you perhaps, I will introduce you. If you won't smoke, you can still have Asta. She would be a minimal risk to you, and you would keep her away from others."

De Gier's large brown eyes dreamed away.

"Sparkly eyes," he whispered, "dominating an intellectual face, alive with sensual unfulfilled longing. A good mouth with the fullness of the lower lip restricted in the tight curve of the upper edge." He shrugged. "Too young."

Grijpstra's finger dropped away.

"Let me tell you what Jurriaans had to say about her."

De Gier listened, then nodded.

"Yes, I see. Drunken driving, indecent exposure, adultery, lesbian cavorting. Not all of it is punishable, but he should watch it all the same, and he shouldn't tell you. The relationship still continues?"

"No," Grijpstra said. "She's all yours." The adjutant's voice trailed away. His feet shuffled.

"Please," de Gier said. "Not again." He pointed at a display window. "Look, adjutant, final sale. Just the store for you, elegant and expensive. See that cap? For ten guilders? A gift. But maybe your head is too fat, you think your head is too fat for that classy cap?"

Grijpstra danced into the store. He tried the cap. The fit was a little tight. He left a ten-guilder note near the register and danced out of the store.

"*Weedeeho. Weedeeha.*"

"Please, Grijpstra, that'll be enough. Let's sit on that nice tree over there. You can't dance on it, for you'll fall into the canal. Let's go look at the geese. A moment of peace and quiet, Grijpstra."

De Gier guided the adjutant to the fallen tree. Grijpstra balanced carefully on the fairly wide trunk. De Gier followed. They sat down.

"What happened is clear," Grijpstra said.

"What happened?"

"You described it yourself when we visited the suspect. Frits and Rea are sitting down together, man and wife. Togetherness in the living room, without harmony. A conflict situation about to change into turmoil. Rea Fortune is a woman of fantasy. She pictures herself in a chauffeured Mercedes automatic, silver sheen finish."

De Gier looked up. "The driver is German."

"If you like."

"Fat? Bald? Rolls of bacon for a neck?"

"Whatever your choice, a chauffeur, may I continue?"

"Yes."

"Rea Fortune, she wants to go out. She wants to eat snails in a wine sauce, brought by waiters with Byzantine profiles. A Gypsy plays the violin, right into her ear. High notes, glassy, harp in the background. Fortune said so himself. A woman of fantasy, unfulfilled."

"He gave no details."

"*I* give you details, so that you can see how it happened. Unfulfilled fantasy leads to frustration, frustration leads to tension, tension translates itself into deeds. *Mis*deeds. She attacks the suspect, sucks the blood from under his fingernails, chips at the last shred of his discipline. I understand both sides. I'll write some of this into my report. A horrifying circle; woman irritates man, man hides in his habits, he works even harder, reads even more, talks even less, irritates her even more. They'll never go on holidays, they'll never have any fun. She becomes more aggressive. Tension increases, becomes unbearable. The woman shrieks her insults. The poodle yaps. The man's nerves snap. *Bam!* Sometime earlier this week. The poodle escapes into the street, while Fortune gets rid of the household goods, beg pardon, the contents of the house, in a hired van, with the help of a couple of illegal migrants, Pakistanis maybe, Turks maybe. The poodle returns. Fortune is pleased; he takes the animal into the house, tries to enjoy its company, but the dog is whining, it looks for Rea. Again, *bam!* Babette gets chucked onto the roof and becomes dinner for the birds. Bear Brom got buried. Habitual behavioral patterns repeat themselves. But where did Rea go? Oh *no!*"

Grijpstra groaned. He looked about him but didn't seem to recognize the sergeant or the familiar surroundings.

"Now what?"

"But of course I know where she went. How stupid of me. Of you too. We could have known it all along. Amsterdam is a city of holes, fenced-in holes. They're always tearing at the street bricks, taking them out, stacking them, digging, fencing, taking the fences down, filling the holes. Aren't they?"

"He buried her in the street?"

"Where else? He didn't have a car and he couldn't give her to the Pakistanis or the Turks. Had to keep her in the house. He looked out of the window and saw the street workers had been at it again. Holes everywhere. He picked up the corpse, nipped outside, buried her, removed the fence. You think the street workers remember where their holes were? Never. They just come in the morning and dig and cover up, whatever comes first. But I've got to get that corpse, Rinus, no corpse, no case. They'll have to tear it all up again."

"You do carry on."

"Hmm?"

"You chatter and prattle. If the commissaris could hear you, he'd water your neck with his little plastic can."

"The commissaris would listen politely," Grijpstra said. "Politely and approvingly."

"Would he now? Think of the base your construction rests on. You're building a tottering tower on the unconfirmed and hearsay gossip that Frits Fortune, in the remote past, as a toddler, whopped a teddy bear. He is, you state, a bear-whopper. I was a smoker. I no longer am. If somebody asks me, 'Do you smoke?' I say, 'No, I do not,' and I speak the truth. If somebody asks Fortune if he is in the habit of whopping bears, he will reply, 'No, I do not whop bears,' and that can be the truth too. It doesn't have to be true, but it could be true."

"*You* carry on," Grijpstra said. "You're suffering withdrawal effects. You're a bit out of your head. Not that it matters. I will do this job alone. Stay with me so you'll be safe. I'll provide distraction by keeping you busy."

"There's Kiran."

The dog stood on the quayside and chewed on a cap.

"Haha," Grijpstra said, "he got hold of somebody's cap. Probably took it from one of the fellows in the sandwich shop. Look at that, he's tearing off the rim."

"That's your cap."

Grijpstra felt his head.

"Where's my cap?"

"Probably fell off when you danced onto the tree. Kiran found it. He's got strong teeth, hasn't he?"

"Miserable hound! Hellish mongrel! Is nothing holy in the city of Sodom? Get away, Rinus, I've got to get by you."

De Gier got up. He tried to turn around Grijpstra's bulk. Grijpstra held on to him.

"What goes on there?" two harsh voices inquired. "Get off that tree, you two."

"Sorry, adjutant," Karate said. "Ketchup thought you were fighting. I thought you were fighting too. You weren't fighting, were you?"

"No. There goes Kiran, Rinus. Escaping into café Beelema. I'm going there too, to ask for immediate compensation. Coming with me?"

"Adjutant," asked Karate, "are we correct in assuming that you left number 33, Emperorscanal, just now?"

"You are," Grijpstra said.

"Were you visiting Mr. and Mrs. Fortune?"

"I was."

"And the man who happened to fall into the canal last night, by accident so to speak, wasn't his name Fortune too?"

"It was."

"Curious," Karate said. "It's a small world. A while ago, maybe a year ago, Ketchup and I also visited the Fortunes."

"Pleasant people," Grijpstra said, "and reliable too. They supplied me with welcome information. And now I will go to café Beelema. I want you to arrest that dog. That dog robbed me of my cap and subsequently destroyed it."

"Did you say reliable, adjutant? Did you say that Mr. and Mrs. Fortune supplied you with reliable information?"

"Yes."

"That couple is not reliable, adjutant. That couple is mad."

"Why do you think so, constable?" de Gier asked. "Please explain your reasoning to the adjutant. Don't bother to explain it to me because I'm mad too. But the adjutant's mind is in perfect order and he has to know everything. Especially as he is now working on his own."

8

"WE VISITED the address officially," Karate said, "following orders as we always do. It was about a year ago; I can check the exact date if you like. We were sent by Headquarters, because of a fight, of sorts. It could have been anything, an exchange of words or missiles, but we didn't know what to make of it because of the address, which is good. Ketchup thought there might be a sex club, there are some around here. We'd been to one before; that was because of a fight too. We found naked ladies up to their ankles in broken glassware. So were some of the clients, and one had lost his eye. I found it for him and he lost it again. Amusing in a way, for the time being, that is. Later it turns to work when you have to write it down. We found a variety at that club, and all of it was bad. There was gambling, and liquor without a license, a bit of junk, some weapons, and a minor. All of it to be reported on, but that would be later, as I said. There was a gentleman there who got away without his clothes in an Alfa Romeo. Nervous he was and he drove into the canal; not at once, for the car stuck on the railing. We watched it and thought maybe it wouldn't go all the way, but it did in the end, and the fire brigade got it out. Very nice."

"The damage," Ketchup said. "Unbelievable indeed. Another client in a Porsche, in a bit of a hurry too and didn't look where he was going. Hit a street full of cars on both sides and all the owners pouring out of their houses. You shouldn't laugh and I didn't. It cracked my jaw, it hurt for days. Endless damage!"

"Right," Grijpstra said. "Well, we'll mosey along."

"Wait, adjutant, please, don't interrupt, Ketchup. As I said, we stood on the steps of thirty-three and the old gent opens up and acts all surprised and says, 'Good evening, constable, anything wrong or are you coming to visit the servant?' and I say, 'No sir, we came to ask *you* what is wrong because we hear there is a fight,' and he says, 'No, you must have been given the wrong number, there are some Negroes further along who play the trumpet,' and he wants to close the door, but his wife comes and holds it and tells us that she was expecting us and to please come in."

"So it gets difficult," Ketchup said. "She is pulling and he is pushing. There was a fight but they don't manhandle each other, they manhandle us. What to do? How to write it down? Do conflicting elements constitute a prosecutable misdemeanor or will it be the easy way out again? Are the officers harassed?"

"Just a moment, Ketchup. As I was saying, adjutant, the lady had phoned but it took half an hour before we found out what for. They served us coffee and a spot of cognac, they threw in cigars, although he said she shouldn't. We are busy, he said, and mentioned the trumpeting Negroes again. Then, in the end, she told us what it was. Would we arrest her husband and take him with us, for she was complaining about being threatened with appreciable physical injury. By him."

"Right," Ketchup said, "and that's unlawful. They were married, but even so. Rape is okay but they didn't do that so much anymore. They got to threatening, he threatening her. We were supposed to take action. I spent a while in the bathroom and checked the situation in my notes; I carry notes for special cases. It was right there, clear enough."

"A moment, Ketchup. See what happened, adjutant? He had threatened her and he had done it every night for years. The judge would like that, for it makes it worse. He'd ask for coffee and she wouldn't want to make it and he'd say, 'Right now, dear, away with you, to the kitchen, or I'll knock you down. I'll wring your neck. I'll batter you to death. Get up, dear, I'll count to three.' And he was serious, she said, he'd pull faces, and count and push himself out of his chair and she'd have to rush to the kitchen or he would do all that. But she wouldn't let him do that anymore because of equal rights, and so she phoned Headquarters and here we were."

"What?" Grijpstra asked.

"Yes, adjutant. Thought you might want to know. Not quite what one would expect, although she was right in a way. Knew the correct terms too. If you don't do it, you aren't *in the legal exercise of your service,* she said. I wonder where she found the term, maybe she was hiding in the classroom when I went to police school. And that's what we would be, not in the legal exercise of our service, if we ignored her complaint."

"Go on, constable," de Gier said.

"We arranged matters in the end, sergeant. There was no way we could have arrested old Mr. Fortune. I don't believe you know our Sergeant Jurriaans. If we had brought that old bird in, he would have pulled our ears and there'd be *ee-ee* again. We couldn't refuse either, for she was out for his blood and would have written to Headquarters. The cognac saved us, and another two hours of patient listening. Disgraceful in a way, and Ketchup got drunk."

"And yourself?"

"Just a little," Ketchup said. "I drove him home. Karate was tired and he couldn't remember where he lived."

De Gier looked at Grijpstra.

"Would you care to go?"

Karate and Ketchup saluted. Grijpstra watched the patrol car drive off. He was whispering and de Gier leaned close to catch the words.

"Good luck comes to those who keep on trying," Grijpstra whispered. "A minor setback. Now I'll find the corpse." The whisper was fierce and de Gier stepped back. "I'll find that corpse, sergeant," Grijpstra shouted, "even if I have to lift the last brick in the last alley!"

De Gier led him away.

"That Sergeant Jurriaans," de Gier said, "maybe you're right. I don't think he's much good. He tortures his subordinates and rapes them when they're female. Didn't you tell me that he made that lovely young cop strip on a garden table and perform on a carpet with another lady?"

"You got that wrong."

"Tell me again then."

"It was the girl, Asta, who caused the trouble, not Sergeant Jurriaans who is a mature man who happened to be off balance that evening, because of his wife who is restless and who watches TV."

"Asta," de Gier said softly.

"Stay away, the girl is horse medicine. You might start smoking again and die peacefully of cancer at a ripe age. That would be better."

"Asta."

"You're not old enough for her," Grijpstra shouted. "She likes older men. Like Sergeant Jurriaans. Like *me.*"

"Yes," de Gier said softly. "I'm sure you're right, adjutant. Maybe I shouldn't interfere."

9

DE GIER STOOD in front of Café Beelema. His head rested against a lamppost.

"How do you feel?" Grijpstra asked.

"Constrained. In my throat, spreading to my lungs. Everything is closing up. My veins are narrowing, the blood no longer flows. I would like to shout, or cry perhaps, at the same time, I think. Do you have cigarettes on you?"

"Cigars. There'll be cigarettes in the café. All brands. Shall I get you some?"

"No, I just thought I'd like to know. I don't smoke anymore. I'll stand here for a while. It'll pass and then it'll come again. I'm in a tunnel; I'm a worm, a pink worm, stretched, pulled on both sides. The sensation is painful and hopeless. I suffer, Grijpstra."

"Poor fellow."

De Gier pushed himself away from the lamppost.

"Right. Hell is not forever. There are pauses. Without intermissions there would be no hell. If the experience were continuous, I'd get used to it. This way I can't. I'll suffer again later. Let's go."

They went into the café and greeted Titania who stood behind the bar, Zhaver who was playing with Kiran between the tables, and Borry who sat at the counter. Zhaver pulled on what was left of the cap and Kiran growled.

"That's my cap," Grijpstra said. "That's an evil dog."

Beelema jumped up.

"I'm sorry, adjutant. Let me reimburse you. What did the cap cost you?"

"Ten guilders, but what's money? Paper with figures printed on it. I just bought that cap. I liked it. Look at it now."

Kiran dropped the slimy rag and grinned. Borry put up all his fingers and pointed at the register with his nose. Titania took out a ten-guilder note and gave it to Grijpstra.

"With my apologies, adjutant," Beelema said, "but the dog is still young. A little playful, eh? I'm glad you could find the time to drop in. The city is empty today, everybody has gone to the beach to annoy the tourists. Those of us who remain should keep each other company. Can I offer you a drink?"

"A beer," Grijpstra said and sank down on a bar stool. The beer soaked into his gulping throat. He replaced the empty glass. Titania refilled it. De Gier wandered about. A well-dressed middle-aged man came in and sat down at a table. He picked up the newspapers and glanced at Titania. Zhaver asked the customer what he would like to drink. The man didn't see Zhaver, he stared at Titania. Titania saw him but seemed unaware of his attention. The man put his hands on the table and raised himself slowly. He staggered to the bar. "Hello." His voice croaked. He was pale and his hands trembled.

"Sir?" asked Titania.

"Hello."

Titania looked at Zhaver.

Zhaver asked the man if he was all right. The man let go of the bar rail and began to rub his stomach.

"Yes," he said. "No. Excuse me." He left, swaying slightly. He had trouble with the door handle.

Grijpstra was impressed.

"And your arms were down," he said to Titania. "You're beautiful indeed. You unnerved that man."

"Maybe he was drunk," Beelema said soothingly. "It sometimes happens. We see it happen every now and then."

"They ask for a drink and we give it to them," Zhaver said. "Then they ask for another. They keep on doing it every day. Slowly they turn into alcoholics. It's sad, but that's the way it sometimes goes."

De Gier stood at the window. "He's going into Hotel Oberon."

"They have a bar too," Titania said.

"He's still on his feet, maybe he's all right."

Several tourists entered the café, South Americans, with mustachios and gleaming teeth; they trailed a woman in a low blouse filled with trembling, soft, fertile flesh.

The blouse's contents did not match the Titania's. Titania wasn't doing anything on purpose; she reached up, she had to, the bottles were on a high shelf. The gesture freed her breasts; the mustachioed gentlemen could see everything from the side, and those who were placed farther along the bar, from the other side. A moment is now, and now lasts forever. The gentlemen saw what they saw through narrow appreciative eyes. The lady saw what the gentlemen saw. Her lower lip tightened and her upper lip moved up just a little, but it changed her face. She hissed while she should have swallowed. The liquor burned her throat. The gentlemen beat her on her back while their eyes rested on the Titania's.

Other customers came in and were served by Zhaver.

"Are you working?" Beelema asked.

Grijpstra pushed his glass to Titania. "A little, we have a question. A simple question. Where is Rea Fortune? Answer the question satisfactorily and we'll be free."

"She is gone."

"Yes, yes."

"Don't you believe me?"

"I believe she's gone."

Borry Beelema thought.

De Gier stopped wandering and leaned against the bar. He studied the embroidered shirt of the café owner, the artificial color of his thick, curly, hairdryer-fluffed sideburns, his golden wrist and neck chains, the well-cut trousers that minimized the bulge of his belly and lengthened his legs. He thought he might find the man's photograph in the police files. He seemed to remember having seen the photograph. Perhaps in the drawer of sexual offenders. What would have been the charge? Shared delight with a minor? Harassing female pedestrians by holding on to these innocent and self-centered beings and, without having been invited, touching, or even kneading, certain of their prominent or hidden parts? Or would it have been the usual display of the pink pecker?

"Rea Fortune has gone," Beelema said, "which is a pity, or isn't it a pity? What do you think, Titania?"

Titania blushed.

"You're blushing," de Gier said. "How becoming. Look, Grijpstra, Titania is blushing."

"Don't," Titania said, "please."

What a lovely closed face the girl has, de Gier thought. Each feature is perfect. Then he forgot what he was looking at. Segments of another face fitted together. This other face was Asta's, but he had only seen her briefly, as she passed him in the patrol car. Yet the face was clear, clearer than Titania's. But what was Asta, apart from Grijpstra's misunderstanding of Sergeant Jurriaans's observations? He concentrated on the tip of Grijpstra's cigar. It smouldered like a pit in a Lilliputian's hell. In the microscopic flames, Asta's face formed itself again. He forced his eyes back to Titania.

"Titania is in love," Beelema said, "with Frits Fortune. It's a drama we have lived with for some time now. Frits Fortune doesn't know what goes on in Titania's heart, because she's a modest girl who resigned herself to the impossibility of her desires. The man was married, wasn't he, and he still is, but Rea has gone, so now the coast is clear."

"Heaven be praised and thanked," said Zhaver, "for we can no longer bear her unhappiness, although we, on our side . . ."

Titania broke into tears. "You dirty . . ." She didn't finish her observation. She ran away. A door slammed. The soles of her shoes rattled on a wooden staircase. Another door slammed.

"That wasn't clever of you, Zhaver," Beelema said. "Now you have to work for two. The gentleman over there has been waiting for service. Why don't you ask him what he wants?"

Zhaver took the fat German's order. The customer wanted two knockwursts on toast with pickles on the side. He also ordered beer. Zhaver dropped the sausages in a pan. Zhaver grumbled.

"What's so dirty about going to bed with Rea? Did you think it was dirty, Borry? You enjoyed it too."

"Did you sleep with Mrs. Fortune?" Grijpstra asked Beelema.

"Now and then."

"Did Mr. Fortune know?"

"I didn't tell him."

"Disgusting."

"There you go," Zhaver said. "She wanted to."

"She was often home alone," Beelema said. "It isn't that bad, is it? Times are freer, you know, and the police are slow to catch up. We did it because we wanted to help. Titania is in love with Fortune. Titania is ours and we fight on her side. Rea didn't even like her husband. A proved point, she ran away, didn't she?"

The German complained, loudly and with a thick accent. He wanted his beer. Beelema brought it to him. He also wanted his knockwurst. Zhaver fished the sausages from the boiling water, popped up the toast, spread the pickles. The German ate, blowing heavily through extended nostrils.

Grijpstra had become busy with sipping his beer, arranging his cigars and his matches on the counter, and moving his bar stool. He found some coasters to be lined up in a square. He studied a number of bottle labels. He scratched the stubble on his chin and felt his navel. In the end he patted the side of his jacket.

The concrete presence of his pistol provided some peace of mind. His body sagged back in the accepting attitude it had assumed before the disturbance of new facts interfering with a theory. Rea Fortune has disappeared, he thought again, as he had thought before forming the theory. Rea Fortune's absence remained the foundation on which all theories would rest. If Rea were there, he, Grijpstra, wouldn't be here, he would be home with his wife and children in the upstairs apartment of the Oilmakerscanal. Streetside view: water displaying floating objects, mainly made of rubber; rear view: windowsills displaying other objects, mainly plates containing scraps of food.

Rea Fortune is not there. Why? Because her husband killed her. Why did he kill her? Because he lost his temper, that's why. Everything thought out and approved, tightly completed. Next step: *find corpse.*

But what if everything changed? If, apart from two new lovers (Rea's), a fallen-in-love girl (with Frits) were added to his collection? How would all this fit the original and tested theory? Grijpstra sweated. His hand dropped and once again patted the textile-hidden pistol. This support did not stop his forehead from sweating. All factual evidence so far obtained danced around the adjutant, including the headless bear Brom and the earless and eyeless Babette, including the lovers and the enamored girl, naked and pornographing.

He left his bar stool, grabbed hold of the wandering de Gier, and pushed him to a corner table.

"I won't pay," the German said loudly. "The beer was warm and the knockwurst was cold."

His statement caused no comment, but the sergeant left his chair and walked to the phone. He dialed, spoke, and returned to the table.

"I'm sorry," Grijpstra said, "I know I've been treating you badly, in a condescending manner, because of your temporary affliction."

The door opened and closed. Two uniformed constables, one male and elderly, one female and young, entered the café. They switched off their electronic communicators and looked at Beelema. Beelema pointed at the German who was staring at his meticulously cleaned plate and empty glass. The girl constable marched up to him.

"You won't pay, sir?"

The German answered her in the affirmative and explained why he had come to his decision.

"You've got to pay, sir."

"I will not."

The elderly constable stood in front of the door, a resigned but heavy presence. He contemplated the floor. Kiran barked and embraced the girl. When he barked again, he was flat on his back in a far corner of the room and appeared to be in pain. The girl resumed her original position. The café became as quiet as before.

The German's eyes, embedded in pale fat, glowed. The girl's eyes sparkled through long lashes. The German took out his wallet, produced a note, and put it on the table.

"Will that be enough?" the girl asked Beelema.

Beelema nodded.

The elderly constable stepped aside. The German waddled through the door. The elderly constable followed him. The girl smiled at de Gier. She saluted. She followed the elderly constable.

"Got to have that corpse," Grijpstra was saying. "And you should help me. Without the corpse there is nothing but vagueness, nothing but . . ."

"A ripped fog in the early morning."

"What?"

De Gier smiled encouragingly.

"A ripped fog in the early morning. I saw that this morning, above the river, when I drove into town. Lovely, but you can't hold on to it. I understand what you are saying, Grijpstra. What a beautiful place this café is. Just look at that paneling, it's rosewood and well joined. Look how Zhaver contrasts against that background of mirrored bottles. Study Kiran, lying on sunlit boards. If I were smoking now, I wouldn't have this awareness. Nicotine narrows the potential of imaginative reception by slowing the blood flow in the brain. It limits the capacity of the senses. I'm close to the essence of creation. I see that everything is glorious indeed. Too glorious in a way, I don't think I can stand it."

"Hold it."

"I will see what I can do for you, Grijpstra. Please tell me how you intend to find that corpse."

"Right. The corpse is close, under the road bricks. But where exactly? I've thought of a method to determine its location. We must have Fortune followed. He will be attracted to the spot where he buried his wife, for marriage creates a link, strengthened in his case by crime. We can't follow him, for he knows us, but he doesn't know Cardozo. Listen carefully while I go into details and tell me what you think."

"No," de Gier said a few minutes later and smiled over Grijpstra's shoulder at the expanse of the Brewerscanal, stretched quietly in the heavy yellow light of the late afternoon.

"I'll do it anyway."

"You won't," de Gier said, "but how did you ever think of it? How wonderful."

Grijpstra inhaled deeply. De Gier cut the adjutant's protest with a loving wave of his arm.

"Not now, Grijpstra, I want to see it again." His eyes rested on the canal's surface while he saw the phantoms raised by Grijpstra. First of all there goes the suspect Fortune, wandering in solitude, a prey to his own bad conscience and his self-inflicted demons. His muffled curses interchange with gnashing of his teeth. At a safe distance follows a detective. He is Cardozo, constable first class, a member of the murder brigade, a small figure, untidy and long haired, blending with the city. He carries a bundle of red flags. Everytime the suspect's behavior changes, whenever Fortune curses or gnashes louder, Cardozo remembers where the change occurred and inserts a flag between the bricks. The flags are small but bright of color and are seen by the laborer who follows the detective. The laborer drives a yellow machine, grumbling on wide crunching tracks, the machine carries a blade, and the blade digs holes. But each hole is always empty.

"Each hole is always empty."

"But where could the corpse be?"

"Each hole is always empty, and how will you defend your decision when you are asked to explain the holes?"

"I do have serious suspicions," Grijpstra said sadly.

"You do not. You have a bizarre construction, resting on what isn't there. You have negatives and you're adding them. No contents of a house, no lady, no life in a dog. Added negatives do not make a positive. You have a no head on a hearsay teddy bear. You have an insufficiency, adjutant, you have a nothing obscured by shapes."

"What can I serve the gentlemen?" Beelema asked. "You're just sitting. You aren't ordering. It's dinnertime. Tell you what? I invite you to come to the sandwich shop with me because my kitchen is closed because Titania is crying upstairs."

"No, no," Grijpstra said. "Can't you send for some food? It's nice here, why leave?"

"Yes," Beelema said, "what will it be?"

"A roll with warm meat, another chopped steak, another with ox sausage and another with *two* meatrolls."

"Yes," Beelema said, "and the sergeant?"

"A roll with meat salad, another with crab salad, another with lobster salad, and another with *two* meatrolls."

"That'll be four meatrolls," Grijpstra said worriedly, "two for him and two for me, that makes four. Not two, not one for him and one for me, but two each, that's four, but only with two rolls, one for him and one for me. Can you remember that?"

"For each?" Beelema asked. "Isn't that a lot? He doesn't smoke anymore and should be careful and you're heavy already. It isn't my concern, of course. I'll get eight, or sixteen, but . . ."

"Two each," Grijpstra said.

"Let Mr. Beelema go," de Gier said, "he understood."

Beelema returned. Zhaver had laid the table. Beelema joined his guests and observed them while they ate.

"I'm proud of you," Beelema said when they were done. "You didn't mess about. Where do we go from here?"

Grijpstra turned slowly. He observed the crowd at the bar. The South American low-cut lady admonished the mustachioed South American gentlemen. Two groups of glass-in-hand locals flanked the foreign element.

"Introduce me to somebody who knows the Fortunes, a reliable somebody. Can you do that?"

"Yes," Beelema said. He walked over to the locals and studied them one by one. He made his choice. "Mr. Hyme," Beelema whispered, "do you see the two men sitting at the corner table? They are police officers. They want to meet you. Please go and talk to them."

10

"SIR," Hyme said and contemplated the foam on his beer. "Sir, your question fascinates me. I asked myself the same question, last night, to be precise, when Beelema told me that Rea had gone and left an empty apartment. A most interesting question. Where is Rea Fortune? Or may we formulate it differently? *Is* Rea Fortune? The *where* could be immaterial, and if we should pursue that side, we might find ourselves in the Hereafter of parapsychology or the Bardo of Tibetan migrants. I believe that I understand the direction of your reasoning, and I agree in anticipation. Especially since I met with Fortune, just now in fact, on my way here. The man's mood is peculiar, victoriously nervous it seemed to me. And the tale he told me does not fit the past, if that past were decent, which we doubt, do we not? He told me that he is now eager to sell his business, while only a week ago the possibility drove him into a frenzy."

Grijpstra smiled cheerfully. Hyme smiled back. De Gier glanced out of the window. Hyme, dressed like a British sportsman of the early twenties and affecting the whiny tone of voice that is respectable in some provinces but antagonizes the denizens of the capital, irritated the sergeant. The view the window offered irritated him too. He had seen the elegant hairy cyclist before, he had heard the clanging pedal before. He forced himself to listen to Hyme and to neither kick nor hit Grijpstra. It was a pity that Grijpstra had so little intelligence, de Gier thought. He found a burned match in the ashtray, inserted it into his mouth, and began to chew slowly and rhythmically.

"Victoriously nervous," repeated Grijpstra, "exactly sir. The very impression the suspect made on me, when we interrogated him earlier today."

"As if he had succeeded in the undertaking of an important project," Hyme continued, "as if he had surmounted certain risks. Do you know what I thought when I reflected on our recent meeting?" ("No?" Grijpstra asked eagerly.) "I thought of the possibility that Frits Fortune is engaged in the Great Clearing. He rids himself of everything. First of all of his home, then of his work. Isn't that what life consists of? Home and work? Aren't both stress situations? Isn't home the worst of the two? Shouldn't home come first? If our lives contain too much hardness, if suffering outbalances pleasure, will we not destroy first the one and then the other?"

"*Right!*" Grijpstra shouted. "A type of suicide?" Grijpstra asked meekly.

"And reincarnation. But not in the hereafter, no, *here*. That was the impression Fortune gave me. Everything goes but he stays here. Remarkable, don't you think?"

Why does he wear a tie? the sergeant thought. That man is an asshole. Why does he wear a blazer? Why is he so happy? De Gier's thoughts colored the atmosphere, weighed it down, but Hyme pushed ahead. Perhaps he noticed the threat, for he spoke both louder and faster, and his hands, which had grabbed at Grijpstra's cigar smoke before, found a more useful occupation in producing a newspaper and folding it artfully so that it became a triangular hat, of the type old-fashioned children will wear.

"Yes, adjutant, the disappearance of Rea Fortune, a charming woman engaged with the short end of the stick throughout her short and unhappy life—she can't have been older than thirty-five when I saw her last—" ("Yes?" Grijpstra asked compassionately) "is surrounded by doubt." Hyme focused his eyes triumphantly. "Doubt!"

De Gier's chewing changed. He abandoned the earlier method of simple chomping and replaced it by repetitive sucking and flattening.

Zhaver, at Grijpstra's request, brought more beer.

Hyme patted his paper headgear into shape and placed it on the table. He stretched both arms and nodded pleasantly.

"Doubt. And why do I doubt Rea's so-called voluntary retreat followed by a complete failure on Frits's part to retrieve her presence? I doubt, for the one-among-other-reasons that this very same Rea practically embraced me when I offered Frits Fortune, at this same table a week ago, a cool million for his assorted rubbish, against my personal inclination, although the urgency of my associates' desire to take over

Frits's business might have warranted such a price." Hyme sighed briefly. "Did Frits accept? He did not. Was he sorry? No, he was angry. Was he very angry? He was furious. An emotion of that caliber is not without its deeper meaning. It isn't necessary to have studied psychology, as I have . . ."

"Really?" Grijpstra asked admiringly.

". . . to conclude that Frits's personality began to split at that moment. A new personality attempted to emerge: new Frits trampled old Frits and confronted me, a once trusted friend."

Zhaver brought more beer, at Hyme's request.

Hyme collapsed. The beer supplied new energy. His voice dropped. His hand touched Grijpstra's knee. "We had been drinking, my guests and I. The stage was set well and I meant to give joy. Was I thanked? I was not. Frits stalked out of here; Rea followed sadly. What happened afterward? Can we surmise?" Hyme took his hand from Grijpstra's knee. "Was Rea a dragon, and did new Frits become a knight without fear?"

"Or blame," de Gier said.

"With blame," Hyme whispered.

De Gier stood up. His chair screeched on the boards. Hyme coughed, shielding his mouth politely. "Suicide and reincarnation, and the new birth financed by a million florins to ease the black knight's future path."

Grijpstra ordered a box of expensive cigars. Hyme accepted a cigar, reached again, and put a handful in his breast pocket.

De Gier combed his hair in the rest room. Except for the detectives and Hyme, there were no clients in the café.

Beelema returned from having walked Kiran in the street. "Titania hasn't come back yet?"

"Not yet," Zhaver said. "I shouldn't have joked about her predicament. True love is admirable. She has loved Fortune since he bought her those flowers."

De Gier came back. "Flowers?"

"Two dozen roses. Beelema and I forgot about Titania's birthday although we remembered the year before, and Titania complained. She cried. Frits Fortune was here and a flower cart happened to pass. He rushed outside and bought the roses. A sentimental gesture and the undoing of Titania."

"Because Fortune is a serious man," Beelema said. "Titania isn't used to his type, she is used to the others."

"Fornicators," Zhaver said, "like us."

"Whom she tries to avoid."

"Not too successfully," Zhaver said.

"Which makes her feel worse," Beelema said.

Zhaver smiled. "Frits Fortune is a serious gentleman left by his wife, a handsome man still in the strength of his late youth and blessed with ample income. Titania is a lonely and beautiful woman looking for appreciation and solidity. If those two could meet, even for a moment, everlasting joy would surely result. I would like to see such bliss. True love, harmonious and lasting. It would encourage me. Why don't you arrange it, Borry? You claim divine parentage, it's your sort of thing."

Beelema nodded, shifted on his stool, bent his elbows on the counter, rested his head in his hands, and closed his eyes.

Grijpstra and de Gier studied Beelema.

Hyme said goodbye and left the café quietly.

Zhaver put his hands to his lips and moved to the far end of the bar. The detectives followed him.

"Sshh," Zhaver whispered, "he's thinking, it may take a while. What will be your pleasure?"

"Coffee," Grijpstra said, "for me and my sergeant." He smiled. "I was glad to meet Mr. Hyme. He argues along sensible lines and he is a reliable gent." He turned to de Gier. "I don't understand your negative attitude, Rinus. I'm going to telephone Cardozo and Public Works. They'll have to produce a digger and be quick about it. Weekend work is healthy and pays double."

"Please, Grijpstra."

"I don't quite know what you're talking about," Zhaver said, "but Mr. Hyme is not a reliable gent."

"No?" Grijpstra asked. "No? A director of the best known publishing house of this country? A gentleman who dresses as a gentleman, who behaves as a gentleman?"

"Don't talk like the American lady in Paris," de Gier said. "A gentleman is a gentleman is a gentleman."

"Rose," Zhaver said. "Rose. Not gentleman. Do me a favor and please look out of that window, so that I can share my suffering. Throughout the week he holds himself together, but the weekends are too much, like now. Again and again. Isn't that type of behavior degenerate? Or am I old-fashioned? I think it is degenerate."

Hyme straddled the bridge railing in feeble but ecstatic balance. The triangular paper hat rested on his elongated skull. His penis rested on the tops of two fingers. A thick foaming jet of sunlit fluid raced to the sky before—gracefully forced by gravity—curving downward to unite with the passive and gleaming canal water.

"*No,*" said Grijpstra.

"Yes," said de Gier. "As if you couldn't have known. Why did you have to force it? Forget your imagination and join the party. Nothing whatsoever is the matter. We are in a café in the inner city of Amsterdam. Life is bad but we can put up with it here. And when we're done, we'll go for a nice little walk and look at the geese if you like. A Hondecoeter theme, remember?" He clenched his fist and shook it in Grijpstra's face. "Cheer up. It's all right."

Beelema opened his eyes.

"It's not all right, but we can rectify the situation. Zhaver, it won't be easy but I can do it, as you say. Fetch Titania and tell her to wear her new jacket and skirt."

"With this heat?"

Beelema sighed. "You want me to do it or not? You want to obstruct or assist? Is it your fate or Titania's?"

"This is *it,*" Grijpstra said. "This is *it* forever. I will no longer do this work. Everybody is quite abnormal in this town. I hereby grant them leave to destroy each other. I will, from now on, be sorting out traffic. No, because then I will still see them. I will be working in the clothing store at Headquarters. Not up front, but in the rear where nobody ever comes."

"I want to assist in achieving Titania's happiness," Zhaver said. "I'm sorry, Beelema."

"Go and fetch her then. She has to wear the long skirt, not that minirag. Her knees, first, will be covered or I won't even get into this. And a simple black blouse and something easy around her neck, that silk cord with the bone ring, she wore it the other day. She has to look neat."

"Neat," said Zhaver.

"Neat. And long silk stockings, no combination, real stockings, with real garters, she'll have some somewhere, and no panties."

Zhaver was at the door but stopped and turned.

"Is that neat?"

"Neat? What neat? What do I care about *neat?* We're concerned with Fortune's mind, and with contrast. What are you delaying the action for, Zhaver?"

"Right away, Borry."

"And I need her make-up kit, and a comb, and a brush."

They heard Zhaver crash up the stairs.

Beelema locked the front door. He closed the curtains and placed a chair in the middle of the room. He arranged the lights.

Titania came in and was directed to the chair. She sobbed pitifully. "I can't help it that I fell in love. And that he never notices me. Never *wants* to notice me. Because I'm a street girl. Heeheehee."

"Don't cry, Titania."

"Heeheehee."

Beelema talked into her ear.

"This is your big day, Titania. The prince is coming."

"What prince, heeheehee?"

"Prince Frits the First. He loves you but he doesn't know that yet, because he doesn't know your true shape. We're going to work on your true shape. You're not what you think you are. You are a princess."

"Yes?"

"Yes. Easy now, Titania. You're an easy princess. Lovable on a high level, as I'm about to indicate. Here, a little here, and a little here too, close your eyes or I'll glue your lashes together, this shit is sticky, and a little there, oops, rub it away a mite. Aren't you incredible now? And you'll have a small accident, and the prince will be there to save you and take you to his castle. It's a bit empty his castle, but never mind, there'll be a mattress I hear, and that's all you need. A round of fah-deefoozle, a shower together, a bowl of soup and a sandwich shared in the main chamber, or in the royal kitchen maybe, and your souls will be linked. You'll never work again, Titania. We'll miss you maybe but nobody is irreplaceable, we'll find another so that the clients can have a fresh view, two fresh views, haha. Don't pull faces, Titania, or I can't do your mouth."

Borry Beelema worked on and continued his monologue. He rubbed color on her cheekbones and wiped most of it away again. He stood back.

"You'll have to be tragic, Titania, and decent, but sensual." He bowed down, adjusting lipstick. "Sit still, I've got to concentrate, or we get nowhere."

"Morons," Grijpstra said, "and not an exception among them. If they're in Amsterdam, they're morons. Sometimes I think I see a normal person, but the fault is mine. I've let myself be persuaded by weakness, by unhealthy idealism, but it won't happen again."

"I'm a little nauseous," de Gier said. "Maybe it's the matches. Don't you have any gum, Zhaver? Who would ever have thought that I would chew gum? And to think that I stopped Seeny on the corridor the other day and bothered her, and now I do it too."

"Here you are," Zhaver said. "This is supposed to taste like sour apples. Who is Seeny?"

"A constable from the radio room," Grijpstra said, "a well-shaped girl, but since he grabbed her by the throat and broke her jaws open and removed the gum from behind her back teeth, she doesn't like him anymore."

"Quiet!" said Beelema. "I've done it, Titania. From here we can proceed. The beginning is easy enough, you'll go outside, and so do we, to take care of you, for you're too lovely to be on your own now. All sorts of types are about and they all have loose hands, my work is not to be spoiled. We'll be with you, although we won't be in sight, and Zhaver will phone Frits. He does have a telephone, I hope, or did she take that too?"

"There was a phone on the wall," de Gier said.

"Splendid, that's all we need. Zhaver phones and says that he has, what do we have? Knockwurst? That he has some nice knockwurst for him, that we're about to close but that he can come in for a moment. He is home, see?" Beelema lifted a curtain. "The light is on." He dropped the curtain. "Frits comes here, and Zhaver feeds him the sausage. Then Zhaver says it's been a long day. Frits leaves again. And then you cross his path, Titania, and have your accident."

The girl smiled.

"Right away?"

Beelema arranged a hair that had jumped free of his careful arrangement.

"No, no, no. No hurry, please. First there'll be some conversation. He never saw you in this outfit, he won't even recognize you. I've changed and exaggerated, your eyes are bigger and your ears are all out. So you say, 'Hello, Frits,' softly and nicely, polite-like, but a little more. Say it, Titania."

"Hello, Frits."

"Okay. That'll stop him but that's not enough. He's got to be *with* you, so you touch his arm. Let's see, I'm Frits, I pass you; say it . . ."

"Hello, Frits."

"Perfect, hold my arm now, see? He's stuck, never to free himself again. And now, a few steps ahead, there's this brick sticking up, and you stumble and fall. Pay attention now, Titania, this is where it goes, you've got to grab him with sex, it's your only weapon in the end. He's got to think of the actual insertion, he's got to really want the ultimate contact. Do you get me?"

"Can't we kiss? I like kissing too."

"Yes, sure. It'll be a start, you can do that too, I don't mind. So you fall *and pull up your dress,* all the way up, he looks right into you, *but only for a moment,* for then it's gone. You pull your dress down again, if you stay there in your full glory, you overdo it, it'll be the end of it. Get me? Let's try. Move up, gentlemen, take your stools. Sit up straight, your heads will have to be on the same level as if you were standing. You're the committee. All set?"

"We're the committee," Grijpstra said.

Titania stumbled and fell. Dress up, dress down.

"No," Grijpstra said. "I didn't see anything. Too fast."

Beelema agreed. "We'll try again."

Later.

"Are you crazy?" Titania said. "I won't fall all night. And I'm not on show for nothing, certainly not underneath. Have you all gone out of your minds?" She took a deep breath.

"Don't say it!" Beelema had raised his arms. "That's it. You're in the right frame of mind now. Let's go."

11

It was Saturday night and the lush heat of summer hung under a clear and starry sky. Two red-beaked geese floated in the Emperorscanal and had almost reached the bridge at the edge of the Brewerscanal. The herringstall on the bridge had closed.

Grijpstra and de Gier stood next to the stall and peered cautiously around it. Kiran sniffed at a tree. Beelema and Zhaver were present but invisible. A couple, arm in arm, approached slowly. The woman, clearly visible in the light of the bridge's lampposts, emitted a serene beauty from every particle of her body and clothing. She talked to the man in a low voice. She stumbled and fell. Frits Fortune reacted in fear and concern, he bent down, his arms reached. Titania groaned. Her skirt, made of pure and delicate wool and matching her long and elegant jacket, slipped up, ignoring the limits of decency.

A gentleman, in a three-piece summer suit and wearing an old-fashioned expensive felt hat, cycled toward the bridge. One of the pedals of his cycle clanged against the metal chain guard. The geese appeared at the other side of the bridge and greeted their new view, honking softly. Titania corrected her unruly skirt. Frits Fortune, with diminishing fear and growing concern, lifted the fallen woman and remembered how, in clear and almost touchable detail, the lady's thighs were soft and pink, and how they held and would still hold a promise of curly down that in turn protected a moist NO, he would think no further. He asked if she had hurt herself. She said she had, poor Titania.

On her feet, she leaned into his arms. The geese honked loudly, the cyclist was close. Beelema and Zhaver stepped back into the shadows between a pickup and a van, Grijpstra and de Gier held on to each other. Titania's lips pursed, opened slightly, her long lashes partly hid her soft and inviting eyes. Frits's mouth drew close to Titania's, the cyclist braked, the cycle fell, the object the cyclist pointed was made of blue steel.

"HO!" Grijpstra shouted.

De Gier was running, no, leaping. The cyclist flew sideward, propelled by the sudden contact with the sergeant's last and far-ranging leap. The shot rang out. The bullet whistled and splashed. The red-beaked geese flapped and blew in anger. The cyclist's hat dropped, and his wig, beard, and mustache moved to the side of her face.

Titania, suddenly released by Frits Fortune, staggered, stumbled, and fell. Her skirt, much higher now, translated the indicated into the obvious until once more corrected, as Titania, unaided, struggled up. Beelema and Zhaver came forward. Kiran waved his long tail. Fortune, Titania, Zhaver, and Beelema stared at the cyclist.

"Hello, Rea," Fortune said.

"Mrs. Fortune," Grijpstra said politely, "I arrest you, under suspicion of repeated attempted murder or manslaughter, as the case may be, of your husband, and of ill treatment of your dog Babette resulting in its death."

De Gier bent his knees and looked into Beelema's eyes.

"Are you the other son of God?"

"It was well meant," Beelema whispered hoarsely.

"It usually is," de Gier said.

"Are you coming with me?" Grijpstra asked Rea Fortune imperatively.

"Coming with me?" de Gier asked Beelema pleasantly.

"Coming?" Fortune asked Titania shyly.

Kiran embraced Zhaver, barking cheerfully.

12

"WELL, WELL," the commissaris said, "and in the weekend too, in the off weekend! Will I ever understand what motivates activity? I do hope your reports will be short and limit the prosecutor's ridicule. A merry display indeed! Will you be holding Rea Fortune, adjutant?"

"I might recommend that to the authorities, sir," Grijpstra said. "I've charged the suspect with the illegal possession of a firearm."

"And the attempted manslaughter, albeit murder?"

"We might drop that part of the charge, sir. The suspect is in a state of shock, the material we've come up with is somewhat garbled, and the lawyer the suspect hired seems to be rather forceful, and, eh, intelligent, sir. It seems that Mrs. Fortune was merely persuading her husband to sell his business, by manipulating circumstances, so to speak. I gather that she thought that the sudden emptiness of their apartment, coupled with her own and the dog's disappearance, would make him change his mind. By weakening his defenses by, as the lawyer puts it, not illegal means, she meant to release the victim of his fear of retirement."

The commissaris harrumphed furiously.

"And the evidence you found? Fortune's weak heart? His susceptibility to sudden shocks? The actual death of that poor little poodle? Can't we show a sinister underground? And what about Beelema, the divine entrepreneur, surely he can be charged with complicity?"

"The evidence could be rather thin, sir."

"And the count? That Zhaver fellow? He was her lover, wasn't he?"

"So was Beelema, sir, but the two of them stood to gain nothing.

They weren't being paid and there was no promise of payment. Neither of them meant to marry Mrs. Fortune or live with her. The relationship was merely physical, it seems."

"So what were they? Friends? Did they help the lady to move the contents of the apartment?"

"No sir."

"Who *did* help her?"

"Illegal immigrants, sir, Turks and Pakistanis. There are quite a few of them in the neighborhood. They're always looking for jobs."

"Are you sure?"

"I have no reason to disbelieve the suspect, sir, but the sergeant and I can check the point if you like."

The commissaris whipped off his spectacles and began to polish them with his handkerchief.

"Ha! No. I won't go against your judgment. You might explain, however, why the lady did dress up as a man and cycle around the area."

"To see how her husband was doing."

"Ah. And the dog?"

"Rea lived in a hotel, sir. The dog was confused. It got away from her and ran home. She picked it up the next day; she still had the key, of course, but it was still nervous, crossed the street and was killed by a car."

The commissaris blew on his glasses.

"Hold it there, adjutant, how did the body get on the roof?"

Grijpstra scratched his chin.

"She put it there, didn't she?" the commissaris asked. "Now why would she do that? She could have dropped it in a garbage can, but she went to a lot of trouble to hide it in an unlikely place. Would she be hoping perhaps that Fortune, who was still doing well and not suffering enough perhaps, might be disturbed by the gulls and crows, climb onto the roof, and find the torn corpse of a pet he was fond of? Another shock to shake the poor fellow's mind perhaps?"

Grijpstra scratched his chin with a little more force.

"Could be, sir."

The commissaris frowned.

"Bad, adjutant, bad. To misuse affection. She had done it before, after all, by running away, thinking that Frits would miss her. Consistent behavior. Do you think the woman is evil?"

Grijpstra sighed.

The commissaris replaced his spectacles and managed to smile.

"Bah. But you're right not to pursue the point. Her lawyer would tell the court that the means justify the end somewhat, and the end was to help. Wives are supposed to help their husbands. They rarely do. And the means never justify the end, but that's between you and me. The lawyer will also mention that the dog was already dead. So what does all this add up to?"

Grijpstra grunted. The commissaris got up, left his desk, and found the center of his carpet.

"Now what caused you two to waste two free days on such a flimsy case, eh? And why didn't you spot the suspect? Isn't it hard for a woman to impersonate a man? If I understand the situation correctly, she must have shown herself to you on several occasions."

The Oriental arrows extended from his shoes. One arrow pointed at Grijpstra, the other at de Gier.

De Gier plotted the course of the arrow. When he realized the danger, he spoke.

"The suspect used to be an actress, sir, possibly a good actress. I believe she was a professional. I saw her too and I never caught on. I only noticed that the cyclist was slender, well dressed, and overhairy. I've seen worse in the city, perhaps my mind no longer registers abnormalities. All sorts of apparitions appear these days. There was a dwarf, for instance, dressed in a yellow cape. He rode a scooter, a monkey sat on the handlebars."

The commissaris's mouth opened as he tried to visualize the yellow-caped dwarf.

"Really? What sort of a scooter, a motor scooter?"

"No sir, a child's scooter."

"And he wasn't a child?"

"No, sir, he had a beard too, and a mustache."

"For heaven's sake."

Grijpstra gestured. "Amsterdam, sir!"

Grijpstra offered a cigar. The commissaris was calmed by the sudden intake of nicotine.

"Dwarf! Well. Ah. Something else. The lady pulled a gun. She actually fired the gun. Did she aim at the kissing couple?"

"She didn't have time, sir, the sergeant knocked her off her feet."

"But the shot went off so she had pressed the safety catch. Did you question her on that point?"

"Yes sir, she said that she intended to fire over their heads. She confesses to being jealous but there was no murderous intent."

"Is she a good shot?"

"No sir, she had never fired a gun, except on the stage where they use blanks."

The commissaris sucked his cigar.

"Yes. Hmpf. So she could have shot them by mistake or she could have got someone else, so perhaps it was a good thing you two were around, to prevent an accident. You know . . ."

A streetcar passed down the Marnixstreet outside and the commissaris had to wait for the noise to subside.

"You two remind me of a farewell speech delivered by my first chief who retired. That was a long time ago, but truth lasts. I wore a saber on my belt then, and performed street duty."

"What did your chief say, sir?"

"You really want to know? Very well. He claimed that the police are by definition stupid, because intelligent men will not apply for boring work at low wages. He also said that stupidity hardly matters in our profession, provided our brainlessness is compensated by zeal."

"Zeal . . . ," Grijpstra muttered.

"Weren't you and the sergeant zealous, by working when you didn't have to?"

De Gier got up.

"Could I bother you for a match, sir?"

The commissaris flicked his golden lighter.

"No, a match. To chew on, sir."

"Chew? Oh, I see. You're still not smoking. No, I don't have a match, sergeant. Grijpstra?"

The adjutant passed a box of matches. De Gier began to chew hungrily. Grijpstra moved his chair. The arrow no longer pointed at his feet. The commissaris stepped off the carpet and yanked a corner. The arrow followed Grijpstra. The commissaris stepped back.

"Perhaps the chief's statement was too abstract, but he accompanied it with a story. Would you like to hear the story too?"

"Yes," de Gier said.

"You too, adjutant?"

"Yes."

"Good, because I would have told it anyway. Listen here."

Grijpstra moaned.

"Adjutant?"

"I *did* have serious suspicions, sir. The sergeant is smiling, and it's true that he hasn't gone along with me much, but I refuse to believe that my theory was silly. Rea Fortune did disappear with her dog and the contents of the house. An exceptional course of events has often provided me with a case. We found nothing but dust specks in that apartment. Unusual, sir, very."

"Yes?"

"There were character witnesses," Grijpstra said sadly. "Several, in fact. They confirmed the suspect's tendency, I'm referring to *Mr.* Fortune now, to destroy what he didn't like. Isn't a character the sum of certain habits, and aren't habits with us forever?"

"I used to smoke," de Gier said, "but I don't anymore."

"Arrgh!"

"Just thought I would mention it."

"Not again!"

"So a man is a slave," de Gier said, "the slave of what he did. For what he did, you say, he does, and what he does, you say, he will always do. There's also liberty, I just thought I would mention liberty."

The commissaris left his carpet and studied a geranium.

Grijpstra glared.

De Gier smiled. "I *did* stop smoking, you know. I chew matches now, different habit altogether."

"We know, we know," the commissaris said to the geranium. "He stopped smoking. Now why would he have done that?"

"For Grijpstra, sir."

Grijpstra jumped up.

"Won't you ever stop saying that? What is it to me whether you smoke or not?"

De Gier moved his match with his tongue.

"To show you that there is still hope."

"Hope. For who?"

"For you."

"Not for me. I'm stuck. I waste my time watching morons because anything is better than to stay home. A situation that can't be changed."

"If I can change, so can you. To smoke is to be addicted. I broke my chain. I'm free." De Gier got up and clutched his belt. "Would you excuse me a minute? Chewing matches doesn't agree with me. I'll be right back."

He looked pale when he came back and there was a sour stench.

"Won't you go back to smoking again?" the commissaris asked.

"Not just yet, sir."

"Then I'll tell you the story to distract you. *A jack rabbit runs through a field. He doesn't pay attention. He runs into a fence. The impact stuns him for a moment. He staggers about for a bit. A few cows are around. The jack rabbit bumps into a cow. The second mishap is*

*too much for him. The jack rabbit faints. He's under the cow. 'Look,'
the cow says to the other cows, 'I actually managed to catch a jack rabbit.'"*

"That's about the way it was," de Gier said.

"Do you agree, adjutant?"

"Yes sir."

"I'm glad to hear it and I'm glad you were good enough to keep me
informed of your activities. You know that I don't have much of a function here, as the journalist of the *Courier* was kind enough to point
out."

More streetcars passed through the Marnixstreet. The commissaris
spent another minute on his geranium.

"And what do you think of our lovers, Grijpstra, do you think that
the affair will last?"

"Frits Fortune and Titania?"

"Yes."

"I think so, sir. Titania is a dear girl and I was mistaken about Mr.
Fortune, I believe he's a good man. She certainly managed to impress
him at the right moment."

"In which case you'll have to find a suitable partner for Rea, we cannot let go of her now. She'll be depressed and slip into even worse
ideas. Perhaps Beelema should exercise his powers again, keeping the
lady's extravagant desires in mind. How about matching her to the
nobleman Xavier Michel d'Ablaing de Batagglia? The capital which will
be returned to her by Frits Fortune could ease her way with him.
Zhaver has gone straight for a long while; perhaps the two of them
could start up a luxurious restaurant."

"Yes sir."

The commissaris rubbed his legs. His lips thinned.

"A change of weather, gentlemen, I feel it in my bones. Perhaps we
should do some real work for a change. I had a call just before you
came in. A well-dressed male corpse was found in the luggage compartment of a stolen Mercedes." He tore a sheet out of his notebook and
gave it to Grijpstra. The sergeant read the notes over the adjutant's
shoulder.

"A corpse!" de Gier said. "Just what is needed."

When the detectives crossed the hall on their way to the elevator, Grijpstra held on to de Gier's arm.

"Didn't you mention a dwarf in a yellow cape on a scooter just
now?"

"I don't smoke anymore," de Gier said.

"With a monkey on the handlebars?"

"A withdrawal monkey," de Gier said, "and a withdrawal dwarf."

"Is that what you see? But that's horrifying. I'll never stop smoking."

"What has that got to do with it?" de Gier asked. "Smoking is fun."

"So you'll start again?"

"Me? No. I don't smoke. Not smoking is becoming a habit and habits are forever."

De Gier walked on. Grijpstra walked after him. De Gier frowned. Grijpstra grinned.

PART II

1

DE GIER crossed the courtyard. His legs bounced, his arms swung, his chin jutted, the sun highlighted his wavy hair. Grijpstra followed heavily, as if the tarmac stuck to his soles, as if the air was viscous, as if his blood was glue, coagulating in every artery and vein. De Gier folded himself into the Volkswagen and waited, drumming his fingertips on the steering wheel. He started the engine as Grijpstra lowered his bulk on the creaking plastic next to him. Grijpstra mumbled.

The car left the courtyard and headed for the inner city, ignoring traffic signals, swerving around jaywalking pedestrians.

"I don't know what you're saying," de Gier said, "but here's your corpse. You looked for it all weekend. You were right, after all; whatever you want will find you in due time." He patted Grijpstra's shoulder. "A solid corpse, adjutant, all ours. No manufactured case this time. We won't have to make excuses to each other and to the good citizens who obstruct our path. We can work by the book. We're following orders. Forward."

"Forward how?" Grijpstra asked and nodded at a gesticulating oversized lady on a bicycle as the car eased through a red light.

"From dream time into actuality," de Gier shouted as he made the Volkswagen shoot ahead. "A real body, quite dead but able to withstand our prodding. Facts instead of a vacuum. Cause and effect instead of conjecture on a transparent tightrope. Connecting events instead of stacking flimsy cards!"

Grijpstra mumbled on.

De Gier parked.

"We can walk from here. We even have an address. Gentleman's Market. Across the canal, see? There's the Mercedes, there's a patrol car. We have all sorts of details. A silver Mercedes with a German registration. Corpse of a forty-five-year-old man, well dressed. Isn't it unbelievable, Grijpstra, after all we've been through?"

Grijpstra grunted, spoke, and grunted again.

"What's that?"

"I'm saying," Grijpstra said in an unnecessarily loud voice, "that we are back where we started, on the Brewerscanal, with nothing in our hands. Once again we will twist misrepresented evidence and be a bother to ourselves and all those who have the misfortune to meet with us. What do we have?" He held up a finger. "A corpse, you're right. From that point on, you're wrong. The corpse was not killed, neither by itself nor by others. There are, according to the commissaris's notes, no wounds. Very likely our man died of natural causes. If we get into this, we'll stumble forever, and there'll be nothing in the end."

De Gier got out of the car, walked around it and opened the passenger door. He reached in, grabbed Grijpstra by the forearm and pulled.

"No. I'm right. We have a case. The corpse was found in the baggage compartment of a car. How did it get there?"

They crossed the nearest bridge. A male and a female constable walked toward the detectives.

"I'll tell you how it got there," Grijpstra said. "It fell in. It was still alive then. The man became unwell, the baggage compartment of the car was open, he lunged toward the car, intending to find support, he was dizzy, fainting, he tumbled into the gaping hole."

"And somebody closed the lid," de Gier said. "No, no. Murder. I tell you it's murder. We're employed by the murder brigade. This is our thing. The hunt is on. Hello, Asta, hello, Karate, where's Ketchup?"

"Do you know my name?" Asta asked.

"Ketchup is on leave," Karate said. "The weekend was too much for him. He scraped some free days together and foul-mouthed Sergeant Jurriaans. The sergeant jumped across the counter, but Ketchup was out on the street by then. He's a good runner. Look what I got in his place."

"I'm not a what," Asta said. "I'm a she. I have my rights. I didn't know you knew my name, sergeant."

"Stay away from him," Grijpstra said. "He's working, but not for long. This corpse is nothing, we'll find something else to do. We could have a late breakfast or an early lunch. Where's the dead man, constable?"

Asta stopped smiling at de Gier. "Taken away, adjutant, there were too many people around, it was causing an obstruction. It has been photographed, and the doctor was here. The ambulance took it to the morgue. The doctor thought the man may have died of natural causes. He suspected a stomach ulcer that broke and caused a bleeding."

"See?" Grijpstra asked. *"See!"* Grijpstra shouted. "Isn't that what I said just now? Let's go, sergeant. We'll visit the morgue, meet with the doctor, and have a meal. I won't waste one unnecessary minute on this routine accident."

"Let's see the car," de Gier said.

"The lid of the baggage compartment was closed," Karate said, "but not quite. The lock had been forced, you see. We have the car on the stolen list, it disappeared sometime during the night. It had been parked in front of Hotel Oberon. The owner of the car stays there. I met him this morning before we went out on patrol. A fat German, wheezing and bubbling. He told us the car cost a lot of money and that we had to drop everything and look for it."

De Gier turned to Asta. "Were you there too?"

"Yes," Asta said, "he was the same man who wouldn't pay his bill at Beelema's. Didn't we do that little job well, sergeant? There can't have been more than two minutes between your telephone call and our arrival. Wasn't it great?"

"No," Grijpstra said.

"What was wrong with the way we handled that incident, adjutant?" Asta asked.

"What? Oh, nothing. You're paid to do your job well, aren't you? I don't want this case, sergeant. It's the same thing again. I got away from it and now we're back. Beelema, I don't want to hear that name again. And that German was obnoxious, he'll still be obnoxious. I'm glad his car was stolen." He hit the trunk with his flat hand. "Is this the only damage, constable? Just a broken lock?"

"Yes."

"Pity. Thieves took the car and forced the baggage compartment. They left, either finding nothing or taking what they found. The car remained. Our fellow staggers along and falls into it. He dies."

"Who closed the lid?"

Grijpstra shrugged.

"Who cares? Some person who passed the car and didn't like the gaping rear end. He pulled the lid down without looking at the possible contents of the baggage compartment. He saw something that shouldn't be and corrected the situation. I'm like that too. Last night, on my way home, I saw the wheel of a bicycle lying in the street. Shouldn't be there, might cause an accident. I picked it up and left it with some garbage cans so that it could be picked up this morning by the collectors. There are many people like me. A passer-by who closed the lid. It was dark, the streetlights are at some distance. Did the lock work when the lid was closed?"

"It held," Karate said, "but it had been tampered with."

"How did the car get here? Did the thieves have a key?"

"No, they hot-wired the engine."

"How did you find the corpse?"

Karate took off his cap and scratched his head.

"Well?"

"I don't want to upset you, adjutant."

De Gier pushed Grijpstra gently aside. "Tell me, Karate. I'm all right this morning. It's a beautiful day. This is a nice case. I'm glad we're working together again. Tell me all you know, Karate."

Karate replaced his cap. "Very well, sergeant. Mrs. Cabbage-Tonto checked in with us this morning. She has a small dog, very small, a Chihuahua, I believe it's called. Looks like the wrong sort of mouse. The dog had to pee, she was taking it for a walk on a leash. The dog pulled her to the Mercedes, peed for a bit and started yelling or squeaking. That kind of dog doesn't bark, I believe. She dragged it away and it went on peeing and it did the other thing too, maybe it even threw up, it was in a proper state, sergeant. It wanted to get back to the car and had another fit. Mrs. Cabbage-Tonto, she claimed to know the adjutant—Sergeant Jurriaans didn't want to listen to her at first—said that she knew somebody really high up in the force and would complain, and she described the adjutant, fat man in a pinstripe suit and big cheeks, she said, so we knew it was Adjutant Grijpstra . . ."

"Ho!" Grijpstra said.

"Yes?" Karate asked.

"Never mind."

"Right," Karate said. "So Mrs. Cabbage-Tonto said she found the dead man. She looked into the baggage compartment. The lock closed but didn't lock, if you see what I mean, because it had been forced. The witness ran all the way to the station, dragging the dog. It had sore paws when it arrived and sort of cried. It had to stand in a tray filled with water for a while to cool its feet."

"Go on."

"The lady didn't strike us as a reliable witness, but as she knew the adjutant and our station has had trouble with the adjutant before, Sergeant Jurriaans thought we might have a look. We found the corpse all right. It looked peaceful, folded into itself, but it was covered with blood."

"Could you ascertain its identity?"

"Yes, sergeant. The doctor gave us the wallet he found in its jacket. The man is called Jim Boronski."

"A foreigner," Grijpstra said, "we don't want that, a foreign corpse isn't easy to deal with."

Karate smiled helpfully. "He was Dutch, adjutant. The wallet contained a passport. Born in Rotterdam, now residing in Colombia, South America. A businessman. He also carried a hotel key, from Hotel Oberon."

Grijpstra groaned.

"Beautiful," de Gier said. "As I thought. We can link facts already. So our man drops dead into the car of a fellow hotel guest. Continue, constable."

Karate spread his small hands. "That's about it, sergeant. The corpse was dressed in a well-made suit of good material. Apart from the blood, it looked well cared for. I don't recall seeing the man in this district."

Grijpstra crossed the quay, studied the green water of the canal for a while, and came back. "Very well, we'll look into this. When did you find the corpse?"

Karate produced his notebook and flipped the pages. "Here, adjutant, 10:04 this morning. The doctor took it away at 10:30, it's 12:30 now, we waited for you."

Grijpstra scribbled in his notebook. De Gier looked at Asta. He remembered Sergeant Jurriaans's tale relayed by Grijpstra. He tried to visualize her as she must have been during that adventurous night but could only see a neatly dressed constable with inordinately sparkly eyes, now smiling politely. "I wish I were a detective," she was saying. "This job is boring, bah, smelly."

De Gier peeked at the bloodstained baggage compartment of the Mercedes. "Smelly? But this is fresh."

Asta peeked too. "The corpse was fine. I meant the chicken remains earlier on. Another complaint we took care of this morning. There's a Chinese in that sidestreet over there who slaughters poultry and dumps the leftovers in the street. The garbage collectors won't pick it up and the stuff rots. The Chinese won't bag it for he says bags are too expensive. Or so he seems to say. I don't speak Chinese."

"Yes," de Gier said.

The girl stood closer. "What will you do now, sergeant? Is this a murder? Is there a killer around? Will you find him?"

"Maybe."

"You will won't you? I hear you always find the killer."

De Gier returned her smile. "Your informants exaggerated." He looked at Grijpstra. "We've been known to fail." He touched his breast, then patted his other pockets.

The girl took a packet of cigarettes from her bag. "Would you like one?"

"No thank you. I don't smoke."

They had to step aside. Municipal workers were trying to park some road machinery and a sooty tank on wheels approached dangerously. An unmuffled engine started up and heavy drills bit into the tarmac.

Grijpstra shouted into de Gier's ear. "Let's go to the morgue and raise Cardozo. If there's any work he can do it."

De Gier shouted back. "Cardozo is sick, didn't you see the note on your desk just now?"

Grijpstra walked to the car, but had to come back to release de Gier from Asta's smile. He pushed the sergeant into a slow walk. "How sick is Cardozo?"

"Flu, may take a few days."

"Useless fellow. Who'll do the routine? That Boronski has no address here, he probably doesn't even have relatives in the city. If he had he wouldn't be staying in a hotel. We'll have to circulate his photograph, see what we can find out about him. We may have some time-consuming sleuthing to do."

"Yes," de Gier said, "but there's no hope of help in the brigade; it's holiday time and we're short-staffed."

"Get help."

"Yes, adjutant. Do you care where I get it?"

"No."

"Wait for me in the car."

Grijpstra smiled as he saw de Gier walk into a tobacconist's store. It took a while before the sergeant came back, but he wasn't smoking.

"What did you do in there?"

"I phoned, of course. I spoke with Sergeant Jurriaans. We have help. He's lending us Asta. He will order her to go home and change into civilian clothes. We are to pick her up later; I have the address."

Grijpstra snorted. "*You* pick her up. You're an idiot, Rinus, I warned you. That girl can't be more than twenty-five years old and Jurriaans is my age, in his fifties. She isn't right in the head, neither are you at this particular time. You sure you didn't buy cigarettes in that store?"

"Yes. To the morgue?"

"To the morgue," Grijpstra said cheerfully and grinned at his thoughts. They were in color and three-dimensional. His jealousy evaporated as he contemplated his vision. The central part of it was Asta without any clothes on, kneeling, her left hand held by Grijpstra who was dressed in a long silk robe. His free hand blessed the girl, who, with downcast eyes, demurely accepted the benediction. Her right hand was stretched out in the direction of a reclining naked male body, peacefully asleep on a well-kept lawn. The body carried a noble face with a full mustache and shiny curly hair.

I'm giving her to him, Grijpstra thought, as he took in more details of the vision. The little group was surrounded by orange trees close to a pond where interesting hard-to-define animals cavorted in pure water. The sky was cloudy, but had opened to frame a mysterious faraway figure shrouded in light. That must be God, Grijpstra thought. That's good, that makes me an angel. I don't want to be God, but to be an angel must be all right. They get to do things.

Like giving away, he thought a little later as the Volkswagen found a place in the small courtyard next to the city's morgue, a low building built out of glowing red bricks that belied the cold finality of its contents. It's better to give than to receive. Besides, he thought as he wrung himself out of the compact, I don't want to be hassled by females, no matter how superior they may be. De Gier still likes it. All I want is . . .

Not quite knowing what he wanted, he didn't finish the thought.

2

"GENTLEMEN," the small man said, "your client is waiting for you. He hasn't been in storage for more than five minutes. The doctor is done with him and is now washing his hands."

He restrained Grijpstra who was about to light a cigar. Grijpstra frowned.

The attendant raised his hands in helpless defense.

"Regulations, adjutant. They still apply to the living. The dead are free, they may do as they like in peace. You're welcome to smoke in my office." He opened a door and pointed at a table where a collection of pipes surrounded a full ashtray.

De Gier looked at the neatly labeled drawers of the massive refrigerator in the back of the room.

"Boronski. Here we are." He pulled. The drawer came faster than he expected and the corpse's face, slightly twisted to the side, looked up at him with an expression of furious surrender.

"Easy," Grijpstra said and put an arm around the sergeant's shoulders. "You should remember that nicotine no longer dulls your fears." He swiveled the sergeant's body and walked him away from the extended drawer.

"Can't stand it, can he?" the attendant asked. "I don't blame him. Took me a while to get used to them too, and I've lived with them for a long time. But they're not here, of course. A few will linger for a while. I can feel that, but I talk to them, polite-like, and they go away. There's nothing here for them and most should have better places to go to. I tell them that I'm just a crazy guy who works here, that I mean no harm. They're frightened, you know, whatever they were used to is no longer there. Alive yesterday, dead today, must be a bit of a change."

De Gier's nausea slipped away as he listened to the attendant's quiet voice. The man's beady eyes behind round little glasses seemed unfocused, his trousers were so short that they showed white skin above the crumpled socks, his green coat was partly unbuttoned. He wore a skull cap.

"Jacobs is the name," the small man said. "You won't remember me, sergeant, but I've seen you here before. Don't feel shy about showing your weakness. There's something wrong with the man who has to show his self-control at all times. If you want to know what your corpse died of you better see the doctor before he gets away."

They were ushered into another room where the doctor was looking at his notebook, circling words with a pencil.

"You're here for Boronski? Interesting case in a way, and so is the other, the one your colleagues brought in yesterday. Have a look at her before you leave. Attractive young gal, also found in the trunk of a car. Had been there awhile, but not long enough for the heroin traces to disappear. The white stuff in the corners of her mouth are maggot eggs, by the way. I thought it was spittle at first, but it wasn't. Maggots breed fast in this kind of hot weather."

"Murdered?" Grijpstra asked.

The doctor laughed. "No, no, that's all you chaps think about. Murder. Manslaughter. Violence. Most people die by accident, you know, out of stupidity. I believe there was a party in a villa somewhere; young people amusing themselves. This gal took an overdose, heroin has to be measured carefully, but she was a young girl, there were people about, dancing, making love. She didn't pay attention, injected herself in a hurry and croaked. Nobody noticed her death for a while, then they found her. Nobody knew who she was either. She was picked up, taken to the party, and there she was, dead. They meant to dump her, put her in a car, and forgot all about the matter. Body started to smell after a few days, the car was parked in the sun. Somebody noticed and stopped a patrol car. The owner of the car was found, and he said he didn't know at first. Later he remembered, vaguely. It all checked out. Your colleagues were upset because they didn't have a case, not even death through negligence. The girl is over twenty-one, she injected herself, she was put in the car without the owner's proper consent, he didn't know what was asked of him, being stoned himself. And then he forgot. Drove her around for days in his brand new supercar. Pleasant young fellow apparently. Bit of an addict. Won't live long himself. Well, gentlemen, what can I do for you?"

"Boronski, sir," Grijpstra said.

"Boronski. What can I tell you? He died around midnight. My original diagnosis was confirmed by the subsequent tests. Man was suffering of a really bad duodenal ulcer, enormous. Must have formed quickly, came to a head, the stomach perforated, and the flow of blood and pus upset his insides. He sort of choked internally. Severe cramps, must have doubled up, literally vomited his guts out and collapsed, I imagine. An extreme case indeed. He might have been saved if he had been taken to hospital immediately. Still a fairly young fellow too and no trace of other ulcers, his first and his last. You chaps know anything about ulcers?"

"No," Grijpstra said.

"Really? Had one myself once, long time ago now. I'm only a corpse cutter, but I'm not altogether out of touch with what the other branches of the profession come up with. Ulcers are psychosomatic, they say. You know what that means?"

"Caused by a malfunctioning of the mind, sir?" de Gier asked.

"Yes. Emotional malfunction. The mind is emotional, so is the rest of the body. I'd have to find the book again, but I think I remember that ulcers, particularly duodenal ulcers, are caused by a sudden loss of faith, in another person or maybe in an idea, a comforting idea that falls away and is no longer comforting. Some frightening insight, caused by something not being there that should be there. Would be true in my case. I thought I had a wife and I didn't; she was still around at that time but not in the way I thought that she should be. She had a lover." He chuckled. "I was young then and thought I had rights. Nobody has rights. We've got what's coming to us. However, I, in my innocence, or ignorance, that's a better word, ignorance, insisted on things to be otherwise than they were. So I was punished by an ulcer. A little one, but it hurt, and I had to eat porridge for a while, yak, porridge, and pudding. The puddings weren't so bad. My wife made them and put cherries on top. Very nice of her. Then she left me altogether. There was another female for a while who comforted me and the ulcer healed. Hasn't bothered me again."

"About Boronski, sir."

"Yes?"

"Any bruises on the body?"

"No. The hands are scratched; he must have toppled over and

scratched them on the cobblestones. I found traces of street dirt; it'll be in my report."

"But he wasn't found on the street, he was in the baggage compartment of a car."

The doctor dropped his notebook into his briefcase. The tiny lock of the case snapped in place.

"Really? Now how did he get there? Well, I've done my job, good luck to you. Have a look at that girl before you leave. Just out of interest. Maggot eggs, amazing."

The doctor left and the attendant came in and presented Grijpstra with a carefully typed list.

"The actual stuff is at Headquarters, adjutant, but this is what we found on him. Wallet, pocketknife, clean handkerchief, and so forth."

"Any money in the wallet?"

"Oh yes, plenty. Notes, cash, credit cards, checkbook, a foreign checkbook, I believe."

Grijpstra nodded at de Gier. "You hear, sergeant? Money. He wasn't even robbed. I tell you, he *fell* into that car. Nobody interfered with him."

"Yes," de Gier said tonelessly.

"You don't agree?"

"No. Look at the corpse again, closely."

Grijpstra walked back into the refrigerated room. The attendant pulled out the large metal drawer. Grijpstra shivered.

"Cold, eh?" the attendant asked. "I'm used to it, and it's nice during summer."

"I'm not cold."

"You recognize him?" de Gier asked from the far corner of the room.

Grijpstra rubbed his chin. "Yes. I didn't before. That's the man who came into Café Beelema on Saturday. We thought he was drunk. Maybe the ulcer was bothering him already."

"I watched him go into Hotel Oberon, after he staggered out of the café."

"Ah," Grijpstra said and continued to rub his chin. "I see. Fat German who owns Mercedes stays at Oberon. So does Jim Boronski. Mr. Boronski is dead in fat German's car. We'd better do something. *You'd* better do something. Find that German. Ask him questions. He's a foreigner without a fixed address and if he won't answer you satisfactorily, you can arrest him. Why don't you do that? Bring him over to Headquarters. By that time I'll have gone through the dead man's papers. You want to see the maggots?"

"Please!" de Gier said, withdrawing farther into his corner.

Grijpstra pulled the next drawer. He didn't look long. As he stepped away, the attendant pushed the drawer back into the wall.

"Did you see them?"

"Just the eggs, clusters in the corners of her mouth, as the doctor said. She's pretty, all right, although corpses never are, really. They're too dead."

"How old?"

"Hard to say. How young, rather. Nineteen, twenty-five, somewhere in between."

"Death," the attendant said. "I was reading about a place; Calcutta. Up there they have men like me who deal with the dead. They've got a name which I forget. They have long hair and a loincloth and when they don't work, they meditate. They sit quietly and reflect on the non-sense of it all. When they work, they burn fires and put the dead on the firewood, carefully, it's a ceremony, every movement has to be right. There are vultures to help the men, they're always there too. They get what falls out of the fire maybe, and they pick through the ashes. It's a better system than what we have. Here it's all mechanical. When the corpses are here awhile and nobody has come and the police don't care, they're cleared out and blasted in a huge oven with pressured fire. It should be done slowly, I think, with care, and there should be birds about."

"Crows and sea gulls," Grijpstra said. "We saw what they do a few days back. You take the car, sergeant, I'll walk. Don't be too long."

Grijpstra thought as he walked. He now knew that the stomach cramps he had been suffering from wouldn't be caused by ulcers. Mrs. Grijpstra was the way she was and had been so for a great many years. He concluded that ulcers could be avoided if nothing is relied on. If there are no points of reference, the framework the mind rests on cannot be destroyed, for there is no framework. He also knew that Jim Boronski died of natural causes; there should be no reason to pursue the search or even start it. However, the German and Boronski lived in the same hotel and they used the same car, be it for different purposes. Grijpstra saw a terrace with a view of a busy thoroughfare. He found a chair and ordered coffee. He promised himself a ten-minute rest while the trusty sergeant worked.

But he can't be trusted, he thought, for he is without his drug. Perhaps Asta would look after him. He remembered that Asta couldn't be trusted either. He forgot his fears while he watched young girls crossing the street, with sharply outlined bodies dressed in tight jeans or in narrow frocks, not quite narrow enough for the wind not to play with.

The adjutant had either picked the wrong place or the wrong time, for suddenly the crossing girls were all fat. He looked at the surrounding buildings and didn't like them either, they were square and gray. The sky was gray too. He sipped his coffee, put the cup down, and closed his eyes. Once again he saw himself bestowing the divine gift on de Gier. He wondered how the sergeant would react to his new companion.

The vision faded, and he got up and found canals and narrow streets lined with old and stately gable houses that rested his mind. He stopped to scratch a cat, spoke to a dog which changed its snarl into a pathetic grin, and picked up a shopping bag dropped by an old lady. While he listened to her complaint about rising prices, he saw the dead face of Jim Boronski again. It hadn't been a pleasant face, although the man was undoubtedly handsome. A villain, Grijpstra thought, and forgot the definition as he had to jump for his life to avoid a careening truck.

3

THE ADDRESS where Asta lived turned out to be a boarding house. The landlady directed the sergeant to the top floor, but when he got there, he had forgotten on which door he should knock. The second, he thought. There was no answer, and he opened the door. He was in a large bathroom and Asta was in the bath on her knees adjusting the faucets, her small, round bottom faced him. She looked over her shoulder.

"Excuse me," de Gier said, "I'll wait downstairs."

He went down and waited awhile, constructing theories to pass the time. None of the possibilities would hold. Why would the fat German kill expatriate Boronski, temporarily back in the old country? Were they businessmen fighting over a deal? What sort of a deal warrants violent death? Were they lovers of the same woman? Why would the German dump his enemy's body in his own Mercedes and then report the car as stolen? The ulcer seemed to rule out all thought of murder, but there were still mysterious and accusing facts. He left the building, bought chewing gum, chewed for a while, spat the gum out, and rang the bell again.

"Third door on the left, sir, but the ladies in this house are not supposed to have male visitors."

"Yes," de Gier said and ran up the stairs. The painful need of nicotine made him forget to knock. He saw Asta in the middle of the room. She still had no clothes on. She was on her knees again, looking over her shoulder into a mirror.

"Excuse me," de Gier said.

The girl jumped up, snatched a towel from the bed, and wrapped her slight body in it.

"For heaven's sake, don't you ever knock?"

"I did the first time, but the water of the bath was running."

"Are you wondering about my strange position?"

"Yes."

"I wanted to know what I look like when I'm on my hands and knees and somebody looks at me from the rear."

"Oh."

"What do I look like from the rear?"

"Nice."

She sighed. "Nice? Is that all?"

"Very nice," de Gier said patiently. "Appetizing. Irresistible. Please dress. The adjutant is waiting at Headquarters for his new detective and we have to see that German. I'll wait outside."

"You'll wait right here. You've seen everything already, but I would prefer you to look out of the window while I dress. What should I put on? I've never worked out of uniform. A dress? Jeans and a blouse?"

"A dress, Hotel Oberon is a classy place."

"Shouldn't you be wearing a tie then?"

"I never wear a tie. Hurry up."

"I like the way you wear your clothes," Asta said while her cotton dress rustled. "A scarf is elegant, you're an elegant man; they are rare in the police, I've never seen one except you. Even Sergeant Jurriaans isn't elegant."

"You like him, do you?"

"Yes."

"Is it true that the two of you went out one night and got drunk and that you stripped on a table and played on an Oriental rug with a girlfriend?"

"*What?*"

"Is it true?"

"Who told you that?"

"I heard," de Gier said.

"Me and Sergeant Jurriaans?"

"That's right."

"I had a drink with him once; he came into Beelema's and was distraught. He had a fight with his wife. I know his wife, she's charming. Jurriaans can be grumpy at times. He shouldn't talk about his private life to another woman, but I didn't mind."

"You didn't go anywhere with him?"

"No."

"Would you have liked to?"

She held his shoulders and pushed him round. "Of course. I love him. I would do anything for him. Even dance on tables and play on rugs."

"With another lady?"

"If he wanted me to. Shall we go? I'm ready."

De Gier was uncomfortable, but the ride didn't take long. The German wasn't in the hotel but pushed his bulk through the revolving glass door as they were ready to leave an invitation for him to come to Headquarters.

"Police? I don't want to speak to the police. Or is it about my car? Did you find my car?"

De Gier's German was slow and painful; the fat man didn't understand until Asta helped out. Her German wasn't much better than the sergeant's, but her pronunciation was better.

"We found the car, but we have to speak with you. Take us to your room."

The room was spacious and well furnished. The German didn't offer them chairs, although he sat down himself. He opened a thermos flask and filled its cup with lemonade.

"You found my car, where is it?"

"Do you know Mr. Boronski, Jim Boronski?"

"Yes. No. What is that to you?"

"What is your name? Show us your passport." De Gier found it impossible to be polite to the man. He caught the passport the German threw at him and opened it. "Karl Müller. What is your profession?"

"My firm imports wood. I buy from Mr. Boronski. He ships me wood from Colombia and Peru. We are men who do business together, no more."

"Mr. Boronski was found dead in your car this morning."

"What?"

De Gier looked at Asta.

"*Tot*," Asta said, "in your car."

Herr Müller's pudgy red hands trembled. He replaced the flask and cup on a side table.

"*Tot, Herr Boronski tot?*"

"Quite dead."

"How did he die? Was he murdered?"

"We don't know yet. We came to ask you if you knew anything."

Müller's cheeks trembled. Sweat ran down his face. He tried to say something but the words stuck in his throat. De Gier pushed his chair closer.

"He died during the night. Where were you last night?"

"I was out. In a bar and a club. I came home late."

"How late?"

"Two o'clock maybe, or a little later."

"You remember where you were?"

"Yes."

"Write down the names of the establishments and the times you were there."

While Müller wrote, de Gier considered the next move. The man's answers were acceptable so far. There was no charge, for if the doctor was right, Boronski wasn't murdered. Müller's passport seemed to be in order. To attempt to arrest the man might cause all sorts of unpleasantness. He looked at the passport again. The man originated in Hamburg. They might check with the Hamburg police.

He took the slip of paper from the table and read the names of the bar and the club. He knew the bar, a fairly respectable place. The club was a sex club, expensive and supposedly high-class. He had never been there and couldn't remember if the place had ever figured in police reports. If Müller said that he'd been there, he was probably speaking the truth.

"I'll have to hold your passport, and I must ask you not to leave this hotel until you hear from us. Tell us all you know about Mr. Boronski."

"Shall I make notes?" Asta asked.

"Please do."

The girl crossed her legs and pointed her ball pen at a new notebook. De Gier smiled and looked away. She had slender legs and slim ankles.

Müller seemed to have come through his crisis and talked easily. He had corresponded with Boronski's firm in Bogotá, Colombia, for years and done regular business with him ever since he began importing wood from that part of the world. Gradually the shipments had grown to sizable proportions, and as even larger deals were envisaged, he had thought that he should meet his supplier. Boronski said that he would go to Amsterdam and they had agreed to stay at the same hotel.

"So you came here specially to meet him?"

No, Müller also had other business in Amsterdam.

"What do you know about Boronski's private life?"

Not much. Boronski wasn't married, had no relatives in Holland, and hadn't been to Holland for many years. He drove a Porsche that he had just bought and meant to take back to Colombia.

Was there anything wrong with him physically?

Yes, he complained about stomachaches.

Did he drink a lot?

Yes, but not to the point of getting very drunk.

Girlfriends?

Not that Müller knew of.

Visiting sex clubs?

Yes.

Had he been seeing a doctor?

Müller didn't know.

Could Müller show any correspondence with Boronski's firm?

No, not here. Müller claimed that the correspondence was on file in his office in Hamburg.

"Where is my car?" Müller asked.

De Gier explained where the car was. "You can have it back. It was shorted and the lock of the trunk was forced, but the door lock wasn't. Did you forget?"

Müller nodded. "I forgot to lock the door. In Amsterdam they steal everything. Bad city, bad food, too expensive."

"You should have stayed home."

"Can I go and pick up my car?"

"Yes, you can move within the city as long as you leave a note at the hotel desk to say where we can find you."

"When do I get my passport back?"

"Soon."

"I was planning to leave. You'll have to pay for any extra time I have to stay at the hotel."

"Let's go," de Gier said and held the door open for Asta. He left without saying goodbye, closing the door behind him with a little too much force.

"A pig," Asta said. "Shall we make inquiries about Boronski at the desk?"

The hotel manager let them into his private office and ordered coffee. He was both polite and precise.

"Mr. Boronski? Dead? How unfortunate."

"Very. He lived in Colombia and had no relatives. It may be difficult for you to collect his bill."

"Perhaps, but it's a risk of the trade."

"Did he do anything that caused special notice?"

"Yes," the manager said, "on several occasions, he bothered us and I contemplated asking him to leave. There was that business with the girl and the trouble about his car. He seemed very upset, and in pain too. I suggested he should see a doctor. There was something wrong with his stomach."

De Gier sat up. "Trouble with a lady. Would you explain?"

"Of course. When was it? Last Thursday, I believe, or Wednesday. It'll be in the register. A lady checked in. I was at the desk that night, I remember her well, a rather lovely lady. She just wanted to stay the night, well dressed, good-quality suitcase, demure, didn't say much, didn't have a credit card, so she paid cash in advance. That night I wasn't on duty, I left shortly after she arrived. The night staff reported in the morning that there had been trouble with Mr. Boronski. A strange tale indeed. It seemed that he tried to get into her room, did get into her room, in fact, and somehow bothered her."

"Attempted rape?" de Gier asked.

"No, no. I tell you, it's a strange tale. He claimed that she was in his room, that he knew her, that he had arranged with her that she would stay the night with him, and the lady claimed that she had never set eyes on the man. She phoned the desk, my assistant went up. Boronski had lost all self-control, man was foaming at the mouth, I believe, and then my assistant discovered that Boronski's room was next door. Quite an upheaval. The lady was so upset that she packed her bag and left. My assistant tried to reassure her and offered excuses, free breakfast and so forth, drinks, anything she liked, but she insisted."

"Did she get her money back?"

"Oh yes."

"And Boronski?"

"He came to see me the next morning and stated that his room had been switched in some devilish manner, for all his belongings were arranged precisely as he had left them, but they were in the other room. I didn't believe him, of course. I even showed him the register. He had room 14, not 12, he had room 14 from the start. Boronski also told me that the lady had been in his room that afternoon. He had met her in the street somewhere, she was a prostitute. The, eh, meeting was most satisfactory and she had promised to come back in the evening at ten. He went to his room before ten and she was there all right but she didn't know him."

"Wouldn't somebody here have noticed her in the company of Mr. Boronski?"

The manager hid a yawn behind a dainty hand. De Gier noticed that he had polished fingernails.

"Excuse me, no, nobody noticed; we have sixty-four rooms here, there's a lot of coming and going."

"How could she have got into his room? Boronski had the key, didn't he?"

The manager yawned again. "Do excuse me, I haven't had much sleep lately. I wouldn't know."

"Amazing," de Gier said. "You also mentioned other trouble, something about a car?"

"Yes, another tall tale. He came to see me and said that his car, a brand new Porsche that he had just bought, tax-free, to take with him to South America suddenly had the steering wheel *on the wrong side*. I ask you. Fortunately, I knew by then that the man wasn't in his right mind; this was after the business with the lady, you see. I didn't want to listen to him, but he practically dragged me into the street. The car was there, a lovely job, silver color, red leather upholstery, must have cost him a fortune. The registration plates were special, Colombian, must have got them through the local consulate. The steering wheel was on the right side, and he said it was on the left when he bought the car the day before. Quite impossible. To change a steering wheel is a major operation, not the sort of thing somebody does with a screwdriver and a couple of wrenches in a few minutes. This was in the morning. He said he had parked the car in front of the hotel, had worked in his room for an hour, come out, and noticed the change. He had phoned the agent where he bought the car and the agent confirmed that the wheel was on the left side. So Boronski said he wanted me to phone the agent but I refused. I didn't want to listen to him. It was his car and his mind. We only provide rooms and meals." The manager laughed. "Anyway, the next day the wheel was back in its correct position so the mishap was taken care of."

De Gier gaped. Asta stopped writing.

"Did I hear you correctly?" de Gier asked. "Or am I going mad too?"

"You heard me correctly, but the man was mad."

"Did you see the car again?"

"No. He wanted to show it to me, but I refused to leave the desk. Damn it all, I'm not a psychiatrist, I'm a hotel manager. There had been all the other nonsense too. His watch disappeared from his bathroom and turned up an hour later in the spot where it should have been all the time. He sent his clothes for dry cleaning and the wrong clothes

came back to his room. One of the girls checked, but by that time they
had changed into the right clothes again. Mr. Boronski was suffering
from some form of paranoia. He hallucinated. He was physically ill too,
he complained of stomach cramps and we had to serve him porridge for
dinner; he exhausted the room service waiter by phoning for milk every
half hour. I'm glad he has left us."

"Yes," de Gier said.

"I'm sorry he is dead, of course, sergeant. Now if there is anything
else I can help you with." The manager looked at his watch. "I'm afraid
I . . ."

De Gier got up. "Thank you."

Asta stumbled in the corridor, the sergeant stooped to catch her arm,
and she turned and kissed him on the mouth.

"Hey!"

"I've been wanting to do that, do you mind?"

"No."

"Kiss me again."

"You kissed me. I don't kiss colleagues during working hours. Would
you like coffee?"

They sat in the coffee shop of the hotel for a while. Asta served the
sergeant, she even stirred his coffee for him. He grinned.

"You're a slave. I thought that young ladies don't do that sort of
thing anymore."

"What sort of thing?"

"Be servile."

"I love to be servile," Asta whispered. "I'm old-fashioned. I like to
be on my back and the man to be on me. I like to oblige. It's a pity you
have nothing to carry, I would carry it for you, even if it was very
heavy."

"Have you had many men?"

She pursed her thick lower lip and a tiny frown appeared on her
smooth forehead. She blew at a curl that hung in her eyes.

"Hmm. Not too many. I tried some young men but they weren't any
good, too quick. The older men are usually married, and when they embrace me, I know that they're looking at their watch behind my neck. I
can see it in their eyes. They're slow and polite, but they go away when
it's over. You wouldn't be like that, would you?"

"I might be. Who did you believe, the manager or Boronski?"

"Boronski."

"Why?"

"I saw his corpse, remember," Asta said. "I didn't like him at all, not with that low forehead and the eyes too close together. I've known men with low foreheads and close eyes that I liked, but Boronski had something nasty about him. But he wouldn't lie like that. And that manager didn't really exist, did you notice that?"

"How do you mean?"

"He was just like the hotel. It looks all right, but once you're in it you can see that it's all hollow. They have tried to recapture the dignity of the past; they've got the right architecture and the right trimmings, but there's nothing in it. Everything is hollow, filled with air. He was too. He's like a doll I once had. I threw it away. Even when I scratched its face and tore its clothes, it wasn't there."

"How do we find out who told us the truth?"

She giggled. De Gier looked up. The giggle was vulgar. It reminded him of the cry of a disheveled parrot in the city's zoo. He would always spend a few moments with it when he strayed into the zoo. The parrot was a jolly common bird, quite unlike its splendid mates eyeing the passing crowd arrogantly from their high perches. So far Asta had impressed him as refined, different from the other policewomen he had worked with.

"Are you testing me or don't you know how to find out whether Boronski saw things that weren't there?"

"Let's say I'm testing you," de Gier said.

She reached into her bag and gave him her notebook and her pen. "No. Write the solution down and fold the paper, then I'll tell you what I suggest doing and we'll see if we have the same solution."

He wrote while she looked the other way. "Okay. Tell me what we do."

"Boronski must have parked his Porsche close to the hotel. We'll find it and see which side the steering wheel is on. We know that it had the wheel on the right side when the manager saw it. If it's on the other side now, Boronski spoke the truth."

"Right," de Gier said.

"Can I see what you wrote?"

"No." He crumpled the paper and put it in his pocket.

"Am I right?"

"Let's find the car."

They found the car a few blocks away on the Princescanal. It had two traffic tickets under the windshield wiper. De Gier made a note of its location, phoned Headquarters from the nearest booth, and told them to tow it away. The car's steering wheel was on the left side.

4

THEIR EYES ARE the same color, Grijpstra thought as he watched the communication between the commissaris and the girl. He still referred to her as the girl, and the memory of the divine vision wherein he had given her to de Gier was clear in his mind. The sunlit antique room which the commissaris used as an office should have comforted him, as it had done so many times when the detectives discussed a case under the benevolent guidance of their chief, but it didn't now. At first he felt good again and easily fell into his role as an archangel handing out a sublimely beautiful girl to a special mortal, his cherished friend. The adjutant mused, and sucked on his cigar, which tasted bad but cost too much to throw away. The spotlight of the vision veered away from Asta, whose crossed legs showed enough of her thighs to stimulate Grijpstra's carnal appetite which he had transferred so successfully to the sergeant, to the pond that had formed part of his original fantasy. At that time, the pond was filled with various animal shapes, pleasurably engaged in play. He could see them more clearly now. There were monstrosities. A reptilian bird had caught something that might be a squirrel but had the legs of a frog. There was an evil glint in the bird's eye; it was relishing the frantic movements of its helpless prey. A winged fish was about to leave the water to attack a many-headed bird of splendor preparing to drink from the water that was no longer clear. Another shape, partly fish, partly animal, with a hooded head, floated about, engaged in reading a small book, a book of spells and curses,

Grijpstra assumed, as he tried to read the text. He shook himself and tuned in to the conversation.

"So we have an indication," the commissaris said, "a concrete fact we may call it. Very good of you, Asta, we should be grateful to Sergeant Jurriaans for lending you to us. You saved us some work, although I think that the value of Boronski's other accusations should be ascertained as well. Perhaps the sergeant can go back to the hotel this evening and find out what name the lady used when she registered. It may be her true name, and that part of Boronski's tale may be untrue, although if one part of his nightmare connects with reality, the others may . . . It was you who suggested finding the car, wasn't it, Asta?"

"Excuse me, sergeant," Asta said and got up. She walked over to where he sat, reached in the side pocket of his jacket and produced a crumpled piece of paper. She read it and laughed.

"The sergeant was teaching me, sir. We played a game. I would say what I thought we should do and he would write his idea down. Here you are."

The commissaris read the note. *"Find the car Boronski referred to."*

"I see." He took off his glasses, blew on them, and rubbed them gently with his handkerchief. "But you shouldn't protect him, dear." He turned to de Gier. "And you shouldn't be smiling. You've been in the game a long time. Credit is . . . Grijpstra, you had a good term for credit, what is it again?"

"A fart in a brown paper bag, sir."

"Exactly. However, we have the Porsche and the hotel manager's statement. We also have a corpse, dead of disease but found in the trunk of a car with the lid down. What else?"

"An obnoxious German, sir," de Gier said.

"Ah yes. I'm glad you qualify him, for there are also good Germans. I mention the point, because it has taken me a long time to admit the existence of intelligent, sensitive, and highly developed Germans. During the war I tended to forget, to my loss, I might say. But we haven't *got* the man. There's no charge. Are you planning to find confirmation of his whereabouts last night?"

"I thought I might go to the nightclub and the bar."

"Can I go, sir?" Asta asked.

The commissaris looked at the slight figure of the girl. He hesitated. Asta's lips pouted. "I'm not as weak as I look."

He nodded. "I know. Sergeant Jurriaans told me, and I heard what you did to the dog at Beelema's. Very well, you can go if you like. In which case Grijpstra can visit the hotel again and de Gier can stay here.

There should be a telex from the Hamburg police, I've asked them to give us any information they may have on Herr Müller. If there's nothing out of the ordinary there, sergeant, you'll have to return his passport. I don't believe in unnecessarily annoying civilians, especially not if they are our guests. I should have an early night, my wife tells me. You can wait here for the reply from Germany and your colleagues can report back to you if anything turns up so that you can plan further actions. Now." He opened a drawer of his desk and held up a wallet.

"I went through the contents of Boronski's wallet. There is a fair amount of cash, here are his credit cards, and there is an alphabetical register of names and phone numbers, mostly in Colombia and Peru, it seems, and some here in Europe. Mr. Müller is included—there is an office number and a private number, so we may assume that the two men had fairly intimate dealings with each other. There are no photographs except one which the photo room was kind enough to duplicate. It's rather small and in black and white, but I would like to study it closely. The photo room provided me with a slide, which I will now project; would Asta perhaps draw the curtains?"

The commissaris busied himself with a projector, and Grijpstra set up a screen. The projection was life-size. It showed a treeless busy street with wide sidewalks. Boronski and a female companion, arms linked, were walking toward the camera; around them were several men in black suits and with dark faces. Street sellers were selling trinkets from shoddy suitcases. Dirty children ran in front of the couple.

"Taken by a street photographer," de Gier said.

"That's what I thought, sergeant. This must be in South America. Please remember that it was the only photograph in the wallet, so Boronski valued it. What do you think of the lady? Study her at your leisure."

The room became silent for a full minute.

"What do you think? Ladies first. Asta?"

"The lady is Dutch, sir. I'm sure of it. The skirt she is wearing is expensive, but it was on sale in Amsterdam two months ago. It's tweed, I remember the C&A stores advertising it. Strange that she would wear tweed in South America; isn't Colombia a warm country?"

"Yes, but Bogotá has a cool climate. I looked it up in my encyclopedia this afternoon. The city is nine thousand feet high and usually chilly. Are you sure about that skirt, constable?"

"Absolutely, sir, the lady is wearing the complete combination C&A advertised. The vest goes with the skirt and is of a special cut, it's called the Groninger style. Originally the style was for men only, but C&A

launched it for women. Even the blouse fits the prescribed combination."

"I would also say the woman is Dutch, sir," de Gier said. "She is about thirty years old and still slim, but she'll soon be heavy and she has a local face. Maybe it's the hair style, but it's also the features."

"What do you think, Grijpstra?"

"She's married, sir. I see the wedding ring, thick, gold, without a stone. An old-fashioned wedding ring on her left hand, that is, if the photograph isn't reversed. Is the traffic on the left or on the right side in Colombia?"

"I don't know. In the photograph the cars drive on the right."

"Right-hand traffic," de Gier said. "I saw a list of left-hand traffic countries, Colombia wasn't on it."

"Good. We know that Boronski isn't married, Herr Müller told us. So this would be an affair. Affairs are quite common but we might try to find out who the woman is. Bogotá is a big city with two million inhabitants, but I don't think there will be too many of our countrymen over there. I can try our embassy out there; I could also try the police, but I hear that it's hard to establish contact with them. We had some illegal Colombian immigrants the other day who had fallen afoul of the law and we couldn't raise any information at all. I'll see if I can contact somebody on the teletyper, perhaps the Ministry of Foreign Affairs can assist; they've been helpful before. Anything else you noticed?"

"Yes," Asta said, "I think I see something. The woman is in love. The man isn't. She is good looking, he's showing her off, but he only wants to bed her and be rid of her again." The girl's voice was flat but trembled slightly on the last part of her sentence. The room became silent.

"Very well," the commissaris said, "you can open the curtains again, dear."

De Gier helped the commissaris to rearrange the projector into its case, and Grijpstra rolled up the screen. The commissaris limped to the door.

"How's your leg, sir?"

"Worse," the commissaris said, "and it shouldn't be in summer. The heat usually stops the pain. And I have my wife after me, she wants me to rest; maybe I should listen to her."

Asta and de Gier had left.

"What do you think of this case, sir?"

"What do I know, Grijpstra? I haven't seen the corpse, I'm not doing my job well these days. What do *you* think?" He closed the door and indicated a chair. "I have a few more minutes before my wife will call."

"Do you know the morgue attendant who is called Jacobs, sir?"

"Yes. He has been with the morgue a long time, but he's often ill. The man survived Auschwitz. It's strange that he selected such a morbid profession after all he went through. He came back alone, all his relatives died. Did you meet him today? I'm glad he is sane again, he was institutionalized for a while."

"He was talking about the dead this morning, sir, when we investigated the corpse. The way he talked interested me. He said that the dead sometimes hang about the morgue and are frightened, and that he talks to them and tries to reassure them and send them on their way. I went to see him again, just before I came here. The morgue is close and there was something I wanted to ask him."

Grijpstra fumbled with a cigar. The commissaris flicked his lighter and waited.

"I didn't like that corpse, sir. I've always paid special attention to corpses, it's part of the job; usually you get some sort of impression that's helpful. Do you remember the case of the blond baboon, sir?"

"Yes. Mrs. Carnet?"

"Yes. She looked victorious, as if she had pulled something off, just before she was killed. There have been other cases where the corpse hinted at something. This Boronski was different, he died of natural causes, but I had a distinct impression of evil, secretive evil, extreme egotism. There was also fear, but you feel that with most corpses. Nobody is courageous when it's all over and he is about to enter the unknown."

"So you went back to Jacobs? Why?"

"I wanted to know what he felt about the corpse."

"Did he tell you?"

"Yes. He said it was giving him trouble. He said Boronski was still around in the morgue; hating, cursing, frantic with rage."

"Was Jacobs bothered by that?"

"Not too much. He had protected himself." Grijpstra smiled. "He said he had made a transparent egg around himself, and that Boronski's spirit wouldn't be able to get through it. He said he always makes the egg when he has a troublesome client. I found him in his little office, peacefully sucking on a pipe and reading some holy book in Hebrew."

"Jacobs is a wise man," the commissaris said.

Grijpstra lumbered to the door. He turned before he left. "You know that we haven't really got a case. We are chasing phantoms again, just as we did during the weekend, but this time de Gier insists on going on."

"Are you with him, adjutant?"

"I am, sir."

"Good. The sergeant is developing, but he should still be watched."

Grijpstra walked back to his office and addressed the empty corridor. "I'm with him," he said loudly, "but I overdo it. I've even given him the loveliest girl I've seen in a long time, a girl, moreover, who prefers men my age to men his age. Now she's all his, to mess up as he likes."

He got into the open elevator, didn't pay attention, and went all the way round before he got off at the proper floor.

He was still mumbling. "A lovely girl with the right perversion. A pearl, for a pig."

He forced himself to think of something else and evoked the thought of hot water and a sharp razor. He found his shaving gear in his desk drawer and walked over to the rest room. Ah, to shave at ease, for there wasn't much to do, just a leisurely walk to Hotel Oberon to find out what the woman's name might be and another pleasant walk back to Headquarters to check her with the computer.

Then his mood changed again. He no longer saw the smooth lines the shaver traced through bubbly foam but the pond that had been in his vision when he was an angel, giving Asta away. The pond was filled with murky water now and sinister tiny animals tore at each other in the greenish slime. The sight unnerved him, the shaver caught his skin and a thick trickle of blood formed a fat drop and stained his shirt.

5

MANAGERS are all the same, Asta thought as she sat opposite the man in an office that could have been any office. The man was still looking at her police card. His face was blank.

"I'm a police officer, as you can see. The photograph is of my face, right? I'm not here to apply for a position in this establishment, I'm here to find out whether a certain Mr. Karl Müller, a fat German businessman, came here last night and I want you to tell me at what time he arrived and at what time he left."

"Yes," the man said.

They make them in a machine, she thought. The other one ran a hotel, this one runs a brothel. They are employees, there are others behind them who may be alive. This man isn't. He either came out of the metal mouth of some fantastic gadget or he grew in a big bowl of warm fluid. When he was done they fished him out, dried him, put him on his legs, slipped him into a plastic envelope, and brought him here. He was already programmed so nothing could go wrong. All he has to do is greet the visiting lechers, take their money, pour them full of alcohol, and steer them to the right girl. I don't fit his formula, and he doesn't know what to do now.

"Are you alone?" the man asked.

"Yes, but don't get any ideas. If you touch me, I'll tie you into a knot with both your feet in your mouth."

The man smiled. "Really?"

Asta smiled too. "Really. Now will you tell me about that German or do you want me to get help? I trust your license is in order. If it is, I could still charge you with living on the profit of prostitution of another person or persons, that article hasn't been revoked, you know. We still use it occasionally."

"Quite," the man said. "I'm sorry, officer. I have been trying to remember that German you mentioned. We had a busy night yesterday, there's a convention in the hotel across the street, of politicians. We were a bit crowded. Quite a few of the gentlemen were fat, and some of them were German. Müller, you said the name was?"

"Karl Müller, man in his forties, obese, bald on top and a long fringe below, a lot of gold teeth, a heavy gold watch, light-color suit and a red tie."

"Ah. Yes. I remember the tie. Red is my favorite color. Let me check the credit card slips."

He opened a neat file and turned small rectangular slips, wetting his finger.

"Here we are, Karl Müller, the address is in Hamburg. Yes, I remember him. He complained, the girl hadn't been cooperative, he wanted a discount. I asked the girl what was wrong and she said she refused to get into the bath with him. The more expensive rooms have baths, you see, with gold-plated faucets, special feature of the house. The baths are king size; even so, there was little room left for the girl. He also complained about the quality of our snacks, we serve free snacks with the drinks. They're good. I've never had anybody criticizing them before."

"What time did he leave?"

The manager closed the file and placed it on the right corner of his desk, tapping it with his finger so that it was parallel to one side and perpendicular to the other.

"He left early. He wanted another girl, but we had so many clients that the girls could make their own choice, and nobody wanted him. Sometimes I'm able to obtain free-lance help but usually not on Mondays; the ladies are resting then after the weekend. I made a few unsuccessful phone calls and the gentleman left."

"What time?"

"Hard to say, there was so much coming and going. Around midnight, I would think."

"You'll have to sign a statement to that effect, and I also need a statement from the girl who wouldn't get into the bath. She'll have to confirm the time he left."

The manager puffed on his cigarette. His eyes evaded the demon that was pestering him.

"I'm afraid that will be impossible."

"As you like," Asta said. "Let me use your phone. I don't care how many sex clubs there are in Amsterdam, they're still illegal. I'm going to get my sergeant and some uniformed cops and we'll go through the place. Don't leave this room until my colleagues have arrived."

There were two telephones on the desk; the smaller model was pseudoantique. He picked it up.

"Ask Willemine to come into my office, will you? It's urgent, I don't care if she is busy."

The knife flashed past Asta and hit the center of the circle that had been painted on the cupboard door. De Gier walked from the other side of the room to retrieve it.

"You might have hit me," Asta said.

"No, I missed you by a foot. I'm accurate within an inch, and I've been practicing for a year. I've always been bad with knives. Grijpstra is better, he's never more than a centimeter off, but he is slow on the draw. That part I've got right, I think, you didn't see me draw the knife, did you?"

"No."

"Good, but not good enough. Your results aren't good enough either. So Müller left the club at midnight, two hours earlier than he told us. The difference doesn't constitute a crime. He had been drinking, didn't know what the time was. We still can't arrest the slob. What happened to Grijpstra?"

"Here," Grijpstra said. The knife came again. Grijpstra took off his jacket and hung it on the knife. "I've been to the hotel; the girl we're looking for gave a false name. It isn't in the computer. The address she gave is in Rotterdam. I telephoned the police there, and a patrol car drove to the street; the street exists but the number doesn't."

"Harassment," de Gier said, "and she had help inside the hotel. Boronski must have stayed in room 12. Did you check the register?"

"Yes. The entries are made with pencil. The pencil hadn't been pressed down and the handwriting wasn't too clear. It's easy to change a 2 into a 4. I took the register with me and the lab looked at it. They say that the 2 of 12 may have been erased and replaced by a 4, but they won't swear to it."

De Gier took Grijpstra's jacket off the knife and hung it on a hook.

He replaced the knife in a sheath that had been sewn to the lining of his jacket.

"Inside help, probably the same person who changed Boronski's dry-cleaned clothes and then changed them again; he or she must also have lifted his watch from the bathroom and replaced it."

Grijpstra walked over to a battered set of drums and picked up two tapered sticks. He played on the side of the largest drum, lightly hitting the center in the middle and at the end of each bar.

"No," Asta said. "Do you often do that here, play drums?"

"Ever since the lost and found department gave him the drums," de Gier said. "Grijpstra gets everything free, I had to pay for this flute." He had taken the flute from his desk and blew a single note. Grijpstra sat up and started a fairly complicated rhythm. Asta couldn't hear who followed whom. The music seemed to become more intricate. The two men played for no more than five minutes. De Gier dropped the flute back into his desk, Grijpstra finished the way he had begun, with slowing taps on the side of the main drum.

"Wow! What was it? An improvisation?"

"Of course," Grijpstra said. "Ibaniz composed this for piano. He never thought of us, we can't play the piano."

Asta shook her head. "Sergeant Jurriaans told me that you two are musicians, but I never believed him. Most of what he says isn't connected with daily life."

"I should hope so," de Gier said. The telephone rang. "Right, I'll come and pick it up."

He was back within minutes, waving paper. "Hear this. In German but I'll try to translate it. *Karl Müller, businessman, import and export of lumber, apart from legitimate business possibly active in unproved drug dealing on large scale. Please let us know immediately if you can produce charge. Hamburg Police, Criminal Investigation Department, Narcotics Branch, signed Inspector Hans Wingel.*"

Grijpstra read the teletype message and gave it to Asta. He began to pace the room.

"So now we have some sort of construction. Ever since I heard that Jim Boronski lived in Colombia, I suspected drugs. We know that the stuff coming from Turkey is being intercepted too often, and the supply is irregular anyway. Colombia is a new source that seems more efficient, and the hashish and marihuana that originates there is of good quality. The Colombians also sell cocaine, and cocaine ranks about as high as heroin, in price, that is. A smart man like Boronski and another smart man like Müller would prefer to deal in cocaine; just a few pounds make a golden deal. So now let's assume that Boronski played foul and that Müller got annoyed. He harasses Boronski to the point where he drops dead."

"In Müller's car," de Gier said.

"RIGHT!" shouted Grijpstra. "That's where we go wrong. Every time. The whole silly thing is impossible. Boronski is sick, he gets sicker, he dies. That's all we have. We should close the case and go home. There's no logic in it. See you tomorrow." He put on his jacket and stamped out of the room.

"I haven't got a car," said de Gier, "but I could walk you home. You'll be safe, your landlady doesn't approve of male visitors."

"You can kiss me here."

De Gier bent down and kissed her.

"Is that the way you kiss? Just smack?"

She embraced him. "Can't you bend your knees? Or shall I stand on a chair?"

"No."

"All right, I'll take *you* home. My car is only two blocks from here and you live in the southside of the city; you have no car and it's a long bus ride."

"Who told you that?"

"Sergeant Jurriaans. I know that you are single and that you live with a cat in a luxurious apartment and that you have no current girlfriend."

"I'm married, I have four kids, and my wife worries about me."

"No."

"Didn't you say that Jurriaans can't be trusted?"

She opened the door. "Let's go, darling."

The car was an old compact Ford, battered and rusty. The inside was cluttered with clothes, cartons of cigarettes, and frayed wicker baskets containing odd objects. She made room on the passenger seat. The dashboard was cluttered too. A faded cloth tiger was glued to the loud-speaker. De Gier counted three boxes of tissues of different brands, all opened.

"How can you look so neat when you drive about in this junk pile?"

"Different parts of my mind manifest themselves in different ways. There's nothing wrong with this car, everything works."

She drove fast and paid little attention to traffic lights. De Gier hardly noticed. Her hand was on his shoulder. I'm in love, he thought. I haven't been in love for years. It's as if I knew the girl since the day I began my first life. He looked at the tiger, rooted solidly in the frame-work of the loudspeaker. Maybe we hunted saber-toothed tigers together when we were still apes. This is absurd. I don't want to be in love.

"This is south, am I going the right way?"

He gave her the address. She turned through a red light and put her foot down. A patrol car's siren howled behind them. She parked in front of the apartment building. The patrol car screeched to a halt and two constables came running up. Asta got out and showed her card. De Gier got out too.

"Evening."

"Evening, sergeant."

"Are you busy tonight?" de Gier asked.

"No, sergeant. Maybe later. There's a thriller on TV, all the crooks are watching it. Maybe later we'll find something to do."

"Good hunting."

"Thank you. You wouldn't be taking this constable home for pleasure, would you, sergeant?"

"He's thinking of it, but he won't get anywhere," Asta said. "Good night."

The patrol car drove off, the constables grinned and waved.

"Would you come up for a drink?" de Gier asked.

"I would."

They drank on the balcony; it was only a small balcony, but she kept away from him. He went inside to feed his cat. The cat purred and ran to the balcony. Asta picked it up. "You're ugly, you have too many colors."

De Gier came out to water his geraniums. "She's got the colors of a Persian carpet, that's why she's called Tabriz. Can I make you a meal? I've got some noodles and frozen soup, they might go well together. I could toss a salad, too."

They ate and washed up together. De Gier thought he should be flirtatious but couldn't think of suitable words. The girl was quiet and efficient. He didn't have to tell her where to put the dishes; she opened the cupboard and found the right places.

"Coffee?" he asked.

"No, sergeant, I think I should go." She raised her head and he kissed her lightly. When he tried to embrace her, she stepped out of his arms. "No. I'll see you tomorrow."

He pulled his only easy chair onto the balcony and sat with the cat on his lap. The cat turned over and he pulled at some hair that had matted together. The cat groaned. "I won't do it if you don't want me to." The cat didn't move. He tugged. Suddenly the cat jumped away and a sizable cluster of hair stayed in his hand. "Bothered you, did it? Used me as a tool, did you? Clever Tabriz." The cat wanted to come back, but he got up. "I don't want to work, Tabriz, I want to stay here and be with you, but I think there may be something to do." He looked at the sky; heavy clouds floated toward each other. "No car and it'll be raining." He put on a round cotton hat and took the elevator down to the basement where he extracted an old bicycle out of the clutch of another.

Half an hour later, a lone cyclist entered the inner city. The dying sun touched the lining of clouds that were lowering themselves on the spires of medieval churches. He left his cycle under a tree at the Brewerscanal and became a pedestrian. The herringstall on the bridge across from Hotel Oberon was doing a brisk business. He bought a herring, liberally sprinkled with chopped onions, and retired under the awning at the side to eat it in peace.

"Evening," a portly gentleman said.

"Evening," de Gier said. "I thought you had gone home."

"I didn't. I've been here for an hour and a half. I've eaten six herrings. He hasn't come out yet. Stay here, I'll have a beer at Beelema's. I'll be right back."

6

"THERE," Grijpstra said.

They moved simultaneously, each taking a side of the man, keeping well back. Müller waddled ahead, carrying a flat case. It was dark by now and the ornamental street lights, spaced far apart, played with the fat man's shadow. They also played with another shadow, slim and sharp, darting in and out of the lights. The shadow was attached to a girl, dressed in faded jeans and a trim jacket, bouncing on high-heeled sneakers. De Gier, on the waterside, and Grijpstra, inconspicuously merging with the walls of small and narrow houses, lagged even farther behind. Two more shadows joined the procession; they had sneaked from a side alley. They moved as gracefully as the girl. They were tall and thin, as black as their owners, who were both in their late teens or early twenties, with shaved skulls, sporting leather jackets and tapered dungarees.

Rapists, Grijpstra thought.

Robbers, de Gier thought.

Can't have that, they both thought. Neither man was concerned about the girl's safety at that moment. They were hunting and Müller was the prey. If the boys caught up with the girl, there would be a scuffle, some noise, a scream maybe. Müller would be distracted and not do what he was supposed to do, or do it in a different manner, adding complications to the simple situation that now faced the original pursuers. One of the muggers followed the line of the trees bordering the canal, the other adopted Grijpstra's tactics. Neither of them was aware of the danger behind. De Gier ran, Grijpstra lumbered. De Gier drew his knife faster than Grijpstra.

"Hey."

The boys stopped and turned. They were well trained. They did the right thing, their knives were out too, but they were at a disadvantage.

"Drop it."

The knives fell. They were light and didn't clatter much on the cobblestones.

Grijpstra's catch muttered four-letter words, the other stared at de Gier. Of the two, the adjutant's prey was the most surprised. Grijpstra could not be in the same profession as the boy, yet he was. This well-dressed elderly man with the kind face, complete with tie, cuff links and neatly folded white handkerchief in his breast pocket, was asking a black street mugger for his money. The boy's deepest mind was disturbed. Facts no longer fitted reality. There was the stiletto, its cruel point pressing against his throat, there was the hand on the shoulder of his leather jacket, there was the pleasant voice, asking for money.

The other boy could accept his particular set of circumstances more easily. The tall man in the round cotton hat looked somewhat odd. He could, if the imagination were stretched just short of the breaking point, perhaps be lurking in dark streets, prowling for loot.

"Give," Grijpstra said.

De Gier didn't speak. He hissed. He supported the boy's bare skull with his left hand, pressed the knife with the other. The skin on the boy's throat was about to break. The boy fumbled in his pocket and came out with crumpled bills. De Gier grabbed the money and swung the boy round. The boy held on to a tree while de Gier patted him down. The sergeant's foot pushed the boy's knife into the water, it splashed softly. Grijpstra picked up the other boy's knife.

"*Give!*"

The boy gave.

"Off with you, that way!" Grijpstra pointed over his shoulder. The other boy was running already.

There was a second splash as the other knife hit the canal's calm surface.

The detectives waited for the boys to slip into the alley that had emitted them a few moments ago and turned.

They should have kept the knives. Müller, alerted by the splashes, looked around. Asta stopped short.

"You?" Müller asked. The arm that carried his case swung back. The girl ducked and pulled her gun, arming the pistol as it came out of her pocketbook. The pistol's click immobilized Müller.

"You're under arrest; drop your case, turn round, and hold your arms behind your back."

Asta shifted the gun to her left hand and produced her handcuffs. She had some trouble trying to fit them around Müller's fat wrists. He kicked twice, forward and backward. The case shot into the canal and Asta staggered.

When Müller turned, clawing at the air separating him from the girl, de Gier jumped. The sergeant's flat hand came down, hitting Müller in the neck. The man's thick skin and spongy blubbery tissue absorbed the impact, but de Gier hit again in a blur of vindictive fury. Müller's breath escaped in a burst of foul air; after that he sobbed. Then he fell, taking his time, spreading his monstrous body between a tree trunk and de Gier's feet. The sergeant stepped back.

Grijpstra was on his knees, holding Asta's leg.

"I'm all right," she said. "He caught me on the side. It hurts but the knee'll still work. Help me up please."

She held on to Grijpstra and hobbled over to de Gier.

"The case, it's floating away, we've got to get it. You can lower me down and I'll pick it up. Here, hold my gun."

De Gier lay down and Grijpstra held his feet. Asta grabbed the low railing at the end of the cobblestones and lowered her body gently. She touched the case with the point of her shoe and maneuvered it toward her.

"Don't drop me, sergeant." The case was between her feet. "Pull me up now."

Grijpstra handcuffed Müller while de Gier and Asta opened the case; it contained sixteen small plastic bags. Asta undid one and sniffed at the powder; she passed the bag to de Gier.

"Probably cocaine, the laboratory'll know. You did well, Asta."

She looked round. Grijpstra was slapping Müller's cheeks slowly and methodically with both hands.

"Is he coming to?"

"In a minute, not yet."

She kissed de Gier, just touching his lips. "Did I really do well? I wasn't sure. The connection between Müller and Boronski was drugs. There would be drugs in the hotel. Müller knew we were after him. He had to get rid of the evidence; he didn't want to leave it in the hotel, for we might have traced it back to him. He thought he would dump it into the canal, a little bag at a time. He would wait until dark. If I could catch him with the drug in his possession, I could arrest him. Right?"

"Wrong, you wanted to do it on your own. We never work by ourselves, not if we can help it. You should have asked me or the adjutant to assist you. We're supposed to work as a team."

"Yes, I'm sorry."

"It's a long road," de Gier whispered, "and there's nothing at the end, but we can have company on the way."

"Yes."

He saw her lower lip tremble and embraced her. She was talking, but her face pressed against his chest, and he couldn't hear what she said. He held her at arm's length. "Say that again?"

She was crying now. "Please don't think I wanted the credit of the arrest. It was that you looked so happy on your balcony with Tabriz. I thought the two of you should rest for a while. Please tell the commissaris you made the arrest."

"That's all right." He gave her her gun and his handkerchief. "Cops don't cry, not much anyway. How's he doing, Grijpstra?"

"Awake, and he wants to get up."

Together they pushed and pulled until Müller was in balance. They led him back, and Grijpstra telephoned for a car at café Beelema. De Gier parked the wheezing Müller against the bridge railing while he bought Asta a herring. The car, a minibus driven by Karate, arrived within minutes.

"Where to, sergeant?"

"To Headquarters. Tell the turnkeys to make him comfortable. We'll interrogate him later tonight."

"Right. If you have a minute, you and the adjutant might go over to our station. Sergeant Jurriaans wants to talk to you."

"No," de Gier said, "I've had enough for tonight. Some other time."

"You'd better go, sergeant, me and the chief did a little work for you tonight."

"Tell me what you did."

"No. The chief wants to tell you himself."

The bus drove off.

Grijpstra came out of the café, wiping beer froth off his mouth.

"Why did you let that bus go? I don't want to walk back to Headquarters."

"I have my bicycle," de Gier said, "but Asta wants to go with me and it won't carry two passengers. There's also a proposition from the station here, which is around the corner. Jurriaans wants to see us."

"Good. He can have us driven home."

They walked slowly, Asta in the middle.

"See?" Asta said, pointing at a disorderly heap of feathers. "This is where the Chinese throws out his garbage, and there's nothing we can do about it. It isn't just feathers, there's blood and meat too."

"Good for rats," Grijpstra said, steering her around a temporary fence. "This part of town'll never get organized. What are they black-topping this area for? What's wrong with cobblestones?"

Asta tried not to limp. De Gier supported her elbow.

"You realize that we are still nowhere," Grijpstra said. "So Herr Müller is a drug dealer and we can prove it. That's nice. But drugs is not our department. That the Hamburg police will be pleased has nothing to do with us either. First we had a murder and no corpse, it added up to zero. Now we have a corpse and no murder. Zero equals zero."

De Gier grinned. His arm slipped around Asta's shoulders. "There's nothing more glorious than zero, adjutant. You can multiply it at will, you can divide it at will, and it will always be the same. We can lose ourselves in nothing and go as far as we like; we'll never hit the other end of it."

The adjutant hadn't thought of a reply yet when Sergeant Jurriaans welcomed his guests with outstretched arms, beaming at the bedraggled group that reluctantly entered his small office.

7

"You look tired," Jurriaans said. "Are they overworking you already?"
Asta lit a cigarette. Her hand trembled.

"No, I fell and hurt my knee; otherwise I'm having a good time."

"How do you like de Gier?"

De Gier reached for the match Grijpstra was about to strike; he put it in his mouth.

"This is not a social call, colleague. Please come to the point."

Asta smiled. "I love him. I love you too. My soul is torn."

Jurriaans nodded. "I'd advise you to lean his way, even if he's short-tempered. Married men are easy to deal with, but they've lost their spunk; the stress of the home situation takes its toll. Married men also carry guilt which clogs up the atmosphere. Take him and come to me for comfort. I'll always be around for I can't get away."

De Gier's teeth snapped through his match and he took another from Grijpstra's hand. Grijpstra gave him his matchbox and took Jurriaans's lighter. He lit his cigar and slipped the lighter into his pocket.

"Why are we here?"

"You're here because your case has come to an end. I've liberated you. If you like, I'll tell you about it, after you return my lighter, of course."

Grijpstra replaced the lighter.

Jurriaans sat back. He cleared his throat.

"Well, where shall I start? I can't start at the beginning, for I don't know where it is. My interference came so much later, and it wasn't even mine, for Karate saw him. He saw the Prime Punk, and we subsequently arrested him. About two hours ago I tried to get hold of you, but I couldn't trace you. I wanted you to hear the Chief Punk confess, but he'll repeat his performance if you like, and if you don't, I have his signed statement."

"Who?" Grijpstra asked.

"He is a mugger and he robs cars. He's quick and sly and an expert, but Karate was quicker. Karate and I were driving about tonight; with Ketchup on leave and Asta in the higher spheres I'm even more shortstaffed than usual and besides I was bored. A bit of active duty cheers me up sometimes. We drove through the Red Mill Alley, and Karate braked and raced out of the car and confronted the Punk. He is twenty years old and leads the other Punks, the second best gang of the district. The best gang is the Black Jackets and I'm sorry we didn't catch their chief for he specializes in perfidity. The Punks will break your bones, the Black Jackets will suck the marrow. They're bad and they're black. This is a racist station and we tend to identify the two ideas. That is a mistake, I know it. I know that the percentage of criminals of our black fellow men is only slightly higher than the white percentage. I'm also aware that the blacks are recent immigrants and are learning to deal with a new environment, but I don't always practice my knowledge."

De Gier selected a fresh match. "You arrested the Prime Punk?"

"I did. He was breaking into a car. Karate caught him red-handed; the Punk was using a wonderbar. A wonderbar is a metal tool and he hit Karate with it. Karate thereupon attacked the Punk and I couldn't stop him in time. The Punk was in a bad state afterward. I admonished Karate for a few minutes and interrogated the Punk for an hour. I said that it was about time that we caught him and that I would make sure that he would receive the maximum punishment. I thereupon appealed to his sense of logic. I implored him to confess all his crimes so that he would only be punished once and not repeatedly. The Punk has never been arrested yet and we don't have his fingerprints. Knowing that he works without gloves, I told him that we found fingerprints on a silver-colored Mercedes with a Hamburg registration yesterday. I said that, if the fingerprints matched his, he would be in more trouble than he was now, but that he could improve his position by confessing right now."

Grijpstra no longer reclined in his chair. De Gier's match broke again, but he didn't take another.

"Ah," Sergeant Jurriaans said, "I see that I have your attention. Yes, my friends, it was him, him and an unidentified helper."

Grijpstra sighed. "He didn't kill Boronski. Our corpse died of natural causes. We'll never break the doctor's statement. A large duodenal ulcer, no human hand. What did the Prime Punk say about Boronski?"

"He said that he and his helper, whose identity he can't remember, hot-wired the Mercedes in front of the Oberon and drove it to the Gentleman's Market. They parked the car and pried the trunk open. There was nothing in the trunk. They closed the lid and got back into the car, intending to go for a joy ride, when the trunk's lid popped open. Because they had forced the lid, it no longer closed easily. They got out to close it again, when a man came staggering along. It was around midnight and there was nobody else about."

"They didn't rob Boronski," Grijpstra said.

"No. They may have intended to, thinking that the man would be drunk and helpless. As they approached Boronski, the man doubled up and vomited blood. He took a few more steps and held on to the trunk's lid. He fell into the trunk."

"As I thought," Grijpstra said. "As I thought all the time."

"Did he fall in altogether?" de Gier asked.

"No, but a patrol car passed on the other side of the canal. The constables in the car weren't paying attention, but the Prime Punk didn't want to be seen with a bleeding drunk. He expected the patrol car to come back on his side of the canal. He pushed Boronski into the trunk, slammed the lid, and walked away. He thought that the man would sleep in the trunk and that there would be enough air, because the lid didn't close properly. He expected the man to be found in the morning."

"Death by guilt," Grijpstra said. "You have a charge. The doctor said that Boronski could have been saved if he had been taken to hospital straightaway."

"The charge has already been laid. Now for the Prime Punk himself." He picked up his phone.

Within a minute the suspect was brought in. The young man's face was made up and his jacket carried a number of gaudy brooches, a bottle opener that had been unscrewed from a bar counter, a framed photograph of Alain Delon, and a German Iron Cross. His short hair was dyed with henna. His fingernails were painted orange. He didn't say anything. His jaw was bruised and his left ear bandaged.

"You can take him away again. Remove his ornamentation so that he can't hurt himself." The elderly constable accompanying the Prime Punk saluted.

"End of the case," Sergeant Jurriaans said when the door closed again. "I didn't mean to fish in your water, I just happened to be around when the fellow could be caught."

"Another cow catches another rabbit," de Gier said. "Here's money." He counted seven twenty-five guilder bills. "How much did you get, Grijpstra?"

Grijpstra put another seven bills on Jurriaans's desk.

"You're not paying me, are you?"

"No, we mugged two muggers. Black Jackets. They were in our way and if we hadn't acted serious, they might have hung about. You probably had a complaint at this station tonight. Somebody must have lost the 350 that the Black Jackets split among themselves. I hope it was only one robbery. If this is the total of several felonies, you may have complications."

Jurriaans laughed. "You must have shaken them. It so happens that I do have a complainant who lost that amount tonight, a parson from the provinces who happened to stray into one of the bad streets around here. Do you remember what your fellows looked like?"

"Perhaps this little matter shouldn't be pursued," Grijpstra said. "Just return the venerable sucker's money, will you?"

"I will," Jurriaans said and tucked the bills into an envelope which he licked carefully. "Perhaps the parson doesn't want to pursue the matter either. He's a married man and the street where he was caught has a prostitute behind every window." He looked at his watch. "Are you free now? I am, and I live close by; I can go home and change. We could meet at Beelema's."

Grijpstra got up. "No, I've been there twice already tonight, and it is a place I'm trying to avoid. We still have some work to do. Some other time, Jurriaans, at another café, and thank you."

"The pleasure is mine."

They met Karate at the door. He looked at Asta. "How're you doing?"

"She's fine," de Gier said.

"I'm not," Asta said. "My knee hurts and needs a compress. A wet towel will do. I should lie on a bed. Do you have a towel?"

"He'll have a bed too," Karate said.

De Gier turned on the small constable. "Just for that, you can drive us to Headquarters and pick up my bicycle on the way, and you can drive me home, too, after we're done."

Karate opened the side door of the minibus.

"Be my guest, sergeant."

Grijpstra sat in front. He pushed away the partitioning between the driver's compartment and the rear of the bus and tapped de Gier on the shoulder.

"Rinus?"

"Yes?"

"We have no murder."

De Gier smiled. "Are you sure?"

"No."

The bus drove off.

Asta's hand slid into the sergeant's. "You mean it isn't over yet?"

"No, but we'll have to start all over again and in a different way."

"Good," she said, "I need more time with you, and my knee hurts."

"I have a towel at home," de Gier said and looked at a window where a tall black woman in white lace underwear stared back at him. She smiled; the mauve neon lighting of the small room made her teeth light up. She pulled a hidden string and her bra opened for a moment, displaying a perfect bosom.

Asta's elbow hit the sergeant's chest.

"Uh."

"Did you like her?"

"So-so."

"Did you like me in the bath today?"

"Yes."

"Good," she said. "Let's not spend too much time on Herr Müller." She tapped on the partitioning and yelled at Karate. "Let's go!"

The minibus's faulty siren howled hesitantly, worn gears ground painfully, a profound rattle shook the vehicle. Karate, jaw set, bent down over the wheel and mumbled encouragingly; the car picked up some speed.

It stopped again for some drunks who tottered from sidewalk to sidewalk in the narrow street.

"Sorry," Karate said, "only civilians can speed in Amsterdam."

"Yes," Grijpstra said, "or no. Never mind. Maybe I see it now, but I don't see all of it."

"Beg pardon, adjutant?"

"A chaos."

"It sure is, adjutant. See that respectable lady over there? With the hat in her eyes? A schoolmistress or a welfare worker. Drunk as a coot. How the hell did she fall into sin?"

"I've never accepted the chaos," Grijpstra said. "Perhaps I should. Turn up that siren, constable, we've got to get out of here."

8

"BUT LOOK HERE," Grijpstra said, "you were seen opening your case, taking out a small plastic bag, and pulling back your arm with the obvious intention of throwing the bag into the canal. We subsequently searched the case, which you closed again when you were arrested and managed to kick into the water. The case contained plastic bags, and each bag, according to our laboratory, was filled with a quarter of a pound of first-class cocaine. All in all, you had four pounds of high-priced junk in there. True or not?"

Müller's chins moved convulsively in a fluid movement upward until his thick lips trembled slightly. Grijpstra wasn't sure how to interpret this facial agitation. "Are you smiling, Herr Müller?"

"I am."

"Why?"

"Because you're wrong."

"You weren't about to throw the cocaine into the canal?"

The fat man's hands shifted slightly on his belly, which was pushed up obscenely and ready to flow over the edge of Grijpstra's desk.

"Your facts are correct but your explanation isn't. The case belonged to Boronski. He left it in my room; perhaps he planted the case on me, I don't know. Boronski was a sick man. He chose my car to die in; perhaps that desire was intentional too, again I don't know. We weren't getting on well; I was displeased with the quality of his shipments. I told him that I might find another supplier. He wasn't in his right mind, he was hallucinating, he was causing trouble in the hotel."

"Really?" Grijpstra asked. "So why would you destroy the cocaine, why didn't you give it to us?"

Müller's face appeared to become more solid. A crafty light flickered in his protruding eyes.

"Tell me, Herr Müller."

"Because you are the police. The police here are no good. The food is no good either. Nothing is good here."

There was a newspaper on Grijpstra's desk. The adjutant glanced at the headlines. *Further moves in drug scandal.* He had read the article earlier that day. The paper claimed that charges would be pressed against several highly placed police officers.

"Yes," Müller said. "I'm from Hamburg, our dialect is similar to Dutch. I can read your newspapers. What would happen if I gave you four pounds of cocaine?"

"It would be confiscated and in due time destroyed."

"Nein."

"Nein?"

"Nein. It would disappear. It would make you rich. I don't want to make you rich. Cocaine is bad. It would still reach the addicts. I decided to do some good work. I'm an honest merchant, I deal in lumber. My material goes into homes and furniture. I protect society. I took the risk to do away with the poison myself, but you prevented my service to society."

Grijpstra nodded pleasantly. "You could also have burned it, or flushed it down the toilet."

"I'm not a chemist. Perhaps cocaine explodes when it burns. Perhaps it does not dissolve easily. I did not want to clog up the hotel plumbing. I thought I was doing the right thing, but you interfered."

Grijpstra got up. "Fine. I will now take you back to your cell."

Müller got up too. "I want some cigarettes and matches."

"But of course. We will get them from the machine on our way to the cell block. By the way, Herr Müller, there's another charge against you. You resisted arrest and attacked an officer. You hurt her knee."

Müller smiled triumphantly.

"This way," Grijpstra said.

He came back a few minutes later, sat down, and dialed.

"No," a female voice said, "the teletyper is in use by your chief."

"My chief is at home."

"He's here."

"Here? Doing what?" Grijpstra looked at his watch. "It's two in the morning."

"He's using the teletyper."

Grijpstra looked at the telephone.

"Will that be all, adjutant?"

"No. Get me the Hamburg Police Headquarters, Inspector Wingel, drugs department. He won't be there, but they'll know where to find him. I'll wait here for his call."

"I don't speak German," the girl said.

"Then just get me the number."

It took twenty minutes before Wingel was on the phone. His voice sounded sleepy but became clipped when he understood what he was told. "Yes," he said. "Yes."

Grijpstra yawned. "I thought you might be interested."

"I am. I'll be right over."

"Here?"

"There. I'll leave now and bring a colleague. There won't be much traffic. We'll be there in three hours."

"Very well," Grijpstra said. "I'll wait for you." He let the telephone drop back on its hook. He yawned again. He picked up the phone again.

"Who is the commissaris talking to? Not to the German police, is he?"

"No, adjutant. To Colombia. It took us forever to make the connection. He's got himself set up in the other office. He's been there for more than an hour; he's speaking to our embassy out there."

Five minutes later the adjutant was asleep, his head against the wall, his feet on his desk. The remnants of a grin eased his face and he burbled placidly through pursed lips. De Gier was asleep, too, at the edge of his bed to give room to Tabriz who had stretched herself on a wet towel. She had come in late and nudged Asta's body aside patiently, pushing the girl with her nose and soft paws. Even Müller was asleep, snoring heavily while he fought shapeless fiends that tore at his lies. Boronski was dead, more dead than when the detectives observed his stiffening features. Perhaps his spirit was about, but the attendant Jacobs no longer cared. He had built his transparent insubstantial egg and sat within it, peacefully puffing on his battered pipe, studying a Hebrew text through his little round glasses.

Only the commissaris was awake, waiting for the teletyper to rattle again and reading through a stack of paper with torn edges that recorded his conversation so far.

9

THE COMMISSARIS had gone home that afternoon and limped up the cracked cement steps to be embraced by his wife, stripped out of his clothes, and lowered into a hot bath. In his bath he was without pain, for his rheumatism was eased by the steam and the swirl of minute soapy waves, as well as the coffee, and the cigar that his wife brought and lit ceremoniously, before placing it carefully between his lips. She hovered about while he read the paper, skipping over the headlines and the editorial and concentrating on two items. Astronomers, an article tucked away into the far corner of an inside page told him, had discovered a new galaxy; it was about the size of the Milky Way and would, therefore, contain the same number of planets that were the size of the earth, at about the same distance from their suns, at more or less the same state of development; approximately a million. The commissaris chuckled. The other item informed him that a Gypsy child on the outskirts of the city died that morning. She had, somehow, fallen into burning rubbish. The identity of the child had not been established; she was about three years old.

"A new galaxy," the commissaris said to his wife. "At three billion inhabitants each, multiplied by one million. How much would that be?"

"I don't know, dear."

"Would their suffering add up to the fear and pain of one child?"

His wife did not hear him, she was letting a little more hot water into the bath. "Are you comfortable, dear?"

"Very."

"Afterward you should have a nap."

He slept, first thinking, then dreaming about Boronski. After a while, he was conscious of waking up but resisted and slipped into no man's land where everything is instantaneously possible and solutions rise up like bubbles, each holding a complete picture.

He dressed and left. His wife accompanied him to the front door.

"You won't work, will you?"

"A little."

"In your office?"

"Oh yes."

His sleek Citroën was respectfully greeted by the old constable in charge of the large courtyard behind Headquarters. He reacted by lifting a finger. He didn't see the old man, he didn't see anybody in the corridors either. In the teletype room he asked to be connected to the Dutch embassy in Bogotá, Colombia. After a good while the machine came to life. He heard the staccato of the keys, saw the words form.

"Please go ahead."

He gave his name and rank and asked for the ambassador.

"He's lunching."

"This is urgent. Please find him."

"It'll take time. He's not in the building. There are some festivities. Perhaps later in the afternoon . . ."

"It's late evening here, the matter cannot wait."

"Yes sir. You'll hear from us."

The commissaris returned to his room and brought out his projector. He unrolled the screen and closed the curtains. He sat and gazed at the slide showing Boronski and the unknown woman. The telephone rang two hours later; he was asked to return to the teletype room.

"This is the ambassador."

"Do you know a man by the name of Jim Boronski?"

"Yes."

"He died here in Amsterdam yesterday. There are some complications. Please describe the man to me, not his body, his mind, please."

The machine hummed. A minute passed.

"Are you there?"

"Yes," the machine wrote, "but remember that I'm a diplomat. I've also consumed a fair quantity of alcohol. This is not the time to make an official statement that is recorded at your and my end."

"Are you dictating this message?"

"I am."

"Can you handle the teletyper yourself?"

"I suppose so."

"Please make direct contact with me. I will ask the lady who's assisting me to leave this room and will write myself. Afterward I will destroy the messages."

The commissaris nodded at the female constable sitting next to him. She got up and left the room.

The machine hesitated. "This is . . ."

"Go ahead."

"The ambassador. Are you alone?"

"I am."

"What's your age?"

"Sixty-three."

"What is your job?"

"Chief of the murder brigade."

"Will you give me some private advice?"

The commissaris sat back. He reread the sentence, then reached for the keys. "Yes."

"I'm in personal trouble. I'm also drunk. The lunch was heavy. I need advice; do I have your word of honor that this correspondence will be destroyed?"

"Yes."

"I'm fifty years old. I'm partly homosexual. I'm married and have children, not yet grown up. My family does not know about my sexual inclinations. I appear to be normal."

"Homosexuality is not abnormal," the commissaris typed slowly.

"So I hear. I don't believe it. I'm ashamed. You understand?"

"Yes."

"I have a lover. A Colombian. Sometimes I visit him. He has had us photographed."

"I see."

"The photographs are revolting."

"So you say."

"I could describe them to you. You would agree then."

"I would not."

"Are you homosexual?"

"No."

"Are you faithful to your wife?"

"Lately yes; I'm old and suffer advanced rheumatism."

"And before?"

"Yes, I was unfaithful."

"Often?"

"There were certain bursts of activity."

"Were you ever blackmailed?"

"No, but it has been tried."

"Photographs?"

"No, correspondence."

"What did you do?"

"I told the lady to go ahead. She did. Photocopies of what I wrote were sent to my wife and my chief."

"What happened?"

"I had some trouble, not too much, the truth is the best lie."

"My trouble is more serious than yours was."

"I don't agree."

The machine hummed for nearly two minutes. The commissaris lit a cigar. He puffed and watched the paper in the machine.

"You know, Colombia is not The Netherlands. Guns are for hire here. My enemy is evil. I was set up. He'll go to the limit."

"Don't."

"The matter could be arranged, I know where to go. A colleague was in the same predicament. His problem was taken care of."

"Don't."

"What if there's a scandal? I will lose my job, my wife, my children. At my age I cannot find other employment, I'll rot somewhere in fear, in misery. I'll be alone."

"You won't, but even so, there is always something worthwhile to do. Murder is a lowly way out and will twist back on you."

The reply was prompt. "Yes." There was a pause. "What would you do in my case?"

The commissaris put his cigar on the edge of the machine. He typed slowly and carefully. "I would sit in my garden and communicate with my friend. Do you have a garden?"

"Yes. Who is your friend?"

"My friend is a turtle."

The machine was quiet.

"You're laughing, aren't you?" the commissaris asked.

"I am. Your advice is good. I have a small dog, I will communicate with him tomorrow morning when I'm sober."

"What sort of dog?"

"Small, white with black spots, ugly. I found him a year ago, starving, covered with vermin."

"He'll confirm my advice."

"Yes."

"Boronski?" the commissaris asked.

The machine picked up speed.

"No good. I know him fairly well. An amoral small-time tycoon. Deals in lumber and anything else that is profitable. Smuggles whisky into the country, on a fairly large scale. Probably exports drugs. Owns a large villa in the suburbs. Originally a ship's steward, worked his way up rapidly. Goes to most of the parties of the foreign community to show off his importance. Unmarried, but attractive to women. There have been unsavory affairs."

"How unsavory?"

"He uses women, then drops them when he feels bothered or as soon as they bore him. There have been divorces and at least one suicide."

The commissaris closed his eyes, opened them again, and typed out a description of the woman in the photograph. "Is she known to you?"

"Yes. She doesn't live here, she came on a South American vacation with her husband. They were due to go to Rio from here, but she stayed behind to continue her affair with Boronski."

"For long?"

"No. Boronski tired of her, he has a lot of choice here. She had no money and came to the embassy for help. We contacted her husband who paid for her ticket. About two months ago. She fell down the stairs in her hotel, slipped a disc and left in a wheelchair."

"Her name?"

"I forget, I'll phone my wife. Hold on."

The commissaris stretched.

"I have her name. Marian Hyme. Her husband works for a publishing company in Amsterdam. Was Boronski killed?"

"Yes."

"How?"

"He was harassed to death."

"Will you be able to prove that?"

"No."

"So why bother?"

The commissaris lit another cigar. He smoked peacefully.

"I see," the machine wrote. "Thank you for your advice. I trust you. Goodbye."

"Goodbye."

The commissaris got up and tore the sheet out of the teletyper. He crumpled it, together with the others that had slipped off the small table attached to the machine. He dropped the paper into a metal wastepaper basket, held the container on its side, and lit a match. The paper burned fiercely and the smoke hurt his eyes, but he held on until the flaming balls fell apart into black crisp shreds. He stirred the ashes with a ruler. Two girls came into the room.

"Is there a fire? Are you all right, sir?"

He coughed. "Yes. I'm sorry I made a mess. I threw a burning match into the trash can, silly habit of mine. My wife keeps warning me and I keep on doing it." He left the room while the constables opened windows and waved the smoke away with a plastic tablecloth.

It was quiet in the building as he walked to the corridor to take the elevator back to his office. He found Grijpstra and two middle-aged men waiting near his door.

"Sir," Grijpstra said, "I'm glad to see you. These gentlemen are Inspector Wingel and Subinspector Roider of the Hamburg Police. I have interrogated the suspect Müller, without success so far. These colleagues now request permission to speak with him. They have met him before and are interested to find out what connections he may have in Germany."

The two men straightened up and clacked their heels as the commissaris shook their hands.

"Why not? We're always happy to oblige."

Grijpstra smiled apologetically. "They want to see him right away, sir. They say it's better when the suspect is tired. We arrested Müller tonight because he was in possession of four pounds of high-grade cocaine and because he kicked and hurt Constable Asta's knee. She was in pain."

The commissaris stiffened. "She was, was she? How is she now?"

"De Gier took care of her, sir. They left together earlier on."

"Nothing serious?"

"Not too serious."

The commissaris looked into the cold eyes of the German inspector. "You may go ahead; my adjutant will find you a suitable office. Do you have a hotel?"

"We'll find a hotel later, Herr Kommissar, we know our way about in Amsterdam." Wingel bowed stiffly.

The commissaris watched the three men walk away, Grijpstra leisurely ahead, the German policemen marching slowly in step. He shuddered and his hand missed the door handle of his room.

10

"Good," the commissaris said while he read through the large menu, handwritten on elegant paper. "A new restaurant, but obviously handled by the right people. Even the chief constable recommends it. Hmmm, oysters. Hmmm, mushrooms. Hmmm, sirloin steak. Yes. Well, have you all made up your mind? I'm sorry I'm late, but I couldn't find a parking place easily and I've forgotten my cane, took a while to get here. Oysters, Grijpstra?"

The waiter took his time writing down the order and the commissaris sipped his drink. Asta sat opposite him.

"How's your knee, dear?"

"The swelling is going down, sir."

"I trust you had a restful night?"

Asta looked at de Gier. "Not quite. The sergeant has a cat. I woke up in the middle of the night because I thought my alarm went off." She pointed at an electronic watch that seemed far too large for her slim wrist. "I switched it off, but the beeping went on. It was the cat and a friend."

"The cat beeped?"

"No sir. The friend. A mouse. I suppose Tabriz wanted to catch the mouse, but the mouse didn't want to play. It got annoyed. When I switched on the light, I saw the mouse jumping, a foot high, right in front of the cat. Every time the mouse faced Tabriz, it beeped. It was a rhythmical sound, that's why I thought my alarm went off."

"I'll have another drink," the commissaris said, holding up his glass. "I see. These are modern times indeed. Not only do you spend the night with a lover, you're telling us about it."

"He didn't love me, sir. My knee still hurt. I didn't want to go home. My landlady doesn't approve of latecomers and I don't have a key for the night lock. There was no choice."

The commissaris offered de Gier a match. "Sergeant?"

"Yes sir. Thank you, sir."

"You'll never learn, will you? Is there a happy end to the tale?"

"Yes sir. She made me get up and take the mouse down to the park. It wasn't hurt. Tabriz couldn't go to sleep after that; she rattled about in the kitchen. Kept me awake."

The meal was served and the commissaris was the first to finish his plate. He sat back and lit a cigar. "The chief constable was right, this is an excellent place to have lunch. Now then, I must congratulate you three on the arrest of Müller. I would like to hear the details. Tell me, adjutant, but eat your potato first."

Grijpstra reported. The salt cellar became Müller, a toothpick was Asta, the Black Jackets turned into two black olives, de Gier was a small cigar, and Grijpstra himself the pepper shaker.

"No," the commissaris said, "you mean to say that you mugged the robbers?"

"There was no other way, sir. We had to keep them away from Asta. We couldn't arrest them because they hadn't done anything yet. If we'd merely stopped them, they might have shouted or interfered with Müller's arrest in some other way."

The commissaris pushed his spectacles to his forehead. He picked up the olives and ate them, then he chuckled. "Hee hee, Grijpstra."

"I'm sorry, sir, but we did a good thing; the parson got his money back."

"Hee hee." The commissaris laughed helplessly. Two tears streamed down his cheeks. He wiped them away with his handkerchief. "How silly, Grijpstra, how *apt*. What splendid fellows you two sometimes are."

"And Müller confessed, sir," de Gier said. "We got his statement this morning in German. Inspector Wingel gave it to us, signed and witnessed by himself and his assistant."

The commissaris was serious again; he blew on his spectacles and wiped them carefully. "Yes? I thought Müller wasn't too cooperative after the arrest."

"He wasn't," Grijpstra said, "but he weakened when the German inspector woke him up somewhat roughly, sir. They had him for two hours after that."

"Were you there?"

"No sir, I waited in my office. They interrogated him in a room on another floor. It was five in the morning then and there wasn't anybody in the building, except the staff of the radio room. I thought I heard Müller scream a few times. When I saw him again, there was a stream of spittle running out of the side of his mouth and he seemed dazed. Subinspector Roider had gloves on; he was taking them off when he escorted the suspect to my office. Müller's face seemed abnormally red."

"Ah."

"The German colleagues were pleased, sir. The suspect had provided them with some names and addresses in Hamburg and other cities. He also made a full confession. Apparently Boronski had brought down the first consignment of cocaine to get the connection started. Future deliveries would be made by couriers, so-called tourists, nice elderly couples who would have their trips paid for and receive an ample fee on top of expenses. This was the first time Müller bought drugs from Boronski. Until now their business was legitimate."

"Where did he buy before?"

"From Turkey through Lebanon and France, but that traffic was stopped by the French police a while back. He was buying heroin then, but cocaine is about as profitable."

"Have the Germans left?"

"Yes. They said Müller was lucky that he was caught here and not in his own country. The penalties in Germany are stiffer, here he'll only get a few years."

"True," the commissaris said. "Did you ask him anything about Boronski's death?"

"Yes, he denies having anything to do with that."

"Do you believe him?"

"Yes sir." Grijpstra was playing with the menu that the waiter had replaced next to the commissaris's plate.

"Yes," the commissaris said, "we'll choose our desserts in a minute. Why don't you believe that Müller killed Boronski?"

Grijpstra put the menu down and held up two fingers. "First, Boronski was Müller's goose that lays the golden eggs. Second, Müller wouldn't have placed the body in his own car, a car reportedly stolen at the time and looked for by the police."

De Gier held up a finger too. "Boronski died of an ulcer, sir."

They ordered and ate their desserts. It took a while, for both Grijpstra and Asta selected the special, which came in a tall glass and had many layers of different ice creams, topped with fruit and whipped cream.

"Boronski was killed," the commissaris said when Asta licked her spoon. "He was attacked by a mind that was more subtle and agile than his own, and manipulated to the point where his fear and uncertainty turned inward and gnawed through his gut. Remember Mr. Fortune, this case is similar. Fortune faltered, became accident prone, fell afoul of the police, and was dumped into the Brewerscanal. But there was some insight in him and he managed to save himself. Fear eventually strengthened Fortune; it destroyed Boronski, understandably, I suppose. Boronski was, I hear, rather a rotter, and Fortune, according to your reports, seems to be a nice fellow."

De Gier deposited the remnants of a match into the ashtray. "Is good stronger than evil, sir?"

"I've often wondered about that," the commissaris said, "and I do believe that I have had some indications that the supposition may be true. The subject is tricky, sergeant. Good is useful and evil destroys. Sometimes it is good to destroy, and useful is often a shallow definition; it's relative, of course." He folded his napkin. "If we imagine that a drug dealer is a bad man and that a publisher ready to retire in solitude to meditate on the center of things is a good man, and if we bring them both into stress situations by playing about with their environment, and if they are both of the same strength, I would say that Boronski will go under and Fortune will come out on top. But the experiment starts at the end and I've built up its base afterward. We know that Fortune is a happy man today and Boronski's spirit is in hell, if I'm to believe Mr. Jacobs, the morgue attendant."

"You seem to have investigated Boronski's death further, sir."

The commissaris wrote a check. He looked up. "I have, Grijpstra. I spoke to an acquaintance of the dead man last night by teletype. The lady in the photograph you studied in my office yesterday is a Marian Hyme, the wife of a local publisher."

"Hyme," Grijpstra said.

"The name is familiar?"

"Back to Beelema, sir. It's the last place I want to go to. I was there twice yesterday. I can't get away from it."

"Tell me what you know about Mr. Hyme," the commissaris said, "and I'll tell you what I know. If we pool our ignorance, Mr. Hyme may turn out to be our missing link."

11

"I MUST ASK you to calm down," the commissaris said. "Please sit down, sir, and don't shout."

Hyme sat down. His pale face framed a flabby and twitching mouth. "Boronski! The bastard! Dropped Marian like a sack of potatoes when he was through with her. Destroyed her dignity. She was a beautiful woman, intelligent, witty. You should see her now. *He* saw her. He came to the hospital to see if she was about to get out. Looking for a free fuck. Man hasn't been in Amsterdam for years and he has no connections here. He let her go in Bogotá, pushed her out of his palace with hardly enough time to pack her suitcase, but here he comes running after her. Marian has just been operated on again; she's flat on her back and in pain. It's the second operation and they don't know yet if they got the disc back in place this time. If it's where it should be, it'll be another six months before she can walk. When Boronski realized there was nothing doing, he shook her hand and left. I'm surprised he didn't take his flowers with him; he could have given them to somebody else. He had wasted his money."

"So you were aware that Boronski was in Amsterdam. Did you meet him at the hospital?"

"No. Marian told me about his visit."

"Did you meet with him here?"

"Briefly, on the Brewerscanal. I ran into him; he stays at Hotel Oberon. When I met him, I couldn't speak. The man has ruined my life. That vacation to South America was the worst hell I've ever lived

through. We were invited to a cocktail party at the embassy and Marian
fell for the bastard immediately. I thought it was a little flirtation, but
she went home with him. She checked out of the hotel. We had a terrible scene; everything was said, everything that has ever been bad between us. I thought it would be the ultimate farewell, but she came back
to me. She probably still loves him."

Hyme hid his face in his hands. Grijpstra sucked patiently on his
cigar. De Gier studied a stain on the wall.

"Would you like some coffee?"

"Yes."

De Gier poured the coffee. The cup rattled on its saucer when Hyme
took it.

"Did you see Boronski at his hotel, Mr. Hyme?"

"No. If I had, I would have killed him. I'm not a violent man, but I
must have changed. I keep on thinking of ways to destroy that devil. I
thought of having him kidnaped, locking him up in some dungeon, tor-
turing him, but what can I do? The days a man could take revenge are
over. I'm not too courageous anyway, that's why Marian got bored with
me. I'm a slave, chained to my desk. My only act of bravery is pissing
off bridges and I can only do that when I'm drunk."

"Yes," Grijpstra said softly.

"With a paper hat on. I'm the knight of the paper hat and the
wooden sword, riding a rocking horse."

"Ah," the commissaris said. "What sort of a car do you have, Mr.
Hyme."

"What?"

"What sort of a car do you drive?"

"A Porsche."

"With the wheel on the right side?"

"How do you know?"

"I guessed."

Hyme drank his coffee. The room was quiet. Grijpstra got up and
left. The telephone on the commissaris's desk rang.

"Yes?"

"It's me, sir, Grijpstra. Can I have a word with you in the corridor?"

"Yes?" the commissaris asked when he had closed the door behind
him.

"We might as well arrest him, don't you think, sir? The car checks
out, he had the opportunity and the motive. He must have paid the employees of the Oberon to play tricks on Boronski."

"You can arrest him, adjutant."

Grijpstra reached for the door handle, but the small almost transparent hand of the commissaris rested lightly on his sleeve.

"I wouldn't advise you to do that, however. Harassment is difficult to prove and hardly punishable. You'll find yourself wasting endless time in a court case where the lawyers will have a field day. Besides, Hyme is not your man."

Grijpstra stepped away from the door. "He isn't?"

"No. I admit that the suspect's nerves are in a bad state and that he may be at the lowest point of his life. But you mustn't forget that he is a director of a large and successful firm. Mr. Hyme is no fool. He's not a genius either. Only a genius would have confirmed, in the way he just did, that his dearest wish is to do away with Boronski, and tried to prove his innocence in such a perverse way."

"Shall we tell him that Boronski is dead, sir?"

"We can do that now."

"Dead?" whispered Hyme. "When?"

"Yesterday. Jim Boronski bled to death internally. A severe duodenal ulcer. Some would-be muggers saw him staggering about on the Gentleman's Market just after midnight on Saturday and, for some reason, dumped him in the trunk of a car. He must have died shortly afterward."

"My God," Hyme said. "But he was still a young man."

"Young men die too, Mr. Hyme. Your enemy must have labored under heavy stress. He suffered, but didn't go to a doctor. His complaint worsened, circumstances were against him, and . . ." The commissaris gestured.

"Dead," Hyme said.

"Where were you last night, sir?"

"I ate in a restaurant, visited Marian at the hospital, went home, and watched TV."

"And the night before, Sunday evening."

"Same thing."

"You weren't at café Beelema last night?"

"No."

"And the night before?"

"No. I was there Saturday and met with your assistants."

Grijpstra raised a hand. "Have you met with Mr. Fortune recently?"

"Yes, yesterday. We arranged for the take-over of his firm. He came to my office. I was glad to hear that his wife turned up after all."

"Did Mr. Fortune tell you about Boronski's death?"

"Frits Fortune? No. Why should he? He doesn't even know Boronski."

"Did Borry Beelema know Boronski?" de Gier asked.

"Yes. I pointed him out to Beelema. Hotel Oberon is just across the street from Beelema's."

"When was that?"

"Last week some time."

"Did you confide in Beelema about your troubles with Boronski?"

Hyme nodded. "Yes. Beelema is a friend. I've known him for years, ever since he bought the café. Before that I was his client at the hair salon, I still go there every fortnight and at the café I see him several times a week. He's my best friend." He smiled. "He's more than a friend, he's an incarnate angel. A lot of people call him the other son of God."

"Did you," de Gier asked, "by any chance, some time last week, lend your . . ."

The commissaris jumped up with such force that his chair hit the wall.

"That'll be all, Mr. Hyme. Thank you for coming here. I hope your wife's condition will soon improve. Adjutant, please escort Mr. Hyme out of the building."

12

"This is the best time of the day," Beelema said. "They've all just got home and there'll be dinner in a minute. The town is quiet. The town is so much more beautiful when there's no bustle, don't you think? Like one of those old prints or glass paintings—they only show the buildings and the water, maybe a boat moored to a tree. People are a nuisance."

"Indeed," the commissaris said. He was leaning over the railing watching a duck. The duck's head was submerged, and it was waving its bright orange feet. A little farther down a swan floated, asleep, its feathers precisely arranged. It bobbed almost imperceptibly on the slow ripple of the canal's weak current.

"It was good of you to come to see me. You're not here professionally, I understand?"

"Oh yes," the commissaris said, "I'm here professionally but not officially. You've committed a crime, but I won't arrest you if that's what you're getting at. My curiosity has brought me; I would like to know the details of what you managed to bring about."

Beelema unclipped a gold toothpick off the chain that spanned his ample stomach and pressed it slowly between his teeth. He took it out and spat. The duck retrieved its head, quacked, and paddled away; the swan looked up sleepily and reinserted its beak between its back-feathers. "But perhaps you could arrest me. Some of my deeds could be proved, I suppose; you might get some sort of case together."

"No. The law we uphold is primitive. I would have to prove intent to kill. Did you intend to kill Boronski?"

Beelema fumbled with the toothpick. Its clip was small and he had to bring out his spectacles to finish the operation. "No, not really, but he died."

"You see, there goes one charge. Yet you killed the man as surely as if you had fired a bullet through his head. Death caused by guilt would be the better charge, but you would have to confess and I would have to produce witnesses who heard you state your intention to bother Boronski."

Beelema's fluffy white curls danced as he shook his head. "I wouldn't confess, and I told nobody, not even Hyme. The favor was a secret."

"Favor," the commissaris said softly.

Beelema smiled, and his golden canines caught the sunlight. "Yes, a favor to a friend. Hyme was harmed and couldn't defend himself. I have a talent; I'm imaginative and energetic. I'm also efficient. But I've reached all my goals. My hair salon is successful, I can live on it in luxury. The café goes well. I have all I want and to spare. I've no need for a car or a boat or an airplane or all the other gadgets rich people go in for. This area is all I care for, I hardly ever move outside it. When I found that I could help people unobtrusively, by pushing factors a little, by fitting parts into a whole, I began to experiment. I've been amazed at what I can do."

"Just amazed? Never frightened?"

"Never frightened. I listen to my friends, I observe them, I see what goes wrong with them, I also see ways to right the wrong. Sometimes I concentrate when I sit at the bar or walk about in my shop or stand on this bridge, but often the thoughts just pop into my head. You've seen two examples of my work. I liberated Frits Fortune and I balanced the scales in Hyme's head. There have been other examples that I won't mention because I'm not trying to impress you. I didn't ask for my talent. It just came to me to be used."

The commissaris was watching a sparrow now, investigating ripening seeds on a weed growing between stones. "Ah."

"You don't approve? You must be doing the same thing, or do you wait until there's a deadlock and the man goes down? Do you kick him when he is down? I've often wondered about the police. In a way I also police this area; I restore order."

The commissaris smiled. "We usually wait until it's too late. *Optima civi cives*. The highest value of a citizen is the citizenry. We'll let them muddle through as best they can and only interfere when they break the law."

"When it's too late."

The commissaris nodded. "When they break the law, it is too late. But they shouldn't break the law."

"Pfff."

"I beg your pardon?"

Beelema turned and found the right place for the railing to support his back. He was of the same size as the commissaris but nearly twice as wide.

"The law. Rules and regulations, I never liked them. As a toddler I took part in a school performance; I had to dance with the other kids in a circle. I kept on leaving the circle and dancing the other way. I don't remember that event, my mother told me about it. She was embarrassed. Everybody laughed and I wasn't allowed to finish the act. I see what goes wrong and I help others to find an original solution, contrary to custom. Fortune was unhappy, he'll be better off in his present position. Hyme was a wreck. He was turning into an alcoholic, swilling beer at my café, making a spectacle of himself on this bridge. Now he can face the world again. Boronski was a scoundrel; he didn't concern me until he crossed Hyme's path and therefore mine. I enjoyed that little game."

"Who was the lady who upset Boronski at Hotel Oberon?"

"Guess."

"Titania?"

"Never," Beelema said, poking the commissaris playfully in the side. "You don't know Titania, so you are excused. She can only perform when I'm right behind her. No, Rea Fortune, of course. She used to be an actress, not a very good one, I think, but good enough for this little drama. I mentioned the matter to her and she accepted immediately. Every woman is half a whore, Shakespeare said. She enjoyed being picked up by Boronski and went to the hotel with him. Sexually she is very capable. He had such a good time that he arranged for her to spend the night with him too at a stiff price, which he paid in advance. Even smart businessmen can be suckers. Rea used the cash to pay her expenses when she ran away from her husband." Beelema giggled. "Wonderful how it all fits together, don't you think? And she'll never breathe a word. She is with Zhaver now and Frits Fortune is going to give her a lot of money. Zhaver wants to open up on his own farther along, a small restaurant, I found it for him. There should always be change. He worked well for me, but it's time to replace him. I've already replaced Titania, too. How do you like the new girl?"

"Beautiful," the commissaris said.

"I've always liked black women. I'm having some white jumpsuits made for her. It'll be fun experimenting with how far the zipper should be pulled down. She has perfect breasts, but they shouldn't be exposed completely, I think."

The commissaris agreed.

"I'll ask the adjutant and that handsome sergeant to be on the committee. They're good men; they have the talent, too, I think. I sometimes recognize it in others. Not too often, though; it must be rare. *You* have it."

"Do I really?" The sparrow flew off. The commissaris turned his back to the railing too. "And the car? How did you arrange that? Hyme didn't know, did he? My sergeant was going to ask him, but I cut the question off. I didn't want Hyme to run to you and prevent this conversation or alter it."

Beelema burped. "Excuse me. Too rich a meal again. It'll be worse when Zhaver opens his restaurant. I should really go on a diet. Hyme? No, he never knew. He has a habit of leaving his car keys on the counter, and that night he had a lot to drink. I slipped out and got the two kitchen boys at Hotel Oberon to help me push Boronski's Porsche away. Then I replaced it with Hyme's Porsche and took all the stuff that Boronski had in his car and rearranged it carefully in Hyme's. The kitchen boys changed the number plates. When I knew that Boronski had seen the car, I changed everything back to normal again. No, Hyme never knew. His Porsche was back where it had been by the time he went home."

"The kitchen boys also arranged the matter of the watch and the laundry?"

Beelema laughed. "You heard about that too? Yes. They were foreign students who have meanwhile left the country. They'll be hard to trace. They helped me with all the other set-ups too. Little things mostly. It's amazing how a man can be shaken by little things. I noticed that a long time ago at school, when I practiced on the teachers. It seems as if each man creates a foundation for himself, a pattern of habits. A teacher I particularly disliked would always hang his hat on a certain hook. I would take it off and hang it on the next hook. It drove him frantic. Nobody could understand why he got so upset. I sat in the hotel lounge sometimes and observed Boronski. I read some of his thoughts, analyzed his mind. He was neat. I arranged that the waitresses would spill on him, just a little, a drop of coffee, a tiny splash of ketchup. Can happen to anybody, they would apologize and pretend to clean his trousers or jacket and then they would worsen the stain somehow; women are very clever at that. There were other instances. I know the traffic attendant who writes out the parking tickets here; he drinks at my café. Boronski got a lot of tickets. My friend would wait for Boronski to come out of the hotel and make him pay in cash. And my dear old lady friend, Mrs. Cabbage-Tonto, pretended that Boronski had stepped on her Chihuahua and made a terrible scene in the street. Much more happened, I won't bore you with it all, but I had Boronski jumping during every waking minute, and I daresay I got into his dreams too."

"True," the commissaris said, "we live in patterns. We make them ourselves, they're our safety, and you dare to interfere with the patterns of others."

"With reason," Beelema said. "I'm entitled to do it; I have both the talent and the right. You don't agree?"

"No," the commissaris said.

"You don't," Beelema said. "I'm sorry to hear it. I thought you would agree. I've studied you a little. I took you for a superior man, like myself. But you're small-minded. You would be, of course, in your official capacity, but I thought you would liberate yourself from prejudice in your spare time. However, no matter, would you care to step into my café and have a drink with me?"

"I would not," the commissaris said, "but I thank you for satisfying my curiosity."

Beelema did not move.

"Is that your last word? I had hoped for a little more."

"There is the law," the commissaris whispered so that Beelema had to lean over to hear him. "I don't mean the law in our books, that's no more than a projection. The true law is in all of us, in our center, in the core of our being, where we are all connected and where the illusion of identity no longer obscures our insight. If you have, as you say, the talent, you are misusing it. Reflect, sir, and take care."

13

SUMMER CHANGED into autumn, the heavy rains had passed, and the air was crisp. It was late at night and Beelema walked by himself. Kiran wasn't with him. The dog had refused to leave the house and snarled when Beelema tried to pet him. The dog's behavior had been gradually changing; he no longer bothered people and seemed tired and listless. The veterinarian could find nothing wrong with the Great Dane. Beelema worried about the dog. If Kiran continued to snarl at him, he might have to get rid of his pet.

Beelema also worried about himself. He was getting fatter. He also drank too much. He had been drinking a lot that particular evening, served by the two lovely barmaids, one black, one Indonesian. Yet everything was going well. The bar was crowded every evening and Zhaver's restaurant, in which he had an interest, was usually booked days in advance. He was busy in his hair salon too.

It's the time of the year, he thought, as he walked on, maneuvering around a corner and bumping his shoulder. It's autumn, nature is dying, the general decline affects me.

He bumped into a tree, softly, for his stomach protected him. Then he stumbled over a low fence. Really, Beelema thought, I must watch myself. I know every square inch of the area. This is where they keep blacktopping the same hole. Every time, it caves in again, and they bring out the machinery and make a new mess. He stepped back and walked around the fence.

A young man, a boy still, but tall and slender, walked toward the stumbling figure.

I still feel sexy, Beelema thought, that's good.

"You're a dear boy," he said aloud. "You're handsome. Walk with me a little way. We'll like each other."

The boy stopped. Beelema caressed his black leather jacket.

"Can I feel your skull? I like bare skulls. I shouldn't because I'm a hairdresser and naughty boys like you spoil my trade. You *are* naughty, aren't you?"

"Sure," the boy said. His teeth shone in a black regularly shaped face. Beelema's fat finger pressed on the aquiline nose.

"Yes, you are beautiful. Would you like some money? First we play together and then I give you some money. How much would you like, naughty boy?"

"He'll want all of your money," a voice said behind Beelema. Beelema tried to turn around but his shoulders were held.

"Let's take his gold too," the first boy said, "everything. He's got some in his mouth. Break it open and I'll knock it out. Use your knife."

"No," Beelema yelled, but his cry was cut short by a hand clasping his mouth. Another hand yanked off his watch chain. There seemed to be many hands, punching him, slapping his face, tugging at the rings on his fingers, removing his wallet, even the loose change from his pocket. The hands hurt him; there were hard feet too that kicked his ankles and shins. Then he felt a sharp pain in his neck.

"Don't say a word, sugar daddy, this is a sharp knife, it'll cut you and you'll bleed like a pig; you ever see a pig bleed?"

"Let's get his teeth," the first boy said.

"Hold him, I'll get my pliers. They're in the car. Don't run away now, sugar daddy, I'll be right back to take your nice teeth."

"And his nice balls," the first boy said. "He has gold balls, too, haven't you, sugar daddy?"

Beelema pulled himself free. The boys allowed him to get away a few steps, then ran after him and pushed him down.

He fell on the fence, knocking it over, and rolled in the tar. The boys removed the top of the fence and pushed him so that he rolled on. He rolled till the tarmac was solid again, scrambled to his feet, and ran on. The boys were close behind, running soundlessly on their rubber-soled halfboots.

"Here," the first boy said.

A hand came down on Beelema's neck. He fell. There was the smell of blood.

"Bah, he's sticky. Give me that two-by-four. We'll roll him through that heap of feathers, maybe we can change him into a bird."

Beelema felt the hard edges of the stick and turned over to get away from it. Then there was nothing for a while. He woke because a light shone into his face.

"What do we have here, Ketchup?"

"Good question, Karate. A ball of feathers with eyes. What are you, sir?"

Beelema crawled away to escape the harsh light.

"Hey, stay here. What happened to you?"

The two policemen stared at each other. "What do we do now? Can't leave him. He's bleeding too."

"Ambulance," Karate said. "They'll fix him up at the hospital. Are you drunk, sir?"

Beelema tried to speak but coughed instead.

The ambulance arrived, but the attendants refused to lift him up. They found a plastic sheet and folded it so that it covered the stretcher.

"You take him in, you found him. It's the least you can do."

Karate went back to the fence and kicked until a thick board snapped free. He stuck the board between Beelema's legs and Ketchup held the other side. They lifted together.

"Right," the attendant said. "Easy now, don't drop him. Get him on the plastic. Yagh, what a mess."

"There you go, sir," Karate said. "We'll see you at the hospital."

14

THE COMMISSARIS sat next to the bed. He held Beelema's hand. De Gier stood at the foot of the bed and agreed. The procedure was proper: always hold the victim's hand. That way he doesn't feel alone. Death is an agony that can be shared, up to a point of course. From there on, the victim is on his own again.

"Is he conscious?" the commissaris asked.

A young man in a white coat bent down.

"Barely."

"What is he dying of?"

"Can't say. The wounds don't appear to be too serious, maybe the tar has interfered with his breathing. I thought we got most of it, but he may have been in that condition for hours. In some places we scraped off more than an inch and we had to use solvents to get rid of the rest. There's a bruise on the head, that may explain his predicament too. And there's fear. People can die of fright. A number of causes, I would say."

"This is the worst mugging I've ever seen," Grijpstra said. "They went all out."

The doctor felt Beelema's pulse and shook his head. "He's out too," the doctor said. "We'll have an autopsy to determine the exact nature of his death. I'll let you know what we come up with."

The commissaris released Beelema's hand. He got up and bowed his head.

"You warned him, didn't you, sir?" de Gier asked as he slid behind the wheel of the Citroën.

"Yes. But I was too late."

"We're always too late," Grijpstra said from the rear of the car.

The Citroën found a place in the heavy morning traffic and coasted slowly back to Headquarters. The commissaris led the way to the canteen.

"Too late," he said to de Gier, "but I think he was entitled to this, it was his right."

"Man has no rights," Grijpstra said, joining the line for the coffee machine, "only duties."

The commissaris held up his mug. "We have one right, adjutant, the right to face the consequences of our deeds."

De Gier mumbled as he shuffled through the crowd of constables and detectives, carrying a plate of apple cake and his coffee.

"What was that, sergeant?"

"What a way to go, sir. A nightmare. And it started out so well. Grijpstra danced and sang. I saw bits of beauty everywhere. We were floating right on top of the whole thing and then we got sucked in again."

The commissaris walked over to the cigarette machine, dropped in some coins and came back.

"It's all in your own mind, sergeant."

De Gier tore the pack open, took out a cigarette, accepted a light from Grijpstra, and sucked in the smoke.

"There," the adjutant said, "you'll feel better."

"Much."

"Everything is all right. Asta will be waiting for you when you come. She is a beautiful girl and she loves you."

"Yes."

"Security will be restored."

"Yes."

The commissaris touched de Gier's hand. "Security is in the mind too, Rinus."

The adjutant got up to reach over to the next table for some sugar. A passing constable didn't notice him and took his chair. When the adjutant tried to sit down again, he fell to the floor.

"I see." De Gier helped Grijpstra to his feet.

"I hope you haven't hurt yourself," the commissaris said and pulled up another chair.

THE BLOND
BABOON

to Alexander Stillman

1

"BIT OF A BREEZE," Detective-Adjutant Grijpstra* said.

Detective-Sergeant de Gier agreed with him but he didn't say so. He didn't have to. The pale gray Volkswagen he was trying to steer through the wide, empty thoroughfare of Spui in the center of Amsterdam had just been pushed onto the sidewalk and had stopped, thanks to his timely braking, at about an inch from a lamppost. The engine was still running and he reversed the car, bumping hard on the uneven pavement. The gale, which had started as a deadly suck of cold air, touching the frightened faces of the capital's citizens around lunchtime, had grown to such strength that it could be called a hurricane. It had forced the inhabitants of Holland's flat, below-sea-level coast to go home early, to watch the worrisome weather from behind the plate glass of apartments or the dainty windows of narrow gable houses. They listened to radios and watched TV and noted the State Weather Bureau's forecasts that grew a little more serious as the minutes ticked by. They knew that the authorities had been taken by surprise but that the emergency was being dealt with, and that the dikes were manned, and that heavy earth-moving machinery was on its way to the danger areas, where high seas were threatening man-made defenses and strengthening their attack methodically, repeating their onslaught every half-minute, raising roaring, foam-topped water mountains in deadly rushes, whipped by shrieking blasts of furious air.

* The ranks of the Amsterdam municipal police are: constable, constable first class, sergeant, adjutant, inspector, chief inspector, commissaris. An adjutant is a noncommissioned officer.

But Sergeant de Gier wasn't concerned with the overall danger of the calamity. He was only trying to do his duty, which, right now, consisted of keeping the Volkswagen moving. He was on normal patrol duty in the city, together with his immediate superior, the large adjutant who was peacefully smoking a small cigar while he held on to the car's roof and commented on the weather.

Grijpstra turned his heavy head, topped by a whitish gray millimetered bristle, and smiled almost apologetically. "Not too many people around, eh?"

The sergeant, who had got the small car back on the road and was preparing for a U-turn, grunted agreeably.

"They are at home," Grijpstra explained, "where they should be. Maybe they are in bed already, it's nearly eleven. Watch it!"

Grijpstra pointed. De Gier's mouth opened in a soundless shout. An elm, a full-grown tree over forty feet high, was ready to break. They could hear the protesting wood creak and saw the trunk split. De Gier shifted into reverse and pressed the accelerator with his toe. The car began to move, whining. The tree fell ponderously, its foliage touching the round nose of the Volkswagen. Grijpstra sighed.

De Gier was ready to say something but the car's radio had come to life. "Three-fourteen," the radio said politely. "Three-fourteen, come in."

"Go on driving," Grijpstra said. "There are other trees." He had grabbed the microphone from under the dashboard. "Three-fourteen."

"A little job for you, adjutant," the well-modulated voice of a female constable in the radio room of Amsterdam's police headquarters said. "A car of the uniformed police is asking for assistance. They are in the Kalverstraat. Where are you, three-fourteen?"

"Spui."

"Good, you are close. A lot of store windows in the Kalverstraat are smashed by garbage cans. A thief had a go at a jeweler's display and was seen but got away. A small fellow, a little over five feet, long black hair, short new leather jacket. In his late twenties. The colleagues think he is still close by."

"Right," Grijpstra said without any enthusiasm. "We'll join the chase on foot so that we can see what is falling on us."

"Good luck, adjutant. Out."

Grijpstra was still clambering out of the Volkswagen when de Gier sprinted away, leaning over to counterbalance the gale's driving force. Grijpstra cursed gently as he moved his bulk into motion. The athletic sergeant was waiting for him on the sidewalk, sheltered behind a parked truck.

"Which way?" de Gier asked. Grijpstra pointed as he ran.

"Let's try the alleys."

De Gier jumped ahead, veering toward the protected side of a side street while the wind howled along storefronts, pulling at signboards and gutters. A lid of a garbage can obstructed his way and he jumped and shouted a warning, but the adjutant had seen it and kicked the rolling disc so that it shot off at a tangent. A few cardboard boxes followed the lid and the policemen avoided them, turning into a passage that would take them to the main shopping center of the Kalverstraat. Grijpstra stopped running.

"In here somewhere," he panted. "He is bound to be somewhere around here. In the Kalverstraat he can be seen—the stores all have glass porches. Let's go."

"Wait," de Gier said softly and put out a restraining hand.

"What?"

"I think I saw a head pop out, over there. I'll go."

Grijpstra grinned as he watched the sergeant's progress.

De Gier was sliding with slow, exaggerated movements. His tall slim shape merged with the alley's shadows. The hunter, the deadly hunter. But Grijpstra stopped grinning. He was sure that de Gier would make his kill. Ferocious, he thought. Very.

As de Gier jumped ahead and flattened himself against the aged, crumbling front of a small house, Grijpstra stepped back and drew out his heavy service pistol, loading it as he jerked it out of its cracked holster. He shook his head. There had been times, not so long ago, that he wouldn't have thought of drawing his gun, but thieves were changing. Hit-and-run thieves were usually armed these days, with knives mostly, with firearms occasionally if they were desperate enough, because the drug habit was forcing them to be desperate. He covered the slow-moving sergeant, edging inch by inch along his wall. The sergeant reached the porch and froze. There was no movement for a little while. The gale seemed to have the alley to itself, wheezing up strength while it rattled windows and doors tentatively. The thief would show himself again. The thief was in there. The thief was nervous. The thief wanted to know what was happening.

Out popped the head. Long shiny black hair framing a furtive eye peeping over the turned-up collar of a leather jacket. The sergeant's hand shot out and grabbed the head by the hair and pulled. The thief tumbled from the porch. A plastic bag dropped and clanged as it hit the pavement's gleaming bricks. A knife flashed.

"*Police*," Grijpstra roared. The knife fell too. The sergeant's thumb had found the thief's wrist and had pressed it cruelly while his fingers twisted. The thief squeaked.

"Handcuffs," de Gier said, and Grijpstra put his gun back and produced the required article. The cuffs clicked. De Gier blew his whistle. The shrill earsplitting sound cut through the gale's roar. Two uniformed constables came running into the alley.

"Ha!" the constables shouted. "Got him!"

"Got him," de Gier said. "Here you are, with the compliments of your CID.* Why didn't you catch him yourselves? We're supposed to drive about quietly and not to interfere."

"We are old men," the constable facing de Gier said, "and we like to give others a chance. Nasty wind, what?"

"Bit of a breeze," Grijpstra agreed. "You don't mind if we go back to our car, do you? If it is still there—an elm nearly got it just now. Did you see this man break in?"

"I didn't break in," the thief said. "The window was all broken and the stuff was spilling out into the street so I picked it up to take it to a police station, but these fools were running and firing their guns so I ran too. I don't want to get killed."

Grijpstra patted the narrow leather shoulder. "Professional, are we?"

The thief looked up. His eyes had widened with fear and he shivered.

"We'll take him. You want your handcuffs back, adjutant?"

"Of course, constable. My private property, I saved up for them."

The cuffs were taken off and the constable brought out another pair. The thief looked unhappy. "Ouch! Too tight!"

"They are not too tight," the constable said, tugging the steel grips gently. "See? Plenty of room. We'll take them off at the station. Come along."

"Home," de Gier said as he twisted his tall body into the Volkswagen's driving seat. "The wind will be hitting my balcony full on. It'll be tearing up my plants and Tabriz will be nervous. She'll be at the marmalade jar again."

"Marmalade jar?" Grijpstra asked. "What does a cat want with a marmalade jar?"

* Criminal Investigation Department.

"Throw it on the floor and break it, what else? So that I can cut my feet and then slither about in the jelly—it has happened twice already. The last time I fell on the table and tried to steady myself on a shelf and I broke just about everything in the kitchen and cut an artery in my ankle."

"I know." The adjutant tried to stretch but gave up the attempt. His shoulder hurt; he had probably bumped it during the chase. "You took a week off, remember? But I still want to know why a cat gets at a marmalade jar."

There were more trees down, and de Gier was maneuvering around their fallen twisted forms. One of the windows of the car didn't close and the wind cried through it, a high-pitched evil wheeze. "They used to have that sound on radio plays. Horrible sound. I would always switch off the program. To accompany young girls raped in attics, as if the crying and sobbing weren't enough."

"Cat," Grijpstra said. "Marmalade jar."

"I don't know why she does it, a way to show her displeasure, I suppose. Cats have their ways. Your household will be a mess too, with your wife and kids rattling all through the place."

Grijpstra frowned. "My wife won't rattle. She'll ooze. She got fatter again, you know, I didn't think she would do it but she did. She's sleeping on the floor now, bed won't hold her weight." He took the microphone out of its clasp.

"Headquarters, Three-fourteen."

"Come in, Three-fourteen."

"We caught your thief and gave him to the constables and we are on our way to the garage."

There was a strange breaking noise and Grijpstra stared at the microphone, which looked small and innocent in his large hand.

"Window got blown in," the female constable said. "That's the second window tonight. It's a mess here. My notebook has blown away. Did you say you are coming back?"

"Yes, we were supposed to go off duty at eleven. It's close to midnight now."

"I *am* sorry, but I have another assignment for you. We're short of staff again—everybody is out helping people who got trapped, there are crushed cars all over the city, and we're having panic calls from people who got their walls blown in or roofs torn off. And people have been blown into the canals and, oh, all sorts of things."

"Is that the sort of job you have for us?" Grijpstra asked, dangling the microphone as if it were a dead mouse.

She tried to laugh. "No, adjutant, the uniformed police and the fire department are around too. I have a proper job for you, a dead lady. A health officer called just now. He was supposed to pick up a corpse, but the doctor hasn't come and the death isn't natural anyway. An accident, according to the lady's daughter. Lady fell down the garden stairs and broke her neck. The ambulance can't take the corpse until they have clearance from us. Mierisstraat Fifty-three. Just a routine call, probably."

Grijpstra showed his teeth. The microphone was still dangling.

"Three-fourteen?"

De Gier stopped the car and tugged the microphone from Grijpstra's hand.

"We'll go, dear. Do you have any additional information? The Mierisstraat is a nice quiet little street. Nobody throws anybody down the stairs of a house in the Mierisstraat."

"That's all I know, sergeant. Dead lady, fell down the garden stairs and presumably broke her neck. The health officer says she is dead."

"Okay."

"Out."

De Gier pulled a knob on the dashboard and a small pale red light came on as the siren began to howl from its hiding place under the hood. Grijpstra lifted the blue sparkle light from the glove compartment and rolled his window down. The magnet clicked the light onto the car's thin roof and its reflection lit up the wet street surface around them, sweeping a ghostly wide beam on the reflecting road. The Volkswagen shot away as de Gier's foot came down. The gale grabbed the car at the next corner and pushed it to the middle of the glimmering tar. It was raining hard suddenly and the wipers had trouble keeping the windshield clear. A streetcar approached from the opposite direction and de Gier twisted the wheel viciously. The streetcar's bell was clanging as its long yellow shape flashed past. Grijpstra closed his eyes and groaned. The driving rain became a solid white spray in the headlights, then it stopped. Another streetcar threw up a sheet of gray liquid dirt that hit the Volkswagen head on. De Gier cursed and braked. The windshield wipers cut through the mud and he could see again. The car skidded around a tree, a huge poplar that had fallen parallel to the sidewalk. A branch got into the right front wheel and wrapped itself around the tire.

De Gier drove on and they could hear twigs snap. Grijpstra opened his eyes.

De Gier was laughing. "Look! We're driving through a forest."

The poplar's leaves were brushing Grijpstra's windows.

"That lady was probably blown down her stairs," he said morosely, "and that fool health officer shouldn't have phoned. Doesn't he know we're busy tonight?" He closed his eyes again. The wind was pushing the car toward a canal and the Volkswagen was skidding. The sergeant pumped the brake and steered with the skid. They stopped a few feet from the rail, a thin rail, about a foot high, meant to stop parked cars from sliding into the water.

"We're all right," de Gier said and reversed. The wind was whipping at the car's rear and they were gathering speed.

The adjutant kept his eyes closed. It'll happen again, he thought, remembering how he had been in a small car that slipped into a canal and sunk slowly and nearly drowned him; he had been saved in the nick of time by a fire brigade's crane. He badly wanted to shout at de Gier, to tell him that the lady was dead, and that they wouldn't revive her by hitting a tree or drowning in a muddy canal or getting under a streetcar. He wanted to ask the sergeant why he had switched the siren on if the din of the gale was so overwhelming that they had hardly been able to hear the streetcar's electric bell clamoring right next to their ears.

Grijpstra opened his eyes when de Gier's hand brushed past him. The sergeant was switching off the siren. They had arrived. Mierisstraat. He recognized it. Quiet, slightly elegant. Wide sidewalks lined with tall plane trees. Tall narrow houses, turn of the century. A street of doctors and lawyers and comfortable upper-middle-class families making their money in gentle leisurely ways. An unlikely street to be stalked by violent death. A street where pedigreed dogs lift their legs daintily before they spray a lamppost. He smiled. The smile didn't come to full bloom.

"Dog," Grijpstra said, and his fist hit de Gier's side softly.

"Dog, damn it. Same address. Day before yesterday. Cardozo was supposed to take care of the complaint. Remember?" De Gier whistled.

"Same address. Poisoned dog. Mierisstraat Fifty-three. Cardozo didn't want to go."

"Right." De Gier's handsome profile was nodding solemnly.

"You had to kick him out of the room. And he was talking about it yesterday. He had a suspect, he said. Man who lives in the rear. The gardens meet. He had some of the dog's puke in a bottle. Very proud of himself. Lab test proved arsenic poisoning."

While de Gier's head nodded Grijpstra's head shook. "Bad. A poisoned dog and a lady with a broken neck. Same address. We'll be busy."

They waited while they thought. Police reasoning. Something small happens, then something big happens. Same place. There would be a connection. They waited until a respectful gloved hand tapped on the windshield.

De Gier got out and the health officer saluted.

"Evening, sergeant. Haven't met for a while, have we? Different routes. My mate is waiting for you inside. The lady's daughter is a bit upset, he is keeping her quiet. The two ladies live by themselves, no man in the house. And there is something with a dog. Poisoned, so the young lady says."

"The wind," Grijpstra said hopefully, "the bloody gale. Sure the gale didn't grab your lady?"

"No, adjutant." The health officer's face showed helpfulness and apology neatly blended. "The gale can't reach into the gardens here. The houses are high, you see. The wind may be getting at the tops of the trees but it can't reach down to the garden stairs. I've been out in the garden awhile, nice and quiet. But maybe she slipped. It had been raining earlier on and the stairs are wet and she was wearing high-heeled shoes and a long dress."

"A party?"

"Could be. There's a smell of alcohol and an empty bottle. The daughter says there was no party. Lady liked to drink by herself."

"Wasn't she with her mother when it happened?"

"No. The young lady has her own apartment, top floor. She said she came down to check if everything was all right before going to bed. The garden door was open and her mother . . . Well, you'll see."

De Gier was looking at the closed door. A good-quality door with simple dignified ornamentation. Varnished oak with a garland of leaves. Two nameplates and two bells. Elaine Carnet. Gabrielle Carnet. Hand-painted nameplates, white on green. Polished brass bells. A polished brass knocker in the shape of a lion's head.

The door moved as his hand reached for the lower bell.

This is a bad night, de Gier thought, and he waited for the door to open altogether. A very bad night. I should be home to safeguard the balcony's plants and to comfort Tabriz and to have a hot shower and several mugs of strong tea. It wouldn't be a bad night if I were home. But I am not, and this is a killing.

He couldn't be sure, of course, but he was. As sure as Grijpstra, who was standing just behind him. Each profession develops its devotees. The detectives of Amsterdam's murder brigade are trained to be suspicious, but that doesn't mean much more than that they are always suspicious. They ask mild questions and they look at faces and dig about in the endless chain of cause and event, but their eyes are quiet and their voices soft and their manners mild. Not always. There are moments when the detectives quiver, when little fiery stabs touch their spines, when they sweat slightly, and when their eyes open and stare fiercely.

Gabrielle Carnet stepped back quickly and nearly stumbled. De Gier's long arm shot out and steadied her.

"Evening, miss," he said, forcing himself to keep his voice down to the prescribed level of politeness. "We are the police."

Grijpstra had walked past the sergeant. He followed the other health officer through a long corridor, a central hall, into an enclosed porch, to the garden door.

Elaine Carnet, a soaked sad shape, lay crumpled at the bottom of the steps. The health officer pulled the blanket away. The head had snapped back at a most unnatural angle. The woman's dead eyes stared out of a messy arrangement of sodden make-up smears. Her double chin was stretched tight by the position of the head. The hair, neatly puffed up into fluffy curls only a few hours before, clung to the wet scalp. The wide mouth was smiling, and the gold fillings of two canines sparkled in the light filtering from the porch windows. The smile seemed genuine, a joyous surrender to an unexpected but welcome visitor.

Grijpstra stepped over the corpse and squatted. The light fell differently now and the smile had become a snarl. The sudden change upset him and he went back to the steps. A smile again, definitely.

It was only later that he remembered a common feature of the two facial expressions. The common denominator was victory. Something had pleased Elaine Carnet, some event had elated her seconds before she died. The thought sparkled through his brain but didn't ripen just then. He had already settled down in his routine. He was observing his surroundings.

"Leave her here?" the health officer asked.

"Sure. I'll get the experts. We want some photographs."

There was a phone on the porch and he dialed. "Commissaris?"

"Yes," a soft voice answered.

"I know you are ill, sir, but I thought I would phone you all the same. We've run into something, Mierisstraat Fifty-three. It's a bad night, sir. Shall I phone the inspector?"

"No. I'm feeling better. Send de Gier to fetch me—there's a tree blocking my garage and there won't be any taxis tonight. What have you got, adjutant?"

"A poisoned dog, sir, and a dead lady." Grijpstra moved to the window and looked out. Big raindrops were clattering down on the corpse. "A very dead lady, sir."

2

"MISS?" DE GIER ASKED as he steadied the girl. "Are you all right?"

"Yes. Gabrielle, that's my name, Gabrielle Carnet. You are the police?"

He showed his card but she wasn't interested. She looked at it, and he put it back into the breast pocket of his tailored denim jacket. The rain had gotten into his silk scarf, and he pulled it free and refolded it before tucking it back into his open shirt. The scarf was a very light shade of blue. The denim jacket and the matching tight trousers were dark blue. She followed his movements dreamily. Her eyes came up to his face, noting the full brushed-up mustache and the high cheekbones and the large glowing brown eyes.

"Are you really a policeman?"

"Yes. I showed you my card just now. Detective-Sergeant de Gier. Rinus de Gier. We answered the health officer's call. Was it you who phoned the ambulance service?"

"Yes." Her voice was low. It had an interesting quality. He tried to determine what it was. Silky? No. Something with texture. Velvety. A purring voice. The voice she would use on men, not on women. She would have a different voice for women.

"What happened, miss? Would you tell me, please?"

She still seemed unsteady on her legs, and he looked around for a place to sit down. The corridor was bare except for a carpet and a small table next to the coat rack. He put a hand under her elbow and guided her to the stairs.

"Sit down, miss. You'll feel better."

He automatically noted her particulars. Small, five foot perhaps, a little over, but that was due to the high heels of her stylish soft leather boots. Dungarees tucked into the boots. Tight dungarees hiding slightly bowed legs. A very short blouse that showed skin at both ends. A narrow waist with a little bellybutton and the shine of a gold chain. A fashionable girl. The blouse's top button was open, he could see the curve of her breasts. Long, dark brown hair, glossy. No jewelry. A pointed small face, uninteresting if it hadn't been for the eyes, but the eyes were cleverly made up, they weren't as large as they seemed. The color was startling, a shiny green. Metallic bright eyes. The possibility of drugs immediately presented itself but he could see her arms. No pricks. Perhaps she sniffed cocaine or took pills. But the feverish shine of her eyes could be just due to anguish. The young lady's mother had died.

When she began to speak he noticed the purr again. It couldn't be natural. She was acting, showing off, so the shock of her mother's death had already worn thin. She had taken time to adjust her make-up. The thin penciled lines around the eyes weren't ten minutes old.

"I live upstairs," Gabrielle Carnet was saying, "in my own apartment. Mother and I split up last year. The house was remodeled. My apartment is self-contained."

"Can you hear your mother's doorbell, miss?"

"Not when I am in my kitchen or bathroom."

"Do you know whether your mother had a visitor?"

"I don't know." She sobbed in between the words and her hands twitched. Her hair had fallen over her eyes and she pushed it away, smearing the mascara. A genuine reaction. But genuine about what? Was she sorry she pushed or kicked her mother down the stairs?

"Go on," he said gently, trying to tune his voice and mood to hers.

"I came down about an hour ago, I always check before I go to sleep. Mother drinks a bit and sometimes she falls asleep in front of the TV and I have to wake her up and take her upstairs."

"I am sorry, I have to ask questions. You know that don't you, Miss Carnet?" She nodded. She was trying to get a handkerchief from her pocket but it stuck and she got up. He got up too. "Do you want to go upstairs, miss?"

"No. It's all right here."

They sat down again. She was sitting very close; he could feel the warmth of her thigh.

"Was your mother an alcoholic, miss?"

"Yes. No."

"How much did she drink, a day, I mean. Did she drink every day?"

"Most days, but only wine. Good wine. A bottle a day perhaps, but I think she was drinking more lately. I didn't see very much of her anymore, we were living separately."

"Because of some trouble? Did you fight?" He kept his voice as low as he could to take the sting out of the key words. Alcoholic. Fight. They weren't good words but he had to use them.

"No, we didn't fight, we just didn't get on. I'm nearly thirty now. I should have a place of my own but I didn't want to live somewhere else, she needed care. Oh, my God."

She was crying and he waited. Her thigh was still pressing against him. He didn't like the girl, but why didn't he? She wasn't pretty but she was certainly attractive. An attractive pushover. He could hear Grijpstra's booming voice dominating the health officers farther down the house. If they weren't around he could make the girl right on the stairs, dead mother or no dead mother. He could feel his lips stretching into a sneer. A most unbecoming thought. A policeman is a public servant. But the fact was that the girl wakened nothing in him, nothing at all. And he was sure she was lying. Gabrielle should have heard her mother scream as she fell down the stairs. But there was the gale. Perhaps its noise had drowned the scream. The gale seemed to have found the street at that very moment, and he could hear its deep, menacing, sonorous whoosh and the rattle of parked cars being pushed into each other.

"Sergeant?"

De Gier looked up. "Yes, Grijpstra?"

"Would you go and fetch the commissaris? I phoned the experts, they'll come down as soon as they get their gear together. The doctor is on his way too."

"Sure."

"And get Cardozo too if you can. He's off duty tonight, he's visiting friends, but his mother gave me the address, it's on the way. He knows you're coming."

The girl was still crying and hiding her face. Grijpstra's eyebrows arched. De Gier shook his head silently. His mouth formed the word "lying." Grijpstra nodded. De Gier got up and gestured invitingly. Grijpstra lowered his body slowly. The girl felt his bulk on the step and edged away.

"You can tell me what you told the sergeant, miss. Do you know what happened?"

The front door clicked behind de Gier. The health officers came and said good-bye. Grijpstra could hear the engines of the Volkswagen and the ambulance start as the gale breathed in for a second only to roar away at full strength.

"Miss?"

"She must have fallen down the stairs," Gabrielle said. "I think she worried about her azaleas and opened the garden door, and then the wind pulled the door out of her hands and she lost her balance."

"Come with me, miss, please."

He pulled her to her feet and she followed him down the corridor and into the large sitting room. He glanced at the room's wall. A bookcase holding a beautifully bound encyclopedia, brand-new and never used. A row of artbooks, just as new. A flower arrangement. A modern painting. There was a thick wall-to-wall carpet under his feet, off-white to set off the darker furniture. A showroom designed by an interior decorator. The porch was more personal, with a battered old TV on a cane table and some easy chairs that looked ugly and comfortable.

"Your mother liked to sit on the porch, miss?"

"Yes. She had it glassed in when she moved here, some ten years ago, I think. She was always here, it's the only part of the house that wasn't redecorated. And my apartment, of course. I did that myself after the carpenters were done."

Grijpstra had opened the garden door. "There's no wind here, miss. These gardens are well protected. The houses won't let the gale in. See?"

"Yes."

"So how did your mother fall down the stairs?" Grijpstra's voice was kind and puzzled. He looked solid, trustworthy, fatherly. He was very concerned. "Now how could such an awful accident have happened? Your mother knew these stairs well, didn't she? Did she like gardening?"

"Yes."

"She planted those bushes over there, didn't she? Those are nice azaleas. Did she plant the hedge in the back as well?"

"Yes."

Gabrielle wandered around the room dreamily. She reached for the wineglass on a low table near the TV. Grijpstra touched her arm. "Don't touch anything, please, miss. We'll have that glass checked for fingerprints. Is this your mother's ring, miss?" He showed her a smooth gold wedding ring that was lying on a bare board near the garden door. She stooped.

"Don't pick it up please, miss."

"Yes, that's my mother's ring."

"Did she play with it? Put it on and take it off when she was nervous?"

"No."

"Did it fit tightly?"

She was crying, fighting the tears, biting on her handkerchief.

"I'm sorry, miss."

The girl had sat down, and he sat down opposite her and rubbed his cheeks. He could do with a shave again, there hadn't been much time that morning. His wife had come into the bathroom and he wanted to get away, so he had done a sloppy job. He would do better later on, she would be asleep by then. The thought of scalding hot water soaking into the stubby folds and the neat strokes of a new razor blade cheered him up somewhat. He didn't like cornering the girl. De Gier thought she was lying, and she very likely was. But there could be extenuating circumstances. A drunken, nagging mother, wailing, screaming. A family fight. A push. Most anything can be explained and understood, if not accepted. But if there had been a struggle it would be better for the girl to admit to it, now, when everything was still fresh. It would look better in court. But he wasn't going to feed her a confession. Perhaps the commissaris would. He would wait.

The girl looked up. "I don't want to cry."

"No, miss, I understand. Perhaps we can have some coffee. I'll make it if you tell me where everything is."

"No. I can do it."

He followed her to the kitchen and stood around while she worked. Her movements were organized, efficient. The percolator began to gurgle, then throb. She was staring out at the garden when he began to look for the garbage container. He found it fitted into a cupboard under the sink, attached to the cupboard door. There was another wineglass in the plastic bag protecting the container. The glass had broken at the stem. It was of the same type as the glass he had seen on the table near the TV. He took a long-handled fork lying on the kitchen counter and poked around in the bag. There were several cigar stubs, each stub connected to a plastic mouthpiece, and some cigar ash. The ashtray stood on the counter. It had been cleaned.

A visitor after all. There was no lipstick on the mouthpieces and both Gabrielle and her mother used lipstick. Women smoked cigars these days, and the cigars would have been long and very thin. De Gier sometimes smoked cigars like that; de Gier was vain. A vain male visitor. But who isn't vain?

I am not vain, Grijpstra thought, looking down at his crumpled suit.

The suit was made of excellent British material, pure wool, dark blue with a fine white stripe. He was vain enough to buy expensive suits, always of the same type, but he treated them badly. All right, he would admit to some vanity. Still, he wouldn't smoke sissy cigars with imitation mouthpieces. No, perhaps he would. If he could afford them. They would go with his suit. He breathed heavily so that the air burbled past his pressed lips. Nothing was ever easy. Suspects lie and hide their emotions. Clues aren't seen or get lost. De Gier thought the girl was lying and he was following the sergeant, but why should he? The sergeant's impressions were sieved through the sergeant's own perceptions, forced into shapes, twisted out of truth perhaps.

A man visits Elaine Carnet. Elaine is all dressed up in a long flowered dress. A summer evening. She has done everything possible to doll herself up. She is a woman and she won't admit to getting old. How old would she be? Early fifties? Yes, most likely. She waits for the man in the intimacy of her porch. She gets up, walks around carefully, her dress rustles. A whiff of perfume pervades the room. The azaleas are blooming behind her. The setting sun touches the tops of the poplars and elms and drooping willows. That's what she had anticipated but instead there is a storm, a horrible oppressive atmosphere that creeps into everything, into her very soul, into the mind of the man. They drink wine together, a strong Beaujolais, and the storm gets into the wine too and turns it into a violent brew that seeps into their thoughts. She talks to him. Her voice is raw and cutting. She talks about the past. She twists off her wedding ring and flings it on the floor. A sudden accusation hurts the man to the quick, and he throws his cigar into the ashtray and jumps up and grabs her by the neck and shakes her. The garden door is open and he sees it and pushes her and lets go. And then he leaves.

The girl's eyes were resting on Grijpstra's face.

"Yes, miss?"

"The coffee is ready. I'll take it to the porch."

"Please, miss."

He sipped the coffee and went through the fabricated scene again. It fitted all the facts. But he wouldn't ask any more questions now. The girl seemed in a steady frame of mind again.

The bell rang and the girl went to open the door. She came back followed by de Gier, who introduced her to the commissaris and Cardozo. Grijpstra got up and offered his chair to the commissaris, who accepted gratefully and lowered his frail body carefully into its rumpled cushions. Cardozo, looking even more boyish and flushed than usual, brought in a chair from the living room and gave it to Grijpstra and went back to fetch stools for de Gier and himself.

"Well, miss. This is a bad business," said the commissaris. "My sergeant has been telling me about it in the car. We are sorry to bother you, but do you feel you are ready to answer some questions? We'll be as quick as we can."

His pale, almost colorless eyes glinted behind the round gold-rimmed spectacles. His thin hands were holding his knees. He looked neat and harmless in his worn but recently pressed three-piece suit. A gold watch chain spanned his slightly protruding stomach, and the perfectly knotted tie and thinning hair combed into two equal halves perfected the image of a kind but exact person of authority, a headmaster, a miniature patriarch even.

"Perhaps you would like some coffee, sir, Miss Carnet has just made some. Excellent coffee."

"That would be very nice but perhaps Miss Carnet shouldn't bother. Cardozo can get it."

Gabrielle got up to show Cardozo the kitchen and the commissaris turned quickly. "Anything of interest, Grijpstra?"

He listened as he was told about the wedding ring, the second wineglass, and the cigar stubs.

"Any theory, adjutant?"

"A visitor, male presumably. An argument. We don't know about Mrs. Carnet's marital status yet."

"You haven't asked?"

"The girl was very nervous, sir. I waited for you."

"Good."

The commissaris's hands moved up and squeezed his thin thighs.

"How are you feeling, sir?"

"It was a bad attack, adjutant, rheumatism in its pure and vilest form, but I think the crisis has passed. The sergeant thought the girl was lying. What do you think?"

"I don't know, sir."

The coffee came. The commissaris talked about the gale. De Gier's car had been the only vehicle on the trip back. Fallen trees and overturned cars everywhere. Capsized trucks even. And the gale still in full force.

"Did you hear the news, sir?"

"Yes, it's bad, but the dikes are holding so far. The army is moving out to help, but we may be flooded by tomorrow. How far are we below sea level here?"

The opinions ranged from ten to thirty feet. The commissaris tittered. He seemed truly amused. The titter loosened the room's murky atmosphere. De Gier laughed and the girl smiled. Cardozo looked surprised and pulled his long curly hair.

"Well. I believe that Detective Constable Cardozo and Miss Carnet have already met. A matter of a poisoned dog. How is your dog now, Miss Carnet?"

It was the right thing to say and the commissaris moved with the girl's welcoming reaction. The dog was upstairs in her apartment and he wanted to see it. The bell rang again.

"That'll be the doctor, or the photographers, perhaps. De Gier, why don't you answer the door. Grijpstra can take charge here, and Cardozo and I will go up with Miss Carnet."

Grijpstra nodded. He had wanted to take the girl upstairs too, to keep her near her mother's corpse was a mistake, she would never talk easily that way, but he had wanted to stay near the front door and to keep the girl in sight at the same time. The commissaris, Cardozo, and the girl were on their way up by the time de Gier let in the photographers and the doctor. The men didn't say much, their usual ribaldry suppressed by the sinister howling of the gale. They all seemed intent to do the job as soon as possible and get away.

"Beautiful, beautiful," the commissaris said as he saw the Oriental rugs, the cushions with simple geometric designs thrown about in charming disorder, the low couch, the modern paintings. A small white terrier, whimpering softly, was trying to get out of its basket. The commissaris bent down and scratched the animal between its pointed ears. "Sick, are we?"

"He's much better now," Gabrielle said softly. "Would you like more coffee? I can make some in my kitchen here."

"Lovely, lovely," the commissaris said, and he sat down on a cushion near the dog's basket. He was still talking to the dog in a low voice. "Feeling better, eh? Somebody gave us some poison, did he? Somebody who isn't right in the head. We'll find him and talk to him."

The dog put out a paw and the commissaris held it. Cardozo had knelt down near the basket too. The dog turned his head and licked the young detective's hand.

"What do you know about this, Cardozo?" the commissaris whispered fiercely.

"Miss Carnet came to see us day before yesterday, sir. I went home with her. The dog was in a bad state, but the vet was taking care of him.

Pumped out his stomach. I took a sample and had it tested by the laboratory. It contained arsenic, a big dose. The particulars are in my report."

"Yes? And then?"

"Miss Carnet said that the dog usually plays by himself in the garden when her mother and she are out. They had been out for lunch, and when she came back she found Paul, that's his name, in the kitchen. He seemed very sick, retching and whining, and she called the vet, who came immediately and told her that Paul had been poisoned and that she should go to the police. She took her car and came to see us at once. When I had spoken to the vet I checked the houses that have gardens bordering the Carnet garden, five in all. Everybody seemed sympathetic and upset about the poor dog except the man who owns the house directly behind this one. A man called de Bree, an engineer, fat fellow, bald head, fifty years old, I think."

"And what did Mr. de Bree say?"

"He didn't say very much, sir. He slammed the door in my face after telling me not to bother him and that he had had nothing to do with the damn dog."

"Hmm." The commissaris still looked fierce. "Ah, there we are. Nice fresh coffee, I can smell it. Just the thing on a horrible night like this."

Gabrielle smiled. Only one shaded light had been switched on and her small shape blended well with the exotic background of the fairly large room. An Arab princess entertaining important visitors. The commissaris smiled too, the thought had cheered him up. She had gone to great trouble to decorate the room; he wondered what her daydreams were like. She seemed to be living by herself, for there was no trace of a man's presence. A very feminine room. He remembered de Gier's remark about drugs, the sergeant could be right. The commissaris had been in the rooms of junkies often, far too often. Junkies like the Middle and Far East and imitate their, to them, bizarre environment. He had noticed the torn Persian carpets and dirty cushions bought at the flea market, but this room looked both expensive and clean. Junkies are messy, Gabrielle was not. Junkies also like a profusion of plants and any number of trinkets, small objects strewn about. No, this room was different. He saw the neat row of potted house plants on the windowsill and a bookcase filled with paperbacks arranged according to their color.

"Tell me about your mother, Miss Carnet, what was she like?"

Gabrielle didn't respond. She was trying to but no words came, her small hands gestured vaguely.

"Your father?"

The hands balled and then relaxed suddenly. "Mother was never married. I don't know who my father is. I don't think she knew either, the subject was never mentioned. If I brought it up she would evade my questions, so I gave up."

"I see. Your name is French, isn't it? Carnet, I can't recall ever having heard it before."

"Belgian. Mother was born in Brussels but she lived in Paris for some time. Her father ran away and she had to support herself and her mother. We haven't been very lucky with men in the family."

Her voice was light, conversational. There seemed to be no grudge in it.

"And how did your mother support herself in Paris?"

"She sang. There's a stack of old records downstairs, she was famous once. She sang chansons in nightclubs, just after the war, for a few years. She did very well until she became pregnant."

The commissaris's brain produced a small question but he didn't ask it. There was no point in asking; Gabrielle wouldn't know the answer. Pregnancy can be solved by abortion. An abortion in Paris wouldn't have presented a large problem. Did Elaine Carnet have hopes of marrying the father of her child? There was a wedding ring on the floor of the porch below. Had the father bought the ring or had Elaine Carnet got it herself, later, after she had given up all hope?

"Yes," he said. "And then your mother came to Holland?"

"Yes, my grandmother had friends here but they are dead now, my grandmother is dead too. Mother liked it here, she never left."

"And she sang again?"

"No. She has a business, Carnet and Company. The company sells furniture, Italian furniture mostly. Mother made some good contacts, and she used to be very energetic. She had saved money from her singing and she was looking around for a way to invest it, and then she saw an advertisement of some Italian firm that wanted to have an agent here. The Italians spoke French and Mother spoke French too, of course, and she went to Milan and got the agency and bought some stock and she was lucky, I think. The firm does very well now. Oh!" The hand had come up suddenly and covered her mouth.

Cardozo jumped up, but the commissaris touched his leg and he sat down again.

"Yes, miss?"

"Mr. Bergen. He will be very upset about Mother. He is her partner, you see. I should have called him."

"Perhaps you should call him tomorrow. With this weather he'll be better off at home. Does Mr. Bergen live in Amsterdam?"

"Yes, but on the other side of the city."

"We shouldn't disturb him then. Did you mother start the business with him?"

"He came in a little later. She started on her own and he was working for another firm selling furniture. I think they met somewhere and she offered him a job on commission and he did well. Later he became a director and a partner; she gave him a quarter of the shares."

"Mr. Bergen is married, is he?"

"Yes."

The commissaris shifted on his cushion. "I am sorry, miss. You don't have to answer the question if you don't want to. Did your mother have any close friends? Men, I mean."

She giggled. Cardozo hunched his shoulders. He had been watching the girl carefully, fascinated by her flowing hair and startling green eyes and firm breasts, but he had reminded himself that he was a police officer and that the girl had just lost her mother, by an accident or otherwise. Her purring voice had set off tiny ripples below the skin of his back. He had been impressed by the room and the way the girl's small body controlled the room. He had had the feeling that he had been venturing out into a new world, a world of beautiful sadness, of delicate shades of emotion that he didn't usually come into contact with. But the girl's giggle broke his rapture. The giggle was almost coarse, exciting on another scale, the excitement of a low bar with a juke box going and beer slopped into cheap straight glasses.

"Yes. Mother had a lover but the affair broke up. He came for several years."

"His name, miss?"

"Vleuten, Jan Vleuten, but everybody calls him the baboon, the blond baboon."

"You liked him?" The question was irrelevant at that point and came up suddenly, but the giggle had shaken the commissaris too.

"Oh, yes."

"But the connection broke up, you said. When was that, miss?"

"About two years ago, I think. She would still see him occasionally but then it stopped altogether. He worked for the company, but when he left the affair ended too."

"I see. Well, I think we can go now. We have to see you a few more times, but that will be later. You need a good rest now. You're sure that your mother didn't have a visitor tonight, aren't you, miss? If we knew she had and we knew who the visitor was our work would be easier and take up less time."

"I don't know, there was only one glass on the table when I came down. I didn't hear the bell, but I may have been in the kitchen here when the bell rang. It isn't a very loud bell."

Cardozo jumped up again. "Shall I check the bell, sir?"

"No, that's all right. Thanks for the coffee, miss." The commissaris was attempting to get up and his face grimaced with pain. Cardozo helped him to his feet.

3

THE COMMISSARIS WOULDN'T let Gabrielle accompany him to the front door but said good-bye at the door of her room. He held her shoulder lightly as he said his good-night, having nudged Cardozo into the direction of the staircase. There was a gentleness in his touch that seemed to reach her. She no longer purred; her voice had become slightly hoarse instead. She left the door open as she walked back into her room and he closed it, for he had heard the constables come in to fetch the corpse. They were maneuvering awkwardly, bumping the stretcher against a wall. A trickle of water ran from the sodden body and the head flopped. The victory that Grijpstra had seen in Elaine Carnet's face earlier in the night was still there, but the joyous expression wasn't very substantial as her head moved past the commissaris. A thin victory, reached through great agony, the agony of a useless life. The commissaris had only a glimpse of the victim, but the moment cut into his perception and the shock bared his long yellowish teeth and aggravated the cold pain in his legs so that he stumbled and had to support himself against a wall.

Death was his game, of course, and as the officer in charge of Amsterdam's murder brigade he dealt with it continuously, but he had never made his peace with death. On a few occasions he had seen people die and seen fear change into surprise, a surprise mingled with horror. This was the first time he had seen surprise mingled with joy, or was joy the wrong definition?

The question stayed in his mind as the car made its way carefully through the southern part of the old city. Grijpstra and Cardozo were on the back seat, both sunk into apathy, and de Gier was steering, trying to see something through the waves of water that the nervous little wipers couldn't deal with. After a few minutes the rain suddenly stopped, and the commissaris saw the torn and broken trunk of a weeping willow that had graced a small square for as long as he could remember. Large puddles of inky water were almost brought to foam by a sweep of the gale. He still saw Elaine Carnet's head, the bedraggled clown's mask of a middle-aged woman. Who cares? he thought. The dead are dumped and we tear into the living flesh of the killer if we can find him and frazzle the nerves of a number of suspects in the process. His gloom, cold edged with razor-blade cuts of the pain in his legs, increased and he braced himself in defense. He had to find refuge in the calm that he knew to be in his mind as well. This was a murder case like any other and it would have to be approached by normal methods. He would go into the mess tomorrow, for a mess it was. He only hoped that it was a simple mess that could be cleared quickly. Like de Gier and Grijpstra, he felt sure that there had been a crime, although he wouldn't forget the easier explanation of a combination of accidental causes.

Gales are known to unsettle people's minds. Mrs. Carnet had probably been a nervous woman, lonely and fearful. Her favorite spot was the porch with the ugly chairs and the TV set and a gramophone and old records that reminded her of her glamorous past. She also drank. The doctor would be able to tell him how much she drank, once he had done his tests. She had been drinking that evening. She might have fallen down her garden stairs, why not? The broken wineglass in the garbage container, the cigar butts with plastic mouthpieces, the wedding ring on the floor . . . clues that might lead to nothing.

But he didn't think so. The meeting with Gabrielle had only deepened his suspicions. De Gier was probably right, she had been acting too well. Grijpstra, as usual, wouldn't commit himself. Cardozo was too young and inexperienced, he would only say what he had heard, seen, smelled, felt, tasted, as a young detective should. But Cardozo's assistance would be important, for he had met Gabrielle before her mother died.

The commissaris was organizing his attack on the knot of lies, schemes, hidden emotions, suppressed fears, that had already shown itself in part, but he got caught up again in the gale and in what the gale was doing to the city that had been his hunting ground for over forty years. He knew Amsterdam as warm, friendly, comforting as a mother. He was used to riding through her streets, recognizing odd corners, feeling the spreading protection of old trees, the cool of waterways nibbling at quays built centuries ago out of cobblestones, each individually faced, each with its own growth of minute, fuzzy plants forming a green border to the small, blue-gray, lapping waves. Now the canals were hellish sewers, covered in yellow spray where they were lit up by swinging streetlights.

The sign of a drugstore came flying, and de Gier turned the wheel so that it sailed past and hit the street and broke, exploding into a cloud of plastic particles. He could hear Grijpstra grunt behind him. Two fire engines hurtled toward the Volkswagen and de Gier drove onto the sidewalk. The engine stalled, and they could hear the sirens of the red trucks, howling emptily.

"Must be on their way to a collapsed house."

The commissaris didn't acknowledge the sergeant's remark but struggled on with his thoughts.

They came to the avenue where the commissaris lived. The sergeant had guided the car onto the sidewalk again to avoid the fallen trees and to minimize the commissaris's exposure to the weather. When de Gier switched the engine off he looked at the commissaris's face and smiled. His chief seemed his usual calm self, slightly amused, neat, gentle. The discipline of a long life of continuous effort had reasserted itself, the commissaris's fear had been forced back into its lair, where it sat, cramped and uncomfortable, wrapped into itself, a black shapeless monstrosity, powerless and pathetic.

"I'll see you three gentlemen tomorrow at nine," the commissaris said cheerfully. "Don't think about the case tonight, we'll tackle it in the morning, it'll still be fresh."

"Sir," the three men said. The sergeant wanted to get out of the car to open the commissaris's door, but the little old man was in the street already, stumbling to the front door that was being held open by his wife, whose housecoat was being blown to the side. They saw her reach out and pull him in.

4

THE LARGE ROOM on the third floor of Amsterdam police headquarters breathed a quiet atmosphere of comfortable respectability. The room had been neutral when the commissaris moved into it, many years back. The service had supplied him with furniture—a desk, some chairs, some tables—a carpet, all noncommittal, gray and brown, well made but without any appreciable style. The commissaris had left the furniture where it had been put down but had built his own feeling around them. There was a profusion of plants on the windowsills now, and on the walls hung magnificent seventeenth-century portraits wangled from the stores of the Rijksmuseum, showing bright-eyed gentlemen dressed in velvet, with hooked noses and flamboyant beards, men of past authority who had helped to form the city and contributed to its splendor of canals reflecting a few thousand ornamental but still simple gables. The faces on the portraits showed an unusual degree of intelligence and insight and a glint of humor, and it was difficult, at first glance, to relate the direct lineage that linked them to the commissaris, the mousy old man who now faced his three assistants. The commissaris's shape could sink away into any crowd, and it would be possible to pass him several times in an hour without retaining the slightest recollection. And yet, by studying his face and the way he carried his sparse frame, much could be seen. The three detectives were seeing more of it now. They were also listening.

"A mess," the commissaris had said. "This case is a mess, and I wish we could leave it alone. We could, easily. The lady had a little too much to drink, she was upset because of the gale, she slipped, she fell, she broke her neck. A report, that's all we have to write. I could catch the whole event in half a page and everybody here would accept my version. What do you think?"

There were some mumbles that evolved into one audible word pronounced by Grijpstra: "No."

"No?"

"No, sir." Grijpstra's bulky body filled the commissaris's chair of honor, a heavy piece of furniture capped by wooden lions' heads snarling on each side of his wide shoulders. Grijpstra felt fine. He had got up early and had been able to shave and have breakfast in peace, and he had found a clean suit and his favorite shirt, light blue with a detachable white collar, bought at half-price at the last sale of Amsterdam's best clothing store.

"Why not?" the commissaris asked. "Do you think we have anything to go on? The clues point at a family fight culminating in manslaughter. We don't have to presuppose ill will or planning. I am reasonably sure that we'll come up with the reconstruction of a situation where tempers ran high because of irritation aggravated by the unusual weather. The lady was shoved and fell. There was no wish to kill. The case may sizzle out in court after a few hundred hours of work on our part, and we may have made some blunders on the way that may increase the suffering of some of our fellow beings we haven't even met so far. You think we should go ahead?"

"Yes, sir."

"De Gier?"

De Gier spread his long muscular hands. His large eyes gleamed; there seemed to be a slight movement in the upswept ends of his mustache. "No, sir, you shouldn't ask me. If you start the investigation I will work on it, with pleasure, I may say. There's a puzzle. The girl was lying, I think, and I would like to know the significance of the clues, of the whole situation. But perhaps there is nothing there; the gale gave a strange impact last night, everything was different. But I have no opinion about whether or not to take the case. Maybe you are right, maybe we'll do more harm than good."

"And maybe we shouldn't concern ourselves with that," Grijpstra said quietly. "We are the police, we are maintaining order, we have rules."

"So if the rules lead to more disorder?" the commissaris asked, but he didn't wait for Grijpstra's reply. "Never mind. We'll take the case. I am not asking you, Cardozo, I will ask you in a few years' time. That

doesn't mean I don't value your opinion but it has to be formed first."
He got up and walked over to the young detective, sitting straight up on
a hard-backed chair. Cardozo got patted on his curly head and the
commissaris retreated behind his glass-topped desk. "Right, so we proceed. This is the way I would want you to start out. We have the following persons involved: Elaine Carnet, dead, but she left her corpse
that has to be investigated. I want to know whether the wedding ring fits
easily on her finger. Cardozo, you can go to the morgue when this conference is over. Does anybody have the ring?"

Grijpstra pointed at a carton standing next to his chair. "In there,
sir."

"Good. I saw the fingerprint report. Surfaces have been wiped clean,
in the expert's opinion anyway. The statement wouldn't hold in court—
doorknobs are often in touch with garments and the result is a finger-
printless doorknob—but for us it is a clue. A suspect hiding tracks, or
somebody else's tracks. There is more information that is of interest.
The doctor claims that Elaine Carnet had been drinking to the point of
intoxication and that she was a habitual drinker but not quite an alcoholic. His report is documented properly and it will hold in court. So
Elaine was drunk last night; her lack of self-control may have made her
say something that invited an attack and got her pushed down the stairs.
Who pushed her? The mysterious cigar smoker? We have Gabrielle
Carnet, Elaine's partner Mr. Bergen, and Elaine's former lover the
blond baboon, a man called Jan Vleuten, and that's all so far, right?"

"Mr. de Bree, sir," Cardozo said. "The suspected dog poisoner, the
man I interviewed or tried to interview but he slammed the door in my
face."

"Good. We have him too, but he doesn't want to see us. We need
more material against him, preferably statements by witnesses who saw
him feeding the dog. Maybe the witnesses can be found; the garden in
which the poisoning took place can be seen by a fairly large number of
people, the inhabitants of the houses next and opposite the Carnet
house, opposite the rear of the Carnet house, that is. Something for you,
Cardozo. Once you have been to the morgue you can do your rounds. If
you produce some evidence, no matter how vague, we have a stronger
case against your nasty Mr. de Bree and we can haul him in for questioning. So far he is out of reach although I could try to bluff him."

"That leaves Gabrielle Carnet, Mr. Bergen, and this blond baboon,
sir."

"Yes, sergeant. We don't know much about Gabrielle yet, in spite of
my questioning last night. She'll have to be seen again, maybe also by

Cardozo, for he has met her twice now and there should be some contact between them. I don't think you should go, de Gier. You said you didn't like her, is that right?"

De Gier nodded.

"Lack of sympathy doesn't make questioning any easier, so Grijpstra can go. You and I can see Mr. Bergen and this blond baboon. It can all be done today. We may come up with other suspects, I hope not, however. There shouldn't be too many suspects. Mrs. Carnet had a glass of wine with her killer and received him on the porch, not in her splendid living room. She knew the killer intimately and she gave me the impression of being a lonely woman, but the impression may be wrong. It *was* a strange night and the gale may have influenced our reasoning. Maybe Elaine Carnet had a lot of intimate friends and maybe all the friends hated her. Who knows, but we should find out today."

The room was silent. A constable brought coffee and Cardozo served.

"Any questions?"

"The safe, sir, and the portrait."

The commissaris rubbed his hands. "The safe and the portrait," he said slowly. "Yes. Um. Um, um, um. Very good of you, adjutant. You said that you and de Gier found a wall safe hidden by a painting while Cardozo and I were upstairs questioning Gabrielle. The safe contained a box, an old-fashioned cigar box, and the box had three hundred guilders* in it and some change. So perhaps it hadn't been opened, for the money was there. But according to the fingerprint expert the safe's handle had been wiped clean. You can ask Gabrielle about the safe when you see her today. Maybe she knows if her mother kept a lot of money in it. And then there was the painting hung over the safe. We don't have it here, do we?"

"No, sir."

"A portrait of Elaine Carnet done when she was young. She was standing next to a piano and she was singing."

"Yes, sir. The painting was signed 'Wertheym.' "

The commissaris half-closed his eyes and breathed out sharply. "Well, what would that mean? Just a portrait done by a painter. But we might visit the painter. There may have been some relationship between him and Elaine and he may be able to tell us about her. Very likely not, but we won't pass it up. Why don't you visit this painter, adjutant, while Cardozo sniffs around the area of the Carnet house, and then you two can meet later to see Gabrielle. Will that do?"

---

* A guilder is $0.40, or £0.25.

"Certainly, sir."

The commissaris looked at his watch. "Ten o'clock, we can finish our coffee in comfort and then all set out. Cardozo?"

Cardozo shot forward on his chair, almost toppling off. His eagerness made de Gier smile and he pulled his mustache to mask his merriment.

"You are the only one who has something to work on. So far all our suspects are too smooth to grab. They have plenty of little hooks where we could fasten a string, but we don't know where to look for them. But you have your Mr. de Bree, and we can be almost sure that he did try to kill that dog. We could hold on to him if you can produce some evidence, the slightest evidence will do. He is our only clear contact with the Carnet household: he knows both Elaine and Gabrielle, his garden borders on theirs, neighbors always know quite a lot about each other. It would be too much to expect that you can find witnesses to the actual death of Elaine—it must have happened late at night, when the gale was having its climax and it was raining heavily. But try anyway, take your time, visit everybody who lives in a house with a view of the Carnet garden."

"Yes, sir."

Grijpstra's eyelids dropped as he looked away from Cardozo's bright face. The young detective reminded him of a fellow pupil at school, a wiry little get-ahead, an eager-beaver pup that would drool whenever he could catch a teacher's attention. The pupil always got straight A's. He was a general now, in charge of Dutch tank brigades, clumsily plowing down fences on German farms. Grijpstra was glad he wasn't a general, but then, perhaps generals can get divorces easily. He stopped the thought. Whatever he tried to think about these days would always lead to divorce.

The commissaris stubbed out his cigar and the detectives got up but sat down again. The cigar hadn't been the right signal. The commissaris had left his desk and was wandering about the room, studying his plants.

He mumbled to himself, took an atomizer from a shelf, and sprayed a large fern that hung from the ceiling on a chain.

"Lovely, look at this new sprout, it's all curled up like a bishop's stave." The detectives stood around the fern and made appropriate remarks. Only de Gier seemed really interested.

"You should have some ferns in your apartment, de Gier, they are both decorative and tranquilizing."

"My cat will jump them and tear their leaves, sir."

"Really? Tabriz? I thought she was a pleasant, sedate female. Well, just hang it high enough. It'll rest your mind as you lie on your bed and it will give you good ideas. The mind really only functions well when it's properly calmed." He walked back to his desk and sat down. His small dried-out, almost yellow hands rested on the tabletop. He didn't hear the detectives as they trooped out of the room.

"Sir?" de Gier asked from the door.

"Hmm? Yes. I'll meet you in the courtyard in fifteen minutes, sergeant. We'll visit Mr. Bergen first, the Carnet partner—find the address of Carnet and Company, please, they deal in furniture. I think I've seen their building, near the Pepperstraat somewhere."

The sergeant closed the door slowly. He heard the last two words the commissaris said. "Messy. Yagh!"

5

THE BUILDING in the Pepperstraat consisted of six small, three-storied houses joined on the inside while still retaining their apparent individualities. Each house had its own ornamentation, very different from the others if observed carefully, but the overall effect created unity again. The commissaris stood in the narrow street while de Gier drove off again to find a parking place, and looked up to get a good view. He wondered why the sixteenth and seventeenth centuries had given rise to so much perfect beauty and how the beauty could have got lost for so long. It was coming back now, there was hope again, but it had been gone for hundreds of years, drab years that had built other parts of the city, long cramped streets of soot-soaked grayness lining up houses that were an insult to humanity with their cramped quarters and stark, forbidding rooflines.

A sign, hung from a cast-iron bar, read CARNET & CO., FURNITURE, IMPORT & WHOLESALE in small neat lettering. Through several open windows on the first floor the clatter of electric typewriters could be heard. An elderly couple, probably a storekeeper and his wife, were received at the narrow green front door of the first gable by a smooth-looking young man in a tailored suit. A salesman welcoming customers. Elaine Carnet had obviously built up a good business. He felt sorry now that he hadn't taken time to study the corpse's face more carefully. From the glimpse he remembered he could detect neither efficiency nor the polite ruthlessness that marks a success in business.

He grinned, maybe he was too hard on the trade. But he had always felt the cutting power of the traders' brains whenever he had dealt with them. There might be more friendliness, more understanding, in the smaller merchants, the dealers who were in direct contact with consumers. When business works on wholesale and factory levels facial expressions change. He would have to base himself on what he had seen during that brief moment when the constables carried Mrs. Carnet's body out to the hearse. He had only seen an elderly woman, lonely, defeated, unconcerned about such matters as turnover and profit margin and cost control. The business would have been built up by others, although she might have owned the lion's share of the company's stock. But he had also seen that extraordinary expression of ghoulish delight.

De Gier came running around the corner. "Sorry, sir, I parked her at some distance."

"It's a pity my legs always trouble me, otherwise I could use a bicycle again. To try and use a car these days is more fuss than pleasure. Let's go in, sergeant."

Bergen came to the door. He had been advised to expect a visit from the police by the commissaris's secretary. The man fitted in with the image the firm presented. Not a young man, somewhere between fifty and sixty—the energetic way in which he carried himself might blur a few years. Short silvery gray hair, brushed till it shone, heavy jowls, close shaven, eyes that shone with nervous energy behind heavy lenses framed in gold. An impeccably dressed man, there was no fantasy in the clothes. A dark blue suit, a white shirt, a tie of exactly the same shade as the suit. The sort of man who is chosen by TV commercials to tell the ladies about a new washing machine or some other expensive item that requires some faith before it can be purchased. Mr. Bergen's voice confirmed the impression he was making, a warm deep sound coming from a wide chest.

"Commissaris, sergeant, please follow me. My office is on the top floor, I'll show the way if you'll excuse my going ahead." He must have said it a thousand times, to customers, to suppliers, to tax inspectors.

De Gier was the last to climb the stairs and the commissaris was some six steps ahead of him. As he watched the commissaris's narrow back he hummed, "Creepy creepy little mouse, Trips into Mr. Bergen's house."

Bergen didn't know what he was up against. De Gier thought of the chief inspector who had been in charge of several murder cases some years before. He had liked to use an innocent, almost stupid approach to lure suspects into talking freely, but he had a sadistic side to his character. He always seemed to take pride in demolishing the suspects' defenses and to show them up, finally, for what they were, and the suspects, being human, invariably showed themselves to be little more than brown paper bags filled with farts, a term the chief inspector liked to use. It had never seemed to occur to him that he himself might also fit that definition, and that he might burst or tear if enough pressure were brought to bear on his flimsy outer shell. The commissaris, although he played the game along the same general lines as his colleague, never enjoyed his kills. De Gier wondered if Bergen were a legal prey. So far they had no reason to expect more than some information.

They were ushered into a vast room, half showroom, half office. There was a profusion of leather furniture, couches and easy chairs, and the commissaris and the sergeant were directed to a low settee apparently made of some very excellent cowhide, a choice piece that was no doubt worth a fortune, a perfect example of contemporary Italian design.

"Gentlemen," Bergen said slowly, keeping his voice on a low pitch that was clearly audible, "some coffee perhaps? A cigar?"

The coffee was served by Gabrielle, dressed in a khaki jumpsuit.

The policemen stood up to shake her hand and Gabrielle smiled and purred. They were asked to be seated again and she bent down to give them their cups. Her breasts were almost entirely visible in the low top of her suit. De Gier was interested, but only mildly. He couldn't understand the girl's preference for trousers, the outfit accentuated her rather short bent legs, the way her jeans had the night before. He noted a glint near her neck and concentrated to see what it was. Gabrielle saw his interest and paused longer than necessary. A plastic thread, de Gier thought, very thin, and some object at the end of it, small and brown and shiny, partly hidden by the breasts, stuck in between. A button, perhaps. Why would she wear a wooden button between her breasts? The thought didn't go deep and hardly registered.

"You work here too, Miss Carnet?"

"Only sometimes, when Mr. Bergen expects important customers in the showroom or when the firm is very busy. We're having a visitor this afternoon who buys for a chain of department stores, and Mr. Pullini is in town, of course."

The commissaris came to life. "Pullini? That's an Italian name, isn't it? Didn't you tell me yesterday that your mother started the business with furniture imported from Italy?"

Bergen had sat down near them, balancing his coffee cup gracefully. "That's right, commissaris. Most of our merchandise still comes from Italy, but in this room we only show the expensive items. We also sell a lot of mass-produced furniture and we have been specializing lately in chairs and tables that can be stacked. We started selling to restaurants and hotels and canteens and so forth, and last year we began doing business with the armed forces."

"You must be doing well, yet we are having a depression, are we not?"

Bergen smiled widely. "That's what the merchants say who fail, they'll always have a depression. I don't think there is any real trouble, apart from the high taxes, of course, that's one factor that may squeeze us all out of existence."

"How much are you selling?" the commissaris asked. "Just a rough idea, you don't have to tell me if you don't want to. I'm being curious, that's all."

"Eight million last year." Bergen beamed. His polite awareness was clearly weakening, the policeman had made a good impression. "But that was a particularly good year, and a lot of that was army and navy business. Even so, we should do well again this year, even without any big contracts. The business is steady, fortunately. There will always be a good demand for furniture and we are well placed in the market."

The commissaris was nodding, a proud father admiring the antics of a child. The conversation flowed along until Bergen interrupted himself. "Mrs. Carnet," he said sadly, "my long-time partner, you are here to investigate her death, I presume?"

"Indeed."

"Do you suspect foul play, commissaris?"

The commissaris's head bent and the gesture reminded de Gier of his cat, Tabriz. Tabriz would drop her head to the side if she wasn't quite sure if she liked what he had heaped on her dish. "Perhaps not. There are some indications we can't explain at this point but they may fall into place and the death may very well be due to an accident. If that is so we would like to come to that conclusion with a minimal delay so that the case can be closed. What can you tell us about Mrs. Carnet, Mr. Bergen? Did she have any close friends, and did any of them visit her, perhaps last night, or did anybody at all visit her last night?"

Bergen's tight mouth curved downward. He appeared to be thinking hard. "No. I don't know what she did last night. I was home, working on a tree in my garden that was bumping against the roof. Elaine didn't come to the office yesterday, but then she hardly ever does these days. She is really semiretired and leaves the running of the business to me. We used to have a lot of contact in the old days, when we were making the firm grow, but that's all over now and has been for several years."

"Mother didn't have much of a routine," Gabrielle said. "She liked to get up late and then she would have breakfast in a restaurant somewhere and do some shopping and go to the hairdresser and she sometimes went to the movies. She only had her evening meal at home."

"I see." The commissaris got up, looked about, and sat down again.

"More coffee?" Gabrielle asked.

"No, erhm, no. I wonder if you would mind very much, Miss Carnet, if I asked you to let us talk to Mr. Bergen alone for a little while. I would like to ask some questions that, well, may embarrass you."

Gabrielle laughed and got up, taking the empty cups from the table. "Of course, but I don't get embarrassed easily. I am a modern girl, you know."

"Yes, yes," the commissaris said, still ill at ease. De Gier's eyes narrowed. He had seen it all before. The situation was shaping up nicely, manipulated detail by detail.

"Now," the commissaris said when Gabrielle had left the room, "I'm sure you know why I asked Miss Carnet to leave us alone for a minute. If Mrs. Carnet was killed last night and didn't just slip and fall down her stairs—she had drunk a fair amount of wine, you know, Beaujolais, a strong wine, we found an empty bottle—she may have been killed by someone she was on intimate terms with. Would you know of such a person, sir?"

Bergen was thinking again. Evidently he wanted to be helpful but he was weighing his words. "Yes. I see what you mean. Well, Elaine did have a lover for several years, an employee of this firm, a man called Vleuten. He left us two years ago, rather suddenly."

"Because of any unpleasantness?"

"Yes." Bergen was scraping his throat industriously. "Yes, you might call it that. A nasty business. You see, Elaine fell in love with the baboon—that's his nickname, he rather looks like an ape, he didn't mind being called baboon. Elaine really fell for him, and he does have a nice personality, I'll say that for him. That was some time ago. Elaine was still in her forties then and rather attractive, she went to pieces later. The wine helped, but that's another matter."

"Related perhaps?" the commissaris suggested.

"Yes, related possibly. But there were other reasons, I think. The firm has grown so much that its mechanics became impossible for her to grasp. She could never understand the computerized bookkeeping and store records for instance; she liked to keep the records herself according to some old-fashioned system that she had mastered. She was hurt, I think, when we modernized our administration and most of her work became superfluous, and she began to withdraw. Her desk is over there. There's nothing on it anymore, not even a telephone. She doesn't really like to come in now. She doesn't know what is happening and she doesn't like to try and deal with anything anymore for fear that it may explode in her face."

"Yes." The commissaris's voice sounded thoughtful. "Yes, quite. A lost lonely woman, that's the impression I got from seeing her corpse."

The word "corpse" made Bergen wince and his hand moved quickly over his left cheek. He had made the gesture before, and de Gier noticed the nervous clasping of the hand after the movement was completed. He looked closely at Bergen's face. The left side seemed affected in some way, the eye looked larger than the right and the corner of the mouth drooped a little. Perhaps the man had survived a stroke. When Bergen spoke again some letters appeared slightly transformed. The *p*'s and *b*'s popped. De Gier shrugged. He was collecting some very useful information, so Bergen had suffered a stroke once, so what.

"An affair with an employee, that must have been unpleasant for you. What was Mr. Vleuten's position in the firm? Was he a salesman?"

"Sales director. He did very well for us. Some of our largest accounts are his work. The baboon was never an administrator and I don't think he could have run Carnet and Company, but he was certainly doing spectacular work in his own field."

The commissaris was lighting a small cigar. His voice had crossed the border between being conversational and amiable; the tension that de Gier had originally felt in Bergen's reactions was easing off.

"Yes, sales," the commissaris said, waving his cigar. "A business can do nothing without them, but good sales can be spoiled by bad administration. Did Mr. Vleuten aspire to become the head of this firm, was he a rival to you in any way?"

"No. The baboon didn't aspire to be anything other than what he was but he was a rival nevertheless, a most powerful rival, because Elaine was pushing the baboon right into my chair. And there wasn't just the business aspect to deal with. The baboon was Elaine's lover and she was cuddling him right here in this office, holding his hands, nibbling his ears, gazing into his eyes. You used the word 'embarrassing' just now, that's what it was, embarrassing. I felt a complete fool in my own office the minute the two came in. The baboon was always polite and charming, of course, but Elaine's behavior made me sick to my stomach. If I brought in some business, and I do that all the time, of course, the matter was completely ignored even if it was a contract involving a million guilders, but if the baboon sold a kitchen table and four matching chairs to a dear old lady running a store in the country we all had to sing the national anthem."

The policemen laughed and Bergen laughed with them, pleased with his little joke.

"So?"

"So I had to drive the matter to its peak. I simply couldn't stand it any longer. We had a meeting, the three of us, and I offered to resign and sell them my shares. It was a big risk, for I could have lost out easily, but I was still gambling on Elaine's insight. She must have known that my experience was important to the company's future and that the baboon had only proved himself as a salesman, never as an administrator. But she didn't blink an eye."

"Really? But the baboon left and you still are here."

Bergen's right hand played with the hem of his jacket.

"Yes. He surprised me. He got up and walked over to that typewriter over there and wrote his letter of resignation. It was very decent of him. He had the whole company in the palm of his hand for a minute but he blew it away. Even if he couldn't have administered the business he could have found somebody else to do that part of the work. We were doing very well. He was, in fact, refusing a fortune."

"And he left with nothing?"

"Just a few months' wages. Elaine offered him a year's income but he refused. I offered to accept his resignation in such a way that he would have qualified for unemployment benefits but he refused that too. He just shook my hand, kissed Elaine's cheek, and left. I haven't seen him since."

"Not even in the street?"

"No."

"And Mrs. Carnet? Did he break with her too then?"

"Yes, but she tried to make contact again. I heard her phone him. He's a good carpenter and she wanted him to fix something in her house. He may have come and the relationship may have continued in some way but I don't know, I always preferred not to ask."

The commissaris got up and walked over to a window. "Not the sort of man who would have pushed her down the garden stairs."

"No. The baboon isn't a violent man."

"Are *you*, sir?" The commissaris had turned to ask the question. It was asked in the same level tone he had used before but his eyes were fixed on Bergen's face.

"Violent?"

"Yes. Are you a violent man?"

Bergen's voice faltered. His left cheek seemed to sag more than before. The underlip had suddenly become slack and he was making an effort to answer the question. "No, no. I don't think so. I got into some fights at school and I had a scrap or two when I was in the army but that's gone now, I think it's not in me anymore."

"We'll have to ask you whether you can prove where you were last night, Mr. Bergen. I realize these are unpleasant questions but we have to ask them."

"I was at home, it wasn't the sort of night to go out."

"Were you alone?"

"Yes, my wife is staying with relatives, she is having a little holiday in the country. My children are married already. I was alone."

"No visitors? Nobody telephoned you?"

"No."

"Well, that was only for the record." The commissaris was going to elaborate on his statement, but the telephone rang and Bergen walked to his desk to answer it.

"Mr. Pullini? Has he come already? Ask Miss Gabrielle to talk to him for a little while, I'm busy now. And don't send any calls through; if you take the numbers I'll phone them back." He put the phone down with some unnecessary force and turned to face his visitors again. "Pullini," he said slowly. "It's a day of problems."

De Gier's eyes hadn't left Bergen's face for the last few minutes. He was studying the deterioration of the left side of the man's head with fascination. The muscles of his cheek and mouth were slackening rapidly and he didn't think that Bergen had modified what was happening to his face. The sergeant thought of drawing the commissaris's attention to the phenomenon in some way when Bergen began to speak again.

"Pullini. If only the man himself had come again, but he sent his darling son."

"You're having trouble with your supplier? Pullini is still your main supplier, isn't that right?"

"Yes, we buy more than half our stocks from him. A good factory, steady and quick deliveries, excellent quality, but his prices are too high these days. That's why young Pullini is here, he has been here for two weeks already. I have found another factory in Milan that can supply us and they are more competitive than the Pullini concern. They also give a little more credit—credit is important to us, we have to hold large inventories."

"And Pullini doesn't want to come down in price?"

"Not so far."

"So why doesn't young Pullini leave? Or is he liking Amsterdam?"

Bergen grinned. The grin was definitely lopsided and de Gier wondered if the commissaris was aware of their suspect's transformation. "Yes, he likes the high life here. Italians are still old-fashioned. The boy is having a good time, but he is hanging on for another reason. Old Pullini is also retired, like Elaine, and his concern is run by Francesco now, and Francesco has done a little underhanded maneuvering, or so I think, I can't prove it."

"Stealing from his father's business?"

"Perhaps. Papa Pullini is a tough old bird. He keeps his son on a short leash and Francesco has expensive ways, a brand-new Porsche, the best hotels, a little gambling—you know how it goes. Since Francesco took over we are given two invoices for every purchase. An official ninety percent invoice and an under-the-table ten percent invoice. I don't mind. On the ten percent invoices we have more credit; we keep them in a stack and pay them at the end of the year, in cash."

"And the ten percent goes into Francesco's pocket. I see. That's probably why he can't lower his prices, he's taking ten percent off already."

Bergen was nodding rapidly. He was evidently pleased that the commissaris saw the point so quickly.

"But," the commissaris said and raised a finger, "you say that you pay at the end of the year and we are in June now."

"I didn't make last year's payment. The money is still here, safely in the bank. I have been complaining about the Pullini price list and I have ignored Francesco when he kept on asking for his ten percent. I'm doing a little blackmailing, I suppose. It isn't nice of me, but we aren't always nice in business. I could switch over to the other company in Milan but I don't really want to do that either. The other company is too big, they might want to start up their own office here sometime and cut me out."

"Difficult," the commissaris agreed.

The interview was over, and the commissaris was near the door when he turned around. "Mrs. Carnet had a safe, Mr. Bergen, a small wall safe. We opened it with a key we found in her bag. There was a small amount in it, some three hundred guilders. You wouldn't know if she kept large amounts in that safe, would you?"

Bergen was holding his cheek and massaging it. "No," he said after awhile. "I know she had a safe and there may have been a lot of money in it from time to time, she did have large amounts of cash sometimes, but I wouldn't know if there was any appreciable quantity in there last night. It's not the sort of thing she would talk to me about. Our conversations of the past few years were mostly about what movies to see, we both like the same sort of films."

"You never had much social contact with Mrs. Carnet, had you?"

"Not really. I am married, my wife has always been rather jealous of Elaine, and later there was the baboon, of course."

"Thank you, Mr. Bergen, you've been most helpful."

"Did you notice his face, sir?" de Gier asked as they walked back to the car.

The commissaris was looking at a garbage boat that was making a sharp corner in the canal. A young man, a boy almost, was turning its large wheel effortlessly and the heavy diesel engine controlling the barge's screw was churning up a perfect arc of thick frothy waves. Workmen were sawing a broken tree on the other side of the canal, with the boat pulling cables so that the thick elm wouldn't fall the wrong way.

"Two million trees down in the country, according to the radio," the commissaris said. "Two million, I wonder how they can guess the number. The whole country is a mess and we have our own to play with. Yes, I noted Bergen's facial paralysis, sergeant. It must have started before we came, but he was going through a crisis while we talked to him."

"A stroke, sir?"

"No, I don't think so, but I am sure he's telephoning his doctor right now. I thought I would have to cut my questioning off, but I had gone too far already."

"But if he got upset to such an extent . . ." De Gier had stopped, but the commissaris kept on walking, and the sergeant had to sprint to catch up with him again.

"He must be guilty?"

"He might be."

"He might be, sure. And he might not be. We don't know how involved he was with the lady. And he may have other worries. That Pullini business may be much worse than he made it appear. I would like to see young Pullini. Try and find out where he's staying after you've dropped me off. Don't ask Mr. Bergen or Gabrielle. Find him through the hotel records. It shouldn't be difficult to run him down. If he doesn't expect us to look for him and if we suddenly show up the questioning may be more, what's the word, 'deadly'."

De Gier steered the commissaris's black Citroën through the narrow alleys near the center of the old city. They got stuck a few times and had to wait for trucks and motorized tricycles unloading, and every now and then they would run into a detour caused by municipal workmen clearing fallen trees. Most of the glass of broken windows had already been swept up. The city still looked desolate, however, and the commissaris's mood fitted in with the general devastation.

"Bah," he said as the car turned into its reserved space on the courtyard of police headquarters. "We'll have to push ourselves, sergeant. I want this case to be over in a few days, in a week at the most. There's still some time before lunch to find Francesco Pullini. I hope Grijpstra and Cardozo will be back soon with something tangible. With four men on the job we should be able to cut through their nonsense quickly. There are other projects I'd like to be working on."

De Gier had switched the Citroën's engine off and was waiting for the car to give its customary sigh before starting to sink down to its lowest point. The vehicle's fluid suspension system always gave him a sensuous sensation, he was grinning in the split second of anticipation.

"You noticed that Mr. Bergen didn't smoke?"

"Yes, sir. He didn't smoke while we were with him but I saw a nicotine stain on his index finger. He smokes cigarettes, I saw a packet of Gauloises on his desk. He's probably trying to give it up."

"Giving it up," the commissaris repeated slowly. "I have been watching the inspector lately. He is also trying to give up smoking but he isn't making much headway. He told me that he is now smoking a brand he doesn't like. Maybe Mr. Bergen doesn't like cigars with plastic mouthpieces, or would that be too far-fetched, sergeant?"

The Citroën had finished its sigh and the sergeant was alert again. He hadn't understood everything the commissaris said, but the sound of his superior's words was still in his ears and he could reconstruct the question.

"He could have been at the Carnet house last night, sir, and he might have a reason for wanting to have Mrs. Carnet out of the way. Maybe she doesn't come to the company often, but she does control it, legally anyway—she had three-quarters of the shares."

"So we'll have to find out if there was any tension between them, some recent disagreement, something to do with the company's policy perhaps. Yes." The commissaris had been talking briskly and he opened the door and almost jumped out, but he had to hold on to the car as a fresh flow of pain burned through his legs.

"I'll find this Pullini man and the baboon, Mr. Vleuten, sir. I'll phone you as soon as I know their addresses."

The commissaris was limping ahead as the building's alarm system came on. Short hysterical bursts of a two-toned horn split the quiet of the yard and a glass door burst open, pushed by a young man in torn jeans and a dirty jacket. He was running toward the gate, where two uniformed constables had lowered the beam and were protecting it, their guns out.

De Gier was running too. He cut the young man off and dived for his legs, bringing him down with such force that the dust of the yard came up in a small cloud. The commissaris had frozen in his tracks and watched the commotion. The constables pulled the prisoner to his feet and handcuffed him. De Gier was sadly inspecting a tear in his jacket. Plainclothes detectives and more constables surrounded the prisoner and half marched, half carried him back to the building. The commissaris stopped a detective.

"What are the charges against your man?"

"Robbery, sir, attempted manslaughter, drug dealing. We may come up with a pimping charge too, a girl brought in a complaint this morning."

"Bad case eh?"

"Yes, sir, a hopeless case. It might have been better if he had got himself shot, he'll spend the rest of his life in jail or the nuthouse. The psychiatrists have been looking at him but they don't seem to be able to classify the trouble. As far as we're concerned he's dangerous. He keeps on attacking the guards, he bit the chief guard just now."

The detective ran after his colleagues; the commissaris turned around. De Gier was still looking at his jacket.

"Are you all right, sergeant?"

"Yes, sir. I'll have to get another jacket, I'll do it now. I have a suit at the dry-cleaning place around the corner. This jacket has had it, I think. Even if I have it repaired the tear will still show."

"The police will pay. I am going to my office, de Gier."

The commissaris's mood didn't improve until he was back behind his desk and looking at his fern, which was catching the sun and showing its leaves in an almost unnatural glitter of sparkling green.

"Very nice," the commissaris said. "But you are one aspect of nature. I am dealing with another, and it's rotten, brown, dog-eared, moldy, smelly with disease."

He made the moves that had never failed to restore his equanimity. He lit a small cigar, telephoned for coffee, and began to walk around his office. He fed his plants after having mixed the right quantity of fertilizer into a plastic watering can. He sprayed the fern with slow bursts of a small glass atomizer. His telephone rang.

"I have the hotel, sir, the Pulitzer. Francesco Pullini is in his room now, according to the desk clerk. I also have the baboon's address, he lives on the Amsteldijk. According to the number he lives on the best part of the dike, where it overlooks the river close to the Thin Bridge."

"You haven't spoken to either of the suspects?"

"No, sir."

"We'll go and surprise them. I'll meet you in the courtyard in a minute. We might tackle young Pullini first."

The commissaris finished his coffee and rested his eyes on the fern again, the central ornament of the bright room.

The sergeant was waiting for him in the Citroën and got out when he saw his chief cross the yard.

"How did the gale treat your balcony last night, de Gier?"

The sergeant smiled ruefully. "Badly, sir. I've lost almost everything. The lobelia bush survived, but it sat on the floor in a concrete box Public Works let me have some time ago. The rest have gone. The geraniums and the begonias are torn to shreds. Some of them were blown away, pots and all, and the window of my bedroom is cracked."

"So?" There was some poignancy to the single word, and the sergeant's expressive eyes stared gently at the commissaris.

"I've ordered new plants, sir, but the greenhouse won't deliver them. The garage sergeant said he could let me have one of his pickups for a few hours, maybe I'll get the plants later in the day. I also ordered a new window but it may take weeks to arrive, the glass merchants are having the time of their lives right now. What about your house, sir?"

"Some damage. My wife is taking care of it."

"And the turtle, sir?"

The commissaris grinned. "The turtle is fine. I saw him trying to plow through the rubbish in the garden this morning. The ground is covered with broken branches and glass and the gardenchairs of the neighbors, but the turtle just plows on. He looked quite cheerful, I thought."

"Maybe he'll be reincarnated as a police detective."

The commissaris touched de Gier's sleeve. "He has the right character. Let's go, sergeant."

"Yes, sir." The Citroën moved to the gate, where the constables were raising the barrier. De Gier braked to give way to a police truck loaded with a platoon of constables dressed in riot uniforms and armed with carbines. The truck had all its lights on and was sounding its siren.

"What's up?" he asked the constables at the barrier.

"Turks, they are having a gunfight somewhere, or Moroccans, I forget now, I heard it on the intercom just now. This is the second truck already. A big fight, automatics and everything."

De Gier sighed. He thought of Gabrielle's bowed legs. There wouldn't be a gunfight in this case. But as he followed in the wake of the screaming riot truck his feeling changed. Something might happen to make the case worthwhile, something usually happened. He looked at the small neat body of the commissaris and had to restrain himself not to pat the old man's shoulder affectionately.

6

CARDOZO SIPPED HIS TEA and smiled politely. He had been listening to the old lady for quite a while now. She was telling him about her recent hospitalization. The old lady's sister was waiting for a chance to say something too. A related subject, no doubt, something to do with varicose veins or the cartilage between the spine's vertebrae that wears away in old age and causes pains. Cardozo put his cup down and picked up a cookie and nibbled on it.

"Yes," he said. He arranged a proper expression of commiseration. It sat on his face like a thin plastic mask. Underneath there was nothing but raw impatience, but the mask fitted well. The ladies' birdlike voices prattled on. He had to go through all of it. He even knew their ages now. Seventy-eight, eighty-two. That's old. They wouldn't live much longer, but they were alive now and they had seen something and their statements would be acceptable to a judge, and Constable First Class Cardozo meant to get those statements.

He felt his pocket. The pen was there, so was his notebook. He would write out two statements and have them signed individually—the judge wouldn't like a joint statement. Whatever the two ladies had seen they had seen on their own, and the judge would want to know what they had seen in their own words. They had said they had seen something. They had seen Mr. de Bree, that nasty, ill-mannered man with the fat face. Men shouldn't have fat faces, didn't the detective think so? Sure, he thought so. As nasty as his cat. Mr. de Bree's cat also had a fat face. And he was always catching the nice little birds; he had even caught the thrush that sang so beautifully, and chomped on the poor little thing and spread its feathers all over Mr. de Bree's garden. The old ladies had watched the onslaught through their binoculars. Weren't they nice binoculars? Alice had specially fetched them to show them to the detective. Beautiful copper binoculars, they don't make them like that anymore these days. She and her sister used to take them to the theater and to the opera. But that was a long time ago.

"Yes," Cardozo said. He wasn't going to ask more questions. He had asked them already, they knew exactly what he wanted, and they would tell him, in their own time. He glanced at his watch. Twenty minutes gone, and another two hours on the rest of his search. He had been everywhere, in any house that had a view of the Carnet garden. Nobody had seen anything, but everybody knew Mr. de Bree. A nasty man, he knew that by now, he knew it by his own experience. He hadn't forgotten the red scowling face glaring at him before the door banged with such force that a particle of plaster from the porch's ceiling had dropped at his feet.

He had been given several descriptions of the de Bree cat, a pampered monstrosity with a half-orange, half-black face, which gave the beast two appearances, depending on which side he was approached, but they were both bad. The cat was the terror of the gardens and the main source of the torn ears and bad wounds of other cats. He had also heard reports on Paul, the Carnet dog. Paul was nice. An intelligent, jolly dog who had successfully defended his domain against the de Bree cat, until he was poisoned.

"There he is," the old lady called Alice said and tugged at Cardozo's sleeve. He saw the cat, jumping leisurely across the liguster hedge dividing the de Bree and Carnet properties. "Big, isn't he? Twenty pounds of bad cat."

And then they told him, whispering, hissing, glancing over their shoulders to see if some mysterious shadow in the room were listening in. They had seen de Bree feeding Paul. Chopped steak, they were sure of it. They had trained their binoculars on him, they had seen every detail of the murderous attempt. Two days ago now, in the afternoon. The Carnet ladies weren't in and Paul was playing by himself in the garden, snapping at flies and dancing about, throwing his little pink rubber ball. And de Bree had come out with the meat and Paul had eaten it.

"But why didn't you tell the Carnet ladies?" Cardozo asked pleasantly, holding a respectful expression that belied the accusation in his question. He was the favorite nephew visiting his two old aunties and he wanted to know why they did things.

"Oh, but that would have been terrible. We *did* think about it but we didn't, you see, because they would have been so unhappy."

"Really?"

"Really."

"But you could have told us, the police."

Yes, they could have, but they didn't have a telephone and it was such a long walk to the nearest station and they weren't so young anymore.

"I am seventy-eight," Alice said.

"And I am eighty-two," Alice's sister said.

Cardozo brought out his notebook and prepared two statements. They didn't want to sign them. They didn't want any trouble.

"But Paul is still alive, he'll be playing in the garden soon. You don't want Mr. de Bree to poison him again, do you?"

"No."

But they still didn't want to sign the statement. Mr. de Bree wouldn't like it. He had bumped Alice's leg once with his car and he hadn't even got out to help her up. He was a *nasty* man, maybe next time he wouldn't just bump Alice, maybe the next time he would *kill* her.

"Never," Cardozo said. "Not with us around. We are the police, you see, we protect you, but we can only protect you if you help us." He waved the ball-point encouragingly. "Just a little signature, right here."

Alice signed, and then the sister signed too. They didn't want to read the statements, they didn't have their spectacles on.

"Where *are* my spectacles, Alice?" the sister asked. "You always mislay them."

"*What?*" Alice asked in a suddenly shrill voice.

"Thank you very much, ladies, thank you *very* much."

The argument went on as he ran down the stairs. He had come up with something, something positive, concrete, undeniable. He whistled as he banged the front door, and turned the corner. He waved at the de Bree door as he ran past it.

He remembered that there was a telephone booth at the end of the street. Grijpstra wasn't in but he was put through to the commissaris's secretary. "You are not to go and see Miss Carnet just now but to report to the commissaris later. He has gone away with the sergeant and the adjutant isn't back yet."

"So what am I to do?" Cardozo's voice shot up in indignation.

"Well, I don't know," the secretary's voice said coolly. "Surely you can find some work? The detectives' city patrols are always short of men, Sergeant Sietsema was asking for you. He's on duty this afternoon and he needs company."

"Oh, very well, I'll be back as soon as I can."

"Good boy." She hung up.

"Aren't I?" Cardozo asked the street. The telephone booth's door slammed behind him. "Aren't I? I got what they wanted me to get and I want to tell them about it and they aren't there. They're drinking coffee and smoking cigars and passing the time of day." He glared at the peaceful street.

But Amsterdam is a helpful city, it provides comfort in subtle ways. A woman came past, pushing a perambulator containing identical twins facing each other solemnly from their pink wraps, vaguely resembling Grijpstra in his better moments. An old man with long hair strode on the opposite pavement whistling a Bach cantata. A girl on a red bicycle came around the corner. She wore a sleeveless blouse, unbuttoned, and nothing underneath. A well-shaped girl. Cardozo winked at the girl and she winked back and he began to walk to his car. Not such a bad day after all.

But he felt a little uptight again when he started the Volkswagen. A constable at the next intersection raised his hand. The Volkswagen drove on slowly. The constable whipped out a whistle and blew it. Cardozo's foot stayed on the accelerator. He crossed the intersection and stopped, watching the constable in his rearview mirror. The constable was running.

"Didn't you see me?"

"Sure. I don't know what's the matter with me. I saw you, I saw you giving the stop sign, but I kept on driving. I must be going crazy."

The constable bent down and peered into Cardozo's face. "It sometimes happens," he whispered confidentially. "I see it every now and then. I've thought of several explanations. Some subconscious protest, perhaps, or a hidden aggression, something like that. Have you done this before?"

"No."

"First time, eh? Well, maybe it means nothing. Maybe you're just tired. But if it happens again you might see a psychiatrist. What do you do for a living?"

"I'm a police detective."

The constable's eyebrows shot up and he stepped back to study the car. He jumped forward and pushed his head into the window. Cardozo pointed at the police radio under the dashboard and fished out his plastic identification.

"Get away," the constable said.

"But . . ."

"Come on, get off. *Off!*" The constable walked back to the intersection. He was looking at the pavement and dragging his feet.

7

WERTHEYM, the plate on the door read, PORTRAIT PAINTER.

There was nothing particular about the door and there was nothing to prevent Adjutant Grijpstra from pressing the bell but he didn't. He stood with his hands folded and waited. He had been enjoying himself so far and he didn't want to interrupt the steady flow of well-being that had begun to soak into him from the moment he had left his little house that morning. There was a small black cloud at the end of the flow and he meant to keep it away for as long as he could, a process that would be possible if he consciously experienced the small moments that his working day would present. The black cloud was his return home. He definitely didn't want to go home.

His wife, the blob of semi-solid fats, dirty and bad-tempered, that had grown slowly out of the girl he had once married, was gradually filling the two floors of their home, pushing him to the wall, seeping into his peace, the peace he built up during the day. One day he wouldn't go home anymore. He didn't want to see her leaning on the kitchen table that squeaked under her weight, leaning on the creaking railing on the stair landing, leaning on the cracked windowsill. It was hard for her to stand now. It was also hard for her to sit down, for the effort of getting up again might break the few chairs that were still in one piece.

But, where could he go if he didn't go home? He was spending afterhours' time in his room at headquarters, he was eating out as much as he could, but he still had to go home to sleep. He cursed slowly, articulating the syllables. But then he promised himself he wouldn't think of the little black cloud; it would come on its own, without him thinking about it. His hand reached out slowly and pressed the bell.

The door opened at once.

"Mr. Wertheym?"

"Yes, I don't . . ."

"I am a police detective, sir, here is my card. Just a few questions, may I come in?"

"Certainly, certainly, I thought you wanted your portrait painted. I don't do men, you see, only women. I was going to tell you that, saves a lot of chatter. Come in."

The man could only be a painter. His appearance was a perfect combination of the number of attributes that make up the idea "painter" in the average perceptive mind. A small goatee, high forehead, bright eyes, a beret on the gray locks, an apron smeared with assorted colors—Wertheym was undoubtedly an artist. But there was nothing artistic about his house. The furniture had been taken straight from the showroom of a lower-middle-class store. The imitation fireplace with its licking gas flames creeping over iron birch logs complete with bark was in the worst possible taste. A calendar showing a plump girl in a glued-on flowery miniskirt that could be lifted up hung next to a triangular arrangement of plastic and tin replicas of Spanish swords. Different types of paper flowers had been matched into a bouquet that had lost both color and resilience.

Grijpstra's lips parted in a thin snarl. He also mumbled, "Home sweet home."

"Pardon?"

"I was just thinking that my wife would like this room."

"Would she now?" Wertheym offered a chair, one of a set of four, chrome framed and upholstered with strips of shiny green vinyl. "Not too hot for you here? This house is on the cold side of the street, never gets any sun. I keep the fire going but people say it's stuffy in here, don't notice it myself."

"Quite all right, thank you."

Grijpstra didn't open the conversation. He almost never did anymore. Deliberate silences formed a new trick that had crept into his arsenal. He was practicing the trick now. He had done the necessary, shown his identification. The other party should be a little rattled by now. He waited. Something might come up and, then again, it might not.

Wertheym had read the wording on Grijpstra's card and remembered his rank. "Cup of tea, adjutant? Or coffee? I was just going to have coffee myself."

"Please."

"Police," Wertheym said slowly. *"Po-lice.* First time I've been visited by a police officer, I think, doesn't happen in my trade. I just paint portraits, a harmless occupation. I've had the taxhounds after me but never the police. The taxman thought I hadn't been declaring my true income. Maybe I hadn't it, but he couldn't prove it so he went away again. So what have I done, adjutant?"

Grijpstra didn't have to answer. Wertheym had darted off but he came back again, carrying a tray with two flowered glasses. "Sorry, it's a bit of a mess in the kitchen. No cups today, but the coffee'll taste the same. Instant coffee, hope you don't mind, adjutant."

Grijpstra did mind.

"Mrs. Elaine Carnet," he said and sipped from the glass. "Does that name mean anything to you?"

"Yes. She is dead. Was in the paper this morning. And I painted her portrait, last year. She didn't model. I painted it from a poster, hell of a job it was. The poster was old and torn, a tear right through the face. A French poster. She used to sing in Paris, she said. I did the portraits and she paid cash and she left. Never saw her again. Nice woman, didn't quibble about the price—they often do, you know. Amazing, their vanity gets in the way of their greed, but I'm greedy too and I never drop my price. The hell with 'em, I always say. And if they argue, they'll pay in advance, all of it, or I won't touch the job."

"Portraits?" Grijpstra had moved and some coffee had spilled on his trousers. It was seeping through to his skin. He put the glass down and rubbed the stain. "Portraits, you said? More than one, you mean?"

"Two portraits, identical—well, they differed a little, they were handmade, after all. She wanted two so I made two. Silly work, I massproduced them. Little blob of blue on the one canvas, little blob of blue on the second canvas. I had never done that before, it was amusing in a way. It gave me ideas but nothing came of them. I specialize in female faces, you see, never do buildings or anything like that. If I could do buildings I could pick a particularly good one and do a whole series of them, just line up a lot of canvases and dance around, fill in the browns, then the reds, and so forth."

"Yes." Grijpstra hadn't listened. "So you did two portraits? Why?"

"I never ask why, adjutant. Why should I? Why should they want their portraits done anyway? There isn't one portrait I have done in the last ten years that I would want on my own wall. The ladies are all ugly as sin. I beautify them, of course, or I would have no business. In a way

Mrs. Carnet's portrait was the best of them all: the poster showed her
as a young woman. Young women aren't as ugly as old women."

"Thank you," Grijpstra said. He left his almost full glass on the
table. He had only taken two sips but the taste of the vile brew hung on
in his mouth. He remembered that he had promised himself that this
would be a good day. Fine, so he would find some real coffee somewhere. There were some pleasant sidewalk cafés in the vicinity. He
would locate one and sit around for an hour and rid himself of the portrait painter's sickening fumes. There was plenty of time. Cardozo
couldn't possibly be finished yet, he had been given a sizable job. He
would make contact with Cardozo later and they could have more
coffee while they thought of the right approach. They had to question
Gabrielle Carnet again, and he didn't know what the suspect had answered to the commissaris's questions. Cardozo would have to fill him
in. It would all take time. No hurry today.

His face looked placid as he ambled in the direction of the old city,
careful not to hurt his toes against the uneven cobblestones and walking
as close to the water of a narrow canal as the parked cars would permit.
There had been a squall of rain, but the sun had come out again and
now lit up a formation of seagulls patrolling the water for spoils and
conversing raucously. A small boy was steering a homemade raft that
was bumping crazily on the choppy waves in the wake of a barge.

He passed several cafés until he found one with the right conditions.
It had a view of the canal, the waiter was an old man with a kind face,
there was a fresh smell of coffee, and its terrace had already attracted
several beautiful women. Fate seemed intent to disprove the portrait
painter's harsh remark, for more beautiful women came just after Grijpstra had sat down. He looked around approvingly. An Oriental girl with
a small finely chiseled face, long straight legs, and a tight bosom had
draped herself in the opposite corner. Two blond girls, of that very light
blond that originates in Scandinavian countries, were exposing their
faces and a good portion of their bodies to the warming sun, and three
black women, so stunningly well-shaped that they had to be models or
ballet dancers, were talking to each other in the throaty melodious
voices that he knew from de Gier's jazz records. He took in as much as
he could stand and closed his eyes. The vision started almost immediately and he concentrated to hold it.

The six women were in a pond, set in a luscious tropical landscape.
They were naked, of course. The Scandinavian and the Oriental girls
were swimming, turning their lovely bodies through the clear water, the
black ladies were climbing out, drops glistening on their ebony skin.

There were rosebushes on the banks of the pond and beyond, a forest of fruit trees. The fruit trees didn't look right and changed into huge palms, their leaves rather similar to the commissaris's fern. Grijpstra himself was in the vision too, both as an objective substantial form and as an observer. He was riding a camel, circling the pond. The camel ride gave the adjutant the double pleasure of being able to look down into the pool and participating in the animal's sensuous sway. There was a close-up of the camel's feet sinking into high grass and lifting up again. A beautiful beast, incongruous to the scene but fitting all the same. The vision became more involved and less lusty. He noted many details in the girls' bodies, but they were of color and shape only and abstracted into a line play that got caught in the camel's slow dance. He smilingly drifted away into sleep when the commissaris entered the vision, running through the tall grass and waving.

The adjutant awoke and grunted. He left some change on the table and went into the café proper. There was a telephone.

"Ah, adjutant," the commissaris's secretary said in her grating voice. "I was waiting for your call. Cardozo has reported. He found witnesses to the attempt of dog poisoning and obtained statements. As we hadn't heard from you I told him to report for patrol duty, and he is with Sergeant Sietsema in a car now."

"No," Grijpstra said.

"Well, we can't let him hang around, can we? But I just had a message from the radio room. It appears that Cardozo forgot to check out a ring, he said you would know about it. The ring is on his desk and you'll have to go to the morgue with it." Grijpstra looked at the phone.

"Adjutant?"

He growled.

"And the commissaris and the sergeant have gone to the Pulitzer Hotel to talk with a Mr. Pullini, they will visit a Mr. Vleuten later today."

"Everything topsy-turvy as usual," Grijpstra said. "I need Cardozo to go and talk with Miss Carnet."

"Shall I get him back to headquarters, adjutant?"

"No. I'll take care of that damned ring first. I'll call you later." He slammed the phone down before remembering that this was going to be a good day.

8

"YOU CAN GO BACK to bed if you like." There was a fatherly note of concern in the commissaris's voice. Francesco Pullini's almond-shaped dark eyes stared at the little old man unbelievingly.

"Police?"

"Yes, sir. Sergeant de Gier and I are police officers investigating the death of Elaine Carnet. May we sit down?"

Francesco gestured dumbly. He undid the knot of the tasseled belt around his dressing gown and tied it again. The commissaris and de Gier had sat down. The room in the Pulitzer Hotel was well furnished—it should be, at the price Pullini was paying. The room was quiet and spacious, high enough not to be bothered by the traffic murmuring below on the canal's narrow quay. An enormous double bed showed a slight dent where Francesco's slim body had been resting.

Francesco had had time to line up some thoughts. "Police, what for you come here?"

The commissaris didn't answer. He was observing the young man. His glasses reflected the sun so that a bright spot danced on Francesco's long, wavy, ink black hair.

De Gier was watching his suspect too. A female man, he had thought at first, but he remembered that Francesco was Italian and that Italians are daintier than the northern European male. There was some strength in the suspect's face, a well-shaped wide mouth and a good nose, straight and firm. The daintiness was mostly in the eyes, partly hidden by long lashes, and in the wave of the hair that touched the striped shoulders of the dressing gown. The door to the bathroom was open, and de Gier saw an array of jars and bottles and several leather cases, one of them would contain a hair dryer.

Francesco sat down. "What for you come see me, yes?" His naked feet crossed, high-arched dancer's feet; a thick mat of dark hair showed on his calves as he moved his legs.

"Mrs. Carnet's death," the commissaris said softly. "You must have heard, you visited the Carnet firm this morning, didn't you?"

Francesco's head came forward so that his hair fell and joined the carefully clipped beard, then shot up again. "Yes, I heard. Everybody very sad. Me, I also sad but, me, I don't know Madame Carnet well. My business always with Franco Bergen. Franco and me, us good friends. Madame Carnet, she somebody I say hello-how-are-you to. Kiss hand, give flowers, that all. What for police come see *me?*"

The commissaris's hands came up slowly and dropped back by their own weight. "Routine, Mr. Pullini. We are seeing everybody who knew Mrs. Carnet. You knew her."

"I knew her." Francesco jumped up from the bed and stood in the middle of the room with his arms spread, a miniature biblical prophet addressing the erring faithful. "So what? So does milkman, yes? Greengrocerman, yes? Man who cleans street?" He pushed an imaginary broom. "Morning, Madame Carnet. Nice day, Madame Carnet. You go and see cleaning man too? What is this, yes? Maybe you should leave this room, this my room."

Francesco was still pushing the broom. De Gier laughed and Francesco swung around, eyeballing the sergeant, poking the broom at him.

"Ha," de Gier said, and Francesco laughed too.

"You think I funny, yes?"

"Very funny, Mr. Pullini. Why don't you lie down? Are you ill?"

Francesco coughed, held his chest, and coughed again. "Yes, cold, the storm yesterday. Make me cough, so today I rest. Today I see Franco Bergen, maybe tomorrow I leave. In Milano much to do, I cannot wait forever for Bergen to change mind. Bah."

"The business isn't going well, Mr. Pullini?"

Francesco turned to face the commissaris. His right hand came up, balled, and made a turning movement. "Ehhhhh. Business, it always the same. Sometimes I screw Franco, sometimes Franco he screw me. Doesn't matter, we still friends. Same name, same character. His name Franciscus, my name Francesco."

"So you didn't know the Carnet family very well, did you, Mr. Pullini?"

Francesco was reading the card the commissaris had given him. "Commissaire, eh? You big shot?"

There was a friendly light in the Italian's liquid eyes and the commissaris responded. He balled his hand, turned it, and pulled up the corner of his mouth. "Ehhhhhhh."

Francesco smiled. "A drink!" There was a sly smile on the noble face. He reached for the telephone. "Gin, yes?"

"Orange juice," the commissaris said.

"One orange juice, two gin?"

"One gin, two orange juice."

The drinks came almost at once and Francesco squatted on the bed, toasting his guests.

"You were out last night and caught a cold?" The commissaris had gone back to his original concern. De Gier's eyes swept over the old man's face. An act again, of course, but he never knew how far the commissaris acted. What was an Italian's cold to the chief of Amsterdam's CID? But the commissaris was always concerned with the health of others and would regularly check the cell block at headquarters and sometimes made sure that prisoners were moved to one of the city's hospitals.

"I walk around, visit some bars, eat something, but then I come back, storm very bad. Cough."

"Did anyone see you come back, Mr. Pullini? The desk clerk? Do you remember who gave you your key? And the time of your return, perhaps?"

"I come back ten, ten-thirty, but I no ask for key. Key he in my pocket, forget to leave at desk, always forget." He pointed at the key on his night table. It was connected to a plastic bar that was only three inches long, it would fit into a pocket.

"Do you know Gabrielle Carnet, Mr. Pullini?"

"Sure." The sly smile moved the clipped beard again. "She nice girl, yes? I take her out once, twice maybe, not now, before. Now I married. Gabrielle, she know. Also bad business. Gabrielle, she daughter of *Madame* Carnet. Madame Carnet, she own Carnet and Company. Franco Bergen, he only owns little bit. He my friend, but he not say yes or no in end. Madame Carnet, she is God, yes? Maybe I better not play around with daughter of God."

"Really? I thought Madame Carnet wasn't very interested in her business anymore, that she was retired."

"Retired?"

"Yes, not work anymore?"

"I know word. Me, I know many words but I forget when I speak, I know when I hear. Madame Carnet, she not retired. She work, she chooses furniture, new models, she says to Franco Bergen 'not buy now, yes buy now.' She sometimes cut order in half. Me, I always get shits when Madame come in. First big order then . . . pfff!" He blew something off his hand. "Then nothing. I go back Milano and tell Papa 'no order,' then maybe order comes later but price is wrong. Low price. Madame Carnet, she clever."

"I believe Carnet and Company owes you some money, Mr. Pullini. Do you think you will get it before you go home?"

A slight tremor moved from the eyes and disappeared into Francesco's beard. "Money? You know, yes? Franco Bergen he tell you, yes?"

"We saw Mr. Bergen this morning. We have to ask questions, Mr. Pullini. A cigar?"

The commissaris got up and presented his flat tin. Francesco's hand moved to the tin but he pulled it back. "No, thank you, bad for cough. I bought cigarettes this morning, low tar, no taste, but something."

He lit a cigarette and puffed. "So you know about money. Yes. Franco Bergen, he no pay. He promise, but he no pay. This time Franco, he cat, me mouse. Little mouse, jump this way jump that way. Still no money."

"How much is involved, Mr. Pullini?"

Francesco held his hands about a meter apart. "In Italian so much." He brought his hands closer together. "In Dutch so much."

"How much exactly?"

"Eighty thousand guilders. Sixteen million lire."

The sergeant whistled and Francesco imitated the whistle. He looked into de Gier's eyes but this time he didn't laugh.

"You were going to be given the money in cash?"

"Yes. Secret money. Goes into suitcase. But honest money, nothing to do with police. Pullini, he sells furniture; Franco Bergen, he pays cash. Bergen, he has invoices. All very nice."

"But you didn't get it."

"No. Franco Bergen he says he maybe buy from other firm in Milano, not from Pullini no more. When I say 'What about eighty thousand?' Bergen, he has dirty ears. So maybe I get lawyer, but that later. First I talk to Franco Bergen again. He old friend, he come to Milano, to Sesto San Giovanni where Pullini business is, he stays many weeks, he goes to mountains where Papa Pullini give him beautiful little house for month. Bergen, he bring family. Bergen, he eat in Pullini restaurant, no bill. Bergen, he remember. We talk some more."

"So you think Mr. Bergen will pay you?"

"Sure. Now he screw me but . . ."

"Good. I am glad to hear it, Mr. Pullini. Do you know where Madame and Gabrielle Carnet live?"

"Yes, before, I pick up Gabrielle. I remember street, Mierisstraat, nice street, big trees, maybe I can find street again."

"And you didn't find it last night?"

"No." Francesco coughed. The cough tore through his chest and he doubled up, holding his mouth into a handkerchief.

The commissaris waited for the attack to finish. They shook hands. De Gier turned around in the corridor and caught the expression on Francesco's face as he closed the door.

"Well?" the commissaris asked in the elevator.

"A sad little man, sir, and worried, but he has a sense of humor."

"The sort of man who will push a lady down her own garden stairs?"

"No." De Gier was watching the little red-orange light of the elevator, jumping down, humming every time it hit the next glass button. "But a push doesn't taken long. He is an excitable man and he wants his money. We may safely assume that the eighty thousand guilders are to be his, cash that he is lifting from his father's till. So he may be a little nervous about it."

"Sufficiently nervous to have pushed Mrs. Carnet last night?"

The commissaris shook his head, answering his own question. "No, I wouldn't think so. The amount may seem vast to us but to a businessman of Pullini's caliber it isn't all that much. Businessmen are usually very concerned about the continuation of their trade. Francesco will get his eighty thousand, now or later, but he won't get anything if he pushes his client into her death. No I can't see it. Still . . ."

"Sir?"

The elevator's sliding door opened and they stepped into the hall and into a crowd of American tourists who had just been delivered by a bus and who were jockeying for position at the hotel's counter.

"You were saying, sir?" de Gier asked again as they found each other under the striped awning of the hotel's entrance.

"Well, he might be lying. Or giving his version of the truth, which would also be lying. The truth is hard to catch. He has no alibi. He visited some bars. He walked around. So he says."

De Gier mumbled agreeably.

"Next!" The commissaris rubbed his hands. "The baboon's turn.

This Mr. Vleuten may be a more interesting suspect. Had an affair with the lady and stepped out of it. Also stepped out of his job. He doesn't have to worry about any continuations for he broke his connection. He isn't expecting us, is he?"

"No, sir. I have his address, that's all. We can jump him the way we jumped Francesco just now."

They got into the car. "Jump him," the commissaris said. "I never know which attack is most effective. Sometimes it may be better to set up an appointment and let them work themselves into a cold sweat. But when we jump them they can't lie so easily." He picked up the microphone.

"CID here, headquarters?"

"Headquarters, sir."

"Any messages for me?"

"Yes, sir. Would you phone your secretary, please?"

The commissaris pushed the microphone back into its clip and got out again. De Gier waited behind the wheel.

"Yes, dear?"

"There was a call just now from Carnet and Company, sir, Miss Gabrielle Carnet, she left two messages. Mr. Bergen has become ill and went to see his doctor. It seems he has some facial paralysis that may be serious and he has gone to a hospital to see a specialist."

"That's bad, dear, but it was very nice of Miss Carnet to let us know. What else?"

"She said that her mother took out eighty thousand guilders in cash from the company's bank account yesterday, sir. Mr. Bergen found out this morning, after you and the sergeant left the Carnet office. He was very upset. Apparently it wasn't customary for Mrs. Carnet to deal with the bank directly. If she wanted anything Mr. Bergen would do the necessary. And Mr. Bergen remembered your saying that you had only found a few hundred guilders in Mrs. Carnet's safe last night."

"Thank you, dear. How did Gabrielle Carnet sound?"

"Cool, sir. A businesslike sort of voice."

"Well, well, well. How are Cardozo and Grijpstra doing? Weren't they supposed to visit Gabrielle? That won't be necessary now for Miss Carnet is at her office, they'll have to wait until this evening."

"They are both out, sir. Cardozo has found witnesses to the dog poisoning and is now on street patrol, and Grijpstra is checking whether Mrs. Carnet's ring fits her finger tightly or not. He'll be in the morgue but he should be back shortly."

"Ha." The commissaris rubbed his nose. "Ha. I think I'll be coming back to headquarters. Grijpstra can take over from me." As he walked back to the car he put out his left hand and said "Eighty thousand," then he put out his right hand and repeated the amount.

"Very simple," he added as he told his findings to de Gier. "Too simple, of course. But murder cases are simple sometimes. So suppose that Francesco went to see Elaine last night after all, and suppose he pushed her down the stairs and took her key from her purse and opened her safe. He did leave the household money, that was very decent of him."

"Yes."

"You don't sound very convinced, sergeant?"

"No, sir. We know now that Mrs. Carnet took out an amount identical to what her firm owed Francesco. Perhaps she took it out to give it to him. She may have taken it for a reason altogether detached from the case. The amount is big enough to buy a house, for instance, and I believe solicitors transacting real estate always demand payment in cash. According to Mr. Bergen, Mrs. Carnet wasn't interested in the day-to-day management of her company, maybe she didn't even know what her firm owed Francesco. But if she did know she must have taken the money to pay him, and if she meant to pay him there was no reason to kill and rob her."

"True."

"But why would Mr. Bergen be suddenly suffering a facial paralysis, sir? Is he going to pieces because the police are questioning him?"

The commissaris grinned. "I knew you would say that, sergeant, and the conclusion isn't so far-fetched, but I think I know what is wrong with Mr. Bergen. I suffered from the same affliction some years ago. It is called Bell's palsy. I thought I had had a stroke and fussed and ran to a specialist, but it wasn't serious at all. An infection of the facial nerve: if the nerve doesn't work half the face becomes paralyzed, the eyelid won't close anymore, it becomes difficult to chew, and half the mouth droops, the way it does when you've been to the dentist. The paralysis wears off by itself, however, and the face becomes normal within a matter of weeks."

"And what causes this palsy, sir? A nervous shock?"

"No, sergeant. A draft. I had been driving with an open window. Did you think the man was having a stroke?"

"Yes, sir."

"Maybe you were hoping that, eh, sergeant? Because you wanted to think that we had found our man."

De Gier smiled apologetically.

They met Grijpstra in one of headquarters' corridors. The adjutant held up the wedding ring. "Not a very tight fit, sir, but not a very loose one, either. The corpse was almost frozen, so maybe the experiment was without value. When I left her, her arms were sticking straight up as if she couldn't bear my walking away. Brr. That morgue is a nasty place, sir. I saw at least ten bodies of young people dead of drug over-doses or malnutrition caused by drugs, and they were bringing in more as I left. The attendant said that they are mostly foreigners and all of them nameless and unclaimed."

"Quite," the commissaris said gently. "Let's go to my office." Cardozo's report with the statements of the two old ladies was on his desk and he read it to the detectives.

"That sounds good enough, sir."

"Yes. Tell you what, sergeant, why don't you and the adjutant go and visit this baboon man now. I'll raise Cardozo on the radio and visit Mr. de Bree with him. Cardozo has done good work so far and a visit may lead to the fruition of his efforts."

They left the commissaris's office together and the detectives watched their chief march to the radio room, a dapper little figure in a long empty corridor.

"There he goes."

"There he goes. He seems a little fiercer than usual. What's bothering him, do you think?"

Grijpstra shrugged. "Let's catch that baboon."

They got into the old-fashioned elevator.

"Now where would this ape fit in?"

"Baboons are randy animals. The ones I have seen in the zoo were always either actually busy with or seemed to be thinking about it. He could represent the sexual aspect of this disorder."

"So could Francesco," de Gier said as they entered the garage. "A beautiful little Italian, they are very popular with our womenfolk."

Grijpstra wasn't listening.

"Baboons are dangerous too, he may rush us. Are you armed?"

"Of course. I'll drop him the minute I see his tail twitch."

They were both grinning when they got into the Volkswagen, but they were discussing lunch by then, and meanwhile, back in the morgue, Elaine Carnet's arms still reached for the ceiling while a grumbling at-tendant was trying to push her box back into the refrigerator.

9

GRIJPSTRA'S MOUTH opened foolishly as he watched the sergeant's body float elegantly through the fresh windswept air above the Amstel River, and it snapped shut as de Gier hit the river's greenish, garbage-littered surface and broke through it and disappeared. A disorganized swirl of bobbing objects remained. Grijpstra saw the bottletops, condoms, beer cans, and torn stems of waterweeds taking position in a more or less defined circle that moved to the quayside, and he cursed. Then he jumped. But he jumped away from the river and when he landed he ran. The Volkswagen wasn't too far off. The radio came on as he poked its button and the microphone's cord nearly broke as he yanked it free.

"Headquarters, Three-fourteen."

"Headquarters," the unperturbable female voice said.

"An emergency. We are on the Amsteldijk and a suspect has just got away in a motor launch. Could you locate the nearest water police vessel and connect me directly?"

"Understood. Wait."

Grijpstra counted. Eleven seconds. A very long time. He looked back at the river and saw the sergeant's head and one of his feet appear above the quayside. The head was crowned with a garland of waterweeds, the foot trailed an unidentified object attached, apparently, to some wire.

"Water police, what can we do for you?"

"Where are you?"

"Amstel River, about to go under the Thin Bridge, heading north."

"Turn around and go as far as the Berlaghe Bridge, stop on the northwest side, and we'll come aboard. Adjutant Grijpstra and Sergeant de Gier. Our suspect has got away in a white launch, going south."

"We can be at the Berlaghe Bridge in about five minutes."

"See you there. Out."

Five minutes, Grijpstra thought, an eternity. Anything can happen in five minutes. But a more cheerful thought interfered with his despair. The white launch had a fairly long stretch of river ahead, a stretch without any side escapes. They might just cut him off, the police boat would be faster than the old-fashioned launch. He slid into the Volkswagen and started its engine, which spluttered to life obediently. His stubby index finger pressed the siren into its first wail of terror. The Volkswagen's front tires squealed through a short U-turn and brought the car on a collision course with de Gier, who came running, leaving a trail of dripping slime.

Grijpstra leaned over and opened the passenger door.

"Shit," de Gier said as the car leaped off. "The bastard! Did you see what he did? He pushed the boat's gear forward and opened the throttle at the exact moment I jumped. I was lucky I fell free, I might have cracked my leg on his tiller."

"I saw it." Grijpstra grunted compassionately.

"And he was smiling, the bloody oaf. I know now why he is called the baboon. Did you see his face?"

Grijpstra had seen the face, split under the flat nose and the low forehead, split into a wide scowl of strong white teeth. The man did indeed look like an ape, a large powerful ape, but not a dangerous ape. Grijpstra's first impression had been quite positive. Yet what the suspect had just done belied the friendliness that Grijpstra had seen in the man's unusual, misshapen face.

The adjutant thought back as the Volkswagen careened through the Amsteldijk's traffic, overtaking cars that veered to the side as the siren howled on. De Gier had found a parking place right in front of Vleuten's house, a tall house, seven stories high, reaching for the overcast sky with the perfect double curve of its ornamental gable topped by a large plaster ball that in turn carried a spike. An ancient Rolls-Royce was parked half on the street, half on the sidewalk, and they had taken a minute to admire the vehicle before climbing the stone steps leading to the house's green-lacquered front door. De Gier was about to press the top bell, which said "Jan Vleuten," when a shout hailed them from the river and they had seen a man waving. The man stood on the cabin of an old-fashioned motor launch, painted bright white.

"I am Vleuten," the baboon shouted. "Do you want me?"

When they got to the launch the baboon stood near his tiller, holding the boat's painter, which had been swung around a large cleat on the quayside in a loose loop.

"Police," de Gier had said, squatting down to show his identification. And while the baboon read de Gier's identification Grijpstra had formed his happy thoughts. A nice man, strange-looking for sure, but nice. And well dressed, in a thick white seaman's jersey that set out his wide chest. Light blond glossy hair caught under a small cap, the visor bent up. Long hair still showing the marks of a comb. Large calm blue eyes, very long arms that contrasted with the short legs. The body of an ape harboring the soul of an intelligent, kindly man. What had struck Grijpstra most, apart from the man's receding forehead and the absence of neck so that the head rested immediately on the potent torso, were Vleuten's arms. He remembered the large apes he had seen in the zoo and in films and how they walked, swinging, resting not only on their feet but equally on the knuckles of their hands. It seemed to him that Vleuten would walk the same way, and he was waiting for an opportunity to confirm his thought when de Gier's identification card was thrown onto the quay and the launch pulled away at full speed.

"Did you pick up your card?"

"Of course."

He still couldn't understand the suspect's response to their polite approach.

"Police?" The baboon had a good voice, deep and quiet.

"Yes, Mr. Vleuten. I am a CID sergeant. My colleague and I would like to ask a few questions."

The baboon had taken the card, a respectable weapon in their continuous warfare on crime—the police badge, the state's authorization decorated with the red, white, and blue of the flag of the Netherlands, an authorization that legalizes police officers to bother citizens, for their own sake, the sake of peace, and the maintenance of the rules of peace. And the fellow had actually had the audacity to throw the card on the street.

"You aren't worried about that damned card, are you?" de Gier asked. "What about me? Look at me!"

"You are wet," Grijpstra said pleasantly.

"Wet! I am probably poisoned. I swallowed some of that liquid shit they keep in the canals these days. I could have got killed on some of that garbage that floats around. I could have got drowned! You didn't even trouble yourself to see what had happened to me. All you were concerned about was your fucking radio."

"Now, now."

"But I still have my card, that's all the adjutant wants to know."

"You can swim," Grijpstra said, "and I would have worried about you but I saw you climbing out. And here we are."

"Where?"

"Here. I radioed a police boat. They're supposed to meet us here. Good, they're coming already, see?"

De Gier saw the gray speedboat pushing a fluffy bow wave but he didn't seem interested. He looked down at his hands and began to wipe them. His right hand had bled a little; the left hand had a long gluey yellow weed stuck between the fingers. He pulled it out and threw it out of the window.

"He took a risk," the adjutant said, forcing the car to take a short turn to the right and to dive under a large bridge, Amsterdam's main thoroughfare, connecting its center to the eastern part of the city. They could hear the bridge's rumble as a convoy of trucks passed overhead. "I could have shot him easily, but only in the chest or the head. His legs were covered by his boat's gunwale. Maybe he knows that we only aim for the legs, provided they are not actually attacking us."

De Gier was wringing out his trouser legs. "That's my second suit today, got it from the dry cleaner's this morning. We'll have to catch him, Grijpstra. I want him in a cell, a bad cell, the corner cell." The police launch was waiting and they jumped in, ignoring the water sergeant's helpful arm.

"CID, sergeant, go south, we are after a white motorboat, one man in it, man with a white jersey and a cap. A good-looking boat, old but well kept. A wooden boat."

The constable in the launch's cabin shifted a small lever next to the steering wheel. The boat roared and began to cut through the river's short bright waves, lifting its nose as it gathered speed. Grijpstra stumbled, but the water sergeant caught him by the shoulders.

"Hold on, your friend took a bath, did he?"

"He did. The suspect removed his boat as my colleague jumped."

Hands were shaken as the policemen introduced themselves.

"What's the chase, Grijpstra? Is your suspect dangerous? Armed?"

Grijpstra explained. De Gier had gone into the cabin and was checking his pistol, breaking it into parts and drying it with a rag. The constable gave him a fresh clip and de Gier inserted it. "It'll work," the constable said, "but you'd better take it to the arms room, there are a lot of little bits and pieces that'll rust eventually. You plan to shoot your man, sergeant?"

"I'd love to but I wouldn't be thanked if I did. I don't even know why he got away."

"You have a charge against him?"

"He used to sleep with a lady we know."

The constable wasn't listening anymore. A towboat had appeared, tugging asthmatically at a line of three gigantic barges. The barges were following unsteadily and the racing police-launch seemed to be attracted by the last vessel's looming, rusty hull. The little lever on the dashboard was pushed further and the boat's engines roared a shade deeper.

"Missed her," the constable said. "That's a charge, sergeant? Sleeping with a lady you know?"

"The lady is dead. We're going around asking questions."

"And you land up in the river. Happened to me too. I was shoved off an ocean liner's gangway last week. Part of the job. We keep dry clothes in that cupboard. Maybe they'll fit you. A sergeant's uniform. It'll fit your rank if not your body."

The river was clear, and the constable relaxed and watched de Gier strip. "There's a towel in there too, and underwear, and I have a pair of rubber boots here somewhere. We keep everything, even a small machine gun I can mount on the foredeck. There's something wrong with the gun's breech but it looks most impressive." De Gier stepped into the boots. "No, thanks, I don't think our man is armed. How do I look, constable?"

The water sergeant and Grijpstra had come into the cabin and de Gier was admired. The uniform fitted.

"Stunning," Grijpstra said. "I prefer the gold trim to our silver. Why do the water police have gold trim anyway?"

"Because gold is noble and so are we," the water sergeant said. "The water may be polluted these days, but it can never be as dirty as the shore."

The sun had found an opening in the low clouds above the city and the river's wide expanse, dotted here and there by the spotless white of floating sea gulls spread all around them. The launch was skimming over the short waves. The water sergeant unscrewed the top of a large thermos. "Fresh coffee, made less than half an hour ago." The four men were grinning as the baboon's boat showed up as a speck near the next bend of the river. "Not a bad life, this," the water sergeant said, pouring the coffee. "I don't know why you chaps prefer to work in the city. Narrow streets, no air, people everywhere. The people are the worst, they always want something."

"Don't you deal with people?" Grijpstra asked.

"Sometimes, but I usually manage to avoid them. I prefer fish. We do a fair bit of fishing, you know. And there are always the birds. Some of the birds are stupid, especially the ducks, but I would still rather deal with ducks than with people. People, bah!"

Grijpstra looked up. "What happened to that boat? It was right in front of us just now."

The constable pointed and turned the wheel at the same time, making the police boat knife through the river's curve. "Over there, moored to the jetty. That's the baboon's launch, I thought I recognized it before but I wasn't sure. Is the baboon your suspect?"

"Yes. You know him evidently."

The water sergeant had stepped to the dashboard and turned the key, cutting the boat's engines so that it settled back into the water. "Yes, Grijpstra, we know the baboon, everybody on the water does. But he doesn't seem to be on board."

"Never mind, go back a little and drop us off on the dike, out of sight of the jetty if possible. It could be that he hasn't spotted us. We can sniff around a little. If we don't catch him today we'll catch him tomorrow."

"Sleuths," the water sergeant said to his constable. "Intelligent hunting hounds. I hope you are observing and learning. We would just go away and take that old boat with us but we don't have brains. Sure, the suspect will come back to his boat and walk into our friends' arms." He turned back to Grijpstra. "Are you certain he's your man?"

"Shouldn't he be?"

"No. Tell me again why you're after him."

Grijpstra wrinkled his nose; he appeared to be lifting something heavy on his flat hands. "We know we are after him but we don't know why exactly. He made my sergeant leap into the river, that's one reason. And he used to sleep with a lady named Elaine Carnet and the lady died under suspicious circumstances. We went after him to ask some questions, routine questions, and he didn't give us a chance to ask them. He took off."

"He's a good man." The water sergeant's eyes seemed to be pleading. "I've known him for a few years now, on the water and in a few pubs. He is an artist in a way, restoring our part of the world. The baboon finds old boats, wrecks, there are plenty of them around, rotting and forgotten. He buys and repairs them. Some old men are working with him, retired men who have nothing to do. The baboon got them interested in living again. The municipality is interested in what he's trying to do. They've given him the use of a small city wharf up north. The old men are very proud of their work. They don't work for money, but the baboon sees to it that they get something, and when a boat is in good order again he will sell it at a fair price to somebody he thinks will appreciate a good boat."

"He does? Does he own that old Rolls we saw parked in front of his address?"

"Yes. Same story. Bought as a wreck, taken apart, and reassembled. Same with his house too. I believe he inherited the house, but it was in poor shape, and he remodeled it completely and lets the six lower stories at reasonable rents. He could be a shark, most house owners are, but he isn't."

Grijpstra was listening intently, softly scratching around in his bristly short hair. De Gier, resplendent in his dark blue uniform, was listening too.

"You hear that?" Grijpstra asked.

"I heard, but I still have some weeds in my ears, so maybe I didn't hear it all. A latter-day saint, eh? So why did this lovable gentleman who looks like an ape make me take a flying leap at the river? I wasn't hustling him, was I? He barely gave me time to state my purpose, then whoosh . . . him away and me . . . In fact, I may have a charge for attempted manslaughter against him, or trying to cause serious injury. What else do you know about him? Nothing bad at all?"

"No. I have no idea why he took off, but I know that if you bother him you'll have everybody against you, everybody out here, the people of the waterways."

The launch rubbed itself against the quayside and Grijpstra held on to a tree stump.

"Give us a push, sergeant. We won't harm your hero, unless we can prove you wrong, and even then we wouldn't be too nasty."

De Gier jumped out too. "Thanks for the assistance, you'll have your uniform back in the morning. I'll try to keep it clean, but maybe your friend will have me in the river again."

The water sergeant grinned. "Not in that uniform, he'll respect the gold."

The launch backed away and the two officers waved. It took the detectives a few minutes to walk to the jetty. The baboon had tied up his launch neatly but he wasn't around.

"You want to snoop around here a bit?"

"May as well."

But they were ready to give up and catch a tram back to their car when Grijpstra suddenly whistled. "Over there, on the terrace."

The baboon was peacefully drinking tea. They stopped in front of his table.

"Afternoon, Mr. Vleuten."

The baboon smiled as if welcoming old friends. "Well, I never. And in a water cop's uniform too. Would you join me?"

They sat down but they didn't say anything, and the silence, awkward at first, lost its tension as the three men gazed at the river. De Gier took off his cap and put it on the table and a girl came and took their order.

"I hope you didn't hurt yourself," the baboon said and offered a cigarette.

"I did."

"Badly?"

"No. A scratch. But I did get very wet and dirty."

The baboon touched de Gier's shoulder. "I'm sorry. You came to see me about the fine, did you? I won't pay it."

"Fine?"

"Yes."

"I didn't come to see you about a fine, we came to ask you some questions. A Mrs. Carnet died. Elaine Carnet. We were told you knew her."

"Ah." The baboon sighed. "I might have known. I read about Elaine's death but the journalist said it was an accident. Wasn't it?"

"Perhaps. What is this business about a fine, Mr. Vleuten?"

"Call me baboon. I don't like the word but it has stuck to me for a long time. That fine is a conglomeration of parking fines. Some parking police constable is irritated by my Rolls-Royce, he goes out of his way to plaster tickets all over it. I've complained to his chief but nothing happens. I don't mind paying an occasional fine like everybody else, but I'm damned if I'll have one every day. There aren't enough parking places in the city and I have a car, so have a hundred thousand others."

"But why associate us with your fines?"

"I've been bothered by you before, not by you personally, but by detectives. They keep ringing my bell in the early morning and shouting at me through the microphone at the front door."

"Different branch, you must be referring to personnel from the court.

They will be after you to try and get you to the court's cashier and they have powers to hold you until you pay—if you open your door to them, that is. They aren't authorized to break it down or to grab you in the street. They'll have to take you from your house and you have to be willing to be taken."

"I am not."

De Gier was watching the baboon's calm face. "You might be in trouble now, you know. You made me suffer a bad fall."

"Can you arrest me?"

"Yes."

"Will you?"

"Not just now. But we'll have to question you. Where do you want to be questioned? Here?"

They had finished their tea and the baboon called the girl and paid. "No, not here. And I am sorry about your fall. I thought you were sent by the parking police and I feel badly about this nonsense. A misunderstanding. I apologize, do you accept?"

De Gier nodded. "Maybe I will."

"Then be my guests a little longer, gentlemen. We can take the boat back to my house and you can question me there, but I may not have much to say. I had no reason to kill Elaine, and I wouldn't have killed her if I'd had a reason. Maybe there's never a reason to kill, except to avoid old age, and Elaine wasn't old."

Grijpstra felt the little hairs in his neck bristle. He had detected the tremendous strength that seemed to come out of the baboon's being, waves of strength that enveloped the detectives and neutralized their own force. Grijpstra remembered other occasions when he had been almost hypnotized by suspects. He had felt it during some arrests and also, once or twice, when he had been a witness for the prosecution in court. He had seen high police officers, lawyers, judges even, wilt while an unruffled criminal pleaded his case, made statements, proved himself to be innocent. But the criminals had been guilty.

They ambled across the quay together and de Gier lowered himself carefully into the launch. He was looking at some rubbish floating under the jetty as the baboon started the launch's engine.

"Bah," de Gier said. "Look at that mess. That water sergeant is a chauvinist. His part of the world is dirtier than ours."

The baboon looked too. "We're making an effort. The river is getting cleaner, it was much worse before."

"Bah. People used to swim in the river."

"They will again."

"I was swimming in it just now."

The baboon laughed. "I said I was sorry."

"Sure," de Gier said. "That was very nice of you."

10

"HE ISN'T IN," the square lady in the flowered dress said, "but he's due back any moment. Could you come again in half an hour, perhaps?"

The commissaris and Cardozo had stood for quite a while on the porch of the de Bree house while Mrs. de Bree peered at them through the door's peephole and tried to make up her mind whether or not to open the door. She had seen Cardozo before and knew he was a policeman. Her husband had told her not to let in the police. But the other man was much older than the boyish detective, and he didn't seem to be the sort of man who could be sent away. She had decided that the commissaris looked, in an unobtrusive way, both dignified and intelligent, and she had taken the risk. But now she was stuck again.

"We won't go away, Mrs. de Bree," the commissaris said softly, "and you will have to let us in."

"My husband says that the home is private and that . . ."

"The home is private, your husband is right."

She faltered and blushed. "So . . . ?"

"But there are exceptions to any rule, madame. A crime has been committed and the police have been asked to investigate. In such circumstances the police have the right to enter any dwelling by force if a warrant has been issued or if an officer of a certain rank wants to visit the home."

"I see." She didn't want to ask for the commissaris's rank, but he had given her a card and she glanced at it. She didn't know anything about police ranks. "Well, would you come in then, please. I hope you'll explain to my husband when he comes . . ."

"We will."

Cardozo stepped aside and the commissaris marched into the corridor and waited for Mrs. de Bree to lead the way. They were taken to a room in the rear of the house, similar to the enclosed porch in the Carnet house. Evidently the same architect had been used for all the homes in the two streets sharing the enclosed garden area. Mrs. de Bree offered tea and gratefully retired to the kitchen.

Cardozo jumped out of his chair the minute they were alone. "My witnesses live over there, sir. They have the top floor of the house, there with the balcony, behind the geraniums. Two old ladies with binoculars, ideal witnesses, they have a full view of both this garden and the Carnet garden opposite. And there's the liguster hedge and Mr. de Bree must have stood next to that rhododendron bush when he fed Paul. With binoculars my witnesses could have seen that he was feeding him chopped meat. With the laboratory test that proves that there was both chopped meat and arsenic in Paul's stomach, and with the matching times of the witnesses' statements and Gabrielle Carnet's complaint plus the statement of the veterinarian we have an airtight case against de Bree."

The commissaris had come to the window. "Yes, good work, Cardozo. I wonder if I can smoke here. Does de Bree smoke?"

Cardozo looked around. "There's a pipe rack on the wall, sir, and several ashtrays."

"Then I'm sure Mrs. de Bree won't mind. Hey!"

A cat had landed on the balcony outside. It had dropped from a tree branch with such a thud that Cardozo, who was still studying the pipe rack, had turned around. The cat was oversize, not only fat but enormous in proportions. A lynx with tufted ears, with thick fur spotted with black and orange and with a cruel square head, bright orange on one side, deep black on the other. The line dividing the two colors didn't run in the exact middle of the face, shortening the black half slightly, with the result that his expression was startlingly weird.

"That's a cat, sir?"

"I think so. But perhaps it has a small panther or an ocelot as an ancestor, although I do believe that some breeds of domesticated cats grow rather large. All of twenty pounds, I would say, more perhaps."

The cat walked to the window and stood up, pressing its face and front paws against the glass. The soles of its feet were heavily haired.

"It's purring," the commissaris said. "Perhaps it means well. Should we let it in, Cardozo?"

Mrs. de Bree was with them again, carrying a tray. "Ah, Tobias. Would you mind opening the door, sir? Poor thing must be hungry. He probably tried to come in before but I was vacuum-cleaning upstairs and didn't hear him. He's been out all morning."

The commissaris released the door's latch and Tobias rushed in, forcing the door out of his hand. He ran across the room and loped off into the corridor.

"An amazing animal, madame. Very big, isn't he?"

"Yes. But he's getting old and is blind in one eye now and not too well. We had him operated on for cancer last year and he recovered, but the vet says that the cancer may still be there and that a second operation wouldn't do any good. My husband is very upset about it. Tobias is like a child and we have had him fourteen years—we don't have any real children, you see. And Tobias is so clever!"

The commissaris stirred his tea. The room was pleasant and quiet; there was no sound in the house except a rattling in the kitchen where Tobias was gulping his food and pushing its container around.

"You know why we came, don't you, Mrs. de Bree?"

She was sitting unnaturally upright and playing with a lace handkerchief. There were tears in her mild eyes, enlarged by the thick lenses of her gold-rimmed spectacles. "Yes, sir, you came about Paul. I'm so saddened about that. I don't know what got into my husband, he's never done anything like that before. He won't admit what he did to Paul, but he knows that I know. He hasn't talked to me much since it happened. And the old ladies opposite saw him do it, Alice came to see me about it an hour ago. She said they had told the police and that they were sorry but they couldn't help it, so I was expecting you, you see."

"What does your husband do, Mrs. de Bree?"

"He's retired in a way. He's an engineer and has invented things, we have an income from royalties. Sometimes I wish he were still working."

They heard a key turn in the front of the house and Mrs. de Bree jumped up and rushed into the corridor, shutting the door behind her. The conversation took a full five minutes and de Bree's voice gradually lost its anger. Mrs. de Bree was crying. He came in alone.

"Mr. de Bree?"

The policemen were on their feet. De Bree pointed at their chairs and thought of something to say. Tobias was bumping the door. "My cat, I'll let him in."

De Bree sat down, he sighed, and all the air appeared to go out of him. The sigh seemed endless.

"I'm sorry," the commissaris said. "But what has to be done has to be done, sir. You weren't getting anywhere when you refused my detective entry, surely you knew that, didn't you?"

"Are you arresting me?"

"No."

De Bree reached for his pipe rack and tobacco tin. The tobacco spilled as his trembling hands tried to fill the pipe. He couldn't find a match and looked about helplessly. The commissaris gave him his lighter.

"So why did you come?" de Bree asked between puffs.

"To obtain your confession, sir. It isn't strictly needed, the evidence against you is conclusive, but a confession might help you, the judge will be better disposed."

"Judge? You'll make me go to court?"

"Yes."

Tobias walked past de Bree's chair and de Bree grabbed the cat's tail. It closed with strength and the cat pulled, finding support in the carpet. De Bree's chair moved an inch but stuck on the carpet's edge. The cat looked around, turned, and put a paw on de Bree's hand. It purred and its good eye opened until it was a large shiny green disk. De Bree grunted and released the tail.

"He must be very fond of you," the commissaris said. "His nails didn't come out."

"He'll never scratch me. He did once, by mistake, and drew blood and he was sorry for a week. He followed me everywhere I went. He loves me, he even hunts for me. He is always bringing me birds and mice, rats even. Once he caught a crow, a big crow. Crows are hard to catch. He brought the bird to my bed, I was ill at the time, and dropped it on the blanket. Made a mess, my wife didn't like that, but he loves her too."

"You like animals, don't you?"

"I like Tobias. I don't get on with other animals, or with people. My wife and I live very much on our own, but we don't mind. If they don't bother us we don't bother them. I have my books. I am an engineer. I have a basement where I can work. I don't need anybody anymore."

The commissaris had been looking at a large framed painting hanging in the shadows of the room.

"That's Tobias," de Bree said. "My wife did it. It isn't painted but embroidered, in very small stitches. We found a store where an artist will do a portrait on canvas and they sell you wool so that you can embroider the portrait yourself. People usually like to make portraits like that of their children but we don't have any. I gave my wife the canvas for her birthday. It took her months to stitch it."

The commissaris had got up to study the gobelin. "Remarkable! An amazing likeness. Your cat has an interesting face."

Cardozo whipped out his handkerchief and began to blow his nose furiously.

De Bree had lost interest. He was staring at the floor, his hand resting limply on the cat's back.

"I'm sorry," he said. "Does that help? If I say I am sorry? I'll pay if you like. The Carnet ladies must have had some expenses, perhaps they want to put in a claim. I'll pay for the vet and whatever you say I should pay on top of the vet's bill for damages. I suppose I owe it to them."

"The judge would like to hear you say that." The commissaris had sat down and was stirring his tea. "But why did you want to kill Paul? Death through arsenic poisoning is very unpleasant, painful. The victim suffers cramps, vomits, he may suffer for a fairly long time until the coma finally sets in. You knew that, didn't you?"

"Yes, I suppose so. I didn't think of it. Arsenic is the only poison I could find, they sell it to kill rats. I would have bought a better poison if it had been available."

"But why kill the dog?"

De Bree shrugged. "There was no choice. Paul is a young strong dog. Terriers are fierce and quick on their feet. So is Tobias, but Tobias can only see on one side. The silly cat doesn't know that the gardens around belong to others, he thinks they are all his private hunting ground. The other cats run away when they see him coming but Paul is a hunter too, and he has been out to kill Tobias for a while now. I have broken up some of their fights, but I can't be in the garden all the time. So . . ."

"No." The commissaris had put down his cup and his hands grabbed the sides of his chair. "No, sir. You should have thought of another solution. A very high fence, for instance, there's a limit to what cats can do. A carpenter could have constructed a fence that couldn't have been scaled by Tobias. The point is that you didn't want to restrict your cat. You can't deny other people the right to have a pet because their pet is a threat to yours. You could also have moved to the country. You are not economically bound to the city. You have alternatives, Mr. de Bree."

De Bree's eyelids sagged. "I said I was sorry."

"Yes."

Cardozo had brought out his notebook. "I'll have to take your statement, sir. Would you describe what you did and tell us exactly when you did it. It can be a short statement, but it'll have to be in your own words."

"On Wednesday, the first of June, at about twelve hundred hours . . ."

De Bree's voice was flat. Cardozo was writing furiously as the voice droned on. De Bree proved that his mind was trained in exactitude and had the ability to report logically connected events.

Cardozo read the statement back and de Bree brought out his fountain pen.

"Thank you," the commissaris said, "and please thank your wife for her hospitality."

"Will I have to go to jail?" de Bree asked as the policemen stepped into the street.

"It's up to the judge, sir. I'm sorry, our task is finished now. Perhaps you should consult your lawyer when you receive the summons."

The door closed with an almost inaudible click.

"A telephone, Cardozo. Is there a public booth around?"

"Any news, dear?"

He held the phone away from his ear as his secretary reported.

"Grijpstra and the sergeant had some trouble, sir. The radio room says that they had to ask the water police for assistance. I've had a report from the water police too, but it isn't very detailed. It only says that they chased a boat belonging to a Mr. Vleuten and that Mr. Vleuten wasn't with his boat when they found it. Sergeant de Gier fell into the river somewhere along the chase but he wasn't harmed."

"Really?"

"Yes, sir. And I've had a call from Gabrielle Carnet, she found a hundred thousand guilders under her mother's mattress and thought you would like to hear about it."

"I would, yes. Anything else? Any news about Mr. Bergen and his facial trouble?"

"Yes, sir, I asked Miss Carnet. The hospital referred Mr. Bergen to a private neurologist and the neurologist detected some serious trouble, it seems. Mr. Bergen will have further tests tomorrow. He is at home now, I have the address. He telephoned his office and Miss Carnet was there when the call came in."

The commissaris wrote down the address and the telephone number, fumbling on the small metal desk provided in the booth, and managed to drop his ball-point and bump his head as he came up again.

"Oh, sir."

"Yes?" He had dropped his ball-point again and was rubbing his head.

"There was a note on your desk that I don't think you've seen. It was brought up from Grijpstra's room as it was addressed to you. A report on the adjutant's visit to a portrait painter called Wertheym?"

"Yes. Go on."

"It only says that Wertheym made two identical portraits for Mrs. Carnet. The 'two' is underlined."

"Thanks." He hung up. Cardozo was staring at him foolishly, his nose pressed against the glass of the booth. The commissaris opened the door, slamming it into Cardozo's arm. "Don't stand there like an idiot, Cardozo, did I hurt you?"

"No, sir."

"Your friend the sergeant got himself into the Amstel River this afternoon, something to do with chasing the baboon, apparently. I wish they'd phoned in. I've no idea where they are now, looks as if I'll have to run after my own assistants. My own fault. I'm pushing this case too hard."

They walked back to the car. The neighborhood was experiencing a short burst of liveliness as heads of families were coming home, welcomed by grateful wives. Everywhere around them car doors slammed, children rushed out of front doors, fathers put down their briefcases to embrace their offspring. The late afternoon sun was pouring a thick, diffuse light into the long, tree-lined street so that each object threw a tapered, clearcut shadow.

The commissaris stopped to admire a creeper, heavily studded with clusters of white flowers, that had covered an entire wall and seemed ready to climb over it. "Beautiful. But we are still stuck, Cardozo. Remember that motive that was thrown at us? Mrs. Carnet's eighty thousand guilders? Taken from the bank yesterday, in cash, in crisp notes? Nowhere to be found now?"

"Yes, sir, you told me."

"Well, it grew to a hundred thousand and it has shown up again, under the lady's mattress. Gabrielle found the money and was good enough to phone my office. Back where we started."

Cardozo, who had been nodding encouragingly, lost his smile. He looked so crestfallen that the commissaris cheered up again. "Never mind. Good luck comes to those who keep on trying. The old chief constable used to say that and he was right. Tell you what, Cardozo, you go to see Gabrielle now, she's around the corner. Find out the details of the lucky find and phone your report to the radio room. You can go home afterward, perhaps you should stay home. If I manage to find the adjutant and the sergeant I'll contact you and we may have a conference to finish off the day."

Cardozo almost came to attention, turned around, and marched down the street. The small figure in its shabby corduroy jacket, bouncing under a mop of curly hair, looked incongruous between the elegant houses. The commissaris nodded approvingly. Cardozo's willingness to do his share showed. The young man was shaping up well, but he wasn't a complete policeman yet. The commissaris remembered words spoken by his superiors, who had, since then, turned into old men and doddered into their graves. A policeman is cunning but moderate. Sly as a snake, innocent as a dove. He said the word aloud. "Sly." A good word. To be sly without malice. He would need his slyness now, to sort out this mess caused by uncontrolled but very human emotions. A poisoned dog and a clownish, frumped-up woman, dead in a pool of rainwater. He wondered what else they would find, for the emotions weren't curbed yet. He knew that his main task was to prevent further manifestations and he would have to solve the present riddle to be able to do so.

A large white motorcycle whizzed past, ridden by what looked to be a mechanical man, completely wrapped in white leather, his face hidden by a plastic visor. The Amsterdam police emblem, a naked sword resting on an open book, was painted on the motorcycle's metal saddlebag. It also showed on the policeman's helmet. The motorcycle's presence kept drivers in line. The commissaris looked at his own image mirrored in a store window. The image peered back at him, a small man dressed in grays with a thin face and a glint of gold-rimmed spectacles. Chief of the murder brigade, gliding through the city almost transparent, completely unnoticed. "A sneak," he said aloud. What could a sneak prevent? But he would do his best, his very best, and his mind was locked on the case again as he opened the door of the Citroën.

11

THE COMMISSARIS POINTED the sleek nose of the Citroën away from the curb and waited patiently for an opening. He sat poised at the wheel. The opening came and the car lurched forward and immediately lost the impact of its leap as it settled sedately, nudged into the homeward stream. The commissaris grinned at the success of his maneuver, but the grin faded away as pain activated the nerves in his thighs. He knew he should be home in bed, with his tube of medication on the night table and his wife hovering around, speaking to him soothingly, fluffing up his cushions, caring. The radio crackled.

"Commissaris?"

"Yes."

"The adjutant has telephoned, sir. They found their suspect, Mr. Vleuten, and are now on the river in the suspect's boat. The interrogation will take place at Mr. Vleuten's house, Amsteldijk One-seven-two."

"Thank you, I'll go there now."

"Do you want your secretary to stay in your office, sir?"

"No. Thank her for her assistance. Over and out."

He was almost home, but he took the first road on the left and headed for the river. To be driving around, straining himself, pushing a case that could just as well be solved by his assistants, was pure idiocy. Or sanity, if his choice was between activity and the slow senseless existence of some delicate plant in a greenhouse. He had been ill for a long time now, with no real hope of recovery, although he kept trying to convince his wife of the opposite. Activity might kill him, but it would keep him alert meanwhile.

The car shot through an orange light, turned again, and began to follow the river. He glanced at the house numbers; another block to go. He found the mooring and parked under a row of elms that had survived the gale. The pain in his thighs had reached a steady level and he could bear with it. He got out, content to wait. A tanker came chugging up the river and he admired its strong sturdy lines under the superstructure of artfully intertwined tubes painted a brilliant white. He leaned against a tree and returned the tanker's greeting, a slow solemn wave of the man at the wheel. A heron, balanced on a partly submerged log saw the commissaris's arm move and lifted a long leg but decided to stay where it was and pointed its beak at the water again. Some fat coots were rowing about busily, only a few yards away, headed for a patch of duckweed, rippling in the river's flow. The commissaris was still leaning against the elm when the baboon's boat arrived and touched the quayside with a tire hung over its gunwale.

An ape man, definitely, the commissaris thought as he watched Vleuten move the tiller. De Gier was standing next to the suspect; the baboon's golden mane stood out against the sergeant's uniform. The commissaris caught the rope thrown by Grijpstra and held it while he waited for the three men to join him.

"Mr. Vleuten, sir. Mr. Vleuten, please meet our chief."

They shook hands and crossed the street in pairs, Grijpstra and the baboon going ahead.

"Have you arrested him, de Gier?"

"No, sir. He has been very well behaved."

"The radio room says that you fell into the river. If that event was caused by your suspect an arrest would be warranted."

De Gier explained and the commissaris nodded. "Good. No vengeance."

The commissaris thought back. He was a young inspector again, long ago, thirty years ago. He had been beaten up by a suspect and the suspect was subsequently caught. When he went to the station a constable had taken him down to the cell block where his man was chained to a pipe, cowering. The constable had told him to go ahead and had turned and left the basement. He had been tempted, but he had released the suspect and taken him to a cell and gone upstairs.

"No vengeance," he said again. "That's very good, de Gier."

Some surprise showed on the sergeant's face. "I thought it would be better not to ruffle him, sir. This way he may talk easier."

"You'll lay charges against him later?"

De Gier looked uncomfortable. "I can't, sir. I more or less accepted his apology. A case of mistaken identity, really. He mistook me for an officer from the court. He has some parking fines he has been protesting and the court constables have been bothering him."

"Good. Is this our man's house?"

"Yes, sir, and that's his car."

The commissaris took a moment to observe the seventeenth-century house and the Rolls-Royce.

"A nineteen thirty-six model I would say, sergeant, but very well kept. It should be worth some money, and the house is very valuable, of course. So he isn't badly off, your baboon. That would explain why he resigned so easily from Carnet and Company. Still, he did refuse unemployment benefits, Mr. Bergen told me. Most unusual. He would qualify and they are eighty percent of previous income and will be paid for several years now, I believe. And he turned it down. Most unusual."

The baboon had opened the door and gone in with Grijpstra, and the commissaris and the sergeant began to climb the stairs slowly, pausing on the landings. Even so the commissaris was exhausted when they finally reached the seventh floor. The baboon's apartment was open and the commissaris sunk into the first chair he saw. The baboon was busying himself at the kitchen counter.

Grijpstra looked at the commissaris. "Do you want to ask the questions, sir?"

The commissaris shook his head. He had closed his eyes, his breath was still coming in gasps. "Go ahead, adjutant."

The baboon served coffee and sat down. "Gentlemen?"

Grijpstra phrased his questions slowly and precisely and the baboon's answers connected promptly.

"Yes, I visited her last night, early in the evening."

"Why, Mr. Vleuten?"

"To repay a loan. I shouldn't have borrowed from her but I didn't want to increase my mortgage on the house. The bank has always been very helpful, it's the same bank Carnet and Company uses and I know the manager well, but even so, mortgages take time and I needed money promptly. I had miscalculated on the remodeling costs of two of the apartments below and the workmen expected to be paid, of course. In a weak moment I asked Elaine to lend the cash to me, that was six months ago. Since then I sold a boat and made some money again, so last night I took the money to her."

"How much?"

"Twenty thousand. She gave me the money in cash and I returned it in cash. She didn't ask for interest. I've often done repairs in her house and I never charged her and I think she wanted to repay the favor."

"You have a receipt, sir?"

"No. It was a loan between friends."

"Were you seeing her regularly?"

"No, not anymore. I hadn't seen her since she lent me the money, and that was half a year ago, as I said."

"Was she expecting you?"

"No."

"Did you have the impression that she was expecting anybody else?"

The baboon got up and stretched. The three policemen looked at the short legs that dwarfed the man; when he dropped his arms they swung loosely.

"Yes, she was very well dressed, overdressed, I would say. At first I thought she was planning to go out and I asked her where she was going. She said she wasn't going anywhere."

"Did she seem nervous?"

"Yes. I thought it was the gale. It was a strange night, the gale had already started up. She talked a good deal, but she didn't exactly make me welcome."

"Did she offer you anything? A drink?"

"No."

"Do you smoke, Mr. Vleuten?"

"I'm trying to give it up. I have cigarettes here but I don't carry them anymore. I only smoke when I have to, about ten cigarettes a day now."

"So you didn't smoke while you were with Mrs. Carnet last night?"

"No."

The commissaris was following the conversation but the words seemed far away; his breathing had slowed down and he was controlling the pain. He noticed that the baboon wasn't asking Grijpstra to explain his questions. He forced himself to sit up and observe the suspect. The baboon's and the commissaris's eyes met for an instant. There was a slight gleam in the man's eyes. He seemed amused but there was also sadness, mainly in the lines of the wide lips.

"What time did you leave?"

"Around eight. I only stayed a quarter of an hour, I think."

Grijpstra sat back and the commissaris raised a hand. "Your money was found, Mr. Vleuten. I had a message, just before I came here, from Gabrielle Carnet. She found a hundred thousand guilders, which must be the sum of your twenty thousand and the eighty thousand Mrs. Carnet collected from her company's bank account recently. Do you have any idea what she may have wanted to do with that eighty thousand?"

"No."

"The hundred thousand was found under her mattress, a strange hiding place, don't you think? She did have a safe."

The baboon's hand reached out to a side table and came back with a pack of cigarettes. He smiled apologetically. "Time to smoke. Under the mattress, you said, that *is* a strange place. I know her safe. It isn't really a safe: it's fireproof but not burglarproof, it opens with a normal key. She never kept much money in there. I made a hiding place in her bedroom, under a loose board. It has a spring lock. You have to press a very small knob near one of the legs of her bed. If she wanted to hide money she would have hidden it in there."

Nothing was said for a while and the commissaris looked around. The apartment seemed to consist of only one room stretching from the front to the rear of the house. The furniture was sparse but of good quality, not from the showrooms of Carnet and Company. Good Victorian furniture and not too much of it. A quiet room, refined, with large empty surfaces, both in floor and wall space. The sergeant had got up and was wandering around.

"Sir?"

The commissaris got up too. The sergeant was looking at a painting. The painting showed a rat realistically drawn, each long brittle hair in place, the mouth half open showing pointed cruel teeth, the red eye glared. It was rearing on its spindly hind legs and its long tail, of an obscene, glaring naked pink, hung down.

"Unusual, don't you think, sir?"

The tail went beyond the painting, curving over its frame and continuing on the wall. The part that protruded from the painting's flat surface had become three-dimensional, molded out of some plastic material but so well shaped that it seemed alive. There was another strange detail in the painter's subject matter. The rat was ridden by a little boy dressed in a dainty suit of dark red velvet.

The childish face sat in a high collar of ruffled lace, and the boy's small pudgy hands held reins that were slipped through the rat's mouth.

"Do you like it?" the baboon's voice asked from the other side of the room.

"It wasn't made to be liked, I think." The commissaris was still studying the painting. "Your work, Mr. Vleuten?"

"In a way. The combination is mine. The original is an illustration to a child's tale and I enlarged it and worked in some of the details. I've done more work like this, more elaborate, but in the same vein, I would think."

The baboon got up and pressed a button at the side of a large cupboard. A deep hum filled the room and the cupboard's door swung open. The apparition that rode out of the cupboard came straight at the sergeant, who jumped out of its way, but it changed direction and he had to jump again. The commissaris wasn't able to determine the nature of the apparition immediately, he only knew he felt nauseated.

He followed it as it moved around and returned to the cupboard.

It was a structure of human bones, clipped together and held upright by a transparent plastic rod. The head seemed to be a cow's skull, very old and moldy, with a gaping hole in its forehead framed in dry moss. Part of the skull was covered by a mask of frayed purple corduroy but the eye sockets and the long mouth with rows of pale yellow teeth had been left bare. The cupboard's door closed and the hum stopped. The commissaris looked at the floor. A pair of rails had been sunk into the smooth polished boards, evidently the specter had ridden on a small cart powered by electricity.

"A toy," the baboon said.

De Gier was staring at the cupboard door, his legs astride. Grijpstra stood next to the sergeant, bent slightly forward. Only the commissaris hadn't moved, not even when the ghoul's weapon, a rusted Sten gun, had brushed the back of his sleeve.

He sat down again. "You are an artist, Mr. Vleuten, and your creations are spectacular. I'm sure the municipal museum would be interested and give you space to exhibit. I'm interested too. What prompted you to make that structure?"

"A vision," the baboon said slowly, "a vision when I was drunk. I don't normally drink much, but I did happen to get very drunk some years ago and I passed out. My body stopped functioning but my mind worked well, too well, perhaps. The sensation was unpleasant. I wanted to go to sleep but I had been caught in a maelstrom. You probably know the experience. Dizziness, increasing until everything turns, not only what the mind experiences but the mind itself joins its reflections. A crazy dance, and in my case also macabre."

The commissaris smiled. "If I remember correctly that particular sensation doesn't last too long. One gets sick and vomits and then there is nothing but sleep until the hangover the following day."

"I didn't get sick. I spent hours being part of the maelstrom, trying not to be sucked into the abyss that lurked at its bottom. I had everything against me that night. There was much to be seen although I didn't want to see it. In the edge of the swirl different scenes were acted out and I was in all of them. The main actors, apart from myself, were a human skeleton with a masked cow's head and a little boy riding his rat."

It was the commissaris's turn to get up and wander around the room and the baboon followed him. They were of about the same height, and Grijpstra leaned out of his chair to keep track of their moving shapes.

"So what have we caught now?" de Gier whispered.

"Shhh!"

"Normally a man would try to get away from his fears," the commissaris was saying, "but you went to great trouble to picture them. It seems that you do the opposite of what is to be expected. The effort is deliberate?"

"Yes."

"Like when you had the Carnet and Company firm in the palm of your hand, so to speak, and you threw it away?"

"Yes."

"Would you mind a personal question?"

"No."

"Patient, isn't he?" de Gier's voice said close to Grijpstra's ear. Grijpstra's hands made an irritated flapping movement in response.

"You have a nickname, Mr. Vleuten. You are called the baboon. It would seem to me that you wouldn't like that nickname. A baboon is an ape. I would have expected pictures of baboons in this room, maybe even skeletons of baboons."

The baboon laughed. "I have several mirrors here, I can see the baboon anytime I wish to, and often when I don't wish to." The laugh was relaxed and spread to the three detectives.

"True. Another question, something that interests me, it has nothing to do with why we are here. Your effort is to do the opposite of what is expected and your effort must require strength. It is easier to glide along the groove. You are exerting yourself to go against that movement, to break out of the groove altogether, perhaps. Does that effort get you anywhere?"

The baboon had come back to his chair and sat down. His flat strong hands rested on his knees. "An intriguing question."

"Yes. Would you answer it?"

"Why not? But I don't think I can. Perhaps the vision I tried to describe just now set me off. Everything was going so well at that time, you see. I was, in a way, making a career. I was selling unbelievable quantities of furniture. My income was based, in part, on commission, so I was earning a fair amount of money. On top of that I could have the business, the control of it, anyway. Bergen had weakened to the point where he was ready to have himself pushed out. Elaine wanted to marry me and it wouldn't have been an impossible match, we are of the same age and I was fond of her. But nothing was happening."

"How do you mean, Mr. Vleuten?"

"I was just driving a car, visiting customers, going home in the evenings, resting during the weekends. I had a boat, of course, and there were other pastimes, hobbies. I read, I painted a little. But still nothing was happening. I just moved along."

"And you were bored?"

"No. I became bored after that drunken night. It seemed there was something else. But whatever that something else was, it was certainly frightening. The rat and the little boy, the skeleton threatening me. I don't know whether you felt threatened just now, as it lunged at you from the cupboard. Perhaps to you it was just a silly shape like something you see at a carnival, something you scream at and then forget again. To me the shapes were much more, they came out of my own mind, out of the hidden part of my mind, and they were very strong. I was frightened throughout the vision, but I was also fascinated even while I was being tortured by the little boy—he isn't as harmless as he looks, you know—and chased by his rat and even as the cow shape attacked me over and over again, hurting me badly every time. And it wasn't just masochism. I don't particularly enjoy being in pain, but yet . . ."

"You decided consciously to live with your fear? To deliberately recreate it?"

"I decided to try that. I'm not original. I'm quite content to follow ways already explored. I assume that you are acquainted with the work of Bosch, Breughel. There have been others, also now, the films of Fellini, for instance. And there are writers, poets, even composers . . ."

"Many who follow those paths go mad, Mr. Vleuten. They commit suicide, are found hanging in alleys, afloat in the canals, lifeless in gutters. We find them, our patrol cars bring them in and dump them in the morgue."

The baboon's chest expanded as he breathed. "No, the corpses you find have a different history. Drug addicts and alcoholics are caught in a groove too, they slip into habits like average citizens. I want to do something else, really *do* something, not to slip into a ready-made pattern that has, at the best, some moments of high perception but leads to utter degeneration eventually. The idea is not so bad perhaps; it's romantic to be a tramp, I thought of that possibility. I even spent some time in Paris studying clochards, but I decided that their way of life is both uncomfortable and unnecessary and leads to what most lives lead to, a half-conscious dream that turns in a half-circle. The clochards I followed around had to beg or steal. I didn't want to do that, even though the idea of being nothing, having nothing, not even a name, did appeal to me. But I wouldn't want to break into some tourist's car to be able to buy my next bottle or teaspoon of drugs. Why should I spoil another man's vacation? The tourist has his rights too. I don't quarrel with the ideals or lack of ideals of others. But it was interesting to live with the clochards for a while. Some of them were as sinister, as horrible, as my vision, but it seemed that I could prick through them. They were shadows, my vision was more real."

"The clochards weren't getting anywhere, you mean?"

"Oh, they were somewhere all right, in hell. A hell of boredom, not so different from my own when I was selling a lot of furniture."

"And now, are you bored now?"

"No."

"Happy?"

The baboon shook his head. "Happy! That's a silly word. It has to do with security, there *is* no security. The only thing we can ever be secure about is the knowledge that we will die."

"Do you feel that you are getting anywhere?"

"No, but perhaps I am approaching . . ."

"Approaching what?"

The sergeant was listening with such concentration that his eyes had become slits. The conversation, intense, almost ominous in its inward direction, sounded familiar. He could understand both the significance of the questions and the penetration of the answers. It seemed, and the possibility didn't appear so ludicrous later when he thought back on it, that the meeting between baboon and commissaris was staged for his own personal benefit. There was an accord between the old man and the bizarre figure opposite him that didn't have to be stressed, they would have understood each other without the question-and-answer game. But some of de Gier's own thoughts were being clarified in a way that made the game seem staged.

He glanced at Grijpstra, but the adjutant's initial fascination had ebbed away. De Gier knew that Grijpstra had gone back to his task, the apprehension of Elaine Carnet's killer. He guessed, and the guess was substantiated later when he talked about the investigation again, that Grijpstra thought that the commissaris was only interested in determining the suspect's character, to see if he could be fitted into the facts they had collected about Elaine's death. No more, no less. The ideal policeman.

"A mystery perhaps." The baboon's answer had a mocking overtone. His hand, each finger moving individually, mocked the answer.

"Yes, a mystery," the commissaris said pleasantly. "A useless word, I agree. Well, sir, we'll be going. Just a last question about Mrs. Carnet's death. Could you think of anyone who would derive some pleasure, some gain, from her death? There are a number of suspects we are interrogating. There is Mr. Bergen, young Mr. Pullini, Gabrielle too, of course. There may be others, people Mrs. Carnet employed, perhaps. We found a man, a certain Mr. de Bree, a neighbor, who tried to poison Gabrielle Carnet's dog some days ago."

The baboon didn't answer.

"You have no ideas that could be of help to us?"

"Only negative ideas. Mr. Bergen is mainly a businessman. He was, when I knew him, quite happy to run the business, I don't think he wanted to own it. And with Elaine's death he will still only own a quarter of the shares, the quarter she gave him years ago, the other three-quarters will go to Gabrielle. Did you mention Pullini?"

"Yes, Francesco Pullini. He is in town just now. We saw him briefly today, he isn't feeling well."

"I know Francesco. He dealt with Bergen, not with Elaine."

The commissaris sat up and massaged his thighs.

"Is that so? I understood that Mrs. Carnet did pay attention to the Pullini connection, chose merchandise, determined the size of the orders, and so on."

The baboon shook his head. "Not really, that was just a charade. Bergen liked to work on Francesco and he sometimes got Elaine to help. Tricks: he would give a very large order to get a good price and then he would later halve it and say that Elaine had made the decision, or he might delay the order altogether, also to get a better price."

"And Gabrielle, she didn't get on too well with her mother, I believe?"

"True, they did argue sometimes, but Gabrielle has had her own apartment for quite a long time now."

"Whose idea was that?"

"Gabrielle's. She is clever, and she certainly loved her mother. She could have moved out altogether but she stayed in the house."

"Did Mrs. Carnet drink compulsively?"

The baboon moved a hand over his face. "Yes, I think so, the drinking was getting worse. Couldn't she have fallen down the stairs?"

The commissaris got up. "Yes, she might have, that would certainly be the best solution."

"Where's your car?" the commissaris asked when they were in the street again.

"A little farther along, sir, near the Berlaghe Bridge."

"I'll give you a ride. Sergeant?"

"Sir."

"I know it's been a long day but I'd like you to go back to the Pulitzer Hotel and get Francesco's passport. If he doesn't want to give it up you can bring him to headquarters and lock him in for the night. I'll clear it with the public prosecutor later on, but if you are tactful that won't be necessary. Grijpstra?"

"Sir."

"Do you want to go home now?"

"Not particularly, sir."

"You can come with me, I want to pay another call on Mr. Bergen. You haven't met him yet."

He opened the door of the Citroën and took out the radio's microphone.

"Headquarters?"

"Headquarters, who is calling?"

"CID, the Carnet case. Any news from Detective Cardozo?"

"Yes, sir, he left a number, wants you to call him."

"Any urgency?"

"No, sir."

He pushed the microphone back. "I'll call him from Bergen's house."

"We might have dinner somewhere, sir," Grijpstra said from the back of the car.

"Later, if you don't mind. I'd like to see Bergen first. Would you like to have dinner with us, sergeant?"

"Thank you, sir, but I'll have to go home first to feed Tabriz and I'd like to get out of this uniform and have a shower."

"Fine, how about nine o'clock at that Chinese restaurant next to the porno cinema in the old city? We've eaten there before, it's a favorite hangout of yours, I believe."

"Cardozo might like to come too, sir. He's been complaining that he is always sent off on his own and that he loses track of what goes on."

The commissaris smiled. "Yes, and he is right, of course. But I have his number and I'll ring him later. He's probably having his dinner now but he can have it again. By nine o'clock our preliminary investigation should be complete. It'll be time to compare our theories, if we have the courage to bring them out, and to move into the next stage."

"Setting up traps, sir?"

The commissaris turned around. "No, Grijpstra, the traps have been set up already and not by us. This time we'll have to do the opposite, if we can. We'll have to release our suspects, they are trapped already."

"The opposite," de Gier murmured. "Interesting."

12

CARDOZO MARCHED ALONG, arms swinging, until he became aware of his own eagerness and dropped back into an exaggerated slouch. He had been out of uniform for some two years now, but he hadn't yet lost the habit of being on patrol during working hours. He was still checking bicycles for proper lights and would start every time he saw a car going through the red. He also missed the protection of his mate. Policemen on the beat are hardly ever alone, detectives often are. His trained eyes were registering.

The neighborhood wasn't known for crime but there were still traces. A young man on the other side of the street was moving about hazily. Drugs? Or just tiredness after a long day at grammar school? A badly dressed foreigner, possibly a Turk, a man with a wide brown face and a heavy coal black mustache, seemed interested in a bicycle thrown against a fence. A thief? Or an unskilled laborer on his way to an over-crowded room in a cheap boarding house in the next quarter, which was only a mile from there. Cardozo shrugged, he shouldn't bother the man, even if he stole a bicycle right in front of his eyes. He was a murder brigade detective, a specialist. But he crossed the street. The Turk had stopped and was bending down to examine the bicycle's lock. Cardozo's hand touched the man's shoulder. He shook his head and pulled back his jacket so that the pistol's butt shone against his white shirt.

"Police. Move along now."

The man's teeth showed in a lopsided grin of fear. "Only looking."

"Sure. Move along."

The man stepped aside and began to run. Cardozo noted the man's shoes, the soles had worn through. The seat of the man's trousers was patched, badly, with a piece of different cloth. Poverty, a rare occurrence in Amsterdam, but the Turk would be outside the cradle of social security. If he starved he starved, there would be nowhere to go. Cardozo had only been introduced to poverty once, when he was on his way back from France during a holiday and had lost his wallet with his money and train ticket, slipped through a tear in his unlined summer jacket. He had noticed the wallet's absence in a restaurant, just before he had begun to read the menu, and had wandered out into the street again. Lunchtime without lunch, in Paris where he didn't know the way and could hardly ask for directions for lack of words. It had taken him all day to walk out of the city and find the expressway, and he had waited for hours at the side of the road as night fell and the traffic's flow began to show gaps, long black lulls that increased as the night crept on. He had drunk from a tap at a gas station, suspiciously eyed by attendants in crisp uniforms. No coffee, no cigarettes. He had bummed a cigarette from another hitchhiker and smoked it hungrily. The hitchhiker was professional, a tanned young man carrying a brand-new shoulder pack stuck on aluminium tubes. A sporting type with muscular legs and high boots and an insulated windbreaker and an American flag sewed on his pack. An efficient traveler who had planned his trip through Europe and who had his money in traveler's checks, folded in a clip and buttoned away in his breast pocket. Cardozo had been carrying an old suitcase, reinforced with a frayed belt, and had shivered in the early morning's chill, a lost little figure who was refused, with an imperative wave of her bejeweled and manicured hand, by the lady who gave the American his lift. Cardozo remembered the loneliness and hunger of the two days he had needed to get home, and the memory showed later when he had to deal with the lost and strayed of his own city.

The Turk disappeared around the corner and Cardozo followed slowly, turning again into the Mierisstraat. He pulled the polished bell handle and waited patiently until he heard Gabrielle's voice behind the heavy oak door that swung open slowly, screening her.

"I'm sorry, I was just about to take a shower when you rang. I saw you through my window."

"It's all right, miss, I've come to ask you about that money you found. We heard about your telephone call through the radio but there were no details."

"Come in, come in, we can talk inside."

She was going up the stairs as he pushed his way through the glass door of the hall. Her bare feet were tripping out of sight at the staircase's curve, they hardly seemed to touch the thick rug. The housecoat had fallen open when she welcomed him in the hall. He had seen the outline of her body as she hastily retied the sash. A small body, the body of a very young girl but with the fully developed breasts of a woman. She had said she was nearly thirty years old.

The terrier was waiting for them in Gabrielle's sitting room. He greeted the visitor and Cardozo bent down and scratched the dog's head and rubbed the firm woolly ears.

"Has he recovered now?"

She laughed. "Yes, completely. We've been for a walk this afternoon, I don't dare to let him out in the garden. Are you still working on Paul's case? Or isn't it important anymore?"

"Yes, miss. We know who gave him the arsenic."

"Who?" Gabrielle's voice had lost its purr and the green eyes were drilling into Cardozo's face.

"I can't tell you yet, miss, not until a summons has been issued, but that won't be long now. I expect that the poisoner will have to go to court. The judge has been rather fierce on cases of this sort lately. Our man will probably have to pay a fine and damages to you, and there may be a suspended jail sentence of a few weeks."

"Good. I think I know who it is. That horrible cat was in the garden again this afternoon. I threw a rock at it but I missed. I can't stand that cat with its two faces. It was the cat's owner, right? Mr. de Bree?"

Cardozo shook his head. "I can't tell you yet, miss, but you will be informed in due time. We have a confession, you see, but a confession on its own means nothing. People have been known to admit all sorts of criminal deeds that they had nothing to do with. The public prosecutor will have to evaluate the case but I think it is pretty clear. We also have statements signed by witnesses."

"Good." Her hand came up shyly and touched his hair. "I'm glad you're with the police, I trusted you from the first time I saw you. How is the investigation about my mother going?"

"We are working."

"Can I get you a drink?"

Cardozo looked at his watch. "Perhaps not, miss. I am still on duty."

"Oh, nonsense, it's after hours now. I'll have a drink with you, and please call me Gabrielle. We don't have to be so formal, this is the third time we've met. Whiskey?"

"You don't have vodka, Gabrielle?"

She giggled. "Vodka doesn't smell, they say. Do you still have to report today?"

He nodded. The gauze undercurtains of the room were drawn and the light was soft and restful. He felt tired and the low couch lured him to lean back and forget. He saw the girl open a cupboard and heard a bottle's gurgle. She left for a moment and came back with a pitcher filled with ice cubes.

Cardozo's lips split in a happy sensuous smirk. This was the true police life, the adventurous scene he had so often dreamed himself into at the movies and in the short but vivid imaginations pressed into pauses between his alarm clock's piercing shrieks. The weary detective enjoying a break. The room was just right. His gaze rested briefly on some delicately arranged flowers, on the rows of books, on the soft orange and brown border of the Oriental carpet covering most of the floor. Gabrielle gave him the glass. The drink was properly prepared with a slice of fresh lemon stuck on the side and the ice tinkling through a blurred mixture of vodka and club soda. He saw Gabrielle's breasts, only for a moment again, for the housecoat closed as she straightened up.

He also saw the small object between her breasts, the skull of a cow carved from a small piece of gleaming walnut. A beautifully chiseled miniature with deep eye sockets and a protruding mouth, each tiny jaw complete with its teeth. Between the minute horns the forehead showed a cavity, perhaps a natural fault of the wood, forming an extra eye and accentuating the skull's ghoulish threat.

She had squatted down at his feet and her eyes sparkled in the semidarkness. A small wave of guilt prompted his question.

"You found some money, I was told. A lot of money? How did that come about?"

"I was cleaning my mother's bedroom and stripping her bed. The bills were under the mattress, stuck in a magazine. You want to see them?"

"Please."

He sat up while she was away. A small painting caught his eye. It was hung in a dark corner near the end of the couch and he bent over to study it closer. A portrait of a young man, head and shoulders. A young man in some medieval costume, a tight tunic that fitted the narrow shoulders closely. A striking face framed in long, dark, flowing hair. A hooked nose, large liquid eyes, a high forehead. A nobleman from the South, Italian, Spanish, perhaps a Spanish don from the time that Spain was trying to conquer the Netherlands. He wondered what had moved Gabrielle to hang the portrait in the intimacy of her room, so close to her bed. Whenever she lay on her right side the young man would be staring at her. He heard her in the corridor and moved to the middle of the couch. She came back with a ladies' magazine and opened it and they counted the notes together, one hundred notes of a thousand guilders each. Eighty were brand-new, twenty slightly used.

"I don't suppose I should keep the money here. Do you need it as an exhibit? You could give me a receipt; I suppose the police would return it later?"

The small hand on his wrist distracted him but he could still think logically. "No. Just hide it until tomorrow and deposit it in your bank account. I have seen the money and I'll make up a report and sign it under oath."

Her purring voice laughed. "Yes, you are an official, a police officer. I can't believe it. You must be very dangerous, nobody would ever expect you to be a detective. How clever of the police to employ you. I am sure people will tell you anything you want to know!"

"You mean I look like a harmless moron?"

Her hand was stroking his neck. "Never mind, I am only teasing. I like you very much. I like men who don't look tall and overpowering and handsome like that other officer who came the night of Mother's death, the beautiful man with the large mustache. Men like that are unbearable."

Cardozo was nodding and smiling, but the little wave of guilt had crept back and he heard himself defending the sergeant. "But he is very good, I have worked with him for a long time now. He is very intelligent and dependable."

"Pff. He is a showoff!" She looked at her watch. "Oh, for heaven's sake. I *must* take my shower. It was such a hot day and I'll have to go work again. If I don't bathe I'll be prickly and irritable and nothing will go right. I promised Mr. Bergen that I would sort out his stock files. We are preparing a statement of what we have in our warehouse for the bank, and so far we come up with a different figure every time. I'll have to check through the invoices again."

She jumped up but held on to his wrist so that he was pulled off the couch. He was in the bathroom before he knew that she had taken him with her and he saw her drop her housecoat and step into the tub and adjust the faucets. He stood, holding his glass, trying to find a harmless object to look at. She laughed. "Silly! Haven't you ever seen a naked woman? Why don't you sit on the toilet and enjoy your drink. I'll be ready in a moment."

The shower came on. The bath had plastic curtains but she didn't draw them. He saw the hot water splash on her shoulders and run down her arms and there was a small rivulet trickling between her breasts, with two sidelines running down and causing a steady drip from her nipples.

"Don't you want to see me like this?"

But he did want to, of course, and he was having trouble with his breathing. He took her by the hand before she had had a chance to reach for the towel.

"But I'm still wet."

He pulled the towel off the rack and wrapped it around her body and swept her off her feet and carried her through the corridor. Her head rested on his shoulder.

On the bed he saw the arrogant eyes of the Spanish nobleman and he pushed the portrait's broad gold frame so that it slid off its hook and got stuck between the couch and the wall. The terrier was watching too, its dark button eyes fixed on the linked, throbbing bodies. The dog's fuzzy ears stood up, quivering with interest, and his short tail tapped on the side of his basket. Cardozo wasn't aware that some of his passion was shared by Paul, and when, after a while, he turned over and looked at the room, the dog had curled himself up in a tight ball and was fast asleep.

13

THE CITROËN'S SMOOTH SHAPE was coasting through the avenues of Amsterdam Old South like a large predator fish patrolling its hunting streams. It had been cruising for twenty-five minutes and it kept on turning the same corners. Grijpstra was studying a small soiled map and gave directions that the commissaris found hard to follow. Every turnoff they tried led into one-way streets and they invariably tried to enter on the wrong side. If Grijpstra had been with de Gier his mood might have turned sour and been edging toward blind fury, but the commissaris's presence had soothed his mind and he continued trying to trace a course while the car floated on.

"It can't be here anyway," the commissaris said quietly. "Look at those vast houses, they were patricians' homes once. Homes for the aged now, adjutant, and private hospitals and maybe a few high-priced sex clubs tucked away here and there. The whole neighborhood is subsidized by the state now." He smiled. "Or lust, and expense accounts that cater to lust. Lovely old places all the same, don't you agree?"

Grijpstra looked up from the map. The heavily wooded gardens lining the curving avenue did indeed offer a spectacle of sedate grandeur. The gardens shielded four- and five-storied villas, decorated with turrets and cantilevered balconies overgrown with creepers, abodes of splendor where merchants had once planned their overseas adventures and enjoyed the benefits of constructive but greedy thoughts.

"Yes, sir. But we should be close, we have been close for a while now. The street behind this one must be the one we want, I'm sure of it.

Some mansions were pulled down and a bungalow park has taken their sites. Bergen probably has one of the bungalows, but I wouldn't know how to get in there with all these damned NO ENTRY signs."

The commissaris tried again. "No. No use. We'll walk."

They heard the evening song of a thrush the minute the engine was shut off and the commissaris pointed at the bird, a small, exact silhouette on an overhead wire. The thrush flew off and a nightingale took over. Grijpstra had folded his map and put it away and began to walk on, but the commissaris restrained him, waiting for the end of the trilling cantata. The nightingale seemed to feel that he had an audience, for he pushed himself into such a brilliant feat of pure artistry, and sang so loudly, that Grijpstra expected him to fall off his branch. When the song broke, and ended, in the middle of a rapidly rising scale of notes, the commissaris was standing on his toes, his small head raised, his eyes closed.

Grijpstra smiled. It was good to be with the old man again. His perception had risen and he became aware of the quiet of the street. The one-way system had effectively blocked all through traffic and the old-fashioned streetlights, adapted gas lanterns spaced far apart, threw a soft light that was held by flowering bushes and freshly mowed lawns and hung between the gnarled branches of old beeches and oaks. They walked on, two contemplative pedestrians enjoying the peace of the evening, and found Bergen's street at the next corner.

Grijpstra checked the house numbers. "This one, sir."

The bungalow's garage doors were open. A new Volvo had been left in the driveway, unable to fit into the garage, where the wreck of a small, fairly new car blocked its way. The compact's nose had been pushed in and its hood stood up, cracked. A refrigerator with its door hanging open leaned against the wreck and parts of a lawn mower littered the floor.

"I'm sure most of that could be fixed," Grijpstra said as he peered into the garage. The commissaris had walked on. "Maybe that's considered to be junk, adjutant, the throwouts of a different lifestyle."

The commissaris pushed the bell. The door swung open and Bergen was staring at them, one eye large and round and menacing, the other almost closed. He was holding his face and his spectacles hung on one ear. He was in his shirtsleeves and his suspenders were slipping off his shoulders.

"Do you mind if we come in, Mr. Bergen? We're sorry having to disturb you again today, but we won't be long."

Bergen stepped back and they walked through a hall, stumbling over a pair of rubber boots and two or three coats dropped on the floor, and stopped in the corridor. The door to the kitchen was ajar, and Grijpstra saw a heap of dirty dishes dumped into the sink. There was a smell of burned meat. Bergen passed them and opened the door to the living room. He was still holding his cheek. His voice sounded muffled and, after he dropped his hand, slurred. Grijpstra sniffed; there was no smell of alcohol.

Bergen shifted a pile of laundry on the settee and motioned for the commissaris to sit down. Grijpstra had found a leather recliner, next to a waste basket overflowing with crumpled newspapers topped by banana peels.

"Your wife isn't back yet, Mr. Bergen?"

Bergen had found a chair too and faced the commissaris dumbly.

The commissaris asked the question again.

"No. It's a mess here. I've been camping out, more or less, waiting for her to come back. She won't. There was a letter in the mail today, a lawyer's letter. She wants a divorce."

"I'm sorry to hear that."

Bergen muttered something.

"Pardon?"

"Can't speak so well, paralysis, you know." The word "paralysis" seemed to be causing him considerable trouble.

"It's all right, sir, we can understand you. I must really apologize for this intrusion, but we're still working on Mrs. Carnet's death, as you will understand."

Bergen's round eye stared fiercely. "Any progress, commissaris?"

"Some, we hope. But what's this about your face? Your office told us that you had some tests done this afternoon. The results are encouraging, I hope?"

"No."

"Oh, dear."

"No. Terrible day. This started last night but I didn't think it was anything serious until this morning, and when I got to the hospital they told me they were busy and wouldn't have time for me for a few days. I found a private clinic and the specialist said that I needed a skull photograph, an X-ray. Here." He got up and rummaged through a stack of papers on a side table, impatiently tossing the top sheets on the ground. "Here. This isn't the photograph but a report that has to do with it. They found a spot, a white spot, chalk, and they said there might be something behind it that they couldn't see. Read it for yourself."

The commissaris took the sheet and put on his glasses. He began to mumble his way through the photocopy's faint print. "Hmm. Technical talk. Let's see. *'The chloroid plexuses are calcified bilaterally, left greater than right. There is a small area of calcification that appears to be in contact with the right frontal calvarium and measured to be greater than one hundred seventy-five EMI density units.'* Hm hm. And here we seem to have some sort of conclusion. *'In spite of this, the presence of a small underlying meningioma cannot be ruled out entirely.'*"

He peered at Bergen over his glasses. "Is that so bad, Mr. Bergen? I'm afraid I don't understand the terminology. It would just seem that they found a little chalk somewhere in your skull. What's a meningioma?"

Bergen's reply was unclear and he repeated it. "A tumor, and a tumor would mean cancer, brain cancer."

The commissaris read on. *"'Further serial studies suggested.'"* He gave the paper back and sat down. "Yes. So what they are saying is that the chalk *could* hide a tumor, and then perhaps we might assume that the tumor *could* indicate cancer. But there is no need to jump to conclusions. Were these further serial tests in fact done?"

"Not all of them. I'll have to go again tomorrow and the neurologist said he would know then. I took this copy with me and showed it to my doctor but he wouldn't say anything. They never do when they suspect cancer."

"I see."

The silence lasted for a while, and Bergen's eye, the lid drawn away by the paralyzed nerve, kept on boring into the commissaris's face.

"This really is not the time to disturb you, Mr. Bergen, and I'm sorry about coming here, but what can we do? You heard that Gabrielle located a hundred thousand guilders under her mother's mattress?"

"Won't do any good," Bergen muttered. "She said she would pay it back into the company's account. Eighty thousand; the rest she'll keep, of course, that's Elaine's private money. But on top of everything else I had this letter delivered by messenger. A letter from the bank."

He jumped up and began to look through the papers on the side table again. "You know what this is?"

"No idea, Mr. Bergen."

"A note to say that the bank is curtailing the company's credit. For a few years now the bank has let us borrow a million, and we have been using that credit, of course, and now they have decided to cut that in half. Any money paid in by us from now on will be taken out of our account until we have paid in half a million. They *would* send the letter today. With Elaine dead they're worried about their pennies."

The commissaris sat up and pushed his glasses back. "Really? They have no faith in your presidency of the company?"

"So it seems." Bergen had dropped the letter on the floor. "The manager has come to see Elaine and me a couple of times this year. He had noticed that we were using our full credit continuously and he wasn't impressed by my last balance sheet. I have been selling large quantities at minimal profit and we have a lot of stocks. I told him it was all right. I'm aiming for government business and the transactions are profitable, so why should he be anxious?"

"But he is, evidently."

"An idiot." Bergen's mouth curved on one side. "A perfect idiot. He even suggested that we should hire the baboon again. I think he is a personal friend of Vleuten's. He sort of suggested that we shouldn't have fired the baboon and I told him that we never did, that the man left by his own free will, that he resigned."

"The profit margin of your business was better when Mr. Vleuten was still on your staff?"

"Yes, but since then we have had more competition. Business always has its ups and downs. I am trying to get better prices from Pullini now and we have a new salesman on the road. The pendulum will swing back again. But it's hard to convince a bank manager, and with Elaine's death . . ."

"I see, a new factor to be considered or, rather, the lack of an old factor. Gabrielle will replace her mother, I imagine?"

"The bank is not impressed by Gabrielle."

The commissaris sighed. "I see you have some problems, sir, but problems can be overcome. I'm sure you'll find a way. Just one question before we go. Do you have any idea why Mrs. Carnet took out that eighty thousand on the day of her death?"

Bergen's hands moved about on his skull. The silvery hair that had been so stately during their interview of the morning stood up in tufts. "No."

"Carnet and Company owe that amount to Pullini, isn't that so?"

"Yes, but that had nothing to do with Elaine. She left the day-to-day management to me, she never interfered anymore. She did read our list of creditors every month and she may have known that eighty thousand was payable to Pullini, but why would she concern herself with that? And even if she did intend to pay that debt, why would she pay it in cash? She could have given Pullini a check and he would have cashed the check himself. We don't like to move banknotes around, nobody does."

Grijpstra had gotten up and was looking out through the garden doors. An untidy collection of clumsily sawed logs was pushed against the low stone wall of the terrace. There were scattered and broken roof tiles on the terrace and red stains of crumbled bricks, knocked out by the tree's falling trunk. He walked back to the center of the room and looked at Bergen's trousers and hands. No, they were clean. Bergen hadn't touched his tree today. But even so, the alibi was thin. The tree wouldn't have taken all evening. He could have used his Volvo to visit Mrs. Carnet, a few minutes' ride.

"Have you seen everybody now?" Bergen asked.

"I think so. We saw your friend Mr. Vleuten this afternoon."

Bergen's right hand waved tiredly. "Not my friend. Perhaps the baboon was right to get out of the business. He's doing very well, isn't he?"

"I thought you had had no contact with him since he left. That was awhile ago, wasn't it?"

"I heard," Bergen said. "We have mutual acquaintants. The baboon is doing well. He restored his house, he deals in boats. Boats are the thing these days, everybody who does well wants one. Old boats, antique launches, flat-bottomed sailing yachts . . . excellent status symbols. The baboon is a businessman still, he hasn't forgotten what he learned when he was selling our furniture. And Elaine must have been providing him with capital, she has been saving her wages and profits for the last five years. She used to put them back into the business but stopped when we obtained good bank credit. And she always loved Vleuten. The baboon is the clever one and I am the sucker. I work and he plays around."

"Well, that's one way of looking at it, no doubt there are other ways. But we did see Mr. Vleuten and we also talked with Mr. Pullini."

Bergen laughed cheerlessly and his hand came up to hold his cheek again. "Pullini!"

"You don't think there's a connection?"

"No, Francesco hardly knew Elaine. His father did business with her and she went to Italy, but that was all such a long time ago. She was still working then."

"We'll have to be on our way again, Mr. Bergen. I wish you good luck with your test tomorrow."

"Poor man," Grijpstra said in the car.

"You think so, adjutant?"

Grijpstra's right eyebrow crept up an eighth of an inch. "Shouldn't I be sorry for the slob, sir? He is in about as perfect a mess as Job on his garbage pile. Bergen has lost it all, hasn't he?"

The commissaris suddenly tittered and Grijpstra's eyebrow stayed where it was. "An absolute fool, adjutant. The man must have a special talent for connecting misunderstandings incorrectly. That medical report didn't indicate cancer, it only said there might be something somewhere. Doctors like to be explorers, especially when they have a lot of expensive equipment around that can be used in their explorations. All they have to do is instill a little fear in the patient's mind and they can switch on their electronic gear and work up a bill of a few thousand guilders. And the insurance pays."

"But there could be a tumor in Bergen's head, sir."

The commissaris shrugged. "Surely, and in my head and in yours, but we haven't thought of that possibility yet. Bergen has."

"So you don't think there is any link between his paralysis and whatever they are looking for in his head?"

"Not necessarily. What Bergen has now I've had too, Bell's palsy, a harmless affliction that will go away by itself. I didn't want to tell Bergen that. I'm not a doctor and perhaps he *is* in serious trouble. I'm only saying that the man is overworrying, about everything."

"His divorce and the bank letter?"

"Exactly. Calamities are only calamities if you define them as such; in reality there are only events and all events can be useful."

Grijpstra's eyebrow came down.

"You should know that simple truth," the commissaris continued. "You've been in the police a long time now, adjutant. We always deal with people, suspects or victims, who have managed to channel their thoughts in such a way that they see no acceptable way out anymore. They think they are suffering because of all sorts of reasons—their rights haven't been respected, they've lost something, they've been robbed or slandered or treated badly, and so they're justified in behaving in such a way that they break the law and meet us. But usually they are drowning in a poisonous pool of their own making. But they'll never blame themselves. Never."

The Citroën was waiting for a green light.

"Sir."

"Ah, thank you. No, Grijpstra, I won't pity our friend Bergen. Pity won't do any good, anyway. Let's hope he can get shocked out of his present state of mind and steer himself into a course that may lead to a little more freedom. And it's time to eat. And Cardozo wants to be telephoned. He must be brooding on the information he collected from his visit to Gabrielle."

The commissaris parked the car at the edge of the old city and, after calling Cardozo from a public telephone booth, they set out for the restaurant on foot. A brightly lit store window attracted the commissaris and he stopped to look in. He was still lecturing on the lack of awareness that causes illusion and misconstruction and didn't appear to notice what he was looking at.

Grijpstra cleared his throat.

"Yes, adjutant?"

Grijpstra pointed at the window. "I don't think this display is of much interest, sir."

The commissaris grinned and they walked on. The window had shown a number of different types of vibrators arranged on a ground of artificial grass that was fenced off by a row of plastic penises.

14

THE FAT GOD was grinning at the mongrel but the mongrel didn't care.
She was lying on the floor of the cheap Chinese eating place, half hidden under a table, which everybody who knew the restaurant avoided
because it wobbled, and was noisily licking her swollen private parts.
She was a particularly ugly mongrel, small and hairy and spotted, but
she did own some endearing features, such as large expressive eyes and
a tail with a stiff curl that pointed at the spot where her neck should
have been. De Gier's foot came out and nudged the dog. She looked up.

"Don't *do* that," de Gier whispered. "People are trying to eat here.
The food is excellent but they won't taste it if you keep on making that
blubbery sucking noise." The dog's tail quivered. She bared her teeth in
an effort to be friendly and rolled over, showing her naked pink belly.
De Gier's foot rubbed the belly softly and the dog whined ingratiatingly.
The restaurant was empty and the owner, a tall thin Cantonese with the
face of a philosopher, was resting his back against the counter; he
hadn't moved in the last ten minutes.

The dog rolled back and went on licking and de Gier's eyes wandered
up to the portrait of the fat god, a portly gentleman being crawled over
by seven well-dressed slit-eyed toddlers equipped with similar smiles.
The god of wealth and health, sitting on a cushion that in turn sat on a
hilltop that overlooked a valley planted with dark green crops stretching
to the horizon.

The restaurant's glass door swung open and Cardozo entered, followed by four street prostitutes coming in for a late dinner. Cardozo

held the door and they thanked him politely. They were off duty now and had lost their inviting smiles and prancing mannerisms. De Gier knew them all: he had listened to them many times, he knew their favorite subjects. They never talked shop when they ate their fried rice or noodles. They liked to talk about knitting and the defects of their cars and about taxes, and they would linger over their meal, unwilling to go back to the street, where tourists, usually a little drunk, were ambling about restlessly, waiting to purchase their services.

"Evening," Cardozo said sadly.

De Gier muttered his reply and moved over to the corner chair so that Cardozo could sit next to him.

"Have you ordered?"

"No, I'm waiting for the commissaris, he should be here in a few minutes. We can have a beer."

He waved to the philosopher and put up two fingers. The Chinese bowed, pushed himself off the counter, and slid behind it, grabbing the handle of the beer pump before he had reached his proper station. His other hand swept two glasses off a shelf and caught them deftly; he had them in position as the first stream of frothy golden liquid poured out of the polished spout. The beer was on their table before de Gier's arm had come down.

"Your very good health. Had any adventures today?"

Cardozo nodded as he drank. "Yes, I saw Gabrielle Carnet just now. The commissaris wanted to know how she found the hundred thousand, you heard about that?"

"No. Tell me."

De Gier listened. "That's very nice, so the obvious motive has gone too, has it? What's this now, a complication or a simplification? I had worked out a theory but the facts may still fit. I'll have to talk to Grijpstra, maybe he thought of the theory first, I forget now."

Cardozo tried to smile. "Does it matter? You won't get any credit for it anyway. The case will be solved by the brigade and the chief constable will shake the commissaris's hand in the end or not. Maybe the public prosecutor will spoil the case, or the judge, or some fool lawyer."

But de Gier hadn't heard him. The glass door swung open again and he was waving at the Chinese while the commissaris and Grijpstra came into the restaurant. Two more beers appeared and another ashtray.

"Sir?"

The commissaris had drunk his beer and was waiting for another. His hands moved restlessly on the bare boards of the table. "No, sergeant, Grijpstra can explain and then you three can fill each other in. I'll listen for a change." More beer appeared and the commissaris hid his face behind it.

Cardozo looked at Grijpstra, but the adjutant was reading the menu. "Roast pork, hmm. Fried noodles with shrimp, hmm. Wonton soup, that's nice but it's crossed out. Thin noodles with lobster, hmm, a little slippery but tasty. Yes."

"Adjutant?"

"Yes. Noodles with fried chicken, I think, as always. I don't know why I bother to read the menu. And you'll have the same, de Gier, for otherwise we'll have to wait too long, and you'll have the same too, Cardozo. Sir?"

"I'll have the same."

There was more beer again and then the food came and was eaten in silence. They listened to the prostitutes. The platinum blonde's little Fiat had lost its muffler and she had been given a ticket for causing excessive noise. The small redhead's Volkswagen had starting problems. The tall beauty with the German accent complained about a rattle in her Renault's front door. There didn't seem to be anything wrong with the black girl's car. De Gier was interested. He leaned over. "Excuse me, miss, what sort of a car do you drive?"

"A small Citroën."

"Aha," the commissaris said.

"But it's brand-new, still under guarantee."

The commissaris turned around. "You won't have any trouble, miss. Citroëns are good cars, I've been driving them all my life. No trouble." The black girl smiled and the commissaris turned back to his fried noodles.

"No, sir?" Grijpstra whispered. "I thought you had a problem with your suspension a few weeks ago."

The commissaris's fork came up and pointed at the adjutant's face. "Minor. Little leak somewhere. They fixed it."

"And aren't they always fiddling around with the timing? The garage sergeant was telling me about that. He said it was driving him crazy."

"Nothing wrong with the timing, the sergeant wanted something to do."

"And . . ."

"Never mind. I think Cardozo wants to ask something, what is it, Cardozo?"

"I want to know everything, sir. I've only been working on the poisoned dog angle. I know nothing about the murder investigation. Who *are* our suspects, sir, and what have we found out?"

"Good. Adjutant, why don't you tell him, and then de Gier can do his bit too. And Cardozo can finish up. I haven't heard about Gabrielle Carnet and the hundred thousand guilders that popped up so conveniently. Go ahead, adjutant."

Grijpstra wanted more beer but was given coffee and the discussion started. It lasted for an hour as more coffee was consumed and Grijpstra's small black cigars smoldered away, making the restaurant's owner cough politely and turn on an electric fan.

"Do we know everything now?" the commissaris asked. "Yes, Cardozo?"

Cardozo seemed very ill at ease. His lips, holding the cigar that Grijpstra had forced on him, twisted spasmodically.

"Eh, sir, I would like to hear about that skeleton in the baboon's apartment again. It had a cow's skull, right?"

"Yes."

"Did, uh, the skull have a hole in its forehead?"

The commissaris thought. "Perhaps it did, yes. It was masked, a purple corduroy mask leaving the eye sockets open, but it seems that there was a sort of tear that exposed part of the forehead, a tear or a hole. Do you remember, sergeant?"

"Yes, sir. There was a hole in the skull's forehead, I remember it exactly, between the eyes but a little higher. The skull must have been very old, there was some dried-out crusted moss around that hole. But why do you ask, Cardozo?" His voice was honey sweet. "You weren't with us, Cardozo, so how do you know about that hole?"

"Uh . . ." Cardozo squeaked.

"Tell us, dear boy."

"Gabrielle was wearing a small object, on a nylon string," Cardozo said rapidly. "The object was a cow's skull, the size of, uh, like that." He pointed to a button on de Gier's denim jacket. "That size. It was carved out of walnut, I think, well done, a lot of detail. The eye sockets were quite deep and there was a third hole, I thought it was a fault of the wood."

"Amazing," de Gier said, still in the same sweet voice. "And how do you know that? I also saw a piece of nylon around the young lady's neck and I also saw a small object dangling on that nylon thread, but it was stuck way down into her blouse. I couldn't see any detail on that object and yet you describe it so accurately."

"I saw her this evening, before I came here. I told you, didn't I?"

"But how did you manage to see something she keeps between her breasts? She must have been naked. Why was she naked, dear boy? Did she strip, or did you forget your manners and rape the young lady?"

Grijpstra's eyes stared; the commissaris was stirring his coffee. Cardozo had picked up a match and was digging at a noodle, stuck between the table's boards.

"Maybe you should tell us what happened exactly," the commissaris said gently.

"I'm sorry, sir. I did have, uh, intimate contact with the suspect. I am very sorry, sir."

"She seduced you, did she?"

"No, sir, it was my own fault. I wasn't alert, I'm afraid. It, uh, just happened. I just slipped into it."

"Into what?" Grijpstra asked, frowning furiously.

"Gentlemen!" the commissaris said sternly and raised a forbidding hand. "Now, constable, you can give us some details. Try and describe exactly what happened. You can spare us the physical details, of course. She *did* seduce you, didn't she? I can't imagine that you instigated the action." The commissaris's voice was gentle again, he was stirring his coffee once more.

Cardozo talked for a while.

"I see, well, never mind. Ah, I forgot to ask, did you see Francesco Pullini, de Gier? I want that passport." De Gier produced the passport and the commissaris opened it and looked at the photograph. "Good, was he upset?"

"Not particularly, sir, just a little, but Italians are rather excitable, I believe."

Cardozo picked up the passport and stared at the photograph. His eyes opened wide. "Sir!"

"What is it now, Cardozo? Don't tell me you know the man, you haven't met him."

"But I *do* know him, sir. There's a small portrait hanging behind the couch Gabrielle uses as a bed. An oil portrait. The face is very similar to this face, sir."

The commissaris breathed out slowly. His small wizened hand came out, reached across the table, and patted Cardozo's shoulder.

"Excellent, detective constable first class. You have now managed to link Gabrielle with both the baboon and Francesco Pullini. Three suspects, one woman, two men, and each man has a sexual relationship with the woman. A lot of loose pieces should fit in now, all we have to do is find out how." He waved for the bill. "Well, Grijpstra, how about your theory? I'm sure you and the sergeant have worked out an angle from which Mrs. Carnet's death could be explained. Is your theory still standing?"

Grijpstra touched de Gier's sleeve. De Gier was staring at the black girl at the other table.

"Yes," de Gier said, "yes, sir. The theory still stands, but it isn't strong enough to hold a suspect. I was thinking of doing some more work, tomorrow morning. I can't do it tonight."

The commissaris paid the bill and complimented the Chinese on the quality of his food. He got up, scraping his chair energetically, but bent down to feel his thigh. His thin lips tightened.

"I won't ask you what your theory is, sergeant. I have my own, but it doesn't stand up too well either as yet. I'll have to go further too. I may be away tomorrow, possibly the day after tomorrow. Meanwhile you can go ahead, but I would appreciate your not making an arrest until I'm back. Ideally our theories should be identical and we should arrive at the same results, but we have been pushing the case and perhaps we should go slower now."

His pale eyes made contact with each of the three men in turn.

"Good."

The dog was licking her private parts again as they left the restaurant. Cardozo tripped over her and stumbled into the prostitutes' table. The black girl caught him.

"Clumsy fellow, aren't you?" de Gier asked.

Grijpstra grinned. "Ignore him, Cardozo. I've seen the sergeant make such a mess here once that it took two waiters an hour to clean up after him." Cardozo looked grateful.

"I was making an arrest then," de Gier said. "You always tell part of the story. We were trying to catch a fellow with a knife as long as your arm."

"Tut-tut-tut."

"Did he have a knife or didn't he?"

"We each had a pistol."

"Gentlemen," the commissaris said from the open doorway, "it's getting late. The door is open, there is a draft, the ladies will catch cold."

"Sir," they said as they trooped into the street.

15

IT WAS NEARLY eleven o'clock when the commissaris came home and his wife was waiting for him in the corridor.

"Dear . . ."

"Yes?"

"You shouldn't be out so late. I wish you would stay in, at least during the evening. You know what the doctor said."

"Yes. Rest. But I did rest."

"Just for two days, he said two weeks. Your bath will be ready in a few minutes."

"Good, any messages?"

"Just one, a telephone call at nine o'clock. A Mr. de Bree."

"You have the number?"

She pointed to the pad next to the telephone and he walked over to it and began to dial.

"Mr. de Bree?"

"Commissaris, I would like to come and see you if possible, something has come up."

"You could tell me over the telephone."

There was a pause. "I would rather come and see you. I have some information."

"Now?"

"I can be with you in five minutes, I have my car."

"Very well."

The commissaris hung up. His wife was standing next to him, her arm around his shoulders. "Please, dear, not now, call him and tell him to come tomorrow. You've had such a long day and you look so pale. Why don't you go and have your bath, surely the matter can wait till tomorrow."

"No, dear, it's a bad case and I've been pushing it, it's my own fault. The man won't stay long, I promise."

The doorbell rang and the commissaris peeked from behind a curtain before he went to open the door. Mr. de Bree had arrived in a brand-new Mercedes and had left the car in the driveway. He had forgotten to close the car door and its lights were on.

The bell rang again. The commissaris didn't hurry. He opened the door and looked down on de Bree's sweaty, bare skull, gleaming under the light of the driveway's lantern.

"Yes, Mr. de Bree?"

"I'm sorry to bother you at this hour, sir, but my information may be of interest to you and I thought . . ."

"That's quite all right, I hadn't gone to bed yet. Please come in."

They walked through the long corridor and the commissaris led the way into his study. It was a hot evening and the garden doors were still open.

"Perhaps we can sit outside, it'll be pleasant in the garden."

They faced each other in two old cane chairs. The commissaris offered his flat tin and lit his visitor's cigar. De Bree puffed nervously.

"You said you had some information?"

"Yes. You remember Paul, the terrier that belongs to the Carnets?"

"The information has to do with the dog?"

"No, but . . ."

De Bree's cigar showed a red-hot end; the commissaris could hear the tobacco crackle as more air was sucked into it.

"Go ahead, Mr. de Bree, take your time."

"The dog. I went to see my lawyer as you suggested and he says it is a bad business . . ."

"It *is* a bad business, Mr. de Bree."

"Yes. Quite. But I have some information, as I said just now, and it has to do with Mrs. Carnet's death. My lawyer said I should give it to you and . . ."

"Maybe I would forget about the bad business with the dog?"

"Yes." De Bree looked much relieved. He was smiling broadly. The glowing cigar hung in his limp hand.

The commissaris's thin eyebrows met above the bridge of his nose.

"No. Absolutely not. We won't forget about Paul. You'll go to court, Mr. de Bree, and get your verdict. And I still want your information. If you don't give it you will be in even more trouble. I am surprised your lawyer didn't tell you that. I am sure he *did* tell you but perhaps you weren't listening. If you have information that concerns the Carnet death, and if a crime is involved in that death—and there *is* a crime involved, I assure you, Mr. de Bree—and if you withhold that information, then you are committing a crime yourself."

De Bree was sucking on his cigar again. "Really?"

"Yes. Absolutely."

"But if I don't tell you about what I saw then there is no information, commissaris. You won't know what I saw. Maybe I saw nothing. You can't accuse me because of something that does not exist."

"Your information does exist. You have told me twice already, once when I opened the door for you and once just now. Beg your pardon, you told me three times. You also told me on the phone. I am a police officer, I don't need witnesses. If I write a report and state that you told me three times that you had information about the Carnet death and that you refused to give it to me afterward, then you are withholding evidence and my report, signed under oath, will be irrefutable proof, acceptable to the court."

"Is that so?" de Bree asked softly.

There was an uneasy silence, accentuated by a slight rustle as a turtle came out of the weeds near the commissaris's feet. De Bree looked down at the small armored creature that was plodding steadily forward. "A turtle!"

"He lives here. Well, Mr. de Bree?"

De Bree breathed out sharply; his nostrils widened and pointed threateningly, like the barrels of a miniature shotgun.

"Very well. That night, the night of the gale, the night of Mrs. Carnet's death, I was in my garden. I was looking for Tobias. He hadn't come in, and I was also worried about the trees, a lot of trees fell that night. While I was outside I heard a terrible screaming and shouting coming from Mrs. Carnet's porch. There were several people shouting at the same time, but her voice was the loudest. I couldn't hear what she said, but she appeared to be hysterical, completely out of control. And then the door of her porch opened and I saw her fall. She had a flowered dress on, which made her body stand out against the lights coming from the porch. Mrs. Carnet fell with such force that she must have been pushed, 'shoved' might be a better word. She came hurtling down and a man fell with her. He rolled over her, it seemed. He was holding on to her, so he must have pushed her to the door and the momentum of his push made him fall with her. I saw the two at the top of the stairs. I couldn't see the complete fall for there were bushes in the way, and the hedge and some small trees, and the gale was blowing everything about. It happened very quickly, of course. There were more than two people in the Carnet house for I saw a shadow, a silhouette, move behind the windows of the porch, not very clearly, again, for there are curtains that are draped in such a way that more than half the surface of the windows is obscured."

"Did you see the man who fell with Mrs. Carnet go back into the house again?"

"Yes. He was in pain. He was dragging himself up."

"Big man? Small man? Did you recognize him?"

"I didn't know him. He didn't seem too big, but there was some distance and I couldn't see too clearly. I had seen enough anyway. I went back into my house after that. Tobias had shown up and I didn't want to hang around."

"Didn't you realize that what you had seen made you a valuable witness to a crime?"

De Bree shrugged. "Who wants to be a witness? It's a lot of bother. You have to go to court and waste a lot of time, and some shyster tries to ask smart questions and show you up for a nitwitted fool. What other people do is other people's concern. I hardly knew the Carnets. Maybe they were having a party. And you musn't forget that I had no idea Mrs. Carnet was dead, I thought she just fell, twisted her ankle perhaps. There aren't all that many steps to the stairs in these gardens. And if she had been in trouble the other people with her would have helped her."

"You knew there had been a crime later, when you learned that we had initiated an investigation."

De Bree wiped his face. "Yes, perhaps, but then you had got to me too, about the dog. I didn't want to attract any more attention to myself until my lawyer suggested . . ."

"I see. How was the man who fell with Mrs. Carnet dressed?"

"I don't remember. I saw a dark shape going down with her. It looked male. I think it wore a dark jacket, but ladies also wear dark jackets. Come to think of it now, I couldn't even swear in court that the shape was male."

"And who was left on the porch? Male or female?"

"Female, I think, but there again I can't be sure, for I only had a glimpse of something moving. But there had been a man involved in the fight, for when the screaming was going on there was a male voice."

"You say you didn't hear any words. Do you remember what language they were screaming in?"

"No. Dutch, I imagine, but I'm not sure. Mrs. Carnet is French, isn't she? Originally, I mean?"

"Belgian, but she did speak French."

De Bree got up. The turtle had reached a large rock and was standing against it, nibbling at a lettuce leaf that had been put out on a tray.

"Your pet?"

"Yes, and it doesn't chase cats, all it does is try to destroy my wife's herb garden."

De Bree smiled ruefully. "I really am sorry about that business with Paul, you know."

The commissaris smiled back. "I am sure, Mr. de Bree, and I hope your regret will show in court. Don't forget to offer to pay damages before the judge mentions it, but I think your lawyer has given you the same advice already."

"Your bath," his wife said as he came back from the front door.

"Yes. But I want to phone the airport. I'll be flying to Italy tomorrow, dear, a nice easy trip. I won't be long, a day and a night at the most."

"Oh . . ."

"Did you run the bath?" He was on his way up the stairs. "And by the way, did you remember to buy that cane?"

"Yes."

"Would you show it to me?"

She went into the living room and came back carrying a bamboo cane with a silver handle.

"Very nice, just what I had in mind. I'll take it to Italy with me. This limp is beginning to be a nuisance. I can still hide it at headquarters where the doctor can see me but I think I'll use the cane whenever I'm sure he isn't around. I'll keep it in the car, it'll be safe there."

His wife began to cry. "You're an invalid now, darling, you should really retire. I can't stand it, the way you're killing yourself. I'll go anywhere with you, I really don't mind leaving Amsterdam. We can go to that strange island, Curaçao, the place you're always talking about. That's in the tropics, isn't it? Your legs won't hurt over there."

He came down the stairs and took the cane from her hand and leaned on it, embracing her with his free arm.

"I love you, but you would be very unhappy if you had to leave Amsterdam now. All your relatives and friends are here. Later, maybe, we'll discuss it. This cane will be a lot of help."

They stood for a while, leaning against each other, until he slipped away and began to climb the stairs again.

"The bath," he said softly, "it'll get cold. And I would love some tea. Let's have tea together. I'll soak and you'll sit and watch me soak."

16

Amsterdam dropped away as the plane banked, and the commissaris admired the pale greens and faded blues of fields and ponds set apart by geometrical patterns of expressways spreading out from the city. He had observed the tall suburban apartment buildings rising from parks as they swept away under the roaring jet engines. Their disappearance evoked some satisfaction. He was traveling, getting away, even if it was only for a moment. His forehead rested against the window as the plane flew above a large swamp. He knew the swamp well. It had been a mysterious world once, an endless maze of lagoons and reed-lined twisted ditches filled with murky water. He remembered the freshwater kelp that waved and intertwined in the depth, moved by hidden currents or the undulating sleek bodies of pikes and eels. The swamp had provided his first real discovery, a first indication that there was more to life than school and trying to find ways to fit in with what grownups wanted him to do in the boring grayness of the small provincial town where he was raised.

He craned his neck but the swamp had gone while the plane gained more height and broke through the clouds and reached the great transparency of the sky. It occurred to him that the sky is an emptiness that sits on a layer of cotton wool and has no limit, an ungraspable manifestation of the mystery that he had also felt as a ten-year-old boy, exploring swamp backwaters in a canoe. The swamp had revealed some of its wonders then, the sky might do the same. And he was in it now, reclining in a first-class seat, reaching the top of a curve that would soon begin to dip down again and take him back to the twisted failings of humanity. Afloat in the universe and free while it lasted. Not a bad thought.

A stewardess bent down and smiled professionally. Did the gentleman want a drink? But surely, a nice cold old Dutch gin. He felt supremely happy as he sipped the icy, syrupy liquid and he grinned, for he had remembered what the blond baboon had said the day before. Happiness is a silly word because it has to do with security and security does not exist. True, of course. There is no absolute security and happiness is silly. How very clever of the baboon to have seen that. But there is temporary security and therefore temporary happiness does exist. Right now he was temporarily happy, and temporarily free of everything that annoyed or threatened him. Afloat in the universe. He mumbled the words, swallowed the gin, smacked his lips, and closed his eyes. He was asleep when the stewardess touched his shoulder.

"Yes?"

"We have arrived, sir."

"Ah."

He followed her, carrying his small overnight bag and the bamboo cane with the silver handle.

Giovanni Pullini's foot kicked an empty matchbox rather viciously. He had been waiting for a while near the airport's security barrier, guarded by two carabinieri. The carabinieri clutched short-barreled machine guns, and their dark eyes, in which passion and ferocity were equally mixed, scanned the crowd of incoming passengers. One of the passengers would be the commissaris de la police municipale d'Amsterdam, whom Giovanni Pullini had been talking to two hours before. He had no idea what the man looked like but knew that the foreign policeman would be carrying a cane. Pullini didn't know what the commissaris wanted although he could guess. Pullini didn't like guessing. A vague but sensuous smile lifted his mouth as a bevy of stewardesses pranced past in high heels, bosoms raised, eyelashes flapping rhythmically.

The smirk faded as his predicament flashed through his mind again. His wide shoulders bulged under his custom-made sharkskin jacket and his short squat body moved a little closer to the barrier. His long eyebrows frowned above the deep-set eyes in a round red face. He felt his balding head. His head wasn't of much use to him now. It was only telling him that he might be in trouble, real trouble, and he hadn't been in real trouble for a long time. The opposite was true, he had been doing very well. And he shouldn't be at the airport now, it was lunchtime, he should be in the country restaurant he owned. He should be listening to Renata, the charming lady who ran the restaurant and who lived in the beautifully furnished apartment on its second floor, an apartment he was getting to know better than his own house. A commissaris with a cane. He saw an old man, a thin little old man, limping toward the barrier. The devil himself, the devil in paradise.

Pullini's smile was soft and charming when he shook hands and took the commissaris's overnight bag.

"You had a good flight, commissaire?"

"Yes, thank you. I slept."

A few minutes later they sat on the rear seat of a large car, a new car of a make the commissaris didn't recognize. The limousine was chauffeured by a dreamy young man in a turtleneck sweater of exactly the same tender blue shade as the car.

Pullini pulled down the armrest and his strong, sun-tanned hand adorned with two rings, each holding a large diamond, dug into its soft upholstery. The commissaris's eyes flitted up and observed Pullini's face. Pullini's heavy thoughts were filling the car. The commissaris was thinking too. He had planned his attack early that morning, in the garden with the turtle rummaging around his feet and his wife fussing in the kitchen, coming out every ten minutes to refill his coffee cup. He had looked forward to meeting Papa Pullini, but now that his prey was next to him, breathing heavily through nostrils bristling with long dark hairs, he didn't feel like upsetting the man. Perhaps some rapport had been established between the two, for Pullini's face turned slowly and his lips formed a single word.

"Non?"

"Non."

Pullini's grip on the armrest loosened.

"We go to hotel now. In Sesto San Giovanni. Saint Giovanni. Same name as me, but me no saint." He laughed and the commissaris laughed too. A joke.

"Small hotel. Comfortable. One night, yes?"

"One night."

"You have bath, sleep a little, go for a walk maybe, and then I come and we drink some wine. Good wine. Later we eat, we talk."

Pullini's smile was innocent, childlike, and hurt the commissaris. He was sure that Pullini had tried to contact his son immediately after their conversation of that morning. But there hadn't been much time. Chances were that Pullini still knew very little. He would know about

Mrs. Carnet's death, for Francesco would have reported such an important event in the connection between the Pullini and Carnet firms.

"Did you speak to your son this morning, Mr. Pullini?"

"I try. I phone hotel. I phone Carnet and Company. Francesco, he
not there. I want to ask Francesco what happened that is so important
that Amsterdam police commissaire comes to see me in Milano. Police,
they do not like to spend money, yes?"

"Yes."

Pullini was holding his smile. The smile displayed a glitter of gold
and very white artificial teeth, well made and suitably irregular. He
raised his hands. "Commissaire, I know nothing."

"Do you know what happened to Mrs. Carnet?"

The red face froze. "Yes. She dead. Francesco, he tell me. An accident, yes? Or maybe no? You do not travel to Italy for accident."

An enormous truck pulling an equally enormous trailer zoomed past
blasting its horn. The limousine's chauffeur flicked his wheel. His employee's equanimity seemed to calm Pullini.

"O.K."

The word was out of place between the gigantic billboards screaming
their advertising in poetic, flowing Italian on both sides of the autostrada.

The car turned off the main road and began to follow a narrow cob-
blestoned path winding through fields planted with ripening corn. The
nondescript office and factory buildings that had lined the autostrada
gave way to long cracked-tiled divisions screening the rustic peace of
the countryside. There were rows of high trees, a dam with a wa-
terwheel, and a high bridge that had to be negotiated in low gear. The
commissaris saw farmhouses built like low, square fortresses defending
themselves behind forbidding walls, centered on courtyards overshad-
owed by umbrella-shaped chestnuts and tall poplars.

Pullini pointed out a low pink and gray building. "There I was born,
not farmer's son, laborer's son, in shed. Shed no longer there. Burned in
war."

The simple elements that formed Pullini's face proved to be capable
of forming fairly complicated expressions, even combinations of oppo-
sites such as sadness and triumph.

"You were happy on the farm, Mr. Pullini?"

"No. My father, he works. My mother, she works. Me, I also work.
Always. Feed pigs, shovel shit, pigshit, cowshit, horseshit. Also chickenshit. Chickenshit, he worse. Chickenshit, he burns. All in same wheelbarrow. Wheelbarrow bad. Push like this."

Pullini leaned over and groaned, trying to hold the wheelbarrow.

"Sometimes it falls over. Then I shovel same shit twice." He held up two fingers. "But I had birds. Pheasants. Partridges. Beautiful birds. They walk around like this: titch-titch-titch. Baby birds."

His hand moved around on the floor of the car, making short, swift movements. "When they grow I sell to farmer. Farmer, he eats my birds. But every year new nests and new birds. One year I buy peacock, but only money for one, so no baby peacocks. Farmer, he takes peacock."

"Did he pay you?"

Pullini laughed, a soft, full bellylaugh that gurgled in his throat. "No. Farmer says peacock eats too much feed so he takes him for courtyard. Farmer looks at peacock, me, I listen. Peacock shouts, 'Giovanni! Giovanni!' and I listen. Then I know one day Pullini must work for Pullini. That better."

The car turned sharply. They had come to a village. A man greeted the car, then two women who came out of a store, then another man from the doorway of a shop. The greetings were elaborate. The subjects waved and inclined their heads respectfully. Pullini raised his hand but he didn't wave. He only showed his hand. The driver also reacted by lifting a finger of the hand holding the wheel. The car's nose pointed at a three-story brick building and stopped. A neon sign above the building's double front door said RISTORANTE PULLINI.

"Very nice." The commissaris pointed at the sign. "You have another restaurant, I hear, in the mountains somewhere, I believe?"

"Who tell you?" Pullini's chest bent over the armrest; a whiff of garlic touched the commissaris's face. "My son?"

"Mr. Bergen told me."

Pullini's gold fillings flashed. "Yes. Bergen, he eats very much, but kitchen has plenty of spaghetti, plenty of sauce, plenty of sausage. Also veal, tender veal from Holland, many lires a gram. Bergen, he likes meat. That restaurant in mountains same as this one here, same kitchen. This cook, he teaches cook in mountains. Before, restaurants were bad, just one dish, spaghetti and tomato sauce and sometimes fish, old fish. Now better. We try later tonight, yes?"

The car moved again, following a narrow side street with only centimeters to spare on each side, and emerged into a small sunlit square. A policeman in an olive uniform and carrying a gigantic sidearm in a dazzlingly white gunbelt came to attention. Pullini got out and shook the constable's hand. The driver slid from behind the wheel. The commissaris rested on his cane. The square was quiet, medievally quiet, paved with gleaming yellow stones, dappled by the light caught and softened in the foliage of protecting oaks. Shrubs grew in enclaves on the narrow pavement and songbirds chirped from cages hung under the arc of a gate.

Pullini's hand nudged his elbow and the commissaris remembered his business.

"Yes, thank you, Mr. Pullini. What do you think about Mr. Bergen?"

"Bergen," Pullini said, feeling the word with his thick lips. "Bergen, he all right. He buyer, I seller. He buys, he pays. Sometimes he pays late, and Francesco telephones and talks about this and that and then Francesco says 'Money' and Bergen, he pays. And sometimes he comes here."

"You think he is a good businessman?"

"Half."

"Half?"

"Half. Bergen is salesman. Big salesman, not big buyer. He, how do you say?" Pullini tried some Italian words and the commissaris held up his hands in apologetic despair. "You don't understand, no? Here." Pullini breathed in and his chest swelled up. He kept his breath. A foolish grin spread over his face and his eyes narrowed.

"I see," the commissaris said gratefully. "A showoff. He tries to impress, is that it?"

Pullini breathed out. "Yes. But Bergen all right as long as he pays. That other man, he better. I forget name of other man." Pullini bent and swung his arms. His lips pouted. He frowned.

"Mr. Vleuten?"

"Yes. The monkeyman. He better. But he gone now. One time Francesco thinks maybe monkeyman he marries Mrs. Carnet and take business. Vleuten, he good businessman. Bergen, he sells, to anybody, any price. Like Francesco, but Francesco, he learns, he changes. Bergen, he never learns."

They had arrived at the hotel. Pullini had puffed himself up again and was strutting around the car's bumper, leading the way to the hotel. The commissaris followed slowly. Pullini waited.

"And Gabrielle Carnet, what do you think of her, Mr. Pullini?"

Pullini's face fell. "Me, I don't know Gabrielle. Francesco, he likes her. Gabrielle, she beautiful, yes?"

The commissaris nodded firmly. "Yes. She is."

Pullini whistled. The butt of the small cigar the commissaris had given him rolled on his underlip. He scratched his nose.

"Now maybe Carnet and Company finished."

"Possibly."

"Never mind. We find other company, Holland has many companies. Pullini furniture is good, good quality, good price. Maybe I go to Holland now. Set up own office. Find good Dutchman, good Dutchman he becomes manager. Holland has many good Dutchmen. Maybe you help me, yes? You and I, do a little business?"

The owner of the hotel had come into the street to meet Pullini and the two men embraced. The commissaris was introduced with a flourish and the owner took the overnight bag from Pullini's hand. His bow to the commissaris showed servility, deep friendship, respect, and a great love. His smile flashed as he straightened up again. They were ushered into the building with another display of exuberant intimacy. The commissaris's room on the second floor was large. It had a floor of marble slabs and deep windows, each window with its own vase holding matched bouquets of wildflowers. The owner pointed at the bed as if he wanted to excuse its poor appearance but the bed was big and sumptuous, with clean crisp sheets and a stack of downy pillows. The posts of the brass frame were crowned with white and blue ceramic balls.

"Lovely," the commissaris said, and Pullini translated and patted the owner on the back. The owner pulled his drooping mustache and hunched in a tremendous effort to comment on the compliment. He found a word: "Happy!"

"Yes. Happy."

The commissaris and the owner beamed at each other. The owner opened a door and showed the bathroom. More marble, once white but aged to a delicate shade of ivory. A tub with brass faucets. A brass tank resting on solid oak.

"Hot," the owner said proudly.

Pullini and the owner linked arms and marched to the door. They bowed together. "I come back seven o'clock. O.K.?"

"O.K., Mr. Pullini."

"Have bath, sleep, then walk. Sesto San Giovanni very small, can't get lost."

"Sure. Thank you."

The commissaris sighed as he lowered himself into the bath. His legs felt like two thin dry sticks that had been thrown into a roaring fire. The steaming water would calm the pain once more. A maid had brought a pot of strong tea and he poured himself a cup that rested on the tiled rim of the bath. He forced himself not to think of further developments and made pleasurable little noises instead as the water swept along his legs and hips and reached his chest and shoulders. He even sang, a wordless song consisting of grunts that lengthened and flowed into each other. He sipped his tea and stopped singing. The case had grabbed his mind again and the image of Papa Pullini dominated the stage of his brain.

If only Papa Pullini had married Elaine Carnet. But perhaps it had been too much to expect. A young Italian businessman romancing with a nightclub singer in Paris. All very well. But she gets pregnant. The young Italian businessman fades away. The months pass. The beautiful nightclub singer doesn't sing anymore. She watches her body grow in an upstairs bedroom in Amsterdam. She writes letters on blue perfumed paper. There is an answer, on the Pullini furniture company's letterhead. It is not a romantic letter. It avoids the subject of pregnancy and it doesn't mention the matter of marriage. It offers an agency in furniture. The commissaris's hand came down and hit the bath water. For God's sake! What a way to handle the problem. But a way that suited Papa Pullini's temperament and it had worked. He didn't know how it had worked and he would probably never find out. Had Elaine left her baby in the care of a relative or paid help and traveled through Holland by train and visited the big stores? Had she shown her prospective customers a catalogue and a price list or had she organized a showroom somewhere and enticed clients to look at her wares? The preposterous fact was that Carnet and Company was born together with Gabrielle. He hit the water again with such force that some of it splashed into his teacup. He put the cup into the tub and pushed it around. Papa Pullini had been very clever and very businesslike but it would have been better if he had married Elaine, for if he had Francesco wouldn't have pushed his father's former mistress down the garden stairs of her house in the Mierisstraat. A long chain of events crinkling through a space of thirty years, but set off by Papa Pullini's brilliant egotism.

He imagined the final scene, knowing that he had to be very close to the truth, that he might as well have been in the room, together with Gabrielle, who saw her lover and half-brother kill her mother. Manslaughter, of course, provoked manslaughter, there had been no premeditation in the act. He saw Elaine Carnet, dowdy and painted to hide the lines and folds caused by loneliness and bitter thoughts and continuous frustration. Drunk, most likely. And angry, vengeful. Convinced of her right, snarling with victory. She had been waiting for Francesco, she had probably telephoned him at his hotel. She had created the situation and was, finally, in charge of her circumstances. Francesco had come for one simple reason, his eighty thousand guilders that Bergen hadn't paid and that he couldn't tell Papa Pullini about, for Papa Pullini didn't know that his son had organized a private commission on all sales to the Dutch firm. Francesco didn't know why Elaine Carnet wanted to give him the money instead of Bergen and he didn't care, all Francesco wanted was his cash.

He had gone as a helpless beggar and he must have been in a foul mood. Bergen had been threatening not to give him any more orders. The business might be ending then and there. His trip to Amsterdam had turned into a nightmare. He wasn't feeling well either, he was sniffling and sneezing. And instead of handing him a discreet brown envelope to be stuffed into his inside pocket Mrs. Carnet had been waving the money at him, a thick wad of thousand-guilder notes, a small fortune that he desperately needed to pay for his expensive private pleasures. She had screamed. It had taken him awhile to understand what she was screaming about, but it became clear soon enough. She was explaining, in French, and at the top of her voice, that Papa Pullini was Gabrielle's father and that he hadn't married her but had made her work for him instead, to enlarge the Pullini business. That there had been no choice. That she had had to give Papa Pullini business to pay for the upbringing and education of his own child, Gabrielle, Francesco's half-sister. That she had known, all along, that Francesco and Gabrielle were having an affair, that history was repeating itself. That she knew that Francesco had married in Italy, a rich girl with the right connections, just as his father had done twenty-odd years ago.

Francesco hadn't answered her. He had sat in his chair, his handsome bearded head resting on his slender hands. He had wanted her to stop screaming. But she went on and on, repeating herself, waving the money, dropping some of it and picking it up again. She wasn't going to give it to him. She was only showing it. She would keep it as a small repayment for a lot of suffering. It was hers. Money squeezed out of the pockets of Italian lovers who took their girls for long walks in the moonlight, who sent flowers and beautifully wrapped presents, who slithered into the girls' beds and who performed so admirably only to slide away in the night if the relationships proved to yield more problems than pleasures.

The gale shrieked around the house as Francesco sat listening and the woman screamed on, her lips bubbling with venom. And when she paused it was only to remember swear words in both French and Italian, flinging them at him as they came to her. She had taken off her wedding ring, wrenching it off her finger. She threw it on the floor and it rolled toward his feet and he stared at it. Francesco was having difficulty understanding Mrs. Carnet. His French was bad, but he did know some words, and he gradually began to fit together what the crazy woman was telling him. His nerves stretched even more tautly as a fresh torrent of abuse burst free. Mrs. Carnet's voice had dropped now; she was whispering and her insults had the sharpness of a dagger. The dagger slid into his feverish, aching brain.

"But times have changed," Mrs. Carnet was whispering. Oh yes, times had changed. Girls were no longer helpless and had woken up to the hardness and cruelty of the male world that would use and manipulate and discard them if it was given half a chance. Papa Pullini hadn't liked to use anything when he made love and neither would Francesco. Men didn't like a film of rubber to come between them and their pleasure. They wanted all their pleasure, and if their pleasure led to their girlfriends' sorrow, well, what of it? They were up and away, hunting for fresh game. But now girls had the pill and they didn't get pregnant unless they wanted to. And girls had many lovers now, as many as they pleased.

Did Francesco know that he was only one of Gabrielle's lovers? That Gabrielle only accepted his embraces because he happened to please her for the time being? Other men were asked to come to Gabrielle's apartment upstairs, and they were told to go when she no longer needed them. Gabrielle didn't care so much about Francesco. Gabrielle didn't even care that Francesco was her half-brother. For she knew. She had been told, just now, just a few days ago. Francesco could go back to Italy and never come back and Gabrielle would replace him, just like *that*. And Mrs. Carnet stepped forward, leering, and snapped her fingers in his face.

And it was the last thing she ever did, for Francesco jumped her and tore the money out of her hand and pushed her to the open garden door. They fell together and Francesco came back alone, to face Gabrielle, who hadn't moved from her corner throughout her mother's final performance. They had probably gone down into the garden together and ascertained Mrs. Carnet's death. Perhaps Francesco had cried and Gabrielle had comforted him, she might have stroked his hair. Perhaps Gabrielle had hated her mother and pitied her half-brother. Perhaps she had always wanted a brother and her love could have changed but not ended.

The commissaris pushed the teacup; it filled with soapy water and sank onto his legs. Gabrielle still had a portrait in her room, close to her pillow, that resembled Francesco's features. What did he know about a woman's love? Gabrielle also loved the baboon, for she carried his omen, his symbol, between her breasts. She might have protected

Francesco out of love, but it could also be that she was levelheaded enough not to want the police to meddle with someone who was her lover, her brother, and an important business contact, the man who controlled the supplies of furniture that her firm depended on. Whatever her motives, she had covered up the mess, removed Francesco's glass, wiped everything his hands might have touched, and sent him back to his hotel. She hadn't telephoned the police but the ambulance service, hoping that her mother's death would be filed away as accidental.

And she had allowed him to leave with the money but had probably contacted him again later, very likely early in the next morning, and had arranged for him to return the cash so that she could pretend to find it. And Francesco had been honest enough to return the full hundred thousand. That Mrs. Carnet had waved a hundred notes at him instead of the eighty she owed would have been due to her state of nerves. She had simply added the twenty notes she had just received from the baboon, perhaps to make the wad thicker and more impressive.

Perhaps Gabrielle was a courageous girl who should be allowed to take care of her own life and not be charged as an accomplice to a serious crime. But as the killer's half-sister she might be excused, although she would be charged. The commissaris looked at the submerged cup and thought of refloating it but began to climb out of the tub instead. He wouldn't let Francesco off, for Francesco had pushed a lady down her own garden stairs and the lady had broken her neck. The young man should have had the sense to confess, but he might still be manipulated into a confession. It would help his case and soften the lesson. And this trip was part of that manipulation, but so far it had only resulted in a pleasant hour in a marble bathtub. He found his watch and began to dress. There was still plenty of time. He would go for a walk.

The commissaris had walked for no more than a quarter of an hour when he found himself on a long narrow road with a low wall on each side. He had come to the end of the village and the road was leading to a confusion of small fields, all carefully planted with vegetables. He had just decided to turn back when he saw a small green truck roaring around the next curve. A disreputable pickup with a snarling, lopsided grille set between rusted headlights that wobbled on dented mudguards. As the truck hurtled toward him he recognized its driver, a young man in a light blue turtleneck sweater, the same imperturbable young man who had driven Pullini's limousine. He thought of raising his hand in greeting when he realized that the pickup was coming straight at him, that its left wheels were on the sidewalk, and that its mudguard was razing the crumbling wall. The pickup was sounding its hoarse little horn, but there was nowhere for the commissaris to go, and he pointed his cane at it in a futile gesture of defiance.

17

SERGEANT DE GIER LOOKED at the square electric wall clock that had been hanging, for as long as he could remember, on an improbably thin and bent nail stuck loosely into the soft plaster of his office wall. The clock had said five to eight and had just moved, with an ominous faint click, to four to eight.

"It's morning," he said, and his voice reverberated through the empty room. The hollow, artificial sound sent a shiver through the base of his neck. "It's *very* early in the morning," he whispered. There had been no coffee in the machine in the washroom and he was out of cigarettes. The cigarette machine in the hall was out of order. The tobacconist's wouldn't open up until after nine. Cardozo and his plastic pouch filled with crumbly, cheap, shag tobacco were nowhere to be seen. Grijpstra and his flat tin of cigars hadn't come in yet. The commissaris's office was securely locked. There was nothing to do but to stare at the clock and at his desk calendar, which showed no entries at all.

"First things first," de Gier said and jumped up. He had heard a sound in the corridor. He pulled the door open and jumped out and collided with a uniformed secretary from the traffic department. Her blue jacket showed the stripes of a constable.

"Darling," de Gier murmured, and he clasped the dumpy girl in his arms and breathed against her thick spectacles. "You smoke, don't you? Tell me you do."

The constable had dropped her shoulderbag; her spectacles were sliding down her short broad nose.

"Yes," she said into de Gier's shoulder. "Yes, I do, sergeant."

"Half a pack," he whispered. "Give me half a pack and maybe I can do some work today. Catch the horrible killer, grab the pernicious poisoner, trap the blond baboon. Please? Beloved?"

Her glasses dropped, but he extended his chest, and they caught on the top button of his jacket. He plucked them away, released the girl, whipped out his handkerchief, and polished them before replacing them gently onto her nose and sliding the stems over her ears.

"You shouldn't do that," the girl said. "You are a pig, sergeant." Her breathing was still irregular but her tight little smile had a hard twist to it. "So you're out of cigarettes?"

"Yes, darling," de Gier said, "and I caught your spectacles. They would have broken if I hadn't caught them and you would have been blind as a bat, they would have smashed to smithereens on the nasty floor."

"I won't give you any cigarettes," she said firmly, "unless . . ."

"I'll kiss you," de Gier said. "How's that?"

"On your knees!"

"What?"

"On your knees!"

De Gier looked around. There was nobody in sight in the long corridor. He dropped onto his knees.

"Repeat after me: 'I am a male chauvinist!'"

"I am a male chauvinist."

She opened her bag and took out a pack of cigarettes. De Gier looked at the brand. It was the wrong brand. Long and thin and low on tar and tasteless and with holed filters that would let the smoke drift away before it could reach his mouth. His lips curled down, but she was watching his face, so he smiled pleasingly.

"I'll give you four, that's all you're worth." She counted them out on his palm.

"Well, well, *well*," Grijpstra said.

The girl was on her way, her heels tapping firmly on the thick linoleum of the corridor. De Gier had got up.

"Well what, adjutant? I was out of cigarettes."

Grijpstra's grin was still spreading. "Ha!"

"Ha what, adjutant?"

"Pity Cardozo wasn't here. There he is! Late again, always late."

Cardozo looked at his watch. "Five to nine, adjutant."

"Never mind."

They went in together. Cardozo was sent out to buy coffee and to pay for it out of his own pocket. De Gier puffed on his cigarette, threw it on the floor, and stamped on it. Cardozo came back.

"Give me your pouch, Cardozo, and some cigarette paper and a light."

Cardozo put the coffee mugs down and fished a crumpled plastic pouch of shag tobacco from his pocket. "Do you want me to smoke it for you too, sergeant?"

De Gier reached out and took the pouch. The three men smoked and drank coffee and stared at each other. Grijpstra sighed. "Well . . ."

"Yes?"

"It seems the case is solved. I saw the commissaris's secretary just now. The old man has gone to Milano, he's due back tomorrow. He telephoned her last night and wanted Papa Pullini's number in Sesto San Giovanni, a little town close to Milano. The round-trip ticket to Milano must cost a bit of money and he wouldn't be wasting it, would he now?"

De Gier stretched and began to cough. He glared at Cardozo. "Terrible tobacco, you should change your brand." Cardozo tried to say something but winced instead.

"Right," de Gier said. "So Francesco is our man, as we thought, but there's still a chance that we're wrong, for the commissaris could be wrong too."

Grijpstra yawned.

"Small chance, but still . . . Let's go through it again: Why did we pick Francesco?"

"We picked Francesco," Grijpstra said patiently, "for a number of reasons, all of them flimsy and none of them good enough to stand up in court."

"Let's have the reasons."

"O.K. We agreed that whoever smokes long thin cigars with plastic mouthpieces made to resemble ivory must be a vain man. We had three suspects, apart from Gabrielle. All the suspects were vain. Bergen is a nicely dressed gentleman if he isn't going to pieces in the privacy of his own home. The baboon is a strange-looking man, but he takes great care about the way he looks, and Francesco dries and sets his lovely hair with a dryer and sports a silk dressing gown. All three suspects are vain, but Francesco wins the race. A very faint hint, but something to go on if we can bring up supporting hints.

"A man who pushes a lady down the stairs is violent. We couldn't picture Bergen pushing Elaine and we had trouble imagining the baboon in that position. The baboon is violent, for he got you in the river, but you are a man, not a nicely dressed lady in her own house. Francesco could be an excitable young fellow and he had some sort of a motive. He thought the Carnet firm owed him eighty thousand guilders and we knew that Elaine Carnet took out eighty thousand in cash from her company's bank account. The figures tally, she had the money the evening of her death, and Francesco could have visited her. Suppose she showed him the money but wouldn't give it to him so he jumps her, right?"

"Hmm."

"It was your idea," Grijpstra said, "and I agreed with it. Eighty thousand guilders form a motive. What motives could Bergen and the baboon have?"

"The wedding ring."

"Yes, sergeant, a powerful indication. A wedding ring on the floor and the lady was never married. Yet she wore a ring. And she threw it on the floor that evening; it didn't just drop off her finger. Marriage, love or the lack of love."

"Humiliation," de Gier said.

"Exactly. Women like to humiliate men these days. You were on the corridor's floor a little while ago, groveling. You wanted a cigarette, I believe, and the girl was using her power."

"What?" Cardozo had jumped up. "The sergeant on the floor? What happened?"

"If you had been on time you would have seen what was happening. A female constable had our sergeant on the floor, on his knees, whining."

"Really?"

"Let it go," de Gier said, "I was only play-acting. You're right about the humiliation. So you're saying that Elaine Carnet had her future killer in a position where he felt silly and his pathetic predicament had something to do with her wedding ring. But Francesco is a young man, he couldn't have made Elaine Carnet pregnant way back in nineteen forty-five or forty-six."

"Papa Pullini could have. Papa Pullini is a businessman and he was a businessman in nineteen forty-five too. He must have traveled. We know he speaks French, Bergen told us so. Maybe he went to Paris, strayed into a nightclub, saw the beautiful singer, bought her a bunch of roses, started a romance."

"So she waits thirty years and revenges herself on Papa Pullini's son, is that what you're saying?"

Grijpstra got up and walked over to the window.

"Very weak," de Gier said softly. "Now what if Bergen was the wicked father? Or the baboon? They're the right age."

Grijpstra turned around. "I know. But the commissaris went to Milano. I thought of Bergen too, but why would she pick him as a business partner? And the same goes for the baboon. She worked with both men for many years. Why would she work with a man, and allow him to share her profits, if she had every reason to despise that man? And where do the eighty thousand guilders fit in? And the twenty thousand that the baboon borrowed and returned? That money does exist. Did you count the money Gabrielle showed to you, Cardozo?"

"Yes, adjutant. There were one hundred thousand guilder notes, eighty new, twenty slightly used."

Grijpstra's index finger came up. "See, sergeant? The money was there. Francesco took the lot and rushed out of the house. He counted the money in his hotel and found more than he expected. He phoned Gabrielle. She told him that she had removed his fingerprints and that he was safe but that he should return the money to her. She probably promised to pay him the eighty later, officially, out of the firm's account —she could make that promise for she inherits the firm, Bergen only owns a quarter of it, she could override all his decisions. I am sure Francesco would have given the twenty back anyway. I don't think he's a robber, he just wanted what was due him."

"And he killed Elaine in anger," de Gier said slowly. "That'll help him in court, if he confesses. He should come and see us and give himself up, that's why the commissaris didn't want us to make an arrest while he was away."

"Exactly."

"Adjutant?"

"Yes, Cardozo?"

"But Elaine was a bit of a bitch, wasn't she? She knew that her daughter was having an affair with Francesco and that Francesco was Gabrielle's half-brother. She could have stopped the affair, couldn't she?"

Grijpstra shrugged. "Perhaps, but Gabrielle might not have cared. I would say that Gabrielle's real feeling is for the baboon and that Francesco was something on the side, strong enough to protect him against us but still . . . She jumped at you at the drop of a hat, didn't she? She probably has lots of sex, here, there, and everywhere."

Cardozo blushed.

De Gier got up too and joined Grijpstra at the window. "I don't know, Grijpstra. Elaine had an affair with the baboon and he got himself out of it, even at the expense of losing his job. Next thing we know is that Gabrielle dives into his bed. Elaine may have known. There may have been a terrific scene between mother and daughter, which would explain the wedding ring on the floor too. Gabrielle kills her mother. That way she has the business and the baboon and is free forever after."

"And who was smoking the cigars that evening?"

De Gier walked back to his desk. "True. It would be nice if we could prove that angle, wouldn't it?"

"Here," Grijpstra said.

They all looked at the long narrow tin of cigars the adjutant had placed on de Gier's desk. "Signorinas, made in Brazil. I found this tin late last night, had to wake up my cousin who owns a tobacco store. Expensive cigars for successful businessmen, my cousin doesn't sell too many of them. He says they are really excellent cigars. Maybe he is right, I tried one and they taste rather perfumed. Cardozo can take the tin and check the cigar counter in the Pulitzer Hotel and all the tobacconists around it. He should be able to come up with a statement that says that a man of Francesco's description bought the cigars on the evening of Mrs. Carnet's death. The statement won't mean too much in court, but it'll mean something. At least we'll be able to prove that Francesco was lying when he said that he didn't visit Elaine Carnet on the evening of her death."

Cardozo took the tin and left.

"Anything else we can do while the commissaris is away?"

Grijpstra grinned. "Sure. We can go to the snack bar around the corner and drink some real coffee and enjoy a quiet twenty minutes. And then we might go and visit the baboon again."

"Why?"

"Why not? He's an interesting man, isn't he?"

"O.K. And Bergen?"

"He's having more tests this morning, but I think we should contact him later in the day. They've all been lying, of course, hiding facts. Everybody has been hoping that we'll give up and consider the easiest way out."

De Gier nodded. "Write it off as an accident. Good, we'll go and shake them, but I don't think it's necessary. The commissaris is bound to come up with something conclusive."

"I think I'll become a mercenary," de Gier said a little later in the snack bar. He held up the paper and showed Grijpstra a photograph of a fat, jolly black man in a general's uniform. "This guy has killed a few hundred thousand people in his country, why don't we go and get him?

Why must we go after a tiny little Italian who doesn't really mean any harm?"

Grijpstra choked on a meat roll. De Gier waited.

"The Italian is here," Grijpstra said finally, when he had finished coughing.

"We could go there, couldn't we?"

"I am here too."

"And if you were there?"

Grijpstra took the paper and looked at the photograph. The fat general was still smiling. Grijpstra stuffed the rest of the meat roll into his mouth. He chewed for another minute.

"Well?"

"I would kill him," Grijpstra said and wiped his mouth. "It would be fun. We could think it out carefully, make it look like an accident, set up some sort of a trap. The commissaris would like that too. He could sit in his bath and build a trap out of subtleties, do it step by step, each step a little more slithery than the one before, create a safety system for the general's protection, for instance, but the system suddenly malfunctions and poof!"

Grijpstra's fingertip tapped the general's forehead. They walked to the counter together. Grijpstra stepped back so that de Gier could pay.

"Yes," de Gier said, "the commissaris would like that."

18

"VERY VERY SORRY," Pullini said. "I will buy new truck for Eraldo. That old truck, he has bad brakes. I warn him many times but Eraldo, he keeps driving truck. Eraldo, he says you broke your cane, yes?"

The commissaris felt in his pocket. He put the handle on the table. Pullini picked it up. He shook his head in silent consternation.

"Nice handle, beautiful handle. Maybe I can get you new cane. Really very sorry. Eraldo, he could have hit you, yes? Fortunately he turned wheel just in time, but say he had not, then what would happen? Commissaire de la police municipale d'Amsterdam dead in Sesto San Giovanni. Accident, of course. Constable here, he says accident. Eraldo, he says accident. Many witnesses say accident. But you, you dead commissaire."

The commissaris took off his glasses and began to polish them. His eyes twinkled. The wine had been excellent, so had the meal. Proper gourmet food, exquisitely cooked. A lovely salad. Even the ice cream had been outstanding, and the service could be called personal, very personal. Renata had served every dish and had hovered around the table in between courses, managing to be both inconspicuous and lovely.

He couldn't argue about Pullini's good taste as he couldn't have argued with Eraldo's little green pickup that had missed him but had taken his cane and crushed it. Eraldo was, indeed, a good driver. Pullini's chauffeur had taken his chances, another fraction of an inch and the commissaris would have been caught by the sleeve, whirled around, and smashed into the cobblestones. As it was he had fallen, but the truck, in spite of its alleged absence of brakes, had stopped a few hundred feet down the road and come back to pick him up. Eraldo had been most apologetic and solicitous. He had brushed the commissaris's jacket and helped him into the truck's cabin and delivered him at the Ristorante Pullini. A good show.

"Now," Pullini said, rubbing his wide hands, "we have eaten and now we talk. Something I understand now. Francesco, he has been silly, Elaine, she has been also silly. Sillier, for now she is dead."

"Did you speak to your son this afternoon?"

"Oh, yes." Pullini smiled benignly. Yes, he had finally got through to Amsterdam. Francesco was quite sure that the police suspected him of having pushed Mrs. Carnet down the stairs, and he was also quite sure that he was caught. His passport had already been taken away, soon he might be in jail.

"And did he kill Mrs. Carnet?"

Pullini's right hand balled up and began to turn. Well, perhaps something did happen. But it was an accident, of course. There had been a scene, a terrible scene. Francesco was very upset, also on the telephone. Perhaps Papa Pullini should have told his son about the romantic adventure so long ago, and so far away, all the way to Paris.

Pullini poured more wine, barola, a rich wine. He spilled a little, and Renata's lithe body came between them to sprinkle salt on the stain. Pullini was talking volubly. He had been in Paris at the time to buy luxuries that could be sold to the American officers in Milano. It had been a good time, but difficult, for he had to learn so much. Fortunately some of the American officers had spoke Italian. That had been a help, but even so. He was gesturing wildly. Even so, a struggle, yes. But he had earned the capital necessary to buy his furniture business. And he had enjoyed himself in Paris.

"Where you met Elaine Carnet?"

"Oh, yes, surely."

"But you didn't marry her. Why not, Mr. Pullini?"

Amazement spread over Pullini's gleaming cheeks. Marry a nightclub singer? A foreigner? When he had just invested his entire capital in a furniture factory? He needed connections in those days. He needed textiles to upholster his furniture, didn't he? And the young lady he married was the daughter of a textile manufacturer.

"So Francesco thinks we may put him in jail?" The commissaris asked the question gently, patting his lips with the snow-white napkin that Renata had just handed him.

He had taken a few seconds to admire Renata. She had noticed his admiration and the raven-black eyes had flashed. Pullini had noticed too. He was grinning.

"You like her, yes?"

"Beautiful," the commissaris agreed.

"Renata, she sleeps upstairs. Perhaps we can have a small glass with her later, yes? Restaurant, he close soon."

"Jail," the commissaris reminded his host.

Pullini laughed. Yes. Francesco is such a dear boy, he imagines things. Pullini suddenly looked sad. He launched into another monologue. Police officers in Italy are very badly paid, so thoughtless of the government, no doubt it was the same in Holland. Police officers are hard-working officials, but who thinks of them as they risk their lives in the middle of the night chasing the bad men? Or nearly get run over by a truck in a foreign country? So many police officers think of themselves sometimes and arrange a little this or that. Pullini's balled hand was turning again as if it wanted to bore a hole into a wall. Police officers know many people. Perhaps some of those people would be connected with the furniture trade. It might be possible that a certain commissaire would like to be connected with a certain furniture business, say, on a monthly basis. Or yearly. Part of the profits. A little more wine, perhaps?

"Yes," the commissaris said and smiled benevolently. Another glass of barola, a majestic wine.

"So?" Pullini asked.

"No, sir. Perhaps Italian police officers are badly paid but the Dutch police cannot complain. The salaries are quite adequate. And they are not so interested in business; business has to do with buying and selling and distribution and so on, a different kettle of fish from what Dutch police officers are used to doing for a living, Monsieur Pullini, very different."

Pullini wiped his face. His eyes, slightly bloodshot, became calm. He picked up his glass but it was empty, and Renata moved closer. He waved her away.

"Your leg," Pullini said quietly, "it hurts, yes?"

"Yes, I suffer from rheumatism."

Ah. Pullini's eyes gleamed again. He knew all about rheumatism. His mother, old Mrs. Pullini, bless her soul, also suffered from rheumatism, but she had gone to the mountains and there, no more pain. She was dead now but her last years were peaceful years. No pain, no pain at all. The mountain air is clean and quiet and known to cure many ailments. And it so happened that he, Pullini, had a little chalet for sale, a beautiful chalet. The price, for a friend, would be very reasonable, almost nothing in fact, maybe even nothing at all. A token payment so that the deed could be passed and registered in the friend's name.

The commissaris held up his glass and Renata filled it.

The raven-black eyes flashed, the hips swung smoothly, the narrow skirt split and there was a glimmer of a firm white thigh.

"Maybe," Pullini said quietly, "maybe we go upstairs now and we talk about chalet, yes?"

But the commissaris was shaking his head. "Non."

Pullini breathed out. The breath took a number of seconds and seemed to take all the air out of his body. He sank back in his chair. When he spoke again his voice was low and precise.

"Commissaire, what can you prove against my son?"

The commissaris put his glass down. "Enough, sir. There are statements by witnesses. Your son has lied to us and we can prove that he lied. My detectives are working now but we don't really need any more proof. The judge will convict your son."

Pullini looked at Renata. He was smiling helplessly.

She held up the bottle and he nodded.

"So, commissaire, why you not arrest my son? My son, he is in hotel, yes? Not in jail."

"Your son must confess, sir. He must come and see us and tell us what he did, how he did it, and exactly why he did it. He must describe everything that happened."

"Why, commissaire?"

"It will be better. Your son did not murder Elaine Carnet, he only killed her. He didn't plan her death. He got angry and he pushed, that's all."

Pullini's heavy body had straightened up. He was staring at his opponent. His hand pressed and pushed the tablecloth.

"Yes? So all right, Francesco, he confesses, then judge, he sends Francesco to jail. How long?"

"Not so long."

"Years?"

"Months. There are extenuating circumstances. Our charges will be modest. But he must come to us, he must tell us what he did."

A cold calculating light had crept into Pullini's eyes. "So he confesses, so very easy for police municipale d'Amsterdam, not so? Police, she maybe know nothing, she maybe guesses, and here stupid Italian boy, he walks right up and he says, 'Me, I guilty, please take me.'"

"No, we know what he did. If he doesn't come we will have to take him from his hotel. The case will be much worse."

Pullini's mouth tried to sneer but the expression trembled away before it had a chance to form itself clearly. The sneer became a joyless smile that did little more than show Pullini's expensive teeth.

"You trap me, yes? Me, I tell you that Francesco, he pushes Elaine. I know because Francesco, he tell me. He also tell me about the eighty thousand guilders. He already confesses, to accident and to stealing from his father. I knew about the stealing, not how much, but that not important. His life different to mine, for Francesco everything easy from beginning, too easy. Maybe better to start off with baby birds and one peacock. Well . . ."

His hands rose slowly from the tablecloth, then dropped from their own weight. "You trap me, yes. But how do you know all this? How you know Gabrielle is Pullini's daughter?"

Once his cleverness had left him Pullini's face changed strangely, perhaps to its truest form. The powerful jaws smoothed into round, innocent lines that continued so that they held the bald skull too, and the eyes, bereft of their cunning glint, became bland and almost transparent.

The commissaris's small thin hand was pointing, and Pullini turned around to see what he was pointing to. A portrait of a young woman singing, the woman's smooth arm resting on the top of an upright piano.

"Elaine," Pullini said. "Yes, that is Elaine. *Was* Elaine, thirty years ago in Paris. But she must be changed in thirty years, Francesco, he did not know her like that. You, you never knew her. How you know that is Elaine? You guessing again, yes?"

"There is another copy of that portrait." The commissaris told Pullini where he had seen it.

Pullini nodded. "Two portraits, eh? Elaine, she keep one, and she send me one. In parcel; no letter, no nothing. Just portrait. I like it and I hang it here, in my restaurant where I eat every day. Me, I don't go home much. But no proof for you, commissaire. You, you do not know that Elaine, she sends portrait to me. You only see portrait when you come here."

"It is proof now," the commissaris said, holding up his glass. Renata brought a new bottle of barola. The other guests had left; the two men had the restaurant and the woman to themselves. Renata locked the door and switched off most of the lights. There was no further conversation until Renata opened the door and the two men entered the narrow street and walked the few blocks to the hotel, arms around each other's shoulders, swaying in unison.

"Tomorrow you go, yes?"

"Yes."

"Me, I go with you. What time your plane he leaves?"

"At ten in the morning."

"Good, we breakfast together, yes?"

"Yes."

Barola is a good wine. It seeps away both aggression and resistance. Their embrace was quiet and dignified.

"Me, I am sorry about Eraldo's truck. But I tried, yes? Eraldo, he good driver. When he is told to miss, he miss."

"Yes," the commissaris said.

"Tomorrow I buy you new cane. I have handle. Same handle, new cane."

"Yes."

They peered into each other's face. A half-moon had dipped the small quiet square into an eerie haze of soft white light that encircled the vast dark mass of a widely branched oak, a comforting central ornament caressing the cobblestones with its deep purple, almost imperceptibly moving shadows. The commissaris watched Pullini's squat body turn ponderously. Pullini could still walk on his own, but he had to find his way slowly in the square's silence, stopping every few steps to make sure of his direction. Three identical little Fiats, pushing their noses into the pavement, provided support in turn until Pullini, with a final lunge of great deliberation, located the gaping dark mouth of the small alley that would take him back to his restaurant and Renata's comforts.

The commissaris shook his head and began to walk to the hotel door. He noted, to his surprise, that he had sobered up again and that he wasn't even tired. It seemed a pity to withdraw from the square's tranquillity and he turned back, feeling the polished surfaces of the cobblestones through the thin soles of his shoes. He rested for a while against the oak's trunk until he began to feel cold and pushed himself free reluctantly.

The case was solved. He had been very sly, basing his attack on shaky proofs and a web of deductions that fitted but could be shaken loose by any lawyer for the defense. If he had given himself more time the proofs would have been substantiated sufficiently to stand up in court, but he had been pushing the case at breakneck speed. But Francesco would no doubt confess now and make further work unnecessary.

The prosecution wouldn't be too hard on the suspect and the punishment would be mild. That, in a way, was a pleasant consequence of the method he had applied.

But why had he been in such an infernal hurry? Yes. His small head nodded firmly at the hotel door's polished brass knob. There was more to the case, and he had better get back to see how the pus, festering out of the wound slashed by Pullini when he refused to marry Elaine, was spreading. Perhaps he should have had the other actors, the baboon, Bergen, and Gabrielle, and Francesco too, locked up. But it isn't the task of the police to lock up citizens who are potentially dangerous to each other. Jail space is limited and reserved for those who have translated their faulty thinking into wrong acts. He had better get back quickly. But he would have to wait for the morning plane. And meanwhile he could have another bath. When nothing can be done it is not a bad idea to do nothing. The profundity of the thought helped him up the hotel's stairs.

19

WHEN GRIJPSTRA TURNED the key of the Volkswagen in the garage of headquarters, a voice grated from a loudspeaker attached to the roof directly above the car.

"Adjutant Grijpstra."

"No," Grijpstra said, but he got out and trotted obediently to the telephone that the garage's sergeant was holding up for him.

"Yes?"

"A message came in for your brigade, adjutant," a radio room constable said. "A certain Dr. Havink called, about a Mr. Bergen. Dr. Havink didn't ask for you in particular, but he mentioned Mr. Bergen, and one of the detectives told me that he had read the name in the Carnet case file."

"Yes, yes, very good of you, thank you, constable. What was the message?"

"This Mr. Bergen has disappeared or something. I didn't really catch on, but I've got Dr. Havink's number here. Would you call him please, adjutant?"

"Yes." Grijpstra wrote the number down, waved at de Gier, and dialed. De Gier picked up the garage's second phone and pressed a button.

"Dr. Havink? CID here. I believe you called just now."

The doctor's voice was quiet, noncommittal. "Yes. I am concerned about a patient, a Mr. Bergen, Mr. Frans Bergen. Does that name mean anything to you?"

"It does, doctor."

"Good, or bad perhaps, I wouldn't know. The point is that Mr. Bergen had a nervous breakdown in my office this morning and left before I had a chance to stop him. According to my nurse, the patient was talking to himself and kept on mentioning the words 'police' and 'killing.' Would you like to come to my office or can I explain over the telephone?"

"You say Mr. Bergen has left, doctor? Did he say where he was going?"

"He left and didn't say where he was going, and he appeared to be very upset. My nurse says that the patient kept on patting his pocket and that it's possible that he was carrying a firearm."

"Go on, doctor."

The doctor's report was clear. Bergen had arrived that morning at eight-thirty for his final test. The test was designed to determine whether or not the patient's skull held a tumor. The patient's blood had been colored and the blood's flow through the brain had been checked. The result was negative, no tumor. The patient had been asked to wait in a small room adjoining the doctor's study. The door between the two rooms was ajar so that Bergen could see what the doctor was doing. Dr. Havink had been looking at the results of another test, nothing to do with Bergen. The results of that particular test had been positive, a case of brain cancer in an advanced state. While Bergen waited, Dr. Havink had telephoned a colleague to discuss the other patient's test.

"Ah," Grijpstra said. "I see, and Mr. Bergen could hear what you were saying on the telephone."

"Yes, most unfortunate, I should have made sure that the door was closed. It usually is, but it wasn't this morning."

"Go on, doctor, what did you tell your colleague?"

Dr. Havink's meticulous voice described the course of events. He had told his colleague that the test's results were of such a definite nature that he didn't think that the patient had more than a week to live and that an operation would be useless. The conversation had taken about five minutes, and during that time Bergen must have left the small waiting room and gone back to the main waiting room, where, according to the nurse, he began to pace about and talk to himself in a loud voice.

"And pat his pocket," Grijpstra said.

Yes, and pat his pocket. Mr. Bergen talked about the police, about money, and about killing. Then he left. The nurse tried to stop him but he pushed her aside. And so Dr. Havink called the police.

"I see, I see. So we may assume that Mr. Bergen understood that your verdict referred to him. He wasn't aware that you were talking about another patient."

"Yes. I am sorry about this. It's an occurrence that has never happened before but it could have, obviously, for it has happened now. My arrangement here is faulty. The door between my office and the little waiting room should have been closed, and I should have told Mr. Bergen that I would be discussing his case with him in a minute but that I had to take care of something else first. The whole thing is pathetic, really. There is nothing the matter with Mr. Bergen. We did three tests on him and they were all negative, although the X-ray did show a small calcification, but this is nothing unusual. Still, we continue checking in such a case, routine, simple routine. All Mr. Bergen has is a facial nerve infection that will cure itself; his face should have some movement again soon, in a few days, I would say. But I didn't have a chance to tell him."

Grijpstra sighed and looked at de Gier. De Gier was shaking his head.

"Yes, doctor. Thank you for letting us know. We'll see if we can find Mr. Bergen. Do you happen to recall what he was wearing?"

"A dark suit, crumpled as if he had slept in it, no tie, open shirt. He hadn't shaved."

"Thank you."

De Gier had put his telephone down and was standing next to the adjutant. "An alert, don't you think? A general alert. Bergen will be running around somewhere. He wouldn't have gone home or to his office, but I'll check."

Bergen's home phone didn't answer. A secretary at his office said he wasn't there. "Miss Gabrielle Carnet?" Gabrielle hadn't arrived yet. De Gier telephoned the Carnet house. No answer.

"O.K., an alert, for what it's worth. The patrol cars never see very much, their windows are all steamed up."

Grijpstra telephoned the radio room. He described Bergen and added that the suspect was in a state of mental breakdown and probably armed. When he put the phone down he was smiling.

"What?"

Grijpstra prodded de Gier's stomach. "Crazy situation, don't you think? As the commissaris said, there is nothing wrong with the man, but Bergen has imagined himself into a terminal position, a good-bye maybe, or a complete breakdown that he hopes will leave him senseless. He must have slipped a pistol into his pocket before he went to Dr. Havink's clinic this morning. A pistol is a very violent instrument. He could have bought sleeping pills—he has a house of his own and a bed."

De Gier was scratching his bottom. "Sleeping pills are never very dramatic."

"Quite." Grijpstra was still smiling.

"But what's so funny?"

"Don't you see? The fellow has made all the mistakes he could make. He gets a letter from the bank that must be negotiable in some way. Banks always threaten, but if you owe them enough their threats don't stick; they can't afford to break your business, for if they do you can't pay them. But Bergen insists that his business is finished. His wife sends him a lawyer's letter and he cracks up. Can't he sit down and figure out whether he really wants her? If he doesn't want her there's no problem, he can sell his house and find a good apartment somewhere, or even a few good rooms. With his money he can find a woman to go with the rooms and state his terms. But if he really wants his wife back, well, he can find her and talk to her, can't he? There may still be an opening for an approach, but no, he chooses to rush around and mess up his house and ruin one of his cars and burn holes in the carpet."

"Very funny, what else?"

"This paralysis, of course. You heard what Dr. Havink said. It's a minor affliction, a nothing. It will go away if he has the patience to wait a few days. But he doesn't even have the patience to wait for the doctor to come out of his office, for he has already convinced himself that he is suffering from brain cancer and has a week to live and he has rushed out into the street, screaming."

"Hilarious. And now we have him wandering around, a raving lunatic with a deadly weapon. Does he have a car with him?"

"Probably. We saw a new Volvo in his driveway last night."

"So he may be anywhere by now."

The loudspeaker in the garage's ceiling croaked again. "Adjutant Grijpstra."

"Oh, for God's sake!" But the adjutant turned and marched back to the phone.

The radio room constable apologized. "We know you're busy, adjutant, but the commissaris isn't here and the inspector is out on an urgent call and I can't raise him. We have a call from a patrol. They were asked to go to an address on the Amsteldijk, Number One-seven-two. Neighbors heard a shot in the top apartment, first an angry male voice, then a shot. The constables broke the apartment's door and found blood on the floor but no one is there. The apartment belongs to a Mr. Vleuten. I have been trying to find Adjutant Geurts, he's probably out having coffee somewhere. Shall I ask him to go to the Amsteldijk when he comes in?"

"No, we'll go."

"Siren?" de Gier asked.

"No."

Grijpstra was sitting behind the wheel, the engine idling.

"Hospitals?" de Gier said. "The baboon is wounded. He isn't the sort of man to wander around. He has a car, perhaps he can still drive it."

"University Hospital," Grijpstra said. "That's where I would go if I lived on the Amsteldijk and got shot. Maybe the Wilhelmina is closer but you get stuck in traffic. Let's have that siren."

The small car dug itself into the heavy morning traffic, howling furiously. A large white Uzzi motorcycle appeared, and de Gier shouted at the constable riding it.

"University Hospital, lead the way."

The constable saluted. The motorcycle's siren joined in, and the Uzzi reared and shot away with the Volkswagen trailing its gleaming suave form while cars stopped and bicycles fled to the pavement.

"Easy," de Gier shouted as the Volkswagen's fender ground past a streetcar's bumper, but Grijpstra didn't react. He sat hunched behind the wheel, twisting it to make the car follow the motorcycle. The car's engine whined and the sirens howled on gleefully.

The dented Volkswagen swung into the hospital's parking lot and came to rest next to the baboon's Rolls-Royce, shining in splendid isolation between a row of mud-spattered compacts. The motorcycle cop waved and rode off as Grijpstra and de Gier clambered out of the car and began to run toward the emergency entrance. A nurse directed them, and they found the victim sitting on a plastic chair in a small white room. Gabrielle sat on the bed, swinging her legs.

"Very good," the baboon said, looking at his watch. "I got shot an hour ago and here you are already. The deadly detectives."

Grijpstra grinned.

"But I'm all right," the baboon said, and he pointed at his bandage. The bandage hid his short neck and his left ear. "A minor wound. If Gabrielle hadn't insisted I would have used a Band-Aid."

"And he would have bled to death, the doctor said so."

"And I would have bled to death."

"Who?" de Gier asked.

The baboon was rolling a cigarette.

"Who?"

The baboon looked up. "A bad man. I won't tell you. He is in enough trouble now without your adding to it."

"Oh," Gabrielle said, "you are such a *fool*, baboon. Sometimes you overdo it, you know. If you don't tell them I will."

"Who?" De Gier's voice hadn't changed. He felt very patient.

"Bergen, of course. He came running into the apartment waving a gun and holding his face. He was such a *mess*."

"But why the aggression? What does Mr. Bergen have against the baboon?"

"Gabrielle being with me didn't help much," the baboon said and felt his bandage. "This scratch hurts, you know. Do you know that the cow's skeleton saved me?" The baboon began to laugh, a pleasant rumbly laugh. "You should have been there. Gabrielle didn't have any clothes on and all I had was a towel, and Bergen kept standing there, shouting away. I pressed the button and the cow came out of the cupboard, directly in his path, so he had to jump aside and he couldn't aim, but the bullet did make contact and I fell, so he probably thought he had got me and ran. And meanwhile the cow had made its full circle and gone back into the cupboard. And Gabrielle was holding her breasts and screaming." The baboon was wiping his eyes.

"Yes," Gabrielle said, "very funny. And I am to blame, of course. Francesco phoned last night and foulmouthed me too. As if it's my fault that I'm his half-sister. He has forgotten that I have been helping him, but I won't help anybody anymore."

"So will you make a statement now, Miss Carnet?"

"About what?"

"That Mr. Pullini pushed your mother down the stairs. We do have some sort of a witness's statement but it isn't enough."

"Anything," Gabrielle said, "anything you like. I'm tired of this tangle. That idiot Bergen thinks he can be jealous too, and that he can use me. *Nobody* can use me." Her voice no longer purred and her eyes seemed to have shrunk and were glittering with fury. De Gier took his chance.

"There was something between you and Mr. Bergen, Miss Carnet?"

"Something? What is something? We have been on business trips together and maybe we had a little too much to drink and maybe I let him get away with being such a powerful male. That was a long time ago, a year maybe. But he fussed. He fussed so much that his wife heard about it and finally left him."

"He thought he loved you?"

"Love." Her eyes narrowed and her lips pouted.

"You didn't love him?"

"Of course not."

The baboon had gotten up and was walking to the door.

"Are you leaving, Mr. Vleuten?"

"I may as well. I was waiting for the nurse to come back but it seems she won't. I have things to do. So have you, I imagine."

"We'll have to find Mr. Bergen."

The baboon stopped near the door. "Where?"

"Exactly. Where could he be?"

The baboon turned and leaned against the wall. "A good question. Have you seen him recently? I was wondering what brought on this sudden attack? He was shouting a lot but I didn't understand him."

Grijpstra explained.

"Cancer?"

"He thinks he has cancer, that he has a week to live."

The baboon fingered his bandage. "I see. So I became the enemy. I've been the enemy before, when he thought I would marry Elaine and take the business away from him. But I didn't and I thought that obstacle was removed. Maybe it wasn't, maybe he kept on blaming me."

Grijpstra leant his bulk against the wall of the sterile little room and smoked peacefully. "For taking Miss Carnet away?"

"Possibly. But there were other reasons. He was manufacturing them, ever since we met, I think. Perhaps it started when I was bringing in a lot of orders."

"Jealousy?"

The baboon was still stroking the bandage. "More than that, I think. Bergen never felt very secure. He didn't want to blame himself so he found me. The fact that he took a shot at me just now may prove that theory."

Grijpstra looked at the smoke crinkling out of his cigar. "You won, he lost. Quite."

"Not quite. Unless you can define what constitutes the ideas 'to win' and 'to lose.'" The baboon's eyes were twinkling.

"Yes, Mr. Vleuten?"

"You should have seen that damned cow. Zooming at him and then turning and disappearing again. I would never have thought that the thing would protect me. I had constructed it for the absolute opposite. It was supposed to frighten me."

"Oh, you're so *crazy*." Gabrielle had snuggled into the baboon's arm. She was looking into his face, touching his cheek gently with her pointed nails.

"I'm not so crazy," the baboon said. "I'm just trying to do things from a different angle. Only trying. It's hard to go against the flow, maybe it's impossible. What happened this morning rather underlines that, doesn't it? I create an object of fear, maybe ridiculous to others but really fearsome to me, and it saves my life. But I won't give in."

"Mr. Bergen," de Gier said firmly, "we've got to find him. Do you have any idea where he is, baboon?"

"Bergen is under great stress. He is wandering around," Grijpstra added. "You must have gotten to know the man fairly well. Can you think of any place Bergen would go if he thought he was in real trouble?"

The baboon was looking out the window. "Yes," he said slowly, "yes, perhaps I know."

"Where?"

"He surprised me once. I always thought the man had no soul, you know, that he was only concerned with selling furniture. But we came back from a trip once, in his car, and we were late, we had been speeding, for he wanted to be home in time for dinner. When we got near the city it was after seven o'clock and he said his wife wouldn't have waited for him and he turned the car off the highway. We went to a little village on the river and had dinner there and some brandy afterward, and later we went for a walk."

"He went to that village on purpose? You didn't just happen to find it on your way?"

"No, he knew the place, he had been there before. He told me that his father used to take him to the village sometimes and that they would always have dinner in that little pub and then go for a walk. We ended up in a small cemetery, very old, with moss-covered stones, and we walked about. He seemed very peaceful that evening. I had never seen him like that before."

"What's the name of the village?"

"Nes. I can take you there. Nes on the Amstel. Only a few houses and a church and the pub. We had to cross the river in a little ferry to get to it."

De Gier had opened the door. "Shall I get the water police?" he asked Grijpstra.

"No. Why don't you go with the baboon and Miss Carnet can come with me. I'll follow the Rolls. Nes is only about a quarter of an hour from here. Perhaps we'll still be in time. If we get assistance we'll delay ourselves unnecessarily. What sort of handgun did Bergen use, baboon?"

"A revolver."

"He only took one shot at you?"

"Yes."

"So he has five bullets left." Grijpstra groaned and sighed simultaneously.

"A nice little job. Shall we go?"

20

IT TOOK AWHILE before Grijpstra had time to talk to Gabrielle. He was busy with his radio while the Volkswagen, gray and inconspicuous, followed the regal backside of the Rolls along the road clinging to the river. The radio room had connected him with the commissaris, and their conversation was linking their separate adventures.

"Very well, sir, so Papa Pullini is now at the hotel talking to his son?" Grijpstra looked at the microphone. He hadn't released the button yet, so the commissaris couldn't reply. "And you expect Francesco to come in sometime today to make his peace with us?"

The button sprang back and the commissaris's soft voice mixed with the high-pitched sound of the car's engine and the squeak of its battered shock absorbers.

"Yes, adjutant, that side of the case should be fixed. Cardozo will be here to take their statement, I think he'll be able to follow Francesco's English. Cardozo tells me that he's found the tobacconist that sold the cigars Francesco smoked when he visited Mrs. Carnet. I think I'll be joining you and the sergeant presently, but I'll probably arrive too late. You have almost reached Nes, you say?"

"Almost, sir, I can see the ferry sign, it should be just around the corner, and the village should be a few hundred yards farther down."

"Right. I'll be there as soon as I can. Out."

Grijpstra replaced the microphone and turned to Gabrielle. "You've had an exciting morning, Miss Carnet."

"It's still going on." She had used the time to adjust her makeup and comb her hair and seemed to have recovered some of her composure. "A real crisis, isn't it? I never expected Bergen to lose himself so completely. He was a raving maniac when he attacked the baboon. I'd gone into the bathroom when the bell rang, but when I heard the shot . . ."

Grijpstra mused. He remembered the young woman who had shot her husband. It had happened a few weeks before, early in the morning. Just after nine, he and de Gier had just gone out on their patrol and were waiting at the first traffic light. The couple was about to get divorced and the man had been ready to go to work when his wife shot him in the face, point-blank, with no more than a foot between the pistol's muzzle and the man's forehead. She had telephoned the police herself, and the detectives had arrived within a matter of minutes. The woman was crying when de Gier took the weapon out of her hand. A hopeless case. The couple had a little son, four years old, wandering about in the apartment. Father dead, mother in jail. They had taken the boy to the crisis center; he hadn't dared to check what they had done with him. The crisis center wasn't a good place to check with, its staff was continuously overworked. He hoped that the center had found good foster parents and that the boy wasn't being shifted around.

Gabrielle was talking and he forced himself to listen.

"Was he really saved by that crazy contraption, miss?"

Gabrielle kept her eyes on the Rolls's rear bumper. "Yes, he must have been. The crazy skeleton, I knew it was there. He never showed it to me but I pressed the cupboard's button once, thinking it was a light switch, and I became hysterical when the horror lunged out at me. Crazy, like the baboon himself. Just look at that car. There's hardly any money, between his mortgage payments on his house and the rents he is collecting and he has to pay for the upkeep, there are always lots of repairs. He is living on a few hundred guilders a month, but if he takes me out he won't let me pay and we go to a sandwich bar somewhere and we sit in the front row of the cinema. But he runs a car like that. When he can't afford to pay for gas he takes the streetcar; often he walks."

"Doesn't he sell boats?"

She shrugged. "There isn't much profit in that, either. I wish he'd come back and work for us, he could have a good income and he'd be worth it too."

The Rolls had parked near the ruins of a mill, and the baboon and de Gier were walking to a small brick building almost hidden under a patched thatch roof. Grijpstra squeezed the Volkswagen between the Rolls and a tree.

A hunchbacked man behind the bar was pumping four beers and listening to de Gier at the same time.

"Yes," he said, deftly wiping the beer's foam into the counter's small sink, "he was here. About an hour ago. Had a few beers and drank them through a straw. First time I've ever seen beer drunk through a straw."

"Was he talking to himself?"

"No. He was quiet. I've seen him here before. A well-behaved gentleman, but he looked somewhat scruffy today. Out on a binge, is he?"

"Yes. Where would he be now?"

"Should I tell you?"

De Gier produced his police card, and the man took a pair of horn-rimmed spectacles from a drawer. He studied the card and tugged on the end of his scraggly mustache. "Police, hmm. Never see police here except the local constable and he's my brother. Nice job if you can avoid the poachers but he can do it. You'll be different, I suppose."

Grijpstra drank his beer and the hunchback left the bar and peered through a side window. "That's his car, I think, so he can't be far. Seems he wanted to hide it, you can't see it from the road."

The baboon came to life at his end of the bar. "There's a cemetery close by, I remember. Where is it again, not far, is it?"

"Out the front door, turn right, first path on your right again, and you'll walk straight into it."

De Gier paid and they left the pub, but Grijpstra paused at the door. "It would be better if you stayed here, miss."

"No."

"Stay here," the baboon said. Gabrielle took a deep breath, but the men were out on the dike and the door had closed in her face.

The sun hung under a ragged edge of heavy clouds and its filtered light seemed to deepen the green of the grasslands all around them. A herd of spotted, light-colored cows was grazing close to the fence and a flock of unusually neat-looking sheep was moving away on the other side of the path.

"An experimental state farm," the baboon said. "I remember Bergen telling me about it. They have imported types of cattle here, special breeds. Bergen seemed to know all about the farm. I remember because he had never expressed any interest in anything that wasn't furniture. He was a different man out here."

A falcon hung above the field, whizzing its wings, its stiff pure white tailfeathers sticking out like a miniature fan.

The baboon pointed. "The cemetery. There's no cover here, he'll be able to see us coming."

Cartridges clicked into the chambers of the policemen's pistols. De Gier had taken the lead, sprinting toward a high gravestone so old that its writing had been eaten away by the weather and overgrown by thick, bristly lichen. The first shot rang out as he reached the stone, and Grijpstra and the baboon dropped into the grass on the sides of the path.

"Bergen!" Grijpstra's booming voice reached into the depth of the soundless cemetery that stretched away from them, aloofly tolerating their intrusion.

"Bergen! Come out of there! We're here to help you. You have misunderstood Dr. Havink. There's nothing the matter with you, Bergen. Come out and let us talk to you." Grijpstra's voice, even with all the air in his lungs behind it, sounded calm and reassuring, but the cows, pushing each other behind a duckweed-covered ditch, mooed mournfully and offset his message. Grijpstra gestured at the baboon. The baboon pushed himself up.

"Down! Stay down there. You'll only be in our way and you are wounded already. Get those cows to shut up."

The baboon crawled back and jumped across the ditch. The cows were still jostling each other, trying to see what was going on, and he grabbed the biggest one by the horns and pushed. The cow didn't move. His attempts startled a pair of peewits that flew up from behind a cluster of swamp reeds, calling shrilly.

Grijpstra got up, ran, and dropped behind a tombstone crowned by three miniature angels that had once played trumpets but were now staring sadly at their broken arms. The closest angel had lost both its nose and chin and weeds were crawling up its chubby legs. Grijpstra peered around the legs.

"Bergen! You're all right. You only have palsy, no tumor. You hear! No tumor. There has been a mistake. Bergen!"

The cows mooed again furiously, irritated by the baboon, who was still shoving their leader.

"Palsy," Grijpstra shouted. "It will go away by it—"

There was another shot, this time aimed at de Gier, who had left his gravestone and was without cover as he jumped to the next. He dropped as the shot cracked, and the bullet whistled away in the general direction of the cows.

"Fool!" Grijpstra roared and de Gier looked around, waving a weed with small pink flowers that he had picked from a spot where the stone had powdered away so that nature could reassert itself. He was close enough to be able to speak to Grijpstra in a normal voice.

"You know what this is?"

"Keep your cover."

"Thousand-guilder weed, Grijpstra, *Centaurium erythraea,* one of the very few I know by its Latin name. Fairly rare, I believe, but it grows near the streetcar stop and I took some to the city's botanical garden the other day. Amazing, don't you think? It grows all over the place here."

"De Gier," Grijpstra said pleadingly, "he must be close. It's hard to hear where the shot came from. These stones echo, I think, but he must be over there."

"Where?"

"There, near that damned prick."

"Prick?"

Grijpstra was pointing at a heavily ornamented phallus, sprouting a poll of withered grass on its crumbling extremity. It was nearly six feet high and throned on a huge granite slab.

De Gier moved and drew another shot. They heard the bullet's dull impact where it hit the earth; a tufted reed sagged and broke with a snap as the tuft touched the ground.

"How many bullets left?" de Gier asked.

"One for the baboon, three for us, two left."

"Can I move again—we'll have to draw the other two—or do you want to sit here all day?"

Grijpstra picked up a rock and threw it at a patch of dandelions that brightened a complicated ruin of several tombs that had tumbled together. The revolver cracked again.

"Bergen! Stop making an ass of yourself. We won't charge you, just get out of there. You're safe. We want to help you."

"Let me be!" Bergen's voice was high-pitched, hysterical with fear and rage.

"No, you're being senseless."

Several cows mooed simultaneously. Grijpstra tried to move and slipped; his face fell into a patch of raw earth and he sat up, spitting out dirt. He saw de Gier take aim carefully, supporting his right arm with his left. The pistol's bark was sharp and was followed immediately by the heavier retort of the revolver.

"Got him," de Gier shouted, "in the arm. And he's out of bullets. Come on, Grijpstra."

They ran but Grijpstra stumbled, and de Gier stopped to help him.

They reached Bergen in time to see him press the revolver against his temple. They were both shouting but the shot drowned their words. Bergen's head snapped to the side as if it had been hit by a sledge-hammer, and his body tumbled against the phallus and slid down slowly until it rested on the grave's rubble. A small pile of cartridges had been stacked neatly into a cavity on the gravestone's surface.

De Gier took out his handkerchief and manipulated Bergen's revolver so that its chamber became detached. Its compartments were empty except for one. He closed the gun again and let the hand drop back.

"He just had enough time to slip in one more cartridge."

"Yes," Grijpstra said. "If I hadn't stumbled we would have got him in time. What a mess." He pointed at the blood seeping out of the corpse's head. It was trickling off the stone and mixing with another little stream pouring out of the man's arm. De Gier looked away. Grijpstra replaced his pistol into the holster on his belt and stretched. His back ached. It was very hot, and he thought of the cool pub on the dike and the cold beer that its polished barpump would splash into a polished glass.

When he turned he saw the commissaris running up the path, and he waved and shouted. The commissaris was supporting himself on a cane with a metal handle; he limped as he ran.

"Don't run, sir, it's all over."

The baboon had jumped back across the ditch and was moving through the fallen gravestones, waddling on his short legs. He reached the corpse at the same time as the commissaris.

"We tried to draw his fire, sir, and rushed him when we were sure the revolver was empty. De Gier had put a bullet in his right arm so we were doubly sure. But he had extra ammunition and he used his left hand."

The commissaris had knelt down and was examining Bergen's head. "Pity," he said quietly. "The skull must be badly damaged on the inside."

"He is quite dead, I think, sir."

"Oh, yes, that's clear. Dead. But there's something else, this case goes on, adjutant. Well, never mind. I'll think of something, but it's a pity about the skull."

21

DE GIER'S BALCONY DOOR was open and the commissaris was sitting close to it, peering contentedly at his mug. De Gier faced him. He was coming to the end of his flute solo, a sixteenth-century drinking song, full of trills and quick runs and occasional short intervals of almost mathematical precision. Grijpstra, his bristly mustache white with beer froth, was rubbing Tabriz's belly, smiling at the cat's droopy look of complete surrender. Cardozo was stretched out on the floor, his head resting on a small cushion propped on a stack of books.

De Gier lowered his flute. The commissaris inclined his head and applauded briefly. "Very good. Get him another beer, Grijpstra. Pity you couldn't bring your drums, it's been a long time since I heard you play together."

Grijpstra lumbered into the small kitchen and came back holding a fresh bottle. De Gier poured the beer, spilling a little. "I won't be able to play anymore, sir, the neighbors will be at my throat tomorrow."

Grijpstra had brought in another bottle but the commissaris shook his head. "I would like to, adjutant, but it's getting late, my wife'll be expecting me. Cardozo, how do you feel?"

Cardozo's eyes opened. He seemed to be thinking. The commissaris smiled. "Go back to sleep. I don't think either of us should drive."

It was past midnight. The lights in the park behind de Gier's apartment building had been switched on sometime before but the opaque white disks, spread among the willows and poplars, couldn't compete with the moon. The apartments around had gone to rest, and there were no sounds except an occasional rumbling from the boulevard on the other side of the building and the confused squeaking of a group of starlings that hadn't found the right tree for the night yet.

"We'll take a taxi. You can drive the Citroën to headquarters tomorrow, sergeant," the commissaris said firmly. "One of my colleagues got arrested for drunken driving last week. It reminded me how vulnerable we are."

"A brandy, sir?"

De Gier had struggled to his feet and was groping about behind his books. His hand came back holding a crystal decanter. Grijpstra's heavily lidded eyes were watching him.

"Just a nip, that would be very nice."

"A bad case," the commissaris said a little later. "But it's over and done with now. I didn't like it. There was too much pettiness in it."

Grijpstra stirred. There was a vague note of admonition in his voice. "We did have the baboon in it, sir."

The commissaris raised a finger. "Indeed. Its one ray of illumination, and he stayed true to type until the very end, you know . . ." He looked at the balcony. Cardozo had begun to snore softly, but his cushion slipped away, and he woke up and pushed it back.

The commissaris sipped his brandy thoughtfully. "You know, I thought he would give in and I didn't want him to give in. The baboon was drifting into a perfect, happy ending."

The commissaris giggled. "But he smartly stepped aside. Good for him. Happy endings are always so sad. I even thought so when I was a little boy and my mother would read fairy tales to me. I would cry when the princes married the princesses and settled down in the beautiful palaces. Whatever were they going to do forever after? Watch football or cartoons? Play cards? But the stories didn't tell, they didn't dare to, of course. Just suppose that the baboon would marry Gabrielle and move into that splendid home on the Mierisstraat with the sheik's tent upstairs. Just imagine."

He put the brandy snifter down and brought out his handkerchief, wheezing into it energetically. "Our baboon, spending his nights on Gabrielle's couch while the young lady gradually sucks his soul away, wasting his days back in the furniture business, lodged safely in Bergen's office, swiveling around on the president's chair, taking care of things."

"The Carnet Company will probably have to declare bankruptcy," Grijpstra said tonelessly, as if he were reading from a report.

"Oh, yes. Unless they have somebody on their staff who can take over, but that's rather doubtful. Or Gabrielle . . . no. I don't think she can do it. But the baboon can, easily. And he would be rich too, I don't think he would need more than a few years to get the company back on its feet and the bank would be sure to back him. Remember what Bergen told us? The bank liked the baboon."

"Why do you think the baboon refused to become the company's president, sir?" De Gier's voice was flat too.

"The *opposite,* dear boy," the commissaris said. "The *opposite.* Surely you've noticed." The commissaris blinked and took off his spectacles. "You *must* have noticed. You are leading an old man on. Or do you want me to confirm what you have already concluded yourself?"

"Please confirm it, sir."

"What would the average man do if something frightened him? He would run away, wouldn't he? He would prefer to get away from whatever was causing him pain or anxiety. And if he could get hold of it he would try to kill it, or hide it somewhere deep in his mind so that he couldn't get close to it again, and so that it wouldn't be able to get at *him.* But the baboon recreated what he feared and kept his enemies in easily accessible places, on the wall of his apartment and in the cupboard. He set up his fear in such a way that it could charge him. You saw the rat's tail hanging out of that painting, de Gier. You must have, for you are frightened of rats yourself. Would you have a painting of a rat in here? And would you make it more gruesome by allowing the hellish fiend to let his tail hang out, right into the intimacy of your home?"

De Gier's face didn't move. His large eyes were staring at the commissaris.

"No. Don't answer me, you don't have to. We are discussing the baboon. He likes to do the opposite of what seems to be expected of him, and perhaps he evades the trap that way. He accepted neither Elaine's nor Gabrielle's offer. And yet he had worked for the Carnet ladies for ten years, had been their chief salesman and their close friend, their lover even. They were offering him the whole caboodle, lock, stock, and barrel, with themselves thrown in. And Gabrielle's offer was even better than her mother's had been, for she is an attractive young woman."

Cardozo had woken and had pushed himself up against the bookcase.

"A most reasonable offer. The intimate pleasures Gabrielle can dispense plus a firm that, if properly managed, should yield half a million profit a year over and above a director's salary."

The commissaris coughed as if he had said too much. His eyes strayed back to the balcony. De Gier had replaced the plants that had been either torn or swept right out by the gale. A profusion of begonias covered the balcony's cast-iron railing and their top leaves shimmered in the moonlight like small, succulent, live coins.

"Another brandy, sir?"

"Just a nip, a small nip, I must really be on my way."

The crystal decanter appeared once more, and the commissaris sniffed the fragrance of the thick liquid pouring into his glass.

"Your health, sergeant. Yes, the baboon was worth meeting. We won't meet him again. He was sucked into the case by a lonely woman's desires, a woman he might not have liked very much once he got to know her too well. I didn't like Elaine Carnet either. Fortunately I didn't have to, she was dead when we began. Bergen was worse. I should have liked him for he needed our help, but I couldn't make the effort. A fool, sergeant, of the worst variety." He looked into his glass. "Perhaps because he lived on the surface, doing what he thought was proper, following the stream without ever bothering to consider where it was taking him. Well . . ."

"Has Mr. Pullini gone back to Italy, sir?"

The commissaris brightened up again. "Oh, yes, I took him to the airport this morning, after we had breakfast in the Pulitzer, a very enjoyable breakfast. You haven't met him, sergeant, have you?"

"No, sir."

"Pity. A dangerous man in a way but good to be with. We had a marvelous time in his hometown together. Papa Pullini visited Francesco in jail last night. Francesco isn't comfortable but he is reasonably contented. Nobody in Italy should ever find out what happened to him here. He is supposed to have gone on an extended business trip and will be back at the end of the year."

"He will only get a few months, sir?"

The commissaris nodded. "Yes, the prosecutor wasn't too impressed with our charges, fortunately. The charges will stick, of course, they are well documented. Mr. de Bree's statement, Gabrielle's statement, Francesco's own confession, Cardozo's report about the cigars. The defense hasn't got a chance, but even so, just a few months, I would say, and we'll be able to escort Francesco to the airport before the year is over. A beautiful case in a way, a textbook example of provoked manslaughter. It will probably be known as 'the Italian furniture dealer's case' and will be used in examinations."

"And Dr. Havink, sir?"

"Dr. Havink? I thought you would ask me about Mr. de Bree. I would think that de Bree's crime was worse than Dr. Havink's. I find it very difficult to feel compassion for a man who tries to kill an animal by poisoning. But he did it out of love for another animal, our good friend Tobias. Interesting, very. I hope the judge will probe the case deeply and I'll be in the court listening. Yes, that would be most interesting. I hope he'll get that elderly female judge, she has a brilliant mind."

"I would like to hear more about Dr. Havink, sir," de Gier said slowly. "I read your reports, but you didn't waste too many words and you made the arrest on your own."

The commissaris drained the rest of his brandy and smacked his lips. De Gier reached for the flask. "No, sergeant, very kind of you, but no more. Well, what can I tell you? A greedy man. It's amazing that medical specialists with high incomes can be that greedy and also that stupid. They can't see their own motivation in spite of all the intelligence they are undoubtedly equipped with. He told me that he practiced his little tricks because he had to pay for his equipment, all that computerized electronic gear he needs for his brain tests. He assured me that the equipment was benefiting humanity. Nonsense. The city doesn't need Dr. Havink's gadgets, our hospitals are overequipped already, and our crippling taxes are partly due to our paranoid fear of death. Why should we have private clinics where already available equipment is duplicated?"

"Yes, sir, but how did you get him?"

The commissaris waved at the begonias. "Ah, the good doctor was so easy to trap. I couldn't use Bergen's skull anymore, it was too badly damaged, so I used my own. I have a friend who is a neurologist and I asked him to arrange for an X-ray of my head. Easy as pie, sergeant, easy as pie. My skull showed no calcifications. Oh, sure, it showed some, but nothing abnormal. Nothing behind which a nasty little tumor could hide. Then I went to Dr. Havink, who had never met me, and registered as a patient suffering from intolerable and chronic headaches. He hemmed and hawed and told me that he would need to photograph my skull. Very well. He did and showed me the photograph. Sure enough, a white spot. And the whole rigamarole about the tumor. Of course it might be nothing, and if it was something it might be harmless, but still, one never knows. Better to be on the safe side. Surely. So would I undergo further tests? Yes, yes, yes. Please. The results of the tests were negative and I was sent on my way again. No mention of money, for I had told him I worked for the municipality and had given him my insurance policy's number. No trouble there."

"And then you asked him for the photograph with the white spot?"

"Yes. And I whipped it off his desk and ran off with it. He was shouting at me, but by that time I was out the door. My neurologist friend compared the two photographs, which were altogether different, of course."

"Falsification and embezzlement."

"Yes, sergeant. And I went back the next day to arrest him. You read my charges, I'm throwing everything at him. He, and some of his colleagues, are manipulating the ignorant by playing on their fears. An old game of the medical profession, it's been with us since the first medicine man went into his trance. They used to charge two pigs and a goat. Now they clean out the insurance companies and the insurance companies grin and raise their premiums. A very old game, sergeant. Cardozo! Rise and shine."

De Gier telephoned for a taxi, which arrived within minutes, and walked his guests to the elevator.

Grijpstra was on the balcony when de Gier came back.

"Closed," de Gier said as he began to gather the debris of the little party.

"What? The bar?"

"Never. No, the Carnet case."

"I'll have a brandy. I saw where you hid that decanter, there's still a good deal left."

"But, of course. But first you can help me wash up and I'll vacuum this room. Cardozo has been sitting on his cheese and crackers and you must have walked that sausage into the carpet."

"You know," Grijpstra said half an hour later when the decanter had appeared again, "that case will still give us a lot of work. Paper shifting. Court sessions. The bloody thing has managed to split itself into three and Bergen's suicide is another inquiry. We'll be running about like ants."

De Gier looked at Grijpstra through the top of his glass. "Yes. And we'll probably be having our skulls photographed. I think the commissaris is all set to attack the doctors, that'll be fun. I wonder how many X-rays my head can stand."

Grijpstra had taken off his jacket and was loosening his tie. "Perhaps. The commissaris seemed very pleased with himself, but I hope the Havink business didn't go the way he described it. He was provoking the doctor, and the judge will throw the case out of court."

De Gier sat up. "Hey. You aren't planning to stay here, are you?"

"Of course. I'm drunk. I'll sleep in that nice big bed of yours and you can bring out the old sleeping bag. Athletes shouldn't sleep in beds anyway."

De Gier poured the rest of the brandy into his glass. "O.K., stay if you like, as long as you fix breakfast in the morning. It's a strange night, I can't get drunk, I'm as sober as when we started. And the commissaris isn't silly. I think I know exactly what he did. He had another X-ray taken after he had been to see Dr. Havink, by a third neurologist. He won't mention the first photograph in court. He'll say that he really suffered from headaches and that he went to Dr. Havink for a diagnosis and, if possible, treatment. But somehow he became suspicious of Dr. Havink's methods and had the results of the tests checked. That first photograph was only to assure himself that there was nothing wrong with his head to start with. He is clever, our chief ant."

The conversation flowed on in bursts and spurts while they had their showers and coffee. De Gier had arranged his sleeping bag so that he could see Grijpstra's face through the open bedroom door.

"Didn't you think the commissaris was rather callous about that Bergen fellow?"

Grijpstra was talking to Tabriz, who had jumped on the bed, and de Gier had to ask again.

"No. He didn't like Bergen, why should he? I didn't like him either. But the slob was dealt with correctly. Shit, we took a hell of a risk on that cemetery when we were drawing his fire, especially you with your thousand-guilder weed."

"I took some home," de Gier said. "It's in a pot on the balcony now. I wonder if it will take; weeds are hard to transplant sometimes, especially rare weeds."

"Bah. You're a detective, not a botanist. You're getting worse all the time. But Bergen can't complain. The commissaris lost all interest once he was dead, but there isn't much we can do for a corpse, especially in the case of suicide. We can't avenge his own stupidity."

"So the commissaris didn't like Bergen," de Gier said.

"Sure."

"So there are people he doesn't like."

Tabriz had put a furry paw into Grijpstra's hand and the adjutant was scratching the cat's chin with the other.

"Sure, sergeant. The commissaris doesn't like fools, certain types of fools. Especially fools who never try. There was a time when he didn't like me and he made my life so hard that I was tempted to ask for a transfer, but that is a little while back now."

"You didn't ask for a transfer, what happened?"

"I started trying again."

Grijpstra switched the light in the bedroom off. They woke up a few hours later with a start.

"What was that?" Grijpstra asked sleepily.

"Tabriz. She has got at the marmalade jar again. It broke and there'll be a mess on the kitchen floor. You better watch your step tomorrow or you'll have ten bleeding toes."

"Why does she do it?"

But de Gier had sunk away again, far beyond the boundaries of his sleeping bag, which curved on the living room floor like a gigantic banana.

"Why?" Grijpstra asked the ceiling. "Why, why, why? There'll never be an end to it, and even when you find the answers they invariably lead to more questions."

He sighed. Tabriz came out of the kitchen, jumped over the sleeping bag, and leaped onto the bed. Grijpstra's hand reached out and the cat put her paw into it. It was sticky.

"Yagh," Grijpstra said.

DEATH OF
A HAWKER

to Lenore Straus

1

"YES, MADAM," the constable said quietly. "Would you mind telling me who you are? And where you are?"

"He is dead," the soft veiled voice said, "dead. He is on the floor. His head is all bloody. When I came into the room he was still breathing but now he is dead."

She had said it three times already.

"Yes, madam," the constable said again. There was patience in the way he said it, understanding. Love, perhaps. But the constable was acting. He had been well trained. He was only concerned about finding out who was speaking to him, and where she might be. The constable had been working in the central radio room of Amsterdam Police Headquarters for some years now. He took a lot of calls. Anybody who dials two six times gets through to the central radio room. Anybody means a lot of people. Some of them are serious citizens, some of them are mad. And some of them are temporarily mad. They have seen something, experienced a sensation. The experience may have knocked them free of their usual routine, perhaps to the point where they are suffering from shock. Or they are drunk. Or they just want to talk to someone, to know that they are not alone, and there is someone amongst the million inhabitants of Holland's capital who cares enough to listen. Someone who is alive, not just a taped voice which tells them that God is Good and All is Well.

"You say he is dead," the constable said quietly. "I am very sorry about that, but I can only come to see you if I know where you are. I can help you, madam, but where do you want me to go and look for you? Where are you, madam?"

The constable wasn't planning to go to see the lady. It was five o'clock in the afternoon and he would be off duty in fifteen minutes. He was planning to go home, have a meal and go to bed. He had put in a lot of hours that day, many more than he was used to. The central radio room was manned by a skeleton staff, short of three senior constables and a sergeant. The constable thought of his colleagues and smiled grimly. He could picture them clearly enough, for he had watched them leaving the large courtyard of Headquarters that morning. White-helmeted, carrying cane shields and long leather sticks, part of one of the many platoons which had roared off in blue armor-plated vans. It was riot time in Amsterdam again. They hadn't had riots for years now and the screaming mobs, flying bricks, howling fanatics leading swaying crowds, exploding gas grenades, bleeding faces, the sirens of ambulances and police vehicles were almost forgotten. Now it had started all over again. The constable had volunteered for riot duty but someone had to man the telephones, so he was still here, listening to the lady. The lady expected him to come and see her. He wouldn't. But once he knew where she was, a car would race out and there would be policemen in the car and the lady was now speaking to the police. Police are police.

The constable was looking at his form. Name and a dotted line. Address, and a dotted line. Subject, dead man. Time, 1700 hours. She had probably gone up to call the dead man for tea, or an early dinner. She had called him from the corridor, or the dining room. He hadn't answered. So she had gone up to his room.

"Your name, please, madam," the constable said again. His voice hadn't changed. He wasn't hurrying her.

"Esther Rogge," the woman said.

"Your address, madam?"

"Straight Tree Ditch Four."

"Who is the dead man, madam?"

"My brother Abe."

"You are sure he is dead, madam?"

"Yes. He is dead. He is on the floor. His head is all bloody." She had said it before.

"Right," the constable said briskly. "We'll be right there, madam. Don't worry about a thing now, madam. We'll be right there."

The constable slipped the little form through a hole in the glass window which separated him from the radio operator. He waved at the operator. The operator nodded, shoving two other forms aside.

"Three one," the operator said.

"Three one," Detective-Sergeant de Gier said.

"Straight Tree Ditch Four. Dead man. Bloody head. Name is Abe Rogge. Ask for his sister, Esther Rogge. Over."

Sergeant de Gier looked at the little loudspeaker underneath the dashboard of the gray VW he was driving.

"Straight Tree Ditch?" he asked in a high voice. "How do you expect me to get there? There are thousands of people milling about in the area. Haven't you heard about the riots?"

The operator shrugged.

"Are you there?" de Gier asked.

"I am here," the operator said. "Just go there. The death has nothing to do with the riots, I think."

"Right," de Gier said, still in the same high voice.

"Good luck," the operator said. "Out."

De Gier accelerated and Adjutant-Detective Grijpstra sat up.

"Easy," Grijpstra said. "We are in an unmarked car and that traffic light is on red. They should have sent a marked car, a car with a siren."

"I don't think there are any left," de Gier said, and stopped at the traffic light. "Everybody is out there, everybody we know and a lot of military police as well. I haven't seen a police car all day." He sighed. "The crowd will clobber us the minute they see us go through the roadblocks."

The light changed and the car shot off.

"Easy," Grijpstra said.

"No," de Gier said. "Let's go home. This isn't the right day to play detectives."

Grijpstra grinned and shifted his heavy body into a more comfortable position, holding on to the car's roof and the dashboard at the same time. "You are all right," he said. "You don't look like a policeman. They'll go for me. Crowds always go for me."

De Gier took a corner and avoided a parked truck by forcing the VW's right wheels onto the sidewalk. They were in a narrow alley leading to the Newmarket, the center of the riots. Nobody was about. The riots had sucked people into their vortex while others stayed inside, preferring the small rooms of their seventeenth-century homes to the raw danger of violent hysteria which stalked the streets, changing apparently normal people into robots swinging fists and primitive weapons, intent on attacking and destroying the State which, through their bloodshot and bulging eyes, showed itself as the Police, rows and rows of blue-uniformed and white-helmeted warriors, nonhuman, machines of oppression. They saw the riot police guarding the exit of the alley and a commanding gloved hand was raised to stop the car. De Gier turned his window down and showed his card.

The face under the helmet was unfamiliar and de Gier could read the words on the badge pinned on the man's jacket. "THE HAGUE," the badge said.

"You from The Hague?" de Gier asked, surprised.

"Yes, sergeant, there are about fifty of us here. We were rushed in this morning."

"Police from The Hague," de Gier said surprised. "What next?"

"Rotterdam, I suppose," the constable said. "There are plenty of cities in Holland. We'll all come and help you on a nice day like this. Just give the word. You want to go through?"

"Yes," de Gier said. "We are supposed to investigate a manslaughter on the other side of the square."

The constable shook his head. "I'll let you through but you'll get stuck anyway. The water cannon has just charged the crowd and they are in a foul mood now. One of my colleagues has caught a brick full in the face and they rushed him when he fell. We got him to the ambulance just in time. Maybe you should try to get there on foot."

De Gier turned and looked at Grijpstra, who smiled reassuringly. Inspired by his superior's calm, de Gier nodded at the constable. "We'll park her here."

"Right," the constable said, and turned. The crowd was coming their way, pushed by a charge of unseen policemen on the other side of the square. The constable braced himself, raising his shield to ward off a brick, a heavy man suddenly lurched forward and the constable hit him on the shoulder with his stick. The blow made a dull sound and the heavy man faltered. There were a dozen policemen between the detectives and the crowd now and Grijpstra pulled de Gier onto a porch.

"We may as well wait for the fight to shift."

Together they watched a brick dent the roof of their car.

"Cigar?" Grijpstra asked.

De Gier shook his head and began to roll a cigarette. His hands trembled. What on earth inspired these people? He knew about the official causes of the riots, everybody knew. The underground, Amsterdam's new means of transport, had tunneled as far as this old and protected part of the inner city and some houses had to come down to make way for the monster eating its way through down below. There would be a station here sometime in the future. Most of Amsterdam accepted the underground; it had to come, to relieve the impossible traffic trying to get through the narrow streets and fouling the air. But the inhabitants of the Newmarket area had put up a protest. They wanted the station to be built somewhere else. They had written to the mayor, they had marched through the city, they had printed tens of thousands of posters and pasted them up everywhere, they had harassed the offices of the Public Works Department. And the mayor and his aldermen had tried to appease the protests. They had said "yes" sometimes and "no" at other times. And then, one day, the demolishing firm that had won the city's contract suddenly arrived and began to tear at the houses, and the citizens had fought with the wreckers and chased them off and had grappled, successfully at first, with the police.

Now the wreckers were back and the police had come out in force. The citizens would lose, of course. But meanwhile they were organized. They had bought two-way radios and put up guard posts. They had coordinated their defense and thrown up barricades. They were wearing motorcycle helmets and had armed themselves with sticks. They were even supposed to have armored trucks. But why? They would lose anyway.

Grijpstra, sucking at his small cigar, listened to the growling of the mob. The mob was very close now, its snout no farther away than ten feet. The policemen were holding their ground, being reinforced by a squad which had rushed up through the alley. Three constables had stopped when they saw the two civilians hiding on the porch but Grijpstra's police card had sent them on their way again.

Why? Grijpstra thought, but he knew the answer. This wasn't just a protest against the building of an underground station. There had always been violence in the city. Amsterdam, by its tolerance for unconventional behavior, attracts crazy people. Holland is a conventional country; crazy people have to go somewhere. They go to the capital, where the lovely canals, thousands and thousands of gable houses, hundreds of bridges of every shape and form, lines of old trees, clusters of offbeat bars and cafés, dozens of small cinemas and theaters encourage and protect the odd. Crazy people are special people. They carry the country's genius, its urge to create, to find new ways. The State smiles and is proud of its crazy people. But the State does not approve of anarchism. It limits the odd.

The Newmarket area is very odd. And now, when the odd tried to argue with the State's choice of an underground station, and lost the argument, and reverted to violence, the State lost its smile and produced its strength, the strength of the blue-uniformed city police, and the black-uniformed military police, resplendent with white and silver braid, and reinforced with steel helmets and truncheons, and backed with armored cars and mechanical carriers equipped with water guns, spouting thousands of gallons of pressurized water on and against the bearded yelling hooligans who, only this morning, were artists and artisans, poets or unemployed intellectuals, gentle misfits and innocent dreamers.

De Gier sighed. A paper bag filled with powdered soapstone had flown into the alley and exploded on the pavement. The right side of his stylish suit, made out of blue denim by a cheap Turkish tailor, was stained with the white sticky substance. De Gier was an elegant man who took pride in his appearance. He was also a handsome man and he didn't like the feel of the powder in his mustache. Some of it would be on his thick curly hair. He didn't relish the idea of having a white mustache for the rest of the day. Grijpstra laughed.

"You caught some of it too," de Gier said.

Grijpstra looked at his trousers but he didn't care. All his suits were the same, baggy and made of English striped material, thin white stripes on a blue background. The suit was old, like the gray tie, and he wouldn't mourn its loss. His shirt was new but the police would replace it if he filled in a report. Grijpstra leaned back against the door at the back of the porch and placed his hands on his stomach. He looked very placid.

"We ought to try and get through," de Gier said. "That lady will be waiting for us."

"In a minute," Grijpstra said. "If we try now we'll only be food for the ambulance. If the hooligans don't get us the police will. They won't take the time to study our cards. They'll be nervous as well."

De Gier smoked and listened. The fight had moved, it seemed. The screams and thuds were a little farther away now.

"Now," he said, and stepped into the alley. The constables let them through. They ran across the square and dodged a heavy motorcycle and sidecar which came straight at them. The sergeant in the sidecar was beating the metal side of his vehicle with his rubber stick. His face had been cut by a woman's nails and blood had run all over his tunic. The constable driving the contraption was gray with dust and sweat streaked his face.

"Police," Grijpstra boomed.

The motorcycle veered and charged the mob which had begun to form again behind the detectives.

Grijpstra fell. Two boys, in their late teens, had heard him shout "Police" and they both attacked at the same time, kicking the adjutant's shins. De Gier was quick, but not quick enough. He hit the nearest boy on the side of the chin and the boy sighed and crumpled up. The other boy had been hit with the same movement, not by de Gier's fist but by his elbow. The elbow's sharp point hit the boy on the side of his face and he howled with pain and ran off.

"All right?" de Gier asked, helping Grijpstra back to his feet.

They ran on but an armored van was in their way now and a spout of water hit them from behind. De Gier fell. Now the water gun changed its position, and was aiming at Grijpstra's large bulk when the gunner saw the red stripes on the police card which the adjutant waved.

"Go away," a police officer shouted at the detectives. "What the hell do you think you are doing here? We don't want any plainclothesmen around."

"Sorry, sir," Grijpstra said. "We have a call from the Straight Tree Ditch; this is the only way to get there."

"Let them wait," the inspector roared, his young face pale with fear.

"Can't. Manslaughter."

"All right, all right. I'll give you an escort although I can't spare anyone. Hey! You and you. Take these men through. They are ours."

Two burly military policemen answered the command, both with torn braid dangling from their shoulders.

"Shit," the nearest of the two said. "We have had everything today short of gunfire and we'll have that too if this goes on much longer."

"Nobody went for his gun so far?" Grijpstra asked.

"One of your young chappies did," the military policeman said, "but we quieted him down. His mate had caught a brick in the face. Upset him a bit. Had to take the gun away from him in the end; said he would shoot the fellow who got his mate."

Grijpstra meant to say something positive but a bag of soapstone powder hit them and he couldn't see for a while.

"Messy, hey?" the military policeman said. "They must have tons of that damned powder. We caught a man on the roof using a heavy catapult; he was our first prisoner. I'd like to see the charge report we'll come up with. It will be crossbows next and mechanical stone throwers. Have you seen their armored trucks?"

"No," de Gier said. "Where?"

"We got them early fortunately, two of them. There's nothing you can do when they come at you. Friend of mine jumped straight into the canal to get away. The crowd was very amused."

"Did you catch the driver?"

"Sure. Pulled him out of the cabin myself, had to smash the window for he had locked himself in. That's one report I am going to write myself. He'll get three months."

"Nice day," Grijpstra said. "Let's go. We have a lady waiting for us."

They got to the lady ten minutes later. They only got into one more fight. Grijpstra was bitten in the hand. De Gier pulled the woman off by the hair. The military policemen arrested the woman. Her artificial teeth fell out as they threw her into a van. They picked up the teeth and threw them in after her.

2

THE STRAIGHT TREE DITCH is a narrow canal flanked by two narrow quays and shadowed by lines of elm trees which, on that spring evening, filtered the light through their haze of fresh pale green leaves. Its lovely old houses, supporting each other in their great age, mirror themselves in the canal's water, and any tourist who strays off the beaten track and suddenly finds himself in the centuries-old peace of this secluded spot will agree that Amsterdam has a genuine claim to beauty.

But our detectives were in no mood to appreciate beauty. Grijpstra's shins hurt him and the wound on his hand was ugly. His short bristly hair was white with soapstone powder and his jacket had been torn by an assailant whom he had never noticed. De Gier limped next to him and snarled at a policeman who told them to be off. There were no civilians about, for the canal offered no room for mobs, but the police had sealed its entrance to prevent access to the Newmarket Square. Red and white wooden fences had been hastily installed and riot police guarded the roadblocks, staring at the curious, who, silently, stood and stared back. There was nothing to see, the fighting in the square being screened by high gable houses. The atmosphere of the canal was heavy, loaded with violence and suspicion, and the policemen, forced into idleness, hit their high leather boots with their truncheons, splitting the silence. Far away the revving engines of motorcycles and trucks could be heard, and the whining of the water cannon, and the subdued yells of the combatants, eerily setting off the clamor of machines. Demolition was still continuing, for the houses had to come down, the sooner the better, and the cranes, bulldozers and automatic steel hammers and drills were adding their racket to the general upheaval.

"We are police, buddy," de Gier said to the cop, and showed his card, which had got cracked when he fell.

"Sorry, sergeant," the constable said, "we trust nobody today. How is it going out there?"

"We are winning," Grijpstra said.

"We always win," the constable said. "It's boring, I'd rather watch football."

"Number four," de Gier said. "Here we are."

The constable wandered off, hitting the canal's cast-iron railing with his stick, and Grijpstra looked up at the four-storied house, which was number four according to a neatly painted sign next to the front door. "Rogge," said another sign.

"Took us three quarters of an hour to get here," de Gier said. "Marvelous service we are giving nowadays, and there's supposed to be a dead man with a bloody face in there."

"Maybe not," Grijpstra said. "People exaggerate, you know. Adjutant Geurts was telling me that he was called to investigate a suicide last night and when he got to the address the old lady was eating nice fresh toast with a raw herring spread on top of it, and there were chopped onions on top of the herring. She had changed her mind. Life wasn't so bad after all."

"A man with a bloody head can't change his mind," de Gier said.

Grijpstra nodded. "True. And he won't be a suicide."

He rang the bell. There was no answer. He rang again. The door opened. The corridor was dark and they couldn't see the woman until the door had closed behind them.

"Upstairs," the woman said. "I'll go first."

They turned into another corridor on the second floor and the woman opened a door leading to a room facing the canal. The man was lying on his back on the floor, his face smashed.

"Dead," the woman said. "He was my brother, Abe Rogge."

Grijpstra pushed the woman gently aside and stooped to look at the dead man's face. "You know what happened?" he asked. The woman covered her face with her hands. Grijpstra put his arm around her shoulders. "Do you know anything, miss?" "No, no. I came in and there he was."

Grijpstra looked at de Gier and pointed at a telephone with his free hand. De Gier dialed. Grijpstra pulled his arm back from the woman's shoulders and took the telephone from de Gier's limp hand.

"Take her outside," he whispered, "and don't look at the body. You two have some coffee, I saw a kitchen downstairs; I'll see you there later."

De Gier was white in the face when he led the woman outside. He had to support himself against the doorpost. Grijpstra smiled. He had seen it before. The sergeant was allergic to blood, but he would be all right soon.

"The man's head is bashed in," he said on the phone. "Do what you have to do and get us the commissaris."

"You are in the riot area, aren't you?" the central radio room asked. "We'll never get the cars through."

"Get a launch from the State Water Police," Grijpstra said. "That's what *we* should have had. Don't forget to get the commissaris. He is at home."

He replaced the phone and put his hands into his pockets. The windows of the room were open and the elm trees outside screened the pale blue sky. He looked at their leaves for a while, resting his eyes on their delicate young green and admiring a blackbird which, unperturbed by the weird atmosphere of his surroundings, had burst into song. A sparrow hopped about on the windowsill and looked at the corpse, its tiny head cocked to one side. Grijpstra walked over to the window. The blackbird and the sparrow flew off but gulls continued swooping down toward the canal's surface, looking for scraps and dead fish. It was the beginning of a spring evening which the occupant of the room would have no part of.

How? Grijpstra thought. The man's face was a mess of broken bones and thick red blood. A big man, some thirty years old perhaps. The body was dressed in jeans and a blue bush jacket. There was a thick golden necklace around the muscular neck and its skin was tanned. He has been on holiday, Grijpstra thought, just returned probably. Spain. North Africa perhaps, or an island somewhere. Must have been in the sun for weeks. Nobody gets a tan from the Dutch spring.

He noted the short yellow curls, bleached by exposure, and the beard of exactly the same texture. The hair fitted the man's head like a helmet. Strong fellow, Grijpstra thought, could lift a horse off the ground. Heavy wrists, bulging arms.

He squatted down, looked at the man's face again and then began to look around the room. Not seeing what he was looking for, he began to walk around, carefully, his hands still in his pockets. But the brick or stone wasn't there. It had seemed such a simple straightforward solution. Man looks out of the window. Riot outside. Someone flings a brick.

Brick hits man in the face. Man falls over backward. Brick falls in the room. But there was no brick. He walked to the window and looked down into the street. He still couldn't see a brick. The helmeted policeman who had stopped them earlier was leaning against a tree staring at the water.

"Hey, you," Grijpstra shouted. The policeman looked up. "Has there been any stone throwing here this afternoon?"

"No," the constable shouted back. "Why?"

"Chap here has his face smashed in, could have been a stone."

The constable scratched his neck. "I'll go and ask the others," he shouted after a while. "I haven't been here all afternoon."

"The stone may have bounced off this man's face here and fallen back into the street. Get some of your friends, please, and search the street, will you?"

The constable waved and ran off. Grijpstra turned around. It could have been a weapon, of course, or perhaps even a fist. Several blows perhaps. No knife. A hammer? A hammer perhaps, Grijpstra thought, and sat down on the only chair he saw, a large cane chair with a high back. He had seen a similar chair in a shop window some days before and he remembered the price. A high price. The table in the room was expensive as well, antique and heavily built with a single ornamental leg. There was a book on the table, a French book. Grijpstra read the title. *Zazie dans le Métro.* It had a picture of a little girl on the cover. Some little girl having an adventure on the underground. Grijpstra didn't read French. There wasn't much more to see in the room. A low table with a telephone, a telephone directory and some more French books in a heap on the floor. The walls of the room had been left bare, with the exception of one fairly large unframed painting. He studied the painting with interest. It took him a while to name what he saw. The picture seemed to consist of no more than a large black dot, or a constellation of dots against a background of blues, but it had to be a boat, he decided in the end. A small boat, a canoe or a dinghy, afloat on a fluorescent sea. And there were two men in the boat. The painting wasn't as sad as it seemed at first glance. The fluorescence of the sea, indicated by stripes of white along the boat, and continuing into its wake, suggested some gaiety. The painting impressed him and he kept on looking back at it. Other objects in the room held his attention for a moment but the painting drew him back. If the corpse hadn't been there, dominating the space by its awkward and grotesque presence, the room would have been a perfect setting for the painting. Grijpstra himself had some talent and he meant to paint seriously one day. He had painted as a young man, but marriage and the family which suddenly began to spread around him, and the small uncomfortable house on the Lijnbaansgracht opposite Police Headquarters, drowned in the holocaust of a TV which his deaf wife would never switch off, and the fat ever-present existence of the flabby woman who shouted at him and the children had frustrated and almost killed his ambition. How would he paint a small boat, afloat on its own on an immense sea? He would use more color, Grijpstra thought, but more color would spoil the dream. For the picture was a dream, a dream dreamed simultaneously by two friends, two men suspended in space, drawn as two small interlinked line structures.

He stretched his legs, leaned back and breathed heavily. This would be a room he could live in. Life would become a pleasure, for a hard day would never be a hard day if he knew he could return to this room. And the dead man had lived in this room. He sighed again; the sigh tapered off into a low groan. He looked at the low bed close to the window. There were three sleeping bags on the bed, one zipped and two unzipped. The man would have slept in the one bag and have used the other two for cover in case he needed it. Very sensible. No fuss with sheets. If a man wants sheets he needs a woman. The woman has to make the bed and change the sheets and take care of the other hundred thousand things a man thinks he needs.

Grijpstra would like to sleep on a stretcher and cover himself with an unzipped sleeping bag. In the morning he gets up and leaves the bed as it is. No vacuum cleaner. Sweep the room once a week. No TV. No newspapers. Just a few books maybe and a few records, not too many. Don't buy anything. Whatever you attract clutters up your life. He might invite a woman to the room, of course, but only if he could be absolutely sure that she would leave again, and would never stick plastic pins into her hair and sleep with them on. He felt his face. There was a scratch which had got there before he had fought his way through the riot. Mrs. Grijpstra had ripped his face with one of her pins; she had turned over and he had screamed with pain but she hadn't awakened. His scream had stopped her snore halfway and she had smacked her lips a few times and finished the snore. And when he had shaken her by the shoulder she had opened one bleary eye and told him to shut up. And no children. There are enough children in Holland.

"Why the hell . . ." he said aloud now but he didn't bother to finish the question. He had slipped into the mess so gradually that he had never been able to stop and twist free. The girl had looked all right when he stumbled across her path, and her parents too, and he was making a bit of a career in the police, and it was all dead right. His oldest son had gradually grown into a lout, with long dirty straight hair and buck teeth and a shiny screaming motorcycle. The two little ones were still very nice. He loved them. No doubt about it. He wouldn't leave them. So he couldn't have a room like this. All very logical. He looked at the corpse again. Had someone come in and hit the giant with a hammer, smack in the face? And had the giant stood there, seeing the hammer come and catching its impact full on the nose, without even trying to defend himself? Drunk perhaps? He got up and went over to the window. Three constables were poking at the cobblestones with their long truncheons.

"Anything there?"

They looked up. "Nothing."

"Did you find out about the stone throwing?"

"Yes," the constable who had been there earlier shouted back. "It has been quiet here all day. We were only here to stop people getting to the trouble spot."

"Have you let anyone through?"

The constables looked at each other, then the first one looked up at Grijpstra again.

"Plenty. Anybody who had business here."

"A man has been killed here," Grijpstra shouted. "Have you noticed anyone running about? Behaving in a funny way?"

The constables shook their heads.

"Thanks," Grijpstra shouted and pulled his head in. He sat down again and closed his eyes, meaning to feel the atmosphere of the room but gradually drifting off into sleep. The sound of a ship's engine woke him. He looked out and saw a low launch of the Water Police moor outside. Some six men got off, the commissaris, a small dapper-looking elderly man first. Grijpstra waved and the men marched up to the door.

"Nice coffee," de Gier had been saying meanwhile. "Thank you very much. Drink some yourself, you need it. Please tell me what happened. Are you all right now?"

The woman sitting opposite him at the kitchen table tried to smile. A slender woman with dark hair, done up in a bun, and dressed in black slacks and a black blouse with a necklace of small red shells. She wore no rings.

"I am his sister," she said. "Esther Rogge. Call me Esther, please, everybody does. We have lived here for five years now. I used to have a flat but Abe bought this house and wanted me to move in with him."

"Looked after your brother," de Gier said. "I see."

"No. Abe didn't need anyone to look after him. We just shared the house. I have the first floor, he has the second. We hardly ever even ate together."

"Why not?" de Gier asked, lighting her cigarette. She had long hands, no lacquer on the nails, one nail was broken.

"We preferred not to fuss with each other. Abe kept the refrigerator stocked and he just ate what he liked. If we happened to be both in I might cook something for him but he would never ask me to. He often ate out. We lived our own lives."

"What did he do for a living?" de Gier asked.

Esther tried to smile again. Her face was still white and the shadows under her eyes showed up as dark purple stains but some life had returned to her mouth, which was no longer a slit in a mask.

"He was a hawker, sold things in the street. In the street market, the Albert Cuyp Market. You know the Albert Cuyp, of course?"

"Yes, miss."

"Please call me Esther. I sometimes went to see him in the Albert Cuyp. I have helped him too when I had a day off. He sold beads, and all types of cloth, and wool and colored string and braid. To people who like to make things themselves."

"Creative," de Gier said.

"Yes. It's fashionable to be creative now."

"You say your brother bought this house? Must have cost him some money or did he get a substantial mortgage?"

"No, it's all his. He made a lot of money. He wasn't just selling things in the street, you see, he dealt in a big way as well. He was always going to Czechoslovakia in a van and he would buy beads by the ton, directly from the factory, and he would sell to other hawkers and to the big stores too. And he bought and sold other things as well. The street market was for fun, he only went there on Mondays."

"And you, what do you do?"

"I work for the university, I have a degree in literature." De Gier looked impressed.

"What's your name?" Esther asked.

"De Gier. Detective-Sergeant de Gier. Rinus de Gier."

"May I call you Rinus?"

"Please," de Gier said, and poured himself more coffee. "Do you have any idea why this happened? Any connection with the riots, you think?"

"No," she said. Her eyes filled with tears and de Gier reached out and held her hand.

"They threw something at him," the commissaris said, looking down at the corpse. "With force, considerable force. From the impact you would almost think they shot something at him. A stone perhaps. But where is it?"

Grijpstra explained what he had been able to deduct from his investigations so far.

"I see," the commissaris said pensively. "No stone, you say. And no bits of brick, I see. They were throwing bricks on the Newmarket Square, I am told. Red bricks. They break and pulverize when they hit something. There is no red dust on the floor here. Could have been a proper stone though and somebody may have found it and thrown it into the canal."

"There would have been a splash, sir, and the street has been patrolled all day."

The commissaris laughed. "Yes. Manslaughter and we are sitting right on top of it, have been sitting on it all day, and we never noticed. Peculiar, isn't it?"

"Yes, sir."

"And he can't have been dead long. Hours, no more. A few hours, I would say. The doctor'll be here in a minute, the launch has gone back to pick him up. He'll know. Where's de Gier?"

"Downstairs, sir, talking to the man's sister."

"Couldn't stand the blood, could he? You think he'll ever get used to it?"

"No sir, not if he is forced to look at it for some time. We were in the middle of the riot and he put up a good fight and he didn't mind the blood on my hand but if blood is combined with death it seems to get him. Makes him vomit. I sent him down just in time."

"Every man has his own fear," the commissaris said softly. "But what caused all this, I wonder? Can't have been a bullet for there is no hole, but every bone in the face seems to have been smashed. Hey! Who are you?"

He had seen a man walking past the door in the corridor, a young man who now entered the room.

"Louis Zilver," the young man said.

"What are you doing here?"

"I live here, I have a room upstairs."

"We are policemen investigating the death of Mr. Rogge here. Can we come to your room? The photographers and print people will want to have a look at this room and we can use the opportunity to ask a few questions."

"Certainly," the young man said.

They followed Zilver up a flight of narrow stairs and were shown into a large room. The commissaris took the only easy chair, Grijpstra sat on the bed, the young man sat on the floor, facing them both.

"I am a friend of Abe and Esther," Louis said. "I have been living in this house for almost a year now."

"Go ahead," the commissaris said. "Tell us all you know. About the house, about what went on, about what everybody does. We know nothing. We have just come in. But first of all I would like you to tell me if you know how Abe died and where you were at the time."

"I was here," Louis said. "I have been in the house all day. Abe was still alive at four o'clock this afternoon. He was here then, right here in this room. And I don't know how he died."

"Go on," the commissaris said pleasantly.

3

LOUIS ZILVER'S room was almost as bare as the dead man's room one floor below, but it had a different quality. The commissaris, who hadn't spent as much time with Abe Rogge's body as Grijpstra had, didn't notice the difference. He just saw another room in the same house, a room with a bare wooden floor and furnished with a neatly made bed and a large desk, cylinder-topped, showing an array of cubicles, stacked with papers in plastic transparent folders, and a bookcase covering an entire wall. Grijpstra defined the difference as a difference between "neat" and "untidy." Zilver had to be an organized man, or boy rather, for he wouldn't be much older than twenty. Grijpstra observed Louis, squatting patiently opposite his interrogators, and noted the large, almost liquid, dark eyes, the delicately hooked nose, the tinge of olive in the color of the skin stretched over high cheekbones, the long blue-black hair. Louis was waiting. Meanwhile he wasn't doing much. He had crossed his legs and lit a cigarette after placing an ashtray in a convenient place so that the commissaris and Grijpstra could tip the ash of their small cigars into it. The ashtray fascinated Grijpstra. It was a human skull, molded in plastic, a large hole had been left in the cranium and a silver cup fitted into the hole.

"Brr," Grijpstra said. "Some ashtray!"

Louis smiled. The smile was arrogant, condescending. "Friend of mine made it. He is a sculptor. Silly thing really, but it's useful so I kept it. And the meaning is obvious. Memento mori."

"Why do you have it if you think it's silly?" the commissaris asked.

"You could have thrown it out and used a saucer instead." The commissaris, who had spent the day in bed to ease the pain in his legs which had almost lamed him during the last few weeks, was rubbing his right leg. The hot needle pricks of his acute chronic rheumatism made his bloodless lips twitch. The commissaris looked very innocent. His shantung suit, complete with waistcoat and watch chain, seemed a little too large for his small dry body, and his wizened face with the carefully brushed, thin colorless hair expressed a gentle exactness.

"The man is a friend of mine, he often comes here. I think it would hurt him if I wasn't using his work of art. Besides, I don't mind having it around. The message of the skull may be obvious but it's true nevertheless. Life is short, seize the day and all that."

"Yes," the commissaris said. "There is a dead man in the house to prove the saying's worth."

The commissaris stopped to listen to the noises downstairs. Feet were clomping up and down the bare steps. The photographers would be setting up their equipment and the doctor would be getting ready to start his examination. A uniformed chief inspector, his jacket soaked and caked with soapstone powder, stomped his way into the room. The commissaris got up.

"Sir," the chief inspector said. "Anything we can do for you?"

"You have done enough today it seems," the commissaris said mildly.

"We haven't had any dead men outside," the chief inspector said. "Not so far, anyway."

"We have one here, one floor below. Got his face bashed in, hit by a stone or something, but we can't find the stone or whatever it was in his room."

"So my constables were telling me. Maybe your man was a reactionary, somebody the red mob outside may have disliked."

"Was he?" the commissaris asked Louis Zilver.

Louis grinned.

"Was he?"

"No," Louis said, carefully stubbing out his cigarette in the skull's silver cranium. "Abe didn't know what politics were. He was an adventurer."

"Adventurers get killed for a number of reasons," the chief inspector said, impatiently tapping his boot with his truncheon. "Do you have any use for me, sir?"

"No," the commissaris said, "no, you go ahead, I hope the situation is getting a bit better on the square."

"It isn't," the officer said. "It's getting worse. We are getting fresh crowds now, young idiots who come in screaming and dancing. I better get back."

Grijpstra watched Louis's face as the officer left the room. Louis was showing his teeth in the way a baboon does when he feels threatened. "It seems you are enjoying yourself," Grijpstra said.

"It's always nice to see the police get a beating," Louis said in a low voice.

Grijpstra bristled. The commissaris made a gesture. "Let's forget the Newmarket for a while. Tell us about the incident in this house. What do you know about it?"

Louis had lit a new cigarette and puffed industriously. "Esther found the body close to five o'clock this afternoon. She screamed. I was here, in my room. I ran downstairs. I told her to phone the police. Abe had been in my room an hour before Esther found him. He was right here, talking to me. There was nothing wrong with him then."

"What's your connection with Abe and Esther?"

"I am a friend. I got to know him on the market, the Albert Cuyp Market. I bought a lot of beads from him once, kept on going back for more. I was trying to make a structure, an abstract figure which I was planning to hang from the ceiling. Abe was interested in what I was doing and came to see me where I lived. I had an uncomfortable room, small, no conveniences, no proper light. He was buying this house and suggested I move in with him. And we used to go sailing together. His boat is outside, moored next to that big houseboat you can see from the window. A clapped-out little yacht. He would take it out when there was a good wind but he found it difficult to handle by himself."

The commissaris and Grijpstra got up to look out of the window. They saw the sixteen-foot plastic sailboat.

"It's half full of water," Grijpstra said.

"Yes. Rainwater. He never bothered, just hosed it out when he wanted to go sailing. The sails are downstairs; it only takes a few minutes to rig the boat."

"What about that houseboat?"

"It's empty," Louis said. "Been for sale for a long time. They want too much money for it and it's rotten."

"Somebody could have stood on the roof and thrown whatever it was that hit Abe," the commissaris said thoughtfully. "Why don't you go down, Grijpstra? Perhaps the police in the street saw somebody on the houseboat."

"What was that nasty remark you made about the police just now?"

the commissaris asked when Grijpstra had left the room. "You told Esther to telephone us when the body was found, didn't you? So we must be useful, why sneer at something which is useful?"

"The body had to be taken care of, hadn't it?" Louis asked, and his eyes sparkled. "We couldn't dump it into the canal, it would foul the water."

"I see. So you called the garbage men?" Louis dropped his eyes.

"But your friend is dead, his face is bashed in. Don't you want us to apprehend the killer?" Louis's face changed. It lost its sparkle and suddenly looked worn and tired. The sensitive face became a study in sadness only kept alive by the luster of the large eyes.

"Yes," Louis said softly. "He is dead, and we are alone."

"We?"

"Esther, me, others, the people he inspired."

"Did he have enemies?"

"No. Friends. Friends and admirers. A lot of people used to come and see him here. He threw parties and they would do anything to be invited. He had lots of friends."

"And in business? Was he popular in business as well?"

"Yes," Louis said, staring at the plastic skull in front of him. "King of the Albert Cuyp street market. Very popular. All the street sellers knew him. Bought from him too. He was a big businessman you know. We used to bring in cargoes from Eastern Europe and a lot of it was sold to the market. Lately we were doing wool, tons of wool, for knitting and rug making. Wool is expensive stuff nowadays."

"We?" the commissaris asked.

"Well, Abe mostly. I just helped."

"Tell us about yourself."

"Why?"

"It may help us to understand the situation."

Louis grinned. "Yes, you are the police. I had almost forgotten. But why should I help the police?"

Grijpstra had slipped into the room and taken his place on the bed again. "You should help the police because you are a citizen," Grijpstra boomed suddenly, "because you are a member of society. Society can only function when there is public order. When order has been disturbed it has to be maintained again. It can only be maintained if the citizens assist the police. The task of the police is to protect the citizens against themselves."

Louis looked up and laughed.

"You think that's funny?" Grijpstra asked indignantly.

"Yes. Very funny. Textbook phrases. And untrue. Why should I, a citizen, benefit by what you, in your stupidity, in your refusal to think, call public order? Couldn't it be that public order is sheer boredom, a heavy weight which throttles the citizens?"

"Your friend is dead downstairs, with a bashed-in face. Does that make you happy?"

Louis stopped laughing.

"You are a student, aren't you?" the commissaris asked.

"Yes. I studied law but I gave it up when I saw how sickening our laws are. I passed my candidate's examinations but that was as far as I could go, I haven't been near the university since."

"What a pity," the commissaris said. "I studied law too and I found it a fascinating discipline. You only have a few years to go. You don't want to finish your studies?"

The boy shrugged. "Why should I? If I become a master at law I may find myself in a concrete office somewhere working for some large company or perhaps even the State. I don't particularly want to join the establishment. It's more fun shouting at the street market or driving a truck through the snow in Czechoslovakia. And I am not after money."

"What would you do," Grijpstra asked, "if somebody rolled your wallet?"

"I wouldn't go to the police if that's what you mean."

"And if someone murdered your friend? Didn't you tell Esther to phone us?"

Louis sat up. "Listen," he said loudly. "Don't philosophize with me, will you? I am not used to arguing. I accept your power and your attempt to maintain order in a madhouse and I'll answer any questions you may ask as long as they relate to the murder."

"You mean that humanity consists of mindless forms groping about?" the commissaris asked dreamily as if he hadn't really been listening. He was looking at the trees outside the window.

"Yes, you've put it very well. We don't do anything, things happen to us. Abe has found his death just now, like a few million black people have found their death in Central Africa because the water ran out. There's nothing anybody can do about it. My grandparents were thrown in a cattle truck during the war and dumped into some camp and gassed. Or maybe they just starved to death, or some SS man bashed their heads in for fun. Same thing happened to Abe and Esther's family. The Rogges stayed alive because they happened to survive; their lives weren't planned, like the deaths of the others weren't planned. And the police are pawns in the game. My grandparents were arrested by the police because they were Jews. By the Amsterdam municipal police, not the German police. They were told to maintain order, like you are now told to maintain order. That officer who was here a minute ago is merrily bashing heads now, on the Newmarket Square, half a kilometer from here."

"Really," Grijpstra said.

"What do you mean, *really?*" Louis shouted. "Are you going to tell me that only part of the police worked for the Germans during the war? And that most of your colleagues were on the queen's side? And what about the queen? Didn't she send troops to Indonesia to bash villagers on the head? What will you do if there's another war? Or a famine? It may happen any minute now." He coughed and looked at Grijpstra's face, ominously, as if he wanted the adjutant to agree with him.

"Or the Russians may invade us and impose communism. They will take over the government in The Hague and some minister will tell you to arrest all dissidents. And you will maintain order. You will send blue-uniformed constables armed with rubber truncheons and automatic pistols, helmeted perhaps, and carrying carbines. You'll have proper razzias with armored trucks blocking the street on each side. It's not unlikely you know. Just go outside and have a look at what's happening on the Newmarket Square right now."

"Who are you blaming?" the commissaris asked, tipping the ash of his cigar into the plastic skull.

"No one," Louis said quietly. "Not even the Germans, not even the Dutch police who took my grandparents away. Things happen, I told you already. I am not blaming things either, it's just that this idealizing, this reasoning, sickens me. If you want to do your job, if you consider your activity to be a job, do it, but don't ask me to clap my hands when you make your arrest. I don't care either way."

"It seems you are disproving your own theory," the commissaris said. "You refuse to do as you are told, don't you? You don't want to fit in. You should perhaps be finishing your studies so that you can join society on the right level, but you are working on the street market instead and driving a truck in some faraway country. But you are still doing something, working toward some goal. If you really believe what you say you believe, it seems to me you should be doing nothing at all. You should be drifting, pushed by circumstances of the moment."

"Exactly," Louis said. "That's what I am doing."

"No, no. You have some freedom, it seems to me, and you are using it. You are deliberately choosing."

"I try," Louis said, disarmed by the commissaris' quiet voice. "Perhaps you are right. Perhaps I am free in a way and trying to do something with my freedom. But I am not even very good at trying. I would never have done anything on my own. I was rotting away in a dark room, sleeping until two o'clock in the afternoon every day and hanging about in silly bars at night, when Abe found me. I just tagged on to Abe. It happened to me. He practically took me by the scruff of the neck and dragged me along."

"Didn't you say that you were making some structure out of beads? You were doing that before you met Abe, weren't you?"

"Yes, nothing ever came of it. I threw the whole mess into a dustbin one day. I had meant to create something really unusual, a human shape which would move in the wind or the draft. I was trying to make a body out of copper wire and connect the wire with thin plastic threads and string beads on the threads. The body would glitter and show life when it moved, but it wouldn't be moving itself, only acting when forces beyond its power played with it. Unfortunately I am no artist. The idea was good but I only managed to string a lot of beads together and waste a year."

"Right," Grijpstra said. "So Abe got you out of your mess. He may have got others out of their messes. But now he has been killed. The killer may want to kill other people like Abe."

"Rubbish."

"Pardon?"

"You heard me," Louis said sweetly. "Rubbish. Rot. Abe got killed because some force moved somebody's arm. The force was a haphazard force, like the wind. You can't catch the wind."

"If there's a draft we can find the crack and block it," the commissaris said.

"You can jail the instrument," Louis said stubbornly, "but you can't jail the force which activated the instrument. It's beyond you and the effort is silly. Why should I help you waste your time? You can waste it on your own."

"I see," the commissaris said, and looked at the trees again. There was no wind and the last rays of the sun were reflected in the small oblong mirrors of the young leaves.

"Do you really? You are an officer, aren't you? You direct the police?"

"I am a commissaris.* But if your theory is right I am only pretend-

* The ranks of the Dutch municipal police are constable, constable first class, sergeant, adjutant, inspector, chief inspector, commissaris, chief constable.

ing to direct a shadow play which doesn't exist in reality. You are not original but you probably know you are not. Other people have thought of what you are thinking now. Plato, for instance, and others before him."

"There have been clever shadows on the planet," Louis said and smiled.

"Yes. But you have helped us nevertheless. We know a little about the dead man now and we know a little about you. We are simple people, deluded probably, as you have pointed out already. We work on the assumption that the State is right and that public order has to be maintained.

"And we work with systems. Someone, some human who meant to harm Abe Rogge, has killed him. He had the opportunity to bash his face in and he thought he had a reason to do it. If we find somebody who had both the opportunity and the motive we will suspect him of a crime and we may arrest him. You, Louis Zilver, had the opportunity. You were in the house at the right time. But from what you have told us we may assume that you had no motive."

"If I was speaking the truth," Louis said.

"Yes. You have told us he was your friend, your savior in a way. He got you out of a rut. You used to spend your time lying in bed all morning and drinking all evening and trying to make a beady man all afternoon. You weren't happy. Abe made your life interesting."

"Yes. He saved me. But perhaps people don't want to be saved. Christ was a savior and they hammered nails through his hands and feet."

"A hammer," Grijpstra said. "I keep on thinking that Abe was killed with a hammer. But a hammer would have made a hole, wouldn't it? The face was bashed in over a large area."

"We'll find out what killed him," the commissaris said. "Go on, Mr. Zilver. You interest me. What else can you tell us?"

"Tell me," de Gier said, still holding Esther's hand, "why was your brother killed? Did he have any enemies?"

Esther had stopped crying and was caressing the table's surface with her free hand.

"Yes. He had enemies. People hated his guts. He was too successful, you see, and too indifferent. He was so full of life. People would worry and be depressed and nervous and he'd just laugh and go to Tunisia for a few weeks to play on the beach or to ride a camel to a little village somewhere. Or he would sail his boat onto the great lake. Or he would take off for the East and buy merchandise and sell it here and make a good profit. He was a dangerous man. He crushed people. Made them feel fools."

"Did he make you feel a fool?"

"I *am* a fool," Esther said.

"Why?"

"Everybody is. You are too, sergeant, whether you want to admit it or not."

"You were going to call me Rinus. O.K., I am a fool. Is that what you want me to say?"

"I don't want you to say anything. If you know you are a fool, Abe wouldn't have been able to hurt you. He used to arrange dinner parties but before anyone was allowed to eat anything, that person had to get up, face the assembled guests and say, 'I am a fool.' "

"Yes?" de Gier asked, surprised. "Whatever for?"

"He enjoyed doing things like that. They had to state that they were fools and then they had to explain why they were fools. Some sort of sensitivity training. A man would say 'Friends, I am a fool. I think I am important but I am not.' But that wouldn't be enough for Abe. He wouldn't let the man eat or drink before he had explained, in detail, why exactly he was a fool. He would have to admit that he was proud because he had some particular success, a business deal for instance, or an examination he had passed, or a woman he had made, and then he would have to explain that it was silly to be proud of such a feat because it had just happened to him. It wasn't his fault or merit, you see. Abe believed that we were just being pushed around by circumstances and that man is an inanimate mechanism, nothing more."

"And people had to admit it to him all the time?"

"Yes, that was the only way to start doing something."

"So they could *do* something after all?"

"Yes, not much. Something. Provided they admitted they were fools."

De Gier lit a cigarette and sat back. "Shit," he said softly.

"Pardon?"

"Never mind," de Gier said. "Your brother must have annoyed a lot of people. Did he ever admit he was a fool himself?"

"Oh, yes."

"And he really thought he was a fool?"

"Yes. He didn't care, you see. He just lived for the moment. A day consisted of a lot of moments to him. I don't think he cared when he died either."

"These friends he had, what sort of people were they? Business friends from the street market?"

Esther adjusted her hair and began to fiddle with the coffee machine. "More coffee, Rinus?"

"Please." She filled the apparatus and spilled some coffee on the floor.

"Allow me," de Gier said, and picked up a dustpan and a brush.

"Thanks. Are you married?"

"No, I live by myself, with my cat. I always clean up immediately when I make a mess."

"Friends, you said. Well, he often had friends from the street market in the house, and students would come, and some artists. And journalists, and girls. Abe attracted women. And Louis, of course, you have seen him in the corridor, haven't you. Where is he anyway?"

"He is upstairs with my colleague, Adjutant Grijpstra, and the commissaris."

"That little old man is your chief?"

"Yes. Can you describe some of his friends to me? I'll need a list of them. Did he have any special friends?"

"They were all special. He would get very involved with people, until he dropped them. He wasn't concerned about friendship, he always said. Friendship is a temporary phenomenon; it depends on circumstances and it starts and ends like the wind. He would annoy people by saying that, for they tried to attach themselves to him."

"Some case," de Gier said.

Esther smiled, a slow tired smile.

"You remind me of the constables who came here a few days ago," she said. "They had the wrong number. Our neighbors had phoned. An old man was visiting them and the man suddenly got ill and collapsed. The neighbors had phoned for an ambulance but the police came as well, to see if there had been any violence, I suppose. The woman next door was very upset and I went there to see if I could be of some help. The old man was obviously dying. I think he had had a heart attack. I overheard the conversation between the constables."

"What did they say?" de Gier asked.

"The one constable said to the other, 'Hell, I hope the old bugger doesn't croak. If he does we'll have to write a report on it,' and the other one said, 'Never mind, he'll die in the ambulance and the health officers can take care of it.'"

"Yes," de Gier said.

"That's the way you people think, isn't it?"

"Not really," de Gier said patiently. "It's the way it sounds to you. You are involved, you see. The dead man is your brother. If a friend of mine dies, or if my cat gets run over, or if my mother gets sick, I'll be upset. I assure you that I will be very upset."

"But when you find my brother in a pool of blood . . ."

"I am upset too, but I keep the feeling down. I won't be of much help if I crack up, will I? And this looks like a strange case. I can't figure out why your brother was killed. Perhaps Grijpstra has seen something. You were here all afternoon, weren't you? Did anybody go up to his room?"

"No. Louis came in but I heard him pass the room and go up the second staircase to his own room."

"The Straight Tree Ditch is not a very busy thoroughfare," de Gier said, "but there must be people moving about in it. It would be possible to climb into the room from the street but it would be a real risk. Nobody has reported anything to the constables in the street, for they would have come in to tell me about it."

"Perhaps someone threw something at Abe," Esther said. "He could have been looking out at the canal. He often does. He stands at the window, the window is open, and he stares. He goes into a trance that way and I have to shout at him to break it. Somebody threw a strone at him perhaps."

"The stone would have fallen in the room or bounced off and got back to the street. The constables would have found it. A bloody stone in the street. I'll go and ask them."

He was back in a minute. "Nothing. I asked the men upstairs as well. There is a man from the fingerprint department. He says there is nothing in the room either. No weapon, no stone."

"Abe was a strange man and he died in a strange way," Esther said, "but there will be some technical explanation. There always is, for anything."

"Nothing is stolen, is there?"

"No. There is no money in the house, except what Abe keeps in his wallet. The wallet is still there, in the side pocket of his bush jacket. I saw the bulge. The pocket is buttoned. He usually has a few thousand guilders in it."

"That's a lot of money to keep in one's pocket."

"Abe always had money. He could make it much faster than he could spend it. He owns the warehouse next door; it's full of merchandise, and it never stays there long. There is cotton cloth in it now, bought just before the cotton price went up, and a whole floor stacked with cartons of wool, which he is selling in the street market."

"There is no connection between this house and the warehouse next door is there?"

"No."

"No secret door?"

"No, sergeant. The only way to get to the warehouse is via the street. The courtyards in the back are separated by a high brick wall, much too high to climb."

Grijpstra and the commissaris were coming down the stairs. De Gier called them in and introduced the commissaris to Esther. Two health officers were maneuvering their stretcher up the stairs, they had come with the Water Police launch.

"I'll go upstairs," de Gier said. "I think we would like to have the contents of the pockets before the body is taken away. You'll be given a receipt, Miss Rogge."

"Yes," the commissaris said. "We'll be off for a while now but we may have to come back later. I hope you don't mind the intrusion on your privacy, miss, but . . ."

"Yes, commissaris," Esther said. "I'll be waiting for you."

The atmosphere in the street was still eerie. A siren wailed in the square nearby. A fresh platoon of riot police came marching up the narrow quay. Two launches of the Water Police, their foredecks packed with leather-coated constables ready to disembark, were navigating carefully between the moored houseboats and the launch preparing to take Abe Rogge's body aboard.

A young man, exhausted, was being run to the ground on the other side of the canal. Gloved hands grabbed his wrists and the detectives could hear the handcuffs' click and the man's sobbing breath.

"Where to, sir?" Grijpstra asked.

The commissaris was watching the arrest. "Hmm?"

"What now, sir?"

"Anywhere, a quiet place somewhere, a pub, a café. You go and find it. I am going back into the house a minute. When you find a good place you can telephone the Rogge house. The number will be in the book. Terrible, isn't it?"

"What, sir?"

"That manhunt just now. These riots bring out the worst in everyone."

"They weren't manhandling him, sir, they only made an arrest. The man has probably wounded a policeman in the square. They wouldn't go to so much trouble to catch him otherwise."

"I know, I know," the commissaris said, "but it's degrading. I have seen men hunted down like that during the war."

Grijpstra had seen it too but he didn't say anything.

"Right, run along."

"Sir," Grijpstra said and tapped de Gier on the shoulder.

"So where to?" de Gier asked. "Do you know anything here? The pubs will all be closed and I wouldn't want a police conference in a pub here right now anyway."

Grijpstra was staring at the policemen across the water. They were marching their prisoner to a Water Police launch. The prisoner wasn't resisting. Three men going for a walk.

"Hey."

"Yes," Grijpstra said. "The only place I can think of is Nellie's bar. It will be closed but she'll open up if she is in."

"Don't know the place."

"Of course you don't."

They read the sign together. It said "If I don't answer the bell don't bang on the door for I won't be in." They read it three times.

"What nonsense," de Gier said finally. "If she isn't in she won't mind us banging on the door."

Grijpstra rang the bell. There was no answer. He banged on the door. A window opened on the second floor.

"Fuck off. Do you want a bucket of dishwater all over you?"

"Nellie," Grijpstra shouted, "it's me."

The window closed and they heard steps.

"It's you," Nellie said. "How nice. And a friend. Very nice. Come in."

The lights were switched on and they found themselves in a small bar. The only color in the bar seemed to be pink. Pink curtains, pink wallpaper, pink lampshades. Nellie was pink too, especially her breasts. De Gier stared at Nellie's breasts.

"You like them, darling?"

"Yes," de Gier said.

"Sit down and have a drink. If you buy me a bottle of champagne I'll give you topless service."

"How much is a bottle of champagne?"

"A hundred and seventy-five guilders."

"I am a policeman," de Gier said.

"I know you are, darling, but the police pay a hundred and seventy-five guilders too. I hate corruption."

"Do you ever have any policemen in here?"

Nellie smiled coyly and looked at Grijpstra.

"You?" de Gier asked.

"Sometimes," Grijpstra said, "but I don't pay. Nellie is an old friend."

"And you get topless service?"

"Of course he does," Nellie said briskly. "What will you have? It's a bit early but I'll mix you a cocktail. I don't serve straight drinks."

"No, Nellie," Grijpstra said. "We want to use your bar for an hour or so. Our commissaris wants a quiet place to talk; there will be some others as well. Do you mind?"

"Of course not, dear." Nellie smiled and bent over the bar and ruffled Grijpstra's hair. The breasts were very close to de Gier now and his hands twitched. "The bar is closed tonight anyway," Nellie crooned. "These damn riots are bad for business. I haven't seen a customer for two days and my runners can't get anyone through the roadblocks."

Her lips framed a snarl. "Not that I would welcome any customers these days, not with all this tension about."

"And you still dress like that?" de Gier asked, and stared.

Nellie giggled. "No. I wear jeans and a jersey, like everybody else, but I don't want Grijpstra to see me in a jersey. He is used to me like this, so I slipped on a dress."

"Wow," de Gier said.

Nellie patted her breasts. "Disqualified me for a Miss Holland contest once. I had too much, they said. But they are good for business."

"Do you have a license for this place?" de Gier asked.

Her face clouded. "I thought you were a friend."

"I am curious, that's all."

"No, I don't have a license. This isn't a real bar. It's private. I only entertain one or two clients at a time. The runners bring them in."

Prostitution, de Gier thought, straight prostitution. He knew there were bars like Nellie's bar but he hadn't come across one yet. Grijpstra had and he hadn't told him. He looked at Grijpstra and Grijpstra grinned. De Gier raised his eyebrows.

"Nellie had trouble once and I happened to answer the call."

"That was a long time ago," Nellie said and pouted. "You were still in uniform then. I haven't seen you for a year; you are lucky I am still here." She groaned. "That's the way it is. The nice ones are busy and they don't pay and the bastards take far too much time, but they pay."

De Gier could imagine what the bastards would be like. The stray tourist, the lonely businessman. "Want a nice woman, sir, something really special? Cozy place? All to yourself? A little champagne? Not too expensive? Let me show you the way, sir." And an hour, two hours maybe, three hours at the most later, the bastard would be in the street again with a stomach full of fuzz and a light head and a light wallet. She would squeeze them in stages. A pink spider in a pink web. And out the minute they were dry, out into the street. And the runner would be waiting and slip in for his cut and rush out again, to catch the next fly.

"How's business, Nellie?"

She pulled in her underlip and bit it. "Not so good. The guilder is too high and the dollar too low. I don't get them as I used to get them. It's Japanese now and they make me work."

A majestic woman, tall and wide-shouldered, with long red hair framing the green slanting eyes. De Gier could feel her strength. The strength of a voluptuous snake.

"Who is your friend, Grijpstra?"

"Sergeant de Gier," Grijpstra said.

"Nice. Very nice. I don't often see handsome men nowadays; they are getting scarce." The green eyes became innocent.

"Careful," Grijpstra said. "He has a way with ladies."

She giggled. "Don't worry, Grijpstra. I prefer your type, warm and heavy and fatherly. Handsome men make me nervous. They don't really need me and I hate it when I am not needed. Well, gentlemen, what can I do for you?"

"Let me use the phone," Grijpstra said.

She pushed the phone across the counter of the small bar and suddenly leaned over and kissed him full on the mouth. Grijpstra returned her kiss and reached out and patted her buttocks. De Gier looked away.

4

THE BELL RANG and de Gier went to open the door. The commissaris came in, followed by the doctor and the fingerprint man.

"Evening," the commissaris said brightly.

Grijpstra was rubbing his lips with a crumpled handkerchief. "Nellie's bar, sir, only place we could find. Very quiet."

"Your ears are red," de Gier said.

Grijpstra mumbled through his handkerchief. "Introduce me to the lady," the commissaris said, and climbed on a bar stool.

Nellie smiled and extended a hand. "A drink, commissaris?"

"A small jenever, if you have it."

Nellie poured six glasses.

"I thought you didn't serve straight drinks," de Gier said and looked at the woman's breasts again. He wasn't the only one who looked. The commissaris was fascinated; so was the doctor, so was the fingerprint man.

"Cleavage," the doctor said. "Lovely word, isn't it? Cleavage?"

The others grunted their agreement.

"Yes," the commissaris said and raised his glass, "but it isn't good manners to discuss a lady's anatomy in her presence. Cheers, Nellie."

The glasses were raised, emptied and plonked down on the counter. Nellie grabbed the bottle and filled them again.

"Lovely," the doctor said stubbornly. "As a doctor I should be immune perhaps but I am not. There is nothing more beautiful in the world. There are sunsets, of course, and sailing ships in a strong wind, and a deer running in a glade in the forest, and flowers growing on an old crumbling wall, and the flight of the blue heron, but nothing compares to the female chest. Nothing at all."

"Right," the fingerprint man said.

Nellie smiled and a slow ripple moved her bosom, a delicate ripple which started almost imperceptibly but gathered force gradually and ebbed away again.

De Gier sighed. The commissaris turned his head and stared at de Gier.

"She charges a hundred and seventy-five guilders for a bottle of champagne," de Gier explained.

The commissaris inclined his small head.

"And then she takes off the top of her dress, sir, there's a zipper at the waist." De Gier pointed at the zipper.

Grijpstra had put his handkerchief away and was fumbling with a black cigar which he had found in a box on the counter. "What do you want the commissaris to do?" he asked gruffly. "Order champagne?"

The commissaris smiled and scraped a match. "Here," he said mildly. "It isn't the right night for champagne."

Grijpstra inhaled and glared at de Gier. The smoke burned Grijpstra's throat and he began to cough, pushing himself away from the bar and upsetting a stool. The smoke was still in his lungs and he couldn't breathe and he was stamping on the floor, making the glasses and bottles, lined up on narrow shelves attached to a large mirror, touch and tinkle.

"Easy," the doctor said, and began to pound Grijpstra's solid back. "Easy, put that cigar away!"

"No. I'll be all right."

"Syrup," Nellie said. "I have some syrup, dear."

The thick liquid filled a liqueur glass and Grijpstra swallowed obediently.

"All of it," Nellie said.

Grijpstra emptied the glass and began to cough again, the cigar smoldering in his hand.

"Stop coughing," de Gier said. "You have had your syrup. Stop it, I say." Grijpstra hiccupped. "That's better."

They drank their second glass of jenever and Grijpstra quieted down.

"We'll have to talk business," the commissaris said to Nellie. "I hope you don't mind, dear."

"Do you want me to go away?"

"Not unless you want to. Now, what did you think, doctor? You had time to study the body, did you?"

The doctor rested his eyes on the lowest point of Nellie's cleavage. "Yes," he said slowly. "Yes, quite. I had enough time although we'll have to do some standard tests later, of course. I have never seen anything like it. He must have been killed this afternoon, at four o'clock perhaps, or four thirty. The blood was fresh. I would think he was hit by a round object, small and round, like an old-fashioned bullet fired by a musket. But it looks as if he was hit several times. There were marks all over the face, or over the remains of the face, I should say. Every bone is smashed, jaws, cheekbones, forehead, nose. The nose is the worst. It seems that the object, whatever it was, hit the nose first and then bounced about."

"A musket," the commissaris said. "Hmm. Somebody could have stood on the roof of that old houseboat opposite the house and shot him from there. But it's unlikely. The Straight Tree Ditch has been patrolled by riot police all afternoon. They would have noticed something, wouldn't they?"

"Your problem, it seems," the doctor said. "All I found was a corpse with a smashed face. Perhaps someone clobbered him with a hammer, jumped about like a madman and kept on hitting him. How about that?"

He looked at the fingerprint man. The fingerprint man was shaking his head.

"No?" the commissaris asked.

"Don't know," the fingerprint man said, "but I found funny prints. There was blood on the windowsill, not much, traces of blood really. But there was also blood on the wall *above* the window, small imprints of a round object, like the doctor said. Round. So the madman must have been banging away at the wall as well, and on the windowsill. With a hammer with a round head. There were imprints on the floorboards too."

"Sha," de Gier said.

"Pardon?" the commissaris asked.

"No," de Gier said, "not a hammer. But I don't know what else."

"A ball," Grijpstra said. "A little ball which bounced about. Elastic, a rubber ball."

"Studded with spikes," the fingerprint man said. "That would explain the imprints. I photographed them and we'll have them enlarged tomorrow. There were marks, groups of red dots. Say you hammer a lot of spikes into a rubber ball, the heads of the spikes will protrude slightly.

We can do a test. Leave some open places so that the rubber can still touch whatever it hits and bounce back."

"But there would have been a lot of balls, wouldn't there?" the commissaris asked. "One ball wouldn't do all that damage, so somebody would be pitching them from the roof of that houseboat, one after another, assuming Abe Rogge was standing in the window and taking them all full in the face. And we found nothing. Or did I miss anything?"

"No sir," Grijpstra said. "There were no balls in the room."

"Silly," de Gier said. "I don't believe a word of it. Balls ha! Somebody was there, right in the room, and hit him and went on hitting him. The first blow knocked him down and the killer couldn't stop himself. Must have been in a rage. Some weapon with spikes. A good-day."

"Yes," the commissaris said thoughtfully, "a good-day. A medieval weapon, a metal ball on the end of a short stick and the ball is spiked. Sometimes the ball was attached to the handle with a short chain. Would explain the marks on the wall and the windowsill, a weapon like that covers a sizable area. The killer swung it and he hit the wall with the backward stroke. What do you say, doctor?"

The doctor nodded.

"So the killer left and took the weapon with him. Nobody saw him, nobody heard him. The riots on the Newmarket may have drowned the noise."

"His sister heard nothing," de Gier said. "She was upstairs part of the time and in the kitchen part of the time. And that young fellow was upstairs too."

"Could have been one of them," Grijpstra said.

"They both benefit by the death," the commissaris said. "His sister inherits and the young man might believe he could take over the business. And we may assume that it was murder as there seems to have been some planning. The riots may have been used as cover and the weapon is unusual."

"Not necessarily," Grijpstra said. "There may have been a good-day on the wall, as a decoration. Someone lost his temper, grabbed it and . . ."

"Yes, yes," the commissaris said. "We'll have to find out, but I don't want to go back now. Tomorrow. You or de Gier, or both of you. There are a lot of suspects. These hawkers live outside the law. They don't pay much tax, sales tax or income tax. They always have more money than they can account for, put away in a tin or hidden in the mattress, or under a loose board. We may be dealing with armed robbery."

"Or a friend had a go at him," de Gier said. "His sister was telling me that he had a lot of arty friends. They would come for meals and drink and talk and he would play games with them, psychological games. They had to admit they were fools."

"What?" the commissaris asked.

De Gier explained.

"I see, I see, I see," the commissaris said, then smiled at Nellie.

"Another glass?" Nellie asked.

"No, coffee perhaps, or would that be too much trouble?"

"Coffee," Nellie said, "yes. It would be the first cup I ever served here. I can make some upstairs and bring it down."

The commissaris looked hopeful. "Does everybody want coffee?"

The five men agreed they all wanted coffee, eagerly, like small children asking for a treat. Nellie changed with them. Her smile was motherly, she wanted to care for them. The feeling in the pink whore's hole changed; the soft-shaded lights, the chintzy chairs, the two low tables with their plastic tops decorated with frilly doilies, the sickening disharmony of pinks, mauves and bloody and fleshy reds no longer inspired the urgency of sex but softened down into an unexpected intimacy; five male disciples adoring the goddess and the goddess cares and gives and flows and oozes and goes upstairs to make coffee in a percolator. Grijpstra reached across the bar and grabbed the stone jar of jenever. The glasses were refilled.

The commissaris sipped. "Yes," he said, and looked over his glass. "Strange place this. So all we have is questions. That remark of yours interested me, de Gier."

De Gier looked up, his thoughts had been far away. "Sir?"

"About Abe Rogge trying to make fools out of his friends. A powerful personality no doubt, even the corpse looked powerful. So he humiliated his entourage. The king and his court. One of the courtiers killed the king."

"We only met one courtier," Grijpstra said, "that young anarchist. Another strong personality."

"Intelligent young man," the commissaris agreed, "and with a grudge. But a grudge against us, the police, the State."

"Against power," Grijpstra said hesitantly.

"And Abe meant power to him?" the commissaris asked. "No, I don't think so. It seemed to me he liked Abe. Did that young lady you talked to like her brother, de Gier?"

De Gier hadn't been listening. The commissaris repeated his question. "Oh yes, sir," de Gier said. "She liked him, and they weren't in each other's way. They lived separate lives, each on a separate floor. They only had an occasional meal together."

"She wasn't dependent on him?"

"No, sir, she works for the university, has a degree."

"We might check her clothes for blood spatters."

"No, no," the commissaris said. "I saw her; she isn't the type to jump about waving a good-day."

"That young fellow you were talking about?"

"No, not him either."

The fingerprint man shrugged.

The commissaris felt obliged to explain. "A man who has killed another man an hour ago will be nervous. Louis *was* nervous. The corpse, the crying sister, the police tramping about. He was suffering from a slight shock, but I didn't see any signs of a real mental crisis."

"You are the man who knows," the fingerprint man said.

"No," the commissaris said, and drained his glass a little too quickly. "I don't know anything. Whoever says he knows is either a fool or a saint, a blithering fool or a holy saint. But I have observed a number of killers in my life. I don't think Louis has killed a man this afternoon, but I could be wrong. In any case, he has handled the corpse, he has been in the room. There'll be some blood on his clothes, explainable blood, not enough to raise a serious suspicion. The judge won't be impressed."

Nellie came back with a full percolator and five mugs. They drank the coffee in silence.

"Thank you," the commissaris said, and wiped his mouth with his hand. "We'll go now. You have been very helpful, Nellie."

"Any time," Nellie said graciously, "but not when I have clients."

"We won't bother you. Grijpstra, would you mind asking about in the street? Perhaps the neighbors saw something. De Gier!"

"Sir."

"You come with me, I have another call to make tonight. I should take Grijpstra but you have more to learn."

They shook hands with Nellie and trooped out. De Gier was last.

"You are lovely," de Gier said quickly. "I would like to come back one evening."

"A hundred and seventy-five guilders," Nellie said, and her face looked cold and closed. "That'll be for the topless service, and the same for another bottle of champagne if you want more."

"Three hundred and fifty guilders?" de Gier whispered incredulously.

"Sure."

He closed the door behind him. The commissaris was waiting for him but at some distance. Grijpstra was closer.

"Did you try?" Grijpstra asked.

"Yes."

"Any luck?"

"Three hundred and fifty guilders."

Grijpstra whistled.

"What's the matter with the woman?" de Gier asked fiercely.

Grijpstra grinned.

"Well?"

"Her husband was a handsome man. Same size as you. Thick curly hair and an air force mustache. Could have been your brother. He invented that bar for her and lived off the spoils. Until he got knifed one night, by a Canadian sailor who wasn't used to jenever."

"De Gier," the commissaris called.

"Coming, sir," de Gier said.

5

THE SUDDEN TRANSITION shocked de Gier into consciously registering his surroundings. The small bar, in spite of its cheap gaudiness, had protected him somewhat and the lush femaleness of the hostess had lulled and excited him simultaneously, but now he was outside again, exposed to the clamor of shrieks and thuds and revving engines on the Newmarket and the plaintive wail of ambulances taking battered bodies to hospitals and racing back again. The clamor was far away, and half a mile of solid buildings, gable houses and warehouses and a few churches and towers shielded him from immediate violence, but the conflict's threat was all around him. His fear surprised him because he had never disliked violence before and he had certainly never run away from a fight, so why should he be glad to be out of it now? There would be plenty of opportunity on the square to practice his judo throws, to dodge attacks and have opponents floor themselves by their own weight and strength.

Perhaps it was the intangibility of the threat that unnerved him; the Straight Tree Ditch was quiet enough, guarded as it was by leather-jacketed riot police in pairs, strolling up and down, respectfully greeting the commissaris by either saluting or lifting their long truncheons. The elm trees were heavy and peaceful, their fresh foliage lit by street lights, and the ducks were asleep, floating about slowly, propelled by subconscious movements of their webbed feet, well out of the way of flying bricks, and the human shapes which had been diving into the cold dirty water to get away from charging constables and the relentless approach of police trucks and patrol cars—a common occurrence that night in the waterways closer to the Newmarket.

Grijpstra had marched away and the doctor and the fingerprint man were already on the launch. The commissaris, limping slightly, was a hundred yards ahead when de Gier finally shook himself free from his muddled thoughts. He sprinted and caught up with the commissaris, who looked approvingly at the sergeant.

"Nice," the commissaris said.

"What's nice, sir?"

"The way you sprint. If I run I get out of breath and the nerves in my legs play up." He looked at his watch. "Ten o'clock, we haven't wasted much time so far."

The commissaris turned into a narrow alley which led to another canal. They crossed a narrow footbridge. The commissaris was now walking briskly and his limp was less noticeable. De Gier ambled along, alert because they were getting closer to the Newmarket and might stumble into trouble, but the canal led nowhere, its water lapping gently at age-old crumbling quays and supporting more ducks, sleeping heaps of feathers emitting an occasional pleasant quack. De Gier remembered having read somewhere that ducks spend some twelve or more hours a day in a dream and he envied their daze, a condition preferable to human sleep on a bed. He was trying to imagine what it would be like to be a dazed duck, bobbing about in one of the city's many harbors or canals, when the commissaris stopped and pointed at a small houseboat.

"That's the one I was looking for," the commissaris whispered. "We are going in there and I want you to grab hold of yourself. A strange person lives on that boat but she is an old friend of mine and perhaps she will be of use. She may shock you perhaps but don't laugh or make a remark, never mind what she says or does. She won't be any good to us if we upset her."

"Yes, sir," de Gier whispered, awed by the unexpected warning. There was no need to whisper, the houseboat was still thirty feet away.

De Gier waited on the quay as the commissaris stepped on the short gangway, stood on the narrow ledge of the boat and knocked on the door. The houseboat looked pretty, freshly painted and its windows decorated with red and white checked curtains, tucked up in the middle and lifted toward the sides by pieces of laced braid, and framing geraniums in Delft blue china pots. Loving care had not been limited to the boat itself but had extended to the quay. A small garden grew on each side of the gangway, hemmed in by low ligustrum hedges and consisting of miniature rock gardens, the dislodged cobblestones piled up and serving as rocks, overgrown with trailers paying homage to the delicate orange laburnum flowers which formed the centerpiece of the arrangement. The entire garden covered no more than some twelve square feet, but de Gier, a dedicated balcony gardener himself, was impressed and promised himself to find the spot again, perhaps just to stand there and gaze or perhaps to see if the designer's artfulness would inspire him to do something more imaginative with his flower boxes than he had been able to do so far.

"Who is it?" a heavy voice asked from within.

"It's me, Elizabeth," the commissaris shouted. "Me and a friend."

"Commissaris!" the voice shouted happily. "Come in! The door is open."

De Gier's eyes were round when he shook the lady's heavy hand. She was old, over seventy, he guessed, and dressed in a black gown which hung to the floor. There was a purse attached by straps to the leather belt which surrounded her ample belly, an embroidered purse with a solid silver handle. Gray hair touched her shoulders and there was a knitted cap on the large head.

"Sergeant de Gier," the commissaris said, "my assistant."

"Welcome, sergeant," Elizabeth said and giggled. "You are looking at my cap, I see. Looks funny, doesn't it? But there is a draft here and I don't want to catch another cold. I have had two already this year. Sit down, sit down. Shall I make coffee or would you prefer something a little stronger? I still have half a bottle of redberry jenever waiting for company but it may be too sweet for your taste. How nice to have visitors! I can't go for my evening walk with all this fuss on the Newmarket and I was just saying to Tabby here that there's nothing on TV tonight and he gets bored just sitting around with me, don't you, Tabby?"

Tabby sat on the floor, looking at de Gier from huge slit eyes, yellow and wicked. De Gier sat down on his haunches and scratched the cat behind the ears. Tabby immediately began to purr, imitating the sound of an outboard engine. He was twice the size of a normal cat and must have weighed between twenty-five and thirty pounds.

Elizabeth lowered her bulk into a rocking chair and pounded her thighs. "Here, Tabby." The cat turned and leaped in one movement, flopping down on his mistress's lap with a dull thud.

"There's a good cat," Elizabeth boomed, and squeezed the animal with both hands so that the air was forced out of its lungs in a full-throated yell, which made the commissaris and de Gier jump, but the cat closed its eyes with sensuous pleasure and continued its interrupted purring. "So? Berry jenever or coffee?"

"Coffee, I think, dear," the commissaris said.

"You make it, sergeant," Elizabeth said. "You'll find everything in the kitchen. I am sure you can make better coffee than I can, and while you are busy the commissaris and I can have a little chat. We haven't seen each other for months and months, have we, darling?"

De Gier busied himself in the kitchen, nearly dropping the heavy coffeepot as he thought of what he had just seen. When Elizabeth sat down he had glimpsed her feet, stuck into boots which would be size thirteen. De Gier had seen travesty before, but always in young people. Only a week ago he had helped to raid a brothel where the prostitutes were men and boys dressed up as females. When he had interrogated them, trying to find a suspect to fit the charge of robbery brought in by a hysterical client, he had been a little disgusted but not much. He knew that the human mind can twist itself into any direction. But de Gier had never met with an old man, an old big man, dressed up as a woman. Elizabeth was a man. Or was she? Was this a real case of a female mind accidentally thrown into the body of a male? The houseboat was definitely female. The small kitchen he was moving about in now showed all the signs of female hands having arranged its pots and pans, having sewed tablecloths and curtains to fit the cramped space, selected crockery in harmony with the neat array of cups on the top shelf of the cupboard and crocheted a small cloth in an attempt to make even the refrigerator look nice and dainty. The room where Elizabeth was now chatting to the commissaris—he could hear her deep voice coming through the thin partition—could be part of a Victorian museum; its armchairs, foot warmers, tea table, framed yellowish photographs of gentlemen with waxed mustaches and high collars had been high fashion, female fashion, a very long time ago.

"Can you manage, sergeant?"

De Gier shuddered. Elizabeth was in the open door, filling it completely; she had to bend her head.

"Yes, Elizabeth." His voice faltered. She was in the kitchen now and he could see the commissaris through the open door. The commissaris was gesticulating frantically. Yes, yes, he wouldn't give the game away, what *was* the silly little man worrying about?

"Yes, Elizabeth, the coffee is perking and I've got sugar, cream, cups, spoons, yes, I've got it all."

"Naughty," Elizabeth said. "You haven't got the saucers. You aren't married, are you, sergeant? Living by yourself, I bet. You weren't planning to serve coffee in cups only, were you? What do you think of these cups? Bought them last week. Just what I've been looking for for years.

My mother had cups like that, cost a few cents when I was a child and now you pay as many guilders, but it doesn't matter, I bought them anyway. And there's a saucer for Tabby too, nasty cat goes on banging it about when I don't keep it filled; he'll crack it if he isn't careful and I'll have to give him an ugly enameled one again. Nasty cat, he got so angry with me yesterday that he didn't watch where he was going and he fell off the roof into the canal and I had to fish him out with a broom and all I got for thanks was a scratch. See here."

She rolled up her sleeve and de Gier saw a thick hairy wrist with a deep scratch on it.

"I have a cat too," and he showed the top of his right hand where Oliver had scratched him that morning.

"Ha," Elizabeth said, whacking him on the shoulder so that he nearly dropped the sugarbowl, which he was refilling from a tin found on the cupboard. "They all do it, but what else can they do, the silly little animals! They can't talk, can they? But they still have to show their tempers. What's your cat? Alley cat or proper aristocracy like my Tabby?"

"Siamese."

"Yes, they are nice too. I had one, years ago now. The neighbor's dog got it when it was still small, grabbed it by the neck and shook it and it was dead when he dropped it. All over in a second. Since then I have always had bigger cats. No dog would try to pick on Tabby. He would be blind and castrated and floating in the canal with his legs up if he only tried to look at my Tabby."

She went back into the living room and de Gier followed, carrying a tray. Elizabeth fussed with the cups and brought out a tin with a Chinese design. "A biscuit, gentlemen?"

De Gier was nibbling his biscuit, inwardly grumbling about its oversweet taste when Elizabeth got up again and opened a drawer. "Here, what do you think of it, commissaris? Didn't I make a nice job of it? A hundred and fifty hours of hard work, I timed it, but it was worth the trouble, wasn't it?"

The commissaris and de Gier admired the bellpull which Elizabeth dangled in front of their eyes. It showed a repeating design of roses, embroidered in cross-stitch. "I have lined it with the material you brought me in that little plastic bag. They are clever nowadays, aren't they? When I was a little girl you had to buy your material by the yard, even when you only needed a little bit, but now it's all supplied in those handy kits. Just the right fit too. All I have to do now is find a set of copper ornaments and sew them on and then I'll hang it over there, next to the door. Just the right place for it. Maybe I'll get a brass bell as well and then I'll pull it and the servant will come. Hahaha."

"Beautifully done, Elizabeth," the commissaris said. "No, don't put it away, I want to see it properly. My wife is doing something like that as well. On linen I think she said it was, pure linen."

"Can't work on linen anymore," Elizabeth said sadly, "not even with a magnifying glass. If the design isn't printed on the cloth I can't follow it; on linen you have to count the stitches, from a chart. I used to like doing that but now I get a headache when I try. We are getting old. It was very thoughtful of you giving me the bellpull kit, commissaris. Good of you not to forget an old woman living by herself."

"I like coming to see you," the commissaris said, "and I would come more often if I wasn't so busy and if my legs didn't make me ill all the time, but this visit tonight isn't a social call. That's why the sergeant came with me. He is a detective and we are working tonight. There's been a manslaughter on the Straight Tree Ditch this afternoon."

"Manslaughter? Nothing to do with the riots, I suppose?"

"No. A man's face got bashed in. Abe Rogge, a hawker. The house is close, perhaps you know the man."

"That handsome man with the blond beard? Big fellow? With a golden necklace?"

"Yes."

"I know him." Elizabeth pursed her lips. "He has spoken to me. Often. He has even visited me here. He's got a stall on the Albert Cuyp street market in town, hasn't he?"

"Had."

"Yes, yes. Got killed, did he? What a shame. We haven't had any crime here for as long as I can remember. Not since those two idiot sailors clobbered each other years and years ago and I don't think they were ever charged. I pulled them apart and one of them slipped and fell into the canal."

She rubbed her hands gleefully. "Maybe I shoved him a little, did I? Hehehehe."

"Ah well, there has to be a first time for everything. Manslaughter, you said? Or murder? I saw some murders when I was on the force, but not too many of them, thank the Lord. Amsterdam isn't a murderous city although it's getting worse now. It's those newfangled drugs, don't you think?"

"You were on the force?" de Gier asked in a sudden high voice. The commissaris kicked him viciously under the table and de Gier began to rub his shin.

"Constable, first class," Elizabeth said proudly, "but that was some years ago, before I retired. My health was a bit weak, you see. But I liked the job, better than being lady of the toilets. Five years on the force and thirty years in the toilets. I think I can remember most of my police days but there wasn't much happening when I was scrubbing floors and polishing taps and carrying towels and cakes of soap. And all these men pissing, piss piss piss all day. I thought in the end that that was all men ever do, hehehehehe."

The commissaris laughed and slapped his thighs and kicked de Gier under the table again. De Gier laughed too.

"I see," he said when he had finished laughing.

"But tell me about Abe Rogge's death, commissaris," Elizabeth said.

The commissaris talked for a long time and Elizabeth nodded and stirred her coffee and poured more coffee and handed out biscuits.

"Yes," she said in the end. "I see. And you want me to find out what I can find out. I see. I'll let you know. I can listen in the shops and I know a lot of people here. It's about time I paid some visits."

The commissaris gave her his card. "You can phone me in the evenings too. My home number is on the card."

"No," Elizabeth said. "I don't like telephoning gentlemen at their homes. The wives don't like it when a spinster like me suddenly wants to talk to hubby."

The commissaris smiled. "No, perhaps you are right. We'll have to be on our way, Elizabeth, thanks for the coffee, and you did a beautiful job on the bellpull."

"Commissaris," de Gier said when they were on the quay again.

"Yes?"

De Gier cleared his throat. "Was that really a friend of yours, commissaris?"

"Sure. I kicked you just in time, didn't I? I thought I had warned you before we went in. *That,* as you put it, once was Constable First Class Herbert Kalff. Served under me for a while, used to patrol this part of the city, but he had a problem as you will understand. He thought he was a woman and the idea got stronger and stronger. We put him on sick leave for a year and he was more or less all right when he came back but it started again. Claimed he was a girl and wanted to be Elizabeth. He was on sick leave again and when there was no change we could only retire him. By that time she was a woman. There wasn't much medical science could do for her then. I imagine they operate on cases like that now. The poor soul has to live in a male body. She got a job as a lavatory lady in a factory but they made fun of her and she didn't last. She thinks that she was there for a long time but it isn't the truth. Her self-respect makes her say that. The truth is that she was declared unemployable and has lived on State money ever since. I've kept in touch and the social workers call on her but there was no need really; she has had a stable personality ever since she chose to be a woman, and she is incredibly healthy. She's over seventy, you know, and her mind is clear."

"Shouldn't she be in a home for the elderly?"

"No, the jokers would make fun of her. Old people are like children sometimes. We'll leave her here as long as possible."

"And you visit her regularly?" De Gier's voice was still unnaturally high.

"Of course. I like her. I like walking about this part of town and she makes a good cup of coffee."

"But he, she's mad!"

"Nonsense," the commissaris said gruffly. "Don't bandy that word about, de Gier."

They walked awhile in silence.

"How's your rheuma, sir? You have been in bed for a while, they tell me."

"Incurable," the commissaris said pleasantly. "Drugs help a bit but not much. I don't like the medicines anyway. Horrible little pills, chemicals, that's all they are. Lying in a hot bath helps but who wants to be in a hot bath all day, like a frog in the tropics?"

"Yes," de Gier said, trying to think of a more helpful remark.

"And she isn't mad," the commissaris said.

"I can't understand it," de Gier said slowly. "The person is unnatural, absolutely, and you go to see her. Aren't you frightened or disgusted?"

"No. She is different, but that's all really. Some invalids look gruesome when you meet them for the first time but you get used to their deformity, especially when they are lovely people, just as Elizabeth is lovely. She is a kind and intelligent person so why would you be frightened of her? You are frightened of your own dreams, it seems to me. You *do* dream, don't you?"

"Yes sir."

"Any nightmares?"

"Yes."

"What happens when you have a nightmare?"

"If it goes wrong I wake up in a sweat and I scream but usually it doesn't come to that. I can control the dreams somehow, get out of the most gruesome parts anyway. I find a weapon in my hand and I kill whoever is chasing me, or there's a car in the right spot and I jump into it and they can't catch up with me."

"Very good," the commissaris said, and laughed. "But you don't always get away, and then you suffer."

"Yes," de Gier said reluctantly.

"But why? The dream is part of you, isn't it? It's your own mind. Why should your own mind frighten you?"

De Gier stopped. They had reached the narrow footbridge again and de Gier was ahead of the commissaris, so the commissaris had to stop as well.

"But I can't avoid my dreams, can I, sir? I *can* avoid that . . . well, apparition in the houseboat. It scares me. I don't have to go there."

"Shouldn't I have taken you, sergeant?" the commissaris asked quietly.

"Well, yes, sir. Maybe it can help us with our investigation. It lives in the area and it has police training. May be useful. Yes, you should have taken me."

"So?"

"But you can't ask me to enjoy the experience."

"I am not aware that I am asking you to enjoy Elizabeth's company." The commissaris was smiling.

"No. Yes. Perhaps you are not. But you won't let me . . ."

"Let you what?"

De Gier raised his hands helplessly and walked on, slowly, so that the commissaris could keep up with him.

"We are all connected," the commissaris said softly. "Elizabeth is part of you, and you are part of her. Better face up to it."

They were passing the Rogges' house and Grijpstra was waiting at the door.

"Nothing, sir," Grijpstra reported. "The house on this side is a warehouse and it belongs to Abe Rogge. It's full of merchandise, wool and various types of cloth. Esther Rogge opened the door for me. Nothing there. The neighbors on the other side saw nothing special but they claim that quite a few people walked about this afternoon. The constables on duty let anybody through who lived here, without asking for any identification."

"Did you check the houseboat, Grijpstra?"

"Yes, sir. It's a wreck as you can see. Windows broken and everything. I found nothing extraordinary. A lot of rubbish, a broken fish knife and a plastic bucket and some rusted fishhooks and the usual collection of used condoms. I checked the roof as well but I had to be careful; the roof is rotten too, full of holes."

"Nobody fired a musket from there, you think? Or threw balls?"

"No, sir."

The launch had come back and was waiting for the commissaris. Grijpstra climbed aboard, de Gier hesitated.

"Don't you want to come, de Gier?" the commissaris asked.

"Perhaps I should have another talk with Esther Rogge and that young fellow, Louis Zilver. I would like to have a list of Abe's friends, and girlfriends."

"Can't it wait till tomorrow?"

"It could wait," de Gier said, "but we are here."

"Grijpstra?" Grijpstra looked noncommittal. "All right," the commissaris said, "but don't overdo it. The woman is tired and that young man isn't very easy to get along with. Don't lose your temper."

"No, sir," de Gier said, and turned on his heels.

6

HIS SUIT was stained with soapstone powder and his right trouser leg smeared with red paint. He hadn't noticed anyone throwing paint but someone had. His socks were still wet, for although the water cannon hadn't hit him full on, he had been forced to run through puddles and mud had oozed into his shoes. He badly wanted to go home and have a hot shower and lounge about his small flat in the kimono he had bought at a department store where they were having a Japanese day. He wanted Oliver to be asleep on his legs while he looked through the paper and smoked and sipped tea. He also wanted a meal, some spaghetti perhaps, a dish he could cook quickly and tastefully, and Oliver would be sitting on the chair, his only chair, while he squatted on his bed and ate the spaghetti from a bowl. And then, afterwards, a cigarette on the balcony. He would have to do something about his flower boxes. He had lobelia in them again, and alyssum, like last year, and a geranium in a pot hanging from the wall. There might be more interesting plants. He stopped and cursed. Elizabeth, the artful gardener. Nellie and her three hundred and fifty guilders. Had he joined the criminal investigation department to meet crazy people? To be with them? To try to understand them? To find, as the commissaris had suggested, his own connection with them? The commissaris! Silly little wizard with his limp?

"Mustn't talk about the commissaris like that, Rinus," he told himself. "You admire the man, remember? You like him. He is an advanced man, he knows far more than you do. He understands. He is on a different level. Higher, Rinus, much higher."

He stood at Esther's front door but he didn't ring the bell. The launch was taking off, the water sergeant was hauling in the mooring rope. The commissaris and Grijpstra were talking on the foredeck. They probably thought he had gone in already. He might not go in at all. What was he doing here anyway? Was he being the efficient policeman, efficient and energetic, going on when others were having a break? Or did he want to hold Esther's hand again?

A lovely woman, Esther. Not a cheap whore like Nellie who had bedazzled him with her big shapeful tits and low oozing voice, a gritty oozing voice. A voice can't be gritty and oozing at the same time but hers *was*. It *was,* damn it. "Easy, Rinus," he told himself. "You are losing control. Today has been too much for you. A battered corpse and a whole square full of dancing idiots throwing soapstone powder and paint and all those uniformed bullies charging the idiots and the sirens, it was too much for you. The commissaris shouldn't have left you, he knew you were cracking up. But he left you all the same, didn't he?"

De Gier listened to the silence of the canal. So he had. And if the commissaris had left him on his own he must have had faith. Policemen don't usually work on their own, they work in pairs. Detectives work in pairs too. So that the one can check the other, restrain him if necessary if he loses his temper, or touches his gun. The one policeman protects the other by restraining him. He protects him against himself. It is the task of the police to protect the civilian against himself. It is the task of the policeman to protect his mate against himself. He was talking aloud now, droning the words.

"Shit," de Gier said and pressed the bell.

Esther opened the door.

"You," Esther said. "Sergeant Rinus de Gier."

De Gier tried to smile.

"Come in, sergeant."

Esther looked better. There was color on her face again and she had made up her lips.

"I am having something to eat. Would you care to join me, sergeant?"

"Please."

She led the way to the kitchen. He was given a plate of soup, hot tomato soup from a tin. De Gier didn't like tomato soup and never ate the bloody-looking fluid but he didn't mind now. She cut him a piece of bread and there were gherkins on the table and olives, and a piece of blue-veined cheese. He ate it all while Esther watched him.

"We can have coffee upstairs."

He hadn't said anything during the meal and now he merely nodded.

"A nice room," de Gier said, from the deep low chair Esther had directed him to, "and you have a lot of books."

Esther waved at the two walls covered by bookcases. "A thousand books and I have learned nothing from them. The piano has been of more use to me."

He got up and walked toward the baby grand. An étude by Chopin was lying on the stand and he put a hand on the keyboard and picked away, trying to read the notes.

"That's very nice," Esther said. "Do you play often?"

"No. I had piano lessons as a child but I switched to the flute. I play with Grijpstra, the adjutant you met today."

"What does he play?"

"Drums," he said and grinned. "Someone left a set of drums in our office at Headquarters, years ago now, we have forgotten why, but Grijpstra remembered that he played drums once and started again and I found my flute. It's a silly combination perhaps but we manage."

"But that's beautiful," Esther said. "Why shouldn't drums and flute go together. I'd love to hear you play. I could play with you too. Why don't you both come one evening and we can try?"

"It's free music," he said. "We have some themes we use, church music mostly, sixteenth and seventeenth century, but then we go off and we play anything. Trills and bangs."

"I'll fit in somehow," Esther said confidently.

He laughed. "O.K. I'll ask Grijpstra."

"What else do you do?" Esther asked.

"I fuss with my cat and I try to do my job. Like tonight. I've come to ask you questions. If you don't mind, of course. I'll come back tomorrow if you mind."

She sat down on the piano stool. "Right, sergeant, go ahead. I feel better now, better than I did this afternoon. I have even slept for an hour. Maybe one shouldn't sleep when one's brother has been murdered, but it seemed the best thing to do. He was my last relative, I am alone now. We are Jewish. Jews think that families are very important; perhaps we are wrong. People are alone, it's better to realize the truth. I never had much contact with Abe, no real contact. You are alone, too, aren't you?"

"Yes."

"You understand perhaps."

"Perhaps. Did your brother have a weapon in his room, a funny weapon? Something with a studded ball at its end, a weapon which can be swung?"

"A good-day?" Esther asked. "You mean that medieval weapon? I know what it is. It is often described in Dutch literature and in history. I took history at university, Dutch history, murder and manslaughter through the ages. Nothing changes."

"Yes, a good-day."

"No, there was no weapon in Abe's room. He used to carry a gun, a Luger I think it was, but he threw it into the canal years ago. He said it no longer fitted his philosophy."

Esther fumbled in her handbag. "Here, I found this, his passport and a notebook."

He looked through the passport and saw visas for Czechoslovakia, Rumania and Poland. There were also entry and exit stamps from Tunisia and Morocco. The notebook contained names and telephone numbers.

"A hundred names," he said. "Too many to investigate. Any close friends? Boyfriends? Girlfriends?"

"Girls," Esther said. "Just girls. Lots and lots and lots. Two a day sometimes, more even. It disgusted me to see them trooping in and out. Last Sunday he had three, just after he had come back from Morocco. They couldn't wait. He had one before each meal. The first came before breakfast. She is a tourist guide and starts early but she had to have her sex first."

De Gier wanted to whistle but rubbed his chin instead. "And he accommodated them all?"

"The pretty ones."

"Were all his contacts as casual as that?"

"No. He would go and see Corin. She works at the university with me. I don't think he just slept with her although perhaps he did. Corin never discussed him much. Her name is in the notebook, I'll mark it. Corin Kops. You can find her address in the telephone directory."

"Anyone else?"

"Yes, a student, a very young girl. Studies medicine. I think he was fascinated by her or perhaps she just annoyed him. Wouldn't give in so easily. I'll mark her name as well. Tilda van Andringa de Kempenaar."

"Beautiful name."

"Yes, she is nobility, perhaps that's why she won't give in. Blue blood."

"Copulation doesn't mean an introduction," de Gier said, and grinned. His sanity had returned, or rather, it was beginning to return. He still felt shaken. He closed his eyes and tried to think.

"You aren't falling asleep, are you?" Esther asked. "You must be very tired. Shall I give you a blanket? You can sleep on the couch if you like. I'll wake you up at any time you say."

"No, no, I have to go home to feed my cat. Thanks anyway. Business, that's what I wanted to ask. Do you have his business records here? I'd like to look through them. I am no expert at bookkeeping but I'd like to have some idea about the size of his transactions."

"Louis takes care of his books, he's got them upstairs. He is in now. I'll ask him if you like."

De Gier had been hearing an irregular buzzing sound for the last ten minutes and a noise which seemed like scraping. It came from the floor above and he looked at the ceiling.

"Is *he* making that noise upstairs?"

She giggled. "No, maybe the killer has returned and is whirring his deadly ball. Why don't you go up and have a look?"

He didn't feel like leaving the comfortable chair but he got up obediently.

"Yes," Louis said, and looked up at de Gier who had opened the door. He was sitting on the floor and picked up a toy mouse, winding its clockwork. De Gier's mouth was half open. He hadn't expected what he saw. The floor was full of small tin animals—mice, birds, turtles, frogs, even moles and giant beetles. Most of them were moving. The mice stood up every two seconds and then fell down again, busily going on with their zigzag tours on the bare boards of the floor. The frogs jumped, the turtles ambled, the birds hopped and waved their tails, the beetles zoomed. Every now and then one of them would stop, and Louis would pick it up and wind the key. Some of them had pushed themselves against the wall and were burring aimlessly. A bird had been stopped by a small carpet and was jumping feebly, trying to pass the obstacle. A beetle had fallen on its side and its motor was whirring at full speed.

"Samples," Louis said loudly. "Abe bought a few thousand of them and I took these from the warehouse. Most of them work. Crazy, isn't it?"

"Yes," de Gier said. "How long have you been playing with them?"

"Only started just now. It's amusing isn't it? I had them when I was a child but never more than one at a time. Businessmen can amuse themselves on a large scale as you see. No child will ever have a collection like this."

De Gier had squatted down and saved the animals who had got stuck at the wall, by pointing them at the center of the room. "Hey," Louis said. "I didn't invite you to join me, did I?"

"No," de Gier said, and wound up a frog.

"Never mind. You can play if you like. Have the police made any progress in the case yet?"

"No. The police are baffled."

"It's human fate to be baffled," Louis said, and began to sweep up the toys, wrapping each animal in tissue paper, and replacing it in a carton.

"I hear you kept Abe Rogge's books. Can I see them?"

Louis pointed at the desk. "It's all there, you can take them with you if you like. I have kept the books up to date, the accounting is simple. Most purchases are covered by invoices and they are all paid. Our sales were mostly for cash and they are entered in a cash book. And there's some wages-administration; only Abe and myself are on the payroll."

"Your warehouse is full of goods, I hear."

"Yes."

"All paid for."

"Yes."

"How much do you have in stock?"

"In money?"

"Yes."

"A hundred and twenty thousand guilders and something."

"That's a lot," de Gier said, "and all paid for. Was Abe financing his own deals?"

Louis laughed. "The bank wouldn't give us a penny, they don't back hawkers. Abe borrowed from friends. Mostly from Bezuur, his oldest and best friend."

"So he had friends," de Gier said and nodded. "Very good."

Louis looked up from his packing. "The police would suspect friends, wouldn't they? Friends are close and friendship can change into hatred. Two sides of the same coin."

"Yes, yes. Who is Bezuur?"

"A rich man, a very rich man. He and Abe went to school together, to school and to the university. They both dropped out. They studied French. They also traveled together, mostly in France, of course, and in French North Africa. They also traded together but Bezuur's father died and left him a big business, earth-moving equipment. He's a millionaire."

"And he lent Abe money?"

"Yes, at bank interest. Eleven percent we are paying now. The firm owes him sixty thousand, to be repaid in three months' time when we have moved the stocks in the warehouse, maybe earlier. Abe was planning a long holiday and I was supposed to go with him."

"North Africa again?"

"No, we planned to sail a boat to the Caribbean."

"And what happens now?"

"I'll sell the stocks. I phoned Bezuur about an hour ago to tell him about Abe's death. He said I can go on with the business if Esther lets me, for she will inherit it. And I can repay the loan as planned."

"Did you speak to Esther?"

"Not yet."

"And what will you do when you have moved the stocks?"

"No idea. Find a partner maybe and go on as before. I like this business, especially the irregularity of it."

"And if Esther won't let you go on?"

Louis shrugged and smiled. "I don't care. Bezuur will sell the stocks and get his money back and the rest will go to Esther. I'll just leave. Nobody depends on me."

"Detached, are you?" de Gier said, offering a cigarette.

"Thanks. Yes. I am detached. To hell with it. But I am sorry Abe died, I enjoyed being with him. He taught me a lot. If he hadn't taught me I would be very upset now but you find me playing happily with clockwork animals. And I am not pretending. Any more questions?"

"Was Abe close to anyone else? Any enemies? Competitors?"

Louis thought, taking his time. "He slept with a lot of girls," he said in the end. "Perhaps he stepped on somebody's toes. I am sure some of those girls had lovers, or husbands even. He behaved like a stud bull at times. And he insulted people, of course. Insulted them by not caring. They could go blue in the face and blow steam out of their ears and he would just laugh, not offensively to annoy them, but because he didn't care. He would tell them they were balloons, or stuffed lifeless animals."

"But he included himself, didn't he?"

"Oh yes, he refused to see any value anywhere."

"So why did he make money then?"

Louis got up and put the carton in a corner of the room. "If nothing matters you can laugh and you can cry, can't you?" De Gier looked blank. "Abe preferred to laugh, with a full belly and a cigar in his mouth and a car parked in the street and a boat in the canal. I don't think he would have minded if he hadn't had any of those things, but he preferred having them."

"Ah yes," de Gier said.

"You don't understand," Louis said. "Never mind."

"You really admired him, didn't you?" de Gier asked viciously.

"Yes, copper, I did. But now he is dead. The balloon has burst. More questions?"

"No."

"Then I'll go to the nearest pub and have six glasses of colored alcohol, and then I'll go and sleep somewhere. There'll be a girl in the pub who'll let me go home with her. I don't want to spend the night here."

De Gier got up from the floor and left the room. He was too tired to think of any suitable repartee. He found the toilet before he returned to Esther's room and washed his face with cold water. There was a small mirror in the lavatory and he saw his own face. His hair was caked with soapstone powder and mud and there were paint spatters on his cheeks; the eyes looked lifeless, even his mustache drooped.

"Well?" Esther asked.

"I heard the name Bezuur."

"Klaas Bezuur," Esther said slowly, inviting him with a gesture to sit in the easy chair again. "Yes, I should have mentioned him but I haven't seen Klaas for such a long time that I have forgotten him. He asked me to marry him once but I don't think he meant it. Abe and he were very close once, but not anymore."

"Did they fall out?"

"No. Klaas became rich and he had to give up working in the street market and traveling about with Abe. He had to take care of his business. He lives in a villa now, in one of the new suburbs, Buitenveldert I think."

"I live in Buitenveldert," de Gier said.

"Are you rich?"

"No, I have a small flat. I expect Bezuur lives in a quarter-of-a-million bungalow."

"That's right. I haven't been to the house although he has asked us but Abe didn't want to go. He never visited anyone unless he had a good reason, sex, or a party, or a business deal, or a book he wanted to discuss. Klaas doesn't read. He's a bit of a slob now; he was very fat and closed up the last time I saw him."

"I'd better go," de Gier said, rubbing his face. "Tomorrow is another day. I can hardly see straight."

She saw him to the door. He said good night and meant to walk away but stopped and stared at the canal's surface. A rat, frightened by the tall looming shape of the detective, left its hiding place and jumped. The sleek body pierced the oily surface with a small splash and de Gier watched the converging circles fading out slowly.

"Aren't you going?" a voice asked, and he looked around. Esther stood at the open window of her room on the second floor.

"Yes," he called back softly, "but don't stand there."

"He can throw his ball," Esther said, "if he wants to. I don't mind." De Gier didn't move.

"Rinus de Gier," Esther said, "if you aren't going you may as well come in again. We can keep each other company." Her voice was calm.

The automatic lock clicked and de Gier climbed the two flights of stairs again. She stood at the window when he came in, and he stood behind her and touched her shoulder. "The killer is a madman," he said softly. "To stand here is to invite him."

She didn't reply.

"You are alone in the house. Louis told me he is sleeping out. If you like, I'll telephone Headquarters and we'll have two constables guarding the house. The riot police have gone."

"Here," he said and gave her the toy mouse he had put in his pocket when Louis wasn't looking. Esther had left the window and was wandering through the room. She was looking at the tin animal as if she didn't know what it was.

"A mouse," de Gier said. "You can wind it up and put it on the floor. It walks and it jumps a bit. It's yours."

She laughed. "What's this? Shock treatment? I didn't know the police had become subtle. Are you trying to unnerve me so that I'll drop my defense and give you a valuable clue?"

"No," de Gier said. "It's a clockwork mouse."

"Abe used to give me things too. Seashells and bits of driftwood and dried plants. He would buy them on the market or find them on the beach somewhere and keep them in his room, and then he would suddenly come into my room, usually when he thought that I was depressed about something or other, and give me a present. I still have some of them."

She pointed at a shelf and de Gier saw some shells, bits of white and pink coral, a twig with dried seedpods.

Esther was crying. "A drink," she said. "We need a drink. He has a bottle of cold jenever in the fridge, I'll go and get it."

"No, Esther. I have to go, but you can't stay here by yourself."

"Do you want me to come home with you?"

De Gier scratched his bottom.

She giggled through her tears. "You are scratching your bottom, are you nervous? Don't you want me to come home with you? I'll go to the police hotel if you have one, or you can lock me in a cell for the night."

De Gier adjusted his scarf and buttoned his jacket.

"You look a bit scruffy," Esther said, "but you have had a hard day. You are still handsome. I'll come home with you if you like. The house makes me nervous. I keep on thinking of Abe's face and that spiked ball you all keep talking about. A good-day you said. It's all too horrible."

De Gier brushed his mustache with his thumb and index finger. The hairs were sticking together, he would have to wash it. He grimaced. He would get soap in his mouth. He always got soap in his mouth when he washed his mustache.

"You aren't a sexual maniac, are you?" Esther asked. "It'll be safe to go home with you?" She laughed. "Never mind. If you are a maniac you'll be a very tired maniac. I'll probably be able to handle you."

"Sure," de Gier said. "Why were you standing at the window?"

"I heard a splash. I thought the killer had come back and that he had dropped his ball into the canal."

"So why go to the window? It's the most dangerous place in the house. Abe got killed at the window, or, rather, we think so now."

"I don't mind."

"You want to die?"

"Why not?"

"You are alive," de Gier said. "You'll die anyway. Why not wait?"

Esther stared at him. He noticed that she had a thick underlip and a wide nicely curved upper lip.

"All right," de Gier said. "I'll take you to my sister's place or anywhere else you want to go. You must have friends in town. This Corin lady you mentioned just now, for instance. Or relatives. Or I can take you to a hotel; there are lots of hotels. I have a car, it's parked near the Newmarket. I'll go and pick it up and you can pack a bag. I'll be back in five minutes."

"I'll go with you and come back tomorrow. Perhaps it'll be better tomorrow. I have washed the floor of Abe's room. I won't stay here tonight."

"I have a cat," de Gier said as he opened the door of the car for her. "He's very jealous. He'll probably want to scratch you and he'll wait for you in the corridor in case you want to go to the toilet. Then he'll jump you suddenly and yowl. He may also piss on your clothes."

"Maybe I should go to a hotel after all."

"If you want to."

"No," she said and laughed. "I don't mind your cat. I'll be nice to him and my clothes will be in my bag. It's a plastic bag and it's got a zip. I'll pick him up and turn him over and cuddle him. Cats like to be cuddled."

"He can't stand it if people are nice to him," de Gier said. "He won't know what to do."

"There'll be two of us," Esther said.

De Gier was on the floor, trying to adjust to the hardness of his camping mattress. Esther was standing in the open door of his small bedroom, her finger on the light switch.

"Good night," Esther said.

"Good night."

"Thanks for the use of your shower."

"You are welcome."

"Your bed looks very comfortable."

"It's an antique," de Gier said from the floor. "I found it at an auction. The man said it came from a hospital."

"I like the frame," Esther said. "All those ornate metal flowers. And it's very nicely painted. Did you do it yourself?"

"Yes. It was a hell of a job. I had to use a very fine brush."

"I am glad you didn't use a lot of colors. Just gold, lovely. I hate these new fads. Some of my friends have used all the colors of the rainbow to decorate their houses, and those horrible transfers! Butterflies in the toilet and animals on the bath and funny pictures in the kitchen and you are forced to read the same jokes over and over again. Bah!"

"Bah!" de Gier said.

"This must be a good place to live in. Just a bed and a bookcase and a lot of cushions and plants. Very good taste. Why do you have the one chair? It doesn't seem to fit in."

"It's Oliver's. He likes to sit on a chair and watch me eat. I sit on the bed."

She smiled.

Beautiful, de Gier thought, she is beautiful. She had turned the switch now and the only light in the room came from a lantern in the park. He could only just make out her shape but the light caught the white of her breasts and face. She was wearing his kimono but she hadn't tightened the sash.

She can't feel like it now, de Gier thought. Her brother died today. She must still be in a state of shock. He closed his eyes, trying to destroy the image in his bedroom door but he could still see her. When she kissed him he groaned.

"What's wrong?" she asked softly.

He groaned again. The commissaris will find out. Grijpstra will find out. And Cardozo, the new detective on the murder squad, will find out and make sly remarks. And Geurts and Sietsema will know. The murder squad will have something to discuss again. De Gier the ladykiller. A detective who goes to bed with suspects. But he hadn't planned it. It had happened. Why will they never accept that things happen? Oliver yowled and Esther jumped.

"He bit me! Your cat bit me! He sneaked up to me from behind and bit me! Ouch! Look at my ankle!"

The light was on again and de Gier rushed to the bathroom and came back with a bandage. Oliver sat on the chair and watched the scene. He looked pleased. His ears pointed straight up and his eyes looked bright. His tail flicked nervously. Esther tickled the cat behind the ears and kissed him on the forehead. "Silly cat, aren't you? Jealous cat! It's all right, I won't take him away from you."

Oliver purred.

She switched the light off and took de Gier by the hand.

The kimono had dropped to the floor. Oliver sighed and curled up.

"He doesn't watch, does he?" Esther whispered on the bed.

De Gier got up and closed the door.

7

"No, DEAR," the commissaris' wife said sleepily, and turned over. "It's still early, it's Sunday. I'll make the coffee a little later, let me sleep awhile, sleep sleep . . ."

The rest of the sentence was a mumble, a mumble which changed into a soft pleasant polite snore. The commissaris patted her shoulder with a thin white hand. He hadn't asked for coffee, he hadn't said anything at all. She had probably noticed that he was awake and her sense of duty had been aroused. Dear Katrien, the commissaris thought, dear excellent soul, soul of souls, you are getting old and weak and tired and there are more lines in your face than I can count. Have you ever shared my thoughts? Perhaps you have.

He patted her shoulder again and the gentle snore changed into deep breathing. He sat up and pushed the blankets away and crossed his legs, straightening his spine. He lit a small cigar and inhaled the first smoke of the day, blowing it away toward the open window. In the garden his turtle would be rowing about in the grass. It was eight o'clock and Sunday morning. The city was silent without the growl and clank of traffic. A thrush sang in the garden, the sparrows had left their nests above the drainpipe and were rummaging about in the hedge, twittering softly, and the magpies were looking for more twigs to reinforce their domed nest in the poplar. He could hear the flap of their wings as they wheeled about just outside his window. He grunted contentedly.

There had been a dream and he was searching for its memory. It had been an interesting dream and he wanted to experience it again. Something to do with the garden, and with the small fishpond at the foot of the poplar, and with a splash. He sucked his cigar and the dream came back to him. He had been in the garden but his garden had been much bigger, spreading far into the distance, and the fishpond had been a vast lake. And the poplar was a forest, and the turtle was close. The turtle was his ordinary size, small, compact, self-contained and friendly, with a lettuce leaf in his mouth. The commissaris had been expecting something and so had the turtle, for it was craning its leathery neck and chewing excitedly. It had been staring at the blue metallic sky and the round white moon flooding the lawn with soft downy pale light.

And then it came. A purple spot growing quickly in size. Mauve and moving. Splitting into two individual but similar shapes. Female, with large wings. They were so close that he could see their long limbs, curved breasts, calm faces. He saw their features, high cheekbones and slanting eyes. Quiet faces but intent, purposeful. Wings fluttered as they turned above him, him and the turtle, who had lost his benign solitude and was trying to dance in the high grass and had dropped his lettuce leaf. The commissaris was squatting down, holding on to the turtle's shield. He recognized the winged shapes' faces. They resembled the Papuan who had once been arrested by the murder-squad detectives and who had escaped again without leaving a trace. Perhaps they were his sisters. Or his messengers. Or his thoughts, reaching out from wherever he was now. The commissaris lost his association. The apparitions were so close above him now that he could have touched their slender ankles if he had reached out. The wings moved again and they were gaining height. They hovered above the lake and then, first one, then the other, folded their wings, and dropped. They hit the surface of the lake like arrows and plunged right through.

The turtle had lost all self-control and was capering about at the commissaris' feet, distracting his attention. When he looked up again the mauve figures were with him on the grass, with spread wings, observing him and showing a glimmer of amusement in their sparkling eyes and softly smiling mouths. That was the dream. He rubbed the bald spot on his skull, amazed that the dream had come back to him. He didn't like purple or mauve and he had never been particularly impressed by naked winged angels. Where had the images come from? He now also remembered the events of the previous evening. Nellie's bar. Nellie's colors had been purple and mauve too, and pink, of course. He saw Nellie's large solid breasts again and the cleavage the doctor had been so poetic about. Had Nellie so impressed him that she had helped form this dream, together with the sympathetic presence of his turtle and the glorified version of his garden and the Papuan, a man he had liked once and whose attitude had puzzled him at the time?

The commissaris sighed. It had been a good dream. He picked up the phone and dialed a number. The phone rang for a long while.

"De Gier." The voice on the phone sounded deep and throaty.

"Morning, de Gier."

"Sir. Good morning, sir."

"Listen," the commissaris said. "It's early and it's Sunday, and judging from the way you talk you were asleep when your phone rang. I want you to get up and wash and have some coffee and shave perhaps. When you are ready you can phone me back. I'll be waiting for you."

"Yes, sir. Ten minutes."

"Make it twenty. You can have breakfast first if you like."

"Right," de Gier said.

The commissaris replaced the phone and stretched out. Then he changed his mind and got up and fetched some lettuce leaves from the kitchen. The turtle was waiting for him in the garden and bravely left the grass and marched ponderously on the flagstones leading to the open door of the commissaris' study.

"Morning sir," de Gier said again.

"Tell me," the commissaris said, "about last night. Anything worthwhile?"

"Yes," de Gier said. "Miss Rogge gave me three names and three addresses. Do you have a pen, sir?"

The commissaris noted the names and addresses. De Gier talked. "Yes, yes, yes," the commissaris said.

"Perhaps Grijpstra and I should call on these people today, sir."

"No. Grijpstra can go and I'll go with him. I have other plans for you. Are you ready?"

"Yes, sir."

"Right. Go to our garage and ask for the gray van. Then go to the stores. We have some confiscated textiles, bales of cloth, a good assortment. They are due for auction next week but we can have them. I'll phone the chief clerk at his home later this morning."

"Textiles?" de Gier asked. "The gray van? Do you want me to take the textiles somewhere?"

"Yes. To the street market tomorrow. A detective should be a good actor; tomorrow you can be a hawker. I'll contact the market master at the Albert Cuyp and he'll give you a stall and a temporary license. You won't need more than a few days. Make friends with the other hawkers. If the killer comes from the market you'll be able to pick up a trail."

"Just me, sir?" De Gier didn't sound pleased.

"No. You can take Sergeant Sietsema with you."

"Can't I have Cardozo?"

"Cardozo?" the commissaris asked. "I thought you didn't like Cardozo. You two are always quarreling."

"Quarreling, sir? We never quarrel. I have been teaching him."

"Teaching. O.K. Take him. Perhaps he's the right choice. Cardozo is Jewish and Jews are supposed to be good traders. Maybe he should be the hawker and you can be his assistant."

"I'll be the hawker, sir."

The commissaris smiled. "Right. Phone Cardozo and get him to join you today. Better phone him right now before he leaves for the day. And what about Esther Rogge, was she in a good state of mind when you left her last night?"

There was no answer.

"De Gier?"

"I have her here with me, sir, in my apartment."

The commissaris looked out of the window. One of the magpies was sitting on the grass, looking at the turtle. The turtle was looking back. He wondered what the two could have in common.

"It isn't what you are thinking, sir."

"I wasn't thinking, de Gier, I was looking at my turtle. I had a dream last night, something to do with the Papuan. Do you remember the Papuan?"

"Yes, sir."

"A strange dream. Something about his two sisters. They had wings and they flew into my garden. There was a full moon and my turtle was in the dream as well. My turtle was excited, jumping about in the grass."

"In your dream, sir?"

"Yes. And it was real, more real than the conversation I am having with you now. You dream too, you told me last night."

"Yes, sir. I'd like to hear more about your dream sometime."

"Sometime," the commissaris said, and stirred the coffee which his wife had put on the little table next to his bed. "Sometime we'll talk about it. I often think about the Papuan, possibly because he was the only suspect who ever got away after we had caught up with him. You'd better get Miss Rogge home, I suppose. I'll phone you tonight and tell you what Grijpstra and I found out, or you can phone me. My wife will know where I am."

"Sir," de Gier said, and rang off.

By eleven o'clock the commissaris' black Citroën was parked outside Grijpstra's house on the Lijnbaansgracht opposite Police Headquarters and the commissaris had his finger on the bell.

"Yes," Mrs. Grijpstra's tousled head shouted from a window on the second floor.

"Is your husband in, madam?"

"Oh, it's you, sir. He'll be right down."

The commissaris coughed. He could hear the woman's voice inside the house and Grijpstra's heavy footsteps on the narrow wooden staircase. The door opened.

"Morning, sir," Grijpstra said. "Excuse my wife, sir. She is getting too fat to move around much and she won't answer the door anymore. Just sits near the window and shouts a lot. Right opposite the TV, but there won't be any TV till this afternoon."

"Never mind," the commissaris said.

"We are going to see this Bezuur fellow first, aren't we, sir? Does he know we are coming?"

They were in the car now and Grijpstra greeted the sleepy-eyed constable at the wheel. The constable wasn't in uniform but sported a dark blue blazer with the emblem of the Amsterdam Municipal Police Sports Club embroidered on the left top pocket.

"Yes. I phoned and he will see us right now. Then we can have lunch somewhere and see if we can raise the two ladies on the phone. I would like to see them later today if possible."

"Good," Grijpstra said and accepted a cigar.

"You don't mind working on a Sunday, do you, Grijpstra?"

"No, sir. Not at all, sir."

"Shouldn't you be taking the little ones out?"

"I took the brats to the zoo only last week, sir, and today they are going to play at a friend's house. And they are not so small anymore. The littlest one is six and the other one eight."

The commissaris mumbled.

"Pardon, sir?"

"Shouldn't have asked you to come," the commissaris repeated. "You are a family man and you were up half the night. Sietsema could have come just as well, I don't think he is working on anything now anyway."

"No, sir. But Sietsema isn't on this case, sir. I am."

The commissaris smiled. "How is your oldest son, by the way? He must be eighteen, right?"

"Right sir, but there's nothing right about the boy."

"Doing badly with his studies?"

"Dropped out altogether and now he wants to leave the house. The army doesn't want him and he'll never find a job, not even if he wanted to, which he doesn't. When he leaves the house he'll be applying for national assistance, he says. I never know where he is these days. Rushing about on that little motorbike, I imagine, and smoking hash with his friends. He's sniffing too, caught him the other day. Cocaine powder."

"That's expensive," the commissaris said.

"Very."

"Any idea where he gets the money?"

"Not from me, sir."

"So?"

"I've been with the police a long time, sir."

"Dealing?"

"Everything, I think," Grijpstra said and pretended to be watching the traffic. "Dealing, motorbike stealing, straight-out burglarizing and a bit of prostitution. He doesn't like girls so he'll never be a pimp, but that's the only bad thing he'll never be."

"Prostitution?" the commissaris asked.

"He goes to the wrong pubs, the sort of places where they pick up the shopkeeper from the provinces and get him to take them to a motel."

"That's bad," the commissaris said. "Anything we can do to stop him?"

"No, sir. I am not going to hunt my own son but one of our colleagues will stumble into him and then it'll be reform school and he'll come back worse. I have written him off. So have the social workers. The boy isn't even interested in watching TV or football."

"Neither is Sergeant de Gier," the commissaris said brightly, "so there's still hope."

"De Gier has a cat to care for, and he reads. He has things to do. Flowerpots on the balcony and flute-playing and judo at least one evening a week and visiting museums on Sundays. And when a woman is after him he gives in. Sometimes anyway."

"Yes," the commissaris cackled. "He's giving in right now."

Grijpstra thought.

"Esther Rogge? Nellie didn't want him."

"Esther Rogge."

"He'll never learn," Grijpstra said gruffly. "Bloody fool he is. The woman is involved in the case."

"She's a lovely woman," the commissaris said. "A refined woman even. She'll do him good."

"You don't mind then, sir?" Grijpstra sounded relieved.

"I want to find the killer," the commissaris said, "and quickly, before he swings his ball at somebody else. The man can't be altogether sane, and he is certainly inventive. We still haven't worked out what weapon he used."

Grijpstra sighed and leaned a little further into the soft upholstery of the car. "It may be a simple case after all, sir. The man was a hawker, a street seller. They usually make a lot more money than the taxman should know about and they hide the difference in tins under the bed, or in a secret place behind the paneling, or under the floor somewhere. One of my informers told me that over a hundred thousand guilders were stolen from an old mate of his, a man selling cheese in the street. The cheese-man never reported the theft because he wasn't supposed to have that much money. If the taxman had heard about it he would have stung the poor fellow for at least half of it, so the poor sucker kept quiet and cried alone. But Abe Rogge may have wanted to defend his cache and he got killed."

"By a spiked ball swung at his face?"

"Yes," Grijpstra said, "why not? Maybe the killer is a man who is clever with his hands. A carpenter, a plumber. Maybe he made his own weapon, invented it."

"But he never took Abe's wallet," the commissaris said. "There was a lot of money in the wallet. If he came for money he wouldn't have left a few thousand right in his victim's pocket. He only had to reach for it. An inventive man, you said. Louis Zilver is inventive. Remember that figure he was trying to create out of beads and wire?"

"He threw it into a dustbin," Grijpstra said, "made a mess of it. But the idea was inventive, true."

Grijpstra looked out of the window of the car. They were in the southern part of Amsterdam now, and gigantic stone-and-steel structures blocked the sky, like enormous bricks dotted with small holes.

And they are full of people, Grijpstra thought. Little people. Little innocent people, preparing their Sunday lunch, lounging about, reading the paper, playing with their kids and with their animals, making plans for the rest of the day. He looked at his watch. Or having a late breakfast. Sunday morning, best time of the week.

The car stopped at a traffic light and he found himself staring at a balcony, populated by a complete family. Father, mother, two small children. There was a dog on the balcony too. One of the children was making the dog stand up by dangling a biscuit just above its head. The toddler and the small dog made a pretty picture. The geraniums in the flower boxes attached to the balcony's railing were in full flower.

And we are chasing a killer, Grijpstra thought.

"Louis Zilver," the commissaris said, "not a very well-adjusted young man perhaps. I had him checked out last night. He has a previous conviction, for resisting arrest when caught making a drunken racket in the street. Happened a few years ago. He attacked the constables who tried to put him into a patrol car. The judge was very easy on him, a fine and a lecture. What do you think, adjutant? Do we put him on the list of prime suspects?"

Grijpstra's thoughts were still with the family on the balcony. The harmonious family. The happy family. He was wondering whether he himself, Adjutant Grijpstra, flat-footed sleuth, bogeyman of the underworld, restless wanderer of canals, alleyways, dark cul-de-sacs, would like to be happy, like the young healthy father enthroned on his geranium-decorated balcony on the second floor of a huge transparent brick, facing a main thoroughfare.

"Grijpstra?"

"Sir," Grijpstra said. "Yes, definitely. Prime suspect. Surely. It's all there. Motive and opportunity. Maybe he was greedy, wanted the business for himself. Or jealous of Rogge's interminable successes. Or he might have wanted Esther and Abe wouldn't let him. Or he was trying to get at Esther through Abe. But I don't know."

"No?" the commissaris asked.

"No, sir. He's a bungler, that's what he is."

"A bungler?" the commissaris asked. "Why? His room seemed well-organized, didn't it? Bookkeeping all neatly stacked on a shelf. The bed was made, the floor was clean. I am sure Esther didn't look after the room for him; he must have done it himself. And his clothes were washed; he even had a crease in his trousers."

"Because of Abe," Grijpstra said. "Abe pulled him together. Before he started hanging on to Rogge he was nothing. Dropout from university, sleeping late, drinking, fooling around with beads. He functioned because Abe made him function. I am sure he can do nothing on his own."

"Can't make a weapon that shoots a spiked ball, you mean."

"Yes sir."

"Yes, yes, yes," the commissaris said.

"I think the killer may be some connection at the street market, sir, and it seems to me you are thinking the same way, or you wouldn't be pushing de Gier and Cardozo into their masquerade tomorrow. They are going to be hawkers, didn't you say so?"

"Yes," the commissaris said, and smiled.

"This is the address, sir," the constable at the wheel said.

Grijpstra hissed admiringly as he looked at the bungalow spread on a low artificial hill, sitting in the middle of at least an acre of freshly mown grass, decorated with bushes and evergreens. The gate was open and the Citroën eased itself into the driveway.

The front door of the bungalow opened as they got out of the car.

"Bezuur," the man said as he pumped the commissaris' hand. "I was waiting for you. Please come in."

8

A PUDDING for a face, Grijpstra thought, turning his head to watch Klaas Bezuur. Nobody had said anything for at least a minute. The commissaris, at the far end of the vast room, which covered almost three quarters of the modern bungalow, had made Grijpstra think of his youngest son's rag doll, a small lost object thrown into a large chair. The commissaris was in pain. Self-propelled white-hot needles were drilling into the bones of his legs. He was breathing deeply and had half-closed his eyes, fighting the temptation to close them completely. He felt very tired, he badly wanted to go to sleep. But he had to keep his mind on the case. Klaas Bezuur, the dead man's friend, was facing him.

A pudding, Grijpstra thought again. They have dropped a pudding on a human skull, a pudding of blubbery fat. The fat has oozed down, from the cranium downward. It covered the cheekbones and then it slowly dripped down to the jaws and clung to the chin.

Bezuur was sitting on the edge of his chair, straight up. His round belly hung over his belt and Grijpstra could see folds of flesh, hairy flesh, embedding the navel. The man was sweating. The sweat from his armpits was staining his striped tailor-made silk shirt. Bezuur's face gleamed and drops were forming on the low forehead, joining each other in miniature streams, gliding down, hesitating near the small pudgy nose. It was very hot, of course. Grijpstra was sweating too.

A big man, Grijpstra thought. Over six feet, he must weigh a ton. He'll eat a hundred guilders a day, easily. Bowlsful of cashew nuts probably, and shrimps, and a bucket or two of potatoes, or spaghetti, and a loaf of bread thrown in, bread covered with fried mushrooms and smoked eel and thick slices of ham.

Bezuur reached out and grabbed a bottle of beer out of a carton placed near his chair. He broke off the cap and filled his glass. The thick foam rose quickly and flowed down the sides of the glass, spilling onto the thick rug.

"More beer, gentlemen?"

The commissaris shook his head. Grijpstra nodded. Bezuur tore the cap off another bottle. More foam was sucked into the rug. "Here you are, adjutant."

They looked each other in the eye and raised their glasses, grunting simultaneously. Bezuur drained his glass. Grijpstra took a carefully measured sip; it was his third glass. Bezuur had had six since they came into the room. Grijpstra put the glass down gingerly.

"He is dead, the bastard," Bezuur said, and viciously replaced the glass on a marble-topped side table. It cracked and he looked at it dolefully. "The silly stupid bastard. Or perhaps he was clever. He always said that death is a trip and he liked traveling. He used to talk a lot about death, even when he was a boy. He talked a lot and he read a lot. Later he drank a lot too. He was an alcoholic when he was seventeen years old. Did anybody tell you?"

"No," Grijpstra said. "You tell us."

"An alcoholic," Bezuur said again. "Became one when we entered the university. We were always together, at school and at the university. We passed our high school examinations when we were sixteen. Wonderkids we were. We never worked but we always passed. I was good at mathematics and he was good at languages. When we did work we worked together. A deadly team we were; nobody and nothing could tear us apart. We only worked when we came to an examination and then we would only put in the bare minimum. It was pride, I think. Showing off. We would pretend we weren't listening at classes but we soaked it all up, and we remembered the stuff too. And we made secret notes, on scraps of paper; we didn't have notebooks like the other kids. And no homework, homework was for the birds. We read. But he read more than I did and at the university he began to drink."

"He did?" Grijpstra asked.

"Yes."

Bezuur's hand shot out and another bottle lost its cap. He looked at the cracked glass, and turned around to look at the kitchen door. He must have had more glasses in the kitchen but it was too far, and he drank from the bottle, tossing the cap on the floor. He looked at Grijp-stra's glass but it was still half full.

"I think he was drinking a bottle a day. Jenever. He would drink any brand as long as it was cold. One day he couldn't get his pants on in the morning, his hands trembled too much. He thought it was funny but I worried and made him see a doctor who told him to lay off. He did too."

"Really?" Grijpstra asked. "He stopped drinking straight off? Just like that?"

"Yes. He was clever. He didn't want to be a drunk; it would compli-cate his routine."

"Stopped drinking straight off, hey," Grijpstra said, shaking his head.

"I told you he was clever," Bezuur said. "He knew it would be difficult to break the habit so he did something drastic. He disappeared for a while, three months I think it was. Went to work on a farm. When he came back he was off it. Later he began drinking again but then he knew when to stop. He would cut out at the third or fourth glass and drink soft stuff."

"Beer?"

"Beer is not so soft. No, lemonades, homemade. He would fuss about, squeezing the fruit, adding sugar. With Abe everything had to be dead right."

Bezuur tipped the bottle again but it was empty and he slammed it on the table. The bottle cracked. He glared at it.

"You seem a little upset," Grijpstra said.

Bezuur was staring at the wall behind Grijpstra's chair. "Yes," he said, "I am upset. So the bastard died. How the hell did he manage that? I spoke to Zilver on the phone. He reckons they threw a ball at him, a metal ball, but nobody can find it. Is that right?"

He was still staring at the wall behind Grijpstra's chair and Grijpstra turned around. There was a painting on the wall, a portrait of a lady. The lady was wearing a long skirt of some velvety material, a hat with a veil, an elaborate necklace, and nothing else. She had very full breasts with the nipples turned upward. The face was quiet, a delicate face with dreaming eyes and lips which opened in the beginning of a smile.

"Beautiful," Grijpstra said.

"My wife."

Grijpstra looked around the room.

Bezuur laughed, the laugh sounded bubbly and gushy, as if a pipe had suddenly burst and water was flowing down the wall.

"My ex-wife, I should say, perhaps, but the divorce isn't through yet.

She left me some months ago now and her lawyers are squeezing me and my lawyers are having a lovely time, writing lots of little notes at a guilder a word."

"Any children?"

"One, but not mine. The fruit of a previous relationship. Some fruit, a little overripe apple, and stupid too—but what do I care, she went too."

"So you are alone."

Bezuur laughed again and the commissaris looked up. He wished the man wouldn't laugh. He had found a way of putting up with the pain in his legs but Bezuur's merriment shook his concentration and the pain attacked again.

"No," Bezuur said, and stretched his right arm. The arm swept in a half circle.

"Girlfriends," Grijpstra said, and nodded.

"Yes. Girls. I used to go to them but now they come here. It's easier. I am getting too heavy to run about."

He looked at the floor, stamping his foot on the sodden rug. "Bah. Beer. Something to do for the cleaning boys. You can't get charwomen anymore you know, not even if you pay them in gold bars. Some cleaning platoon comes here on weekdays, old men in white uniforms. They have a truck and the biggest vacuum cleaner you ever saw. Whip through the whole place in an hour. But the girls come on Fridays or Saturdays and they leave a mess and I sit in it. Bah."

His arm made a sweeping movement again and Grijpstra followed the movement. He counted five empty champagne bottles. Someone had forgotten her lipstick on the couch. There was a stain on the white wall, just below the painting of Bezuur's wife.

"Turtle soup," Bezuur said. "Silly bitch lost her balance and the soup hit the wall. Good thing it missed the painting."

"Who did the painting?"

"You like it?"

"Yes," Grijpstra said. "Yes. I think it is very well done. Like that picture of the two men in a small boat I saw on Abe Rogge's wall."

Bezuur looked at the carton next to his chair, took out a bottle but put it back again.

"Two men in a boat? You saw that painting too, eh? Same artist. Old friend of ours, a Russian Jew born in Mexico, used to go boating with us and he came to the house. Interesting fellow, but he wandered off again. I think he is in Israel now."

"Who were the two men in the boat?"

"Abe and me," Bezuur said heavily. "Abe and me. Two friends. The Mexican fellow said that we belonged together, he saw it that night. We were on the big lake, the boat was anchored and we had taken the dinghy into the harbor. We came back late that night. The sea was fluorescent and the Mexican was wandering about on deck. He left the next day, he should have stayed a few more days, but he was so inspired by what he saw that night that he had to get back to his studio to paint it. Abe bought the painting and I commissioned this one later. That Mexican was very expensive, even if you were his friend, but he was pretty good."

"Friends," the commissaris said. "Close friends. You were close friends with Abe, weren't you, Mr. Bezuur?"

"Was," Bezuur said, and there was the same blubbery note in his voice again, but now he seemed close to tears. "The bastard is dead."

"You were close friends right up to yesterday?"

"No," Bezuur said. "Lost touch. Went his way, I went my way. I have a big business now and no time to play about on the street market, but I enjoyed it while it lasted."

"When did you each go your own way?"

"Wasshit matter?" Bezuur said, and that was all they could get out of him for a while. He was crying now, and had opened another bottle, slopping half of it on the floor. The fit took a few minutes.

"Shorry," Bezuur said.

"That's all right," the commissaris said, and rubbed his legs. "We understand. And I am sorry we are bothering you."

"What did Mr. Rogge and yourself study at the university?" Grijpstra asked. Bezuur looked up, there seemed to be some strength in him again and he was no longer slurring his words.

"French. We studied French."

"But you weren't so good at languages. Didn't you say so before?" the commissaris asked.

"Not too bad either," Bezuur said. "Good enough. French is a logical language, very exact. Maybe I would have preferred science but it would have meant breaking from Abe, I wasn't ready for that then."

"Did you study hard?"

"Same way we got through high school, in my case anyway. Abe was more enthusiastic. He read everything he could find at the university library, starting at the top shelf on the left and finishing on the bottom shelf on the right. If the books didn't interest him he would flip the pages, reading a little here and there but often he would read the whole book. I just read what he selected for me, books he talked about."

"And what else did you two do?"

Bezuur was staring at the portrait and the commissaris had to ask again.

"What else? Oh, we ran about. And I had a big boat in those days; we'd go sailing on the lakes. And we traveled. Abe had a little truck and we went to France and North Africa and once I talked my father into buying us tickets on an old tramp which went to Haiti in the Caribbean. The language is French over there and I said we needed the experience for our study."

"Your father paid for Abe's ticket as well? Didn't Abe have any money himself?"

"He had some. German love-money. The Germans paid up after the war, you know, and they had killed both his parents. He got quite a bit; so did Esther. Abe knew how to handle money. He was doing a little business on the side. He was buying and selling antique weapons in those days."

"Weapons?" the commissaris asked. "He didn't happen to have a good-day, did he?"

"No," Bezuur said, when the question had got through to him. "No, no, cavalry sabers and bayonets, that sort of stuff. You think he was killed with a good-day?"

"Never mind," the commissaris said. "Did he ever live out of your pocket?"

Bezuur shook his head. "No, not really. He accepted that ticket to Haiti but he made up for it in other ways. He only relied on himself. He would borrow money sometimes but he always paid up on time and later, when I was lending him big money, he paid full bank interest. The interest was his idea, I never asked for it but he said I had a right to it."

"Why didn't he borrow from the bank?"

"He didn't want his transactions on record. He borrowed cash and he paid cash. He was pretending to be a small hawker, a fellow who lived off his stall."

The commissaris looked at Grijpstra and Grijpstra asked the next question.

"Why did you both drop out of the university?"

Bezuur looked at his beer bottle and shook it. "Yes, we dropped out, right at the end. Abe's idea, that was. He said the degree would be pure silliness, it would qualify us to become schoolteachers. We had learned all we wanted to learn anyway. We went into business instead."

"The street market?"

"Yes. I started importing from the communist countries. In Rumania a lot of people speak French and we went there to see what we could find. The East Bloc started exporting cheaply in those days, to get hard currency. You could pick up all sorts of bargains. They offered wool and buttons and zippers, so we found ourselves in the street market. The big stores wouldn't buy at first and we had to unload the goods. We made good money, but then my dad died and left the roadworking machinery business so I had to switch."

"Were you sorry?"

"Yes," Bezuur said and drained the bottle. "I am still sorry. Wrong choice, but there was nothing else to do. There's more money in bulldozers than in colored string."

"You cared about money?"

Bezuur nodded gravely. "I did."

"You still do?"

Bezuur didn't appear to hear.

"One last question," Grijpstra said brightly. "About this party last night. When did it begin and when did it end?"

Bezuur scratched the stubbles on his bloated cheeks. The small eyes looked sly in their greasy sockets. "Alibi, hey? And I don't even know when Abe was killed. Zilver didn't tell me. Party started at about nine in the evening. I can get the girls to testify if you like. I should have their names and phone numbers somewhere."

"Callgirls?"

"Yes. Sure. Whores."

He was looking through the pockets of a jacket which he had taken from the couch. "Here you are, telephone numbers, you can copy them. The names are fancy, of course. Minette and Alice, they call themselves, but they answer their phones if you need them. Better try tomorrow, they'll be asleep now. I had them driven home in a taxi at five o'clock this morning. They had a gallon of champagne each, and another gallon of food."

Grijpstra jotted down the numbers. "Thank you."

"Excuse me, sir," the constable said. He had been standing in the open door for some time.

"Yes, constable?"

"You are wanted on the radio sir."

"Well, we have finished here, I think," the commissaris said. "Thank you for your hospitality, Mr. Bezuur. Contact me if you think I should know something which you haven't mentioned now. Here is my card. We would like to solve the case."

"I'll let you know," Bezuur said and got up. "God knows I'll be thinking about it all the time. I have done nothing else since Zilver phoned."

"I thought you were having a little party here, sir," Grijpstra said, keeping his voice flat.

"I can think while I have a party," Bezuur said, taking the commissaris' card.

"Another dead body in the Straight Tree Ditch, sir," the female constable from the radio room said. "Water Police found it. It was dangling from a rope tied to a tree, half in the water and partly hidden by a moored boat. The Water Police suggested we should contact you. They had seen the telegrams* reporting the other murder last night. Same area, sir. Sergeant de Gier is there now. He's got Detective-Constable Cardozo with him. They are in their car waiting for instructions. Would you like to speak to them, sir?"

"Put them on," the commissaris said, gloomily looking at the microphone which Grijpstra was holding for him.

"Cardozo here, sir."

"We are on our way to you now," the commissaris said, nodding to the constable at the wheel who started the car. The constable pointed at the roof and raised his eyebrows. "Yes," the commissaris mouthed silently. The siren began to howl and the blue light flashed as the car shot away. "Anything you can tell us at this stage, Cardozo?"

"Sergeant de Gier knows the dead person, sir. An old man dressed up as a lady. Used to be on the force, sir." Cardozo's voice had gone up, as if he was framing a question.

"Yes, I know her, Cardozo. How did she die?"

"Knife in his back sir. He must have been killed in a public telephone booth here; we found a track. He was dragged across the street and dumped into the canal. The killer used a short rope, strung under the corpse's armpits and attached to an old elm tree. The rope didn't kill him. The knife did."

"Do you have the knife?"

"No, sir. But the doctor said it was a knife wound. Penetrated the heart from the back. A long knife."

"When did she die?"

"Early this morning, sir, the doctor thinks."

---

* All Amsterdam police stations are connected by teletype. Important events are immediately recorded and distributed. The messages are known as "telegrams."

"We'll be there soon."

"The Water Police want to have the corpse, sir. Can they take it? It's quiet now but the riots may start any minute again and we are blocking the street with our cars."

"Yes," the commissaris said tiredly, looking at a city bus which was trying to get out of the Citroën's way. The constable at the wheel was attempting to pass the bus and several cars were coming from the opposite direction. The siren was screaming ominously directly above them. The commissaris put a restraining hand on the constable's shoulder and the car slowed down obediently.

"They can have the body, Cardozo. Over and out."

Grijpstra was watching the oncoming traffic too and sighed happily when the Citroën nosed back behind the bus. "Bloody fool," he said to the constable. "What are you trying to do, be a hero?"

The constable didn't hear him. The bus pulled to the side of the road, having finally found a spot free of cyclists, and the Citroën jumped off again, careening wildly.

"Oh, shit," Grijpstra said softly.

"Quite," the commissaris said.

"Pardon, sir?"

"That wasn't very clever of me," the commissaris said, "asking that poor old lady to be on the force again. I might as well have shot her on the spot."

9

"YOU'LL HAVE TO GET OUT of here, sir," de Gier said. He had gotten into the car as Grijpstra got out. "The riots will be starting all over today. I don't know what's gotten into these people but they are thronging about again and warming each other up. The riot police will be out any minute now."

The commissaris was leaning back into his seat.

"Are you all right, sir?"

"No," the commissaris said softly, so that de Gier had to bend over to hear him. "It's this pain. It's been with me all day and it isn't getting any better. Riots, you say. The riot police will only make it worse. We don't want a show of force, sergeant."

"No, sir. But what else can we do? They'll be throwing bricks and there are some bulldozers in the Newmarket Square, and cranes and machines. They can destroy a fortune's worth in a few minutes."

"Yes," the commissaris said softly.

A platoon of riot police came tramping past. The commissaris shuddered.

"There they are," de Gier said.

"I hate that sound, tramping boots. We heard it during the war. All the time. A stupid sound. We ought to be more intelligent now."

"Yes, sir," de Gier said. He was watching the commissaris' gray tired face. A spasm moved both cheeks and the commissaris' yellowish teeth were bared for a moment in a grin of agony. "You'd better take him home, constable," de Gier said to the driver. The constable nodded.

"In a minute," the commissaris said. "Tell me what happened, sergeant. Is the corpse still here? Did you manage to organize yourself for tomorrow's marketing?"

"We'll take care of that later today sir. I was at home when the Water Police telephoned. I came straight out. Cardozo happened to phone as I was leaving, so he came out as well. I have had the corpse moved to the mortuary. There may be street fighting here soon and I didn't want them to trample all over it. Cardozo said that it would be O.K. with you. He spoke to you on the radio."

"Yes, yes. Did you find out anything? And have you taken Miss Rogge home?"

"Esther Rogge should be home by now, sir, she caught a bus."

"She stayed at your apartment all night, de Gier?"

"Yes, sir."

"I see. And the corpse, did you get any clues?"

"Just what Cardozo must have told you, sir. A knife killed him. I think he was trying to contact you by telephone, in the booth over there. It must have been early this morning, around four o'clock, the doctor said. Maybe he saw the killer walking about in the street here. Perhaps he thought he was safe, dressed up like an old lady, and all. He got into the telephone booth and got a knife in his back."

"Yes," the commissaris said. "She was trying to telephone me but she didn't get through. Poor Elizabeth. She must have been dialing my number as the killer knifed her. Elizabeth was a 'she,' de Gier, you shouldn't refer to her as a 'he.' She was a nice old lady, and courageous too. I should never have asked her to help us. She should have been in bed last night, with Tabby warming her old feet."

"She wasn't," de Gier said. "She was right here, watching the killer return to the scene of the crime. And I should have been here too. And Grijpstra. She was dragged from that booth to the water; we found blood traces on the cobblestones. The killer had all the time in the world. He didn't just dump the body. If he had it would have floated and somebody would have found it almost immediately. He tied it up with a bit of string. It's amazing the Water Police found it so quickly. It was well hidden between the quay and that houseboat over there."

"So you didn't notice anything special, did you? Apart from the blood traces?"

"Yes, sir. The knots in the string. They were professional knots, made by a sailor or an experienced fisherman. Which reminds me, sir . . ."

"Yes?"

"I think I know a little more about the spiked rubber ball which killed Abe Rogge."

"Tell me."

"I saw some kids playing with a ball attached to an elastic string once, sir. The string was held by a weight placed on the street. I think the ball which killed Rogge was attached to a string too. The killer pulled it back afterward, which explains why we didn't find it. And I think the killer wasn't in the street; he was on the roof of the old houseboat moored opposite the Rogges' house. Perhaps he had hidden himself behind the chimney. You can see it over there, sir." De Gier pointed to the other side of the Straight Tree Ditch.

"Yes," the commissaris said. "So the riot police in the street didn't see him maybe. That's what you mean, don't you? But there were riot police patrolling this side of the canal too. Shouldn't they have seen him?"

"He must have been quick, sir. Hid himself in the houseboat, sneaked through one of its windows at the right moment, threw the ball, pulled it back, sneaked back into the boat's window and disappeared later when the constables were at the other end of the street. They would have let him through easily enough. He probably looked like an ordinary citizen and they wouldn't have thought that he was a rioter. I think they took him for someone who lived in the street and who had come out to do a little shopping or go somewhere."

"The killer could have been a woman," the commissaris said. "Abe Rogge had a lot of girlfriends. A jealous woman or a humiliated woman. I am supposed to see two of them today. You gave me the names and addresses, remember? I am sure they are both young and strong and capable of throwing balls."

De Gier shook his head.

"You don't think the killer might have been a woman, sergeant?"

"Could be, sir, why not? But I can't understand the deadly aim of the ball. Even from the roof of that houseboat there's quite a distance to cover and the ball hit Rogge smack in the face. Now if the ball had been shot . . . I think we are dealing with a hellish machine, sir."

The commissaris grimaced.

"Well, it could be, couldn't it, sir?"

The commissaris nodded.

"But a machine which throws or shoots a ball makes a sound. Or would it have used a spring perhaps? A crossbow maybe? But then there is still some sort of twang. A loud sound, I would say. The patrolling constables should have heard it."

"A person on the roof of a houseboat handling some strange noisy device while riot police are close . . ." The commissaris' voice sounded doubtful.

"Perhaps not," de Gier agreed.

"But I agree with your thought of the ball being connected to string, elastic or otherwise," the commissaris said. "Very clever to think of that, sergeant. You started off right, all you have to do now is continue your line of reasoning. I'll help. And so should Grijpstra and Cardozo. It's probably quite simple. Everything is simple once you understand it." He grimaced again.

"Something funny sir?"

The commissaris groaned and rubbed his thighs. "Yes. I was thinking of something which happened the other day. My wife bought a newfangled type of folding chair and brought it home. She had forgotten how it worked and I fussed with it for a while but it only squeezed my hand. Then the neighbor's daughter came in. She is retarded but her lack of brain didn't stop her from having a go at the damned chair and she had it standing up in no time at all. I asked her to show me how she had done it but she didn't know. Evidently she could only solve a problem very quickly, without thinking about it."

"You think this killing device is like your folding chair, sir?"

"Perhaps," the commissaris said. "Maybe we should just concentrate on the problem and the solution will pop up. Thinking might take too long. We haven't got much time."

"Yes," de Gier said. "You are looking ill, sir, shouldn't you go home?"

"I'll go home now. I want you to check out two women sometime this afternoon or tonight. Grijpstra has their names and telephone numbers. They are callgirls and they were with Klaas Bezuur from about nine o'clock last night till about five o'clock this morning. Grijpstra!"

Grijpstra came ambling up.

"Sir?"

"I am going home for a while, I don't feel so well. Telephone the two ladies we are supposed to see today; set up appointments for late this afternoon or this evening. Once you have set up the appointments you can contact my driver and he'll pick you up and then you can come and fetch me. It would be best if one of the girls is available before dinner and the other after dinner. That way you and I can eat together sometime. I want to make up for calling you out today."

Grijpstra brought out his notebook and wrote down the names and addresses of the two girls.

"Yes, sir. They used to be Mr. Rogge's girlfriends, right, sir?"

"Right."

"Constable," the commissaris shouted.

"Sir."

"Home," the commissaris whispered. It was all he could say. He was almost fainting with pain.

Grijpstra found de Gier contemplating a tree trunk. The lithe body of the sergeant swayed slightly as he stood, hands folded on his back, staring moodily at the elm's green bark.

Cardozo was watching the sergeant too. "Don't disturb him," Cardozo said, holding Grijpstra back. "He is busy. He is swaying. Look."

"So he is," the adjutant said.

"He isn't Jewish, is he?" Cardozo asked.

"Not that I know of," Grijpstra said. "Although, yes, I think he told me once that he has a Jewish grandmother."

"You see," Cardozo said. "He is Jewish. If his grandmother was Jewish his mother was too and that makes him a Jew. It goes via the female line, very wisely. Nobody ever knows who his father was but you can be sure about your mother. And Jews sway, they always sway. When they have a problem, that is, or when they are concentrating on something. They do it during prayer. Back and forth, back and forth. The Spanish Inquisition used to catch us because we swayed. We couldn't help ourselves. And they'd burn us. A strange habit, isn't it?"

"No," Grijpstra said. "The sergeant is an ordinary man, like me. He is swaying because he feels like swaying. Not because he has Jewish blood. Maybe he hasn't got any, maybe somebody else told me he had a Jewish grandmother."

"Holland had only one philosopher," Cardozo said, speaking very slowly, articulating every syllable. "Spinoza. He was a Jew, and he didn't even write in Dutch, he wrote in Latin."

"Why didn't he write in Dutch?"

"He couldn't do it. Have you ever tried to express subtle thoughts in Dutch?"

"I never have subtle thoughts," Grijpstra said, "but it's about time we had some."

"Yes," de Gier said and stopped swaying. "You'd better do something for a change, Cardozo, instead of proving the superiority of your race. The commissaris wants you to help me. Listen."

He explained his theory about the weapon.

"A ball and an elastic thread," Cardozo said. "Yes."

"So how did it manage to hit Rogge square in the face, from that distance?"

Cardozo folded his hands on his back, closed his eyes and began to sway. After a while he opened his eyes again.

"I'll tell you, sergeant, when I know. It'll come to me. But not when you rush me."

"Bah," de Gier said. He remembered how he had helped the Water Police constables to haul the old lady's soggy corpse from the canal. He also remembered the expression on the corpse's face. She had been killed while she was trying to pass on some information. The face had looked eager, and also rather sweet. She had been about to speak to the commissaris, her old and close friend. She had looked coy. Coy and eager.

Grijpstra's hand was on the sergeant's shoulder.

"Let's go," Grijpstra said. "You and I have things to do. You have to check out two whores and I have to telephone some nice ladies. But we have a little time. Stop looking at that tree, it has nothing to say to you. Fancy tying a corpse to a tree and then throwing it into the water. I am going to have a drink, care to join me?"

"Can I come too?" Cardozo asked.

"No. You are too young. We are going to visit a friend of mine and you won't be able to work once you have seen her. You need your strength for tomorrow. Aren't you two going to be street sellers tomorrow?"

"Then de Gier can't go either," Cardozo said. "He'll also be a street seller."

"You're right," Grijpstra said. "I'll go alone."

"Nellie?" de Gier asked.

"Yes." Grijpstra was grinning. "I'll go and see her by myself. She'll change my mood. Some day this is. Another corpse. Two corpses too many. Amsterdam is a quiet city. Holland has the lowest crime rate in the world. You went to that lecture too, didn't you? That slob should be with us now. Silly bald-headed dwarf. I can't stand criminologists. Statistics, that's all they know. When that kid got raped and slaughtered last year he said that the percentage of children killed by rapists is so low that it is almost negligible. You remember what that boy looked like when he was found?"

"According to statistics we'll have another five corpses this year," Cardozo said. "There's nothing we can do about it. They'll happen."

"The hell with you both," Grijpstra said and stamped off.

De Gier ran after him.

"Hey," Cardozo shouted.

"He's not going to drink by himself," de Gier shouted back. "Come and pick me up tomorrow at eight-thirty, and make sure that van is in order and that you have the merchandise."

"Yes, sergeant," Cardozo said loudly. "I hope you choke on your drink," he added softly.

10

"HELLO," de Gier said.

"Hello-oh," a sugary voice answered.

"Minette?"

"Yes, darling."

"I am not your darling," de Gier said and frowned at Nellie, who was watching him from the other end of the small bar. Nellie was smiling delightedly and Grijpstra was grinning. Grijpstra had taken off his coat and tie and was sitting in a corner of the room, near a window which he had opened and which showed a view of a small courtyard where a row of sparrows were lolling about on a wall, their tiny beaks open and their wings half-spread. Grijpstra was puffing and wiping his face with a large dirty white handkerchief. He looked happy, in spite of the heat. He had set up the two appointments with Abe Rogge's girlfriends and would be off in a little while to fetch the commissaris, and meanwhile he had nothing to do but watch de Gier.

"I am not your darling," de Gier was saying. "I am Detective-Sergeant de Gier, Amsterdam Municipal Police, and I am coming out to see you to ask you a few questions. Nothing serious, strictly routine."

"Police?" the sugary voice asked. "They are darlings too. I have a nice client who is a police officer. Maybe you are like him. When are you coming to see me, darling? Right now?"

"Right now," de Gier said and made a face at the telephone, "and I want to see your friend Alice too. Would you ask her to come over to

your place? I have her telephone number here and the first three numbers are the same as yours. She must live close to you."

"But surely," Minette said. "She lives in the same building, two
floors up. I'll ask her to come and we'll do a double number for you."

"No," de Gier said, "don't put yourself out, dear. I just want some
simple answers to some simple questions. I'll be there in fifteen minutes.
Put some clothes on."

Grijpstra chuckled and de Gier made a gesture to shut him up.

"What sort of clothes, darling? I have a nice uniform with shiny buttons and leather boots, and a little whip. Or would you prefer me to
dress up in lace? Or my black evening dress perhaps? It has a beautiful
zipper and it comes off if you . . ."

"NO," de Gier almost shouted. "What's the address?"

"Alkemalaan Five-O-Three, darling, don't shout at me." The voice
was still dripping with sweetness.

"I'll be there," de Gier said.

"An idiot," Minette said to herself, as she daintily replaced the dark
red plastic telephone on her bedside table, "and rude too. Now what
does *he* want? He wouldn't be hunting whores, would he? That other
policeman also said he wanted to ask questions, but he came for the
usual thing and stayed the night. They are all idiots."

"Afternoon," de Gier said. "I am Sergeant de Gier. I phoned about a
quarter of an hour ago. Are you Minette?"

"No, honey," the small girl said. "I am Alice, Minette is waiting for
you inside. Come in, dear."

She put a hand on his arm and tugged gently. "My," she sighed,
"aren't you handsome!"

"Yes," de Gier said. "I am a beautiful man." He looked into the
smiling eyes and noted they were green. Cat's eyes. The face was triangular, like a praying mantis'. He had been looking at a color photograph
of a praying mantis in a book he had found in the Public Library. The
insect had looked weirdly attractive, the materialization of a subconscious fear with a lovely face but with long arms and claws. A preda-
tory insect, the caption had said. An entity to be careful with.

The girl turned and he followed her into the small hall. A little girl,
she wouldn't be much more than five feet high, but well shaped and well
dressed in short velvet pants and a loose flowing blouse. Her bare feet
were tiny. An imp, a prancing imp. He guessed her to be in her late
twenties but the smooth face hadn't shown signs of wear and tear.

Maybe she hadn't been in the game too long. He admired the round tight bottom and the black glossy hair, done up in a bun.

"Now *that* is Minette," Alice said, turning around and stepping back, so that he would enter the room ahead of her. "Here's your sergeant, Minette."

"Woo," Minette said. "Isn't he lovely?"

De Gier felt relieved. Minette was nothing special. A plump girl, rather wide in the hips and with a painted doll's face. Minette sat on a low settee, dressed in a wrap which slipped a little; one breast was visible. De Gier shuddered imperceptibly. The breast looked like the gelatin puddings his mother used to serve on birthdays. They came on a white plate, dripping with a thick cream sauce.

"Take your coat off, sergeant," Minette said in the same voice she had used on the telephone. "You were so abrupt when you rang up. Relax, that's what this place is for. Have a drink, come and sit next to me. What would you like? Get him a beer, Alice. We have some really cold beer in the fridge."

"No," de Gier said. "No drink. I am working. Thanks."

"Have a cigar," Minette said. "Do we still have those long thick cigars, Alice? They were in a big box, with an Indian on the lid, remember?"

Alice brought the box, opened it, put it on a low table next to the corner chair, which de Gier had chosen judging it to be the safest place in the room, and sat down on the carpet, within touching distance of his leg.

"You will have a cigar, won't you, sergeant?"

"Yes," de Gier said. "Please."

The small white hand touched the box, slid over it and picked out a cigar. She caressed it, looking at him languidly, and then rapidly peeled off its plastic skin and licked its end, darting the tip of her tongue in and out. Her small regular teeth showed when she saw that he was watching her. Her long eyelashes came down slowly and then, smiling wickedly, she stuck the cigar into her mouth, turned it around and bit off its end.

"Here you are, sergeant." She lit a match.

"Yes," de Gier said, "thanks. You two girls were with a Mr. Bezuur last night we were told."

"It's hot in here," Alice said. "The air conditioner is on the blink. They keep on fiddling with it but it never works when you want it to. You should get a new one, Minette. Do you mind if I take off my blouse, sergeant?"

She took it off before he could say anything. She wore nothing underneath. The breasts were pretty, very small and firm. She stretched and untied her hair, which flowed down her shoulders, and she adjusted the strands so that her nipples were covered. De Gier stared.

"Yes," he said. "It's rather hot in here. Outside too. Putting the windows down doesn't help much either. Now how long were you two with Mr. Bezuur, yesterday? Do you remember the exact times? When did you get to his house and when did you leave?"

"Bezuur?" Alice asked. "Who is Bezuur?"

"That's Klaas, of course," Minette said. "The fat fellow. You were all over him all night, remember?"

"Oh," Alice said. "The piggy man. *You* were all over him, not me. I only danced about while he drank, and ate. He ate a whole ham. Bah. I am glad he wasn't pawing *me*. Why don't you get some of your clothes off, sergeant? I can sit on your lap, you'll hardly feel my weight."

"You don't need me in here," Minette said and pouted. "Do you want me to go into the other room?"

"No," de Gier said quickly, "no, no. Stay right here, and I am not taking my clothes off either. For God's sake, can't you two answer a simple question? When did you get to his house and when did you leave?"

"Now, now," Alice said, and moved closer. "Don't be uptight, sergeant. We won't make you pay, you are safe in here. Nobody will mind if you stay an hour. It isn't the right day for work, is it?"

"WHEN . . ." de Gier asked, and half-rose from his chair.

"We got there about nine last night and we left early this morning. Around five o'clock it was, I think. A taxi took us home."

"And Bezuur was with you all the time?"

"Sure."

"Weren't you asleep some of the time?"

"He was there while I slept," Minette said. "Right next to me."

"Sure?"

"Yes. He put his fat leg on me, I couldn't get it off. It stopped the circulation in my ankle and I had to massage it."

De Gier looked down. Alice had been inching herself toward him and was now rubbing herself against his leg.

"Yes," she said. "He was there. I was asleep on the couch some of the time but I saw him when I woke up. He was there just like you are here now. Sit back, sergeant, I am going to sit on your lap."

"No," de Gier said, and got up.

She followed him to the door. He was standing with his back against the wall, holding his notebook.

"I want your full name and Minette's name. I'll have to write a report."

"Is that piggy man in any sort of trouble?" Alice was standing very close again.

"Not really. We just want to know where he was last night."

She waited while he was making his notes, gave him their names and dates of birth.

"Profession?" de Gier asked.

"You know!" Alice said. "We are callgirls."

"Prostitutes," de Gier wrote down. "I've got to go now. Thanks for the information."

"Come back," Alice whispered quickly. "I live two floors up, number five-seven-four. Give me a ring first. I won't charge you."

"Sure," de Gier said and slipped through the door.

"Like hell," he said a little later, cruelly pushing the gear lever of the Volkswagen. Like bloody hell, a policeman-friend to help her out when she gets into trouble. But she made me feel randy, the little bitch. Just the sort of thing for a day like this.

He had to stop for a traffic light and gloomily watched a big Mercedes which had pulled up next to the Volkswagen. There were two middle-aged men in the back of the car, dressed in suits and ties. They were both smoking cigars. De Gier saw one of them blow out a little cloud of smoke, which disappeared immediately, sucked away by the airconditioning in the car. He looked at the soggy end of his own cigar, and tossed it out of the window, watching it spark as it hit the tarmac. The driver of the Mercedes winked at him. He had pushed his cap to the back of his head and was loosening his tie.

"Hot, eh?" he asked.

De Gier nodded.

The two men in the back of the car were laughing about something.

"Your passengers are cool enough," de Gier said.

"They are cool," the driver said, indicating the glass partitioning with his thumb. "I am not."

The light changed and the Mercedes accelerated.

"Bounders," de Gier thought. "Two bounders and one little sucker to whizz 'em around."

He was thinking about Alice again. Grijpstra had his Nellie. He forced himself to think about something else. He saw the spiked ball, trying to visualize its flight as it approached Abe Rogge's window. Someone was directing the ball, using a device. But what was it? He tried to visualize the device but it blurred as he focused.

11

THE COMMISSARIS looked at the young woman who, red-eyed, perched on a highbacked chair, was studying a stain on the wallpaper. They had dispensed with courtesies and he would have to make an opening.

"We were informed that you were friendly with Abe Rogge, miss. Perhaps you can tell us something about him. Any information will help. We know a little about the way he was, but not enough. Someone went to a lot of trouble to kill him. There usually is a strong connection between killer and victim. Perhaps you can help us to find out what bound the two together."

"Yes," the woman said, and sniffled. "I understand. Poor Abe. How did he die? I didn't know until the police phoned me this morning. I didn't dare to phone Esther. She must be very upset."

Grijpstra gave her an abridged version of what the police knew. He left out the gory details.

"Horrible," the woman said.

She calmed down after a while. Her two visitors looked harmless enough and were sipping coffee and smoking cigars, careful to tip their ash into the saucers of their cups. She remembered that she hadn't put an ashtray on the table and got up to fetch one. The two men didn't look out of place in the small modern flat on the top floor of an apartment building. The commissaris commented on the view. He identified some of the church towers and when he made a mistake, she corrected him.

"Yes," she said. "I understand now. You have come to me because I was his girlfriend, or one of his girlfriends rather. I didn't mind, not very much anyway. Abe could be charming, he knew how to flatter me, and perhaps I didn't want him all for myself. I am reasonably content with my routine. Abe would have upset it if he had moved in. It wasn't just sex either; he often came to talk, about books or about films he had seen and he took me out sometimes."

"What was he like?" the commissaris asked.

"Crazy."

"How do you mean, miss?" Grijpstra asked.

"Crazy," she repeated.

"In what way?" the commissaris asked. "He didn't pull faces or jump about on all fours, did he?"

"No, no. How can I explain? He had an unusual idea of values. Most people have set values, or no values at all. Abe seemed to change his values all the time, but without being weak. He thought from an angle nobody could grasp. I didn't understand him either and I often tried."

The commissaris had come a little forward in his chair. "That isn't enough, miss. You have to tell us a little more. I can't see the man; we only met him as a corpse, you see. You knew him well . . ."

"Yes. I'll try. Well . . . he was courageous. Perhaps that's the word. No fear, no fear of anything. When he thought of something he did it or tried to do it and most of the things he did seemed absolutely pointless. They weren't getting him anywhere but he didn't mind. Perhaps he didn't want to get anywhere. You have heard about his business, have you?"

"Beads," the commissaris said, "and wool."

"Yes. Funny things. He could have been a big businessman, a manager of a large firm perhaps but he preferred to shout on the market, on the Albert Cuyp street market. I wouldn't believe it at first, not until I went there. A showman, hypnotizing the poor housewives, telling them they were creative, and admiring the ugly sweaters and the horrible dolls they had made out of his yarn. It was pathetic to see those inane dumpy women swarming around his stall. And he almost graduated in French. I knew him at the university; he was the best student of our year, the pride of the professors. His essays were brilliant, anything he did was original, but . . ."

"You make him sound as if he were a failure," the commissaris said, "but it seemed he was a great success. His business did well, he was a wealthy man, he traveled a great deal, and he was only in his early thirties . . ."

"He was a silly man," the woman, whom the commissaris had in his notebook as Corin Kops, said.

"It's not so silly to be successful in business," the commissaris said. "For many people it is still the optimal goal."

"I didn't mean it in that way. I mean he was wasting his talents. He could have contributed something to society. Most people just live, like toadstools. They grow and after a while they begin to die. They are living objects, but Abe was much more than that."

"Yes," the commissaris said and slumped back. "Quite. You said you and he discussed books. What sort of books did he like?"

She pursed her lips, as if she were going to whistle. Grijpstra looked at his watch. His stomach rumbled. "Peckish," Grijpstra thought. "I am feeling a bit peckish. I hope he'll take me to one of those bistros. I could do with a rare steak and a baked potato. A large baked potato."

"Books without a moral. He read some travel books, written by adventurers. People who just roamed about and wrote down their thoughts. And he liked surrealist books."

"Surrealist?" Grijpstra stirred.

"It's a philosophy. Surrealist writers go deeper than the average novelist, by using dreams and unusual associations. They don't bother about surface logic or try to describe daily events but aim for the roots of human behavior."

"They do?" Grijpstra asked.

The commissaris brightened. "Like Nellie's bar, Grijpstra," he said and grinned. "Like what you think when you are fishing, or when you wake up in the morning."

"When I shave?" Grijpstra asked, and grinned too. "Lots of hot water and lather and a new razor blade and nobody in the bathroom and the door locked and swash, swash with the brush."

"What do you think about when you shave?" the commissaris asked. Grijpstra rubbed the short hairs on his skull energetically. "Hard to say, sir."

The woman showed interest. She was on her way to the kitchen, carrying the dirty coffee cups, but she stopped and turned.

"Try to describe your thoughts," Corin Kops said.

"About the sea," Grijpstra said. "Mostly about the sea, and I have never been a sailor, so that's strange, I suppose. But I think about the sea when I shave. Big waves and a blue sky."

"Could you give an example from Abe's life, miss?" the commissaris asked.

"Something surrealistic, you mean? But his whole life was like that.

He lived a dream, even when he was being practical. He never gave expectable answers to sensible questions and he always seemed to be changing his mind. There was no set pattern in his life. The man was like a wet bar of soap."

She suddenly sounded exasperated. She looked at the commissaris in desperation. "Once he was here, at night, in the early hours of the morning. There was a gale on. The windows were rattling and I couldn't sleep. I saw him get up and told him to get back to bed. A hard wind always makes me nervous and I wanted him to be with me. But he said he was going sailing, and Louis Zilver told me later that the two of them took that small plastic yacht right out onto the big lake and they very nearly drowned."

She put down the tray. "The Germans killed his parents during the war, you know. Dragged them across the street and threw them into a cattle truck and gassed them. But he didn't seem to blame the Germans; he even took German as a second language at the university."

"The Germans must have meant to get him too," Grijpstra said.

"Yes, but the SS patrol missed him. He happened to be playing at a friend's house that morning. He didn't blame the Germans, he blamed the planets."

"Planets?"

"Yes. He thought that the planets, Mercury and Neptune and especially Uranus—he was very interested in Uranus, and all the others, I forget their names—control our lives. If the planets form certain constellations there is war on earth, and when the constellations change again war stops and there is peace for a while. He had a very low opinion of human endeavor. He thought we are witless creatures, pushed into motion by forces entirely beyond our control. He often told me that there is nothing we can do about anything except perhaps to stop fighting fate and to try and move with it."

"But he was a very active person himself," the commissaris said.

"Exactly. I would say that to him too, but he only laughed and said his activity was due to Uranus, which happened to be very powerful at the time of his birth. Uranus is the planet of change."

"So he was hit by a cosmic ray when he was born and it made him the sort of person he was," the commissaris said. "I see."

"Made him jump about like a squirrel, eh?" Grijpstra asked.

She laughed. "More like an ape, a large hairy mad ape. An ape with strange gleaming eyes."

"Your friend must have been rather unreliable," the commissaris said.

She picked up the tray again but the commissaris' question seemed to sting her. "No. Not at all. He was trustworthy. He always paid his debts and kept his appointments. If he promised anything he would do it."

"Well, we've got to know him a little better," the commissaris said. "Thank you very much. We are ready now. All I would like to ask before we leave is if you remember where you were yesterday afternoon and last night."

She looked frightened. "You don't suspect *me* do you?"

"Not necessarily, but we'd like to know all the same."

"I was here, all afternoon and all evening. By myself. I was working on some examination papers."

"Did you see anyone? Speak to anyone? Did anyone phone you?"

"No."

"Would you have any idea who could have wanted to kill Abe Rogge?"

"No."

"Do you know *what* killed him?" Grijpstra asked.

"*What?* What do you mean?"

"Was it jealousy? Revenge? Greed?"

She shook her head.

"I am sorry," the commissaris said. "One more question has occurred to me. You have described your friend as a rather negative sort of superman. Never got upset, thought that nothing mattered, did everything well, sailed in storms and came back safely, read unusual books, and in French of all languages. Was he really that marvelous? No weaknesses at all?"

The woman's facial muscles, which had been working nervously, suddenly slacked.

"Yes," she said. "He had his weakness. He cried in my arms once, and he cursed himself while he was shaving, here in my bathroom. He had left the door open and I could hear him."

"Why?"

"I asked him on both occasions and he gave the same answer. He said it was very close to him, so close that he could reach it, he thought, but then he couldn't."

"What?"

"He said he didn't know what it was."

They were almost at the door when Grijpstra, feeling that he hadn't been very helpful, tried again. "We met two of Mr. Rogge's friends, miss. Louis Zilver and Klaas Bezuur. Do you know how he was involved with them?"

She sighed. "He spent a lot of time with Louis. He even used to bring him here for dinner. Mr. Bezuur, I don't know very well. Abe used to talk about him. They were partners once, I think, but Bezuur has his own business now. Abe took me to Bezuur's factory one day, or his garage. I don't think they make the machinery over there; they just keep it around and rent it out, I think. Heavy trucks and all sorts of mobile machinery to make roads and move earth and so on. Abe was driving a bulldozer that afternoon, all over the yard. Louis was there too; he had a tractor. They were racing each other. Very spectacular. Later on Klaas joined them; he also drove a machine, with a big blade attached to it. He was rushing them, pretending to attack but he would reverse at the last moment. They frightened me."

"There was no bad feeling between Abe and Klaas?"

"No, apparently they had drifted apart but that was all. They were very affectionate when they met that afternoon. Embracing each other and shouting and calling each other names."

"When was that?"

"A few months ago, I think."

"Did he have any other close friends?"

She sighed again. "He knew thousands of people. Whenever we were in town together he seemed to be greeting every other person. Girls he had slept with, suppliers, customers, arty types, people he knew from the street market or the university or boating trips. It made me feel on edge, like I was escorting a TV star."

"Probably annoyed them all at some time or other," Grijpstra said gloomily, holding the door open for the commissaris. Corin was crying when he closed the door behind him.

12

"LET'S EAT," the commissaris said.

"They always cry, don't they?" Grijpstra said. "Or they just look dumb, like animals, stupid animals. Toads, snails . . ." He was going to mention more stupid and slippery animals but the commissaris interrupted him.

"Snails," the commissaris said and leaned back into the foam rubber seat. "Yes, snails. I wouldn't mind having some snails for dinner. Constable!"

"Sir," the constable said.

"Do you remember that old windmill, the restaurant you took me to some time ago, with the public prosecutor?"

"Yes, sir."

"We'll go there again, that is, if the adjutant has nothing against eating snails."

Grijpstra looked dubious. "Never ate them before, sir."

"Oh, you'll like them. The French have been eating them for thousands of years and they are supposed to be more intelligent than we are. Did you say the lady struck you as stupid?"

"Not the lady in particular, sir. Most people behave stupidly when they connect with death."

"You aren't criticizing, you mean, you are observing."

Grijpstra looked hurt. "The police never criticize."

The commissaris reached out and patted Grijpstra's solid shoulder with his thin almost lifeless hand.

"Right, adjutant. You've remembered your lessons. We observe, connect, conclude and apprehend. If we can. The suspect always tries to get away, and when we do manage to catch him the lawyers will criticize and excuse him in turns and our observations will be made to fit in with whatever the lawyers say, and in the end nobody will really know what happened or why it happened." The commissaris' hand was back in his lap again. It suddenly became a fist and hit the seat.

"This is a silly case, Grijpstra. I don't understand how all these people link up. Take the lady we saw just now, for instance. Abe slept with her, but he slept with a number of women. What did he see in her? She isn't especially attractive either. Did you think she was attractive?"

Grijpstra's thick lips curled derisively and he shook his head. "No, sir. Thin legs, not a very good figure, a lot of fluffy curls on a round head. But there is no accounting for a man's taste."

"Her mind?" the commissaris asked, but Grijpstra's expression didn't change.

"A bookworm, sir."

"Right," the commissaris said. "Exactly. Living on her theories, or on what she thinks are her theories, on something other people and maybe a few books have droned into her. Surrealism indeed! And *that's* what the link between her and our corpse is supposed to be, a mutual interest in French surrealist novels."

"You don't believe in surrealism, sir?"

The commissaris shrugged and looked out of the window. The car was following the narrow road past the Amstel River and they had a clear view of a wide expanse of water, hardly ruffled by a quiet breeze which had lost most of its force in the river's protecting belt of reeds and bushes.

"Yes, yes," he said slowly, "but the word irritates me. No meaning. It's like saying 'God,' or the 'infinite' or 'the point where two parallel lines meet.' They'll say those words and wipe away a tear. What would a girl like Corin Kops, a brittle stale bunch of bones topped by an unspectacular brain, know about surrealism!"

Grijpstra looked away. He pretended to rub his mouth to hide his smile, remembering that he had once described the commissaris to de Gier as a dry stick topped by a razor blade.

"Hasn't understood anything at all," the commissaris continued. "She just doesn't know. They try to define something that can never be caught in a word, but they'll think of a word all the same and then use it as if it had real meaning. Like the Dutch Reformed preachers holding forth about God. In the old days anyway. They have learned a little more modesty now, and there aren't so many of them left, thank heaven. What do we know about reality? Maybe we do at moments. Like early this morning, with my half-witted turtle pottering about in the grass and a thrush singing away. Maybe I understood something then but it was gone when I tried to put my hand on it. But a woman like Miss Kops thinks she catches it and coins a word, and before you know it the word is in the dictionaries. Hey!"

Grijpstra, whose eyes had been closing, looked up.

"Constable!" the commissaris shouted. "Stop the car!"

The constable stood on the brakes and Grijpstra lurched forward.

"Back the car up," the commissaris said softly, "but slowly. Very slowly. We mustn't disturb him."

"There," the commissaris said. "See?"

Grijpstra saw the heron, a majestic specimen of its race, well over four feet high, standing under a willow on the right side of the road, its plume crowning the thin delicate head. A huge goldfish was held in its beak, tail and head hanging down.

The constable laughed. "He doesn't know what to do with it, sir. That fish must weigh a few pounds."

"That's right," Grijpstra said. "Herons catch small fish and swallow them. He'll never get that whopper through his throat. But how did he manage to catch a goldfish? There aren't any goldfish in the river and he's on the wrong side of the road anyway, the river is behind us."

"Must be a fishpond behind that mansion," the constable said. "The bugger sneaked in there and took his chance."

"Let's go," the commissaris said.

Grijpstra caught on five minutes later. The commissaris hadn't said anything and seemed half asleep, hands on knees, head reclining against the top of his seat.

"A heron is a lovely bird," Grijpstra said, "and that heron was a beauty."

"Indeed," the commissaris said.

"One doesn't often see a heron with a goldfish in his beak."

"Quite," the commissaris said.

Grijpstra tried once more. "I am glad you stopped the car, sir."

"Why?"

"The beauty of it, sir."

The commissaris waved at the river. "The river is beautiful too, Grijpstra, and it's there all the time. So are the trees, so is that old windmill over there. We are surrounded by beauty. Even the new blocks of apartments we saw this morning are beautiful, and not only at sunset or early in the morning."

"It's not the same," Grijpstra said.

"Yes. The heron was different. He had a goldfish in his beak. Most unusual. Maybe the sudden unlikely image shocked something free in you. It's only when we get shocked that we can see something, but it's tricky. Like a man suddenly being knocked down by a car. He is crossing the street, dreaming away, and wham, there he is, flat on his back, with a wound somewhere or a broken bone. I've seen it dozens of times. They cry, they hold your hand, they are all upset. So they are rushed to the hospital and are shot full of dope, and whatever they were able to understand, because their world broke up, is drugged away again."

"The bird looked pretty stupid, sir," the constable at the wheel said gleefully.

"Like us," the commissaris said. "We've got a beautiful case, stuck right up our throat, but we are damned if we know what to do with it."

Dinner took an hour. They had half a dozen snails each and fresh toast and strong red wine from an unlabeled bottle. Grijpstra poked about suspiciously, extracting the small black rubbery lumps from their shells, frowning while he slowly chewed them.

"Well?" the commissaris asked.

"Very nice," Grijpstra said, carefully cleaning his plate with a piece of toast. "Good sauce this."

"More?"

Grijpstra thought. The commissaris nodded encouragingly.

"Yes."

Grijpstra ate another half dozen. He also ate half a chicken and a plateful of strawberries and asked the waiter for more whipped cream.

"If I can get it on your plate," the waiter said.

"Try."

The waiter ladled on more whipped cream.

"You can leave that pitcher on the table," the commissaris said, "and put it on the bill."

"You'd better not kiss your wife tonight," the commissaris said as they left the restaurant. "That sauce you liked so much was solid garlic."

"I never kiss my wife," Grijpstra said and burped. "Excuse me, sir."

"Never mind, but don't burp in the car. You'll knock out the driver and we still have to see that other girl."

Grijpstra nodded gravely but he wasn't listening. A second burp was forming itself at the bottom of his gullet and seemed stuck sideways,

sideways and askew. It burned and cut simultaneously and he began to pat his chest anxiously in a vain attempt to dislodge the bubbly obstacle. The commissaris was still talking and the Citroën waited for them at the end of the path with the constable at the door.

"Funny fellow, don't you think?" the commissaris asked. "He always refuses to eat with me, poor chap still lives in the last century. He probably had a cup of coffee and fried eggs on toast on the terrace while we stuffed ourselves inside. I'll see if I can get his bill. Can't let him pay for himself, can I?"

Grijpstra was still patting his chest.

"What's wrong?"

"I'll be right back," Grijpstra said and turned off the path. Hidden behind a thicket of young ash trees he thumped his chest and wriggled his large body but the burp stayed where it was, obstinately lodged below an invisible impediment. Determined to free himself Grijpstra jumped up and down, flapping his arms and suddenly the burp, having grown meanwhile into a full-grown belch, roared out and touched his vocal cords, vibrating first into a growl and reaching the impact of a thunderclap at its summit.

Grijpstra dropped his arms and staggered back.

"Well done," the waiter said. He had been watching Grijpstra ever since he turned off the path.

"Beautiful," the waiter said now. "Never heard anything like it. I am surprised there are still leaves on the trees. Try a fart now. Go on."

Grijpstra felt too relieved to be hurt. "Shouldn't you be inside working?" he asked mildly.

"I should be," the waiter said, "but I am not. I am here, taking five minutes off and smoking a cigarette. It's my last day at this establishment. I am starting a little snack bar in town next week."

"Where? Maybe I'll come and try it."

"Not you," the waiter said, threw down his cigarette, stamped on it, and walked away.

13

"WE ARE EARLY," the commissaris said to the constable. "You can drive about for half an hour if you like. There's a nature reserve close by. I've been there before, I even have a special pass. It isn't open to the public."

He fished around in his wallet and gave the pass to the driver. The constable turned it around and studied the little map on its reverse side.

"I can find it, sir. It shouldn't be more than a few kilometers from here."

Grijpstra was still exhausted and happy to let events take their course. The soft suspension of the car was lulling him to sleep and when he woke up because the commissaris touched his arm they were in the reserve. Once a graveyard, the place had lain untended for a hundred years or so; then the municipal authorities had discovered it again and promoted it into a special area, enlarging the land by buying the surrounding farms and a small estate, complete with the ruins of a castle and a moat leading into an artificial lake. The city had dipped into a wildlife fund for the money, and botanists and biologists now roamed the reserve, trying to find out what supposedly extinct flora and fauna they might run into.

"Untouched by filthy hands," the commissaris mumbled as he gazed at the landscape. The constable was driving slowly so that they could enjoy the sight of beeches and oaks grown to gigantic sizes, a glade, covered with the lush yellow of gorse, undergrowth bustling with rabbits and a lone pheasant standing on a rock. "Look," the commissaris said, and pointed at a spotted deer, watching them quietly from the cover of a broken gravestone.

"I could hit him easily from here," the constable said and touched the automatic pistol, resting in its holster under his blazer. "A perfect shot sir."

"You're joking," Grijpstra said grumpily.

"A policeman is a hunter," the commissaris said good-naturedly. "Don't scold the constable, adjutant. The thought occurred to me too."

He pointed his index finger at the buck. "Bam," the commissaris said. "You are dead. We'll have venison for dinner tomorrow."

The car was moving again. They were getting close to the lake and at a turn of the path they saw a flock of coots landing. The fat black little birds came in with their flat webbed feet spread, clumsily hitting the lake's still surface and splashing heavily before they flopped down, like puddings thrown in a comic movie.

"Ha," the constable said, but he wasn't laughing a minute later when the wide tires of the Citroën were crushing the first toads.

"What now?" the constable asked, and stopped the car, alarmed by the squashing noise which had suddenly burst on his eardrums. He got out and looked at the tarmac. Some ten flattened baby toads showed themselves on the hot tar of the path.

The commissaris and Grijpstra had got out too.

"You should have avoided them," Grijpstra said. "Toads are getting scarce nowadays."

"He couldn't have," the commissaris said. "He didn't see them, did you, constable?"

"No, sir. I heard them when they squashed. Bah. Horrible sound, wasn't it? Like popping balloons."

"There are lots of them," Grijpstra said.

The grass on both sides of the path was alive with toads. They were coming from the lake, and the car and the three men were in their way. The path became covered with their small slimy bodies and there seemed no way of avoiding their hopping progress. They were every-where, crawling over the policemen's shoes, pushing against the car's tires. They could hear them too now, an oozing sound, as if thick wet sticky mud were being pumped through countless drainpipes.

"Let's get out of here," the commissaris said, shaking the animals off his shoes and inadvertently stepping on them.

The constable slipped and would have fallen if Grijpstra's heavy hand hadn't caught his elbow. They got back into the car.

"If we drive away I'll kill thousands of them," the constable said.

The commissaris looked at the lake. "They are still coming, they may be coming all day. This must be their hatching time. Perhaps there is a plague of toads. That damned gatekeeper shouldn't have let us in. Get us out of here, constable, we have an appointment to keep."

The toads crawled and sucked and squashed for hundreds of yards and the Citroën kept on crushing them. The constable was cursing, holding the wheel as if he wanted to wrench it out of its socket. The slime of the small corpses filled the grooves of the tires, forcing the car to slide crazily, and twice they slipped off the path with spinning wheels. Grijpstra felt sick and blocked his ears to drown the continuous slushing and squeezing. He was trying not to think of the snails, which he imagined sliding about in his stomach in a sea of whipped cream, and was breathing deeply. He could see the constable's wide staring eyes in the rearview mirror.

"That's it," the commissaris said cheerfully. "We are through. Go forward and reverse a couple of times on that sandy spot over there, it'll clean out the tires."

"That girl will be our last suspect for the time being," the commissaris was saying, "but Abe Rogge must have had a lot of close relationships. We are facing a crowd, Grijpstra. Maybe we haven't even started yet."

Grijpstra didn't answer and the commissaris leaned forward to get a closer look. Grijpstra's state of nerves didn't seem improved at all; if anything it seemed worse. The adjutant's skin looked gray and he wasn't able to control his hands, which were fidgeting with the end of his tie.

"Sir," the constable said, and pointed at a small freshly painted houseboat.

Grijpstra grunted and got out of the car. The commissaris wanted to follow but checked himself. Grijpstra was hopping about on one foot on the way, yelling.

"Now what?" the commissaris asked.

"Careful, sir," Grijpstra shouted. "The pavement is full of shit."

The commissaris looked. It must have been a large dog, a large sick dog perhaps. The turds, of a greenish yellow color, covered several cobblestones and Grijpstra had stepped right in the middle. The constable closed his eyes, opened them again and forced his body to move. He walked around the car, opened the trunk and found a hard brush with a long handle. Grijpstra held on to a lamppost while the constable set to work.

"You *are* an excitable fellow," the commissaris said. "Haven't you ever stepped into dog turds before, adjutant?"

"Often," Grijpstra said irritably. "Every day of my life, I think. I attract dogshit. If there's one turd in a street I plow right through it. Some people think it's funny. I amuse them."

"I don't think it's funny," the commissaris said, "and neither does the constable."

"De Gier thinks it's funny. Yesterday, when we went to fetch the car in the police yard, I stepped into a turd and I was running so I slithered all over the pavement. He laughed, the bastard laughed! Tears in his eyes! Slapping his thighs! But dogshit is the same to me as a bleeding corpse to him. *I* don't laugh when he is leaning against walls and fainting and carrying on!"

"Hmm," the commissaris said, "but you are clean now. Thank you, constable. Let's get into that boat before anything else happens."

The girl was waiting for them in the doorway.

"Anything wrong?" she asked the adjutant. "Why were you jumping about?"

"Stepped in some dog droppings, miss."

"The German shepherd next door did that. He hasn't been feeling well lately. I meant to clean it up today but I forgot. Take your shoes off, my boat is all spick and span for once."

Grijpstra knelt down obediently. The commissaris slipped past him, found a comfortable-looking chair and sat down. The girl stayed with Grijpstra until both shoes, upside down, were placed in a corner near the door.

"Are you police officers?" the girl asked. "I always thought they wore raincoats and felt hats."

"You've been watching old movies," the commissaris said.

"Coffee?" the girl asked.

"No, thanks, miss."

The commissaris approved of the girl. Large lively eyes in a freckled face. Stiff pigtails with blue ribbons to keep them together. A dress, reaching down to her ankles, made out of gaily printed cotton. Irregular but very white teeth, a strong mouth. A ray of sunshine, the commissaris thought happily, just what we need to finish off a day's work.

"You've come about Abe?" the girl asked and looked at Grijpstra, who was standing about forlornly. "Why don't you sit down?"

"Where?" Grijpstra asked.

"Right here." She pointed at a shapeless leather bag next to the commissaris' chair, got down on her haunches and thumped the bag. "It's quite comfortable, it's filled with pebbles. I bought it in Spain. Try it." Grijpstra sat down. "You see?"

"Yes, miss," Grijpstra said and screwed his wide bottom into the bag. Its back came up and supported his bulk; the pebbles were crunching inside.

"Yes," the commissaris said. "We've come about Abe. He was killed yesterday, as you know. We were told you were friendly with Mr. Rogge."

"Yes," the girl said. "Very friendly. We slept together."

"Yes, yes," the commissaris said.

"I like to be exact," the girl said brightly.

Why is she so damned cheerful? Grijpstra thought. The man is dead, isn't he? Can't she be upset? He moved and the pebbles crunched again.

"Don't look so worried. That bag won't break. Hundreds of people have sat on it."

"So Abe was your lover, eh?" he asked.

"He was my lover but I wasn't his mistress."

"I see," Grijpstra said doubtfully.

"I don't," the commissaris said. "If Mr. Rogge was your lover you were his mistress. Surely that's the right way of describing the relationship, isn't it?"

"No," the girl said, and smiled. "No, not at all. Abe slept with lots of girls; they came to him when he flicked his fingers—and wagged their tails. He didn't even have to seduce them, they just expected him to take his pants off and do the job. Not me. He came when *I* wanted him to come and he left me when *I* wanted him to leave and he had to talk to me and to listen to me. I never tried to fit into his schedule. I am a busy girl, I've got my own schedule. I study and the State is paying me to study; they gave me a nice grant. I intend to finish my studies in time, ahead of time preferably. I don't play around."

It was a long speech and she delivered it almost vehemently, standing in the middle of the small room. Grijpstra was impressed. The commissaris appeared not to be listening. He had been looking around him. The interior of the boat looked as neat as its outside. She hadn't cluttered the room; everything which it contained seemed to fulfill a function. A large low table, stacked with books and paper and a typewriter. A few plants and a vase filled with freshly cut flowers.

He got up, and walked to the end of the room, stopping at a work bench. "Are you working on something, miss?"

"Tilda," the girl said, "Tilda van Andringa de Kempenaar. Just call me Tilda. That's a bird feeder, or, rather, it will be one day. I am having a little trouble with it."

"Van Andringa de Kempenaar," the commissaris said, and narrowed his eyes. The puckered forehead showed that he was thinking, trying to remember. "A noble name, it shows in our history books, doesn't it?"

"Yes," she said briskly, "a noble name, a noble family."

"I should address you as 'freule' perhaps."

"Not really," she said. "Tilda will do." She picked up her long dress, bent her knees and straightened up again. "We had estates once, and influence at court, and I don't think we paid taxes in those days, but my great-great-grandfather blew it all in Paris and ever since then we've been like the rest and worked for a living."

"I see," the commissaris said and bared his teeth mechanically. "A bird feeder, you said?"

"Yes. I like making things but this is more work than I anticipated. It still has to be covered with sheet metal and glass but I've got to get the inside right first. It's supposed to be ingenious you see. The bird has to sit on this little rod and then some feed will flow into that tray over there. There's a small trapdoor here connected to the rod. But it isn't working properly. There should be just enough feed going into the tray; I don't want to keep refilling the container. The whole thing will be hung outside when it's ready and the only way I can get at it will be via the roof. The windows on that side don't open."

"I see, I see," the commissaris said, replacing the structure. "Very clever. Did you design it yourself?"

"I had some help but not much. I like inventing. I was always making soap box carts when I was a child. One of them got a prize at school. I won a race in it. Want to see it?"

"Please," the commissaris and Grijpstra said.

She brought it in and went into a long technical explanation.

"Very clever," the commissaris said again.

"What do you study, Tilda?" Grijpstra asked.

"Medicine. I am in my third year. I want to be a surgeon."

"But you are still very young," Grijpstra said in an awed voice.

"Twenty-one."

"You'll have your degree in four years' time." Grijpstra was almost whispering. He couldn't imagine the girl as a graduate in medicine. He suddenly saw himself tied to a table in a white room. The girl was bending over him. She had a knife, the knife would cut into his skin, slicing a deep wound. Her fingers were touching exposed muscles, nerves, vital organs. A shiver touched the hairs on his neck.

"Nothing special," the girl said. She had seen Grijpstra's reaction and grinned wickedly. "Anybody who isn't downright stupid and who is willing to work hard for eight or ten hours a day can become a doctor."

"But you want to be a surgeon," Grijpstra said.

"Yes. I'll have to work in a hospital somewhere for another seven years or so. But it'll be worth it."

"Yes," the commissaris said. "Do you have any idea who killed your friend, Tilda?"

The grin froze on her face. She suddenly seemed to become aware of herself, standing halfway between her interrogators. "No. No, I have no idea. He was always so happy and full of life. I am sure nobody disliked him. Esther said that he was killed in some mysterious way? Is that right?"

"That's right," the commissaris said. "You wouldn't have any photographs, would you? We only saw him dead."

Her eyes were moist now. "Yes, holiday snapshots. I'll get them."

They looked at the album. Abe Rogge at the helm of his boat, and running in the surf, and leaning over the railing of a ferry, and at the wheel of an antique motorcar. Louis Zilver was in some of the photographs, and Tilda herself, looking healthy and attractive.

"Fishing," the commissaris said. "Did he fish a lot?" He pointed at a photo showing Abe struggling with a fishing rod, bent backward, pulling with all his might.

"That was in North Africa," the girl said, "last year. Just the two of us went. He had some gamefish on the hook, took him all afternoon to bring it in. It was such a lovely fish that I made him throw it back. It must have weighed a hundred kilos."

"Where were you yesterday afternoon and last night?" Grijpstra asked.

"Here."

"Anyone with you?"

"No, several people knocked on the door and the telephone rang but I didn't answer. I am working on a test. I should be working at it now too. They didn't give me much time and it's an important credit."

"Yes," the commissaris said. "We must be going."

"Hard-boiled little thing," Grijpstra said in the car. "It won't be easy to shake her. She almost broke down when you asked her to show the photographs but that was the only time she weakened. I bet she is the local chairman of some red women's organization."

"Yes, and a proper freule too," the commissaris said. "I think one of her ancestors was a general who fought Napoleon. I forget what he did now but it was something brave and original. She'll be a good surgeon. Maybe she'll invent a way to cut hemorrhoids painlessly."

Grijpstra looked up. "Do you have hemorrhoids, sir?"

"Not anymore, but it hurt when they took them out. Did you see that bird feeder?"

"Yes, sir. A well-designed construction. Do you think she could manufacture a deadly weapon, sir? Something which can shoot a spiked ball?"

"I am sure she can," the commissaris said. "It would work with a powerful spring. I counted six springs in her bird thing."

"It's a thought," Grijpstra said, "but that's all it is. Whatever she had going with Rogge must have been going well, so why would she go to a lot of trouble to kill him?"

"The female mind," the commissaris said. "A great mystery. My wife went to a lot of trouble because she didn't like the man who delivered oil for our central heating. She phoned his boss and said that if they couldn't send someone else she would close the account. I was never able to find out what she had against the man; he seemed a pleasant rather witless fellow to me. But now we are buying oil from some other company. And my wife hardly ever gets upset. This girl would fly into a rage at the slightest provocation. Made that great hulking fellow throw back a fish he had fought with for hours. Made you take off your shoes. Knows exactly what she wants. Studies like mad. Builds involved gadgets just for fun. Has her sex life arranged all *her* way."

"A nasty bundle of energy," Grijpstra said. "Perhaps we should go back tomorrow, sir, take her to the morgue and confront her with the corpse. Interrogate her for a few hours. She has no alibi, she could easily have sneaked out to the Rogge house. She is a small girl. The riot police would have let her through. Maybe she was carrying a parcel containing the device that shot the ball. She climbed onto the roof of that old ship lying opposite the house, called Abe . . ."

"Could be," the commissaris said, "but I am taking you home now. We'll see tomorrow. Maybe de Gier and Cardozo will pick up a clue at the street market. You and I can sit and think for a day, or you can go out to the market too."

The car stopped in front of Grijpstra's house. The constable looked back as he drove away.

"He isn't going home, sir," the constable said. "He hesitated at the door and walked away."

"Really?" the commissaris asked.

"Well, he's right, I think," the constable said. "Some wife the adjutant has. Did you see that woman popping her head out of the window this morning, sir?"

"I did," the commissaris said.

14

WHEN DE GIER turned the key he could hear Oliver's nails scratching the inside of the door. He also heard the telephone.

"It never stops," he said to Esther, stepping aside so that she could enter first, and bending down. Oliver ran straight into his hand, pressed low to the floor, intent on escape. "Here," de Gier said and caught him. "Don't run away, there's nothing outside there. Just a lot of fast cars and a hot street. Here! And don't scratch."

The telephone was still ringing. "Yes, yes, yes," de Gier said, and picked it up. Esther had taken the cat out of his arms and was nuzzling it, whispering into its ear. Oliver closed his eyes, went limp and purred. The nails slid back and his paws became soft playthings of fur. He pushed a paw against her nose, and kept it there.

"That's nice," de Gier said. "I have never seen him do that to anyone except myself. Silly cat loves you."

"Is it silly to love me?" Esther asked, and before he had time to think of an answer, "Who was that on the telephone? You look all grumpy."

"The commissaris."

"I thought he was a very pleasant man."

"He is not," de Gier said, "and he shouldn't phone me. He is fussing. Did I get the schedule for tomorrow organized? Did I speak to Cardozo about it? Did I do this? Did I do that? Of course I did it all. I always do everything he tells me. Why doesn't he fuss with Grijpstra? But he had

Grijpstra with him all day, they had dinner together, while I was sent on an inane errand."

"What errand?"

"Never mind," de Gier said. "Take your coat off and I'll make tea. Or I can open a can of shrimp soup, I have had it in the fridge for ages, waiting for the right occasion. We can have a drop of Madeira in it and eat some hot buttered toast and a salad. And we can look at the geraniums while we eat. The one in the middle is doing very well. I've been feeding it expensive drops and it is responding. See?"

"You like your balcony, don't you?"

"It's better than a garden. I don't have to wear myself out in it. I am growing some cabbage seed now, in that pot in the corner. The little boy in the flat upstairs gave me the seeds and they came up in a few weeks, just as he said. They are in flower too now. I used to study the buds through a magnifying glass; I could almost see them swell."

"I thought you would be more interested in fingerprints."

"No," de Gier said. "Fingerprints don't grow, they are just there, left by a fool who didn't mind what he was doing. We hardly ever find fingerprints anyway and if we find them they belong to a sweet innocent."

She was helping him in the kitchen and sent him out, once she knew where everything was. He sat down on his bed and talked to her through the open door. She didn't take long and served the meal on a detachable board, which he pulled from the wall and which came down to about a foot from the bed's surface, suspended by hinges on one side and a chain on the other.

"Very ingenious," she said. "This is a very small apartment but it looks quite spacious somehow."

"Because I have no furniture," he said. "Just the bed, and the chair in the other room. I don't really like having people here, they make the place overflow. Grijpstra is O.K., he doesn't move. And you, of course. It's marvelous having you here."

She leaned over and kissed his cheek. The telephone rang again.

"It never stops," de Gier said. "It. The whole thing. It's still moving and I want to be out of it. There should be a way of dropping out of activity. Smashing the telephone would be a good start."

"Answer it," she said, "and then come back to me. And to the toast, it's still hot."

"Cardozo?" de Gier asked.

"Yes," Cardozo said, "your faithful assistant is reporting. I am about to start organizing the truck and the merchandise and the permit for the street market and everything, but I thought I'd better run through all the details with you once more before I started."

De Gier sighed. "Cardozo?"

"Yes."

"Cardozo, it's all yours. I want you to prove yourself. Get the whole rigmarole going, Cardozo. Do more than we are asking you to do. Find out what the textiles are worth. We have to sell them at the right price tomorrow. We can't give state property away, can we?"

"No," Cardozo said.

"Right. Besides we don't want the other hawkers to be suspicious. We have to be just right. Think about this business. Try and *become* a hawker. Think yourself into it. Get the thought into your subconscious. Try and dream about it tonight."

"What are *you* going to do?" Cardozo asked.

"I am going to be here, right here in my flat and think with you. Don't feel alone, I am with you, right behind you, Cardozo. Every step of the way."

"When I am carrying those heavy bales out of the police store?"

"Yes."

"Heaving them into the van?"

"Yes."

"That'll be nice."

"Yes. And if there's any problem you can't solve—I don't think there will be any, for you are competent and well trained and an asset to the force—then grab the nearest telephone and dial my number. I'll advise you."

"About how to carry those heavy bales into the van?"

"Yes. Take a deep breath before you lift them. Then stop your breath while you move your arms. Get your shoulder and stomach muscles to help. Heave-ho! You'll find it easy if you go about it the right way."

"I am glad you have faith in me," Cardozo said. "Maybe I will tell the commissaris about your faith in me, sometime when I happen to run into him and we'll be chatting about this and that."

"Oh, no, you won't," de Gier said. "I read the report in your file. The character report. You were picked for the murder squad because you have all the right qualities. Initiative for instance. And an inquisitive and secretive mind. And you are ambitious. You can be trusted to react properly when in a difficult spot. And you are reliable. Did you know all those things about yourself?"

"No," Cardozo said, "and I don't believe that report. It must have been made up by the psychologist who interviewed me. A rat-faced long-haired nervous wreck. I thought he was a suspect when I met him and I was watching him very carefully."

"Psychology is a new science, a long-haired rat-faced science. They all look like that. They have to, or they are no good. And please stop arguing, Cardozo. Haven't you learned by now that nothing is gained by arguing?"

"Yes, sergeant," Cardozo said. "Sorry, sergeant. Forgot myself a moment, sergeant. Won't happen again, sergeant. Do you want me to report when I've got it all arranged, sergeant?"

"No," de Gier said. "That won't be necessary. I'll see you tomorrow morning, at the police garage at eight-thirty sharp. Good luck."

He put down the telephone and went back to the bed.

"Excellent young man," he said to Esther, "and clever too."

"Aren't you clever?"

"No," de Gier said.

"Are you a good detective?"

"No."

"Do you try to be?"

"Yes."

"Why?" He laughed, leaned over and kissed her.

"No. I want to know. Why do you try to be a good detective?"

He kissed her again. He said something about her hair and how well the kimono looked on her and how glad he was that she had changed her clothes while he was talking on the telephone. And how slender her body was.

"Yes," she said. "You are a charmer. But why do you try to be a good detective?"

"To please the commissaris," he said, trying to make the remark pass off as a joke.

"Yes," Esther said seriously. "I had a professor once I wanted to please. He seemed a very advanced little old man to me, and I loved him because he was so ugly and because he had such a big bald head. His mind was very quick but it was also deep, and I was sure he knew things that I should know. He was a strangely happy man and yet I knew that he had lost everything he cherished during the war and lived by himself in an old, untidy and very depressing house. I did very well in his class although his subject hardly interested me when I began. He taught medieval French and he made it come alive again."

"Crime interests me," de Gier said. "It interested me before I began to work under the commissaris."

"Why?" He lay back, stretching out an amorous arm which she didn't resist. "Why do you like crime?"

"I didn't say I liked crime, I said it interested me. Crime is sometimes a single mistake, more often a series of mistakes. I try to understand why criminals make mistakes."

"Why? To catch them?"

"I am not a hunter," de Gier said. "I hunt, because it is part of my work but I don't really enjoy it."

"So what are you?"

He sat up, looking for his pack of cigarettes. She gave him the pack and flicked her lighter. Her kimono opened and she adjusted it.

"Must we talk?" de Gier said. "I can think of better things to do."

She laughed. "Yes. Let's talk for a little while, I'll shut up in a minute."

"I don't know what I am," de Gier said, "but I am trying to find out. Criminals are also trying to find out what they are. It's a game we share with them."

His voice had gone up and Oliver woke and yowled.

"Oliver!" Esther said.

The cat turned its head and looked at her. He made a series of sounds, low sounds in the back of his throat, and stretched, putting a forepaw on her thigh.

"Go and catch a bird," de Gier said, as he picked him up and put him on the balcony, closing the door after him.

"Don't be jealous," Esther said.

"I *am* jealous," de Gier said.

"Don't you have any idea what you are?"

"Yes," he said and lay down on the bed, pulling her down, "a vague idea. A feeling rather. But it will have to become a lot clearer."

"And you became a policeman to find out?"

"No. I happened to become a policeman. I wasn't planning anything when I left school. I have an uncle in the police and he mentioned the possibility to my father and before I knew what I was doing I had signed a form and was answering questions and saying 'yes' to all of them and then suddenly I was in uniform, with a stripe on my arm, and eight hours a day of classes."

"My brother also wanted to find out what he was," Esther said. "It's dangerous to be like that. You'll get yourself killed."

"I don't think I would mind," de Gier said and tugged at her kimono.

They fell asleep afterward and de Gier woke up an hour later because

Oliver was throwing his body against the glass balcony door, making it rattle. He got up and fed the cat, cutting the meat carefully into thin slices. He lay down again, without disturbing Esther, who lay on her side, gently breathing. Her breathing excited him again. He turned over and looked at the geraniums and forced his mind to concentrate. He wanted to think about the spiked ball, the ball which had smashed the life out of Esther's powerful brother. He knew this was the best time to think, when his body was almost all asleep, leaving his brain to function on its own. It had made him conclude, early that morning, that the ball had been connected to a line, probably an elastic line. He had remembered some little boys playing ball on the balcony of a hotel in France. He had been watching them from the lounge, several years ago now, during a holiday shared with a police secretary, who had turned out to be very high-strung and possessive and who had changed the promised pleasure of the trip into a series of fights and withdrawals. He had been trying to get away from her that day and had been on his way out through the lounge when he saw the kids. They had a ball attached to some heavy weight and they were hitting it with miniature bats. They couldn't lose the ball for it could only travel a certain length. He hadn't been trying to think of kids playing, he had only concentrated on the mystery of the spiked ball and the picture of the kids and their gadget had suddenly popped up.

The ball had been thrown or shot into Abe's room but it hadn't stayed there. He was sure that the killer had never been in the room. If he had, there would have been a fight. Esther and Louis Zilver were in the house at the time. They would have heard the fight. There would have been shouts, furniture would have been pushed around, bodies would have struggled and fallen. The killer would have had to leave the house after Abe's death. He would have had to take the risk that either Esther or Louis would see him. De Gier was sure that the murder had been planned. Planned with a hellish machine. He had seen an exhibition of hellish machines at the police museum. Fountain pens that spout poison, rings with hidden steel thorns moved by a spring, very involved machines that will trigger off an explosion, trapdoors, heavy weights that will fall at the right moment. But not a spiked ball that disappears after it has done its work. And yet he knew that he knew the answer. He had seen something once, something that was capable of moving a spiked ball. Where had he seen it?

It would have to be something ordinary, innocuous. Something the riot policemen could see without having second thoughts. And it had to be noiseless. A bang would have alarmed the constables who were uneasy anyway that day. Something the killer could carry through the Straight Tree Ditch and smile at the constables as he carried it.

His eyes were closing. He struggled. The answer was close; all he had to do was grab it.

He fell asleep and woke up two hours later. Esther wasn't on the bed. He heard her in the kitchen. She was stirring something in a pot. The smell reached him, a good smell which touched his stomach. A stew. She must have found the minced meat and the fresh vegetables. He got up and stuck his head into the small kitchen. She had some rice at the boil too.

They ate, and listened to records. De Gier felt happy, unbelievably and completely happy. He also felt guilty and he opened a can of sardines for Oliver.

15

THE ALBERT CUYP is a long narrow street cutting through one of Amsterdam's uglier parts, where houses are thin high slabs of bricks pushed together in endless rows, where trees won't grow and where traffic is eternally congested. The street market is the heart of an area consisting of stone and tar, and its splash of color and sound feeds some life into what otherwise wouldn't be much other than a hell of boredom, in which the human ant lives out its sixty or seventy years of getting up and going to bed, being busy in between with factory and office work, and TV programs and a bit of drinking at the corner bar. It was an area that both de Gier and Cardozo knew well, for it breeds crime, mostly sad and always nonspectacular. The neighborhood is known for its family fights, drug pushing in a small way, burglaries and a bit of robbery, committed by youth gangs who swagger about, waylaying the elderly passerby, stealing cars and motorized bicycles, and molesting lonely homosexuals. The area is doomed, for city planning will do away with it, blow it up with dynamite to make room for blocks of apartments set in parks, but the city works slowly and the street market will be there for many years to come, functioning as a gigantic department store, selling food and household goods cheaply, providing an outlet for the national industry's unsalable goods and for adventurer-merchants who import for their own account, or smuggle, or, rarely, buy stolen goods.

Cardozo had managed to force the gray van on to the sidewalk and was unloading bale after bale of gaily printed textiles, which de Gier stacked on the worn planks of a corner stall, assigned to them for the day by the market master, who had given them a knowing wink when de Gier, waving his license, looked him up in his little office.

"Good luck," the market master said. "You'll be after Rogge's killer, I bet. You'd better get him. Abe Rogge was a popular man here and he'll be missed."

"Don't tell anyone," de Gier said.

The market master was shaking his head energetically.

"I don't tell on the police. I need the police here. I wish you would patrol the market more regularly. Two uniformed constables can't cover a mile of market."

"There are plainclothes police as well."

"Yes," the market master said, "but not enough. There's always a bit of trouble here, especially on a hot day like this. We need more uniforms. If they see a shiny cap and nicely polished buttons they quiet down quickly. I have been writing to the chief constable's office. He always answers, but it's the same answer. Short of staff."

"Complain, complain, complain!" de Gier said.

"What do you mean?"

"What I say. Go on complaining. It helps. You'll get more constables."

"But they'll come from some other part of town and there'll be trouble down *there*."

"So someone else can start complaining."

"Yes," the market master said, and laughed. "I am only concerned about my own troubles. What about you? Will you catch your man?"

"Sure," de Gier said, and left.

But he wasn't so sure when he got back to the stall. Cardozo was complaining too. The bales were too heavy.

"I'll get you some coffee," de Gier said.

"I can get my own coffee. I want you to help me unload these bales."

"Sugar and milk?"

"Yes. But help me first."

"No," de Gier said and left the stall. He found a girl carrying a tray with empty glasses, who took his order. He ordered meat rolls too and hot dogs.

"You are new, aren't you?" The girl was pretty and de Gier smiled at her.

"Yes. First day here. We've been on other markets, never down here."

"Best market in the country. What do you sell?"

"Lovely fabrics for dressmaking and curtains."

"Will you give me a special price?" The girl reached out with her free hand and patted his cheek.

"Sure." He smiled again and she swung her hip at him in response. He wasn't in a hurry to get back to the stall, but Cardozo saw him and shouted and jumped up and down, waving his arms.

Together they finished the stall, draping some of the textiles in what they thought to be an attractive display.

"This is no good," Cardozo muttered as he worked. "That fellow on the other side of the street knows who we are. He keeps on looking at us. Who is he anyway?"

De Gier looked and waved. "Louis Zilver. I asked the market master to give us a place close to him. He was Abe Rogge's partner. He's selling beads and wool and embroidery silk and all that sort of thing."

"But if he knows us he'll spread the news, won't he?"

"No, he won't, why should he?"

"Why shouldn't he?"

"Because he is the dead man's friend."

"He may be the dead man's killer."

De Gier sipped his coffee and stared at Cardozo, who was glaring at him from between two bales of cloth. "What are you so excited about? If he is the killer we are wasting our time here for we'll have to get at him in some other way. But if he isn't he'll protect us. He knows he is a suspect and if we find the killer he'll be cleared; besides, he may really want us to catch the murderer. He's supposed to be Rogge's friend, isn't he? There is such a thing as friendship."

Cardozo snorted.

"Don't you believe in friendship?"

Cardozo didn't answer.

"Don't you?"

"I am a Jew," Cardozo said, "and Jews believe in friendship because they wouldn't have survived without it."

"That isn't what I mean."

"What do you mean?"

"Friendship," de Gier said. "You know, love. One man loves another. He is glad when the other man is glad and sad when the other man is sad. He identifies with the other man. They are together, and together they are more than two individuals added up."

"You don't have to spell it out for me," Cardozo said. "I won't believe you anyway. There's such a thing as a shared interest and the idea that two men can do more than one. I can understand that but I won't go for love. I have been in the police for some time now. The friends we catch always rat on each other after a while."

"Love your neighbor," de Gier said.

"Are you religious?"

"No."

"So why preach at me?"

De Gier touched Cardozo's shoulder gingerly. "I am not preaching at you. Love your neighbor; it makes sense, doesn't it? Even if it happens to be a religious command."

"But we don't love our neighbors," Cardozo said, furiously pushing at a bale of lining which had fallen over. "We are envious of our neighbors, we try to grab things from them, we annoy them. And we make fun of them if we can get away with it and we kill them too if they don't want to put up with our demands. You can't prove history wrong. I was too young to have been in the last war but I've seen the documentaries, and I've heard the stories and seen the numbers burned into people's arms. We have an army to make sure that the neighbors across the frontier behave themselves and we have a police force to make sure that we behave ourselves within the frontiers. You know what the place would be like if the police didn't patrol it?"

"Stop kicking that bale," de Gier said. "You are spoiling the merchandise."

"Without the police society would be a mad shambles, sergeant, a free fight for all. I am sure that Zilver fellow doesn't care two hoots if we catch the killer or not, and if he does care he has a personal interest."

"Revenge, for instance," de Gier said.

"Revenge is selfish too," Cardozo said, "but I was thinking of money. He'll want us to make an arrest if he can profit by the arrest."

"You've been drinking with Grijpstra," de Gier said, and helped to lift the bale.

"No. *You* have. Last night."

De Gier looked hurt. "Last night, dear friend, I was at home. I only spent a few minutes with Grijpstra at Nellie's bar and half that time went on a telephone call. He didn't want me around so I left. Nellie didn't want me around either."

"Nellie?" Cardozo asked.

De Gier explained.

"Boy!" Cardozo said. "As big as that? Boy!"

"As big as that," de Gier said, "and Grijpstra wanted them all to himself. So I left. I checked out two prostitutes who were supposed to be Bezuur's alibi and after that I went home."

"Bezuur?" Cardozo asked. "Who is he? I am supposed to help you and the adjutant but nobody tells me anything. Who is Bezuur?"

"A friend of Abe Rogge."

Cardozo asked more questions and de Gier explained.

"I see," Cardozo said. "What about the callgirls? Had they been with him all night?"

"So they said."

"Did you believe them?"

"According to Grijpstra there were six empty champagne bottles lying about in Bezuur's bungalow, and there were cigarette burns on the furniture and stains on the walls. An orgy. Who remembers what happens during an orgy? Maybe they were out on the floor half the night."

"Did they look as if they had been?"

"They looked O.K.," de Gier said. "One of them even looked pretty nice. But they had had time for their beauty sleep and they knew I was coming. I didn't know the address so I couldn't jump them."

"Couldn't you have checked with the telephone company?"

"I could have but it would have been difficult. It was Sunday, remember? And maybe I was too lazy to try and jump them."

"So what did you do afterward?"

"I went home and I went to bed. And in between I was weeding the flower boxes on my balcony. And I had a late supper with my cat."

Cardozo smiled. "You are a lucky man, sergeant."

"Don't call me sergeant. Why am I lucky?"

Cardozo shrugged. "I don't know. You are older than I am but you are like a child sometimes. You enjoy yourself, don't you? You and that silly cat."

"He isn't a silly cat. And he loves me."

"There we go again," Cardozo said and began to tug at another bale. "Love. I saw a poster in a bookshop last week. A love poster. Half-naked girls with frizzy hair sitting under a beautiful tree chanting away while birds fly around and angels gaze down. It's a craze. When I was still in uniform we had one of these love places a block away from the station. We had complaints every night. The girls would have their bags stolen and the boys had their wallets rolled and they were buying hash which turned out to be caked rubbish and they had knives pulled on them and they got the clap and crabs and the itch. I've been in there dozens of times and it was the same thing every night, dirty and smoky and silly and hazy. Some of them would catch on and drift away, but there were always others who hadn't learned yet and who were begging to get in."

"The wrong place," de Gier said. "Brothels are the wrong place too. And Nellie's bar unless your name is Grijpstra and Nellie falls for you. But love exists." He patted his pockets.

"Cigarette?" Cardozo asked, and offered his tobacco pouch and packet of cigarette papers.

"Thanks," de Gier said. "You see, you are giving me something I haven't asked for. So you care for my well-being."

"So I love you," Cardozo said. De Gier felt embarrassed and Cardozo grinned.

"I only offered you a cigarette because I know that I won't have any cigarettes sometime and I will want you to give me one. It's an investment for the future."

"And if I was dying?" de Gier asked. "Say I was going to be shot in five minutes' time and I asked you for a cigarette. Would you give me one? I would never be in a position to return the gift, would I?"

Cardozo thought.

"Well?"

"Yes, I would give you a cigarette, but I am sure I would have some selfish reason, although I can't think of the reason now."

"How much?" a voice asked. An old lady had come to the stall and was fingering a piece of cloth.

"Twelve guilders a meter, darling," Cardozo said, "and ten percent off if you buy five meters. That's lovely curtain material. It'll brighten up your room and it's guaranteed not to fade."

"Expensive," the old lady said.

"What do you mean, dear? It's two meters wide. They'll charge you three times as much in any store, and it won't be as nice as this. This came from Sweden and the Swedish designers are the best in the world. Look at those flowers. Fuchsias. You'll be sitting in your room and you'll draw the curtains and the light will filter through the material and you'll be able to see the nice red flowers. Aren't they pretty? See, every petal is printed beautifully."

"Yes," the old lady said dreamily.

"Take five yards, dear, ten guilders a yard."

"I haven't got fifty guilders on me."

"How much have you got?"

"Thirty, and I only need three yards."

"For you I will do everything, darling. Give me the scissors, mate."

But he didn't start cutting until the lady had counted out her thirty guilders.

"I thought you said we should get eight guilders for that cloth," de Gier said.

"Start high, you can always come down. And she's got a bargain anyway."

"I wouldn't have that material in my flat if you paid me."

"Stop fussing," Cardozo said. "She selected the cloth herself, didn't she? And it's first-class material, confiscated from a first-class smuggler who tried to bring it in without paying duty and sales tax."

Other customers came and bought. Cardozo was yelling and waving and de Gier handled the scissors. After a while de Gier was selling too, joking and flirting with an odd assortment of females.

"Maybe we should do this for a living," he said during a short pause. A juggler on a collection of soap boxes was attracting everybody's attention and they had time to breathe.

"We have made more than we would normally make in a week working as policemen," Cardozo admitted, "but we have the right goods. It takes time and money to find this type of merchandise."

"I am sure we could do it."

"Yes, we'll find the right goods and we might get rich. A lot of these hawkers are rich. Abe Rogge was rich, or so you told me anyway. You want to get rich, de Gier?"

"Perhaps."

"You would have to leave the police."

"I wouldn't mind."

"Right," Cardozo said, trying to smooth down a piece of machine-made lace. "I'll join you if you want to become a merchant, but I don't think you ever will. I think you were born to become a policeman, like me. Maybe it's a vocation."

The juggler came to collect. He had drawn a lot of people to their corner of the market. Cardozo gave him some coins.

"Thanks," de Gier said. The juggler, an old man with a sun-tanned bald head smiled, showing a messy array of broken brown teeth.

"Thanks for nothing, buddy," the juggler said. "I'll be performing a hundred yards down now and drawing the crowd away from you again, but maybe I'll put them in a good mood and they'll be free with their money. You'd better hurry up though; we'll have rain in a minute and they'll melt away like whores who have seen the patrol car."

"Did you hear that?" de Gier asked. "He mentioned the police. Do you think he knows about us?"

"Maybe."

"Maybe not," de Gier said, and looked at the sky. It had become very hot and sweat prickled under his shirt. The clouds were lead-colored and low. The street sellers were putting up sheets of transparent plastic and pulling in their goods.

The clouds burst suddenly and cold heavy rain drowned the market, catching women and small children in midstreet, forcing them to scatter for cover. Sheets of water blocked de Gier's view and roared down, splashing up again from the pavement over his feet and trouser legs, dribbling down from the canvas roof and hitting him in the neck. Cardozo was shouting something and pointing at the stall next to them, but de Gier couldn't make out the words. He vaguely saw the old hawker and his wife scrambling about, but couldn't work out what was expected of him until Cardozo pulled him over and handed him a carton of vegetables and pointed at a VW bus parked on the sidewalk. Together they filled the small bus with their neighbor's merchandise, which the old man had stored under his stall and which was now in danger of being swept down the street by the torrent. De Gier was wet through and cursing but there seemed no end to the potatoes, cucumbers, baby squashes, bananas and cabbages.

"Thanks, mate," the old man and his wife kept on saying. De Gier muttered in reply. Cardozo was grinning like a monkey.

"Lovely to see you working for a change," Cardozo screamed right into de Gier's ear, so that it needed rubbing to make it function again.

"Don't shout," he shouted and Cardozo grinned again, his sharp face alight with devilish mirth.

The rain stopped when they had filled the bus and the sun was back suddenly, brightening a dismal scene of floating cartons and cases and sodden merchants splashing around their stalls mumbling and cursing, and shaking themselves like dogs climbing out of a canal.

"Hell," de Gier said, trying to dry his hair and face with a crumpled handkerchief. "Why did we have to help those fools? They could see the rain was coming, couldn't they?"

"Friendship," Cardozo said, rubbing his hands and waving at the coffee girl, who came staggering toward them carrying her tray filled with glasses of hot coffee and a dish of meat rolls and sausages smeared with mustard. "Love your neighbor, I remembered. There's nothing those old people can ever do to repay us, is there?"

De Gier smiled in spite of his discomfort. Cold drops were running down his back, touching his buttocks, the only dry part of his body. "Yes," he said, and nodded. "Thanks."

"Thanks for what?" Cardozo asked, suddenly cautious.

"For the lesson, I like to learn."

Cardozo studied de Gier's face. De Gier's smile seemed genuine. Cardozo sipped his coffee, shoving his tobacco and paper toward the sergeant, who immediately rolled two cigarettes, placing one between Cardozo's lips. He struck a match.

"No," Cardozo said. "I don't trust you, sergeant."

"What *are* you talking about?" de Gier asked pleasantly.

"Ah, there you are," Grijpstra said. "Loafing about as I expected. I thought you were supposed to be street sellers. Shouldn't you be trying to sell something? If you hang about in the back of your stall drinking coffee and exchanging the news of the day, you'll never get anywhere."

"Cardozo," de Gier said. "Get the adjutant a nice glass of coffee and a couple of sausages."

"Don't call me adjutant down here, de Gier, and I'll have three sausages, Cardozo."

"That'll be five guilders," Cardozo said.

"That'll be nothing, take it out of the till. You must have collected some money this morning while we were running around catching Turks."

"Turks?" de Gier and Cardozo asked in one voice.

"Turks, two of them, shot them both and took them to the hospital. I hope the one fellow won't die. He got a bullet through the left lung."

"Run along, Cardozo," de Gier said. "What's with the Turks, Grijpstra?"

Grijpstra sat down on a bale of cloth and lit a small cigar. "Yes. Turks. Silly fools held up a bank using toy pistols, beautiful toys, indistinguishable from the real thing. The one had a Luger and the other a big army-model Browning, made of plastic. The bank has an alarm and they managed to push the button. A sixteen-year-old girl pushed it while she was smiling at the robbers. The manager was too busy filling his pants. I happened to be at a station close by and got there on foot, as the patrol cars arrived. The fools threatened us with their toys and they got shot, one in the leg, the other in the chest. It was over in two minutes."

"Did you shoot them?" de Gier asked.

"No. I had my gun out but I didn't even have time to load. The constables fired as soon as they arrived."

"They shouldn't have."

"No, but they lost a man some months ago, remember? He stopped a stolen car and got shot dead before he could open his mouth. These were the dead man's friends. They remembered. And the toys looked real enough."

"I thought those toys weren't sold anymore in the shops?"

"The Turks bought them in England," Grijpstra said, and shrugged. "Some happy shopkeeper made a few shillings in London and now we have two bleeding Turks in Amsterdam."

Cardozo came back and offered a plate of sausages. Grijpstra's hand shot out and grabbed the fattest sausage, stuffing it into his mouth in one movement.

"Vrgrmpf," Grijpstra said.

"They are hot," Cardozo said. "I would have told you if you had waited one second."

"Rashf," Grijpstra said.

"Has he come to help us, de Gier?"

"Ask him when he has finished burning his mouth."

Grijpstra was nodding.

"He has come to help us, Cardozo."

"Are you selling this stuff or are you just showing it?" an old woman with a face like a hatchet was asking.

"We are selling it, dearest," de Gier said, and came forward.

"I am not your dearest, and I don't like that lace much. Haven't you got any better?"

"It's handmade in Belgium, lady, handmade by farm women who have done nothing but lace-making since they were four years old. Look at the detail, see here."

De Gier unrolled the bale, holding the material up.

"Nonsense," the old woman said. "Rubbish, that's machine-made. How much is it anyway?"

De Gier was going to tell her the price when the wind caught the underpart of their canvas roof and pushed it straight up. Several bucketloads of ice-cold water shot off the top, and all of it hit the old woman, soaking her, frilly green hat first, black flat-soled clumpy shoes last.

Grijpstra, de Gier and Cardozo froze. They couldn't believe their eyes. What had been an aggressive body of sharp-tongued fury had changed into a sodden lump of wet flesh, and the lump stared at them. The old woman's face had been heavily made up and mascara was now running down each cheek, mixing with powder in reddish black-edged streaks which were getting closer and closer to her thin chiseled lips.

The silence was awkward.

Their neighbor, the vegetable man, had been staring at the woman too.

"Laugh, lady," the vegetable man said. "For God's sake, laugh, or we'll all cry."

The old woman looked up and glared at the vegetable man. "You . . ."

"Don't say it, lady," Grijpstra said, and jumped close to her, taking her by the shoulders and carrying her with him. "Go home and change. We are sorry about the water but it was the wind. You can blame the wind. Go along, lady, go home." The old woman wanted to free herself and stop, but Grijpstra went on pushing her, patting her shoulder and keeping up his monologue. "There now, dear, go home and have a nice bath. You'll feel fine afterward. Get yourself a big cup of hot tea and a biscuit. You'll be fine. Where do you live, dear?"

The old woman pointed at a side street.

"I'll walk you home."

She smiled. Grijpstra was very concerned. She leaned against the big solid man who was taking an interest in her, the first man she had been close to in years, ever since her son had died and she had been left alone in the city where nobody remembered her first name, living off her old age pension and her savings, and wondering when the social workers would catch her and stick her into a home.

"There you are," Grijpstra said at the door. "Don't forget your hot bath now, dear."

"Thank you," the old woman said. "You don't want to come up, do you? I have some good tea left, in a sealed tin, I have had it for years but it won't have lost its taste."

"Some other day, dear," Grijpstra said. "I have to help my mates. The sun has come back and we'll be busy this afternoon. Thanks anyway."

"You saved us all," de Gier said when Grijpstra returned. "The old cow would have murdered us. She had a wicked-looking umbrella."

"She never bought the lace," Cardozo said.

They were busy all afternoon, selling most of the cloth they had brought. Grijpstra and de Gier wandered about, leaving Cardozo to do the work, only coming back to the stall when the young detective's screams for help became too frantic. Grijpstra talked to Louis Zilver and de Gier followed up on their contact with the vegetable man. The hawkers were talking about Abe Rogge's death and the detectives listened but no new suggestions were given. There seemed to be a general feeling of surprise. The street sellers had all liked Rogge and were telling tall stories about him, stories which showed their admiration. The detectives were trying to find traces of envy in the conversation but there didn't seem to be any. The hawkers had enjoyed Rogge's success, success as a merchant, success with women. They mentioned his good breeding and his knowledge. They talked about the parties he had thrown in bars and at his home. They had lost a friend, a friend who had lent them money in times of stress, who had drawn customers to their corner of the market, who had listened to their troubles and who had cheered them up by his funny stories and extravagant way of behavior.

"We ought to do something tonight," the vegetable man said. "Have a few drinks together in his honor. Least we can do."

"Shouldn't we wait for the funeral?" the vegetable man's wife asked.

"The body is still with the police," Louis Zilver said. "I phoned them this morning. They won't release it for a few more days."

"Let's have the party tonight," the vegetable man said. "I live close by. You can all come at about nine o'clock if my wife is willing. All right, wife?" The fat little woman agreed.

"We'll bring a bottle," Grijpstra said.

"Yes. It'll be in your honor too then," the vegetable man said. "You helped me out today and I hope you'll keep on coming here. I'll ask all the others around here. It'll be a big party, forty or fifty people maybe."

His wife sighed. He leaned over and kissed her cheek. "I'll help you clean up, darling, and we won't work tomorrow. We have cleared our stocks and we shouldn't work every day."

"Right," the vegetable man's wife said, prodding him affectionately.

16

THERE WEREN'T too many buyers around at four o'clock that afternoon and the street sellers began to clear their stalls, pleased with the day's results. The rain hadn't lasted long enough to spoil sales, the puddles had drained away and were dried by the hot sun, vegetables and flowers had sold well and the date was close enough to payday to create demand for durable goods. Even antiques and high-priced electrical appliances hadn't done badly. The hawkers were smiling as they loaded their minibuses, vans and trailers, and were feeling the weight of their wallets, tins and linen moneybags with some satisfaction.

"Right," Cardozo said, and lifted the remnants of a bale of cloth with a gesture of exuberance, but he overdid it and the end of the bale knocked a glass of coffee over, spilling the foaming liquid into the tin till which de Gier was about to close, having counted its contents.

"No," de Gier said.

"Silly," Grijpstra said as he bent down to survey the damage. "There's close to two thousand guilders in small notes in there. I have counted it too. Police money."

"No," de Gier said again. "We'll never get it dry and if it sticks together too much the bank won't accept it. You're a fool, Cardozo."

"Yes," Cardozo said. "You are right. You are always right. It's very annoying for other people, you know. You should learn to be wrong sometimes."

"You did it, you fix it," Grijpstra said. "Take it home and dry it somehow. You're still living with your parents, aren't you?"

"What's that got to do with it, adjutant?"

"Your mother may know of a way to dry it. Hang it on a line maybe, in the kitchen, with clothes pins. Or she can put it in the dryer. You've got a dryer at home?"

"The dryer may shred it," Cardozo said and dug about in the mess with his fingers. "It's all soddy now, it's only paper, you know."

"Your problem," de Gier said cheerfully. "You take care of it, constable. You can go home now and take the tin. We'll take care of the van. See you tonight at the party. Off you go."

"But . . ." Cardozo said, using the whining voice which he reserved for desperate occasions.

"Off," Grijpstra said. "Shoo! You heard what the sergeant said."

"He's only one rank above me. I am a constable first class."

"An adjutant is telling you too," de Gier said, "and an adjutant is two ranks above you. Off!"

"Yes, sir," Cardozo said.

"Don't cringe," de Gier said.

"No, sir."

"He always overdoes everything," Grijpstra said as they watched Cardozo's small shape, the till clutched in his arm, strutting away into the crowd.

De Gier agreed. "He hasn't been in the police long enough. The police underdo things."

"As long as they are ruled by a democratic government."

De Gier turned around. "I thought you secretly preferred communism, Grijpstra."

"Ssh," Grijpstra said, looking around him stealthily. "I do, but the communism I like is very advanced. By the time society is ripe for it we won't need any police."

"You think the day will ever come?"

"No," Grijpstra said firmly, "but I can dream, can't I?"

"What will you do when the dream comes true?"

"I'll paint," Grijpstra said, and heaved the last bale of cloth into the gray van.

They were driving through Amsterdam's thick late-afternoon traffic when Grijpstra touched de Gier's forearm.

"Over there, on the right, near that lamppost."

A man was staggering about, trying to reach the wall. As de Gier watched he saw the man going down on his knees, crumpling up on the pavement. The man was well dressed, about fifty years old. They were close when the man's head hit the ground. They saw the top plate of his dentures fall out; they could almost hear the click when the plastic teeth touched the stone tile.

"Drunk?" de Gier asked.

"No," Grijpstra said. "He doesn't look drunk. Ill, I would say."

De Gier felt under the dashboard for the van's microphone and switched the radio on as Grijpstra put up its volume. The radio began to crackle.

"Headquarters," de Gier said.

"Headquarters," the radio voice said. "Come in, who are you, haven't you got a number?"

"No. We are in a special car, on special duty. Van Wou Street number 187. A man has collapsed in the street. Send an ambulance and a patrol car."

"Ambulance alerted. Is that you, de Gier?"

De Gier held the microphone away from his mouth.

"Stupid bugger," he said softly, "knows my name. I've got nothing to do with this."

"Yes, de Gier here."

"You take care of it, sergeant. We don't have a patrol car available right now. The traffic lights in your area aren't working properly and all available men are directing traffic."

"O.K.," de Gier said sadly, "we'll take care of this."

They could hear the ambulance's siren as they double-parked the van, obstructing traffic and drawing shouts from bicyclists who had to try to get around it.

"Park the van somewhere else," Grijpstra said, opening his door. "I'll see to this and you can join me later."

The man was trying to get back to his feet as Grijpstra knelt down, supporting his shoulders.

"What's wrong with you?"

"Nothing," the man said, slurring his words. "Felt a bit faint, that's all. I'll be all right. Who are you?"

"Police."

"Leave me alone, I don't need the police."

The man picked up his teeth and put them back into his mouth. He was trying to focus his eyes but Grijpstra's bulky shape wasn't more than a blur.

"What do we have here?" the health officer was asking, bending down to sniff the man's breath. "Haven't been drinking, have we?"

"Don't drink," the man said. "Stopped years ago, only a glass of wine with my meals now. Felt a bit faint, that's all. Want to go home."

The health officer felt the man's pulse, counting and looking at Grijpstra at the same time.

"Police," Grijpstra said. "We happened to see this man staggering about and then he fell. What's wrong with him, you think?"

The health officer pointed at his heart and shook his head.

"Serious?"

The health officer nodded.

"You'd better go into the ambulance, sir," Grijpstra said.

"Never. I want to go home."

"Can't take him if he doesn't want to go, you know."

"Hell," Grijpstra said. "He is ill, isn't he?"

"Very ill."

"Well, take him then."

"If you say so," the health officer said, "and I'll want to see your identification."

Grijpstra produced his wallet, searched about in it and found his card.

"Adjutant H. Grijpstra, Municipal Police," the health officer read.

"What happens if we leave him here? "

"He may die and he may not. Most probably he will die."

"As bad as that?"

"Yes."

The man was on his feet now, looking perfectly all right.

"You are sure?"

"I am sure he is in very bad shape."

"Into the ambulance with you," Grijpstra snapped at the man. "I am ordering you to go into the ambulance. I am a police officer. Hurry up."

The man glared. "Are you arresting me?"

"I am ordering you to get into the ambulance."

"You'll hear about this," the man snarled. "I'll lodge a protest. I am going into the ambulance against my will. You hear?"

Together with the health officer Grijpstra pushed the man into the car.

"You'd better follow us in case we have complications," the health officer said. "You have a car with you?"

"Yes. What hospital are you taking him to?"

"Wilhelmina."

"We'll be there."

De Gier turned up and together they walked to the van. They arrived at the hospital a quarter of an hour later. The man was sitting on a wooden bench in the outpatients' department. He looked healthy and angry.

"There you are. You'll hear about this. There's nothing wrong with me. Now will you let me go home or not?"

"When the doctor has examined you," Grijpstra said, sitting down next to the man.

The man turned around to say something but seemed to change his mind, grabbing the back of his neck with both hands and going pale.

"Doctor," Grijpstra shouted. "Help! Nurse! Doctor!"

The man had fallen over his lap. A man in a white coat came rushing through a pair of swinging doors. "Here," Grijpstra shouted. The man was pulled to his legs with a nurse supporting him. The shirt was ripped off his chest and he was thumped, with all the force the man in the white coat could muster. He was thumped again and again and life seemed to return briefly before it ebbed away completely.

"Too late," the white-coated man said, looking at the body, which now slumped in Grijpstra's arms.

"Dead?" de Gier asked from the other corner of the room. The white-coated man nodded.

But another attempt was made to revive him. The body was roughly lifted and dumped on a bed. A cumbersome apparatus appeared, pushed in on wheels. The man's tattered shirt was torn off completely and the machine's long rubber-lined arms connected with the man's chest. The white-coated man turned dials and the body jumped, flinging its limbs away and up and down. The face seemed alive again for a brief moment but when the dial was turned again the body fell back, the eyelids no longer fluttered and the mouth sagged.

"No good," the white-coated man said, looking at Grijpstra. He pointed at a door. "In there, please. There are some forms to be filled in, about where you located him and how and so on. I'll see if we can find them. You are police officers, I assume."

"Yes!"

"I won't be a minute."

But he was several minutes, close to half an hour in fact. De Gier paced the room and Grijpstra studied a poster showing a sailboat with two men in it. The photograph was taken from a helicopter or a plane for it showed the boat from above, a white boat in a vast expanse of water. De Gier came to look at the poster too.

"Some people sail boats," de Gier said. "Other people wait in rooms."

"Yes," Grijpstra said slowly. "Two men in a boat. It looks as if they are in the middle of the ocean. They must be good friends, very close. Depending on each other. The boat is too big for one man to handle. A schooner, I think it is."

"Yes?" de Gier asked. "Are you interested in boats?"

"I am interested in solving our case," Grijpstra said. "Do you remember that painting in Abe Rogge's room? We saw it two days ago when we were taken by his sister to see the corpse. There were two men in that boat."

"So?"

The white-coated man came in with the forms and they filled them in carefully, signing them with a flourish.

"The man was a lawyer," the white-coated man said. "We identified him from the papers he had in his wallet. A pretty famous lawyer, or infamous if you prefer because he handled nasty cases only, charging a lot of money."

"Died of natural causes, did he?" de Gier asked.

"Perfectly natural," the white-coated man said. "Weak heart. Started to fibrillate. May have lived a heavy life, overworked perhaps and too many rich meals and expensive wines."

"And callgirls," de Gier said.

"Could be," the white-coated man said.

17

"BERT," the vegetable man said. "My name is Bert. They started calling me Uncle Bert some years ago but that isn't really my name. My name is Bert."

The detectives were shaking their host's scaly right hand in turns, mumbling their first names. "Henk," Grijpstra said. "Rinus," de Gier said. "Isaac," Cardozo said. They had arrived a little late and the house was full, filled with sweating street sellers and liquor fumes and the harsh acrid smoke of black shag tobacco rolled into handmade cigarettes. The house was close to the wide IJ River, right in the center of Amsterdam. A huge oil tanker was coming past, filling each window with its rusty bulk, honking its high-powered hooter moodily, like a lonely male whale complaining about its solitude.

"Beautiful house you've got here, Bert," Grijpstra said. "There won't be too many people in the city who've got such a clear view of the river as you have here."

"Not bad, hey? The house has been in the family since my great-grandfather built it. Could get a good price for it now, but why sell if you don't have to? The vegetable business is bringing in the daily penny and the wife and I've got a bit in the bank and no mortgage to worry about and the children all gone and settled. What ho! Like a beer?"

"Yes," Grijpstra said.

"Or a shot from the big gun? I've got some jenever that will make your ears wave and it's nice and cold too. You won't be able to drink it all night but a snort to set you off maybe?"

"I'll have a snort," Grijpstra said, *"and* a beer."

Bert slapped his thigh. "That's what I like. You're like me. I always want everything. If they give me a choice, that is."

"If I may," Grijpstra said, remembering the manners which his mother had once tried to hammer into him.

"You may, you may," Bert said, and steered his guest to a large trestle table loaded with bottles and plates heaped with large green gherkins, shining white onions, fat hot sausages and small dishes filled with at least ten varieties of nuts.

"Nuts," Grijpstra shouted. "Nice."

"You like nuts?"

"Favorite food. I am always buying them but they never reach my house. I eat them from the bag on the way."

"Eat them all," Bert said. "I've got more in the kitchen. Heaps of them."

Grijpstra ate, and drank, and was grateful he had been too late for his dinner and had refused Mrs. Grijpstra's grumpy offer to warm up the cheap dried beef and glassy potatoes she had fed her family that night. The jenever burned in his throat and the nuts filled his round cheeks as he studied the room where de Gier, immaculate in a freshly laundered denim suit and a pale blue shirt, smoking a long thin cigar which accentuated his aristocratic nose and full upswept mustache, was listening to a middle-aged woman, flapping her artificial eyelashes. Cardozo was studying a TV set which showed a dainty little girl being pursued by a tall thin black-haired man through an endless and overgrown garden.

The room was as full of furniture as it was of people and it was only after his third glass of jenever that Grijpstra could accept its wallpaper, gold foil printed with roses the size of cauliflowers. There was no doubt about it, Uncle Bert was well off. It was also clear that he wasn't paying his taxes. Grijpstra turned and flattened his left hand and picked half a dozen nuts each from the ten small dishes with his right. The job took some time, and as the time passed Grijpstra thought and when Grijpstra had finished thinking he had decided that he didn't care about Uncle Bert's tax paying. His left hand was full now and he swept its contents into his mouth and chewed.

"You like music?"

Grijpstra nodded.

"I bought a record player the other day," Uncle Bert said, and pointed at a corner of the room. The corner was filled with a collection of electronic boxes, each one with its own set of knobs and dials, and connected to loudspeakers, which were pointed out one by one.

"I'll put on a record," Uncle Bert said. "The sound is magnificent. You can hear the conductor scratch his arse."

"Is that all he does?" Grijpstra asked.

"That's what he does before the music starts. Scratch, scratch and then 'tick' (that's his baton, his little stick you know) and then VRRAMMM, that's the tuba. It's nice music, Russian. Lots of brass and then voices. They sing fighting songs. I like the Russians. They'll come one day and do away with the capitalists here. I've been a member of the party all my life. I've been to Moscow too, six times."

"What's Moscow like?" Grijpstra asked.

"Beautiful, beautiful," Uncle Bert said, and spread his large hands. "The metro stations are like palaces, and all for the people, like you and me, and they play good football down there, and the market is better."

"But you can't make a profit."

Uncle Bert's eyes clouded as he refused to let the thought in. "Yes, yes."

"No," Grijpstra said. "They won't let you make a profit. They all get the same wage. No private initiative."

"It's a good street market, and the vegetables are better. Here. I'll play that record for you."

The record started. There was too much noise around for them to hear the conductor's scratching but when the tuba broke loose the room was drowned in sound and the guests were looking at each other, still moving their mouths, dazed by the unexpected clamor and wondering what was hitting them.

"KAROOMPF KAROOMPF," the tuba grumped, and the tall thin man was still chasing the dainty girl through the endless overgrown garden, in glaring color, on a screen the size of a small tablecloth. Grijpstra put his glass down and shook his head. His spine seemed suddenly disconnected, each vertebra rattled free by the combined attack of raw alcohol and brass explosions. A choir of heavy voices had come in now, chanting a bloodcurdling song in words which seemed to consist of vowels linked by soft *zylee*'s and *zylaa*'s. Uncle Bert was dancing by himself in the middle of the room, his eyes closed and his mouth stretched in a smile of pure ecstatic bliss.

"What . . ." Grijpstra began, but he let the question go. He would have a beer, he thought, and drink it slowly.

Cardozo thumped de Gier's back. He thumped too hard and the

whisky which de Gier had been holding spilled down the dress of the middle-aged woman, who was still trying to talk to him. There had been ice cubes in the whisky and the woman shrieked merrily, trying to dislodge the ice cubes between her large breasts and mouthing some inviting words which nobody could hear.

De Gier spun around, drawing back his fist, but Cardozo smiled and pointed at the window, beckoning to de Gier to follow him. They passed the TV on their way. The tall thin man had caught the girl and had his hands around her slim lovely neck. The man and the girl were still in the overgrown endless garden, close to a stone outhouse, greenish white and lit up by the moon. The girl struggled and the man leered. The warrior's chant was swelling into a gigantic crescendo and tubas, trumpets, bassoons and clarinets honked and wailed shrilly in turn, framing the voices which were coming closer and closer as the girl's lace collar was being slowly torn away.

They had arrived at the window and de Gier saw two large parrots, one gray and one red, each in its own cage.

"Listen," Cardozo shouted.

De Gier went closer to the cages. Both parrots were jumping on their narrow wooden swings. The gray parrot seemed to be singing but the other was throwing up.

"He is puking," de Gier shouted.

"No. He is only making the sound. Uncle Bert told me. Uncle Bert was sick some days ago and the red parrot has been imitating him ever since. He does it very well, I think. Listen."

But de Gier had escaped. He didn't want to hear a parrot vomit. He was in the corridor, away from the noise, wiping his face with his handkerchief.

"I am getting drunk," de Gier thought. "I don't want to get drunk. Must drink water from now on. Lemonade. Cola. Anything."

There was a telephone in the corridor and he dialed his own number, steadying himself against the wall with his other hand.

"This is the house of Mr. de Gier," the telephone said.

"Esther?"

"Rinus."

"I am glad you came. I am at a mad party but I'll try to get home as quick as I can. How are you feeling?"

"Fine," Esther's low voice said. "I am waiting for you. Oliver has vomited all over the house. He must have been eating the geranium leaves, but I have cleared it all up now. He was asleep on my lap when you phoned."

"He always eats the geranium leaves. I am sorry he made a mess."

"I don't mind, Rinus. Will you be very long? Are you drunk?"

"I will be if I go on drinking but I won't. I'll be as quick as I can. I wouldn't be here if it wasn't work."

"Do you love me?"

"Yes. I love you. I love you more than I have ever loved anything or anybody. I love you more than I love Oliver. I'll marry you if you want me to."

He was still wiping his face with his handkerchief.

"You say that to all the girls."

"I've never said it before in my life."

"You say that to all the girls too."

"No, no. I have never said it. I've always explained that I don't want to marry, before I got too close. And I didn't want to marry. Now I do."

"You are crazy."

"Yes."

"Come home quickly."

"Yes, dear," de Gier said and hung up.

"Talking business?" Louis Zilver asked. He had just come into the corridor. Zilver was shaking his head, vainly trying to get rid of the noise in the room.

"Some party," de Gier said. "They are driving me mad in there. Are their parties always like that?"

"First time I have been to a party outside Abe Rogge's house for a long time. Abe's parties were always well organized, and he would have live music. A few jazz musicians who followed the mood of the evening, not like this canned stuff they are pouring out now. And the drinking was slower. They fill up your glass in here when the last drop is still on your lips. I haven't been going for more than an hour and I am sloshed already."

"They scare me in there," de Gier said. "I had to get away for a minute and speak to some sane person."

"I am sane," Zilver said. "Talk to me. You said they scare you. Do you really get scared sometimes?"

"Often."

"Anything in particular that scares you?"

"Blood," de Gier said, "and rats. Rats I can stand now. I saw one the other night when we were chasing someone near the river and I didn't mind so much. A big brown brute, he jumped into the water as I was almost on top of him. I wasn't really afraid then, but blood always gets me, I don't know why."

"You'll grow out of it," Zilver said and smiled at a girl who passed them to go to the toilet. "I am scared of things I can't define. I dream of them but I can't remember them when I wake up. I think I'll go back in there and chase a few girls."

"Switch the TV off," de Gier said. "They have some horror movie on. I would switch it off myself but I don't want to be rude. You know Uncle Bert better than I do."

"I will. I'll change the record too. We want some rock music if we are going to chase the girls. Some pretty ones came in just now. You want me to introduce you?"

"No, thanks. I am here to work."

"Good luck. Got any idea yet?"

"Lots of ideas," de Gier said, "but I want more than ideas."

Zilver smiled and closed the door behind him.

The girl had come out of the toilet and de Gier nipped in, locking the door with exaggerated care. He washed his hands carefully and combed his hair. He adjusted the silk scarf which was just the right color to go with his shirt. He sat down on the toilet seat and took out his pistol from its shoulder holster. He pulled out the clip and checked the cartridges. Six. He put the clip back and loaded, checking the breech. He could see the cartridge gleaming inside the steel of the barrel. He pulled the breech back and made the cartridge jump free. What am I doing this for? he thought. I never do this. He put the cartridge into the clip, replaced the clip and stuck the pistol back into its holster, washed his face, sat down again and lit a cigarette. Two corpses in two days. Three, counting the lawyer. But the lawyer had died because he had died. The others had been robbed of their lives. Robbery is a crime. Theft of the greatest good. The greatest good is life. And here he was, in a house filled with people thumping the floor with their great ungainly feet to the beat of doped long-haired young men, tearing at the atmosphere with their electric sound boxes and magnified drums. The killer might be in the room, thumping the floor too, drinking high-powered jenever and sucking a fat cigar, with his red hand on some woman's eagerly trembling bottom. Or would he be somewhere else in town, grinning to himself? Or herself? He hadn't seen the two women whom Grijpstra and the commissaris had interviewed. He had asked Grijpstra about them but he had only been given the gist of the conversation and a description of the women. He had a feeling that Grijpstra was following some other line of thinking and getting nowhere, for he was saying even less than usual. De Gier got back into his own line of thought. A ball, attached to a string. And the string attached to what? How could the ball have found its mark with such deadly precision?

And the commissaris? Did he know anything yet? The case was only a few days old. No need to rush. Work along the rules. Follow each possibility as far as it will go. Turn back if there is no result.

Someone knocked on the door.

"Coming," de Gier shouted and opened the door.

It was the middle-aged lady who had been talking to him before.

"Are you all right?" the woman asked, touching his shoulder. Her eyelashes shot up and came down slowly. "I was missing you in there."

"I am fine," de Gier said quickly. "Go ahead, dear. The toilet is all yours." He ran back into the room.

Zilver was talking to Grijpstra. Grijpstra's face was flushed and there was a full glass of beer in his hand.

"Rinus," roared Grijpstra, "how are you my boy? Jolly party this. Eat some of the nuts. Delicious nuts."

Zilver wandered off.

"I'll be going soon," de Gier said. "Will you be staying long?"

"Yes, I don't have anything else to do tonight and this isn't a bad way to spend the time."

"You are getting drunk."

"Yes." Grijpstra nodded gravely. "Drunk as a coot. Maybe I'd better go too. How is Cardozo?"

"Drinking lemonade and watching the parrots."

"Disgusting birds," Grijpstra said solemnly. "That red one is throwing up all the time."

"I know. What happened to the girl who was being throttled by the bad man?"

"Police came. Just in time. They always come just in time. To catch the bad man."

"Yes. We don't. Poor Elizabeth."

"Elizabeth?"

"The policeman who was an old lady."

"Oh, him. Transsexual fellow." Grijpstra had some trouble with the word. "Trans-sexual." He tried again.

"I met her," de Gier said, grabbing a glass of jenever from the table without being aware of it. "Nice person. Great friend of the commissaris. She had just finished a bellpull in half cross-stitch."

"Really?" Grijpstra's eyes were round and kind. "Half cross-stitch?"

"You are drunk," de Gier said. "Let's get out of here. I'll tip off Cardozo as we leave."

"Right," Grijpstra said, putting his glass down with such force that it broke. "Home. Or maybe I'll go to Nellie."

"Phone first. She may have a customer."

Grijpstra phoned twice. Nellie was free and a taxi was on its way. He came back looking so happy that de Gier ruffled his superior's short graying hair.

"Nice," Grijpstra said. "Very nishe. Nice, I mean."

Cardozo nodded when de Gier had finished whispering.

"What are you going to do?" Cardozo asked.

"Home. To bed."

"And the adjutant?"

"To bed."

"It's always me," Cardozo said. "Always. I spent an hour hanging all that money on the clothesline. My mother is furious with me for she's got to sit in the kitchen watching it dry. She thinks someone will come and steal it."

De Gier grinned.

"Not funny, sergeant. How long do you want me to stay here?"

"Till it's all over."

"Can I drink?"

"If you are careful. Don't blab. Just listen."

The red parrot had begun to throw up again. Cardozo closed his eyes.

"You'll be a sergeant one day, Cardozo, and then you can push another constable around."

"I will," Cardozo said. "Oh, I will!"

18

"TELL ME," the commissaris said.

The commissaris looked fresh, almost jolly, and surprisingly elegant, for he had finally given in to his wife's constant urging and put on his new linen suit to go with the warm weather. It was specially cut for him by a very old tailor who, in his young days, had designed suits for the great merchants who made their wealth in what was once called the Dutch East Indies. The suit fitted him perfectly, somehow managing to look loose and soft, and the thick golden watch chain spanning his waistcoat added to his general aura of luxury. The commissaris had spent an evening, two nights and a full day in bed, leaving it only to soak in a scaldingly hot bath; and his wife had fussed over him continuously, supplying him with coffee and orange juice and at least five different soups, served in bowls with a plate of hot toast on the side, and lighting his cigars for him (even biting off the ends and spitting them out with a look of gentle disgust); and the pain had finally left him so that he could now sit in his oversized office and stretch out his legs without having to worry about sudden stabs and pricks and cramps, and take care of whatever came his way. De Gier had come his way that morning, at nine sharp, the earliest anybody could bother the commissaris in his secluded room. De Gier was upset, pale in the face, and unusually nervous.

"What happened, de Gier?" the commissaris asked again.

"A rat," de Gier said. "A large dead white rat. Its belly was ripped open and its inside hung out and it was covered in blood, and it was lying on my doormat when I wanted to leave this morning. I would have stepped on it if Oliver hadn't warned me. Oliver went out of his mind when he saw the rat. His fur was all up. He was twice his ordinary size. Like this."

De Gier indicated the size of Oliver. His hand was about four feet off the floor.

"Really?" the commissaris asked. "That's very big for a cat. Was he jumping up and down perhaps?"

"No. Neither was the rat. It just lay there. It had been put there to annoy me. We don't have rats in the building and if we did have rats they would be brown. This was a white rat, the kind they use in laboratories. I've got it with me, in a shoebox. Shall I show it to you?"

"Later," the commissaris said.

The commissaris picked up his phone, dialed two numbers and ordered coffee. He also offered de Gier a cigarette and lit it for him. De Gier didn't thank the commissaris; he was staring at the floor.

"Right," the commissaris said cheerfully. "So why would anyone put a dead rat on your doormat, and kill it first, and rip its entrails out? Do you have any disturbed friends who would play a prank on you? Only your friends know that you are upset by the sight of blood and corpses. Is there anyone in the police who would do that to you? Think."

"Yes, sir."

"Perhaps you irritated someone."

"Cardozo," de Gier said. "I annoyed him yesterday. Twice I annoyed him. I made him take the money from the market home because he had spilled coffee over it. It had to be dried, and last night at the party I made him stay after Grijpstra and I left."

The commissaris picked up the phone again. "Cardozo? Good morning, Cardozo, would you care to step into my room a minute?"

"No," Cardozo said, sitting on the edge of his chair. "Never. I wouldn't do that. I have never killed anything. I shot a man in the legs three years ago and I still have dreams about it. Bad dreams. I wouldn't kill an animal. And I like the sergeant."

De Gier looked up. "You do?" he asked in a tired voice. Cardozo didn't look at him.

"I am frightened of rats," de Gier said. "Blood upsets me, and rats too. A bloody rat is about the worst thing I can imagine. And there it was, right on my doormat. I only bought that doormat a few days ago. The old one was getting tatty. I can throw this one away too now."

"Yes," the commissaris called, answering a knock on the door.

"Morning, sir." Grijpstra closed the door carefully behind him and ambled into the room, waiting for the commissaris to ask him to sit down. The commissaris indicated a chair. Grijpstra didn't sit down, he fell into the chair. The chair creaked.

"Shit," Grijpstra said.

The commissaris looked up irritably.

"I beg your pardon," he asked sharply.

"Shit, sir," Grijpstra said, "all over my doorstep this morning. Dogshit. Somebody must have gone to a lot of trouble collecting dogshit, with a little spade I suppose, and a bucket. Very early this morning when nobody was about. It was heaped in front of my doorstep, I was in it up to my ankles before I knew what I was doing. They had even pushed it under the door but my corridor is very dark and I didn't notice it as I left the house. Whoever did that must hate my guts."

"De Gier had a bloody rat on his doorstep," the commissaris said. Grijpstra looked at de Gier who was smiling faintly.

"Shit?" de Gier asked.

"You think that's funny, don't you?" Grijpstra asked and half rose from his chair. "You're an idiot, de Gier. You are always laughing and rolling about with mirth when I step into it. Do you remember when the sea gulls shat all over me some months ago? You were laughing so much you nearly fell over. I have never laughed when you went into your tantrums because there was a drop of blood somewhere. Never!"

The commissaris got up and stood between them. "Now, now, gentlemen, let's not get more nervous than we are already. The day hasn't even started yet. Who do you think could have done this to you, Grijpstra? Who knows that a dog's droppings will upset you and, mind you, whoever it is has a reason to shake de Gier as well, for he had a similar occurrence this morning. It must be somebody who knows you both very well and who has a good reason to get even with you."

Grijpstra had turned around and was looking at Cardozo. Grijpstra's brows had sunk low and there was an angry glint in his otherwise quiet and harmless blue eyes.

"No," Cardozo said. "Not me, adjutant. I wouldn't be scraping the street to collect dogshit. This is not like me at all. I assure you." Cardozo was on his feet too, gesturing wildly.

"Right. It wasn't you, Cardozo," the commissaris said pleasantly. "Why don't you order some coffee for the adjutant and yourself. Use the phone. My coffee machine is out of order."

It took the commissaris twenty minutes of patient questioning before they connected blood, rat and dog droppings to Louis Zilver and the party the previous night. De Gier, who had been fairly drunk, had to force his memory before he recalled Zilver's questions in the corridor of Uncle Bert's house, and Grijpstra was only prepared to admit a similar conversation with Louis Zilver after de Gier had mentioned his incident.

"Yes," Grijpstra said reluctantly. "I was in my cups a bit. Shouldn't have been but I was. That jenever knocked me off straightaway. He must have gotten it from an illegal distillery somewhere, pure alcohol with a bit of a taste, nearly burned my guts out. And that young fellow seemed harmless. We were talking about the horror movie which was on the TV and about what scares people and I said that I can't bear shit. He laughed, the silly bastard laughed, and he said that it would be unlikely that they would ever show a shit-film on TV."

"And then you said that that's all they show on the telly," de Gier said. De Gier was looking much better.

"How do you know? You weren't there when Zilver was talking to me."

"It's the obvious thing to say."

"Oh, so I only say the obvious, hey? You have exclusive rights to intellectual conversation?"

"That'll be enough of that," the commissaris said, and selected a cigar from the small tin on his desk. He bent down so that Grijpstra had to search his pockets for his lighter.

"Thank you, Grijpstra. So our idea to have a sniff at the street market paid off. I am glad you got yourselves invited to that party. Zilver must have underestimated your drunkenness last night. Obviously he thought you would have forgotten what you said to him. This is a direct link. We may as well try to follow it up."

"Not much to charge the man with, sir," Grijpstra said, "if we can ever prove it was he. Dirtying the public thoroughfare is a minor offense. We can't even arrest him if we do prove the charge. He must have done it in the early hours, after he went home from the party."

"He wanted to shake you," the commissaris said. "He knows you and de Gier are charged with the Rogge case, and poor Elizabeth's death as well. The two cases go together, of course. If he can shake the hounds the fox will get away."

"He must be the fox himself," de Gier said.

"Possibly," the commissaris said, "but not necessarily. Louis Zilver dislikes the police. He told me that his grandparents were taken from their house by the Dutch police, during the war. The police must have handed them over to the Germans and the Germans put them on transport to Germany and eventually killed them. But he blames us, the Amsterdam Municipal Police, and rightly so. If he can get at you and the adjutant, he repays some of the debt he thinks he has to his grandparents."

"I was a boy at the time, sir."

"Yes, but your personal guilt has nothing to do with it. Hatred is never rational, especially a deep hatred such as Zilver must be suffering from. I was jailed and tortured by the Germans during the war and I have to force myself now to give directions to young German students who have lost their way. I associate the way they speak and behave with the young SS soldiers who once knocked six of my teeth out. That was over thirty years ago; the students weren't even born then."

"But we are trying to solve the murder of his friend," Grijpstra said. "If he bothers us it must be because he has killed Abe himself."

The commissaris shook his head and raised a finger. "He was in the house when Abe died, wasn't he? Esther Rogge said so. And Zilver said Esther was in the house. If Zilver killed Abe Rogge, Esther, the victim's sister, must have been his associate. I think we all agree by now that the killer was outside, most probably on the roof of that wrecked houseboat opposite the Rogge house."

"Zilver could have nipped out, sir," de Gier said, "and nipped in again afterward. I would like your permission to arrest him and hold him for questioning. We have a serious reason to suspect him now. We can hold him for six hours if you give the word."

"Yes," Grijpstra said. "I agree, sir."

"Just because of the dog droppings and the bloody rat?"

"I have another reason, sir," Grijpstra said slowly. They all looked at the adjutant, who had stood up and was staring out of the window, his hands deep in his pockets.

"You can tell us, Grijpstra," the commissaris said.

"The painting in Abe Rogge's room, sir. Perhaps you remember the painting. It shows two men in a boat, a small boat surrounded by foamy water. It must have been late at night, the sky is nearly as blue as the sea, a blackish blue. Maybe there was a moon—sky and sea almost merge and the boat is the central point in the painting."

"Yes, yes," the commissaris said. "Go on, and look at us when you are talking."

"Sorry, sir." Grijpstra turned around. "But the main point of that painting is not the boat or the sea or the light, but the feeling of friendship. Those two men are very close, as close as people can get. They are drawn as two lines, but the lines join."

"So?"

"I don't mean a homosexual relationship."

"No," the commissaris said. "I know what you mean, and you are right, I think. I saw that painting too."

"Bezuur told us that the two men were himself and Rogge. He got all blubbery about it. Do you remember sir?"

"Yes. Yes, he was obviously suffering. Quite genuinely I thought."

"Yes, sir. Rogge had dropped him or fought with him or broken the relationship in some other way. I believe Esther told de Gier that her brother just stopped seeing him. But Bezuur didn't crack up, for he had other interests, his father's business, which he inherited, and great wealth. But Zilver would have had nothing if Rogge had dropped him."

"Yes," the commissaris said. "True. A mentally disturbed young man who relied completely on his stronger partner. But did we have any suggestion that Rogge was going to, or had already, broken his relationship with Zilver?"

"No, sir," de Gier suddenly said. "Or at least, not that I know of. But if he *had* it would certainly have upset Louis Zilver, and Zilver is capable of extraordinary activity when he gets upset. He proved that this morning, didn't he?"

"So," the commissaris said slowly. "You two are suggesting that Rogge told Zilver to go away, leave the house, get out of the partnership on the street market, and so forth. Esther said that Rogge would drop people the minute they began to bore him. He didn't need anybody apparently, and he could always find new company. A throng of admiring women, for instance. Flicked his fingers and they wagged their tails, so Tilda told us. The other lady confirmed the fact too. That Kops woman, the surrealist, huh!" He shuddered. "Silly woman that. But never mind. So he told Zilver to get lost and Zilver reacted drastically!"

"Indeed," Grijpstra said. "Esther also told us that Rogge liked to upset people, show them up for what they really are, prick their vanity. He must have done that to Zilver too. Maybe he did it once too often. And suddenly, without anyone being around to notice it. A single remark perhaps. Esther apparently doesn't suspect Zilver, because she didn't know that Abe had told him off. Zilver must have killed Rogge almost immediately after the incident happened."

"Now, now," the commissaris said. "And what about the device? He must have used a hellish machine, as de Gier pointed out before. An ingenious unusual weapon. Did he have it in his cupboard? And did he run to his room after Abe told him off? Did he grab the weapon, rush outside, use it and run back to his room again?"

"Sir," de Gier said.

"Yes, de Gier?"

"It must have been an ordinary thing, sir. A hellish machine which looks like an ordinary utensil."

The commissaris thought. He also grunted. "Yes. Because he had it outside in the street and the riot police didn't notice anything amiss," the commissaris said slowly.

"Zilver isn't normal, sir," Grijpstra said. "He is probably insane. This dogshit and bloody rat business proves it. No sane person would go to such lengths as he must have done early this morning. Poor fellow can't be blamed, I suppose. The war, and what happened to his grandparents and all that. If he is our man we'll have to turn him over to the city psychiatrists. But I think this is the moment to grab him. He'll probably know we are after him and he'll be defensive and frightened and ready to talk."

"True," the commissaris said.

"So can we have a warrant for his arrest, sir?"

"No," the commissaris said. "I am not convinced that he committed a murder, or two murders. Whoever killed Rogge killed Elizabeth. And whoever killed Elizabeth is ready to kill again. Maybe you are right, but I doubt it."

"So do we forget the incident, sir?" There was no emotion in Grijpstra's voice. He was rubbing the stubbles on his chin.

"Certainly not. You and I are going to see him."

"Excuse me, sir," Cardozo said.

"Yes?"

"Just a suggestion, sir. Why don't you let me go and find him. I won't spill anything, just that I was told to take him to Headquarters. Maybe he'll say something to me on the way. He has nothing against me so far and we are about the same age. We even have the same background."

"Very well," the commissaris said. "Bring him in by public transport. But make sure someone is following you. And watch him. We don't know under what stress he is laboring. And perhaps you and I should question him. Grijpstra may provoke him into another tirade about the police. On your way, Cardozo. Bring him straight up to my room when you come back."

"Sir," Cardozo said, and left.

"That's better," Grijpstra said. "You are right, sir. I am ready to wring his neck. And so are you," he added, looking at de Gier.

"Yes," de Gier said. "I've got that dead rat in a carton on my desk. I'll show it to you."

"Never," Grijpstra said. "Put that box in an ashcan. I am not showing you that dogshit, am I?"

"Gentlemen, gentlemen," the commissaris said. "I am sure there's something useful to do. Find out what it is and then do it. I'll let you know as soon as I know something."

19

"AM I UNDER ARREST?" Louis Zilver asked. He was sitting in a low leather chair, close to the window of the commissaris' office, and was frantically sucking smoke from a cigarette he had taken out of his own packet, after having refused the small cigar which the commissaris had offered him. Cardozo was in the chair next to him and the commissaris faced the two young men. The commissaris was sitting on his desk. He had had to jump to reach its top and his feet were off the ground.

"No," the commissaris said.

"So I can go if I want to?"

"Surely."

Louis jumped up and walked to the door. Cardozo followed him with his eyes, the commissaris looked at his cigar.

Louis waited at the door.

"Why don't you go?" the commissaris asked after a while.

Louis didn't answer.

"If you are going to stay you may as well sit down again."

"Yes," Louis said and returned to his chair.

"Well, now. You have upset two of my men this morning and I would like to know why you went to such trouble as you must have gone to. The rat, for instance."

"The rat?" Louis asked in a high voice.

"The rat," the commissaris repeated. "There are a lot of dog droppings in our streets, too many of them in spite of all our efforts to educate dog-owners to train their animals to use the gutters. I can see how you got the dog droppings, but the rat puzzles me."

"I didn't kill the rat. I found him in the courtyard. Esther's cat brought him in. I think he belonged to the little boy next door. I found him when I came back from the party and I remembered the sergeant's remark about rats. I took Abe's car and went to the sergeant's apartment. The address is in the phone book. I knew I had the right address, for Esther's bicycle was there."

"Esther Rogge?"

"Yes, the two of them have something going. I think the sergeant is making use of Esther, pumping her for information most probably, while he is putting on the charm. He's a very handsome man, your sergeant."

Cardozo grinned and the commissaris looked at him. Cardozo stopped grinning.

"Yes," the commissaris said, "de Gier has a way with women. But it never seems to get him anywhere. His only real contact is his cat, I think. But why bother the adjutant too? I can understand that you may think that you dislike the sergeant but the adjutant has given you no reason to . . ."

Zilver laughed. "It happened during the party. Both of them told me about their fears. I thought that I should finish the job properly."

"You certainly succeeded."

Zilver rubbed out his cigarette. "Are you going to do something about this? If you do I'll gladly pay the fine."

"No," the commissaris said and adjusted his watch chain. "No, I think not. We are investigating two killings. I still think you may help us."

"You are the police," Zilver said, and looked at the Persian rug which dominated the center of the large room. "I see no reason why I should help the police."

"I see your point. Well, you are free to leave, as I have said before."

"Where were you during the war?" Zilver asked suddenly, sitting down again after he had half risen from his chair.

"I was in jail for three years."

"Where?"

"In Scheveningen jail."

"That's where they put the people from the Resistance, isn't it?"

"That's right, but I wasn't really in the Resistance. I was accused of disorganizing one of their transports to Germany and helping to hide deportees."

"Jews?"

"That's correct."

"And had you disorganized the transport?"

"Yes. They couldn't prove it but nobody asked for proof in those days."

"And you were in a cell for three years?"

"Yes."

"By yourself."

"For about seven months."

"Seven months, that's a long time."

"Fairly, and it wasn't a comfortable cell. There was some water in it. Caused my rheumatism, I think. But that's all over and done with now."

"No," Zilver said. "It isn't and it never will be. You still have your rheuma, don't you? I noticed you were rubbing your legs when you interrogated me before. You must still be in pain."

"Not today, and when I die the pain will go forever."

"Possibly," Zilver said.

"I didn't bring you here to discuss the commissaris' rheuma," Cardozo said irritably. "Your friend has been killed and a harmless old lady has been killed, and both by the same killer."

"Yes?" Zilver asked.

"Yes," the commissaris said. "We don't have many killings in the city and these two are linked. You knew Abe well. You knew the people Abe knew. You know the killer."

"You are only assuming things, you know."

"We don't know for sure," the commissaris admitted. "Would you like some coffee? Human thought is incapable of coming to absolute conclusions. You studied law and you know that. But sometimes we can assume with a certain degree of certitude. Like in this case."

"I'd like some coffee."

The commissaris looked at Cardozo who jumped to his feet and grabbed the telephone.

"Three coffees, please," Cardozo said, "in the commissaris' room."

"All right," Zilver said. "I know the killer. You know him too. And I know how Abe was killed but I only found out yesterday, by chance."

"You did?"

"He was killed by means of a fishing rod, a rod with a reel. A weight was attached to the end of the line."

Cardozo clapped his hands and Zilver looked at him.

"You couldn't figure it out, could you?"

"No," the commissaris said. "We got as far as a rubber ball, spiked

with nails most probably, and attached to a string. Sergeant de Gier
thought of it. He remembered having seen some little boys playing on
the beach. They were hitting a ball with wooden bats and the ball was
attached to a weight by an elastic band so that it couldn't get away,
even if the boys missed it. How did you come to think of a fishing rod?"

The coffee was brought in and Zilver stirred his cup industriously.

"It's a new sport. I have a friend who fishes and he was telling me
that he joined a club where they play with fishing rods. They attach a
dart to the end of their line and then throw it, at a bull's-eye set up at
some considerable distance. It's an official sport apparently and they
even have tournaments. He said he was getting very good at it."

"Never heard of it," the commissaris said.

"I hadn't either. But it solved the crime for me. The killer must have
stood on the houseboat opposite our house. He pretended to be fishing
and the riot police who were patrolling the street took no notice of him.
There are always people fishing in the Straight Tree Ditch and there
were people fishing there right through the riots. When he saw his
chance clear he turned around, flicked the rod and hit Abe. Abe may
not have seen him, and if he did he may not have recognized him. The
killer may have worn one of those shapeless plastic coats and a hat to
go with it. Dressed like that and seen from the back, he would be
unrecognizable, just another fisherman."

"So Abe knew the killer, did he?"

"Of course."

"Who was he?"

"Klaas Bezuur."

"You are sure, are you?"

"The human mind is incapable of coming to absolute conclusions,"
Zilver said, "but sometimes we can assume with a certain degree of certitude. Like in this case."

The commissaris smiled. "Yes. But you must have some information
we don't have. We were told, by Esther, by you, and by Bezuur himself
that Abe and Bezuur were close friends."

"They *were*," Zilver corrected.

"What happened?"

"Nothing specific. Abe dropped Bezuur because Bezuur dropped his
freedom. He left Abe to become a millionaire in the earth-moving machine business. He got his big house and his Mercedes motorcar and
his wife and his girl friends and his expensive holidays in three-star hotels and lived the high life. He stopped thinking and questioning."

"Did they fight? Or argue?"

"Abe never fought. He just dropped him. He was still borrowing money from Bezuur to finance his bigger transactions and paying it back and borrowing again, but that was purely business. Bezuur charged a stiff rate of interest. But there was no further real contact between them. Bezuur kept on trying, but Abe would laugh at him and tell him that he couldn't have it all. Rogge didn't mind Bezuur's wealth and expensive ways, but he minded Bezuur's weakness. They dropped out of the university together because they had decided that they were only being trained to accept an establishment which was incredibly foolish and wrong. They were going to find a new way of life, an adventure, a joint adventure. They would do crazy things together, like sailing a leaking boat through a full gale, and riding camels through North African deserts, and reading and discussing strange books, and traveling about in the Eastern European countries in an old truck. Abe told me once that they lost their first truck on their first trip. They had been tipped off that a Czechoslovakian factory was selling beads cheaply and they went out there, in winter. They bought all the beads the truck could hold, but the packing wasn't very good. The factory gave them some flimsy cartons, tied together with paper string. On the way back the roads were icy and the truck went into a spin and turned over. Abe said the beads stretched to the horizon and caught the light of the setting sun. He and Bezuur had jumped up and down and laughed and cried, the sight was so beautiful."

"And?" the commissaris asked.

"Well, they lost the merchandise and they lost the truck and they had to hitchhike back. Bezuur said that the moment had been very important to him. It had been some sort of awakening to the nonsense of human endeavor and the beauty of the creation. But he said that words couldn't describe the sensation."

"Hmm," the commissaris said doubtfully. "I met Bezuur, you know, and he didn't seem to have that quality. I can't imagine him jumping up and down in a white landscape covered with reflecting beads."

"No," Zilver said. "Exactly. He lost it. Abe said that Bezuur had been awake a little but he had managed to fall asleep again. He called him a hopeless case."

"And he dropped him?"

"Yes. Bezuur was still coming to the house but Abe would chase him away. He wouldn't even let him in, but would talk to him at the door. Abe could be very nasty if he wanted to. And there may have been other reasons. Bezuur loved Esther once and tried to get her. I think they did sleep together a few times but Esther didn't really want him, especially when he started trying to impress her with his motorcar and bungalow and the rest of it. He married a friend of hers but she couldn't stand him either. She is in France somewhere now, living in a hippie commune, I believe."

"So why didn't he kill Esther?"

"He could hurt her more by killing her brother. Abe was the sun in Esther's life."

"She's got another sun in her life now," Cardozo said.

"The sergeant?"

"Looks like it," the commissaris said.

"A policeman?" Zilver asked.

The commissaris and Cardozo studied Zilver's face and Zilver squirmed.

"Never mind," the commissaris said. "When did you find out that it must have been Bezuur?"

"Last night at the party. The friend who told me about the fishing-rod sport is a street seller. He came to the party and told me that Bezuur is in their club and that he is the champion. Bezuur is a good shot too. Abe kept an old rifle in his boat and he shot at floating bottles, out on the lake. I like doing that too. Abe always said that Bezuur was the best shot he ever met."

"Having a firearm nowadays is a crime," Cardozo said.

"Is that so?" Zilver asked. "Well, I never."

"Would you have told us about Bezuur?" the commissaris asked.

"No. But now I have anyway. I told you I would never help the police, and certainly not deliberately."

"Bezuur has now killed twice," the commissaris said, "and his other victim was an old lady who must have seen him hanging about the Straight Tree Ditch, some hours after he had killed Abe. He probably came back to see what the police were doing. He had even gone to the trouble of providing himself with an alibi. He had two callgirls at his house, poured full of champagne and fast asleep, but willing to swear that he had been with them. Perhaps he went back to kill Esther, or yourself. You took his place. To let a man like him wander about is to ask for trouble, serious trouble. A very dangerous man, highly intelligent and skilled in unusual ways and tottering on the verge of his sanity."

"The Germans are still wandering about," Cardozo said pleasantly. "Millions and millions of them. They are highly skilled and highly intelligent. They've started two major wars and they have killed so many innocent people that I couldn't visualize the figure, or even pronounce it.

It's not only the Germans. The Dutch killed a lot of innocent Indonesians. Killing seems to be part of the human mind. Maybe Abe was right when he said that we don't control ourselves but are moved by outside forces, by cosmic rays perhaps. Maybe the planets are to blame, and should be arrested and destroyed."

The commissaris moved his feet, which were about a foot above the floor. Cardozo smiled. The commissaris reminded him of a small boy, at ease on a garden wall, engaged in playing his own game, which happened to be moving his feet at that particular moment.

"Interesting," the commissaris said, "and not as far-fetched as it seems, maybe. But still, we are here and we have our disciplines, and even if they lead nowhere in the end we can still pretend that we are doing something worth doing, especially if we are doing the best we can."

It was quiet in the room. The commissaris moved his feet together.

"Yes," he said. "We'll have to go and arrest Mr. Bezuur. Where would he be right now, do you think, Mr. Zilver?"

"Any of a dozen places," Zilver said. "I can give you a list. He may be at his office, or at home, or in any of the four yards where he keeps his machinery, or he may be wandering about in the Straight Tree Ditch area again."

"Would you like to come with us?" Cardozo asked, looking at the commissaris for approval. The commissaris nodded.

"Yes. I shouldn't have told you but I have, and now I wouldn't mind seeing the end of it."

The commissaris was telephoning. He spoke to Grijpstra, and to the police garage.

"We'll go in two cars," he said. "You and Cardozo can come with me in the Citroën. Grijpstra and de Gier will follow in their VW. Are you armed, Cardozo?"

Cardozo opened his jacket. The butt of his FN pistol gleamed.

"Don't touch it unless you absolutely have to," the commissaris said. "I hope he hasn't got his fishing rod with him. Its accuracy and reach will be about as much as those of our pistols."

"Mr. Zilver?"

Louis looked up.

"You can come with us on one condition. Stay in the background."

"All right," Zilver said.

20

THE TWO CARS left Police Headquarters at about eleven that morning and managed to lose contact almost immediately, as the constable at the wheel of the Citroën beat a traffic light just as it changed, leaving de Gier cursing in the battered VW, stuck behind a three-wheeled bicycle ridden by an invalid.

Grijpstra grunted.

"*You* should drive this car for a change," de Gier said, turning up the radio's volume.

"Yes?" the radio voice asked as de Gier gave his number.

"Put me on relay," de Gier said, "and give us another frequency. Your third channel is free, is it?"

"Fourth channel is free," the voice said. "I'll tell the commissaris' car to change into it."

"Yes?" the constable in the Citroën asked.

"Don't drive so spectacularly, constable," de Gier said. "We are still in Marnix Street and we have lost you already. Which way are you going?"

"East, through Weteringschans. We are headed for a yard in the industrial part on the other side of the Amstel."

"Wait for us, I'll try to catch up, and don't rush off when you see us."

They found the Citroën again and tagged on. Bezuur wasn't in the yard. He wasn't in the next yard either. They tried his office. They went to the south but he wasn't at home. De Gier's initial impatience disappeared. Grijpstra sat next to him, smoked his small black cigars and said nothing, not even when a Mercedes, coming from the left, ignored their right of way and made them lunge forward as de Gier kicked his brake.

The radio came to life again. Cardozo's voice, flattened strangely, mentioned that it was past lunchtime.

"So?" de Gier asked.

"So the commissaris wants lunch."

Grijpstra broke his silence and grabbed the microphone from de Gier's hand.

"Excellent thought, Cardozo. Tell your driver to turn right at the next traffic light, second right after that."

"What's there, adjutant?"

"A Turkish snack bar. They serve hot rolls with some sort of a meat stew inside, and tomatoes and onions."

The radio crackled for a while and the commissaris' voice came through.

"These Turkish rolls you mentioned, Grijpstra, what are they like?"

"Delicious, sir, but a little foreign."

"Spicy?"

"Not too much, sir."

"What's the restaurant's name?"

"A Turkish name, sir. Couldn't pronounce it if I could remember it, but you can't miss it. They have a stuffed donkey on the sidewalk and there's a Turkish lady on the donkey, with a veil and wide trousers and lots of necklaces."

"Yes?" the commissaris asked. "She's got to sit on that carcass all day?"

"A dummy, sir, a window display model. Not alive."

"I see," the commissaris said.

They sat on the restaurant terrace and ate. The commissaris complimented Grijpstra on his good taste and ordered another helping. Zilver began to talk to de Gier and de Gier, after breathing deeply, managed to look friendly. Cardozo looked at the lady on the donkey. She seemed to be slipping off and he wanted to get up and adjust her, but then the commissaris asked for the bill.

"So where shall we go now, Mr. Zilver?"

"There's another yard in Amstelveen where he keeps some of his larger earthmovers and a few bulldozers and tractors. I've been there but I got the impression that he doesn't often go there himself, so I was keeping it as a last possibility."

"What were you doing there?" the commissaris asked. "You weren't particularly friendly with Klaas Bezuur, were you?"

"I wasn't," Louis said, "but I had nothing against the man either. He was lending us a lot of money after all. I went to the yard that time with Abe. Bezuur had phoned to tell us about a new bulldozer he had bought and which he wanted to demonstrate. I thought Abe wouldn't be interested, but he went straight off and I went with him. Corin Kops, one of Abe's girlfriends, went too. We played around all afternoon. He let us drive some of the machines. We even chased each other."

"Must be nice," de Gier said, "like playing with toy cars at the fair."

"Those machines aren't exactly toy cars," Zilver said. "Some of them must weigh a few tons. I was driving a mechanical digger that afternoon which had a mouth the size of a killer whale's."

"The yard is in Amstelveen, you say," the commissaris said. "Amstelveen isn't a suburb of Amsterdam. It's another city and outside our territory. Well, we can always plead that we were in hot pursuit."

Grijpstra looked doubtful.

"Yes, perhaps we shouldn't. If Mr. Zilver gives us the address we can alert the Amstelveen police. They can send a car out too. We'll make them feel they are in it as well."

Bezuur saw them coming, which was unfortunate. The yard was big, fifty by a hundred meters, and surrounded by a high brick wall, partly overgrown by a profusion of plants. Bezuur was standing right in the middle of the yard as Grijpstra and de Gier came in through the large swinging gates.

"Good day," de Gier shouted, and Bezuur was about to return the greeting when he caught a glimpse of Louis Zilver, getting out the black Citroën's rear door. He also saw the nose of the white police van which the Amstelveen constables were parking on the other side of the street.

Bezuur stopped, turned and ran.

"Halt," Grijpstra boomed, but Bezuur was already climbing onto a bulldozer. As the bulldozer's diesel engine started up, Grijpstra drew his pistol.

"Halt! Police! We'll shoot!"

The commissaris was with them now. The constable had come with him but turned and ran toward the Citroën as he saw the bulldozer coming closer. The constable opened the trunk of the Citroën and grabbed a carbine. He loaded and knelt near the swinging doors. Grijpstra had pointed his gun at the sky and fired. The constable fired too, but the bulldozer's great blade had come up and the bullet hit the blade and ricocheted wildly, burying itself in the brick wall and disturbing the leaves of a creeper, which shook its red flowers in feeble protest. De Gier was firing too but his bullets missed as the bulldozer spun around on its left track. The Amstelveen uniformed constables were hesitating near the gate, seeing little point in using their firearms with so much movement in front of them. The bulldozer roared and kept on turning, its gleaming heavy steel blade moving up and down. The blade stopped in a horizontal position, bare and menacing, and the machine sprang forward. De Gier broke out in a sweat. The bulldozer's blade was aimed at the commissaris, a small lost figure in the vast yard. He inserted his spare clip into the pistol and fired again. He saw Bezuur's fat bulk shake as the bullet hit him but the machine didn't falter, plodding on steadily toward the commissaris, who was running to the yard's nearest corner where, panting, he meant to find refuge by flattening himself against the wall bricks.

De Gier felt a hand on his shoulder and looked around. Cardozo was squatting next to him, pointing at the other side of the yard. Another engine had come to life, a great mechanical digger was coming forward, grinding the gravel with its huge tracks.

"Zilver," Cardozo shouted.

"What?"

"Zilver! He's in the cabin of the digger. I asked him to do something. He said he could handle the digger, didn't he?"

De Gier nodded, but he wasn't interested. He looked again at the commissaris, who had now reached the corner and seemed to be tearing at the creepers in a vain attempt to put more distance between his small body and the approaching blade. The corner seemed safe, for the blade scraped the walls at each side without being able to touch him. Creepers and trailers were being torn off the walls and fell on the blade and on Bezuur's seat, decorating the bulldozer with its red and orange flowers and dark green leaves. The bulldozer reversed and jumped forward again, grazing the wall this time, forcing the commissaris to give up his refuge. As the bulldozer turned to pursue the running old man, de Gier almost closed his eyes to blot out the scene. The commissaris didn't have a chance on open ground, he would never be able to outrun the bulldozer. De Gier emptied his clip but the bullets hit the machine, not the man directing its onslaught. When de Gier's pistol clicked he snarled at Cardozo. "Fire, you fool, fire."

Cardozo shook his head. "Grijpstra is behind there somewhere, look!"

The digger had found the bulldozer and its closed steel-toothed mouth was aimed at Bezuur's body. The digger's engine growled and they could see Zilver in his glass-covered cabin at the rear of the machine, frantically pushing levers. Bezuur felt the danger and made the bulldozer change direction. De Gier jumped up and raced toward the commissaris, who collapsed against him. De Gier picked the old man up and ran to the gate. A constable opened the rear door of the Citroën and de Gier lowered the commissaris onto the back seat.

"I am all right," the commissaris said. "Go back, sergeant. Bezuur is wounded already, we don't want to kill him. See if you can't get the digger to overthrow Bezuur's machine."

"Sir," de Gier said and ran back. When he got to the yard he saw the digger's teeth hit the back of Bezuur's head. Zilver had pushed his lever suddenly and moved it right over. The pointed spearlike teeth hit Bezuur with the full power of the diesel engine roaring away under Zilver's cabin. The head snapped free and was shot across the yard, hitting the stone wall and exploding against it. De Gier's legs weakened and he found himself lying in the yard with Cardozo tugging at his shoulders, for the bulldozer kept going along slowly and they were in its way.

"Up, up," Cardozo shouted and de Gier dumbly obeyed, dragging himself away. Grijpstra ran after the bulldozer, swung himself onto its saddle and turned the key on the small dashboard. Zilver had switched off the digger's engine. It was very quiet in the yard. De Gier heard the sparrows twittering among the creepers.

"Sparrows," de Gier said. "They have lost their nests in there."

"Sparrows?" Grijpstra asked. "What sparrows?"

De Gier pointed at the wall. The creepers were all down on one side, meshed into the ground by the bulldozer's tracks.

"Who cares about sparrows? That fool has lost his head."

Grijpstra pointed at Bezuur's fat body, lying on its back where it had fallen after the digger's mouth had hit it. Blood was still oozing out of its rump and they could see the heavy neck muscles, torn into a ragged circular edge.

De Gier's legs faltered again and Grijpstra's arm caught his shoulders.

A uniformed constable came running up.

"Are you in charge of this arrest?" the constable asked.

"The commissaris is in the car, constable," Grijpstra said, "in the

Citroën. He is in charge, but I think you will have to write the report; this is your territory. You witnessed the proceedings, didn't you?"

"Proceedings," the constable muttered. "Proceedings! I've never seen anything like it in my life. What are we going to do about the fellow's head?"

"Scrape it off the yard and the wall and put it in a box," Grijpstra said. "And the man who handled the digger isn't ours but a civilian. We've got his name and particulars. Don't charge him, we have reason to be grateful; he saved the commissaris' life. I also have the name of the dead man for you."

Grijpstra took out his notebook, opened it and scribbled. He tore out the page and gave it to the constable. "If you want me you can reach me at Amsterdam Headquarters. Grijpstra is the name. Adjutant Grijpstra."

"I'll be wanting you," the constable said. "You'll have me on your back for the rest of the week. What a show! If we staged an arrest like this in Amsterdam, we would never hear the end of it."

"We're from the big city, constable," Grijpstra said. "Be grateful you live in the province."

Another constable had arrived.

"You," the first constable said, "get a knife or a small spade or something and a box. I want you to collect whatever you can find of the head."

"Bah," the other constable said.

Cardozo grinned. The first constable had three stripes, the second only two. Grijpstra grinned too.

"Poor fellow," Cardozo said.

The sparrows were still twittering as they left the courtyard.

21

"My dear," she said, as the commissaris limped into his house. "Has it got worse again? I thought it had gone when you left this morning; you looked positively spry when you got into the car."

The commissaris mumbled something in which only the word "tea" stood out. "I am fine," he answered, "bumped into something, that's all."

"I'll make the tea in a minute. Oh, your *suit!*"

The suit was stained, it was also torn. A creeper had stuck to one of the sleeves as he had tried to pull himself free when the bulldozer came at him. He tried to cover the tear with his hand as she pulled him into the light near the window.

"And what's that? Blood?"

He remembered that he had stood close to the corpse.

"Yes," he said, "blood, dear, but it'll come off again and I am sure the old tailor can repair the suit. I would like some tea, and a bath. Will you bring up a tray?"

"Yes. Will you be long? You do remember that my sister and her husband are coming tonight? They phoned this morning and I said you were much better."

The commissaris was halfway up the stairs. He stopped, turned and sat down.

"You won't mind, will you? They are always so nice and he wants to tell us about the firm he took over, a factory somewhere in the South. He's very excited about it."

"I do mind," the commissaris said. "Phone them and tell them I am ill. I want to smoke cigars tonight and sit in the garden and I want you to sit with me. We can listen to the turtle. He's very nice too, and he never takes over anything."

"My dear, you know I hate to tell lies."

The commissaris had got up again and was climbing the rest of the stairs. His wife sighed and picked up the telephone in the hall. She could hear the hot water being turned on in the bathroom.

"I am so sorry, Annie," she said, "but Jan's legs are much worse again. He's feeling terrible and I thought it might be better if we . . ."

Mrs. Grijpstra glared as the adjutant bit off the end of a small black cigar and spat it in the direction of the large copper ashtray standing on a side table in the corridor. He missed it by about a foot.

"The smoke is bad enough," she said, her voice rising dangerously. "You don't have to mess up the house as well. I've told you a thousand times . . ."

"Enough," Grijpstra said quietly.

"You are late again," she said. "Won't you ever be on time? I fried up the potatoes we had left over from yesterday. There are some in the pan. Do you want them?"

"Yes," Grijpstra said, "and some bread. And make a pot of coffee." His voice was low and she switched on the light in the corridor to be able to see his face.

"You are very pale. You aren't sick, are you?"

"I am not sick."

"You look sick."

"I am sick of my job," Grijpstra said, and stood. His arms dangled and his cheeks sagged. His wife's bloated face moved into what, twenty years ago, would have been a smile of compassion.

"Go and shave, Henk," she said. "You always feel better when you have shaved. I got a new stick of soap yesterday and there's a packet of blades I found behind the night table. They are extra sharp or something, it's that brand you couldn't get the other day when we went to the supermarket."

"Ah," Grijpstra said. "Good. I'll be ten minutes." He watched her waddling to the kitchen.

"Horrible blob of fat," he said as he opened the bathroom door. He was smiling.

"Ah, there you are," Mrs. Cardozo said, as her son came into the kitchen. "Did you deliver that money to the station?"

"Yes, mother."

"Did they count it?"

"Yes, mother."

"Was it all there?"

"Yes, mother."

"We're having fish for supper and sour beet roots."

"Yagh!" Cardozo said.

"Your father likes it and what's good enough for your father should be good enough for you."

"I hate sour beet roots, don't you have something else? A nice salad?"

"No. Did you have a good day?"

"We tried to arrest a man who was driving a bulldozer but his head got chopped off by a mechanical digger."

"Don't tell stories. You know I don't like you to tell stories."

"It's true. It'll be all over the front page of the *Telegraph* tomorrow."

"I don't read the *Telegraph*," his mother said. "Go and wash your hands. Your father will be home any minute now."

Cardozo washed his hands in the kitchen sink. His mother watched his back.

"Man driving a bulldozer indeed," she said.

Cardozo's back stiffened but he didn't turn around.

"You are late," Esther said. "I have to go home to feed *my* cat. I am sure Louis will forget."

De Gier embraced her, squeezing Oliver, who was upside down in Esther's arms and purring sleepily.

"You'll come again later, will you?"

"Yes, but it'll take me at least two hours. It's a long way and I only have my bicycle."

"I'll buy a car," de Gier said, "but it will be easier if you move in with me. You won't have to rush up and down all the time."

She kissed him back.

"I may, but this flat is awfully small for two people and two cats, and the cats won't like each other. It may be better if you move in with me."

"O.K.," de Gier said, "anything you say."

Esther stepped back. "Will you really give up your life here for me, Rinus? You are so comfortable in this flat. Won't it be better if I keep on coming here?"

"Marry me," de Gier said.

She giggled and pushed back her glasses, which had slipped down her nose.

"You're so old-fashioned, darling. Nobody wants to get married anymore these days. People live together now, haven't you noticed?"

"We'll have a child," de Gier said. "A son, or a daughter if you like. Twins, one of each."

"I'll think about it, dear, don't rush me. And I must go now. Did you have a pleasant day?"

"No."

"What happened?"

"Everything happened. I'll go with you. I can tell you about it in the bus. Leave your bicycle here. Then I'll be sure you're coming back."

She put Oliver down and de Gier picked him up, wrapping the cat around his neck and pulling its paws with both hands. Oliver yowled and tried to bite him but got his mouth full of hair and blew furiously.

"It's been a bad day," he said, "and I'll tell you all about it. But it will be the last time I ever tell you about my job. Police work should never be discussed."

"No, darling," she said as she brushed her hair.

"No, darling," he repeated and dropped Oliver, who forgot to turn over and landed on his side with a thud.

"Stupid cat," de Gier said.

DATE DUE
